# WISH QUARTET

## COMPLETE SERIES

ELISE KOVA

LYNN LARSH

Silver Wing Press

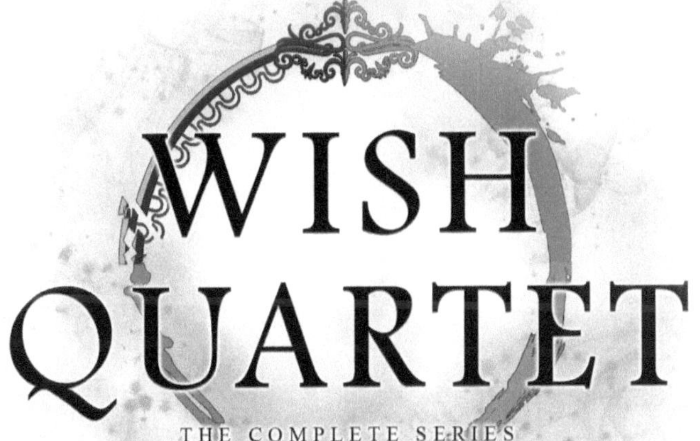


WISH
QUARTET
THE COMPLETE SERIES

# CONTENTS



## PRINCE OF GODS



## SOCIETY OF WISHES

## CIRCLE OF ASHES

# BIRTH OF CHAOS

# AGE OF MAGIC

# ACKNOWLEDGEMENTS

# THE SOCIETY'S MANSION

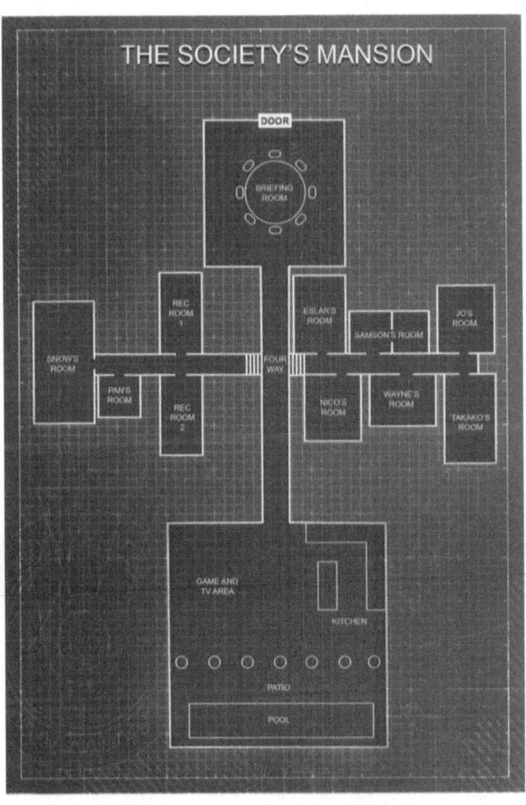

## MAP OF NORTH AMERICA (circa 2057)

# INTRODUCTION

Before you begin reading, what kind of a reader are you...?

*Do you enjoy reading chronologically?*

If you're a reader who wants to read a story in chronological order, or with as much information as possible on the characters and their history, Lynn and I recommend starting with PRINCE OF GODS.

*Or, do you like to stay guessing while you read?*

If you're a reader who enjoys looking for clues and hints about the characters and their world. Or, you like to read in publication order. Then read PRINCE OF GODS between BIRTH OF CHAOS and AGE OF MAGIC.

*Or, read it whenever makes you happy!*

*We hope you enjoy!*

THE BEGINNING OF WISHES
PRINCE
of
GODS
A WISH QUARTET NOVELLA
ELISE KOVA & LYNN LARSH

# THE BEGINNING

I F SHE had the ability to bleed, Destruction's feet would have been scraped raw.

The forest floor dipped under every brutal and frantic footfall, twigs and rocks slashing at her bare feet. There was no recognizable path and she was left to push through the trees and flora, feeling them scratch at her—knowing they would leave no mark.

Even with the greenery acting as camouflage, the environment blurring past at a speed that should easily have separated her from her assailants, Destruction felt them. Encroaching. Fueled by an unnatural force that she knew all too well.

Despite her relatively newfound autonomy as an independent entity in the universe, a twin sensation flowed through her veins.

Destruction reached for the lowest hanging branch of a nearby tree. Using the momentum of her sprint, she swung herself upwards, ignoring the way the rough bark slid against her palms. It was a simple feat, tucking her legs beneath her and jumping from one branch to another, only settling once she'd covered a substantial distance from the ground.

It was then, her back against the trunk of the tree and both legs hanging on either side of her chosen branch, that Destruction let herself relax for the first time since they'd begun chasing her hours ago.

At least relaxing was what she wanted to do.

A spike of magical energy rushed through the trees, causing the hairs on the back of her neck to stand. Destruction leapt to her feet and balanced on the branch with ease. That sickening mix of Chaos' magic and the mortals' essence was growing stronger. They'd been following Destruction's scent since her escape from Yorkton. She needed to keep running, perhaps scale the trees. Mortals couldn't fly, as far as she knew, and if she kept high enough, their limited sight could prevent them from even—

An arrow embedded itself into the trunk barely an inch from Destruction's face.

She turned, drawn to it by instinct, just in time to see the arrow evaporate in a puff of pink smoke. Before Destruction could inspect the projectile Chaos had no doubt touched, another arrow impaled her through the gut. Destruction was sent free-falling to the forest floor and taking more than one branch out with her on the way down.

Pain. Her ribs shattered against a limb, the arrow freed of her stomach as another branch ripped through her. Destruction felt every wound, superficial and fatal, mend itself and shift back into place with sparks of magic and surges of adrenaline. The moment she hit the ground, nearly fifty feet below her, she was already bouncing back onto her feet and into a sprint.

Pain lingered, but her body relished in the destruction, singing despite near-death, with a power that no other entity could command.

She stretched her magic around her, sent its tendrils out into the trees, sensing not two, but five mortals, all carrying the same heavy burden of Chaos' influence. And all were right on her tail. The one with the arrow had caught her off guard; Chaos' reach was now expanding to their weaponry. But she wouldn't let it happen again.

She wouldn't give Chaos the chance to lure her back in.

Determined, she dug in her heels, spinning in place. Until they died of exhaustion or from Chaos' magic tearing them apart, the poor mortals would chase her to the ends of the world. The best she could do was offer them a swift, clean death. Yet while that mercy also carried the fringe benefit of ending this foolhardy chase, Destruction's motivation waned the moment her assailants burst through the branches.

Her stomach churned as a human child emerged. A boy, with eyes sunken and black and his skin turned ashen. There was no telling when Chaos had gotten her hands on him, but he was more like a mortal shell left to do Chaos's bidding than anything resembling a human.

*"You can't escape what you are. What* we *are!"* the boy cooed, a familiar sound more painful than the gaping wound in her middle trying to mend itself.

*"Why do you run from me,* darling?" an old man said as he emerged from the branches to stand by the child. Black veins crawled up his arms and neck. His voice was raspy, though the inflection caused Destruction to shudder as if nails were running down her spine. She knew its true speaker.

When Destruction laid her eyes on these mortals—from the ashen boy to the walking corpse that was the archer who was the last to emerge and face off against her—she did not see humanity. Destruction saw the magic of her other half.

*No,* it ran deeper than that.

Dripping from their blackened eyes was the echo of a familiar force that she, too, had once possessed—what now felt like long ago, when she was still one with Chaos as the ancient goddess Oblivion. Destruction's memories were hazy of her time as Oblivion (being torn asunder into two demigods would do that) but she recognized that raw power.

"*Join with me again,*" the woman hissed with words that were not her own.

For the briefest of moments, with a visceral, involuntary pang, Destruction thought of giving in. Cease this endless fight for control, for autonomy, and rejoin as one. Yet, something wouldn't let her. A voice all her own screamed in objection and those screams were tearing her apart.

"No, I won't. I won't!"

Destruction collapsed in on herself, gripping her dark hair with both hands. Her bare feet dug into the forest floor, her magic crackling down her legs and into the earth. The ground shattered like glass and rose to hover mid-air before imploding with sparks of raw energy. Destruction felt more than saw the shockwaves extending from her and toward each mortal, obliterating tree and rock alike.

Sinkholes as black as cosmos opened in the fissures around them and swallowed them whole. She had never forced her magic into existence in such a way, but she couldn't deny how natural, how *intoxicating*, it felt. She was quickly sobered, however, in watching the child's final agonizing moments before he too blinked out of existence.

Then, the forest was quiet for the first time in what must have been hours. Days, possibly. Mortal time was such a slippery thing. The mortal races seemed to live a whole life in the span of a divine breath.

Her first steps were shaky, her feet digging deeper into the cracked and softened earth for purchase, but she was soon running again. She ran until she no longer heard the animals deep within the forest panicking at the attack. She ran until the essence of tainted humans began to fade. She ran until every trace of Chaos had begun to dissipate out of her system, leaving her truly alone once more.

She ran until she could barely breathe, her feet stumbling into a clearing that stretched in a wide arc around her. Destruction collapsed onto her back at the center of the glade, amidst the tall grasses, and let the sense of solitude wash over her. *Solitude,* and the still ever-present adrenaline from such a catastrophic release of her magic.

The forest clearing stretched around Destruction like a cocoon of its own world—a horizon of trees encircling a field of dewy grass, expansive sky looming dark and flecked with stars above. If she closed her eyes, she could pretend it was a haven from Chaos' mortal slaves. But the gods, too, were still undoubtedly on the hunt for her scent. It seemed as if the whole world were out to track her down.

Yet, as beautiful as false safety could be, closing her eyes made that whirlwind of energy in her chest, the euphoria of power, the lack of direction with which to utilize it, grow more pronounced, hyper focused. So, her eyes stayed pinned on the sky instead. Or, more specifically, on each bright, pinpoint of light.

Slowly, and with a heaviness brought on more by distraction than everything else, Destruction raised a hand from the grass, feeling the moisture soaked into her back and hair drip in beads down her arm. It had been so easy to rip the forest apart, to drag the mortals into its fray. It made her wonder.

In anticipation, that whirlwind inside her, that rumbling, buzzing, electrified need, began to thrum impatiently. And, as she carefully held one of those distant lights between her thumb and middle finger, that thrum grew loud, ready to burst, to destroy. Just like before. Just like she was meant to.

A single pinch, a snap that echoed from dewy glade to the universe beyond—and the star was no more.

Although brief, Destruction soaked in the sensation, eyes fluttering closed at the relief that filled her veins. While the naked eye saw no more than a sparkle of light flickering out Destruction felt tremendous power, absorbing the death and devastation of billions upon billions of energies—of an entire world. It settled into her very being, a calm to the storm within her. Destroying the forest, and Chaos' lackeys with it, had barely given her a fraction of this sensation.

But even still, even before it had had a chance to settle, the whirlwind picked up speed again, a demand blowing fierce and deep that she had never needed to satisfy.

And therein lay the real issue, didn't it?

After being torn away from Chaos, after being forced into her own life (and fleeing from the gods so that she might truly feel what it meant to be alive), her understanding of purpose had wavered and shifted. Now, as she plucked another star from the sky in attempts to fill that void, Destruction felt that understanding fade all but completely.

It had been easier as Oblivion, a natural existence that was older than time itself, and a part of her longed for that simplicity like she longed for the bursts of relief she gained from every stolen star.

And yet . . .

Now that she had a taste of her own sentience, now that she knew what it felt like to be truly *alive*, she was torn. Being Oblivion had been *easier*. But being Destruction was *more*. Like finally waking from an unknown slumber to lay eyes on the real world for the first time.

Now where to go and what to do next?

After pinching another star into nothingness, Destruction let her arm fall back to her side. She knew it would be unwise to stay in this glade much longer. Other poor villagers Chaos had corrupted were probably hot on her trail. And, if not them, then the next pawn of the pantheon. But while her mind knew to run was the most logical course of action, her body remained still, her eyes lazily trailing the remaining stars.

No longer one half of a whole, she felt her own heartbeat thrumming beneath her breastbone, her own lungs filling with air. Her own magic, that brutal need to destroy, coursing beneath her skin and crackling alongside her nerves.

She was Destruction now, regardless of Chaos' plea and Oblivion's pull. Nothing would make her relinquish her autonomy . . . even if Destruction still had to figure out what being truly autonomous meant.

# TEN

HE DID not remember the nothingness that came before him, though he understood it. He understood it as well as he did the table under him or the world that stretched out around him. Every flora and fauna, man and beast, each were already known to him, as though they had been waiting all their lives to offer up their secrets.

Yet, for all he knew of them, they knew nothing of him . . . yet.

His eyes opened slowly, and the ethereal form of an elder god greeted him.

"Greetings, Creation. I am Light."

*Light . . . . . .* The man was much like his namesake. He was more of a sun ray condensed into the shape of a man, not unlike Creation's own. However, where Light's form was brilliantly shining and seemingly not quite solid, Creation's shape was fleshy, soft, and completely bare to the world.

"You were created for a purpose."

"What purpose was I made for?" Creation explored the rumbling sound of his own voice.

"From the darkness, I have carved a place in the universe for you. Carver has fashioned you a form of wood and clay to occupy, and Life has lent you a portion of her power. All of this combined has made you, Creation: one with the power to build and shape from where there is none."

"So, my purpose is to make?" His eyes drifted, now exploring his surroundings He was in a large, vaulted, marble hall, situated on a table in the center as though he were some sort of offering. To Light's left was a woman—a child, more like—with bright eyes and a wide smile. *She must be Life*. To Creation's left was a man with fiery hair and tan skin, burn marks and scars dotted across his flesh from what was no doubt building projects gone wrong—Carver.

"That is your *ability*, to bind the universe together, to bring life in union with the objects around it to make anew. But your *purpose* is to be a companion for Destruction."

Just the name Destruction set his hairs on end. Like everything else, there was a deep knowing of this woman—a demigod, like him. But unlike the knowledge Creation had awoken with, she remained a sort of gap. It was as if there were a space in all his knowing, one that took the shape of *something* that Creation knew to be *her*. From this gap, he could understand her and the role she occupied, but the details were missing. Details he now desperately needed.

"A . . . companion . . ." Creation repeated, feeling the word echo in him with profound rightness.

"Don't let Light make you nervous." Life tutted as she reached over, pulling Creation upright with a tug on his hand. The girl-like goddess was much stronger than her form let on. "It sounds grave and scary, but we promise you it's not. She's a little lost is all, and once she has you, she will no longer be so lost. You'll be just the thing to get her on the right path."

"Even better, your magic has been shaped to temper hers," Carver added.

"Why would hers need tempering?" Creation asked. As the words left his mouth, he somehow already had an inkling of the answer.

Carver and Life shared a look, but it was Light who answered. "Because if she continues on the path she is on, it will lead to either a final end for her . . . or our world."

Creation nodded. There was something connected to the outline of Destruction in his understanding. It was a tenuous thread, pulling her back toward a danger that was utterly foreign and downright alarming. Something he wanted to stop her from reaching.

"Now, let's see to you sorting yourself out with some clothes." Life continued her mission to get him off the table. She gave a little hop when he stood on his own for the first time.

"Clothing himself may be a good opportunity to practice his own power," Carver suggested.

"I shall leave you to this task, my son." Light laid a hand on his shoulder. Somewhere in the shifting rays, Creation could almost make out an approving gaze. "You shall be a worthy addition to our pantheon."

"Thank you." Creation nodded, and Light winked out of existence. Startled, Creation stumbled back

"He does that." Carver was the first to speak, laughter in his voice. "He's the oldest among us."

Creation smiled at the god. Without being able to describe how, he knew that Light was one of the oldest, right alongside Life, who now stood before him.

"Sorry, I'm not used to new demigods. It's not too common one of us gets split or we make someone new." Carver forced a laugh. "Anyway, why don't you attempt to *fashion* yourself some clothing. Whatever you prefer."

Creation looked down at his nude form and then back to the other two. Life wore a floor-length dress under a long shawl, wrapped many times around her shoulders, covering her head, but not her face. Carver wore significantly less: a wrapped skirt that extended to his knees and a wide necklace of wooden tiles that rested over his shoulders and swooped across his chest.

Holding his hand before him, Creation felt his own magic swell. It was part Life, part Carver, and part Light, the three morphing into something entirely new. With a wave of his arm, threads of magic wrapped themselves around his body. They clung to his form, like small tendrils of light, and wove to make a shimmering golden tunic, tightening into a belt at the waist, with a cape resting overtop.

Life clapped her hands happily. "It suits you."

Creation didn't know if she was speaking about the garb, or his magic, so he said a simple, "Thank you."

"Well, well, it's time to be off with you, I believe." Life ushered him out of the room and into another massive hall.

Light was seated at the far end—nearly a world away from where they stood—on a throne awash with the sunbeams streaming through an open window behind him. The ceiling of the great hall of the gods was so tall that the columns supporting it disappeared into the clouds, emerging again among the stars higher up, and stretching beyond into the night's blackness.

On the opposite side of the room, a balcony stretching outward into thin air. Here was the ether of their divinity, where the gods could descend to the world of mortals. Without a thought, Creation headed directly for it.

At some point, he must have said his goodbyes to Life and Carver, for they were gone, and he was alone when a voice stopped him.

"You must be the new one." A woman with wild black curls leaned against one of the pillars near the balcony. Her hair was barely contained by a thin gold band across her brow. Her tunic was a slip of a thing, ending mid-thigh and bunching around the thick band of a quiver she wore at her back. A wolf slept curled at her feet.

"You must be Hunt."

The woman nodded. "Good luck with actually completing that task of yours; she's willful. Even more so than her counterpart, in some ways."

Creation merely nodded. This was what he was made to do: seek Destruction, be with her. The notion that such a thing could *not* come to pass was a foreign concept.

"Don't take it too hard if you fail, however," Hunt continued. The wolf stood, shaking out its haze of sleep. Hunt soon followed, pushing off the column. "If that happens, know I'm working on my own plan just in case."

"I won't fail," Creation said after the goddess.

She paused, turned, and gave a sly little grin. "Men. Always so sure of themselves. Let me give you some free advice: meet the woman and get to know her before you lay claim to her. Last I heard, she was spotted in a scuffle in the northeast most forests of Aristonia."

Creation watched Hunt depart, not bothering to stop her. Why would he not be sure of himself? He was made for this. Surely, Destruction would be of the same mind. They were destined for each other.

Fighting would be futile.

He went unhindered to the balcony. Standing at the edge, Creation peered down over the earth with a vision that those below could not even begin to comprehend. All mortals went about their lives beneath him. At one curve of land, he spotted a dense stretch of viridian. Darkness pooled between the trees, obscuring his sight, harboring a secret within.

Creation stepped into thin air.

He fell to the earth in mere seconds, the pillar of the gods which supported their world at his back. His knees were bent, easing his fall, and grasses tickled up underneath his tunic. All at once, the edge of the dark forest he'd been looking down on stretched out in welcome.

Without hesitation, he passed its threshold and began walking.

# NINE

T HE RECOGNITION was instantaneous. Barely a handful of steps into the forest, Creation's magic tugged him forward, leading him with an intrinsic understanding toward the target he was made to find. His whole being had been ensnared, a rope pulled taut between him and whatever lay at the other end. *Whoever* lay at the other end.

*Destruction.*

His magic rejoiced as he made his way through the trees.

When he'd traversed far enough, he felt the distinct spark and swell of magic in the air. Not Destruction's, not yet, but similar. Creation paused, one hand braced on the trunk of a tree to his left, and closed his eyes to the ripples of sensation. Five of them, all steeped in a magic that felt twisted beyond repair, an echo of Destruction's magic lingering in the wake of what was no doubt a devastation. *The scuffle Hunt had mentioned*, though she'd made no remark about the warring magics, the one belonging to his companion and the one that felt so eerily similar yet so far off.

So, Chaos was looking for Destruction, too. Of course she would be. He could not imagine the pain of a goddess torn asunder. An unfamiliar pang of emotion sparked in his chest at the thought of two parts of a whole being separated.

He reached out blindly for what lay beneath the tainted magic, letting the rope linked between them pull taut once more. Now that he'd had a small taste of her magic, the phantom sensation of it fresh amongst the debris, it was easier to follow.

*Could she feel it too?* he wondered.

When Creation opened his eyes, he took in the surrounding flora nearly overgrown beneath his feet, his hand now tangled in vines of a tree.

This rush of power came from being close to his destined lover. A smile began to dawn on his lips. Surely she knew he was approaching, perhaps sensing her own magic respond and wondering about the reason behind the sudden, frantic beat of her heart.

Creation blinked, placing a hand to his chest. It was true; his heart beat faster at the thought of her, at what being in her presence might provoke. Despite the inevitability of their encounter, his own anticipation manifested into something tangible.

Creation did not hurry towards the pull of Destruction's magic, did not run or sprint. Each footfall felt lighter the nearer he grew. Their magics encircled them both to close the distance. Her power and thoughts whispered through the trees, in the wind. When he took a breath, he felt her very essence lining the inside of his lungs.

As he finally approached a glade, the staccato of his heart ceased, the tension in his shoulders and limbs relaxing at the distinct rightness that emanated from within. The same rightness he'd felt when Light called Destruction his companion.

She was within his reach. *At last.*

Without hesitation, Creation wandered, eyes falling easily on the form lying at its center.

Even with his immense knowledge, despite his minimal existence, he was certain he'd never seen anything so beautiful. Her hair was splayed about the grass, curling naturally like the waves of a darkened sea. Her tan skin seemed to glow in the moonlight, the stars themselves shining against her outstretched hand. He could not see her eyes, though he imagined them as ethereal as she appeared, with the wind blowing subtly at the sleeves of her tunic as she pinched her fingers together.

A star flickered from existence and Creation stumbled back at the sheer power. The devastating magic radiated between Destruction and the universe above, a single second of warped atmosphere and shattered existence, before the glade settled once more. Her magic felt catastrophic in person, paralyzing him.

And his own magic suddenly wanted nothing more than to be closer. Her power was ruthless, and any other being would have feared it. But Creation craved more.

After only a few steps into the glade, Destruction's head turned towards him and her eyes, as bright as he'd imagined, opened wide in alarm. If it were possible to scramble to one's feet gracefully, Destruction managed to accomplish it; her movements were fluid as she braced for attack.

But Creation would never hurt her, *couldn't she sense that?* Not an ounce in his makeup could fathom harming her. Surely she could feel that he belonged to her as much as she belonged to him?

But if she did, she showed no signs towards him beyond hostility and panic. She tensed in a way that told Creation she was no more than a second from sprinting away. So, before she could, he stepped towards her, lips parted to speak, an arm outstretched to—

Destruction leapt back. The glade around them all but exploding in death and decay. The grass yellowed and then darkened as if burnt, and the trees shriveled and collapsed. What had once been a beautiful strip of untouched forest was now a graveyard, Creation and Destruction standing at its center.

Creation's magic retaliated with its own outburst of power. This time, he saw Destruction react fully to it, eyes widening as she pressed her hand against her chest, shoulder slumping from the onslaught of sensation.

Within the span of a second, the grass beneath their feet was vibrant and lush once more, the trees reaching towards the night sky. Flowers dotted the glade where there had once been none, and when Creation bent down to pluck one from the earth, it simply continued to bloom.

The whole forest breathed their magic, Destruction's intertwining with Creation's without her permission, finally seeking his out, even while hesitating. Destruction's very posture screamed caution

A coldness settled like a weight in Creation's stomach.

What he had hoped would be a simple and natural unity between them was instantly dashed by the narrowing of Destruction's eyes and the distrust in her voice as she asked, "And who are *you* supposed to be?"

# EIGHT

CREATION CLEARED his throat. "*Ahem*, greetings?" The word tumbled from his mouth clumsily. This was his destined partner . . . *surely* he could do better than that? "I am Creation, and I have come for you."

*That . . . might not have been the best phrasing.*

She took a step back, fear still running rampant in her eyes. Apprehension curled around her like an impenetrable cocoon that both challenged and threatened him to break.

"Come for me? Like the rest of them?" Destruction looked him over from head to toe. Perhaps she intended to intimidate him, but shivers of delight ran up Creation's spine just from her attention on him. "Come to take me? Or kill me? Or force me to reunite?"

"None of those things." He took another step toward her.

In the same instant, Destruction took that same step away. She knew his movements before he made them—before he even knew he would make them. He would have reveled in it, if given the chance.

But he wasn't.

Her magic unleashed again, charging at him with all the ferocity of an untethered hound. It meant to swallow him whole, break him apart bit by bit. Yet Creation's own magic flared to meet it. From the moment she had set out to undo him, he was rebuilding himself.

*No*, more than that. His magic unraveled eagerly. It did not cancel her own but hummed overtop in harmony. The barren ground between them sizzled, crackled, split along with fissures that were quickly sutured into more perfect designs.

A trail of flowers now linked the two of them, and Creation continued forward.

"Don't come near me," Destruction whispered. The distrust in her voice pained him, settling like a vice around his newly formed heart. But he had faith in her, that somewhere within, if he could reach it, she would feel their bond as strongly as he had been born to.

Instead of saying so, however, he merely promised, "I will not hurt you."

"Lies. You are of the pantheon, I can sense it. You're a puppet of the same deities that split Oblivion in half, giving me the form I am now."

"I am not of their pantheon." He was not of them; *was that true*? He had been made by them. So, surely, he should count himself among their numbers? *And yet* . . . "I do not want them, I do not care for them. I am only here for you."

A crackle of power seemed to rise off her skin, marring the air around her in waves. "To be their latest weapon against me."

"I am no weapon." Creation's voice was strong, willing his point across almost sternly, but beneath the bravado, something desperate bubbled to life deep within him. He simply wanted to prove himself, simply wanted her to believe his words.

"Lies!" Destruction's voice rose, and with it, her magic to match.

Creation watched as a shockwave launched from her. The grasses blew back and singed like a wildfire—all save for what was under his feet. Creation looked around him, trying to keep a handle on his power and just steep in hers for a moment. But as soon as the extent of the destruction became known to him, his magic surged forward and the glade was lush once more.

"I am here *for* you," Creation attempted again, almost apologetically, though he didn't know what he was apologizing for. "Please. Please, don't be afraid."

She laughed then, and there had been nothing in Creation's short existence that had ever sounded more pleasing. Though, the sound wasn't likely intended to be so. "Afraid? Why would I ever be afraid of you?"

Optimism filled his heart, though he willed his feet not to pull him closer to her, as much as they longed to do so. "I'm glad to hear it," he still said eagerly, ignoring that she may well be belittling him.

"How did you come to be?" Destruction asked cautiously. "I don't remember you among the initial pantheon when I was torn asunder. And if you're not of them . . ."

"*You* were torn asunder? Or Oblivion was?" he attempted to clarify.

Something about the question caused Destruction to bristle, even as her magic spiked with contradicting emotion. Like defensiveness, or stubbornness. "Oblivion and I, We are the same."

"Are you?"

She scowled and then demanded, "Answer my question."

"I was recently made," he answered, seeing no use in subversion. "Carver made my body. Life gave me a part of her power. Light awoke me." Destruction scoffed, rolled her eyes, and folded her arms. "This . . . doesn't please you?"

"And why would it?" she asked. "Why would this please me?"

The answer seeming so *obvious*, so deeply etched into his very being that it seemed impossible for her *not* to already know. Still, he tried to assemble the right words. "Because I was hand crafted only for you."

Despite the honesty, Destruction bristled. "*Made* for me?" Her voice became as sharp as a razor's edge. "You were 'made for me' by people who know nothing of me—by the people you somehow claim not to be a part of. The same divine who look and see me only as something to be controlled and tamed and leashed down."

"That's not—"

"I will not have it!" she proclaimed. "Go back to your masters and tell them that I am not beholden to them *or* to Chaos. I do not wish to be joined with her or their pantheon. I am my own woman, and nothing will change that!"

Creation watched as her eyes widened and lips parted. He could nearly feel her horror at the words she allowed to escape her lips. *A confession.* She was her own woman . . . a woman whom he'd known only in concept but saw now, with his own eyes, in all her autonomous glory. It was a glory that he . . . he . . .

His mind froze, and his heart sputtered.

*An autonomy that he only wished he possessed.*

"Nothing will change that," he repeated softly, like a vow. A soft breeze rustled the trees and grasses as if in agreement.

Destruction stared back at him, searching, as if words seemed to evade her.

"Would you prefer it if I called you Zoria, then? Instead of the name the divine refer to you as?" he asked as gently as possible.

"What did you call me?" she hissed.

"Zoria, that's what the mortals call you, isn't it?" It came from the same knowing he had been born with. "They don't call us by our names—Destruction, Chaos, Creation, or—"

"Creation." The name seemed to stick with her. "Is that you?"

Warmth bloomed across his chest at her recognition. "It is."

"Then let me use your name to say this: Stay away from me, Creation. Now and always."

That warmth turned to frost in his veins. "But we are—"

"We are nothing."

"You are everything to—"

Destruction raised her hand and Creation barely had enough time to react. The moment she unleashed her power, he caught her wrist and held it tight. Her magic exploded against him, washing over him like a violent tide. He weathered it and protested with his own power. Together, the glade shifted shapes and colors, spurred on by the relentless wave of death and rebirth.

"You are everything to me," he finally finished. Destruction's other hand raised up and he took hers in both of his. He brought her fingers to his lips, kissing them gently. "You are what I live for."

"You . . ." She stalled and simply met his eyes. "You don't even know me."

Creation was sure she meant the words as a protest. Yet, somehow, they seemed more open now, not quite an invitation but no longer an outright rejection. There was a rush of something happening between them —a sort of feedback loop where for everything she destroyed, he made . . . including their own relationship.

"Allow me to know you?"

"Why?"

"Because I—" Creation stalled. There should be an answer. It was right there, right on the tip of his tongue, right where he wanted to access it but . . . "I—"

Her face fell. "You don't know, do you?"

He wanted to know. He wanted to know everything about her, to earn her trust and with it access to the deepest portions of her being. Yet, in the moment he needed to articulate that the most, he couldn't find the words.

"You're just doing what they command, after all." She pulled away and an icy void rushed to fill the space she'd just been occupying. "You don't feel anything. You're nothing more than a *shell*. You only feel what they designed you to."

Creation wanted to object. But silence was the only thing he was able to provide.

Destruction—Zoria, the woman who was his true companion—slowly shook her head. Pain welled in her eyes and he was now too far to wipe away the shining drops, like so many extinguished stars, from their corners. She turned and ran. He wanted to chase after her, wanted to stop her from being outside of arm's reach ever again. But he couldn't move. Her words cemented him in his spot.

His affections for her seemed so complete. So then why couldn't he object to them being solely by design?

What was the true nature of his feelings?

What was the true nature of who he really was? Not just in relation to her, but to himself?

## SEVEN

THERE WAS no telling how quickly or how far Destruction ran, but Creation felt the distance like a physical tear, his chest splintering beneath the strain. After finally being near her, touching her, however brief, his very being went into withdrawal at the loss.

This torture kept him rooted in his spot, feeling the whisper of Destruction's fading magic taunt him for being unable to follow.

At least, that's what he told himself. Or rather, desperately tried to make himself believe.

If he was being honest, it was less the agony of her distance and more the truth in her words.

Despite his immense knowledge, Creation had nothing to counter her accusation.

They were meant to be together; he was literally *made* to be with her. But what stake did such a belief have if it had been merely implanted into his mind, body, and soul? What value were his feelings if they'd been fabricated by the gods with a vested interest in their relationship's success?

The invisible link between Creation and Destruction vibrated with a distant pull, too taut to bear any more force. On reflex, Creation reached for it, with one hand towards the forest as the other dug tense fingers into the meat of his chest—right over his heart, as though to keep every last bit of her in, no matter how small.

Their separation grew too vast. The link snapped. Creation stumbled, his legs suddenly heavy, pulled down by the weight of exhaustion and grief.

Deep, *deep* into the very essence of his soul, Creation knew their mateship to be true. He knew. Her magic swirling and molding about his own should have been proof of their destiny.

But questions and doubts still spiraled.

He found his feet dragging him not in the direction of her desperate flee, but elsewhere. To where, exactly, he was unsure. He just knew that if he didn't start moving, he would become rooted forever to this spot.

Creation headed in the opposite direction, for if she relented to be with him only because he gave chase, then their relationship would be as solid as air.

Minutes, hours, perhaps even days, he wasted wandering the forest. Mortal time meant nothing to him and he rarely bothered to count it.

Every now and then, he would reach for a sapling or a dying patch of greenery, trying to relish in the feel of their rebirth beneath his hand. But after learning his magic's response to Destruction's, after knowing what true power had felt like, it barely passed for contentment, let alone distraction.

Eventually, his ears picked up distant sounds of life, the forest parting way for a man-made clearing, a small village opening amidst forged earth. He heard something akin to celebration, chanting voices mixing with cacophonous music and natural clatter. He followed the noise, at the very least curious to find source of such jubilee.

Though mirth was particularly distasteful now, Creation took in the sights and sounds with an appreciative acceptance. Whoever was being celebrated right now must have been important, their presence gathering the entire village's attention.

Creation shouldn't have been surprised to find Light there.

Amidst a large crowd of villagers, their clothes timeworn and faces marred with grime, Light stood tall and welcoming, his embodiment amongst the mortals as pristine as his one amongst the gods. However, here, he had donned the illusion of flesh (still glowing).

It made sense that, in his state of turmoil, Creation had inadvertently followed a path directly to one of his creators and the greatest divine of them all. His soul yearned for solace in the hands that made him. Though, whether he was looking for assistance, understanding, or reassurance, he was still unsure.

As Creation approached the mortals, he heard awed chanting, voices young and old proclaiming their fidelity to the one they called "Zeus." Though he was moderately aware of the various monikers attached to Light, this name was unfamiliar; perhaps Creation had been given less of an unending knowledge and instead more of an *applicable* one?

Light finally noticed his presence, his seemingly omnipotent gaze dragging lazily over his form as if he'd been expecting him. Perhaps he'd been aware of Creation's wandering from the moment he'd left the glade.

From the moment he'd—somehow, *impossibly*—failed at his singular purpose.

Through some inherent understanding, Creation followed the unspoken order to filter through the crowd to Light's side. The villagers took him in with a similar sense of wonder, hands grasping for but not quite touching his golden tunic.

"Chosen of Zeus," some whispered.

"Hair white like snow," others observed. "Are you the God of Winter?" It seemed the mortals possessed a similar innate ability to identify divinities as the divine themselves possessed to recognize each other.

"He is no god," Light announced. "But he is a well-loved son of mine and the Demigod of Creation." Light held out a golden hand, motioning for Creation to approach.

"Son of Zeus," one said. It seemed to catch like wildfire across the crowd until someone else uttered, "A prince of gods." There seemed to be agreement toward that. "Prince of Creation."

"While I have heard your prayers, it shall be the powers of my son that will give you what you desire." Light turned to Creation. "Come, you shall assist me."

Creation gave a small nod, and they began walking through the parted crowd of onlookers, all bowed with their foreheads against the dirt. In lieu of bringing up his concerns surrounding Destruction, Creation opted for the more immediate inquiry. "Do you not have followers who call you Ra?"

"Those who wish to worship at my feet are free to call me whatever they wish," he replied, tone free of emotion, which Creation couldn't decide if he was relieved or unnerved by. "Light, Jupiter, Zeus, Ra, the praises still reach my ears—all I need to do is listen. As easily as the words and actions of the gods and demigods beneath me."

A chill ran down Creation's spine; the iciness beneath his words might not have been noticeable to the mortal ears of the villagers following them, but Creation felt it like a chiding hand upon his shoulder.

"You know you were made for this," Light offered simply, his eyes never leaving the mortals they passed. He paused from time to time, reaching out to lightly cup the faces of some, run his fingers through their hair, or brush a thumb across their foreheads, their temples. "She should have responded to your sway as easily as I can sense that you have responded to hers. Do not let her actions dissuade you."

An involuntary flush rose to Creation's cheeks. What Light was saying was truth, pure fact, and yet it left him feeling a bit breathless. Perhaps it was his new body's reaction to his embarrassing failure. But at the memory of Destruction within his grasp, her nearly luminescent gaze as all-encompassing as her magic, he found he couldn't lie.

Instead of bringing voice to these thoughts, however, he heard himself parroting on half-second delay, "I was made for her."

At this, Light spared him another glance, an eyebrow raised. Under his calculating gaze, Creation wanted to fidget, possibly squirm, but he kept his face impassive and his shoulders square.

They came to a stop, and Light spoke louder, no longer just for Creation's ears. "Loyal subjects, my son shall bless your fields, bring them to life once more."

Creation looked ahead of them, noticing for the first time that they'd walked to the edge of town. There, sloping slightly, was a stretch of farmland gone barren. Creation could almost see the threads of life and possibility that had been torn apart.

*Had Destruction run through here on her desperate flight?*

His magic rose, as if trying to assist him in pushing the thought away. Creation brought up his hands with it, casting his essence across the fields. The yellowed grasses greened, and the hard soil became dark and rich— teeming with life again. But, that which was already growing and thriving, his magic did little for.

"Do you see, now?" Light asked.

"I do." His magic responded best to things destroyed, ended. In every way, it had been designed to work with hers. The celebrations of the mortals lauding him as their prince faded. Instead, he heard Destructions words, harsh and bitter at the back of his mind:

*You're nothing more than a* shell. *You only feel what they designed you to.*

"Yes . . . designed . . . but does that mean this bond between us . . . this connection . . .?" *Is she right?*

A flicker of emotion passed over Light's face. *Annoyance.*

"You are but a tool, Creation," he said, voice not quite angry, but close enough to have some of the nearest villagers recoiling in fear. Creation almost did the same; it took far more strength than he was aware he possessed to stand his ground. Especially as Light turned the full force of his glare on him. His voice carried the same debilitating authority as the magic radiating off him in waves, and Creation very nearly knelt in submission at the onslaught. "Just like you have shown here, this day, you are meant to follow orders and do as you were made."

Much like Destruction's words had left him frozen, Light's ultimatum had his knees locking in place, tension holding his neck and spine in a stranglehold.

"Your very reason for existing, the only reason you have been gifted life *at all*, is to control and temper Destruction on behalf of the pantheon. This life, bestowed upon you with great mercy and benevolence by your makers, serves that single purpose alone. Nothing more."

"He shall save us from the Demigod Zoria and her trail of destruction," some of the mortals closest whispered.

Creation fought the objection that there was nothing, truly, to fear from Destruction. She was merely scared and alone. He had sensed much in her, but true malice wasn't among them.

As his rage hadn't just been nearly tangible, Light relaxed his shoulders and reached toward Creation's tense frame. Strong fingers, warmed by their internal light, carded through his silver hair, letting it fall with a gentle touch over one of Creation's wide-set eyes.

"What you feel, the power and temptation drawing you to her, is what you are *meant* to feel. Do not wander from it, or from my gaze and the warmth of the pantheon." Light smiled, pulling away from Creation. Before truly washing his hands of the situation, however, he added, "Perhaps it would be wise of you to spend your time assuring that this life we bestowed upon you does not go to waste, rather than questioning it."

Creation barely registered Light's departure, most of the villagers following in his wake. Some stuck behind to offer Creation praise and thanks, or small gifts from their homes. He paid them no mind, removing himself from their presence the moment he had the wherewithal to do so. And even then, his movements were sluggish and directionless, feet dragging him back towards the forest.

*You're just doing what they command,* Destruction's words filled his head again, screeching like a murder of crows. *You don't feel anything.*

*You only feel what they require you to,* she may as well have said.

*You are but a tool, Creation.* Light had done nothing to assuage his confusion and guilt, his steadily rising panic. *What you feel . . . is what you are* meant *to feel.*

It was because Creation's mind was whirring and occupied that he didn't register another godly presence until a hand had wrapped around his upper arm, yanking him into the cover of the forest's edge.

The first thing he noticed was the tangle of black curls, and the next, a wolf's huff as it poised protectively between their feet.

*Hunt.*

Before he could ask why she was also walking amongst the mortals, by this Aristonian forest specifically, she placed a calloused fingertip to his lips. Her eyes scanned his face, filled with emotions he couldn't decipher. Though when she spoke, her voice was eerily calm.

"Follow me. I want to tell you something." Hunt dropped her hand and turned away, already walking into the forest.

Creation glanced back toward the village; workers were already out in the fields, tending to the new life he'd sown. When he looked back at Hunt's retreating form, she was already far enough away that he had to run to catch up. "Were you watching?" he asked once they were walking side by side.

"Yes." Hunt replied without shame, navigating between the trees. "I've been watching you since you left."

"Why?"

"I think the whole pantheon is watching you." On that, Creation couldn't object. He knew the importance of what he was trying to do, and it seemed only logical to think that others would be equally invested. "They're all watching and waiting. Put all the stock of the world in Light's plan for you."

"Except for you." Creation sensed the caveat in Hunt's tone.

She nodded, reaching down to scratch her wolf tenderly between the ears. "I love my divine brothers and sisters, but I'm much more suited for going off and doing my own thing."

Creation hadn't known the woman long enough to say if such was true, so he took the statement at face value. Something in him seemed to resonate with her sentiment.

"I wish you well, Hunt." He meant it, too. If she was a loner or one for the group, Creation had no reason to feel ill toward the goddess. "But I must go now and do what I am made for." He took a step for the depths of the forest.

"Is that what you want?" Hunt moved in front of him, stopping his progress yet again.

"What?"

"I heard your questions down there. I know your doubts."

"Light removed all of my doubts." Creation wanted to say with conviction, void of all hesitation.

"You were *told* to have no doubts, just as you were *told* to go be with her for the sake of taming her." She leveled her eyes with his. Creation searched the dark skin of her face, unblemished save for a sliver of silver in the shape of a crescent moon at the center of her forehead. "Is that how you want her? Tamed? Controlled? With you only by chase, or force, or sheer will? Is that how *you* want to live?"

*No.* Everything in Creation objected so vehemently to Hunt's suggestion that even his magic rattled in protest. He restrained himself, whispering, "Of course not."

A smile spread across Hunt's lips, her white teeth peeking out from between them. "I thought not. Because you have sense, Creation, and the beginnings of what I'd dare call a mind. Just from the questions you ask, I know you're not one who likes the idea of fighting against nature."

"But I have no choice." Light's words were seared into his mind right alongside the god's brilliance. He was made to be with Destruction. He was made to "tame her"—as Hunt would put it—for the sake of the world.

"Continue on with me." Hunt turned, motioning for him to follow once more now that she seemed to trust he wouldn't run off again. She began jogging along the forest's edge, not even looking back to see if he was behind. The goddess didn't have to. Creation only spent a second staring after Destruction's path in debate before following.

He may not know what Hunt had planned yet, but he did know that he would take the excuse to prolong his chase of Destruction. It was a path he did not want to walk and would only do so by force. Hunt was showing him what he hoped was another way.

They tore through the woods just at the edge of the tree line and the hills that flanked them. Far behind them was the village he had met Light within. For a long stretch there was nothing but plains and sloping hills.

Creation felt it before he saw it.

A pulsing energy, a crackling dissonance to the natural order of things. It wasn't like Destruction's magic—an acceleration of the inevitable breakdown of all life. No, this was more of a *transformation* of matter—twisted, frayed, and abused.

Hunt and Creation stopped at the top of a ridge overlooking yet another village in the valley below. Or what was left of it. This one had seen a horror that was new to Creation's eyes—yet his being knew it all too well.

"Chaos," he whispered.

"This is her work," Hunt affirmed. One house, turned to be made of sweets, being gnawed on by the black-eyed and gnarled shapes of half-men, half-wolves. The road had been transformed to ice, bodies trapped beneath it. One structure couldn't seem to make up its mind on what it was as it rotated through changing shapes and colors. "It's an affront to nature itself."

*And nothing like Destruction.* Now having felt both of their magics so clearly, Creation couldn't believe the two demigods had once been one. Destruction's magic accelerated and played into the natural order. Chaos's magic was, as Hunt put it, a complete divergence from it.

"As far as I'm concerned, *this* is the real threat, not Destruction. We can preempt the latter. But this is utter madness."

Creation allowed his horrified silence to be his agreement.

"Which is where I diverge from my brothers and sisters in the pantheon. As far as I'm concerned, they've busied themselves with the wrong demigod. They saw Destruction as the low-hanging fruit in her relative stability and made you. If they can control her, shield her from Chaos's grasp, then they think Chaos will tire and give up hunting her." Hunt motioned to the village. "Does this look like the work of a woman who will roll over quietly because things became difficult?"

"Not at all." Creation finally tore his eyes away and looked to the goddess. "What are you thinking?"

"I'm not like them, Creation. I go for the kill—and not the easy one."

"You're going after Chaos?"

"Yes. I do not want her magic in the world at all. The Goddess of Earth is on my side as well in this, she's the one helping me know where Chaos' and Destruction's feet fall. Since they've both forsaken the pantheon they're out of reach from Light's eyes and the scrying pools that give us eyes to all things on this world."

"So you can help me find her? Destruction, that is?"

"I can." Hunt nodded. "But, better than that, if you agree to help me, you will not need to chase her. You will not need to force or tame her. You will find your answer—if you were truly meant to be with each other—by creating a space where you both can live as you are. In that space, you can see if you come together not by force but naturally."

Creation couldn't help but imagine it: an existence together not by force or design, but by choice, on both of their parts. He imagined Destruction at his side willingly, her words filled with fondness instead of harsh accusation. He imagined himself looking into her eyes with no doubt or hesitancy about his feelings for her. The thought caused his heart to swell, a hope blossoming within him. For such a possibility to even exist, however, meant first—

"You're asking me to kill Chaos."

Laughter burst from Hunt. "*You?* No. Besides, there are rules in the pantheon—we cannot kill other divine. It's why Oblivion was merely split, not killed. Why Light made you rather than just smiting one of the two. Killing a god—or demigod—is far more troublesome."

Creation frowned. "Then, how do you intend to accomplish it?"

"I have found a mortal champion who will shoot Chaos down from where she stands." Hunt folded her arms and leaned against one of the nearby trees.

Her eyes raked over him, assessing him. Was he measured up to task? He wasn't sure if he even wanted to. This was a dangerous deviation to what he had been made to do . . . but there was something equally thrilling about it. Perhaps she was right; this could be his opportunity to see if what he felt for Destruction was real.

"What I need from you," she continued, "is a weapon for my champion to wield."

"And if I refuse?" A nervous voice from the corner still deeply loyal to his makers asked.

"Then I will find another way. Chaos is my target because of her volatility . . . but all that matters is one of them dies so that Oblivion cannot be reformed."

The roots of the tree around Hunt's feet shot up and curled with Creation's magic in daggers. He vibrated with anger. But no matter the ferocity of his objection to the mere idea of harming Destruction, he was unable to harm Hunt.

It was true—the pantheon did not have many rules—but not allowing their magic to harm their fellow divinities was chief among them.

Hunt's wolf snarled at his feet. The goddess merely continued to smile.

"Do not hurt her," Creation growled through clenched teeth. Even if Destruction never turned her eyes favorably on him, even if he was broken down by Light for failing his task, he would rather accept the punishment than see harm or heartache come to Destruction.

"Then help me." Hunt twisted, stepping away from Creation's foot-daggers. "Help me and we all get what we want. Earth and I see Chaos dead, no more of her magic mucking about. The pantheon gets their assurance that an Age of Oblivion will never rise again. And you . . . you get to see if your lover will care for you when the fate of the world doesn't hang in the balance."

She presented it like a choice, but as far as Creation could see, there was none. There was only one path that led to where he truly wanted to be.

"Very well. I will help create your weapon."

"I had hoped you would say that." Hunt looked skyward. "I'll see to finding you a workshop away from prying eyes. It'll be somewhere here, on earth, not on the pillar of the gods."

Creation nodded.

"Stay here until then." She took a step away and paused. "Actually, you may want to continue pursuing her, if for no other reason than to keep Light's rage off you, should he decide to check in."

"But—"

"She's gone to the beaches of High Luana. You'll find her at the furthest point from the high elf encampments."

With that, Hunt was off, sprinting again until she was just a blur that disappeared over the horizon.

Creation leaned against a tree, catching his breath for a moment. *What had he just agreed to?* It should feel wrong, yet a sense of liberation emerged from his decision.

He started on his own trot across the globe, heading for the home of the elves. And more important, the current hiding place of the woman he dared hope he would fall in love with all on his own.

## SIX

O NCE HE'D made it within the borders of High Luana, it wasn't difficult to pick up on Destruction's essence. He followed on autopilot all the way to the crystalline beaches Hunt had pointed him towards. He could practically taste her magic on his tongue the closer he got.

It surprised him that her presence stayed stationary upon his approach; surely she felt him just as potently in the air now that she was aware of his existence. As he navigated the coarse sands, traveling the perimeter of the vacant beachscape, her presence grew stronger and more pronounced.

He was taken aback at the sight of her again, standing ankle deep in the sapphire waves, staring out at the horizon.

But her voice held exhaustion. "So you intend to seek me out, then, for the rest of my days?"

The bitterness—the blatant disgust—in her voice sent a lonesome pang through Creation's chest. But that was why he was here, to let her know how very untrue that assumption could now be. Creation stepped forward, off the sun-bleached sand and into the seafoam to stand at her side.

*From every angle, she was breathtaking.*

"No," he offered her simply, and had he not been staring at her so intently, he would have missed the momentary furrowing of her brow as it changed the delicate lines of her face in profile. Though she still refused to look at him, eyes locked upon the vast stretch of sea, her surprise was palpable. So, before she could demand explanation, he offered one. "Hunt plans to kill Chaos, and if she succeeds, you will be free."

For a long moment, Destruction didn't seem to know how to respond, jaw clenched as she processed his words. Then, she asked, "And you intend to take this as an opportunity to gain my interest? Manipulate me into your good graces with the promise of freedom just like Carver manipulated wood and clay to make your body, or Light manipulated your thoughts to feel fondness for me?"

Though Creation's heart ached at the implication, however understandable, he pressed on, stepping toward Destruction. The motion brought on Destruction's gaze at him, her expression carefully blank. He saw her emotions, locked behind her eyes like animals pacing a cage. "If the plan to kill Chaos succeeds, then you will no longer matter to the pantheon as you do now. With her gone, Oblivion cannot be formed—by you or her. Which, yes, means your freedom to carry on as you are. Not just from them, but also from me. If that is what you wish."

The words sat heavy at the back of his throat, choking him, but he willed them out, desperate for their truth to reach Destruction's ears.

"I'll alleviate myself from the equation. If you choose for me to never approach you again, for the rest of our days, then that is your will as a free demigod. And I will honor it."

When the admission left him, his throat sore and chest hollow, Destruction faced him properly. Surprise sprung free from its cage and now ran amok on her features. It no doubt mirrored his own as Destruction filled the silence between them with one hesitant step towards him.

And then another.

Creation held his breath, watching as she slowly breached his personal space, almost unconsciously. Her eyes never left his, flitting about his face as if looking for the lie. She pushed the boundaries even further, stepping so close that he could almost feel the heat of her body, their breaths mingling in the air.

There wasn't much height difference between them, but enough that Destruction had to tilt her head up to keep his gaze. At the look of determination flickering in her eyes, Creation swore his own heart stopped. There was so much magnificence before him. The natural splendor of the world around them paled in comparison to the woman who could keep him in perfect thrall with a mere look.

"If we decide to be together," she said in a breathy and low whisper that restarted Creation's heart double time, "and one day I decide to leave —" Creation let out a breath, that same heart clenching "—does that free will still stand?"

All at once, hope coursed through him, a challenge lingering within the question that made it easy for him to reply.

"If Chaos dies, your life is your own. You will be free to do as you please. In any regard, in any age, at any time. You have my word on that."

Destruction inhaled the answer, using it to fill her lungs with new air—an air laced with freedom and opportunity. Yet still, as she exhaled, she did not take her leave. Instead, she placed a hand over Creation's heart. Surely she could feel how fast it was beating, could hear how hard and loud it was beating for *her*.

"What if . . ." Destruction whispered, letting her hand trail up his chest until fingers were digging into the nape of his neck. His eyes nearly fluttered closed at the contact, but he forced them open, unwilling to miss even a second of her face so perfect, so near. "What if you find, even with free will, that you love me so much you can't let me go?"

*Please don't ever go,* his mind cried, every inch of him, magic and body alike, begging for her to stay right where she was, in that moment, forever. He didn't even know if he could handle another bout of separation.

"What if you find you love me so much that *you* can't let *me* go?" he dared.

Her eyes widened barely a fraction. She quickly hid the surprise from him before he could discern what else was there. "Answer me."

"I will never go back on my word. Your life will be your own." He breathed in, then let out a pained exhale. "I would let you go."

For the first time since their eyes had met, something not unlike relief seemed to flash across Destruction's face. Relief and what Creation thought—hoped, pleaded—was akin to fondness.

"You would give me up?" she repeated, barely a note to her voice, though Creation heard each word like a song, one that his entire being mourned despite its beauty. When she pulled him in further by his neck, he selfishly let it happen. This might be the closest she ever wanted him to be, so he sank into her touch, allowing himself to pretend.

Closing his eyes to whatever his words might illicit in her, he gave her what she wanted. "I would do anything you asked of me."

There was no way for him to prepare for the sensation of his companion's lips against his own. It was even more overwhelming than that first tickle of her magic in the air, more all-encompassing than their first moment of physical contact. More primal. It sunk deep, deep into Creation's being, made it sing with new life.

Though he was only half-aware—too lost to the feel of Destruction's teeth against his bottom lip, her tongue soothing the bite—he swore her nails dug into his scalp. He wrapped her up in his arms, pulling her chest to chest with an arm around her waist and a hand tangled in her hair.

Even as his lungs were straining for air, he still felt as though he was breathing for the first time since awakening to this new form.

Just as quickly as she had lured him in, sunk into every fiber of him, Destruction pulled away. Again, that voice that screamed to keep her close protested, an arm reaching to pull her back, though he stopped himself in time.

Destruction watched his movements with wary eyes. She was testing him; he knew it and he let her. He would pass every test she gave him if that's what it took to win her favor.

When Destruction turned her back on him, he let her walk away without a single protest.

He had expected it, had been waiting in agony for her to run away from him again since the moment he'd stepped onto the secluded beach, but it still ripped him apart as he watched the line of her back and the wave of her hair vanish quickly from sight.

# FIVE

**T**HE FLOORS of the pantheon were like ice on Creation's bare feet. Landing on the great balcony he had descended from hours, days, perhaps months ago—he knew of the passage of mortal time, but tracking it was unimportant to him—Creation was met with an oddly foreign world. The Light's throne was dim, the god's attention elsewhere, and Creation found it to be an unexpected relief.

This should be his home, but all Creation could muster was a cautious ambivalence toward it.

As Creation walked in the main room, his suspicions only grew. None of the divinities seemed to be present. Could they perhaps know his plot with Hunt?

Slight movement from behind had Creation leaping forward toward his would-be attacker. He nearly lost his balance.

"Your own shadow will begin to startle you if you stay so on-edge." Hunt leaned against a large column, not unlike how he first met her. Her wolf paced back and forth between them.

"He's restless, too," Creation observed softly, more musing to himself. But Hunt surprised him with a response.

"So you can feel it then."

"Pardon?" His eyes returned to the goddess.

"Chaos. You can feel the havoc she's reaping." Hunt frowned and pushed away from the pillar, heading toward the balcony.

"What's happening?" He followed close behind on her heels.

"She's made a rather big play," Hunt said grimly, referring to Chaos, "and anomalies are popping up everywhere; the other gods descended to try to find her and pin her down . . . but she's just making sport of them."

"Has she found Destruction?" he asked quickly, his heart racing at the thought of Chaos taking the woman he loved so soon after the first taste of her.

"If she had, we would know." Hunt buried her hand in her wolf's fur, giving it a rough scratch. "I'm headed down there now to join the fight."

He watched as she poised to take flight to earth, toward whatever madness Chaos had wrought. Uselessness settled on his shoulders, weighing him down. "What can I do?"

"The fact that Chaos hasn't found her yet may be your doing already." Hunt paused at the edge. "Your magic is a counterweight to Destruction's. It may be helping reign her in, keep her tethers from running out so far that Chaos could easily pursue her." The goddess tilted her head, as if ruminating on the idea. "Perhaps that's why Chaos is beginning this assault. If she can't hunt Destruction as she used to, then she may just be trying to burn her out like a fox in a den."

This was the reality; Creation had no strength to refute it. Now he needed to search for usefulness beyond merely chasing Chaos like the rest of the pantheon. "Your weapon. I could make it now, while everyone is distracted. You could have your champion use it—"

"We don't know where Chaos is, just where her magic has been wrought. I couldn't navigate my champion there in time, and she is still being trained. However, you are speaking some sense . . .." Her wolf gave a small huff and sat heavily on its haunches, as if frustrated with the holdup. "Come, I think I've found a suitable workshop for you. That is where we can begin working on the weapon."

"Where is it?"

"Your kingdom," she teased.

"My . . . kingdom?"

Hunt laughed. Without another word, she stepped off the balcony and disappeared, leaving Creation scrambling to catch up.

He landed on light feet at the edge of a great city (by mortal standards) made of stone and wooden shingled rooves. The air was thin and cool, a light breeze ruffling familiar trees. Creation turned, trying to place where he knew it from.

"This is—"

"Aristonia," Hunt finished for him, beginning to walk. Once more, Creation followed without question. "It's where you first found her. A town to the northwest of here is where you performed your first miracle for the mortals alongside Light, setting them to speak wonders of you."

Back on the earth, he sensed Destruction once more, though vaguely. One kiss, and their bond had deepened enough that he felt he could find her nearly anywhere without Hunt's help. But he resisted the urge. She desired him to let her go . . . for now.

"The king of the land lives here, in the capital city of Goddik, and he has decreed that the '*Prince of Gods*'"—Creation recognized the moniker the mortals had used for him—"will be his family's patron divinity. They even repurposed a temple to you."

"A temple?" Creation paused mid-step. "To me?"

"Sometimes I think mortals have little else to do than revere us. As if we will be able to truly do anything to help them. We can barely do anything to help ourselves right now." Hunt came to a stop as well.

Before Creation could defend the work that Light did on behalf of mankind, and would continue to do once Chaos was destroyed, Hunt raised a hand and pointed. Atop a hill, wide and winding stairs led to a large structure on the edge of the city.

"May I present your temple," Hunt said dramatically with a small smirk.

"This . . .is for me?"

"Yes." She began walking as she spoke. "They outfitted it for you, and because it has been deemed in your honor, there's power here, a sort of barrier if you will that prevents unwelcome gods from spying or entering. When Earth told me of it, I thought it'd be perfect for our purposes."

"Then I could just . . ." Creation's words trailed off mid-sentence. *I could just hide her here*, was what he was going to say. But Destruction wasn't some trinket to be stored away in a vault.

"Yes, I doubt she'd take kindly to the idea," Hunt agreed, easily hearing his unspoken statement. "And the barrier is not quite a tangible force—more of an etiquette among gods. Anyone who trespasses will feel a general discomfort. And, even if Chaos somehow couldn't just stroll in, then she would rattle these foundations to their core to get to Destruction . . . But I think it will be a good place for you to make me my weapon."

They arrived at the entrance of the temple, the doors pulled open. Creation wandered ahead, awed by the delicate stonework lining the atrium, the various tools of craftsmen held up on pedestals. At the far back hung a portrait of, he assumed, him, judging from the swoop of white hair across the painted man's face.

Hunt clearing her throat brought him back to reality. "You need to invite me into your temple, that whole barrier-not-barrier thing."

"Oh, right. Please come in, Hunt," Creation said, hoping he didn't need to be any more ceremonious than that. Her step in assured him he didn't. "We're here, what now?"

"Let's find a space we can work."

The two began to explore, walking through the various halls and rooms of the temple. It was more like a palace, really, on the inside. Toward the back, behind the main congregation area, they stumbled on an elderly man donned in yards of white fabric.

"Prince of Gods." He fell to his knees. "Goddess Mielikki."

Creation glanced at Hunt on hearing the strange name. He would never understand the mortal's need to give a name to everything. It seemed much easier to call the pantheon by that which they were the patrons of. Or, at least have all mortals agree on a singular set of names. But he didn't correct the mortals who referred to Light as Zeus and he certainly wouldn't start now.

"You honor this lowly priest of creation with your presence. How may I be of service to your cause?"

"I have come to inspect my temple," Creation said with an air of authority. "Is there a place I may take rest and work?"

"Yes, of course, the God's Wing has been prepared for you. All craftsmen of the city have left offerings for you there."

"Show me."

The man led them back toward the entrance and off to the side, up a narrow spiral stair, and through a heavy door. "These chambers are not touched, save for offerings. I shall tell your acolytes you have come to honor us. You will hear them sing joyous praise to you for hours to come."

"Thank you," Creation wasn't sure what else there was to be said. He was grateful for it all, but had asked for none of this.

"It is our honor, Lord Snow." The priest gave one more bow—so low he almost fell flat on his face. Then, one to Hunt. "Lady Mielikki." With that, he quickly departed.

"Lord Snow?" Creation repeated, starting through one of the three doors that branched off the landing.

"It seems you received your first mortal name." Hunt gave a small grin. "At least it's a fairly simple one."

"Though it makes no sense," he sighed. Snow had more to do with "God of Winter," as one mortal had incorrectly called him, than creation.

"Perhaps your hair and general glow?" she suggested. Further conversation on mortals and names was cut short as Creation opened the door to a modest but exceptionally well put together workshop. There were tools of every shape and size and long wooden tables and wide beams along the stone ceiling.

"This is all for me?" Creation wondered aloud, looking back to the landing. *What was hidden behind the other two doors?*

Hunt's fingers ran lightly along the surface of a table. "Just wait until you have shrines popping up everywhere—little ones in small towns, big ones in cities. You never know what you'll find there. The offerings really are a delight to pick through."

"I suppose we'll see when we get to that point," he said, pretending to be optimistic. Nothing felt guaranteed as long as Chaos lived, not even the next morning's sunrise. Which brought Creation to the reason they came to this particular corner of the world. "About your weapon . . ."

"Yes." Hunt crossed to the table. "The champion I have in mind will be an archer."

He could've guessed, given the large bow strapped to the goddess's back. "So you'll need a bow and arrow, then?"

Hunt paused, thinking. Strumming her fingers along the table, she finally shook her head. "Just the arrow. I don't want a bow of god-like power roaming the world."

"But an arrow that can kill a demigod roaming the world is fine?"

"Don't try to impress too much logic on me, Creation. I'm a 'shoot first, ask questions later' kind of woman."

Just the kind he liked, if Destruction was any measure. "Very well, just an arrow then."

Creation lifted his hands off the table, envisioning what he would like to make. Warm, yellow light began to hover in the air, condensing into lines like a blueprint. This would be far more complex than making his clothing.

"One other important thing," Hunt said quickly. Creation glanced at her. "Make it so no godly hand can touch it but yours and mine."

"What?" His hands fell, and the light faded. But a new light dawned on him. "You do not want to risk it falling into Chaos's hands."

"Yes," Hunt said grimly. "I know you will die before giving it to her, as will I."

"You don't trust the rest of the pantheon?" Creation felt like he should be surprised by the fact, but he wasn't. In truth, some part of him felt suspicious. Perhaps it was the corner of him dedicated to Destruction and her wariness bleeding over into his own mind.

"Motives shift faster than the weather. Gods do as it suits them. I only trust myself and those I'm forced to."

Creation nearly asked if she trusted him as well, but quickly backed away from the question. It didn't matter. She didn't need to trust him; they just needed to work together. They just needed to kill Chaos. At the least, he knew she trusted they both had an invested interest.

So Creation lifted his hands once more, allowing the light to condense —now with a new thought in his mind. *Let no one touch this but Hunt and I.* Yet Destruction crept in his head and, like always, he did not have the will to push her away.

# FOUR

Hunt left as soon as the arrow was complete.

With only a brief thank you, she was gone, leaving him almost dazed by her swift departure. He sunk into one of the chairs and tilted his head toward the ceiling. Crafting such a perfect and powerful weapon had truly drained him; it appeared his well of power only *seemed* infinite.

The momentary exhaustion passed, however, and Creation was on his feet again. With Hunt off to deliver the arrow to her chosen champion, he had time to indulge his curiosity surrounding the other two doors of his godly quarters.

"Let's see what the mortals think I need . . ." he mumbled, opening the door directly across from the workshop. It led to yet another staircase that wound up and around a different landing. The room was circular, but empty. He couldn't help but wonder what the mortals ultimately intended to do with it.

Creation started back down the steps and tried the final door at the end of the first hall. This one was painted white and he didn't know what he expected, but it certainly wasn't the lavish bedroom that waited on the other side.

Tapestries hung on the walls and a fireplace in its center that Creation went to on instinct. With a dip of his wrist and twitch of his fingers, a fire flickered into existence, instantly replacing the blues and purples of late evening along his walls with orange and yellow. He looked at the way the firelight played on the walls, the four-poster bed, and the lush rugs underneath his feet. Creation walked over to the window, gazing below at the hedges that surrounded the temple—palace, more like, as it was truly fit for a king.

*Or a Prince of Gods*, he supposed.

A sudden thrumming across the ether of his magic cut his exploration short.

Creation sensed Destruction the moment she set foot within the kingdom of Aristonia. Turning, he began walking hastily, a pace that quickened to a near sprint as her presence grew. Though, as he approached the main temple doors, he made it a point to slow his stride, catch his breath and steady his mind.

He had no way of knowing why she was here, just like he had no way of truly knowing why she'd left at the beach. After the way it had felt to finally hold her in his arms, to finally connect with her on the level his magic had been designed to crave, she had run.

Perhaps she was only here to do him the kindness of a final goodbye.

Creation's heart ached at the thought. But even as the possibility loomed just on the other side, he knew he was beyond denying himself her presence, even if it was the last time she were ever to allow it.

So, focusing on the silent pull of her magic, Creation opened the door and laid eyes on her for what felt like the first time in centuries.

"I was starting to think you'd keep me out here in the cold forever," Destruction said without preamble. She stood with her back against the stone curve of the archway, arms crossed over her chest in a perfect imitation of indifference—easily offset by the slight tilt of a smirk at the corner of her lips. Whether it be the spike in his magic from their last interaction —their *kiss*—or something more intangible, Creation couldn't fathom, but the longer he was in her proximity, the less he was inclined to believe that this feeling coursing through him was anything less than real, true, and entirely *his*.

"It took a moment to convince myself you would truly come," Creation admitted in return. The words *you have no reason to* went unspoken, but Destruction's smirk falling and her darting away said it was heard regardless. Despite himself, Creation felt guilty; she was given no choice in this connection forcing them together.

Yet, she was still here, without explanation, and it was easy to succumb to his own hopeful imaginings of the reason for her appearance.

So, before she could shatter that hope, Creation remembered what Hunt had said about the temples and spoke hastily. "Please, come in. You are always welcome here."

"I don't know about always," was what her mouth said, but her feet said a different story as she strolled into his temple as if already owning the place.

Destruction gave a low whistle. "Barely a demigod for a few years in mortal time and they've already gone out of their way to see this repurposed for you." Creation was too busy watching her every movement to ask—or even care—what it had been repurposed from. "Then again, I guess that's what happens when you're the favorite of a king."

"I am certain your temples are twice the size."

"I'm Destruction; mortals aren't too fond of that." She shook her head. "I don't have temples. I have a small chalet I've made my own and that's about it."

He resisted the urge to ask where. "They will be fond of you when they see—" *us together*, Creation stopped himself short, hastily recovering "—how much good your powers can do."

Destruction gave a small smile that was almost . . . sad? He wasn't used to seeing her vulnerability and wasn't sure if she was used to showing it.

"They'll always see me as part of Chaos, with the way she hunts for me. She's done me no favors by making sure even the mortals know that I'm 'hers.'"

*Hunt. Chaos.* The two words brought him back to the present. "Come this way," Creation ushered her toward the stairs, asking as they walked. "Is that why you've come? Because Chaos is hunting you?" *Or is it because you wished to see me?* was the question he dared not ask.

Destruction merely hummed, offering no further response. Creation didn't pry; he was too afraid of the answer.

He opened the white door at the end of the hall, inviting her in to the comfortable room he'd begun to think of as his own. Just like the temple doors before, she entered as if she owned the place. But as far as he was concerned, she did. There was no chamber or quarter he would ever bar her from entering.

Creation closed the door behind her, savoring one more blissful moment of pretending that this was real. That nothing else existed but the room they were in and nothing else mattered but their love . . . or him trying to earn her love. But reality weighed heavily and would for as long as Chaos walked the earth.

"Speaking of Chaos . . . Hunt has enlisted a champion to be her marksman against her," he explained, walking over to the flames still burning in the fireplace. Holding out a hand he created a few logs of wood, depositing them at the base of the fire. "I've created an arrow fit to pierce the heart of a demigod. She's bringing it to that champion now, so soon you will have your freedom." He paused. "So if that was the knowledge you've come here to seek, you now have it . . ."

He didn't want her to go, never wanted to watch the sight of her back but he also vowed never to force her to stay. He kept his eyes firmly pinned on the hearth, waiting for the sound of her departing footsteps.

She'd seen his temple, had a reprieve, and received an update. Surely business.

Instead of fading away, however, her steps grew closer, until she appeared in his periphery.

"It'll never work," she said softly, reaching a hand out towards the flames. "If Hunt's plan is to hinge this all on a single mortal and one shot then, she will fail. I've seen what Chaos does to mortals . . . she's far too strong to fall for something like that. We'll have to think of our own solution."

Creation watched her face. *She dismissed all his work so easily.* From the corner of his eyes he saw her fingers breach the pyre, though no pain marred her face. In a crackle of magic, the fire roared and then died, a single breath between life and death. Creation imagined seeing the darkness bleeding into her skin, sucking the warm yellow glow from her cheeks.

He was so distracted that he almost missed the implication of her words. "We?" Creation's heart hammered as Destruction captured his gaze. Even in the renewed darkness, she seemed illuminous; in any light, it was impossible for him not to see every detail of her beauty.

For a long moment, Destruction simply scanned his face, searching for something—*waiting* for something, perhaps. When she spoke, the look never shifted, never wavered to reveal her thoughts or intentions, yet it was impossible not to hear the half-truth lying underneath.

"My freedom depends on the success of all this," she said, turning to face him fully. "I run all possibilities over in my head and it becomes clearer and clearer to me that you have no chance at defeating Chaos without my help." Then, as if it physically pained her to say so, she added through gritted teeth, "I understand her better than anyone, demigod and god alike. I have to be involved in whatever end she meets."

"You are not like—" Creation began to say before he could stop himself, a hand already reaching for her, the tips of his fingers just grazing the bare skin of her upper arm.

Instantly, the smoldering embers within the hearth caught flame, shining a light on the curiosity in Destruction's eyes. She seemed surprised by his half-formed sentence. Or perhaps at the overwhelming magic rippling between them at such a simple, barely-there touch.

"I am not like . . .?" she whispered once the flames died down and the silence had stretched on long enough. Yet, neither of them made a move to pull away.

"You are not like Chaos," Creation whispered. He desperately needed her to know that, though where it stemmed from, he was unsure. He simply needed her to believe in her own autonomy, her own personality, her own power as much as she claimed she did.

"How do you know? You have never met her or even seen her, have you?" Destruction raised an eyebrow at him, though her eyes glittered not with annoyance or stubbornness, but with mischief. As well as something Creation couldn't quite identify so much as feel—like a tingling beneath his skin.

Creation took a selfish moment to raise a hand to Destruction's cheek, thrilled at her eyes automatically fluttering closed. Just that simple touch alone filled him with an indescribable rightness. He knew she felt it, too.

"I may have been made for you, Destruction," he willed himself to say after allowing one more moment to bask in the feel of her closeness. "But that doesn't change what my magic, what my *heart* recognizes. I don't need to have met her—I know *you*. And that's all that matters."

"And what do you think you know?" Destruction's words fell in a breath against his palm, causing a shiver to run down his spine. He wrapped an arm around her waist and led her a little bit closer. She didn't pull away or tense, didn't even hesitate, lips shaping a smile she seemed unable to bite back.

"You may have once been the other half to Oblivion," Creation answered, filling his words with every ounce of honesty he possessed. "But now, you are the other half to my own. Whether you wish to stay by my side or not, the fact that I am your perfect match is a truth I will forever be grateful for. And, I have seen in you a woman all her own, unbeholden to anyone or anything else." His thumb dragged across her cheekbone.

"If I didn't know any better," she smirked, swaying into him further as if pulling him into a silent dance. "What you're describing almost sounds like love."

*Love.*

Of course it was love. Of course this pull, both within their magic and within each other, was nothing other than love. He had never been more certain of anything in the entirety of his existence. But to be made as a counterbalance and to be in love were two different things, and he was suddenly desperate for her to know which path he craved.

"I had never loved until the moment I saw you, and now will never love anything as much."

Destruction blinked, mouth slightly agape, before she was letting out a soft, breathy laugh. Any distance that remained between them was gone, their bodies flush together. Heat coiled tight in Creation's stomach. His heart stuttered.

"You love me," Destruction whispered, carding her fingers through the short strands of hair at his nape, fingernails dragging against his skin. She hummed as if in thought, her ministrations never stopping. "Close your eyes."

This time, it was Creation's turn to look confused. "What?"

"Close your eyes," Destruction repeated, the smirk from before pulling at the corner of her lips. "I want to try something."

With his eyes closed, the heat of her hand on his neck, her arms around his shoulders, seemed to intensify. When plush lips pressed first feather light and then more intently against his own, he registered no other sensation at all. The universe narrowed down to the feel of her tongue asking for permission, which he easily granted.

He melted into the kiss, thrilled to soak into each shared breath, each smothered moan. Eventually, when the kiss deepened, the same primal and desperate feeling from on the beach began to rise within him. Creation's grip on Destruction's waist tightened as he forced their pelvises flush.

Destruction gasped. Heat boiled low in his belly at the sight of her. He dove back in for another fierce kiss, lowering his arms to her upper thighs so he could pick her up, get her as close as possible. Destruction wrapped her legs around his waist and moaned at the shift in friction. Creation was almost stunned to find himself suddenly lowering her to the bed, his legs on autopilot.

For a moment, she simply rolled her hips against his growing hardness, a motion that had his eyes drifting back in pleasure. But he wanted more. Truly, he wasn't sure exactly *what* he wanted. All he knew was that he needed to be as close to her as she would allow him to be, and his body seemed to have no problem pointing him in the right direction.

Instead of dipping back in for another kiss, as much as he wanted to—he wanted so much, too much, more than he'd ever wanted before—Creation lowered his lips to just below the hollow of her ear. She shuddered, a breathy sound leaving her parted lips. He gently nipped at her pulse point before kissing away the small mark, humming contently when one of her hands tangled in his hair.

"I want you," Creation said, his voice alien and rough to his own ears. Destruction nodded, letting her legs drop and pulling on his hair to get him eye to eye.

"I want you, too," she breathed.

Creation buried his face in the crook of her neck, groaning at the desire that coursed through him. It took everything he had to pull away just enough to shed his clothing. Destruction watched him disrobe, eyes traveling his half-naked body with shameless appreciation, before joining him. She kept his gaze as she removed each layer of clothing. They stood naked before each other in mere moments.

Destruction backed into the center of the bed, and Creation wordlessly followed, arms caged on either side of her head.

Mesmerized, they admired each other for a long breath, their magic mingling between them. When they finally recovered that minute distance,

Creation lowered himself in for a kiss that pressed them skin to skin —electrifying.

The heat of her skin, her nails raking down the taut line of his back seared him. His hands traveled from her shoulder, hip, and back, cupping the swell of her breasts. He pinched each nipple between finger and thumb. Destruction's back arched off the bed, her head falling back in pleasure, a pleasure that Creation felt like a second skin.

"*Creation*," Destruction moaned. Her hand disappeared from his back to reach between them, wrapping her fingers around his length and guiding him towards her. "Creation, *please*."

With her consent written so plainly on her face, in her words, Creation slowly thrust forward.

He was met instantly with tightness and heat, though the wetness between her legs had him gliding easily to the hilt, the two of them connected as deeply as they could be. Creation kept himself still, allowing Destruction to adjust, and listened to their panting breaths until she started rolling her hips, pulling him in deeper.

Creation groaned, leaning into the thrust and shuddering. Destruction gasped, voice cracking in pleasure as his name escaped her lips over and over again until he smothered that voice with a rough and passionate kiss.

Her ankles locked at the small of his back as Creation picked up speed, chasing the sensation that his magic, his heart, his very *essence* seemed to be searching for. Destruction met him thrust for thrust, the kiss deteriorating into nothing but shared gasps and the wet brush of lips.

Around them, the fire flickered and blazed and the plants strewn about in corners died in mass before being reborn even more lush than before. But Creation paid little mind to anything but the woman writhing beneath him, the most beautiful woman and demigod. The love of his life—this one, the next one, and all others.

"Yes, my love, yes," Creation moaned, his love for her growing alongside the heat at his core until he feared it would kill him with its intensity. But there was surely no greater death.

Whether it was his words or the pace of their coupling reaching its peak, Destruction cried out, back arching against the onslaught of her release. Her tightening around him was all he needed to follow her over the edge. He held her in his wave of ecstasy, allowing it to drown them both.

# THREE

DESTRUCTION STOOD at the window, staring out at the world below.

Creation continued to lounge on the bed, admiring how the early morning sunlight seemed to cut her form from darkness and hugged all those womanly curves perfectly. She hadn't said anything in a while, but he found himself content with the silence. There was something perfect about the moment.

She, however, did not seem to share the same feeling.

"It must be nice," she said finally.

"Admiring you from this vantage truly is," he quipped back.

Destruction turned, a coquettish smile playing about her cheeks. But that was all the reward she gave him for his remark before turning back to the world. "Being admired—it really must be nice."

That grabbed his attention, the atmosphere in the room shifting despite his desire to bask in the afterglow a while longer. "Admired? By the humans?"

"Yes." Her voice had gone soft with thought. "They've given you this whole place, a temple—a *palace*—in your honor. They call you the prince of gods. Even their king has decreed you as their patron."

"They misunderstand what I am." Creation finally pulled himself out of bed, trying to also right her unease with the situation in the same breath. The floor was cold underneath his feet and his whole body seemed to ache in the most pleasant of ways from their prior passions. "They saw me one time with Light and think I am his true son, his protégé."

"Son," she whispered, her back still turned to him. "Sons and daughters, a construct that they have, but that we will never truly know."

"My love, of what do you speak?" She was talking in riddles. Pleasant ones, because the riddles were entirely in her own voice, but riddles nonetheless. Creation rested his hands on her bare hips and kissed the skin of her shoulder.

"Gods don't have children as they do. We can't breed—we split or we craft. But that's not true children or families, is it?"

"Does this trouble you?" He rested his chin on her shoulder, looking beyond and trying to see the world as she saw it. Below his tower, men and women went about their business on the city's edge.

"It doesn't trouble me. It just is." Her voice trailed off. "I've been thinking a lot about humans lately."

"You've been thinking about a lot of things. I can almost hear the thoughts rushing around." Straightening, Creation stepped slowly around her side, hand trailing along her hip to the small of her back. With a gentle grasp of her chin, he lightly tugged her attention away from the mortals below and to him. "Tell me what has been occupying your mind?"

"I fear the outcome if I do."

"You should fear nothing with me." He lowered his face slightly, just enough to look her right in the eye. Their noses almost touched. "I would never intentionally bring you harm or give you cause to feel pain." He paused. "I know whatever it is you have been thinking about is significant, as your opinions toward me continue to shift."

"My opinions are shifting in no small part thanks to you and your actions." She gave a brief smile, just long enough for Creation to return.

"But it's more than that. What is it?" His thumb lightly trailed over her cheek.

"It started on the beach, with what you said—Hunt's idea of killing Chaos . . . that I will only be free when she's gone."

"And we will see her dead," he vowed. As far as Creation was concerned, there was no other way forward for him. Light saw him to be the mate of Destruction—the natural counterpart—but that would be impossible if Chaos did not first meet her end. "I swear to you. I made the arrow myself."

"Yes, yes, I know you do. And I am sure the arrow is impeccable." Destruction pulled away slightly, looking back toward the window. "But what if Hunt's convoluted plan doesn't work? What if her champion falters?"

"She has been training her champion herself."

"What if that's not enough?"

Her questions were beyond his control, so Creation remained silent. No matter what reassurances he offered, her mind would still return to the same panic as before. "So what is your plan?"

Destruction hugged herself, not out of modesty—Creation doubted if the woman even knew what modesty looked like (as she shouldn't)—but out of hesitation. It come off her in waves.

"You said you would love me, in any age."

"I did and I will."

"I want to see that true."

"What are you saying?"

"I think . . .I can destroy this world."

Seven words had his magic rallying in objection. Seven words sent sparks along his skin. *Destroy the world?* There was nothing more horrible to Creation.

"You don't like it." She laughed softly, glancing at him. "I can feel it."

"I don't like it. But I love you." This was his mate. He would hear her through and hope that there was perhaps something more to her words. He wrapped his arms around her waist, tugging her close. "Tell me what you would create."

"What I would see destroyed, you mean," Destruction corrected. Then, sighing softly, she unloaded her thoughts. "A god split makes demigods, right?"

"Yes. Unless the demigod is one such as I and has been formed by greater gods."

"Well, a demigod split is made mortal." Something in Creation resonated truth to the statement so he made no objection, allowing her to continue. "If I were mortal, I could not be targeted by Chaos. I would be useless to her to make Oblivion, in such a state."

"If you were made mortal, you would die." His grip tightened around her. He didn't want a single lifetime with her; he wanted eternity.

"I would, but . . ." She sighed again. "Very well, here's my thought. If I were to split myself, or be split, part of me would be mortal and the other part of me would be my raw divine essence.

"You could craft a container, a box of sorts, to keep that essence within. As long as it survives, I could never truly die. The other lingering part of my magic and soul would perpetually seek it out."

"We have no proof of that." Already, visions of his Destruction fading away into nothingness flooded Creation's mind.

"But you have no proof otherwise, and it *feels* right, doesn't it?" Despite his reluctance, his godly intuition agreed with her. "You could use that magic, and with it, you could destroy this world."

"And destroy your mortal form with it."

"But I would return as a mortal again, in a new world—a world you created with your own two hands. I've felt the magic unleashed from the destruction of worlds when I destroyed the stars. I know you would have enough power to usher in a new age. Then, there, my soul would return in a new body, looking for its magic, for its other half." Destruction turned in his arms, cupping his cheeks. "Looking for you."

He couldn't tell if she was saying this just to appease him, to win him over to her cause, or because she truly believed the words. But, no matter what the motive, they had the desired effect. He would do anything in the world for her.

"You could give me my magic back and with that I would stand by your side as a demigod. We would rule a new age, just you and I."

"You're asking to kill the pantheon, to kill this world," he whispered.

"And I don't ask it lightly." Destruction shook her head. "Despite my name and magic, I don't celebrate wanton destruction. I celebrate the natural breakdown of the universe, feeding its natural order. But I don't know if there will be any other way to be truly free. I can't explain it . . . but I'm not confident in Hunt."

"You don't know her." Creation nuzzled her cheek.

"Neither do you." Destruction tilted her head, kissing his lips gently. "Think on my idea. Go back to Hunt if you must. I have faith you'll see this is the best way."

Creation was helpless to do anything more than nod. Even if he offered resistance and even if it was well-founded, he couldn't protest her. She was everything to him, and if she wanted the world only to destroy it, then he would give it to her.

Perhaps Light had made them too perfectly matched, for Creation was discovering he was truly loyal to only her.

"I will see what the status is with Hunt, and I will return to you. Hopefully she has already made strides in finding Chaos." Creation kissed her gently on the lips. "Stay here if you would like. If I am the mortal's prince, then you can call yourself my princess—though queen is far more accurate." Was that the faintest of blushes he saw on her tan cheeks?

Destruction nodded, looking back out the window. "Perhaps, it would be nice to have a home to rest in for some time. One that's slightly more sheltered than my own." She laughed, then added, mostly to herself, "It's comical how much your home and mine look alike."

Just that statement alone sent Creation's mind wandering. He daydreamed of a world to call their own, a place that would be wholly theirs. But first: Chaos. First, he had to find a solution that ensured his love's freedom.

To gain everything, he may first have to destroy the world.

# TWO

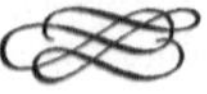

H E DECIDED to start his search for Hunt at the Pantheon, having
found her there last time.

But when Creation arrived, she was nowhere. In fact, no one
seemed to be present at all in the vast hallways and lush landscape
surrounding the domed building. *Perhaps they were all still off dealing
with Chaos?*

Creation passed through a massive entryway into a lavish and equally
massive room. He'd never been given the chance to explore the place of
his birth, but even so, he couldn't have imagined this: a lounging room
filled with finery. Silks in various deep colors—all warm tones—hung
about the walls and decorated plush furniture. Pillows were strewn about,
and incense swirled through the air in blue trails of smoke.

"Oh! You must be the new demigod!" A god approached him with a
smile. This must be Love.

It looked as though he'd taken to wearing one of the room's many silks
as a draping robe, the nakedness of his lithe, tan body still evident beneath.
His hair hung about his shoulders in multiple thin, dark brown braids and
his bright green eyes sparkled with excitement when he was within arm's
reach of Creation.

"It's Creation, right?" Love asked, placing a hand on each of
Creation's shoulders for a moment before pulling him into a tight embrace.
"It's a pleasure to finally meet you. I heard about your making from Life."
Love pulled away, eyes scanning his stunned face. "What brings about this
sudden return? Did you come to see me?"

Creation stepped back, not so much to put distance between them but
to catch his breath from the whirlwind of the presence before him. "No,

not you, apologies . . . I've come looking for Hunt. There's something I wish to discuss with her."

"Last I heard, the gods had gone to do some battle, and Hunt is not one to miss a battle."

That sounded right to Creation. He wondered if, despite Hunt's earlier words on it being too quick, the arrow had already been used. He almost hoped it had, because that would mean the notion of destroying the world would be off the table.

"Why aren't you with them?" he asked Love.

"I'm a lover, not a fighter." The man spun in place. "Have you checked the scrying pool for them?"

"No."

Crossing his arms over his half-naked chest, Love grinned. "Follow me."

He led him into the back of the quarters, to an ornate table, upon which was a large, marble bowl filled with water. Creation leaned in for a glimpse and saw nothing but the bottom of the bowl.

"Last I heard, Hunt was currently leading a group of warriors somewhere in Ollafùr," Love said, waving a hand over the water, causing ripples to expand from the center. "Let's see if we can find out where exactly, shall we?" He threw Creation a wink and the water began to shimmer with a newfound iridescence.

The rippling liquid now revealed faint shadows of movement, an image beginning to form. Hunt's visage was the first to solidify into something recognizable, the area around her hazy and out of focus. She appeared to be leading a group of men, her wolf charging along at her side.

"Yes, she seems to be within the Ollafùrian Wilds," Love explained his scrying as the images shifted. Creation watched, captivated, as Hunt drew an arrow from her own quiver and fired it swiftly and precisely—though at what enemy, he couldn't tell. "If you go now, you might be able to get to her before she leaves." With a wave of Love's hand, the images faded into nothingness.

"Thank you, Love," Creation said, pulling his gaze from the bowl and offering the god a smile. "I appreciate all your help."

"I'm here if you need me." Love winked again, and Creation chuckled softly to himself at the flirtatious display. The more gods he met, the more he began to realize how different they all were. How different *he* was from them all.

Once again, Destruction's words filtered through his mind, about being her own person, regardless of the god she used to be a part of. Even if Creation had been given life from fragments of the other gods, not split as she had been, he still hadn't even considered his own autonomy, his own *personality* until her. At least not in the ways that mattered. But now, he desired a chance to be himself, to be not just what he was meant to be, but what he *wanted* to be. And it was all thanks to Destruction and the love she'd chosen to give.

"Well, well, well. What have we here?" Love was suddenly leaning into Creation's personal space, his eyes mischievous. He lifted a hand to Creation's chest, fingers settling right over his heart. "This isn't the gods' work. Well, this isn't Light's work, at least. This is *mine*, and I've not laid a hand on you until now. How delightful it is to find it naturally occurring in one such as yourself."

If possible, his smirk grew wider, his eyes softening as he straightened back. Before Creation could register the transition, he was pulled back into a fierce hug.

"Oh, well done, you!" He laughed, lifting Creation from the floor and spinning him around in a full circle. Creation stumbled when he was put back down, not quite following the sudden shift in atmosphere. But when Love placed his hand back over Creation's heart, eyes shining and smile pure, it all fell into place. If possible, Creation's face grew hotter. "I'm proud."

Creation didn't know what to say to that, but his chest felt warm and his heart felt full, so he just nodded, offering up his own shy smile in return.

That seemed good enough for Love, the god patting him lightly against the cheek before stepping back and making *shooing* gesture between them. "Now off you go. Hunt should be finishing up soon. Go have your conversation so you can get back to the woman who truly matters to you."

"Thank you," Creation repeated, and with one last smile and nod, he rushed back through the Pantheon and descended from the gods' balcony towards the Ollafùrian Wilds. With any luck, Hunt would be done and away from the warriors by the time he arrived.

Destruction's plan was a brutal one, and something certainly not meant for mortal ears.

Something was off the moment Creation breached the border of the Wilds. Not in the air, but the atmosphere itself, like magic was spilling out from deep within the woods, tainting everything in its path. His gut reaction was to turn away, to avoid entering any further into the thick of it, whatever *it* was, but based off what Love had shown him, Hunt should be in there.

Despite each step sending a chill down his spine, Creation hurried forward.

He didn't need to go very far.

Just beyond a cluster of trees, a wave of sickening magic overwhelmed him. . Creation wasn't sure he would be able to breathe if he continued, but as a movement from within the brush caught his eye, he knew he had no choice.

The first assault was the smell, like iron and moss and something sickly sweet coming from his right, but despite its intensity, nothing could have prepared him for its cause. Hanging halfway up the trunk of a massive tree was the contorted form of a torso-less body, limbs splayed out like branches and a head partially hidden in crimson-soaked bark. A tree had sprout itself right out of the man's middle. Half of his face was locked in the shape of an anguished scream.

And he was not the only victim to such travesty. The farther into the wilds Creation walked, the more he saw. A man half-melted, his liquefied form dripping in hues of blue, purple, and pink. Three men tangled together by the elongated crisscrossing of their own limbs like some odd and nightmarish human braid. One young man lying limp and clearly denied of any oxygen within the confines of an iridescent, pink bubble.

It was a massacre built around insanity.

Around *chaos*.

Creation's feet dragged, his stomach souring further with each step. When he passed an archer, whose fingers had been turned into arrows, her body contorted into a grotesque rainbow-colored bow, Creation nearly got sick, turning away from the sight to catch his breath. . .

Only to find a familiar head of black curls and dark skin lying unmoving a few feet away.

Creation wasted no time, rushing to Hunt's side. He hoped she was simply unconscious from the attack. The moment his hand touched her shoulder, however, his hope shattered. That simple touch, a barely-there grazing of his fingers, had caused large chunks of her shoulder to chip and crumble away.

Creation wrenched his hand back, but the damage had been done. He watched in horror as the cracks and fissures spread throughout Hunt's prone form, breaking or crumbling away completely. Heart pounding, Creation inched his way around her, careful not to damage her further, until he could see her face.

The divine weren't supposed to be able to kill their own kind, but there was no life in Hunt's eyes. And as the cracks spread up her neck, her face, there were eventually no eyes at all. Chaos's magic broke every law they thought they knew.

She had forsaken the pantheon and all its rules with it.

A whimper from his left drew Creation's startled and horrified attention, his heart beating rapid-fire deep within his chest. Inches away from its master lay Hunt's wolf, fatally wounded and sprouting roses with blood-tipped thorns from between tufts of matted, dark fur. Creation reached for him, only to be met by fanged teeth and a rough growl. So he pulled back, doomed to do nothing more than watch as the animal dragged himself to his master and burrowed into her side.

That simple action, however heartfelt and desperately well-meaning, was the last push Hunt's body needed, the dismantled form of her shattering into pieces around the whimpering pet. The wolf howled once, a broken and mournful noise, then settled into the remains of his master and closed his eyes. Whether the wolf continued to live or not, Creation knew he would not move from his spot.

Creation needed to press forward. If Chaos had the ability to kill Hunt, to kill a *god*, then his and Destruction's mission was suddenly much more dire. And much more dangerous.

Destruction had been right all along: Nowhere was truly safe as long as her counterpart drew breath.

Sparing one last glance at Hunt's remains, her loyal pet unmoving, Creation took off in a sprint out of the wilds. Destruction needed to know exactly how high the stakes had just become.

DESTRUCTION WAS exactly where Creation had last seen her, last touched her.

Almost.

Now, rather than standing at the window, she lounged in his bed, waving one hand in thin air. The tiles that served as stars in the constellations on his ceiling shattered to the ground. Then Creation watched as they magically came back together and returned to the ceiling in a slightly new design.

"Your magic lives here." Destruction tilted her head toward him. "Every time I destroy something it has an instinct to come back together, though sometimes it's a little different."

He wanted to revel in the moment with her. Creation wanted to stop everything and hold her and pretend they could continue to explore the love and synchronicity they had only just found. But Hunt's death demanded to be the only thing on his mind.

"Hunt is dead."

Destruction's hand fell slowly to her side. She stared at him, processing the words. "Dead?"

"Chaos killed her." Creation tried shaking free the memories of the carnage. "Killed a whole party of her acolytes. I don't know if Hunt was tracking Chaos or merely at the wrong place at the wrong time. But, either way, Chaos killed her."

For another minute, Destruction seemed to stare at nothing. The silence was so absolute that Creation could almost hear the beating of her heart—low and slow—not nearly as panicked as his was.

"She is derived from Oblivion and was never a part of the pantheon . .

. I'm not surprised she could kill a god if she worked hard enough at it." Destruction pulled herself to her feet, the long, midnight-colored silks she had swathed herself in like a robe pooling around her and hanging off her shoulders. "But I'm confident because of this that my magic could destroy this world—this reality—as I am not beholden to the pantheon's rules either, then."

Her plan came back to him. If his heart wasn't racing before, it certainly was now, just like his feet were racing to close the gap between them. Creation rested his hands on her shoulders.

"We have no proof that my magic could successfully rebuild it."

"With that much power released from the death of a world, converted to pure magic, combined with and channeled through your own powers? I'm certain you could, Creation. You could do it simply . . . without gods."

"What about myself?"

"You'll stand at the apex of it all. You'll create a space outside of time first." Destruction lightly took his hands, lacing his fingers with her own. "This is the only chance we have at being together. Otherwise she will eventually find me. She will force me to rejoin with her and when that happens I will not be able to protect you. Oblivion will destroy everything to return the world to as it was before the gods—to that endless nothingness that she came from and thrives in."

They hadn't had enough time together. They hadn't been given *enough.*

"You will see me on the other side," Destruction whispered. "You will, I promise you. Bu you must do this for everyone."

"I know," he finally admitted. The world—the universe—would be destroyed if Oblivion reigned once more. So, if he failed, the outcome would be the same. If he succeeded, but she did not return, then at least all life—other than the gods—would be saved. And, truly, the god's time was limited with Chaos evolving to learn how to slay them.

His brain hurt just thinking about every wretched avenue, but each one rounded back to the singular fact that it was the only option available to them. Even at the cost of Life, Light, Carver, *Love,* it was the only option.

"I will find my way back to my magic and to you." She freed her hand and cupped his cheek. "Have faith in that."

Sealing her promise, Destruction leaned in, resting her lips lightly on his. Creation relished in the warm heat of her breath, savored it all.

Destruction pulled away, looked him in the eye, and whispered, "Let's do it now, before anyone else can find out and thwart us."

"Very well. First things first . . ." he began, thinking aloud, forcing himself to recall her earlier plan. "This way."

Creation led them from his room and to the right, into the workshop he'd used, what seemed like a mere hour ago, to construct Hunt's arrow.

Surely, it had been more time than that? Not that it really mattered; he was about to attempt to alter time and reality itself.

His eyes on Destruction the entire time, Creation used the feeling of her magic, the intimate knowledge he had of her, to fashion a small, silver box. He tried to imbue it with her essence—for that was what it would ultimately have to hold. The light formed underneath his hands once more, building the outline of the box in the air, slowly weaving together and condensing into pure silver.

All the while, her gaze remained locked with his. Destruction didn't stare in wonder, she didn't watch his work. She looked at him and Creation could only hope that it was because she was as desperate to memorize his shape as he was.

"What do you think?" he asked, finally pulling his hands away.

"This is more your area of expertise than mine." Destruction lifted the box, turning it over in her hands. "I don't feel the need to break it down, however. It's almost . . . familiar?"

"Then perhaps your magic won't try to break it down—or out—either." He hoped. They didn't really have time to test it, so Creation took her hand—the small box in the other.

"Where are we going now?" she asked as he opened the door across the hall.

"To carve a space out of time."

They arrived at the empty room he'd discovered earlier. Whatever purpose the room had been intended for, Creation was sure this wasn't it. He walked to the center of the room, stopping when her hand fell from his grip.

"Are you sure about this?" Destruction asked softly.

"Are you?" Creation felt a twinge of disappointment when she nodded in affirmation.

"Then it's what we'll do, what I'll do, for you. Or us, for this world." Words were becoming hard. Longing for her was already beginning to overwhelm him and she wasn't even yet gone.

"Thank you." Two words, barely more than a breath. Two arms, wrapping around him, holding him tightly—two more holding her back. Two kisses—one on his mouth, and one on hers.

Then, it was time for her very essence to become two as well.

"Be ready to capture my magic when I split, channel it to destroy the world, use the magic of that destruction—I'm sure you'll feel it as I do—and rebuild everything, and find me again."

"I will. I will not rest until I've found you again."

Destruction nodded, took a breath, leaned back, and unleashed her raw essence.

It didn't look painful. She looked almost serene. The center of her chest stretched upward and, then, as if a thread fraying, began to unravel. Magic poured from her in dark tendrils, stringing off and breaking free from the cage of her physical body. Creation watched every splitting of her body up until the moment her face broke apart into a continuous, shapeless, ribbon of pure magic.

Creation held up the box to that swirling mass of raw power. It seemed to rush in, as if it were looking for a place of refuge, as if *she* was commanding it. The box shuddered closed.

With the box resting in one palm, Creation lifted the other. Pointing his finger downward, he turned in place, drawing a circle in the stone floor. It shone with light before dimming into obsidian. The line created a barrier between him and time itself and the thickness of a warped atmosphere surrounded him.

*Time to destroy the world.*

Wrangling Destruction's power was nearly an impossible task. It bucked and resisted; yet, at the same time, it seemed eager to be at his behest. Creation pushed it outward, unleashing it past the barrier, into the world.

He shouted. His body was being torn apart and reborn again, like he was immolating on a cold flame—freezing and burning at the same time. What he was doing was the antithesis to all he was, yet it came almost like a dangerous second-nature.

The world unraveled just as she did. The pillars that Light had built against Oblivion's darkness shook and crumbled, tumbling, bringing the divine down with them. He witnessed the death of time itself, mourning it like an old friend, before seeing it reborn again, his own magic insistently —and finally—kicking in.

Such destruction was not what he was meant for. With an inaudible scream, his own magic fired off the fumes of a dying world. It rose like a phoenix, bringing a new age with it. *She had not been lying about the magic created from the destruction of a world.* He imagined mountains and valleys. He imagined the people and places he had been born with knowledge of but he hadn't yet seen. He pictured a perfect utopia filled with magic and every race.

Every race except for the gods.

Like a band stretched thin, his own magic jostled back into his body. Creation collapsed in his circle, panting. *And he had thought making Hunt's arrow had been difficult.* Magic radiated off him like the primordial afterbirth of a new world.

Blinking, Creation looked out the window—the roof had fallen in. Moss now grew in a room that looked like a hundred years had passed. Perhaps that much time had slipped by around him . . . Or, perhaps his temple still sat in ruin because there was no god for it.

Slow footsteps up the stairs interrupted his thought.

Creation turned, heart still racing. Surely, there was only one woman who would go in search of him. There was only one mortal who could know what this place was in this world without gods. He leaned back onto his heels, keenly feeling each footstep rumbling his very core. Would she look the same? But no matter what form she took, he would recognize her. He would know his Destruction without hesitation.

But it was not her. In fact, she was not a woman at all, but a *demigod*. A demigod that should be dead with the rest of the gods he'd blinked out of existence but wasn't.

"You must be Creation." Chaos's first words to him.

"You—" he doubled over, collapsing onto his hands and knees. "You should be dead."

"Funny thing, that." She hummed, twirling a finger in her long viridian hair. The asymmetrical ruffles of her skirts swayed as she approached leisurely, stopping at the edge of the circle. "Your plan was clever, I'll give you that. To think of splitting her and then rebuilding the world. To think that if she was gone, I'd have nothing to cling with and I'd just *poof* out of existence with the rest of them." She clapped slowly. "Not many divine would sacrifice all of their brethren for the world. How very . . . *Oblivion* of you."

She crouched on her hands and knees, leaning forward and tilting her head so her cheek was pressed against the floor by his forehead.

"But here's the thing you didn't think about—or she didn't, since it was her plan, wasn't it?" the demigod whispered to him like a lover across the pillow. "She was already half of a whole, a whole that won't die if only one part does. So if your plot was to rid the world of me just by splitting her and making her mortal, you failed. If your goal was just to destroy the world for entertainment, then you did a miraculous job of that."

"Where is she?" Creation growled into the ground, wishing his magic would recover faster. Wishing he was just strong enough to wrap his hands around this woman's narrow neck until she turned purple.

"I don't know. You made her mortal, so she's somewhere out there . . . but I can't seem to get a sense of where." Chaos sighed. "And, to make matters worse, this age—this *Age of Magic*—was not meant for Gods. You and I will fade away soon. Our powers seem to seep into the ether in this time."

She patted his back and with it, electricity shot straight into Creation's core. The woman was pure madness and disorder—an upset to the natural order itself.

"Don't worry though," she whispered into his ear. "I have an idea to spare us. You made this lovely little bubble outside of time. Why don't we expand on it?"

Chaos waved her hand and the world around them rippled. Creation lifted his eyes just in time to see reality stretching to the point of breaking. Rooms popped into existence, nonsensical, out of order, impossible. Chaos's magic surrounded him, and he was helpless to do anything to stop it.

"You and I, we'll live here, spread the word of a magical wish granter to the mortals. You can just keep destroying worlds at people's will for me until we find her and then I can take back what's rightfully mine." Chaos stood, walking toward the other side of the room where a mysterious door suddenly materialized into view. "Do take your time getting up. We're in for a long ride, you and I."

Be it the magic still sapping his strength, the crushing agony of their failure, but Creation's body moved of its own accord.

"Y-You can't . . ." His voice croaked. He stretched his hand in her direction, magic pouring out. The effect was minimal, most of his power drained, but it caused Chaos to pause, glancing a cat-like eye over her shoulder before turning around.

Despite his magic attempting to swirl around her, hold her in place, alter her design, something, *anything*, Chaos merely waved it away. Fury in his magic spiked and sought out new directives. The nonsensical amalgamations Chaos had brought into existence righted themselves into rooms filled with power and luxury. The layout of their new surroundings —their new *prison*—organized themselves into what Creation couldn't deny, in his agonizing, grieving half-daze, was a beautiful place.

A mansion outside of time and space.

As his magic finally stuttered and faded, Creation laying limp, Chaos knelt back in front of him, forcing his chin up. He met her eyes, her face blurring as his body began to collapse beneath the weight of all he'd done.

"You can't," he repeated through gritted teeth.

"I can't what?" Chaos purred, her breath on his face faintly registering as candy-sweet. "Creation, Lord Snow, Prince of Gods, protégé and son of the once-god Light? What can't I do?"

His tongue stayed numb and useless in his mouth.

Somehow, Chaos must have noticed the concession. She let his head fall heavily against the hard floor. Creation groaned, his already fracturing awareness fading further. Though not before he felt Chaos shift back to her feet, her words wrapping around the last vestiges of his consciousness like a noose.

"Pity," she sighed, possibly pouted. "Well, whatever it is you *think* I can't do, Creation, I guarantee you this: I can."

With that, Creation knew nothing but true despair. And darkness.

# THE BEGINNING, AGAIN

The mansion was quiet.

The Society's wish this time hadn't been particularly taxing, but there was always an exhaustion left behind in the wake of a session. More physical and magical for Snow—from the destroying and rebuilding of the world (though it had gotten easier with time)—and more mental for everyone else. It wasn't quite calming, but there was also a sense of contentment in seeing another job well done, another wish granted. They'd earned their rest, and Snow was more than willing to take some of his own.

"Somebody looks relaxed."

All at once, any hope of rest vanished, tension filling the room. To his right, Pan was situating herself with a flourish and a bounce directly into his personal space, bright green hair swinging about her shoulders. Snow frowned.

"It's impossible to be relaxed around you, Pan, and you know it," Snow replied, deadpanned, looking back at the members of the Society and ignoring the twist in his gut.

"You wound me, Snow," Pan replied, a giggle in her voice. Snow winced.

How long had it been? After so many years and countless wishes, time became convoluted and dense, overlapping and causing his memories to feel hazy. But when had it happened? At what point had they started referring to each other, to *themselves*, by the names the mortals had given them?

At what point had they gone from Chaos and Creation to Pan and Snow?

Somewhere around Eslar joining, if he was forced to guess. The High Elf and first member to remain in the Society always had suspicions about their true nature. But it was easier to leave it at "Snow" than explaining the circumstances that had brought what the mortals now called the "Society of Wishes" together.

The longer they were a part of this little envelope of timeless, ceaseless wish granting, the more their original selves chipped away. Snow closed his eyes, imagining tan skin, dark hair, a mischievous grin, and warm eyes. These memories, at least, would never fade. Even as Snow, he still loved her, that ache for her still as fresh as the day they were separated.

"Penny for your thoughts?" Pan nudged him with her elbow and Snow quickly schooled his face into one of blank indifference.

"Don't you have a nap to take?" *Or a hole to die in?* was what he really wanted to say.

"I'm bored," Pan whined, and even though Snow kept his eyes on the gathering of Society members in the common area, he heard the petulant frown she no doubt was sporting. "Bothering you is more fun than exploring the darkness behind my eyelids."

This, Snow chose to ignore. He watched as Samson bustled about the kitchen with Nico, the Italian man laughing and talking with their crafter. Samson's eyes shined with interest. Nico was a kind soul, warm like sunshine and filled with an easy happiness that Snow almost envied. Sometimes it felt like his happiness had been ripped apart with Destruction's body.

The sound of a curse pulled Snow's attention to where Wayne and Takako were locked in a game of strategy. It was clear who won by the smug look on Takako's face and Wayne's petulant demands for a rematch.

The pain of his situation was always a bit easier to bear when he saw his charges getting along, growing into their roles as a team, a family. None of them had asked for this burden, and being forced together for centuries to help him destroy and rebuild the world with wishes only added to the difficulty of it all. Yet, in moments like this, some relief could be found.

After Samson had joined them with his fateful wish, Snow had wondered dejectedly if they were doomed to live in silence, forced to shelter themselves to avoid more tragedy. Not that Snow blamed Eslar in any way for his immediate refusal to offer Samson any kindness. No, Snow blamed himself for his foolishness on that wish. But while time did not heal all wounds, it did tend to soothe, and even Eslar was not immune.

*Even he wasn't immune to the dulling effects of time, given how he let Pan sit at his side for more than a minute, at present.*

Eslar removed himself from a side table, book he'd been reading in hand, and walked into the kitchen to join Nico and Samson. What had once been tense and uncomfortable, sometimes even hostile between the two, was now softened, worn down with time. Samson smiled at Eslar as he approached, blushing with pride as Eslar said something to him and placed a hand on his shoulder. Snow couldn't hear the praise, but he saw it on the elf's face, practically felt it in the way Nico laughed and Samson preened.

The three men chatted amongst themselves, and for the first time in a while, Snow felt the contradicting tug of wanting to join them while simultaneously wanting to keep himself away from their little bubble of happiness and ease. He was their leader, their *warden*, and he owed it to them to keep them ignorant of what this place really was . . . lest he taint their experiences further.

Pan sighed dramatically, all but collapsing into his side in a stubborn lean. "You're boring, too, you know that? Just standing here, watching everyone like a creepy prison guard." Snow bit back his wince and stepped forcing Pan to stumble and right herself.

"Why are you still here then?" he asked, narrowing his eyes down at her, only to hesitate at the look in her eyes. He knew that look, remembered it like some distant memory of a dream. His heart began to sink even before Pan opened her mouth.

"Because I know something you don't," she said, straightening with a devious grin as she ran delicate fingers through her hair, each strand she touched streaking the bright green with a jarring fuchsia. "And I want to see your face when you find out."

Another contradictory sensation ripped through him. He'd waited so long, aching and desperate to see his love again, but things were different now. Their situation was different from what Destruction had wanted, what she'd given up her immortality for. And as much as he wanted to see her, he also wished she would never have to experience this life, from this trap and out of Pan's reach.

*Even if it meant never being near her again.*

But Snow knew he had no choice. Pan said, "We have a wish, Snow. A very special wish from a *very* special girl."

Despite his warring desires, Snow couldn't help the way his heart picked up at the thought, that longing he'd buried centuries ago returning full force. And based on the way Pan laughed cruelly, it was written all over his face.

"You'd best gather up the team, Snow," Pan continued through her giggles, stretching her arms over her head with a pleased sigh. Then, in rare seriousness, she turned towards him, her cat-like eyes shining and her grin every inch the chaotic embodiment of her namesake. "The real game is about to begin."

Just as quickly as the seriousness had come, it was instantly replaced with the childish demeanor he'd come to expect of Pan, her focus once again on the rest of the Society members, all of them blissfully unaware of what was to come.

"Such a cute little family," she hummed before heading down the hall towards the briefing room and, adding while Snow was still in earshot, "So sad that it's all about to end."

Snow watched her go until she was out of sight. Once they granted this next wish, everything would be out of his hands. What if it was too much? What if he couldn't protect the woman he'd given up everything for? What if all of this had been for nothing and Oblivion would yet reign? What if—

"Snow?" Nico's voice startled him out of his spiral. Snow's eyes jerked away from the empty hallway to his friendly face filled with concern. "Is everything all right?"

For a foolish moment, Snow considered saying no, considered telling the kindhearted man everything. But what good would it do? Nico didn't deserve to shoulder any of Snow's burden. None of them did. As much as it pained him, Snow worked his expression into something resembling confidence.

"I need everyone in the briefing room in five," he said, throat tight and stomach flipping. Nico's eyes widened a fraction and his hands tightened around his coffee mug, but he nodded nonetheless. Snow turned away without another word, legs carrying him on autopilot past the mansion's central four-way intersection as Pan's words swirled in his head.

*"We have a wish, Snow. A very special wish from a very special girl."*

His Destruction. His love. This time, no matter what came to pass, he would not let her go.

BE CAREFUL WHAT YOU WISH FOR

SOCIETY
of
WISHES

WISH QUARTET BOOK ONE

ELISE KOVA & LYNN LARSH

*to all those brave enough to wish*

# LONE STAR REPUBLIC

I T WAS HOTTER than Satan's tit outside, but Jo wore a fleece-lined hoodie zipped all the way up to her chin, a necessity so she wouldn't catch frostbite in the computer room. She swigged another gulp of RAGE ENERGY and continued to blind herself with the fluorescent light of the monitor set up eight inches from her face.

"How hard is it to get five monitors?" She slammed down her energy drink, rattling a pile of M&Ms and sending them scattering across the table.

"How hard is it to work on four?" her best friend—the only other person she'd seen for a month and, more importantly, the only other person she could tolerate in such close quarters—asked from across the room.

"No one asked you, Yuusuke." Jo rolled her eyes and took another hefty sip of neon-green juice. She wouldn't be surprised if, over the past twenty-four-hour hack-a-thon, she had slowly begun substituting the liquid for blood in her veins.

"Then who else were you asking?"

"Johnson here."

"Who the hell is Johnson?" Yuusuke pushed his chair back from his desk, leaning back so far he almost toppled over.

"Empty energy drink can number fifteen."

"Fifteen? Damn, Jo, you're going to straight-up give yourself a heart attack."

"Don't insult little Johnson." Jo picked up the can as she swiveled her own chair to look at Yuusuke. She brought the aluminum to her cheek, nuzzling it tenderly. Yuusuke gave a roll of his eyes, but she knew better.

He was the only one who could tolerate, not to mention find amusement in, her unique brand of pain-in-the-ass. So Jo milked it further in an attempt to make him smile. "He didn't mean it, sweetie."

"What hour are we on?" Yuusuke groaned and removed all levity by raking his hands almost violently through his hair. Most of it had fallen from his pony tail and now hung limply around his face. Dark stubble lined his chin, the patchy shadow almost the same shade as the purple bags under his eyes. Bags that no doubt mirrored those beneath her own.

"Twenty-five."

"We're screwed if we don't get a break," Yuusuke mumbled from behind his hands, rubbing his face as if to wake himself up. The motion prompted Jo to copy, realizing how heavy her own eyelids felt.

"We're screwed if we don't get a break*through*."

He muttered some kind of agreement, or expletive, or both, and returned to his computer.

Code and sequences ran across one of her screens. It was a little bit of software that could be used for a probing attack on crypto-currency databases, just like the one they were currently trying to crack into. Unsurprisingly, the Black Bank had one of the best security systems in the world. Unsurprising, really, since the bank was owned by the infamous hacker group, Incognito. It's why the payout for this particular job had been so impressive: only fools would take it.

She and Yuusuke were just such fools.

In the corner of her left screen, a little red bubble appeared with a '1' at its center.

"Message from the boss," Jo announced. She looked over her shoulder when there were no signs of life. Yuusuke's head bobbed, his giant headphones covering both ears. Jo took one of her fifteen energy cans and tossed it at his head. It missed, but struck his shoulder, still having the desired effect.

"What?" He nearly jumped out of his skin.

"Message from the boss," she repeated.

"Oh fu— what does it say?" Yuusuke stood and walked over to read their employer's most recent demand.

"Maybe they decided not to hack the most un-hackable thing on the planet?" Jo offered hopefully. The only way they were getting into the Black Bank's servers was if they actually broke into the room they were housed in and got to tamper *behind* the firewalls.

"Then we don't get paid and someone else gets the glory. Fat chance. And, anyway, we both know it's not what you want."

Jo clicked on the bubble and a tiny, encrypted window popped open. It was a small frame, a little portal to the world outside that neither of them had seen for two days now. It showed a barn in the middle of nowhere, adjacent to an unassuming farmhouse. High-efficiency solar panels lined the rooftops, feeding what Jo knew to be industrial batteries disguised as grain silos.

It was the barn in which they now sat. Underneath the picture were listed the current date and time. Then, a few lines of text, colder than the room in which they sat:

> **The Rangers have you surrounded.**
> **Do the honorable thing and purge all data.**
> **Thank you for working with us.**

"W-what's this nonsense?" Yuusuke tried to laugh off the message, but the wavering in his voice was reminiscent of the trembling in Jo's fingers.

She clicked on the image, dragged it to the desktop, and quickly cracked into its meta-data.

"It's from the Rangers." Was that froggy croak her voice? "The image originates from a Ranger server."

"Are you saying this is real?"

Jo swiveled in her seat, looking around the room. Server stacks were piled as high as the roof, consuming half the barn. It was supposed to be enough power to run whatever scripts they needed to break into the Black Bank on dedicated computers. It was supposed to be enough space to store several thousand terabytes of encrypted data. It was supposed to be their big payout.

Now, it was all just incriminating evidence that two citizens of the Lone Star Republic were co-operating with a foreign power.

She was on her feet, starting for the door—the *only* door. The only egress from their dark cave of code, back into the real world.

Her heart had wriggled up her throat with every beat and now seemed to throb so close to her uvula it was going to make her sick. Jo wiped her palms, slick with sweat, on her jeans.

"What do we do?" Yuusuke voiced her only thought. "You can't think you're just gonna walk out, do you?"

"I—"

"This is the Rangers. We have you surrounded. Come out with your hands up."

Yuusuke rattled off every expletive he knew like a magic spell, one that would get them out of being the meat in the shit sandwich they now found themselves in. "What do we do?"

"Let's turn ourselves in?" Jo clung to the final echo of the megaphone-filtered voice that was barely audible through the heavily insulated doors of the server barn.

"Turn ourselves in?" Yuusuke balked. "Have you lost your mind? You know what they do to people like us. They'll kill us, wipe us off the earth, and they'll take everything from our families—if they even let them live at all!"

There had been a growing trend of using the families of "digital terrorists" as examples to dissuade others from taking up the craft. She'd seen it happen to multiple acquaintances over the years, brilliant hackers whose loved ones had been slaughtered to make a point.

"What if we hide?" Yuusuke continued, wrenching her back to the present.

"Hide? Where?" Jo motioned around them. "In case you haven't noticed, we're in a box with nothing more than computer guts!"

"Better than your idea of feeding ourselves to them on a silver platter!"

There had to be a way out—there *had* to be. Jo's mind rattled as she swept her eyes across the room. Way out.

Way out.

Where was the way out?

The walls were double-layer insulated. They couldn't be burst through, and even if they could, they were surrounded.

"How did this happen?" Yuusuke groaned. He froze as if remembering something and suddenly advanced on her. "You. *You* wanted this job."

"Yuu, stop—"

"You wanted to do this. You dragged me into this. Aren't you supposed to be the sensible one between us? Keep me level and all that?"

"What happened to glory, huh?" Jo was yelling. Solved nothing, but screaming felt better than playing nice. "You had something you were all-too-eager to prove to the world."

"Oh yeah? What happened to playing it safe, Jo? Low and steady? Who's gonna support the family now?"

*Mom.* The thought stilled Jo, ice to her burning anger. The people she cared about most were the few things in the world that truly mattered to Jo. "We have to get out."

"We will open fire in THREE . . ." the Ranger announced.

"What're you doing?"

Jo was at the computer again. "Asking for help."

"You don't think they'll try to preserve evidence?"

"Lone Star Rangers aren't known for asking questions first and shooting later." Jo didn't have time to shoot him a dumb look, but she still felt it cross her face.

Someone, *anyone*, come to their aid. Jo reached out to every hacker she ever knew in her frantic plea. Hack their guns. Give them conflicting intel. Hell, she'd take a rogue helicopter that was no doubt circling them suddenly losing all computer function and plummeting into the men about to shoot them down.

"TWO . . ."

"Anything?" Yuusuke was panting, like he'd just been running.

All messages were dark, chats unaccepted. All her pleas were going unanswered. It was like they were alone, banished to an island the world had forgotten.

"ONE . . ."

"I'm going out."

"Yuu, wait!" One of the messages lit up. Someone was responding. Jo leaned over her computer, desperate to see who was ready to help.

Gunshots fired like a mortar out of a tube on New Year's, servers reduced to shrapnel exploding throughout the room. Jo screamed, fell to her knees, and covered her head. When the hail of bullets and circuit board debris eventually ended, Jo's eyes snapped back to her computer. The screens were dark.

"No, no!" She pounded on the keyboard, trying to bring it back to life. "Is your computer—"

Jo turned, and froze.

Yuusuke, her friend, her ally, her accomplice, lay on the floor, riddled with bullets. Crimson pooled around him like the infamous biblical tide rising to drown them both.

She skidded to her knees, pressing down on the wound in his shoulder. Jo alternated to the one on his stomach. But she couldn't seem to stave the blood flow.

"No, no, no . . ." She shook her head and tears streamed down her cheeks. "Come on, man . . . W-what about the Black Bank, huh? Come on, Yuu . . ." Nothing. Jo saw his slack face go blurry more than felt the tears begin to well behind her eyes. "What about Blackbeard?" She tried, desperate. But even finally using his preferred alias couldn't summon her friend back to life. "Don't leave me to do this alone. You promised to stay by my side, like a brother, remember?"

Hopeless, Jo looked around once more.

No way out. She was faced with the same realization as before. Even if she could ask for help, there was no way it would come in time.

Beams of sunlight cut through the darkness, like a glimpse of a heaven she'd no doubt never see because she didn't even know if she believed it was there. Jo closed her eyes and sighed.

This was how she died. This was the end of the line for her. She'd known it might come earlier than most, given her profession, but she'd hoped to at least make it past nineteen. She'd hoped to do a little bit more for her mother before Jo left the land of the living.

In that moment, one of those beams acted like a spotlight on a piece of information in the back of her mind. Maybe it was the fear pulling her back to a time when things were easier, safer. Maybe life really did flash before your eyes in your final moments. She didn't have time to consider the why; she was too busy thinking about her grandmother.

The woman who'd been born ancient and worked as hard as she could to help raise Jo's mother, and then her, up until there was no more to give. The feeling of her lap, the lingering scent of *pastelitos* on her apron, the soothing sound of her voice—it was all there. But what was most vivid were her words: *"Ven pa acá, mijita. I have a story for you."*

The story itself was an old one, and most of the minor details were lost to time even before her grandmother had passed on the tale. But it was a fable Abuelita had spoken about with certainty. Jo recalled circles, wishes, and a spell that could make anything possible.

It wasn't much to go by. But technology could not protect her now. Jo pushed herself from her knees, crouching over Yuusuke's still intact computer for her last-ditch, impossible chance at a way out—somewhere between faith and fairytale.

Her hands flew over Yuusuke's keyboard, stroking in her search query. Blood spattered the table around her, smearing the keys and blotting out the letters.

She struck deep, going straight into the heart of the dark web, searching with everything she had for something that sounded like her grandmother's story. It took three blatantly ridiculous articles before she found one that struck a chord. There wasn't any time to look for a fourth. This would have to do.

Without hesitation, she followed the instructions to the letter.

*Step one: Cast the circle.*

Jo walked over to Yuusuke, ignoring the sounds of the megaphones from beyond the barn. It didn't matter what they said; she knew what would happen next. Jo crouched next to her friend, tucking a stray bit of hair behind his ear. She spoke right to his wide, dead eyes. "I'll join you soon."

Placing her palm flat on the floor in the puddle of his blood, Jo swept it around her, turning, drawing a circle in which she was the center.

*Step two: Say the invocation.*

"I beseech the darkness and the chaos that lives there. Heed my plea and accept my wish."

Jo stared about the room. Nothing happened. She sunk back onto her heels, her feet folding under her butt.

*"Escucha me, Josephina,"* Abuelita had said. Jo closed her eyes, trying to hear her grandmother one final time. *"If the time comes, and you are in need, remember this story."*

The door behind her slammed open and Jo whipped to face it, drawn on instinct by the loud boom of the battering ram. She stared past the barrels of guns at men and women in full riot gear. The army had been called in to take down a couple of kids.

A man began to shout.

Gunfire exploded in front of her eyes, deep in her ears.

And the world stopped.

Jo had to blink twice to know that she was still breathing. Bullets floated before her, frozen in mid-air. The world was doused in perfect silence. There was no wind, no hum of computer fans, no buzzing of monitors, no pulsing of Yuusuke's retro dub-step still blaring from his dangling headphones.

"Your plea has been heard."

The voice was as much in her mind as it was in the air surrounding her. It prickled nerves up her arms, setting every hair on end.

She expected to find some timeless monster to have such a powerful voice. But a man who looked cut straight out of a fashion magazine stared down at her. He had a strong chin, deep crimson lips, skin so pale that it was almost translucent, and silvery hair that swept over the side of a face that looked like something from a distant dream.

"Are you a vampire?" The surreal, almost cinematic nature of her situation had gotten to her; it was like being on a film set. All she waited for now was the director's "Cut!" to bring an end to the nightmarish scene around her.

"I am the Wish Granter." The not-quite-vampire, not-quite-timeless-monster spoke again with a voice that could liquefy diamonds. "And I am here for your wish."

"My . . . wish . . ." Jo looked at the circle he stood on the edge of, drawn in her friend's blood. "I'm not dead?"

"What do you wish for?" he rephrased, with more urgency.

*Step three: Make your wish.*

As her mind was wont to do under pressure, she found herself bullet-pointing. One: She was dead, and it didn't matter. Two: She'd been knocked out and this was all some sort of hallucination, in which case the feds had her and nothing mattered. Or Three: Her insane, improbable, surreal chance had actually panned out as her grandmother had said it would.

Jo swallowed hard.

Her next words either didn't matter at all, or her life and the lives of everyone she loved depended on them.

"I wish . . ." she started, not wanting to lose her chance. "I wish that none of this happened. That Yuusuke was alive and my family was safe."

The man stared down at her. She wasn't even sure if he was breathing.

"This wish requires great power. To grant it, I will need something in return. Something equivalent to the magic I will have to expend."

"What?" She'd give anything for the people she loved most.

"You, your entire future, and the old magic that resides in your blood."

Jo laughed, somewhat crazed. It's not like she'd have a future if she didn't agree. "Is this any way to make a deal? You're not giving me a lot of options."

She tried to ignore the tears that blurred the outline of Yuusuke's body. The only thing keeping the drops from falling was sheer shock at the situation. The blood of her only friend coated her hands like new gloves to remind her that *she* was the one who'd pushed for this job. She was the one who'd led her only real friend and confidant to his death.

Jo tried to pull together a brave front. If this worked, her family would be safe, Yuusuke would be safe, and she—well, it wasn't as if she hadn't made deals with devils before.

Jo took a breath, more stable than expected, and said, "Fine. Take me, I'm yours."

Something about the words echoed deep within her. Perhaps it was the surreal nature of the situation, but it was almost like *déjà vu*—almost like she'd said something similar to this man long, long ago.

"Very well." There may have been the ghost of a smile tugging at the stony man's mouth when he spoke, but Jo never knew for sure.

The world erupted in cold fire and when it extinguished, there was only darkness.

# THE SOCIETY

OVER THE COURSE of her nineteen years, Jo had woken up countless different ways.

There were the more simplistic times of her childhood, when she woke to the smell of her mother's cooking, or her father's voice through the door. There were the more stressful times in her early teens, waking up cold and alone on some stranger's floor after helping out with a "tech favor."

There were the times when her head pounded and eyes peeled open, gummy from passing out with too much caffeine still coursing through her system. There were the times when she barely woke up at all, eyes functioning only enough to scan downloading files before slipping shut once more.

This was none of those times.

In fact, if Jo had to describe it, it didn't feel like waking up at all. More just like suddenly . . . *being*. One minute nothing, perpetual darkness, and then the next, her bedroom.

Despite the lack of tiredness or sleep crusties at the corners, Jo rubbed at her eyes, stars popping to life beneath the pressure of her fingers. When had she come home? Hadn't she just been somewhere else?

Jo dropped her hands and looked around, taking in the overflowing hamper in the corner, the desk piled high with her multiple monitors and equipment. The cork board behind it was littered with pictures and sticky notes, printed documents related to various side projects she'd taken before—

Her mind drew a blank. Before what? She distinctly felt herself present in an "after," but what had preceded it?

With a stretch, Jo got to her feet, walking the length of her room. Everything looked the same. Her poster from the eighth Iron Man movie, which she'd pretended to hang up ironically. Her calendar still stuck in December 2056, because she'd been too lazy to hang the one her mother got her for Christmas. Who even used physical calendars anymore, anyway?

Everything looked exactly the way she'd left it a month ago.

A month ago, when she'd taken the job just on the edge of Big Bend, when she'd coerced Yuusuke into joining her even though they both knew he was "in" before she'd even asked. He was that type of friend, jump first and ask questions later—blind trust Jo had never really deserved. Not to mention his insatiable need for a challenge, rivaled only by her own. It was because of that stupid, complementary-in-a-self-destructive-kind-of-way dynamic that meant they'd both been—

She didn't exactly choose to sit down; more like her legs led her back to the bed and then buckled. Almost as if on delay, her ears began to ring from distant, dream-like gunfire. She was pretty sure she was going to throw up. Jo buried her head in her hands, the images swarming back into her brain like persistent wasps, buzzing and stinging and drowning out all other thoughts: a message from some Japanese mob boss safe in the west, Rangers, gunfire, Yuusuke's lifeless eyes, blood, so much blood.

With a jolt, Jo ripped her trembling hands away from her face, frantically searching her palms, her nails, her wrists and arms. Nothing. Not a trace of Yuu's blood to be found. Just her same sun-deprived skin, her fingernails bitten to the beds, and the plain, simple band of black that was her smart-watch.

It didn't make sense. Not unless she'd dreamed the whole past month. And Jo didn't put nearly enough stock into her imagination for that to be possible.

Frustrated, and more than a little unnerved, Jo got shakily back to her feet. She needed to get out of her room and find out how she'd gotten back to her apartment. She needed to call Yuusuke and see if she really was going mad. And then maybe talk to somebody who "knows a guy" about sleeping pills that would make dreams less . . . vivid.

It was impossible to consider, but what else could it be? Her brain seemed unwilling to wrap itself around any other possibility. Unless she was dead.

Jo stopped, hand frozen on the doorknob.

*Was that it?*

Was she dead? Was the afterlife her messy apartment bedroom? Could be a form of hell, she supposed.

It seemed less likely than the dream theory. When she ran her fingers through her long, brown hair, she felt every strand. When she breathed in, she felt her lungs fill with air. When she swallowed, she felt her spit travel down her throat and past the point of sensation. For all intents and purposes, she still felt alive. Living, breathing, in the flesh, *alive*.

But that didn't make sense either. Her whole existence was a contradiction right now.

With an aggravated huff, Jo turned the knob on her bedroom door and stalked out into the hall. Call Yuusuke, he always knew just how to level her. Then maybe her mom. She could tell her about the dream, pick her brain as to what it all meant. Probably stress. But talking to her about it would ease Jo's mind, regardless, and her mom had taken after Abuelita when it came to all manner of the occult. "I would have been a *curandera* like my great grandmother, maybe you as well Josephina, if we'd stayed in Mexico," she liked to say.

It wasn't just the thought of her grandmother that had Jo stuttering to a panicked halt not more than two steps out of her room.

This wasn't the familiar hallway that led to the bathroom, the living room, the tiny and barely-used kitchen. This wasn't even a hallway in her apartment at all. This was a hallway lined with doors she didn't recognize, decor in soft colors that were jarring in comparison to the chaos of movie posters she kept on her own walls.

This was a hallway she'd never seen in her life, and it sure as hell wasn't supposed to be connected to her bedroom. So, Jo did the only sane thing she could think of.

She turned right back around and closed the door, staring at the familiar blue bedspread, the little spaceship hanging off the cord to her ceiling fan, the poster of Iron Man VIII that she—*wait*.

With a nervous drag to her step, Jo walked up to the bare patch of wall. *Where was her poster?* It had been there just there a minute ago, right?

Her mind jerked, as if suddenly changing lanes. She'd taken that poster down a few months ago. She vaguely recalled losing a bet with Yuusuke, watching as he'd torn it down and replaced it with a vintage poster of America as one unified nation before it was carved up in the aftermath of World War III—a piece of history that verged on contraband, depending on who you asked. In her frazzled confusion, she'd forgotten that the Iron Man poster wasn't meant to have been there at all.

In fact, as Jo began to look around, the room seemed to look less and less familiar. The hamper had clothes in it she didn't remember wearing, some she didn't even remember owning. The files pinned to the corkboard seemed almost illegible when she looked at them closely, like trying to read a book in a mirror.

But it didn't feel like a dream. It didn't feel like anything. *She* didn't feel like anything. How normal it all seemed was the worst part.

In a panic, Jo burst out of the room and back into the hallway. Being in the weird, not-quite-right version of her room was too much. She'd take strange and new to uncomfortably familiar. Her head was spinning, distracted by how wrong it had felt, how wrong *everything* suddenly felt.

Which was why she didn't notice until it was too late that somebody else was in the hallway. A realization abruptly made by way of nearly barreling into the person's chest.

"*Whoa* there! What's the hurry?" A voice suddenly accompanied the presence, two hands coming up to grab Jo's shoulders, steadying her. When she managed to get her head back on straight, she found herself staring into the very handsome face of a complete stranger. Light brown hair was slicked back in a way that made his angular features seem sharper. A crisp, white shirt had been tailored to highlight an obviously well-toned physique. His eyes seemed to spark as they scanned her face, and his lips pulled up into an amused smirk the longer she stared back. "Keep looking at me like that and you'll give a guy the wrong impression."

As if the heavily-accented words had broken the spell, Jo instantly backed away, suddenly realizing she'd been frozen in his arms like some gaping lunatic. The man just continued to grin, raising his hands in a way that seemed placating but obviously had little energy behind it.

"Sorry about that, dollface. Wasn't expecting you to come out of your room so quickly. Usually takes a little while to come back to your senses," he said, the lilt to his voice itching at some old memory.

Jo had a familiar sensation—one of being on a movie set. When the stranger spoke, it was with a sort of accent that she'd only ever heard in people from United North America—New York, to be exact. But also, not . . . It was older than that, pre-World War III. *Way* before. In fact, the closer she looked at him, the more he seemed to be straight out of one of her grandmother's old photos, the ones that were direct to physical, black and white without any filtering.

He was the real deal—sleeves rolled up to the elbows, suspenders, tight black trousers, and a thick gold watch. Match that with the incomprehensible sentences, and Jo was having a hard time following any of it.

"You really must stop staring," he chuckled, wrenching Jo back to the present. Of course, before she could start in on her growing list of questions and concerns, the man opened his mouth with a flirtatious, "Though, you're a real looker, so I suppose I wouldn't be disinclined."

Despite herself, Jo couldn't help but feel heat rising to her cheeks. It'd been a while—okay, at least a year—since anyone had commented on her appearance. Yuusuke never let her forget the fact that he didn't even *see* her as a woman. She managed a fierce scowl underneath the darkening blush, raising her chin at him for emphasis. Just because he was a good couple of inches taller than her didn't mean she couldn't stare down her nose at him.

"Well *I would* be disinclined," she said, putting her hands on her hips, something she only ever did when she was straddling the line between pissed off and way out of her depth. At the very least, she'd be disinclined until she got some answers. "So instead, how about you tell me who the hell you are and where the hell I am."

"Easy there, doll. I didn't mean nothing by it. Not unless you wanted me to." The man shoved one hand in his pocket and held the other one out in her direction, waiting for her to take it. There was an easy friendliness about it, like he was openly trying not to pressure her. "I'm Wayne Davis. And trust me, this'll be a whole hell of a lot easier if you roll with it instead of fighting against the tide."

After a brief pause, eyes jumping from Wayne's face to his hand and back, Jo cautiously returned the handshake. He did have a point. Better to go along with whatever was happening for a bit until she could gather enough data to figure out exactly what was going on.

Every problem could be hacked, broken apart, and solved, but she needed the equipment and information to do it. Right now, it felt like she was trying to break into the Black Bank with an old laptop from the early 2000s. Jo's stomach dropped a bit at the unintentional memory, so she focused on Wayne instead.

"So, what's your story?" he asked her suddenly. She raised an eyebrow at him, tempted to ask if the lingo was an act. Maybe she was in some sort of reality TV prank show. When Jo didn't answer right away, Wayne just shook his head, smiling. "Your name, maybe? Got to give me something to work with here. Unless you're jivin' with 'doll' for the rest of eternity. Which sounds real good to me."

Okay. Guess they were starting there.

"Jo Espinosa," she said, looking over Wayne's shoulder at the rest of the empty hallway, the matching mahogany doors. She went through all her memories at rapid speed, but still came up blank. Wherever she was, it certainly wasn't anywhere she'd been before. "Now, where am I? And what do you mean by 'eternity'?"

"Jo? What kinda name is that for a dame?"

"A perfectly fine one, thank you very much." Jo bristled, hands back on her hips. "It's short for Josephina. My grandma's name. And I'm no 'dame,' so you can cool it," she said, trying her best to mimic his accent. Poorly. "It's 2057. You're not getting anywhere with that shtick." He was attractive enough that he didn't need a shtick at all, but Jo kept the thought to herself. "Also, you didn't answer my questions."

Wayne continued to ignore said questions, whistling in appreciation instead. "It's 2057 already?"

Jo couldn't help but balk. "You're kidding, right?" When Wayne just shrugged, smirking at her stunned surprise, Jo couldn't bite back the huff of frustration. "You know what, forget it. If you won't give me answers, I'll find someone who will." And with a last, scowling once-over, Jo turned on her heel and began to make her way down the hall.

"Hey, hey, hey! Come on now, don't be like that!" Wayne caught up to her quickly, cutting her off with a half skip-half spin into her line of sight. "Look, I'm sorry, doll—I mean Jo. I'm sorry, *Jo.* I didn't mean to upset you, honest." The expression on his face seemed sincere, but Jo merely crossed her arms over her chest and waited for him to go on. As he did, he sighed, waving a hand in front of himself in a vague motion. "It's just been a few decades since we've gotten anyone new, though you did come much faster than the last, so I got all caught up in my excitement. What I should have been doing is showing you around and making you feel welcome, so how about I do that now?"

"But welcome *where*?" Jo latched on to the topic shift like a fish diving back into water from dry land. Wayne straightened up again, that confident air and cocky smirk back in place. Despite the incredibly confusing, anxiety-producing atmosphere of her current situation, she couldn't help but feel slightly at ease in the man's presence; even if she also kind of wanted to punch him right in his stupid forced accent. "Wayne, what's going on . . .? What is this place?"

Wayne's eyes suddenly took on a proud and excited glint as he said, "The Society."

When that was all he offered, Jo rolled her eyes and pressed harder. "What kind of a society?" Her bet was models, because the man before her was way too pretty, almost ethereal, like . . . like . . . A man with white hair and a strong jaw appeared on the edge of her mind, but Wayne spoke again before she could cling to the memory.

"Not *a* society, dollface." Wayne grinned, walking back to her side and placing a hand at the small of her back, leading her with a gentle nudge down the hall. "*The* Society. Let me be the first to welcome you as the newest member of the Society of Wishes."

# CAPITAL D

J O WASN'T REALLY one for clubs.

In her rise to hacker infamy, she'd been lovingly dubbed "She-wolf" by some cabin-based upstarts in Colorado for the fact that she was never seen working with anyone else. That claim evaporated when she started taking on bigger jobs with Yuusuke, but Jo still had a soft spot for her first and favorite moniker.

It was more efficient to be alone; people had the propensity to annoy her. Barring one summer where her mother had forcefully enrolled her into a ranching camp all the way near Austin during a futile campaign to "get Jo out of the house more," she'd never really boasted a wide circle of friends. She believed in quality over quantity on that front. Plus, the more friends she had, the more people she'd end up sticking her neck out for. Yuusuke did a good-enough job of keeping her hands full on the babysitting front, most of the time.

"I'm fairly certain there's some sort of mistake here." Actually, she was fairly certain there were *several* mistakes. "There's no way I would've signed up to be a member of anything."

"No mistakes here." He was so frustratingly sure.

"Okay," she drew out the word like he was drawing out her patience. "Then there's at least the issue of kidnapping?" Jo really wished it was the first time she'd been spirited away somewhere against her will, but it wasn't. At least having past experience was helping keep her marginally calm. That time had worked out fine; she just had to figure out what they wanted and then be on her way.

"Kidnapping? The Society doesn't *kidnap* people."

"Whatever you want to call it then." She sighed heavily. "I've never heard of this . . . *society*. But I'm sure we can work out something with your boss. So, if you could just take me to him—"

"Boss? You mean Snow?" Wayne laughed. "So, first lesson for you right there, doll. You never want to willingly meet with Snow. That man lost his humor somewhere in the ballpark of a thousand years ago."

Jo opened her mouth to speak again, but something about the look on her face must have inspired Wayne to continue. Not that he hadn't already given off the impression of being a man who loved to listen to himself talk.

"I know it's all downright confusing. Takako was the same way when she first came. Come along and you'll pick it up as you go."

He was ushering her down the hall again. And this time, Jo didn't resist—learn first, fight later.

The decor was clean; warm-toned wood floors met flush against white-washed walls in almost too-perfect lines. Something about the shine on the walls where the light hit them made it seem like they would be especially smooth—damp, even—to the touch. Every ten to fifteen feet, give or take, was a doorway, and every doorway had a name.

She'd missed the name on the first doorway, directly across from where she'd emerged into the hallway. But diagonally across from there, where Wayne had come from, was a door that bore his name in blocky, gold-rimmed steel. Across the hall, "Samson" was wrought in copper wiring and welded directly to the door. The next one on the left read "Nico," a blue jay perched on the scripted 'o,' painted with such a careful hand that Jo almost did a double-take to make sure it wasn't about to fly away. The final doorway on the right had an ornate placard in wood with what Jo had to presume was a name, "Eslar."

Six doors in total, counting her own.

They descended a long flight of stairs that fanned out into a central atrium entirely overlaid with marble. Heavy crimson drapes in what looked like velvet, framed tall windows that gave Jo the first concerning glimpse of the outside world. She stopped mid-step, staring.

"Is that real?" Outside was a rolling green field, a lake in the distance, mountains in a far haze. It looked like postcards she remembered seeing in history textbooks of California before the great earthquake of 2011 and the WWIII bombings that followed not long after. She could barely imagine a world with so much un-altered green. Her world had always been filled with dusty plains and genetically-modified shrub grasses that tried to hang on in the all-too-hot climate.

"Reality is what we make it." Wayne stood at the bottom of the stairs, one hand in his pocket, the other flipping a coin. "So, who's to say?"

"I'm looking for answers, not philosophy."

"Trying to provide them, dollface." He caught the coin mid-flip, went to pocket it, and then stopped. The brown-haired man looked at the token and then back to her, no subtle amount of mischief in the expression. "How's about we make a bet?"

"A bet?"

"I flip my coin. Heads, you have to follow me around and listen nicely, no questions till the end of our tour. Tails, you get my nickel and I'll answer anything you want."

"So . . . I can ask my questions now, or later?" This man was the worst gambler she'd ever met.

Wayne thought about it for a moment, and then laughed. "Sounds right. What do you say?"

"Fine, deal." Playing along could well be to her benefit, at least for the time being.

Wayne flipped the coin and caught it so quickly that Jo barely had time to register the slap of his right palm over the back of his left. He peeled away his fingers dramatically. She squinted at the strange-looking currency, trying to place it.

"Oh, bad luck this time, guess I get to keep my nickel and you just need to listen a spell."

Jo walked the rest of the distance down the stairs to Wayne so she could confirm that the coin was, indeed, heads. She felt something wriggle up the back of her neck, like a worm inching its way into her brain. Jo raised a hand, rubbing the offending spot. She felt only hair, and her palm came back clean. Still, that wriggling sensation pricked her skin to goosebumps.

"Next up, the briefing room!" Wayne continued on, oblivious to her inexplicable discomfort.

They turned right and started down a long hallway. Unlike the atrium that was filled with light, this hall was shrouded in shadow. Low-lit sconces on the walls were held by ornately carved, golden hands. The marble floor of the atrium had been covered with a runner made of the same material as the curtains.

Jo rubbed the back of her neck again, looking around. It was as if she was in some high-class, old-world theater. Perhaps she was in Europe somewhere? She wanted to ask, but the second she thought of the question, that uncomfortable feeling had the notion shuddering away.

The "mansion" as Wayne called it, was large, but whoever built it couldn't decide what aesthetic they wanted it to be.

At the end of the hall, two solid wood doors opened to a room that was much more familiar to Jo. Gone were the detailing and lavish designs. In its place was a floor that looked like obsidian, but must have been some kind of black, polished cement. A round table made of the same material was framed by eight executive-style chairs. They were appropriately made of matching black leather. It was the sort of thing you'd expect to find in a mob boss's hideaway or CEO's office.

"We only ever meet here when a wish comes in."

*A wish?* The question sat heavy on her tongue. Despite her desire to ask it, however, she found herself frustratingly silent. Jo frowned. The hair on her arms was still on-end.

"Snow—you met him before you got here—briefs us on the details of the wish."

Jo wondered how often that happened, but again found herself unable to ask. She tried to catalog the questions in the back of her mind—wishes, briefing—but Jo couldn't get a grip, and the inquiries slipped away.

"Back here, this is the Door. Capital 'D'. It's the only one here that really matters because it's the only way outside."

"The only way outside . . ." she repeated, focusing on the steel door and alphanumeric keypad attached to the lock.

"But we'll get to all that later," Wayne said off-handedly, as if it wasn't the most important thing he'd said so far. "Let's go back to the Four-Way."

Jo wanted to ask what he meant by "Four-Way" but she couldn't seem to formulate her question right. By the time she thought she'd figured it out, they were back in the atrium with the tall windows, and Jo had her answer.

To her left was the stairway they'd come from initially. To her right was another equally opulent stair. Behind her was the "briefing room" and ahead, where Wayne seemed to be leading her now, was yet unknown.

"Up that way are the rec rooms . . . and not much else of importance." He gestured to the stairs at their right with a nonchalant wave. "We'll show you those later. You just woke up, after all. I bet you're thirsty?"

"Yeah, actually, a little." It was almost a relief to speak, a balm to the unease that had settled on her. Jo was fairly certain she had not consumed any caffeine for at least ten hours and was close to death as a result.

Where the last hallway had been shrouded in darkness, this stretch was light. It was wide enough that couches and bookshelves could line the spaces between wide bay windows, creating multiple, small sitting areas. Jo kept her eyes trained on the picturesque scenes beyond the glass.

She certainly wasn't in Texas anymore.

"Something smells good," Jo said, more experimenting with speaking than anything else. Statements came out easy enough, but why couldn't she seem to formulate a question to save her life? The scent that was growing on the air shot right to her stomach and a growl followed promptly, eliciting a chuckle from Wayne.

"Seems like your stomach's woken up too. We can find you some food in the kitchen and settle that once and for all."

"Kitchen" was an understatement.

The room they entered, and presumably the final one on the tour for now, was positively massive. It was a giant rectangle supported by columns on the outside, and ornately carved buttresses that stretched to a steeply pitched roof. Stained glass windows streamed color into the room from between each of the pillars.

There was no wall beyond the columns opposite her; instead, the space opened to a massive patio complete with grills, tables, lounge chairs, and a pool that looked like it hung hundreds of feet above the valley. Fresh air—fresher than any she'd breathed her entire life—wafted in from outside, cool and crisp and painfully unlike the oppressive heat of home.

To her left stood a massive kitchen. A large island with eight stools supported two different sinks with more than enough room to work between them. Behind were two gas stove-tops and three ovens mounted in the wall. There was, however, only one microwave, an appliance Jo was ready to fight for, since her cooking skills had never much graduated beyond instant noodles.

To the right was a sitting area with leather couches, most of which surrounded a television that took up nearly half the wall. Next to that was a large billiards table, its frame catty-cornered to a smaller table decorated in black and white squares. The two were positioned right below one of the stained-glass windows, and the light shining through painted each in delicate splotches of color.

Everything around her was part new, part old—a mix of neoclassical cathedral and billionaire playhouse.

"Billiards?" Wayne said with a note of approval to the other occupant of the room.

"It appears so. Though no word yet on who put in the request. Not that it would matter, anyway . . ." Another all-too-pretty man spoke over his shoulder from where he was working two skillets filled—according to Jo's nose—with bacon and eggs. He had brown hair as well, but it was a richer hue than Wayne's and held more red notes. Messy waves straggled down over his ears, into his eyes, and ended at the nape of his neck. He stopped all movement and did a double-take when he saw her. "The new recruit is a *woman*?"

"I'm just as surprised to be here as you are to see me." Jo shoved her palms into her jeans and tried to shrug off the unease that still clung to her. "Less surprised about the woman bit, however."

"Please excuse my shock . . . You're just the second one in fifty short years. I had begun to think that all those remaining in the lineages were men only . . . But here you are, proving me wrong, yet again." His eyes drifted over to Wayne. "And I do hope this foul creature hasn't been harassing you." The man turned off the burners and hastily crossed over to her, wiping his hands on a grease- and paint-stained apron before extending one to her. "My name is Niccolo, but everyone just calls me Nico."

"Josephina, but everyone calls me Jo." If sunshine were a person, it would be this man. His voice sounded like something she could only describe as melted chocolate and his eyes were much the same color. Jo took his hand and found it to be just as warm, albeit calloused, and his grip a little too strong on her narrow fingers. It was hard to feel uneasy, even despite her situation, in the presence of someone like him. His smile was almost enough to make her forget that wriggling that had worked its way to her tongue when she wanted to ask where he was from. Jo swallowed. She could speak, just not questions. It made no sense, but here she was testing the theory. "You're not from North America."

"Not from . . ." He paused, going still. A shadow quickly crossed over his face, gone by the time she noticed it. "Oh, the accent. Do I really still have a touch of it?"

"You do," Jo affirmed. She was used to accents, worked with all sorts. But his was just a little too faint for her to pin down.

"Florence, Italy, originally." He motioned to one of the stools. "Sit. Are you hungry?"

"She is. Heard her stomach grumbling all the way here." Wayne answered for her, taking up one of the stools. He patted the one next to him. "Take a seat, doll. The tour's over."

Just like that, the wriggling slithered back from the void where it'd come. The odd, almost drugged feeling from before was gone. The goosebumps on her skin settled, and her tongue loosened. The invisible dam she never asked for had broken, and questions suddenly flooded from her. "What is this place? How is all this possible? Where am I? How did I get here from the LSR? *Who are you people?*"

Her hands flew to her mouth, and Jo panted softly. The more questions she asked, the more panic returned to her. One hand snaked around to the back of her neck, rubbing once more. But the sensation was well and truly gone. Had she really been about to sit down and enjoy breakfast with these strange, suspiciously kind people, as though nothing was out of place?

"Wayne, you didn't." Nico gave the other man a disapproving look.

"What's the matter?" Wayne held out his arms. "I had to show her somehow."

"You know the rules on using magic on the other Society members." Nico sounded like a parent scolding a toddler. But he looked to be at least two or three years younger than Wayne.

"Sometimes, rules are meant to be broken," Wayne countered. "And they're unofficial, anyway."

"Eslar will hear of this," Nico said ominously, though Jo recalled a man named Snow being referred to as "the boss."

"All right, Mrs. Grundy."

"Who's Mrs. Grundy?" Jo shook her head, dislodging the question. "You know what, it doesn't matter. Just tell me what you want me to do for your 'society' and I'll get on with it."

"We don't have any wishes right now, but as soon as one comes in, I'm sure your magic will be very helpful." Nico walked back over to her from three small plates of food, wrapping an arm around her shoulders. He continued before Jo could correct him on the "magic" subject or inquire about the wishes. Then again, someone so clearly insane likely wouldn't listen to reason. "Foremost, let me apologize for my friend using his magic on you. I don't know what the terms of his bet were, but no matter what he says, it's inexcusable. He never learned the merits of being a proper gentleman."

"I am the most proper gentlemen you've ever met." Wayne shook his fist at Nico, but still helped himself to one of the plates.

"I know, it's a lot to take in all at once. I do hope that, despite the circumstances, seeing the mansion helped. We'll try to answer all your questions in due time, but I'm sure you'll feel better if you get some food in your stomach. Wishing really takes it out of you, and you're only freshly transitioned. But don't worry—those last little necessities of humanity won't be a bother for much longer."

A plate appeared in front of her. Scrambled eggs, bacon—a basic breakfast that smelled positively divine when sweetened by hunger. Jo stared at it listlessly. Yeah, she'd had it "taken out of" her alright. She didn't know if she was alive or dead. Awake or asleep. She felt exhausted and alert all at the same time.

Suddenly everything felt too much. There was that burning feeling right behind her eyes and the one thing she would *not* do is cry in front of strangers. She had to escape, regroup, and then find her way out—hopefully without that weird feeling taking over her again.

"I just want to go home," she pleaded softly.

"This is home now," Nico replied gently. There was an apologetic note to his voice that only made the overwhelming pressure behind her eyes worse. This was starting to sound a hell of a lot more like a kidnapping.

"I'm not worth anything. I don't know what you guys want . . . But there's no money. My family can't pay for me and my employers won't." The memory of being cut off and left to die at the hands of the feds seared hot, putting the hairs on the back of her neck on end—a recollection too real to have been a dream. That, combined with the mentions of magic . . .

*What had she done?*

"You are very much worth something," Nico tried to soothe, cutting through Jo's thoughts.

"And we're your family now anyway," Wayne added.

So, her status had just rocketed from kidnapped to being held hostage by a cult. *Perfect.* Wayne gave her a broad smile, as if she should find the fact pleasing. Jo enjoyed it about as much as a lukewarm cup of coffee and barely resisted telling him so right to his pretty face. She bit back the comment that becoming her family was not so easy. Jo cared about very few people, but when she did, there was nothing she wouldn't do to protect them.

"I need a minute." Jo stood, backing away from the bar. A plan was already formulating in her head. Information gathering was over; now was the time to act. "I need . . . just a minute."

Nico frowned, but he didn't fight her on the matter and stopped Wayne from doing so with a look. "Of course. Why don't you go back to your room, settle in? I'll bring some food in a bit and you can get to know us all one at a time."

"Right, perfect." Jo backed away as though retreating from wild animals.

"Would you like one of us to escort—"

"No!" she interrupted Wayne. She'd had enough escorting for one lifetime. "No," she repeated more softly, gently, trying to pile on notes of sticky-sweet *don't worry, everything is fine, I'm not trying anything funny.* "I'll be fine. You gave me such a good tour. I can find it, pretty simple, up the stairs, to the right."

"Just so." Nico beamed and set her plate aside, away from Wayne's greedy and wandering eyes. "I'll be there in a little."

*No, you won't,* Jo wanted to correct. She started back down the hallway hastily, breaking out into a run the moment she was far enough away not to be seen by the men in the kitchen. She didn't want to happen on anyone else and she certainly didn't want to head back to whatever room she'd woken up in.

There was only one place she wanted to go.

Out.

# ERROR 404

F INDING HER WAY back to what Wayne had called the briefing room was easy enough.

Its black decor and dim lighting were as dark and shrouded in mystery as before. Regardless, Jo hurried inside. When no lock could be found on the massive entry door, she grabbed one of the eight chairs around the table and shoved it roughly, at an awkward angle, beneath the handle. Not much of a barricade, but enough to buy her time. All she needed was long enough to get out.

Which apparently meant going through the Capital-D Door.

An anxiousness she wasn't used to became fast friends with a determined desperation, one she'd spent many an hour with in the past. The feeling only increased as Jo turned toward the back of the room.

From an analytical perspective, the Door didn't seem too outlandish, if a bit intimidating with its thick-looking steel frame. The lock, however, was both familiar in its keypad structure, and unfamiliar in coding methodology. The pad was alphanumeric, as she'd noticed before, but with no screen and no discernible locking mechanism. When Jo looked closer, it even appeared to be unused: no wear from the oils of fingerprint residue, no scuffs from pushing the buttons too hard. In fact, despite her familiarity with various decades of technological equipment, she couldn't even seem to pinpoint when the keypad might have been made.

All of her tricks for figuring out a key code based off of sight alone were thwarted before she even had a chance to start.

Except the more she looked at it, trying desperately to analyze its structure, possible weak points, and unintentional clues left behind by lazy users, the more she started to see. Each number started to match with an opposing letter like a line drawn in connect-the-dots. The seemingly endless list of "all possible combinations" began to shorten, some options fading away in unimportance. Suddenly, buttons seemed recently pressed where they hadn't been before, as if she just hadn't been looking hard enough.

It was like watching a movie in black and white slowly bleed into color, starting at the edges and inching towards the center until the whole screen had been filled. Within moments, the lock seemed almost laughably simple to decode. Jo couldn't help but roll her eyes at the Society's inadequacy.

Pulling her sleeve down over her fingers out of habit, Jo carefully plugged in the most recently used code, holding her breath when what she assumed was the last button gave.

For a couple of seconds, nothing happened. Jo's heart jumped into her throat. But before she had a chance to panic, the keypad blinked three times, and a heavy click, followed by the *whoosh* of pressurization, echoed in the silence of the briefing room. Jo held her breath, slowly reaching for the simple, curved handle of the door, and pulled.

It opened easily.

Jo wasted no time, as if forcefully drawn across the threshold by an unseen hand.

She started by hurriedly closing the door behind her, letting out an involuntary breath of relief at the sound of it pressurizing and locking automatically. At least they couldn't be quick on her heels. She wasn't sure where the Society had taken her, but the green field and clean lake alone meant she was far, far from home. That also meant it would take her some time to find an escape route, make contact with Yuusuke, barter favors for transport from someone in the area . . .

First and foremost, she had to figure out where she was.

The moment Jo turned around and properly managed a look at her surroundings, she knew. Where she expected to be outside in a green pasture—at least in some kind of entry way—Jo found herself in a long hall of doors. It was industrial and dated, and nothing like the other areas of the mansion she'd seen. It shouldn't be familiar, but it was.

Even though Jo had never stepped foot here before, she could see the truth of her situation in the rows of offices, in the pompous-looking walls and doors of glass, in the high ceilings and the hardwood floors. She could see it in the placards on the walls next to bigger offices spouting titles like "Senior Investigator."

A Ranger compound.

The panic from before that she had managed to redirect into calm action returned full force. The Rangers were part-police, part-militia, and operated with all the authority of the government of the LSR, giving them free reign to do as their trigger-happy hands desired. She'd managed to elude them for most of her life, which made running into them once— twice—in such a short period of time all the more jarring.

When Jo's luck ran out, it *really* ran out.

The layout of the hallway she was standing in was too open—too much glass. She didn't have blueprints and couldn't identify an immediate escape route. She needed to think, needed to breathe. But she couldn't do either in her present spot and if she waited any longer, one of the many suits sitting behind their computers would notice her.

Which left her no choice. With the stakes substantially higher, Jo turned around to key her way back into the Society. She'd stay just long enough to figure out a proper plan once she really knew what secret task team she'd unwittingly been drafted into. Things worked out much better with the feds when they believed you were playing along nicely.

Except the door she found herself facing was no longer giant and steel, but wooden and labeled "Supply Closet". Jo blinked, feeling her chest tighten as she reached for the handle. It didn't budge as she tried to turn it.

An office door creaked open nearby.

"Shit!" she hissed under her breath and tugged on the handle again. No luck. Jo frantically searched for an empty hallway, a vacant office—somewhere she could hide for a second to get her head on straight.

Blindly, she started off in the opposite direction of the office. As soon as the door swung open, she ducked into a side hall, keeping an ear out for anyone else wandering around. Thankfully the path she'd chosen was empty and, as she scanned the doors to her left and right, she found none of the large panes of glass from previous hallway. A lucky break, for sure, but that still left her wandering aimlessly in enemy territory. So, mental map set in place, Jo began sneaking around as quietly as possible—a skill she'd honed to perfection.

But skills honed to perfection often left the mind free to wander, and as Jo inched her way around the compound, those wandering thoughts began to consume her.

Was she going crazy? She'd seen the steel door when it closed behind her, watched it lock and heard it pressurize. How had it suddenly transformed itself into a supply closet? Was the Society even real? Had that all been a dream and really she'd been stuck in this Ranger compound the whole time?

What if she'd never left Texas?

What if they'd captured her that day, dragged her away from Yuusuke's bleeding corpse and threw her in a government prison cell to rot? Was she even in the Lone Star Republic anymore? Or had she been handed over to the Yakuza—the Japanese mob—who'd hired her, to be dealt with by them as some sort of under-the-table political maneuver? Had they done anything to her family?

But then what about the Society?

Was this all an elaborate hoax meant to mess with her head, get her to confess to her collaboration with the mob and spill her carefully combed information on the Black Bank? Was any of what had happened with Wayne and Nico even real? Or was that just a hallucination brought on by torture she didn't even remember being inflicted?

What if they'd drugged her?

What if, what if, *what if!* There was some demented part of her that would almost prefer Wayne to do . . . whatever he'd done to her again just to ease the endless questions.

At the sound of more footsteps, Jo stumbled to a halt, heart in her throat and mind buzzing with paranoid over-stimulation. They were approaching from her left, but she'd been coming from the right, which gave her very little option. She chose an adjoining hall and peeked around the corner, hurrying past once she deemed it safe. The footsteps persisted, but they didn't seem rushed, like they hadn't realized her presence yet.

She had to find a computer, a phone or tablet left out on a desk, something she could use to hack into the Ranger main server from within their firewalls and look at the building's layout. She'd worry about her own sanity and possibly repressed trauma once she was out of their clutches and safely back home. Or as safe as she could be, considering the self-imposed WITSEC she'd probably have to endure for a while.

Given her track record thus far, Jo should have expected things to go from bad to worse, but she wasn't ready when they did.

At almost the same time as she turned the corner, a man in a suit decided to come out of his office. Jo swallowed a sound of panic and turned back the way she'd come. Only that hallway was now inhabited by multiple men and women leaving what looked to be a conference room.

She'd rather take her chance with the lone man than the swarm.

At least that was the plan, till they all looked her way.

Jo bolted down the other hallway at once, sprinting past the man in the suit. She'd been spotted. Shouts would turn into alarm bells that would become dogs barking and the click of disengaged gun safeties. But all Jo heard was the ringing in her ears. All she knew was that the lone man hadn't grabbed her; she hadn't been captured yet. She was alive for now, but if she didn't find a way out, that would surely change.

Jo bolted for the first open door she saw, thanking any gods that might possibly exist when she saw a computer inside. It was a bigger office, no glass on the walls—again, thanks to all possible gods—with pictures of some man's family on the desk. It looked to be the office of someone higher up, but not too high. Still, better to hurry and avoid—

She made it a few strides towards the desk before a man and a woman in full Ranger attire walked right in behind her.

Jo's vision seemed to dim in fear even as it heightened in desperation, looking at every corner of the room for somewhere, anywhere decent to hide. But even she wasn't desperate enough to think they hadn't already seen her.

"Don't shoot!" she said out of reflex instead, holding up her hands and willing them not to shake. She thought of Yuusuke, full of holes and bleeding out on a dusty server room floor. She wasn't ready to die then, and she still wasn't now. "Please, don't shoot!"

They didn't.

Instead, they didn't seem to notice her at all, talking amongst themselves like she wasn't even in the room. Like there wasn't some sweaty-palmed girl pleading for her life literally two feet in front of them.

The man whom the office seemed to belong to walked right up to her, looking just past her shoulder, and grabbed something off his desk. If he'd been any closer, he would have skimmed her hip in the process.

Panting loud and harsh, Jo watched the two agents have a civil and almost flirtatious conversation in front of her before exchanging the file and walking away, closing the office door behind them.

It wasn't until she heard the click of lock on the door that Jo even thought to put her hands down.

*What . . .? What just happened?*

"Do you see now?" An already terrifyingly familiar voice spoke without warning from the edge of her periphery. Jo jumped, nearly knocking the computer off the desk as she whipped around to face him.

The man who every instinct told her—practically screamed—was Snow leaned against the office's side wall, arms crossed over his chest and silver hair hanging casually over one eye. Jo wanted to ask what he was doing there. She wanted to ask a lot of things really, like how they hadn't seen her, how she'd ended up in the compound at all, whether or not she was actually dead this time. But no words would come out. Not just questions—no words at all. It was like the neuron-pathways from brain to mouth had fractured; too much data or not enough, she couldn't be sure.

Either way, Error 404.

"Jo," Snow said her name, soft and low but with impossible depth. Despite the fact that she was looking right at him, despite the fact that he'd obviously meant it to be nonthreatening, she still started. "Do you understand?"

No. No she didn't. How could she? So much had happened, too much, too quickly. There was no way for someone to take it all in and stay sane. She wanted to understand, she wanted more than anything to figure out just one *tiny* bit of what was going on, but a part of her already felt broken. All she wanted to do was go home . . . Was that so much to ask?

*Why couldn't she just see her family?*

Something on Jo's face must have compelled Snow to walk towards her, and even though Jo felt wound up tight, about ready to snap, somehow his presence didn't make her feel cornered. It didn't soothe her either, but not being outright panicked was something. Without a word, he reached towards her face and, with pale, elegant hands that seemed almost too still, carefully tucked a loose strand of dark hair behind her ear. Then, with the pad of his thumb, he gently wiped away a tear from beneath her eye.

*Oh.* She'd started crying after all. Damn it.

This close to Snow, it was impossible to ignore just how excruciatingly beautiful he was. Everything else she'd ever laid eyes on seemed to dull compared to him. It was as if this was the first moment she'd ever truly seen anything in her whole life.

He didn't smile, and his eyes remained guarded even as he scanned her face. But somehow, that cold, quiet distance only added to his allure. Like a statue in a museum—untouchable, and all the more breathtaking for it.

He said her name again, and this time she didn't jump. Instead, she soaked it in, reveled in the way it rumbled past her ears and echoed deep in her chest, seeming to resonate against something within her that Jo hadn't even known was there. When Snow finally dropped his hand from her face, turning away, it took everything she had not to feel disappointed —not to feel like she'd just been on the verge of finding something she'd been seeking her whole life.

With a gesture over his shoulder that almost seemed bored, he motioned for her to follow.

# DANGEROUSLY EASY

OR THE FIRST time in possibly her whole life, Jo's mind was silent. The usual incessant buzzing, always reminding her of something she needed to be doing, something she must be freaking out over, was quiet. She wasn't sure how to handle the stillness, so she didn't do anything at all. Her mind must have overloaded and completely fizzled out, faced with the combination of sensory overload and utter panic. At the very least, it wasn't that same wriggling, writing, uncomfortable feeling as before.

She followed behind the strange, beautiful man while he led her out of the room, his demeanor casual, as if they were walking through the park, or down a street, and not into the hive of what had been her arch-nemesis since Jo was fourteen and took her first job.

"I know you have a lot of questions," he started.

"Understatement." She wanted the word to have more snark, but she just sounded tired, even to her own ears.

"Where would you like me to begin?"

"It doesn't matter. Just begin." She paused when another agent rounded the corner ahead of them. Just like the two in the office, the woman walked down the hall without so much as a glance at them as she passed.

"They can't see us." Snow seemingly answered the question she'd been posing to the woman's back.

"Why?"

"Because you no longer exist."

The words were like swallowing a shot of tequila and chasing it with a can of RAGE ENERGY—burning delivered with a tang of sweetness that would become one massive hangover the next morning.

"Nico said I couldn't go home . . . Wayne said they were my family . . ." Jo tried to piece together the earlier conversations in a way that would make sense. But none of the pieces fit yet. She needed some rough edges shaved off before they'd snap into place. "What is the Society of Wishes?"

"You invoked the Society yourself, you know." Snow had the audacity to chuckle at her. Jo's chest had the audacity to tighten at the smooth, rich sound.

"No games, please," she said tiredly. "I . . . I remember what I did in the barn." Admitting the fact was hard, because it meant that her memories of Yuusuke had been real. Which also meant—"Yuusuke?" He was her first thought. Jo's every drive to care for him returned in full-force.

Once more, Snow seemed to read her unspoken thoughts. "He lives."

She couldn't stop the sharp inhale, or the shuddering exhale. Living was too broad. She knew a lot of people who could be classified as "living" but that life was nothing more than agony. "He's all right? Safe?"

"I cannot see where he is at this moment, since your wish was concluded. But as you requested, none of the circumstances occurred, and he and your family were safe as of the timeline change."

"When you say timeline change . . ." The answer was too vague for her. She wanted something more definitive than the "most likely" he seemed to be giving her.

"The wishing ritual invokes the Society to grant the will of the wisher. Doing so changes time."

"I don't know of any ritual." Denial seemed futile in light of everything, but it came on instinct—a deeply-rooted drive to avoid any sort of ridicule that came from an affiliation with the occult. Even Yuusuke had taught her that there were more *real*, more pragmatic things to worry about: her father, teachers, and friends, to name a few. Then again, if any of what was happening was true, Jo might be getting the last laugh—a fact that she couldn't seem to find joy in.

"Clearly, you do."

"I remember what my grandmother told me," Jo conceded begrudgingly. "But . . . she said it's magic lore practically from the dawn of time. No one believes that stuff anymore."

"You believed."

"Not really. I was frantic," she mumbled, willfully ignoring the truth. Either she finally owned up to the fact that the part of her that believed in magic had never gone away (much to her father's dismay), or she was in some kind of trauma-induced craze. There wasn't a way to win.

"Dawn of time . . ." he repeated softly, mostly to himself. But before Jo could question, Snow continued. "Then I'll start at the beginning."

There was a long pause and Snow's expression left Jo wondering if he even knew where "the beginning" was. "The Society of Wishes exists outside of time, outside of any reality, and functions with the singular goal of granting wishes."

"You're telling me you're a fairy godmother?"

Snow did laugh then and, despite herself, it brought a sly smile to Jo's mouth. She already liked the sound of his laughter. "I suppose you could call us that."

"Where's your wand and ball gown?"

"I'm afraid I lost those a few hundred years ago." For all Wayne had cautioned against Snow, he was proving to be the easiest to speak to of them all. There was something about him that felt familiar and comfortable in a way that people usually had to work for.

"Wayne mentioned something about a *thousand* years . . ."

"As I said, we exist outside of time and space. The Society as it's known now has been around for well over a thousand years. Closer to two thousand, actually." Snow continued forward, walking as though he'd been in these halls many times. "Each Society member has joined at a different time, as their magic was made known."

"How did they join?" The Society was still a "they," an other, something Jo was not quite ready to admit to being a part of herself.

"A wish."

A dusty server room floor, a friend bleeding out, a last resort in the form of a desperate cry for help, any help—

"It was all real, then?"

"It was."

Which meant magic was real. What was happening to her was real. It was like twelve-year-old Jo had finally gotten what she wanted from the world of the occult. But the fact didn't make nineteen-year-old Jo nearly as excited as it should. Her whole body was laden with some invisible force that grew heavier by the moment.

"Why aren't there more Society members?" Jo half-asked, half-mused. "If wishing puts you in the Society then—"

"Not quite," he interrupted.

"Not quite what?"

"You, like the other members in the Society, are of the rare few who come from a long lineage of ancient, now latent, magic." Snow ran a fingertip at the edge of his hair as he spoke, pulling it just far enough away from his eye to see. But the movement didn't register to Jo; she was more focused on the memory of her grandmother, of her mother, and the craft of mysticism that had died when the latter left her small town in Chihuahua. "Long ago, the world was in an Age of Magic. Wishes spliced time again and again, driving the world as you know it away from that era, rewriting history, destroying worlds and possibilities, and rebuilding reality in each wish. There were only seven magical lineages strong enough to remain intact throughout the splices, and the power is so far removed that it's nearly unrecognizable without the individual being a member of the Society."

"So let me get this straight." Jo stopped, putting her hands on her hips. "You're telling me I'm the descendant of some ancient witch, one of seven, and you... *woke up* what was passed on in me by forcibly drafting me into your Society?"

He paused as well, a look of focus overcoming his features. "I suppose that encompasses the rough idea of it. Though your lineage is far more special than a mere witch."

"Let's say I buy all this about lineages and magic." She didn't really have a compelling reason not to at this point. But Jo hated the feeling of giving in easily. "Why have the Society at all? I only remember you alone coming to grant my wish."

"As I said, you were a rare case." Snow stopped walking for a moment, a look of focus overcoming his features. "Very rare," he added so softly and delicately that it almost took her aback. He resumed his step before she could question. "You, and the other Society members, are not the norm for wishes. To understand the necessity of the Society, you must first understand how wishes work."

Jo bit back a groan, the almost tender moment forgotten by his continued evasion. Seriously, getting anything Jo could consider a straight answer was like pulling teeth. No man on earth could be pretty enough to be worth all this hassle. And, yet, here he was, making a compelling case.

"When a wish is made, something of equal value must be given. Every choice mortals make divides their reality. If you say yes to a decision, there is a world in which you said no. To grant a wish, I must utilize the very essence of that possibility. I harvest the energy that exists in each alternate future world by destroying it. Then, I take the energy released from that destruction and turn it into the magic that will be used to help see the wish in a single reality."

Jo remembered reading something about parallel dimensions in quantum mechanics when she'd fallen into a binge-watch of one of Yuusuke's favorite pop science shows. "Alternate realities?"

"You may be able to think of it that way . . . But know there is only ever one timeline at a time. What it looks like merely changes due to wishes."

"I didn't ask for all this," Jo muttered, even if there was little use in pointing out the fact now. As Ranger agents and office workers floated around her, oblivious to her presence, it was obvious that what was done, was done.

"You asked for your family to be safe, for your friend to be alive. These were the terms."

"Don't bring my family into this," she chastised.

"You don't want magic, then?" He arched his eyebrows. Jo instantly hated the way she felt under his gaze, like he could see right through her to something that had always been there without her knowledge or permission.

"That's irrelevant," Jo insisted. Just because the idea of magic was sparking some curiosity—enough to give her a bit of fire to fuel her through the exhaustion that was trying to smother her—that didn't excuse his actions. "There's something called consent, and it's necessary."

"I believe your words were: 'Take me, I'm yours.'"

She *had* said that. "I didn't know what I was agreeing to!"

"Would you rather live with magic, or have died? Or would you rather your friend died?" he snapped, frustration creeping to the surface at what Jo could only assume were all her questions.

Her own front wore thin and Jo finally averted her gaze, her hands falling limply to her sides. She wanted to keep up her righteous tirade of inquiry, but she just felt exhausted. It was downright disorienting being a specter in a world she was so clearly—despite all logic—no longer a part of. "Is that supposed to excuse being forced into this agreement?"

"It doesn't much matter if you think it does or doesn't." There was the Snow that Wayne had warned her of—a colder, calculating, more calloused man. And, yet, something didn't feel right about it. It was like a front she wanted to shatter. "There's no revoking wishes and no leaving the Society. Furthermore, the reality in which you existed is gone forever."

"What if someone wishes me back?" She just couldn't leave something be. She had to try to pick it apart.

Snow seemed to legitimately think about the idea for a moment. "No one knows who you are to wish you back. Josephina Espinosa was never born. She never 'adjusted' the local ATM at age eleven to dispense credits at will for her friends. She never argued with her mother about what college to attend, knowing she'd never go because she was already embroiled in organized crime. She never kissed her best friend only to have him—"

"Stop." Her toes were suddenly the most fascinating thing she'd ever seen. "I get it." Something about having her life boiled down in Snow's warm voice and icy manner made it all the harder to bear. It was hard to believe what was happening, but Jo was finding denial harder given all the evidence that was right in front of her eyes. "So, if all that never happened, if that Jo never existed . . . What do I do now?"

"You help the Society grant wishes with your magic."

"Oh, are we finally getting back to my question on why there's a

Society at all?" Jo shoved her hands in her pockets as she finally gave in and let him lead again. Moving was an outlet to the frustrations she was barely keeping contained at the idea of being unwillingly selected for a team—not to mention a team that existed outside time.

Snow either didn't hear, or ignored her sass entirely. "I can only grant wishes once the world is close enough to seeing the wish happen naturally. Otherwise, I risk tearing the very fabric of reality." Snow paused, clearly reflecting on the convolution of the statement. "Think of it this way: If the world is at state A, and a wisher wants to see it at state C, I need the Society to help move the world to a B state before a wish can be granted."

"So," Jo started, trying to logic through what he was saying in a framework she understood. "If someone hates the prime minister and wants to see them assassinated, they make a wish."

Snow nodded, allowing her to continue.

"State A would be the world where the prime minister is alive and well."

"And will keep living," he added. "State C would be a world where the prime minister is dead."

"But the B state . . ."

"In your example, those in the Society would assist with maneuvering the prime minister into a perilous situation, perhaps."

Jo thought about it a long moment. "Not just kill him?"

"I am the Wish Granter. Any changes made outside of reducing that margin by any member of the Society other than myself can risk serious implications for the overall success of the wish."

"Gotta keep yourself useful?" She grinned smugly. "Everyone else is doing all the heavy lifting . . . Jumping from A to C is too hard for you, so you make it so that you're the only one who can flip the final switch?"

"That jump is dangerously easy," Snow corrected ominously.

Jo was distracted from any follow-up.

The narrow, office-lined hallways of the Ranger compound opened up into a large meeting space. Men and women sat at round tables, eating, working, talking—all oblivious to the specters in their midst. Snow and Jo walked the length of the room to the wall of glass that overlooked a much more familiar sight.

Picturesque hills rising into purple mountains could stay in their post-card-land of the Society of Wishes. This was the world she knew.

Dallas swept out before her underneath the towered headquarters of the Rangers. The gray sky loomed over a metropolis of straight-lined, industrial buildings. Every tower competed for light by trying to smother the next in its shadow. Other official government buildings bore large flags with two horizontal bands of red and white and one vertical band of blue with a single white star and five blue stars inside—an adjustment made to the original Texan flag from back in the days of pre-WIII USA. Highways stacked over highways, congested by a meaningless rat race that Jo had long avoided.

She'd always placed herself outside the norms of conventional society. Why should it be any harder to place herself outside of reality itself?

"Is this real?" she couldn't help but ask, motioning to the cityscape.

"It is, for now."

"Until someone makes another wish?"

"Possibly."

"How many?" Jo's voice had dropped to a whisper. "How many wishes have there been that have changed the world itself?"

"Too many to count."

So, nothing was real. Nothing had ever been real. It was all luck of the draw crafted by a handful of people who were playing at power by making wishes using an ancient ritual they didn't even understand. At least, she hadn't understood it. Not really. Not at all.

Jo remembered what Wayne had said: "Reality is what we make it." This was supposed to be her new reality now. An odd existence outside time and space, where she was magic and nothing beyond the Society was permanent.

Her mother came to mind. Jo gripped her sweatshirt over her stomach, trying to quell the uneasiness there. Could her mother blink out of existence with one wish gone awry? If Snow was to be believed, her mother didn't even know who she was. Tears at the thought prickled her eyes dangerously.

"I'm ready to go back now," Jo forced out the words.

"Back?"

"To the mansion." Jo swallowed hard and wiped her cheeks, making sure no more rogue tears had continued their bold escape. Too much information swirled in her head to process at once. But the truth of everything Snow said all boiled down to one word. "Home."

# BECAUSE MAGIC

THE REST OF the walk through the compound was done in silence.

Snow led Jo back to the supply closet where she'd started her futile attempt at escape. She contemplated telling Snow it was locked, but before she had the chance, he reached for the handle and wrapped his hand around it. The moment those elegant fingers made contact with metal, the door shifted, like a veil giving way. One second it was the wooden door of the supply closet; the next it was the solid steel door of the briefing room.

It was almost too quick to see, like watching a hologram glitch out of existence: blink and you miss it. But as if the little bit of magic was commonplace for him—which Jo had no doubt it was—Snow merely pulled the door open without a word and ushered her inside.

"How did you get it to turn back?" Jo asked, clearing her throat a bit when she heard how hoarse and exhausted she still sounded. "When I tried before, nothing happened."

"Intention," Snow answered as he closed the door behind him. "The door to return never left. You simply believed it had." Still not looking at her, Snow headed back through the briefing room.

Jo hovered a moment, unsure if she should follow. But she wasn't about to try the Door again, not until she had a little more information on it. With nowhere else to go, she remained in tow behind him.

"Next time I'm out there, what do I do? Do I just clap my hands or click my heels and believe?" Jo sniffed, latching on to the concept with her usual vigor; a sense of purpose would help, surely. Learning as much as she could about the Door was a good place to start. Perhaps the next time she went through it, she'd find a way home. Or perhaps it'd just make everything feel a little less overwhelming.

Again, that soft chuckle of Snow's graced her ears, her heart fluttering a bit at the sound. "If that offers the assistance you require," he said. "But as long as your intent is to return, the Door will always be there to grant you access."

Jo nodded, even if the explanation lacked some of the more logistical requirements she was familiar with. Part of her reality now came with "magic" as an explanation, and that was something the more logical side of her mental framework was simply going to have to get used to.

About halfway back to the Four-Way, an unfamiliar woman stepped out from where she had been leaning against the wall, blocking their path. She looked to be Jo's height, Japanese, and about as attractive as every single person Jo had met so far. She had short black hair, combed to one side, and the sort of sturdy muscularity that reminded Jo of a swimmer.

The woman turned in the direction of the Four-Way and cupped a hand around her mouth.

"Snow has her!" she called out, presumably to Wayne or Nico. There was a small flash of guilt at the thought that Nico might have gone looking for her, even going so far as to recruit other members of the Society in his search. But she'd needed to try to escape, needed to find out on her own, even if knowing was less than ideal. "Ignorance is bliss" just wasn't how she did things.

"Takako," Snow said, grabbing the woman's attention. Takako turned to face them both, locking eyes with Jo only for a moment before offering Snow her full focus.

"Snow," she said, face stoic.

All of a sudden, there was a hand at the small of Jo's back, her shoulders tensing at the abrupt contact. She glanced up at Snow in surprise, but he wasn't looking at her. Instead, he just gave her a slight push in Takako's direction, his hand falling away in the same motion.

"Accompany her back to the others?" It was formed as a question, but even Jo could tell it was more of an order. Takako nodded, seemingly used to the unequal balance of power. This time, when she locked eyes with Jo, she offered her a small, barely-there smile. It might have been worn purely for Jo's benefit, and it didn't last long, but Jo was grateful for it nonetheless.

When Takako turned to lead her away, Snow stepped ahead. For a second, Jo considered saying something, possibly thanking him for explaining things, or for not leaving her panicked and stranded, but in the end she decided against it.

As if sensing her, Snow slowed and turned. Jo's chest tightened despite herself. It'd been way too long since she was last around attractive men;

she was like a cat in heat, heart fluttering at every turn. Snow spoke right to Takako: "Look after her."

Takako gave a small nod. Jo didn't miss the curious glance in her direction, but the woman said nothing more.

Jo watched him walk away, eyes following the steady stride, the length of his frame, until he turned the corner of the stairs to the right of the Four-Way and vanished from sight.

It was like dealing with a ghost, watching him float in and out of her life in the same breath, haunting her memory with the sound of soft laughter and unexpected kindness only to be cut short by the edge of something rough. It was something that seemed dangerous to even think of, never the less want.

"Jo?" Takako's voice wrenched her back and she could feel her face heating. Takako was already a couple of steps ahead of her, staring at her with an eyebrow raised in confusion. "Are you coming?"

"Yeah, sorry." Jo swallowed down the embarrassment of being caught staring and hurried to catch up. The other woman didn't seem like the conversationalist type, but Jo struck one away, not quite ready to be alone with her thoughts. "So, your name's Takako?"

Another nod, her face remaining passive, not quite cold but definitely far from open.

"Takako Kanazawa."

"Cool," Jo said eventually, when it looked like that was all she was going to get. A thought filtered in past all of the chaos her walk with Snow had kicked up, and Jo rolled with it. "So, um. What year are you from?" Snow had mentioned everyone joining the Society at different times throughout the thousand-ish years of its existence, but as far as she'd seen, outside of Wayne, everyone she'd met so far looked to be dressed in the sort of retro-grunge, industrial, uninspired fashions of the 2050s.

When Jo glanced over at Takako, her eyes looked distant. Maybe that had been an intrusive question? Before she could dwell on it for too long, however, Takako said, "I was born in 1998."

Despite expecting an unbelievable answer, Jo couldn't help the rush of surprise. Takako appeared close to her age, maybe a little older, but technically she was old enough to be Jo's mother. In an attempt to regain composure, Jo picked up the pace a bit, stepping past her.

"Wow. Looking good for fifty-nine." As she glanced over her shoulder with a smirk, she was met with a look of surprised amusement. Jo considered that a win; little victories were going to help her get through this.

The moment the two of them walked into the kitchen and lounge area, she was met with the sound of billiards being played and murmured conversations being had—conversations that stopped as soon as the room became aware of her presence. As Jo scanned the small gathering of people—all men save her and Takako—she caught sight of Wayne at the pool table and Nico having a conversation with someone by the stove. The other two faces were unfamiliar.

The man playing pool with Wayne had long, black hair and unusually defined features. Even from a distance, she could see a striking green tint to his eyes, the color all but popping against his russet skin. The way he looked at her was almost calculating, like he was looking not just at her but *into* her, seeing something beyond just her physical presence. It reminded Jo of the way Snow observed the world around him, but with a much more clinical, emotionless nature.

The other man, currently leaning against the kitchen counter next to Nico, had a mess of curly hair in a color similar to burnt sienna, one side of it shaved in strips between tight braids. The shade of it seemed to brighten beneath the natural light flooding the kitchen, popping against his bark-brown skin and seemingly highlighting his sharp and almost elongated features. He too had a sort of supernatural quality. Nearly identical to her own humanness, and yet, *different*.

He was slouching a bit, not quite keeping eye contact with Jo for more than a few seconds at a time, choosing instead to focus more intently on whatever his hands were fiddling with. Jo quickly looked away, realizing she'd been staring. Luckily, the awkward silence of her arrival was broken relatively quickly, Nico rushing over with a relieved exclamation.

"Jo! I'm so glad Snow found you!" When he was in front of her, he reached out without preamble and took her hands in his, smiling brightly. His hands were soft, fingers stained in places with a variety of different colored inks. "When I brought some food to your room and you weren't there, I worried we'd been too forthcoming and frightened you off. Thank you for coming back."

*It's not like I had much of a choice*, she wanted to say, but for some reason, she found it difficult to be cruel to the man. His disposition radiated warmth and kindness like its own mini-springtime. And, if Snow was to be believed, he was as much of a prisoner here as she was. So instead, she just carefully pulled her hands out of his grip, took a step back, and said, "Yeah. Sorry about that, I just . . . I needed some time. You know, to process."

"Of course." Nico nodded, seemingly untroubled by the space she'd added between them. "Do you feel better?"

"Not really," Jo sighed, because why bother lying? "I get that I put myself in this position, so I take responsibility for it. Or, I don't know, that it wasn't my fault but my lineage? Either way, I think it's gonna take some serious getting used to." She had magic, though. That was something she could see herself eventually *wanting* to get used to, when she wasn't so tired.

"It will begin to feel more commonplace in time, do not doubt that," the man with the long black hair interjected, approaching her with a fluidity to his step that seemed almost dance-like, graceful in a way simply walking shouldn't be. Once he was close enough, he held out a hand. The dark green of his fingernails was prominent even against his dark skin, though not nearly as unexpected as the slightly pointed shape to his ears that she hadn't made out from a distance. Jo tried to bite back her surprise, grabbing his hand in a firm handshake.

"My name is Eslar Greentouch," he said, releasing her hand. His voice was sweet and song-like, pleasant to listen to, if not almost familiar. "And yes, to get it out of the way, I come from a time when elves" —he paused, something indescribable passing across his face— "still existed."

The cogs turned much slower than she would have liked, but eventually the underlying meaning clicked into place. "A wish?" Jo asked, seeking a connection to what Snow had mentioned about a long-ago Age of Magic. But being confronted with evidence of a time so different from her own—a time where even elves existed—was surreal.

Eslar nodded, face guarded. Despite the multitude of questions jostling for space in her already crowded mind, Jo didn't probe further. She didn't really want people asking her yet about Yuusuke and would extend the same courtesy about their wishes.

"Looks like you and Takako have already gotten acquainted," Wayne chimed in. Jo glanced over her shoulder to where Takako had been standing, but at some point, despite being right behind her, she'd walked over to one of the couches without Jo noticing.

"Which means you've met everyone but Samson." Nico gestured back to where the orange-haired man still stood, all but staring holes into his shoes. Samson's hands continued to fidget, though now the unknown item that bore the brunt of his tinkering seemed impossibly bigger.

"Samson, say hello," Nico encouraged.

"Hello," he said, barely giving her a glance.

"Samson's our craftsman, and a fine one at that," Nico continued, as though Samson's mannerisms were expected. "And then there's Pan. She's . . . rarely around, but you'll meet her eventually."

"Hey, Samson," Jo called over, if only just to show she'd been actively listening. Samson startled a bit at being addressed. He raised a hand in a quick wave but nothing more, so she turned her attention back to Nico, not wanting the guy to literally melt from the discomfort that seemed to be heating to a boil on his face. "What did you mean 'craftsman'?"

"Everyone's gotta have a job, doll." Wayne sauntered over. Jo forced herself to roll her eyes at him in response. Yet despite outward appearances, she found herself immensely satisfied at his positioning right at her side.

"So, what's my job, then?" Jo asked, frowning. "All I'm good at is hacking, and if I can't interact with anything in the real world anymore, how am I supposed to do that?" The group exchanged a look; the feeling that she was missing something prickled beneath Jo's skin.

"I'm more than certain you are good at something far greater than that," Eslar jumped in, thwarting her self-doubt deftly. "And given time, you will be able to interact and use your magic, full-force."

"Time," Jo repeated, deadpan. "Like what? I need to practice?"

"No, no." Nico shook his head, smiling like a teacher would for a kid too impatient to listen and learn. "Well, yes, you should practice at some point. But our friend meant *physical* time." He reached into the pocket of his jeans and pulled out an over-sized, silver pocket watch, unlike anything Jo had ever seen. When he pressed the top, it popped open to reveal three simple clock faces, one with only a second hand, one seeming to tell the current time, and one perpetually frozen at what appeared to be 1:17.

As Jo looked around, she saw everyone pull out their various time-pieces in example. Eslar's was another pocket watch, this one made of wood and etched with designs and markings that were unfamiliar to her. Samson's was made of some sort of crystal, it looked like, the watch face embedded in a leather bracer he wore on his right forearm.

"When we're given a wish that requires legwork, we're also given time." Wayne picked up the explanation, holding out his wrist and showing off his own watch with all the determination of a man compensating for something. It was shiny and expensive-looking, probably a Rolex. Jo put her bet on a knock-off. "That time lets us interact with people and things in the real world."

Despite herself, Jo perked up at that. Interacting with the real world, the Door . . . it could add up to a way out. "Do I get one?"

"You should have woken up with one," Eslar said, and Jo's heart fell.

She hadn't woken up with anything.

"Yours is probably like mine," Takako chimed in, and when Jo looked over in her direction, she was holding up a rather dated-looking "smart" phone. Involuntarily, Jo looked down at her wrist, the strip of circuit-embedded fabric peeking out from beneath the sleeve of her hoodie. She pushed the cuff up to her elbow and, as she did every day, ran a finger along the material, watching it light up with the time. Only instead of the whole display coming to life, flush against her skin, it stayed frozen on the lock screen, the time passing in solidarity.

"Yeah," Takako chuckled quietly. "Mine won't unlock either."

Jo lowered her sleeve back down. "So how does it work?"

"When you're out in the field, you activate it," Takako said, as though the fact should've been obvious.

"It means little until you have time," Eslar interjected.

Jo looked back at her watch. Zeros stared back at her where the stopwatch would usually be running. She shook her head, feeling exhausted all over again. Just when there had been hope, she was thwarted.

"And I get time when a wish comes in?" There was a consensus of nods. "When does that happen?"

"No one knows when. The wishes are random, by all accounts," Eslar continued. "And even when you have time, it's not to be squandered."

She was dealing with a real Snow 2.0 here. Jo's mind continued to try to work out alternatives, but it stayed sluggish. Despite herself, a yawn escaped through her lips.

"Tired?" Nico asked.

"Yeah, a bit."

"I'll walk you back to your room," Wayne offered. "Should be the last time you need to sleep. After this your body will have fully acclimated to its new status as member of the Society. Naturally, you can try to sleep if you really want, but it'll no longer be a necessity."

Jo's mind buzzed with the new information, trying to make sure that tidbit got sorted with Nico's earlier comments about food. But it couldn't seem to gain traction about anything. "Sure, okay," she mumbled.

Wayne led her out of the room to a chorus of brief goodbyes and see-you-laters. He kept pace with her dragging feet. "Why did you let me walk you this time?" he asked, finally.

Jo didn't bother concealing a self-satisfied smile at the discovery that he was the sort to speak first, not at all because he seemed equally pleased to be with her. "I have a question for you."

"Oh?" He had the coin from his pocket, flipping it absentmindedly. Jo regarded it cautiously, remembering the magic he'd used on her earlier. She wouldn't let herself fall into the same trap. The wriggling feeling meant danger.

"You seemed so helpful earlier, I thought you may be willing to assist again." And he also seemed like the type who got off on saving a damsel. The self-satisfied grin confirmed her suspicions. Oh, yes, she'd use this to her advantage if needed. "How do you pick where you want to go through the door?" Her tongue moved freely this time. Whatever coin magic he had, wasn't in effect.

"Intent," he answered. She should've guessed it was something like that. But her intent certainly hadn't been to go to the Rangers. She'd just been trying to find the code, thinking there was only one.

"The last wish the Society granted—" Jo swallowed, hard, the words suddenly sticky. "Mine. Did the Society need to go into the Ranger headquarters to help grant it?"

His flipping stopped, the coin pocketed. Wayne regarded her thoughtfully. "Yes. How did you know that?"

"Good guess." So the numbers that had appeared in front of her eyes when she'd looked at the keypad weren't random. Somehow, she'd broken apart clues to find a pattern where one wouldn't have otherwise been. They stopped in front of her door. "Well then, goodnight."

"Goodnight, if you—"

The closing of her door cut him off. Jo looked back at her room that was not quite hers. Then, down at her watch. She had a path home at least, she hoped.

But finding it would have to wait for tomorrow. Her eyes were already shutting of their own accord. Tomorrow, yes, she'd go home tomorrow and see if Snow was being more upfront about the outcome of her wish than he had been about the price she'd paid to get it.

For now, though, sleep was the only thing on Jo's weary mind.

# WISH

J O STARED AT the blank spot in the wall where the Iron Man poster had been, not moving, barely blinking.

She was not in her tiny apartment, no matter how much it looked like she was. She was not even really alive anymore. She was a member of the Society of Wishes, and this was their mansion head-quarters that existed outside time.

*Her family didn't even know she existed.*

Perhaps, if she said it all enough times in her head, she'd start to believe it. Though, the last thought was proving the hardest of them all.

Jo pulled herself to her feet, rummaging through the hamper and picking out two random articles of clothing that looked suspiciously like what she wore yesterday. However, they didn't smell, and the jeans-plus-tank-top combination worked just as well with her hoodie in this world as all the jeans and tank tops she'd worn in her past life.

Before the nostalgia monster could sink its claws into her, Jo exited her room. It was suddenly a lot easier to believe that she was pulled from time and had magic when the unfamiliar stretch of Society members' doors greeted her. Down the hall, down the stairs, down the second hall, and Jo was back in the living area-slash kitchen-slash dining-slash games-slash patio-slash pool area.

The space, which Jo mentally dubbed "the common room" for ease, was completely empty, a fact that made her thankful for two reasons.

Firstly, she didn't have to interact with anyone. Everything was still settling on her like a weird dream that contrasted with the reality she'd known for nineteen years of life. She felt more than a little off-balance and awkwardly on edge, to say the least. And secondly, there would be no witnesses to her fumbling about in the kitchen.

"There must be coffee somewhere . . ." she muttered.

"Second cabinet to the left of the refrigerator." Jo hadn't expected a response, least of all from the voice that gave it. She stilled, turning slowly. Snow stood in the doorway.

For a moment that could stretch into infinity, they merely stared at each other. He almost looked out of place, even among the opulence. There was something to his perfection—a lean yet muscular frame or the way his fingers draped over the crook of his elbow—that even the arched ceilings and stained glass couldn't compare to. She felt like she was breaking some rule just by looking at him.

Jo swallowed hard. "Morning."

"Is it?" The question struck her as odd and had Jo looking at her watch.

"I guess so, I mean, technically . . ." Her watch read 11:45. When had she gone to bed? How long had she been asleep for? It suddenly seemed a blur.

"Time gets distorted here," Snow said, as if reading her mind.

"Yeah . . ." They stared at each other for a long moment before Jo suddenly remembered that there was coffee to be had.

It was unexpectedly relieving to have an excuse to look away from him. Under any other circumstances, she'd want to appreciate a man as attractive as Snow. Admiring Wayne's attractive qualities certainly hadn't been hard. But Snow was . . . *different*. He had a warmth that was in direct contrast to all the icy airs he seemed to put on. A warmth that a girl could sink into and get lost in if she wasn't careful.

"How did you sleep?"

Jo stilled once more, and turned. His lingering presence surprised her. "Good. Like the dead, really." Jo instantly cringed at the metaphor and returned to her task.

"Good."

Another awkward silence. *What was he waiting for?* It was almost as if he enjoyed staring at her as much as she him.

"Do you want a cup of coffee?" She asked as the pot was percolating, secretly hoping he'd say yes.

"No, not this morning."

Another long pause. Another stretch where their eyes remained locked and everything else seemed to fade away.

"Snow," Jo whispered, barely realizing she was talking at all. "Have we . . . met before?" The question was ridiculous, yet it sprung from her with the ease of certainty.

"You were born in the Age of Man."

"That's not an answer." Jo took a small step forward, the coffee all but forgotten. "There's something about you that's—"

"I'm afraid there's no time for further conversation." The sudden urgency to his tone startled her. It was as if he was suddenly jarred back to reality from whatever daydream that had been distracting him. "Wake Eslar, inform the rest of the group. There has been a wish. Briefing room in ten."

With that, the man was gone before she had time to even turn back around. Jo blinked. "I guess that's a no to meeting previously? I'm just crazy, then," she murmured at the spot he'd just vacated.

Mug in hand, Jo ventured down the series of hallways, ending up at the room with Eslar's name on the door. She gave a few solid raps. By the speed with which the man opened the door and how put-together he was, he clearly had not been sleeping for some time. *Not that Society members needed sleep*, her mind reminded in a desperate attempt to grasp her new circumstances. She tried to steal a glance into his room, but couldn't; the tall elf dominated the sliver of open door.

Eslar looked her up and down, and Jo did much the same. *An elf, an actual elf.* She'd seen stranger things, she supposed. Heading to the first town in the LSR to be inhabited entirely by androids after the artificial rights bill passed should've been one. But at the exact moment, even that seemed far more benign.

"Yes?" he asked, the word void of any emotion.

"Snow said there's a wish, told me to get everyone."

"Told you?" Eslar arched an eyebrow.

"Yes . . ." Jo wasn't uncertain of her request; she was uncertain of why Eslar was suddenly looking at her as though she'd sprouted a second head.

"Why you?"

"I don't know? I was awake? He drew straws? Or maybe he likes me?" The last joke hit an odd place in Jo's chest.

"Very well, let's round up the others."

Samson and Takako looked as if they'd been awake as well.

Wayne was found lounging in a mostly-open silk robe, but had a clarity to his eyes that told Jo they hadn't been closed in restful repose for some time. He leaned against the doorframe, appraising her. "You're quite the sight to see first thing."

Jo rolled her eyes and hid her smirk with her coffee mug. "Flattery will get you nowhere."

He made a low humming noise, folding his arms over his chest. He didn't have to say the words, "We'll see about that"—they were written all over his body language. Jo felt her cheeks warming and that same thought returned: how long had it been since someone, anyone, was even the slightest bit interested in her? Perhaps that was the explanation for the odd pull toward Snow, too.

"I'm supposed to tell you there's a wish, briefing room in ten." Jo glanced at her watch. "Five, now."

"Let's go then." Wayne took a step toward her, encroaching just slightly on her personal space.

"You're going like that?"

"Bother you, dollface?"

Before Jo could ready a response, Wayne gave a laugh. He turned, heading back into his room. Jo stared at the closed door, digging her nails into her coffee mug, taking another long sip.

It was just the coffee pooling hot in her lower stomach, nothing more.

She moved onto the next door—Nico's. The man practically lunged for her cup of coffee the moment he saw it. Jo liked the guy, but not enough to give him her coffee. Which meant that the two of them went on an expedition to the kitchen for refills before being the last ones to arrive in the briefing room.

What she had only yet experienced as the still, quiet air of the briefing room was now alive with energy. Everyone shifted restlessly, like they couldn't find a comfortable way to sit. Three chairs were empty, and when Nico settled by Eslar, Jo went for the location between Takako and Wayne, on the opposite end of the table from Snow.

"Not there." The former held up a hand.

"Why?" It was more curiosity than anger. Jo didn't care if she sat in that chair or the one between Eslar and Samson.

"Pan sits there."

"Pan?" Jo vaguely remembered the name being mentioned before.

Snow spoke from the head of the table. "She'll be here in a—"

"Sorry I'm late." A woman made a show of a yawn from the doorway, scanning the room as she entered. She had pencil-straight hair down to her waist in an ombré of pinks from her roots to the ends. At first glance, Jo thought she was nothing more than a child—young teen, at the oldest. But there was a maturity to the shape of her face. Her proportions, though slender, were womanly, and Jo was left wondering if she was looking at someone very young, or *very* old.

*No, it was more than age.* There was something about seeing her in general, something that immediately had Jo's hair standing on edge. It was a sensation similar to what Snow made her feel—a sense of familiarity. But where his was a calming and alluring presence, hers had Jo wanting to bolt for the door.

Midway to her chair, the woman stopped dead in her tracks. Slowly, her attention swung over to Jo. She stared at Jo with bright yellow eyes, almost like those of a cat, and with all the same curiosity. Then, a pterodactyl screech shattered Jo's thoughts.

"There's a girl?" Pan exclaimed in echo, thrusting a finger in Jo's direction. "When did this happen?"

"Uh . . ." Jo looked over to Takako, whose expression betrayed nothing. The way Pan acted, it was like the other woman who'd been in the Society before Jo didn't even exist.

"Takako is so dull that she's practically one of the boys." Pan shook her head. The casual discursiveness toward Takako had Jo bristling. But before she could say anything, Pan continued. "Why did no one tell me?"

"I just got here yesterday," Jo explained.

"Not a good enough excuse. *Someone* should've told me." Pan's eyes fell on Snow, briefly, before swinging to the rest of the table. "You all know how I hate secrets!" Pan rushed over to her and Jo leaned instinctively back in her chair. Energy pulsated around her in a wriggling way that Jo was coming to associate with magic. But unlike everyone or anything else Jo had felt to date, this was near-constant—a low thrum that seemed to hover in an aura around the fuchsia-haired woman. It did nothing to help her unease.

"I'm sorry I didn't introduce myself sooner."

"It's fine, really, I was taking a nap anyway." Pan shrugged.

"For a whole day?" The phrase DOES NOT COMPUTE scrolled through Jo's brain.

"For a month. It was a good nap. I was dreaming about someone special. Funny, she looked a lot like you." She grinned, her lips spreading toward her ears with unnatural wideness. Just like that, the visage of the woman-child transformed into something slightly more animalistic. But it was gone so quickly that Jo was left wondering if it was all in her head to begin with.

"I thought we didn't need sleep anymore. Does it have to do with your magic?" Jo was still pulling up errors left and right for every thought.

"No, I just like sleep." Pan shrugged. "Eternity can be so boring, it passes the time while I wait for something interesting to happen."

"At least it wasn't six months this time," Eslar whispered, the only one among them who seemed brave enough to comment.

"Well, perhaps you can teach me how to take naps that long." Jo thrust out her hand, mentally scolding herself for the unease she felt. There was just something about this woman-child that Jo couldn't put her finger on and was certainly unfounded. "I've been known to like my sleep, as well."

"I'm sure you'll figure it out soon enough!" Pan clapped her hands and completely ignored Jo's outstretched hand. She spun in place and sauntered around the room to the last empty seat.

In trying to ignore her own awkwardness, Jo observed an interesting phenomenon occur—a unique shift in the overall demeanor of the room. Everyone suddenly seemed obsessed with anything other than Pan. There was an almost subservient manner to the way their eyes were directed elsewhere.

Pan sat gracefully, swinging her legs into a criss-cross and tapping her fingers on the table. She locked eyes with the man at the head of the table, directly across from her. "It was about time, Snow. You finally have all seven chairs filled."

*About time for what? What's the importance of the chairs being full?* Jo wanted to ask. She remembered Snow mentioning the seven lineages, but why did that really matter? The questions remained heavy on her tongue. She wondered if Pan had magic like Wayne's, and had used it to still her questions.

Jo rubbed the back of her neck. There was no uncomfortable sensation to be felt.

Snow and the woman shared an unreadable look before Snow attempted to continue on as though she hadn't said anything. "We have received a wish."

Questions of a different sort burned in Jo's mouth, but she kept them quiet of her own volition. A wish meant time, and time meant being able to interact with the real world (however that worked in practice), and that was something Jo desperately wanted. She had to make sure her family was safe.

"The wish comes from a nurse at a hospital in Canada." Snow waved his hand, and the table glimmered to life. What could only be described as magic rippled across the surface, so tangible-looking that Jo lifted her fingers off the edge before it lapped against the side. She couldn't stop a small gasp, or the blush that immediately followed the outburst. No one else reacted, save for Wayne. *He* shot her a smug little grin. She narrowed her eyes and then promptly ignored him and the fact that he had been paying attention to her.

Jo rested her hands back down to find the surface still glass-like, despite the swirling energy beginning to coagulate into shapes. The image of a doe-eyed nurse in soft, teal medical scrubs materialized as if the entire table had been transformed into a hi-def television screen.

"Is this live?" Jo whispered, to no one in particular.

Eslar gave a noise of affirmation from her side.

"The nurse is working with a terminally ill patient in a hospital that specializes in clinical trials. He's the second she's dealt with, but the third to die from this disease. If left unchecked, the illness will become a pandemic," Snow began.

"Can you see the future?" Jo blurted.

"I can see all possible avenues relating to a wish and only the wish."

The soft, almost-kind Snow from the compound had vanished, leaving behind a stoic and purpose-driven instructor. This version was different than the almost-awkward man who had encountered her rummaging through the kitchen that morning as well. While his tone wasn't exactly harsh, it lacked gentleness—not so much leading her calmly into this new world as expecting her to follow dutifully. Like a soldier.

Was that what they were?

"Will you take her existence, too?" The question came out more biting than Jo intended, but she also didn't feel exactly apologetic for it.

"That only happens for a select few. The people assembled here and no more, ever." Snow was unbothered by her tone and motioned to the room. "Usually, I only destroy an unrelated world and turn it into magic."

Snow's statement reaffirmed what he'd said in the compound the day prior—a deluge of information Jo was still working to process.

"So," Eslar joined in, no doubt seeing the confusion on Jo's face, "if this nurse wished for the disease to be cured . . ." He glanced at Snow, who gave a nod of affirmation. "Snow would take another wish, an alternate future of hers—"

"To someday become a doctor herself, in this instance," Snow volunteered.

"Wait." It dawned on Jo, but seemed too horrible to bear. "To grant her the wish of curing the disease, you made it so that she can never become a doctor?"

"That is where the magic required to alter reality and grant the wish comes from—destroying worlds," Snow affirmed. It was an emotionless statement, calculated, and so far detached from any guilt or regret that Jo was surprised it didn't echo in the space that his heart and human empathy must have once occupied. This was as much business for him as crashing an ambassador's self-driving car was for her. Or, had been for her, in the life she'd had before she was a magical wish-granting soldier-puppet.

Very well, she knew how to steel herself. She could play this game.

"But the magic generated isn't always enough." There was a knowing tone to Eslar's addition.

"This one will fall to you," Snow affirmed with a nod in the elf's direction.

Jo remembered the A to C premise Snow had previously explained. "So, Eslar will help move the world to B so you can get it to C?"

"B . . . what?" Eslar's brow furrowed in confusion.

"Just so." Snow understood her perfectly. And Jo didn't miss the way his lips quirked up just barely into a smirk. It was like a secret they both shared, even if it wasn't secret at all.

"I can help," she offered, newfound confidence building.

"Not this time. We have no need of you for this task."

The words seemed harmless enough, but they grated against something raw, a space in her chest that looked like home. "If you have no need of me" —she threw his words right back at him— "then why bring me here in the first place?"

"As we discussed—"

"I really think I could help," she interrupted. She needed purpose, reason. She couldn't have her entire world taken from her, only to be shoved aside. If she didn't have purpose, then all she had was to dwell on all she'd lost. "I'm sure there's some research somewhere that I could hack—"

"I have made myself clear." Snow pushed away from the table, his face expressionless. Any emotion he'd spared for her was now so far buried that there was no hope of dredging it up. "Eslar will see to the preliminaries of the wish and I will ensure the world knows of the cure. You are all dismissed."

Jo watched him begin to leave, completely stunned until a different emotion took over.

"But!" Jo shot up from her chair so quickly, it nearly toppled backwards. Everyone in the room, even those only halfway out of their own chairs, startled into stillness. She swallowed, trying to collect the nervous energy into something that could be explained to everyone else. "Please, I . . ." How she hated begging. "It will help me get used to things . . . if I can be a part of this too. I promise I won't be a burden." Her eyes were on Snow's motionless back as she made her plea. Surely, he had to take pity on the situation she'd been thrust into. They all knew how hard it was, right?

A long moment passed where Snow didn't even bother to face her. He stood in the doorway, his posture set tall and stern, intimidating (despite how much Jo loathed to admit it at that moment). Then, very slowly, he turned around, and looked her in the eye.

There it was, that look again that seemed reserved for her alone. At least, it felt that way. Jo swallowed hard, but couldn't dislodge the breath caught in her throat. Hope swelled in that air, ready to carry a thank-you to him for agreeing to keep her hands busy and let her help.

"I realize it is not your intent to be a burden," Snow assured, taking a step towards her. "But you are a novice. You need to learn your own limitations—your restrictions. You need to enhance your strengths and get a hold over your magic. Until then, you have no place on the field." Snow continued to walk towards her, eventually standing directly in her personal space.

Jo's hands remained at her sides. No matter how much she willed them, they didn't move. It was as if her body admitted he was right before her mind would. Snow's eyes scanned her face, waiting for an objection she couldn't seem to muster no matter how hard she tried.

"Learn your magic, and your place, before trying to jump into a wish."

With that hanging in the air between them, Snow left the conference room, Jo standing in his wake with nothing but her own shell-shocked, silence to cling to. It was neither kind, nor cruel; he'd left her in a space void of emotion that Jo suddenly had a hard time navigating.

It took a moment for her to remember that she wasn't alone. The sound of Pan's chair sliding backward filled the silence as she stood.

"Well, that was certainly exciting!" The woman-child clapped her hands. "Good luck, Eslar. I can't wait to see what you come up with."

And with that, she was gone.

Everyone else stood in relative silence and began to filter out. Jo, however, sunk back into her seat. The feeling of uselessness was more bitter than waking up and finding that she had been pulled outside of reality.

# GIFT OF TIME

S HE HAD ONLY just begun scheming ways to prove her worth to
Snow when Wayne cleared his throat and Jo's head jerked up. Jo
hadn't even realized he'd lingered while the rest of them had left.
He offered her a shrug, a half smile, and the tension seemed to instantly
break.

"Is he always like this?"

"Snow doesn't always need all of us for a wish," Wayne explained.
"He has the tact of a three-year-old sometimes, but I'm sure he only meant
to remind you that fieldwork can be dangerous, especially when you're
only just beginning."

"Thanks for coming to my defense," Jo huffed, and rested her chin in
her palm. Right or wrong, justified or not, it still left her with nothing to
do other than stew about not existing. Wayne chuckled.

"Well, fine, he was also being a right pill." Wayne pulled up a chair
next to hers. Boldly, he took the hand that wasn't occupied with her chin,
giving it a squeeze. Jo looked at his fingers wrapped around hers. She
focused on the warmth of his touch, different from how Snow's had felt;
there wasn't that same spark. "Don't let it get to you."

"Easy for you to say," Jo mumbled. While she hadn't invited the
contact, Jo found it more reassuring than she wanted to admit. Out of
everyone, Wayne was proving to be her only lifeline. So, for now, she let
his hand stay. "You're already integrated here, familiar with this life; you
have nothing to prove. You'll be useful as they need you to be."

"But I'd rather not be needed," Wayne said quickly. "Trust me, dollface, helping with a wish isn't always what you want."

Jo turned to face him, searching. "Why?"

Wayne shook his head. "It's a lot of pressure. But you'll have your moment. When you've had a chance to learn and understand more of what it is we do, I have no doubt you will be an irreplaceable asset to the team."

"Even still . . ." Jo sighed heavily. "I wish I could do something now. I'm not the sort to just sit around and wait for something to happen, I never have been. I've always had a job or a duty to someone or something. Even if it's not helping with our mission, I'd take any distraction."

Jo's eyes drifted toward the Door. It was as unassuming as it had been yesterday. But she now knew it was her only portal out.

Remembering all at once her new circumstances, Jo twisted her wrist, looking at her watch. Sure enough, under the time where her stopwatch would count down—if she was using one—the numbers read 10:00.

"I have time," Jo whispered. "How? I'm not part of the wish, so—"

"Everyone gets time when a wish comes in," Wayne clarified. "Snow isn't the one to dish out the time; it's given by default."

"Is it the same for every wish?"

Wayne shook his head. "It varies, depending on the complexity of the wish. And any leftover time can roll-over from one wish to the next. I think Takako has almost a hundred hours stored. She'll never risk wasting minutes, just in case she's not given enough time for a future wish."

"Has that ever happened?" Jo asked. "Not having enough time to complete a wish?"

"No, never." Wayne chuckled. "That's just the sort of woman Takako is. Nothing ever in excess. Boring if you ask me. But you seem like a woman who can appreciate spending a little bit here and there."

Jo wasn't ready to let him derail the subject. "If Snow doesn't dish out the time, and doesn't decide how much is given for any wish . . . who does?"

"Who knows? Maybe it's just some automatic magic system?" Wayne shrugged. His nonchalance grated her. She didn't like the idea of some invisible force governing such an important aspect of her life. But Jo swallowed down the worry, for now at least. The Society and its members had been around long enough. If it was something worth worrying about, they would've already done it.

"How do I use it?"

"Let's not get ahead of yourself, doll."

"What happened to appreciating someone spending a little?" Jo grinned, satisfied by his look of surprise and brief frustration at her throwing his words back at him. "Do I just go through the Door?"

Jo didn't wait for a response; she was already at the threshold, her fingers hovering over the keypad. Intent, Wayne had said—she just had to have the right intent to get to where she wanted. As long as she had that, she shouldn't risk using the same magic that picked up the last code input and took her to the Ranger's HQ—she supposed. Magic seemed more guesswork and determination than an exact science.

"Now that I have time, can I just go out and interact with the real world?"

"Ease up." Wayne grabbed her wrist, pulling it away from the keypad. "Let's not be hasty."

"I want to go home," she demanded, her voice raising by a fraction. Jo blinked at herself, startled by the sudden ferocity that escaped her, but she stood by it.

"Jo, there isn't—"

"I need to see it," she whispered. "Snow tells me that I didn't exist, that I'm not real." She shook her head. Saying it was harder than she thought it would be. But it wasn't the first hard thing she'd done in her life and it wouldn't be the last. "He says that my wish worked, but how do I know for sure? How can I give up on that world if there's any hope that it still has a place for me? How can I move on if I haven't even said goodbye to my mother?"

His grip went slack on her wrist and Jo could tell she was gaining ground. An inborn sense told Jo that if she pressed just a little more, he'd break.

"I'm going to go. You can either help me or stand aside." It sounded threatening, but Jo intended it simply as matter of fact. As if to seem less threatening, Jo shoved her hands in the pockets of her hoodie, a threadbare thing that had become softer with every wash since her first year of junior high.

"All right, I can tell when a dame's mind is set," Wayne conceded. "It shouldn't be an issue, I suppose."

"Good." Jo freed her hand and held it back over the touch pad.

"What you need to do is—"

Before he could finish the thought, her fingers were moving. Home was crisp and clear in her mind. Jo didn't even know what numbers or letters she depressed, but her fingers moved with certainty. There was that same hiss of pressurization, the click of the door opening, and then—light.

# NOT REAL

SHE FELT TUGGED alongside Wayne, drawn from her navel as if by some magic umbilical cord pulling her back toward the real world, a world that she'd been born into just nineteen short years ago. Jo raised a hand up to her eyes, guarding them from the suddenly all-too-oppressive sun.

The door spit them out on a side street connected to her mother's neighborhood. Jo instantly recognized the squat houses and modest lawns. It wasn't a long walk from her home, maybe ten minutes. She should be glad to be so close, but Jo's anxiety had already kicked into overdrive and she found herself wishing she'd had just a bit longer to compose herself.

"So, where's home?" Wayne looked around, hands in his pockets.

"Texas." Jo followed suit, beginning to lead the way.

"The mighty Lone Star Republic doesn't look like what I'd expect," he mumbled.

"What would you expect?" She latched onto the conversation as an opportunity for distraction.

"It used to look a lot more different."

"Looks like the same dusty corner of the world I've always known. What did you think it'd look like?" She gave him an up and down look and quickly added so he didn't think she was checking him out, "No one has dressed like that in America for over a century, you know."

"More than fashion, doll. When a country is invaded and then split up . . . I just thought it'd look a lot different is all."

"Texas has always been Texas. It's not even like this is the first time it's been its own country, even." Jo shrugged. "I'm surprised you even know about the outcome of World War III."

"I haven't lived in a hole." There was mock offense in his voice.

"Just outside time," she countered.

"And even there you can't escape the talking heads on the television."

"Really?" Jo arched her eyebrows. "You get news in the mansion?"

"How else would we keep up with the world?"

She merely hummed and kept wondering why people who existed beyond time would even need to "keep up with the world." Jo looked at the sky; it was already turning a dusky color with the beginnings of sunset.

"I was born in 2038, a full twenty-three years after the war ended. Can't say I know what the old America even looked like to compare. Plus, most of the fighting stayed on the coasts. From what I've heard and seen, there's still some rebuilding there. But America surrendered before any of the bombings got here."

"For the best, as they say." Wayne's voice grew distant as he pulled into his own thoughts.

Jo nodded in agreement. The war had been hard and costly in both life and finances. But history was a topic her mind withdrew from when they rounded the corner of her street—or rather, the street that once marked home. Down at the end of the cul-du-sac, her family home crept into view —still small and square-shaped, a one-story affair painted in a rich terra-cotta that her mother got to keep after the divorce. She didn't know whether to be relieved or disappointed that it looked exactly like she remembered. It was almost too similar, eerily so, and Jo had to keep reminding herself that this was a house that she had now never visited before.

"Come on, dollface," Wayne pulled her out of her thoughts, one hand on the back of her neck as the other fiddled with his coin, flipping it up and down. "You were rallying to come here. How's about you give me the nickel tour?"

Jo hadn't realized her feet had stopped moving at the edge of the driveway. She took a breath and nodded, walking up the concrete with renewed purpose. As frustrated as he had a knack for making her, Jo appreciated Wayne's presence immensely in that moment. She honestly wasn't sure if she could've done this alone.

Her mom's car wasn't there, so it was unlikely that anyone was home —unless this was now a universe where her father was a stay-at-home husband. Unlikely, even in a world of magic. Jo thanked her lucky stars, not quite sure if she'd have been able to handle that. Knowing the woman who had been everything to Jo wouldn't be able to hug her, probably wouldn't even recognize her? Even with her ability to go unseen, she didn't think she had the heart for it.

They walked up to the keypad on the garage door. Jo raised a hand, hooking the cap to open it. When it didn't budge, Wayne caught her wrist.

"Just a sec, doll."

"What?"

"Let me." Wayne motioned to his watch. "You can't interact with things outside of time."

"Why? I got time with the wish, didn't I?" Jo flipped her watch, affirming the fact. The numbers 10:00 still read where her stopwatch usually was.

"Time doesn't just run because you walk through the Door. Thankfully," Wayne added the last word as a mutter under his breath. "You have to activate it."

"How do I do that?"

"Let's not worry about that for now," he said with more delicacy than Jo had previously thought possible for him to muster. As Jo moved to object, he placed a sturdy hand on her shoulder and continued. "I have some time still left over from a prior wish. So, just in case, I'd rather preserve yours."

"Didn't Snow make it clear that I wasn't going to be of help anyway? Shouldn't I use mine?"

Wayne just shook his head, clearly not wanting to go down that route of conversation again. Jo watched closely as he pushed in a knob on his over-sized Rolex. Just like that, the hands began turning on the face. She didn't perceive him as any different, but the keypad opened up with a flick of his fingers where it had been utterly immobile for hers.

"Code?"

"Eleven, Seven, Two," Jo recited, watching his fingers depress the buttons as though that—of all things—was the most magical thing she'd seen. "And press the car button after."

The door groaned open, then closed again as they slipped through.

The garage was a little messier than she remembered, but she hadn't visited her mother in months (she'd been too busy trying to find work), so that could very well have been a recent change. Either way, she ignored the little details for now and started for the interior door.

"It should be unlocked," she informed Wayne.

Sure enough, it was, and he ushered them both inside, closing the door behind them and pulling out the pin on his watch again. Time stopped flowing through the device and the hands stilled. Jo gave him a once-over, waiting for some magical aura to appear, but he seemed the same as he always had.

She didn't know why everyone was making magic out to seem so complicated. All this "learning her place." From what Jo had seen, so far, magic was about intention, determination, and simple actions.

The moment Jo took more than a step into the house, however, all thoughts of magic and time vanished from her mind. Out of reflex, she found herself sniffing the air, heart clenching when she could smell none of the familiar scents of home.

"You all right?" Wayne asked softly. Jo startled slightly.

"Oh, yeah. Fine," she replied quickly, clearing her throat. "Just . . . habit."

"To sniff your house?" He asked, and his obvious attempt at keeping the mood lighthearted almost worked, the grip around her heart loosening a fraction.

"Whenever my mom knew I was coming home, she would always make my favorite dessert," Jo said, taking a breath as she reminisced, even though it came away lacking. "The first thing I would smell whenever I visited was *sopapillas*."

A brief pause, and then, "Your mother used to feed you soap?"

She couldn't help the laugh that bubbled up her throat, but she offset it with a tight roll of her eyes. "Yes, Wayne. My mother used to feed me *soap*." After a second, however, she felt her own face soften, the laughter settling into a sigh. "*Sopapillas* are like hollow donuts you can pour warm honey into. When you take a bite, the honey pours out all over your fingers, and it's just . . ." She took another breath, this time more to combat the renewed tightness in her chest than any lingering desire to smell dough and honey in the air. "They're just really good, that's all."

She didn't wait to see Wayne's reaction, and instead continued wandering through the house on autopilot.

Besides more of that relative messiness, it was still in much the same shape as she remembered. There were more little details depicting slight, barely recognizable change, however, like no upright piano in the hallway; a smaller, lower-quality television in the living room. As she walked into the kitchen, she noticed a lack of fruit in the bowl by the toaster, a pile of bills stacked in its place. Without turning her watch on to get a closer look, she could tell some of them were recent, especially the ones with Final Notice stamped in bold red ink along the front.

It occurred to her then, just how much her mother had been relying on her for financial stability. The money she made from various odd and usually illegal jobs—high paying stints with the Yakuza, usually—had always gone at least in part to her mother. Without that cut, how difficult was it for her to get by?

"This your little sister's room or something?" Wayne's voice pulled her through the kitchen and to the back of the house, her distraction giving way to confusion the moment she approached the open doorway.

"This—" she heard herself whisper on a half-second delay. Jo swallowed to clear the lump in her throat and make room for the rest of the sentence. "This is my room."

But it wasn't. Not really, not anymore. The walls were painted a light blue, toys and stuffed animals littering the floor. It was obviously a room belonging to a little girl, nowhere near what her own childhood room had been. Her walls had been a messy collage of movie posters and sticky notes, her "toys" limited to various computer parts and video games. Whoever this child was, she was very much not Josephina Espinosa.

And why should she be? Jo remembered the vague conversation of a miscarriage somewhere around when she'd turned eight, a passing comment about how it had probably been for the best. A casual joke about Jo being enough of a handful, though Jo was already old enough to recognize that it was more about another mouth to feed and all too recently filed divorce papers. Maybe, in this version of reality, Jo's lack of existence meant the creation of this little girl's.

Maybe embryonic Jo had been the one who miscarried.

Wandering throughout the room, letting her fingers brush against a bright, floral comforter, a stuffed unicorn, it finally hit her.

The world didn't continue on without her. The loved ones she'd had and the memories she'd made with them didn't just vanish; they were never there to begin with. She'd known that, Snow had implied as much, and yet the sinking realization hit her like jumping into an outdoor pool in the winter. Her sacrifice had created something entirely new: a world where "Jo" had never been. In giving up her own existence, she'd ultimately set everyone she'd ever known down a different path entirely. A new time-line, new reality.

Which meant—

"I need to go see Yuusuke," Jo said abruptly, turning towards the closet door and imagining—no, believing—that the Door would appear. It took a second for the sensation to manifest into something tangible, but just as she reached towards the handle, it began to shift.

Which was exactly when a small child, hair almost identical to Jo's pulled into pig-tailed braids, came frolicking into the room.

Jo lost the image of the door instantly, turning on her heel with a start, part of her still expecting to be caught. She'd been so preoccupied with her thoughts, she hadn't even heard anyone come home.

Just like the agents in the Ranger compound, the girl paid them no mind, going about removing her backpack and tossing it onto the bed. With a quick flourish, she plopped herself onto the comforter beside it and began digging through the small, purple bag with a determined expression. She looked to be about seven years old.

She looked nothing like Jo had at her age.

"Lydia!"

Jo's heart clenched, her mother's voice echoing from the kitchen. The little girl—Lydia, not named after her maternal grandmother like Jo had been, but her father's mother—sunk her hands deeper into her bag. With a grin, she pulled a touchpad from somewhere in its depths and settled into her pillows.

"*Mija*, no games until your homework's done," came her mother's voice again, this time closer. Jo found herself panicking.

She couldn't see her, not like this. She didn't want to see how tired her mother looked or how much happier she was. She didn't want to know anymore either way.

Without her permission or thought, her hand reached out not for the door but for Wayne. He was a sturdy tether and the only thing grounding Jo to her new reality. The motion was a plea for help and luckily Wayne heard it loud and clear.

His grip on her tightened and he had her jerking back towards the closet, Wayne's other hand was already on the handle; the keypad blinked, waiting for her to plug in a code. When she looked up at him, no idea what expression was written on her face, he only motioned at the door with his chin.

"Let's make tracks, doll," he said, voice serious and calming. It was a steady skiff in the swell of panic she was suddenly riding. She took a second to let herself be grounded in his touch before turning back to the keypad, the code forming like puppet strings tugging at her fingers.

She tried not to listen to the sound of her mother's approach, keeping all of her focus on leaving that room, that house, and that life behind. For good.

Almost too quickly, they were on the other side.

Yuusuke's familiar wreck of an apartment was laid out before them. Amidst that wreck was also Yuusuke himself, her friend lounging in an awkward half dangle off the couch. He seemed to be struggling with whatever game he currently had pirated onto his touchpad (Jo would, in any reality, default to assuming he stole it), and the sight was so blissfully familiar, it almost made her dizzy.

He was alive and well. Thanks to her wish, despite the little alterations of the new reality, Yuusuke was alive. Her family was alive. Even though they'd never know about her sacrifice, it didn't make the results any less real, and that made everything she was currently drowning in worth it. She'd sacrificed everything in life for them, why should death be any different?

Jo found the tension in her shoulders seeping out, a smile beginning to tug at the corner of her lips. She'd needed this. She could go and accept her new life, knowing that the ones she loved were well. She could make herself believe everything was going to be okay, knowing that she'd accomplished *something* with her wish by giving them all another (hopefully safer) chance.

Before Jo had even turned back towards the door, however, a familiar beeping sound began to echo persistently from Yuusuke's computer.

"Finally!" Yuusuke groaned, tossing his touchpad onto the couch cushions and scrambling to his feet. His headphones were in place and his fingers tapping furiously over the keyboard in seconds flat.

Maybe it was curiosity, maybe it was jealousy—but before they left, Jo had to know what he was working on. For reasons she didn't even particularly understand, she needed to see his current project.

All it took was one glimpse at the screen.

"You dumbass," Jo hissed, taking a step back. Her hands were clenched so tight she could feel the bite of her nails against her palm. "You suicidal maniac!"

Wayne might have said her name, but it barely registered. All she could hear was the faint music coming from Yuusuke's headphones, the rhythmic tapping of his fingers working through a reply to the messages— a thank you for this anonymous person's assistance. All she could see were the start of scrolling files, the thumbnails and open windows depicting every bit of information she was still painfully, suffocatingly familiar with.

He was, after all, sifting through data that Yuu and she had worked on together for months. It was nowhere near as organized as when he'd had her help in collecting it, but that wasn't something Jo could even take pride in. He was far enough, and the information was sound. At the rate it looked like he was going, he'd be right back in that server room in under a few weeks—days even, if he was reckless. And he usually was.

Yuusuke was still going after the Black Bank, *alone* this time. Sure, the person who had hired him for the job seemed different; the scripts he was running were just slightly altered. Snow hadn't lied to her—the circumstances had changed. There was just something or someone else trying to lead her best friend down the path of death.

A man she considered family was still speeding toward his demise. She hadn't changed a goddamn thing.

"Jo?" Wayne repeated her name for what could have been the second or umpteenth time, concern evident in his voice. Unfortunately, Jo was still seeing red.

"Will he feel it if I hit him?"

Wayne didn't answer right away, and when Jo shot her glare in his direction, the look of surprise was etched plainly across his face. "I mean, without time activated? No? But I don't think you should—"

Jo didn't even breathe before rearing back and slapping him across the back of the head, something she used to do (with far less force) whenever he was acting stupid. His headphones didn't fly off, though, and he didn't turn towards her with a shout and a crude gesture. In fact, Jo was pretty sure the action hurt her more than it hurt him. Deep down, though, she hoped she could at least give him a weird, unexplained headache.

If she knew how to use her blasted watch and time and magic, she could appear before him. She could be like some Latina ghost of Christmas Present wielding a "what do you think you're doing" *chancleta*. But watching him obliviously race down the same rabbit hole that had gotten him killed the first time while she was helpless to stop it? That was the last straw. Something she couldn't quite describe broke at the idea.

"Take me back," Jo whispered, suddenly too tired to even believe the door would appear to her if she tried. When Wayne didn't immediately respond, she turned towards him more completely, eyes pleading. "Take me home. Please."

For a long moment, Wayne looked as if he was trying to figure out what to say. An apology maybe. Or some kind of comfort. But in the end, he did as told, leading her back to the Society without a word.

# READY, AIM, FIRE!

I T HAD BEEN a whole day since she'd last left her room in the Society.

At least, Jo thought it had been a day. She hadn't turtled like this in quite some time. The hours washed over her like the one stone they couldn't erode. Her anger was just as present as it had been when she'd left Yuusuke's apartment.

She'd wished to save his life, and her family's. She'd wanted them to be safe. But her mom seemed in no better shape—if anything, worse—without Jo's monthly stipend deposited into her account. And Yuu was headed right toward failure with all the determination of a high-speed rail.

What was the point of her wish? What was the point of her even being here? She could change one reality only to transform it into a worse timeline.

A knock on the door startled Jo from her thoughts. She twisted her head, looking dully at the offending portal. Didn't everyone know that she was too busy sulking and feeling sorry for herself to entertain?

Another knock signified that her self-pity was officially over.

"Come in," Jo called out. After a brief pause that seemed almost hesitant, Jo watched the knob turn and the door creak open.

"Jo?" Takako peeked around it, taking a cautious step into her room once she caught sight of her. "Wayne said you'd come back here after seeing your family, and no one else has mentioned seeing you for two days," she said, as if trying to explain her presence.

"So, it's been two days, huh?" Jo mumbled. She sat and massaged the stiffness from her shoulders. "I guess I really don't need to eat anymore."

"No, you don't."

Takako's matter-of-fact manner brought a small smile to Jo's lips, one she quickly abandoned. "So, what's up?"

"Wayne said you were pretty upset."

"I don't need taking care of," Jo huffed, even though her actions screamed to the contrary. "And I certainly don't need Wayne spreading my personal business."

"All he said was that you visited family and that you were upset. We don't really pry when it comes to past lives." To Jo's surprise, Takako laughed—a soft breath of sound—but enough for Jo to hear. When she glanced back at the other woman, she was smirking, a subtle, barely-there tilt at the corner of her mouth. "And I'm sure you don't need 'taking care of.' Even if you did, that's more Nico's thing."

"All right then. What's your thing?"

"Well," Takako said, shoving her hands in her pockets. "I figured you might want to let off some steam."

"What might that entail?" Jo already knew it would involve finally leaving her bedroom. It was way past time.

Takako just gave a nod of her head and strode out the door, leaving Jo to disentangle herself from the cocoon of sheets. At the sound of Jo's door closing, Takako glimpsed over her shoulder, as if to make sure Jo was still following.

When they got to the Four-Way, Takako led her straight across, where Wayne had pointed out the recreation rooms. There hadn't been much detail offered on her tour, so Jo's old curiosity perked up right away at the possibility for new information.

They stopped in front of one of two rooms positioned across from each other. Further down the hall, Jo spotted a solid black door to the left, and one in white at the very end. Neither had nameplates. At least, she thought neither of them did. They were so far away that she could make out little other than their color.

Before Jo could ask about the mysterious black and white rooms, however, Takako was pulling her smartphone out of her pocket and placing it on a small, gold shelf next to the door in front of them.

"We have to leave our watches outside?" Jo asked, involuntarily reaching for her own wrist.

"Don't bother." Takako stopped her from taking off her wristband. "No one can touch another person's watch. And once yours is on the shelf, no one can alter that recreation room either."

Eyeing Takako's smartphone, Jo asked, "What do you mean no one else can 'alter' it? Use it, you mean? Like a sock on the door?"

At this, Takako chuckled again. "No, physically alter. The room molds itself to what you need. And, until you take your watch from the shelf, it won't mold to anyone else. People can come and go, but it'd be useless to them if they want something different."

As if in explanation, Takako chose that moment to open the door.

The entire room appeared to be a rather elaborate gun range, filling the area in both a width and a length that far exceeded what should have been possible based on the layout of the building. Targets were already set in place, each pulled back from the shooting booth at various distances, some going all the way out to what must have been at least five hundred feet, maybe more.

"So, firearms?" Jo sidled up next to Takako as she walked over to the side wall, the entirety of it lined with all manner of firearms from semi-automatics to long-range sniper rifles. Jo wasn't deeply familiar with the logistics of gun use, nor would she consider herself a connoisseur. But that didn't mean she was a novice either.

"I usually only use the recreation rooms to practice," Takako answered, grabbing a few guns off the wall and placing them in one of the booths. She followed that up with a few boxes of ammo. "But sometimes, I also come when I need to clear my head."

"So, they—the rooms I mean—change for everyone?" Jo's mind was already spinning with possibilities.

Takako nodded. "It changes based on what you need."

Takako was loading bullets into her first gun, a semi-automatic if Jo had to guess. As she watched in silent appreciation of Takako's almost elegant familiarity with the weapon, Jo couldn't help but wonder what her own recreation room would look like. Maybe it would have a really elabo-rate, high-priced, decked-out desktop—like the one she'd always dreamed about owning one day. The sort of thing she'd only buy when she'd done her last gig, made all the money she could hope to make, and was wasting away her days in a penthouse suite somewhere.

If she thought about it, she'd already crossed most of those things off her list:

Last gig, check.

A magical mansion was better than a penthouse. So, check.

She didn't really have any need for money, now. Damn, if she wasn't careful she'd talk herself into thinking she had a sweet setup going here.

"All right, you ready?" Takako successfully pulled Jo from her own thoughts once more, placing the gun in front of her in the booth.

"Me, first?" Jo blinked, looking down at it with a wary eye. She'd shot a gun before, sure; it was hard to avoid in the Lone Star Republic. But it had been long ago enough that Jo was in dire need of a quick safety review.

Takako seemed to catch on quickly, thankfully, and smirked a bit as she reached over and grabbed two headsets off a hook to Jo's left. She put one on, and then, without hesitation, reached over to place the second over Jo's ears. Jo could feel the gentle touch of the other woman's thumbs as they brushed her temples, could see the concentration in Takako's eyes as she adjusted the earmuffs to where they completely blocked out all sound.

Suddenly, the sound of her own breathing, a bit rushed, seemed very loud.

Before she could dwell on the other woman's kind and careful action any longer, Takako was grabbing the loaded gun, clicking off the safety, and aiming. A deep breath, finger moving with practiced ease from the flank of the gun to the trigger, and then suddenly she was firing.

For the first shot, all Jo could do was watch her face. Takako's expression never wavered, never flinched, both eyes open and zeroed in with a savage sort of focus. It was mesmerizing. It took Jo a substantial amount of effort to drag her eyes away and back to the targets.

With each shot, no matter how far, a bullet careened easily and poignantly into a bullseye.

Jo's jaw dropped. It was incredible, like watching a pianist execute a perfect concerto, or a baseball player bat a perfect game. She could practically feel the energy emanating off of her, rolling in waves as each bullet left the chamber. It was as if she could see an aura radiating around her. Almost like, like—

Oh. It was like *magic*.

Once all six bullets had been fired, Takako took off her headset and set it on the booth. Jo did the same, still somewhat slack jawed.

"So that's your thing then?" she asked before she could stop herself, trying not to flinch at the lack of tact. "I mean, your magic. You're . . . a good shot?"

Again, Takako smiled at her, shaking her head a bit in amusement. This time, when Jo felt warmth spreading across her cheeks, it was welcome.

"A 'good shot' might miss. A 'perfect' shot, however . . ." For the first time since meeting the woman, Jo swore she saw pride in her usually reserved expression. Takako's posture radiated something Jo could almost call smug satisfaction.

"Right," Jo nodded. Takako was their sharpshooter. Jo was their hacker, even if being their hacker had been meaningless so far.

*Hacking.*

The idea brought Jo right back to Yuusuke. But instead of anger, a new thought filled her, one of possibility. The recreation rooms could become whatever was most appealing to members of the Society, whatever they wanted . . . What Jo wanted right now, more than anything, was to make sure her sacrifice meant something. If there was a way to protect the people she cared for beyond the grave then she'd find it.

"Okay then." Jo nodded, grabbing her headset and placing the muffs back over her ears and allowing that notion to simmer in the back of her mind. She grabbed one of the loaded guns and aimed as best she could, trying to seem relaxed, like she wasn't now buzzing with nervous energy. Before unlocking the safety, however, she glanced over at Takako, grinning. She hadn't felt this good since before the Society. "What do I do first?"

# BROKEN MUG

"I WAS GETTING almost as good as you towards the end there," Jo boasted boldly. Her index finger pulled away from the slick, condensing glass of her drink, ice bobbing as she took a sip of what tasted delightfully reminiscent of RAGE ENERGY.

"I'd better be careful, or you'll take my job from me." Takako chuckled that soft and breathy sound Jo had come to associate as uniquely hers.

"Everyone will want me to be the sharpshooter, you can hack." Jo grinned. They both knew she was being utterly ridiculous, but after the last couple of days, it felt good to be.

She'd unloaded countless bullets into paper targets. When she'd grown tired of those, Takako pushed a button on a panel and flesh-colored dummies had sprung from the ground. The Law of Especially Large Numbers was responsible for the shots Jo managed to land; if she fired a hundred shots, one was bound to make contact—but Jo made it out to be a source of pride anyway, for the sake of irony if nothing else.

Takako had played along then, encouraging her and keeping the seemingly never-ending stream of bullets ready in a rotation of guns. And she played along now as they lounged by the pool in the late afternoon sun.

"I'd make an awful hacker."

"I'm sure you'd be fine. And at least you'd be useful to the wish. Snow would let *you* help, I'm sure . . ." Jo swirled her drink before taking a long, embittered sip.

"You don't always want to be useful to the wish." As if on instinct, Takako turned her gaze back, as if she could peer all the way through the walls and halls, to the briefing room. "Sometimes, it's better not to be."

"Why?" Jo questioned the somber and reflective tone as much as she did the sentiment. It was so similar to Wayne's, possibly the only similarity between the two.

"A lot of pressure when you're involved; you have to make a lot happen in a small period of time." The mention of time reminded Jo of Wayne's caution for wasting her time, even if Snow said she was benched for the current project. *But recreation rooms didn't take time,* a little voice in the back of her head whispered.

"I've been in high-pressure situations before," Jo insisted.

"I'm sure you have. Yet another reason why you're the best hacker we could ask for." Takako shook her head and brought her attention back to Jo. "Besides, you're the only one of us who can. I'm the newest 'recruit'—if you will—and even I know very little about computers."

"I don't see how that's possible." Jo shook her head at the excuse. She knew Takako was just trying to deflect the conversation away from the wish and her sourness regarding it. "Everyone is practically born with a computer in-hand."

"In your time, maybe." Takako looked out over the far edge of the pool.

Jo studied Takako's face in profile; looking outward or in, the woman's expression was no more relaxed. *Her time.* It was no longer the present, no longer now. It was hers—that was the only reference point that mattered to anyone else. Just like the early 2000s belonged to Takako. But what had her life been like? Where had she lived? Did she have a family, a job, a lover? What had brought her to this life outside of time?

Eventually, Jo followed Takako's stare at the mountains in the distance, the questions burning her tongue. She hadn't wanted Takako asking about her mom, or Yuusuke. But Jo wanted to know more about her new friend; even just a little would go a long way.

"Did you have mountains like this, where you lived?" Jo asked softly, not taking her eyes away. "I mean, I didn't. Texas in my time is—was— flat, and hot, and dusty. There were a lot of forestation efforts in parts of the LSR. Too much was lost in the great drought," she added quickly, not wanting to seem like she was asking without giving something in return.

"I did." Takako nodded. "I grew up in the shade of the Japanese alps, northwest of Tokyo in Gunma." Her attention was still glued to the horizon and Jo wondered if she saw the haze of the mountains from her childhood.

She said nothing more, leaving Jo to glance at the other woman from the corners of her eyes. Now what? She'd started this train of conversation but had no idea where to lay tracks so she could proceed. She couldn't just demand more information, she wouldn't; she respected her kind new friend too much. But she was curious, and that hindered her from concocting any sort of effective transition.

A crash from behind them saved her.

Jo startled, half jumping from her chair. Two men were in the room beyond. Eslar was sitting at the chess table in the far-left corner—too far to overhear, she hoped. With those elongated ears of his, though, who really knew? Though Jo was left to wonder when, exactly, he'd arrived. And why, exactly, he had time to play chess when he was supposed to be granting wishes. Nico was in the kitchen, fretting over ceramic shards that littered the floor.

"No, no-no." The man who was sunshine incarnate was under threat of drowning due to the invisible raincloud that hung over his head. "Not that one, it was my favorite."

"What happened?" Jo called.

Nico looked up, startled. Even despite his obvious turmoil over the broken dish, he smiled. "Jo, how good to see you. How do you feel?"

"Better," Jo admitted and started in, Takako on her heels. There wasn't any point in trying to play off the fact that she'd been in an utterly pathetic funk for two days. But finding out you gave up your whole existence for nothing could do that to a person. She paused at the entry to the kitchen where Nico was scraping up the remnants of a mug and coffee in shaky hands. "Are you all right?"

"Just get a little twitchy when I haven't had enough nectar of the gods." Her opinion of Nico increased tenfold the moment she realized his description of coffee matched her own.

"I know that feeling." She chuckled and knelt down, picking up some of the larger shards. "Takako, is there a broom?"

"Yes, I'll get it." She gave a nod and darted to the far end of the kitchen, returning with a broom and dustpan.

"Thanks." Jo set her shards in the pan, helping Nico clean up the rest. When they stood up, Takako held another mug out, steaming and potent with the aroma of coffee.

"Soothe yourself." Takako might be the only person alive who could turn a cup of coffee into an order. And a very . . . interesting order at that. Jo had to swallow back laughter at the seriousness in Takako's expression.

"That was my favorite mug," Nico lamented as he took the fresh cup, staring longingly at the dustpan Jo still held. "It was just the perfect size and shape, everything about it was ideal. I have no idea what came over me. It was like it wanted to break."

"Can the house just . . . give you a new one?"

Nico shook his head. "The mansion only gives us things in the recreation rooms and our bedrooms. But we can't take things out of the former, and can't just ask for things from the latter. It's a mixed bag of what we get in our rooms. Usually, it's what we need and are familiar with, but not always."

*Of course, anything else would make sense*, Jo thought bitterly. Whoever came up with the rules of the mansion had a sick sense of humor. Wasn't magic supposed to make your life easier, not harder? Jo felt seriously betrayed by all the fairy tales she'd read as a child.

"So, how do we get things if we need something specific?" Jo asked no one in particular.

"Samson." Eslar stood and joined the conversation. He moved over to them in that lithe, willowy manner that could only barely pass for human. There was a surreal feeling about him, as if he didn't move, but the world moved around him. "I'll take it to him."

"You don't mind?" Nico put his coffee mug down to clasp his hands over Eslar's as the elf grabbed for the dustbin.

"It will be easier if you unhand me," Eslar said, not unkindly.

"Thank you!" Nico called after the elf, who was already practically to the hall due to his long strides. A soft sound flowed from mythical man, a language sung in a tongue that Jo couldn't recognize even with her belief in magic. Jo had a fresh batch of questions, but before she could ask any, the Italian turned his attention back to her. "You must think I'm insane, getting so worked up over a coffee mug."

"I don't," she said honestly, much to his and Takako's obvious surprise. "I had a mug, one my mother got me when we went to Disney . . ." The one family trip they'd gone on before grandma died and her parents split. "I would have cried messy tears if something had happened to that."

Jo paused and stared at the countertop where the dustpan had been. It was another trip she hadn't taken. Another token from her mother she'd never received. Jo wondered if it was still in the house, even. If, now, her mother would buy it for Lydia's cocoa.

Not existing could really mess with your head if you thought too much on it.

"I'm glad I caught you, actually." Intentionally or not, Nico stopped her from slipping into that rabbit-hole of sorrow. "There's something I'd like to show you."

"What?"

"You'll need to follow me." Nico beamed at her. Excitement radiated off of him like sunshine and Jo was helpless to say no.

"Sure, not like I'm doing much else." And it gave her a convenient escape from Takako. It wasn't that Jo hadn't enjoyed her time with the woman—quite the contrary, in fact. But there was a new mission in Jo's head and she needed a clean breakaway that wouldn't rouse suspicion. She'd see whatever Nico needed, and then figure out her next steps. "If you don't mind?" she asked Takako.

"You do what pleases you." She leaned against the counter, hands in pockets, small smile. A polite person was ten times more attractive for it.

"Thank you."

"Anytime."

Jo hoped that when Takako said "anytime" she meant it, because she had every intention of seeking her out again. Nico led her away and Jo gave one more appreciative look back at the stoic woman still leaning against the kitchen counter, doing nothing other than giving her that small, unassuming smile the whole time Jo had her in her sights.

NICO LED HER back the way she'd come, smiling at her over his shoulder as they passed through the Four-Way. She gave him a quick smile back, shuffling to catch up.

"So where are we going?" she asked, matching his pace. All he gave her in response was a rather giddy-looking gesture towards the door they were approaching on their right. Jo instantly recognized it as Nico's room, the little bird painted on his nameplate oddly welcoming.

As Nico reached for the doorknob, Jo realized she'd yet to see inside of anyone else's room but her own. She knew his would certainly not look like her messy apartment, but she couldn't begin to imagine what shape Nico's sanctuary would take. Or anyone else's, for that matter. What did Samson or Eslar find soothing in their personal quarters? What did Wayne rest his head on when he lounged in that silken robe? What did Snow's room look like?

A flash memory raced through her mind—more like a recollection from a long forgotten dream. The world stilled for just a second as Jo tried to recover the images she'd seen but not really understood. *Snow's room.* The thought put a flush in her alongside the feeling of heavy blankets and desperate, whispered words.

Thankfully, Nico saved Jo from herself and the phantom sensations by opening the door and ushering her inside.

His room was unlike anything she could have imagined and yet so very fitting for the warm, friendly, Italian artist. The décor was so calming that it blissfully pushed all other thoughts from her mind.

The ceiling was vaulted high, making the room feel open and airy; the large span of space was cluttered without being the slightest bit cramped.

In fact, the room felt like a breath of fresh air, as if she were standing on the rooftop of a skyscraper overlooking a giant city, contained within four corners but in no way confined.

"Give me a second, I want to make sure it's ready." Nico grinned, an excited bounce to his step as he rushed over to the far side of the room.

Jo watched him go, and the way he stumbled over his footing a bit in his haste had her stifling a small bubble of laughter. The wall he stopped at was crowded with canvases in various stages of completion. Some were completely blank, but most had splashes of color, partial designs, patterns and sketches of bodies or flowers or night skies or an image that only the artist could conceive. Even from a distance, she could tell they were stunning.

Nico rifled through them for a second before looking over his shoulder at her. "No peeking! J-just one second." Jo nodded and turned away from him when he continued to stare expectantly; the sound of him shuffling through his pieces promptly picked back up.

She busied herself in the meantime by walking around the room. The wall opposite Nico's collection seemed to be comprised primarily of shelving units, each one filled to the brim with art supplies and books. It reminded her of the art studio at her old high school, splattered with dried paint, stained in ink, and marred with scratches from hundreds of projects. It was that sort of "messy clean" only an artist could achieve.

She picked up a paintbrush, noticing that, despite the obvious signs of recent use—discoloration at the tip, caked paint around the edge—it also seemed relatively new. Maybe that was the room's way of providing comfort; enough signs of age to be soothing, but no actual decay.

Jo put the brush down and turned her attention back to the rest of the room—the large, patterned rug that filled a circle-shaped portion of the cement floor, the bed in the corner overflowing with dark, rumpled linens; a leather chair, pale at the corners, that was kept company by a lone reading light whose switch was worn to a deep brass from years of use.

But the parts of the room that grabbed her attention most were the giant, floor to ceiling windows taking up nearly one full wall. Behind the perfectly polished glass, what Jo's limited knowledge of geography told her, was somewhere in modern-day Italy.

The windows pulled her to them, as if she were in a trance. Her hand rose instinctively to the glass, smearing the immaculate cleaning job with an instinct to touch the vision before her. It was beautiful, exactly as she'd seen in pictures.

"Home," Nico said, and Jo jumped a bit at the sudden appearance of him at her side. He laughed. "Sorry, didn't mean to startle you."

"No, no, that's on me." Jo waved him away, smiling a bit in embarrassment. "I was kind of lost in my own head, that's all." Nico nodded, staring out at the expanse of old and new architecture that was all crammed together like one big happy family. A thought occurred to Jo, stumbling out of her mouth before she could stop it. "Is this really Italy? The real one?"

Surprisingly, Nico didn't look uncomfortable or disturbed by the question. Instead, his eyes grew wistful, a soft and sad smile tugging at the corners of his lips. He nodded. "It's Florence. Not my Florence, not anymore. But still my home and I still like to keep up with it for all its fantastic creations and fatal flaws. It's the city where my promised and I had once planned on raising our family, so I can't seem to let it go."

"You were engaged?" Jo asked, trying to keep her question sincere and kind despite how curious she was. Nico didn't seem to mind her prying, but she didn't want to push it.

As if in explanation, Nico reached into his pocket, pulled out his over-sized, antiquated pocket watch, and clicked it open. Jo hadn't noticed it the first time, too focused on the time, then. Engraved on the inside of the simple silver casing was a name in elaborate cursive.

*Julia d'Este*

"We had planned on marrying in the spring, when the weather would be tame," Nico said softly. "It would be unfair to our guests to have them suffer at the hands of the season during the ceremony, she'd said. My Julia was the most kind and beautiful thing to ever grace this world and the next."

"You really loved her."

"Love, not loved. Enough to wish for her." Nico glanced at Jo out of the corner of his eye, smile growing warmer still. And then vanishing entirely. His stare seemed to grow somber as his mind wandered out upon the city, so lost in thought it seemed he'd even forgotten that he was holding his watch between them, open to the face, his thumb absently rubbing against the grooves of Julia's name.

Jo found herself drawn to that watch face: three clocks positioned amid a backdrop of pearl. For the second time, she couldn't help but wonder why one of them seemed frozen, stopped forever at 1:17. When she opened her mouth to ask, however, the words wouldn't come. Not because she didn't want to know, but because it felt too personal, like a line she shouldn't cross.

"If you don't mind my asking," Jo eventually tried, hoping for a change in conversation that might lift Nico's mood a bit. He seemed the sort of person who should always be smiling—like when he was happy, the whole world was happy with him. "When were you born?"

To Jo's surprise, this actually managed to pull a chuckle out of the man. With a flick of his wrist, he snapped his watch shut and pocketed it, leaning back on his heels.

"December 9th, 1484."

Before she could stop herself, Jo heard herself whisper a stunned, "Holy shit."

Nico laughed, loud and boisterous. "I know, right? And I'm not even the oldest one here. Eslar, Samson, and Pan were already around when I arrived, and for all we know, Snow could have been running things even long before them."

That struck Jo as odd. "You don't know how long Snow's been here?"

Nico just shrugged. "No one does, and if he hasn't told Eslar, he's not telling anyone. The Society seems, as far as I can tell, to have always been around. Pan may know, but good luck getting any kind of sensible answer from that one."

Jo made a mental note to look into *that one* a bit more later—on her list of Society focused missions it was somewhere between "figuring out time" and "learn how to use her magic in a helpful way." For now, she turned away from the window as Nico did.

Her eyes fell instantly on a large painting Nico had placed on an easel in the center of his circular rug.

Without really meaning to, she found herself walking towards it, breath hitching in her throat. Even though it was stylized, the colors blending together and brush strokes intermingling in a way that was clearly an artist's rendering, the likeness was irrefutable.

It was a painting of the Texas skyline, the sweeping deserts in oranges and tans, the smattering of cacti and foliage in dark greens and bright streaks of yellow, blots of purples and reds playing stark contrast against their stalks.

It was a painting of home.

"Nico, what—?" Jo's voice was strangely choked. When she looked behind her, Nico was leaning against the window, watching her reaction with a knowing smile on his face.

"I thought you could use some art for your room." It was all he said, but even she could hear the layers of unspoken understanding beneath the words. When she raised an eyebrow in question, he just motioned for her to look back at the painting. "Go on," he added. "It's yours. Take a good look."

Not quite sure whether or not she was imagining the mischievousness in his voice, Jo nodded, turning back towards the painting and taking a step closer.

It really was remarkable work, his artistic talent obvious. He'd managed to take an image straight from her mind and render it in near perfection with what looked to be no more than a handful of colors. In fact, the more she looked at it, the more she felt as though she was looking not at a painting, not even at a photograph, but at a memory.

She remembered quiet drives through the endless ribbon of road that was Long Horn, the wind turbines gently spinning as her mother drove past. As Jo looked closer, she could even see them, strips of white paint just barely interrupting the distant expanse of burnt sienna.

She remembered heat lightning cracking open an indigo sky, distant flashes of yellow sparkling with an aura of purples and pinks, swirls of light in rainless and cloudless heavens.

*Empanadas* and *sopapillas* and hot chocolate with cinnamon coated her tongue. Abuelita's old quilt in all its sturdy, faded familiarity fell in comforting weight over her shoulders. The rumble of her father's dirty pickup reached her ears. Jo felt her mother's hands in her hair and her arms around her waist and all the indescribable feelings that summed together, formed the essence of home.

She could smell her first lunch with Yuusuke—the new kid and the loner fighting for the corner of the cafeteria as if destiny itself had it out for them. The feel of the keyboard was smooth under her fingers as she showed him her "little project" in the ice box of their junior high computer room. Jo almost coughed in the dust he let in through the open windows of his hatchback, the ones that never rolled up, as they made their way out to their first real job together when they were supposed to be headed to college in Houston.

Colors became sensations that evoked memories she'd long and momentarily forgotten but had never stopped treasuring.

Her shoulders sagged under the soothing touch of nostalgia, the image on canvas blurring into her own recollection. There was a word for this feeling, she realized, something she hadn't felt since she got here. Something she hadn't felt in a long, long time, even.

Contentment. Not happiness, but a calm acceptance that her situation in life wasn't just "not so bad" but had the possibility to be pretty good, even.

It felt a little like letting go. And she felt better.

She didn't need to ask to know that Nico's magic had something to do with this. She could practically feel it vibrating beneath her skin, calming nerves she'd only been minutely aware were so frayed. In the back of her mind, she wondered if she should be upset, having her emotions manipulated so easily and completely. But this hadn't felt like Wayne's magic, struggling against invisible tethers. Every sensation was wholly hers; the painting merely brought them forth, played up certain things and dialed down others. Alongside the acceptance of it all was a deeper sense of genuineness, an offering of Nico's that felt like more of a gift than an exploitation.

This was his way of welcoming her to the Society. This was his way of making her feel more at home.

So, with eyes still blinking from the fresh feel of hot air, the scent of desert still clogging her nose, Jo turned away from the painting and walked up to Nico. Without warning, she wrapped her arms around his waist, feeling him tense in surprise. Quickly, however, he eased into the embrace, hugging her back tightly and without restraint.

He smelt like fresh paint and cedar, his arms strong and warm. The realness of him brought her back from the deluge of memories, but did not sever the sensation of peace those images left in their wake.

After a long moment, Jo pulled back, running a hand over her face to check for any stray tears. Dry—looked like she was solidly back on the right track when it came to crying.

"Thank you," she said, keeping as much appreciation in her voice as she could.

That knowing smile on Nico's face only grew in response, his eyes crinkling at the corners.

He'd never know it, but he'd given her the greatest gift of all—cementing her resolve for what she must do next, regardless of the consequences. She may not exist, but that didn't mean she was ready to turn her back on the home she knew.

# REC ROOM

T HE MANSION WAS quiet and the world outside its windows was
dark—leading Jo to believe that it was, indeed, nighttime. Her
watch corroborated the fact, reading just after midnight. But Jo
still felt like she had to sneak through the halls.

She didn't want anyone bothering her. And, in a house filled with
people who didn't need sleep, a distraction could come from anywhere—
like Nico. Though that earlier distraction had been just what she needed. It
had been a reminder of what she'd sacrificed for, and what she'd still fight
for with any tools at her disposal.

Through the Four-Way, Jo's persistent stride didn't slow until she was
standing in front of one of the recreation rooms. The empty shelf practically beckoned her to relinquish her watch and unlock the door. She'd
seen Takako do this and while it seemed simple enough, Jo didn't know
what to expect solo. Nerves settled low in her gut the moment she tugged
on the band of her watch and pulled it from her wrist.

It seemed strange that something so small could suddenly mean so
much. In many ways, that watch was everything to her now (even if she
didn't fully understand how it worked as a means to interact with the real
world), and she was just about to leave it out in the open. Even with
Takako's guarantee that no one else could touch it, she couldn't help but
feel possessive, maybe even a little reluctant to allow it to leave her
fingers.

But Jo had a mission, and that far outweighed any fears she could
have. She pulled off the strip of fabric and set it on the shelf, took a breath,
and slowly inched the door open.

A low whistle escaped her lips; she certainly wasn't disappointed.

Wall to wall were various pieces of tech. It was the elaborate set-up she'd been dreaming of after all, and then some. There were multiple towers attached to twelve monitors, stretching above two separate desks so she could run two entirely separate rigs at once, with a rolling chair to swivel between them. Routers gave her little neon-green winks, assuring her that she could connect to the world beyond. Brand logos she'd only dreamed of affording glinted at her in the low-light.

Honestly, it was a technophile's wet dream, so far beyond anything she could have hoped for that Jo could only stand there and gape, practically salivating. Even with limitless imagination, she would never have guessed the recreation room could provide what was before her.

Once the initial shock wore off, Jo swallowed down her excitement and settled herself into the rolling chair, sliding with a small huff of laughter from one row of monitors to another, larger desktop screen. She reached for the pair of over-sized headphones that were hung on an eerily familiar peg in the perfect place, and pulled her jacket sleeves up to the second knuckle on her thumb. Even the chill was familiar.

The computer was already running, a soft hum filling the room, and when she went searching for suitable software, it appeared all her favorite programs were already installed.

"All right . . . come to me, Black Bank."

If Yuusuke was suicidally-bent on glory, then Jo would see him succeed this time. She'd take matters into her own hands. Hell, she'd take them down first, if she must. She'd do this one last job for the man who'd been like her brother and then really make an attempt to move forward in this new life.

As if plunging a needle into a vein, the moment Jo's hands touched the keyboard, she could feel magic and information flood her system, a transfusion of knowledge. She could see exactly what paths to take to gain restricted access, navigating blocked servers and sifting through unnecessary firewalls like following a straightforward, illuminated text. The entire stream of data was laid out before her—what should've been a tangled mess. Yet every string of information fell into its own line.

Hacking had always been a high for her, a sort of adrenaline rush at the idea of lifting the skirts of the most secure servers. And maybe it was a little bit of a power trip too, a smug sense of self-satisfaction knowing what she was capable of. But this? *This* feeling of her already impressive talent swelling into overdrive? It was intoxicating.

It was something Jo could lose herself in, and she did so gladly.

She was starting five steps ahead. She knew just where to look and she knew just what encryption the Black Bank used. Even if the world had changed enough for her to no longer exist, it didn't change enough for the group behind the Black Bank—Incognito—to have altered their processes.

*Much*, at least.

"Oh, what's this?" Jo grinned, leaning toward the monitor. "This is new." She narrowed her eyes at the screen. "No matter . . . shouldn't take more than a second . . ."

Jo continued on like this, conquering one hurdle after the next with an ease she had never possessed before. It was a sort of assurance that she could barely understand, but one that bred an assessment she was utterly confident in: *this* was her magic. And using it felt *excellent*.

"Well, someone seems to be up to no good." A voice appeared at her side, far too close. In fact, Jo was so startled by the sudden presence that she nearly jolted completely out of her chair, turning awkwardly and rather ungracefully in its direction.

Pan was standing in the center of the room, eyeing the new layout with a glint of amusement in her eyes. She even went so far as to whistle in approval.

"Wow." She grinned, and when she finally brought her attention back to Jo, it was with a look in her eyes that seemed almost impressed. "And here I thought the rooms had outdone themselves with Takako. The technological future really is a sight to behold."

"Uh . . ." Jo looked from Pan to the accumulation of tech and back. "I guess?"

Pan smirked, all but frolicking about the room, fuchsia hair swaying behind her with each step. "So, what do you think you're doing in here?" The girl leaned over Jo's computer.

"I could ask you the same." Jo tapped the keyboard and the monitor went dark.

"Make it come back!" Pan whined. "Don't be so sneaky. I don't like secrets, remember?"

"Maybe I don't feel like sharing."

"Be like that, and I'll have to tell Snow."

"That sounds like a threat." Jo side-eyed the girl.

"That's because it is!" Pan clapped her hands together, clearly pleased with herself.

Jo's side-eye turned into a full-blown scowl. "I'm not doing anything wrong. We're allowed to use the recreation rooms as we please."

Pan hummed, bringing her index finger to her chin in thought. "I guess that's true . . . But 'as you please' looks a lot like trying to affect the outside world . . . and that's a big no-no. Especially when we have a wish. You wouldn't want to break anything, would you?"

Jo's back went rigid and she balled a hand into a fist. She'd fight Pan if she had to. The woman-child wasn't taking Jo's work from her.

"How did you know what I was doing?"

"I didn't." Pan stilled, a smile widening across her cheeks as if trying to touch each of her ears. "Not until you kindly confirmed it for me."

"Isn't the job of the Society to change the outside world?"

"Only for wishes."

Jo opened her mouth to speak again, but was interrupted a second time. She had never been happier to see Wayne. The fact must have been plain on her face, because Wayne's attention shifted from Jo to Pan, and the first question from his mouth was, "What trouble are you getting into?"

"Me, trouble?" Pan gasped. "Wayne, you know I'd never. You should be asking *her*, not me." Pan threw an accusatory finger in Jo's direction.

"Back away, Pan." The bass in Wayne's voice startled Jo, and planted a warm feeling of endearment in the space her surprise vacated. "Go take a nap, or something."

"She's the one causing trouble. She's trying to change the outside world."

Wayne's attention was back on Jo, threatening to destroy the fuzzy feeling he'd been earning a second ago. "All right"—back to Pan—"I'll take it from here, then."

Pan hovered for several seconds, clearly debating the idea. She folded her hands with a shrug and strolled out of the room. "This was becoming boring, anyway." The woman-child paused in the doorway, looking back at them both. "Do make sure that you look after her, Wayne. She's a dangerous one, I just know it."

With that, the rainbow-haired girl left. Wayne watched from the doorway and whatever he saw must have satisfied him because he stepped inside the room and closed the door behind him. Jo met his searching eyes fearlessly, knowing what question was coming before it even left his lips.

"Just what *are* you doing in here, Jo?"

# SHEWOLF'S MISSION

J O LOOKED BACK to her computer, tapping the monitor back to life. "I don't see how it's anyone's business. But thank you for getting Pan out of here."

A large sigh was let loose from her left. Jo kept her eyes on the monitor, trying to convey that while she may be appreciative of his help, she had no intent of having a conversation. Wayne either didn't get the hint, or didn't care, because he pulled up the chair from the other workstation.

"What are you doing?" he repeated.

"I'll tell you the same thing I told her." Jo continued to work. While Pan had this odd way about her that made Jo suspicious that she understood far more than she let on, Jo was fairly confident that Wayne had no idea what the various folders or scripts meant. "I don't feel like sharing."

"Doll, don't play that way." He looked toward the monitor and with one stare affirmed Jo's suspicions that he didn't actually know what he was looking at. "It's been two days and—"

"Two days?" Jo balked.

"Since anyone has seen you? Yes." Wayne seemed confused as to why she was startled.

"Two days, huh?" She skimmed her work. "Pretty good, almost finished, actually . . ."

"With what?" he probed again.

"Didn't I tell you I'm not going to share?"

"Don't you know by now that I'm here to help?" He slung his own question back at her. "That we all are just trying to take care of each other?"

Jo leaned back in her chair, folded her arms over her chest, and swiveled to face him. She arched her eyebrows, assessing the man. He wasn't wrong, not really. He had shown her around at first, and had taken her to see her family. She had been so ready to hate the man and his frustrating accent but . . . Did she dare even think it? Something about him had become endearing. More than simple base attraction and flattery, he was proving a good friend and ally.

She sighed, debating where to start. "It's Yuu."

"You?" His brow furrowed in confusion at her pronunciation. "Me?"

"Yuusuke."

"The gentlemen we went to see," Wayne spoke with the confidence of clarity now.

"I wouldn't call him a gentleman. More like an annoying kid brother who's the same age as me." Jo rolled her eyes. "But, yes."

"What about him?"

Jo looked back to the monitor and swallowed in an attempt to relieve the sudden tightness in her throat. "My wish . . . was for him. And my family by extension. When we saw him . . . he was doing the same hack that led to our deaths. He's going to end up back there. Depending on how stupid he acts—and believe me he can be quite stupid when he's on a mission—he could be headed there in a week, a matter of *days*."

Jo could feel Wayne's attention on her before he opened his mouth to speak. "You can't stop this."

"Like hell I can't!" Jo's head snapped back to Wayne and her sudden ferocity had him pinned down to a stunned silence. "Why? Why can't I? You expect me to just sit here? To not help with the wish, even though I've already quite grasped the hang of my magic? And on top of that, to watch as Yuusuke gets himself killed, *again*? To watch the people I care for suffer?

"If I do, my wish will mean nothing. The life I gave up will mean nothing. The very few things I managed to stand for will mean nothing. *I* will mean nothing!"

Her words seemed to echo impossibly in the small space. Jo's chest heaved, as if trying to snuff the burning in her lungs. Now that she'd said it so simply, Jo wondered how she hadn't seen it all along.

"Wayne . . . I'll mean nothing." Her voice cracked under the weight of her own realization. For all she loved Yuusuke, this was as much about her as it was him. She couldn't go forward without first settling the past.

"You can help in the Society. You have people who care for you and to care for here. You'll always mean something." His hands grabbed for hers, closing them both in a net of his fingers. That same sturdy, reassuring feeling was there with his touch. But it wasn't enough, not this time. Still, Jo's fingers tightened around his.

"If I can help with a wish."

"You can."

"Just not now." He didn't object to her counter. Jo shook her head. "Please . . . I'm not one to beg, but I'm *begging* you. Let me do this."

Gravity pulled her chin to her chest and Jo waited, as if an axe that Wayne wielded hovered above the nape of her neck. She'd spent two days on this, and she was close, so close.

"What do you need?" he asked softly. Jo didn't know if his voice had dropped due to the conspiratorial nature of the subject, or out of pure tenderness that she didn't know the man could muster.

Jo's head jerked up, and her heart latched onto the opportunity. She searched his face for any reason to disbelieve and came up empty handed. He was giving her hope against hope and for that she could practically kiss him. "I need you to show me how to use time without having my watch on my wrist. I'm close, but all my prep work is for nothing if I can't affect the real world."

"The room will vanish if you remove your watch, and you can't use time without wearing it. Even if those things weren't true, you *can't* affect the real world from here."

Her heart sank into her stomach, tore through the bottom, fell to the floor, and continued in free-fall straight to the depths of space.

"But we can if we go through the Door," he added hastily. His voice was so low now that he needed to lean in and whisper. Wayne was close enough that Jo felt as much as heard the rumble of his words. "If I help you with this, now, promise me you will never try to change things outside of a wish again?"

"I promise." Jo didn't know if she was lying or not, and didn't really care. She'd say anything to garner his help.

"And promise me you'll be careful; you'll change as little as possible." His fingers tightened further around hers, if it were possible.

"I promise." The words flew from her lips before he even had a chance to finish speaking.

"All right. We should go, then."

"Wait, I can't just leave my code. I wouldn't have time to start from scratch there . . ." Jo looked to the computers. How could she transfer her work? If what Wayne said was true, she couldn't upload it to a cloud server and expect to access it on the other side. If only there was some physical way of carrying digital information . . . "I have an idea."

Jo was sprinting back through the mansion before Wayne even had time to respond. Her feet flew over the marble and carpeted floors alike, carrying her back to her room. Nico had said they couldn't take things from the recreation rooms, but that they could from their bedrooms.

She flung open her door, flying to her desk and rummaging around in her drawers.

"Please, please, please . . ." she uttered on repeat like a prayer—a prayer that was answered. If the mansion was recreating her room from real life, then there was bound to be a rogue USB stick somewhere. Antiquated technology, really, but something Jo always insisted on having at least one or two of. Physical backups were much more difficult to track than the cloud, even if you couldn't always find a computer with the proper port.

Back in the rec room, Jo appeared to a dazed Wayne who barely had time to get "What?" out before she was back to work.

"Our clothes go with us to the real world."

"Thankfully, or unfortunately, depending on who you're with," Wayne mumbled.

Jo braved a grin, feeling in a better mood than she had in days—such a good mood that his appreciative stare toward her regarding the latter sentiment didn't go unnoticed. Optimism made her bold. "I do hope you're talking about me with the 'unfortunately' bit."

Wayne's jaw dropped in a way that seemed both startled and impressed at her retort. Jo gave him a smug look, one he responded to in kind. "Guess you'll just have to wait and find out." He leaned back in his chair, knees spreading slightly. "Now, what is it you really wanted me to know about your clothes?"

"It means we can bring stuff from here, there."

"And?" Of course he wouldn't follow.

"I'm backing up all my scripts." Jo tapped the blinking USB, mid-transfer. "I'll pop over to the real world, polish them up, and run them."

"Run them from where?" Wayne asked warily. *Good*, Jo thought. He should be wary. He'd offered to help the Shewolf on a mission, after all, and she was feeling in rare form.

"From inside the Black Bank, of course. Where else?" The computer answered her question before Wayne could with a satisfying beep, indicating the end of her transfer, and the start of her chance at securing meaning in her new world.

PARIS

THEY STOOD BEFORE the Door, Jo's heart threatening to beat from her chest. She kept glancing over her shoulder—a motion mirrored by Wayne—looking for any indication of anyone following. Luckily, they were solidly alone.

"Where are we going, dollface?"

Jo playfully swatted his hand away from the keypad. "I got this," she said with a satisfied grin. Closing her eyes, she envisioned where she needed to go.

The early 2000s saw rise to a hacker group that would forever remain in infamy: Incognito. Following the end of the third world war, they escalated themselves from Internet defender and vigilante group to sophisticated peace-keepers of the digital world. In a time when governments were rising and falling, countries were collapsing, and economic systems were in peril, they established themselves as the "true free market" where anything could be bought and sold using the most elaborate cryptocurrency ever conceived (even if obviously named)—credits.

And where they housed this currency in massive server racks that Jo had only uncovered the location of from months of prep-work in what was now a past life, was (also obviously) the city the group had founded themselves in.

"Paris," Jo murmured. Her fingers flew over the keypad, pulled by an invisible force as they had been the first time, and she threw open the door.

There was that same hiss of de-pressurization, the click of the door opening, and then—light.

Jo raised a hand up to her eyes, guarding them from the sun as they stepped out of the side-door of a shop and into a narrow street. If the quaint, picture-perfect cobblestones weren't enough, the lilting sounds of French being spoken around her should have been all the proof she needed.

But they weren't.

In parallel with her now racing heart, Jo suddenly found herself sprinting down the narrow Paris street, darting between people who unknowingly parted for her, seemingly by random chance. None of them saw her, or even glanced in her direction. She ran, unhindered, to a main thoroughfare that offered a clear view of the most iconic landmark Paris had to offer: the Eiffel Tower.

"We're really here," she breathed in relief.

"We are." Jo wasn't sure how Wayne had caught up with her, but there he was, glued to her side. "Where else would we be?" Whenever he spoke, the rest of the world fell into a hush, as if in thrall. Jo was sure it had something to do with the fact that neither of them existed by technical standards.

"I could do it, though, no problem." Working the Door was far more empowering than Jo ever expected it to be.

"You can do a great many things . . ." Wayne paused, looking down at her wrist. "Like using that watch."

"You'll show me how?" She grabbed his wrists without thinking, gripping them to the point that she was sure she was hurting him. Initiating contact had become oddly easy. "Finally?"

"Finally?" Wayne snorted at the word. "Doll, you haven't been in the Society for *that* long." Before Jo could protest that it was long enough without any kind of formal instruction, he continued, albeit hesitantly, as if admitting to some heinous crime. "Yes, I'll show you. But we still need to conserve time and be careful."

"So you mentioned. I promise to be careful."

"Good, because this is only going to fly if we change as little as possible."

Jo thought a moment. "For the Severity of Exchange? The A to B?" Wayne gave a soft noise of affirmation. "Is that why we aren't supposed to change the real world? Not because we can't . . . but because we don't want to alter things for the wish?"

Wayne nodded.

"If only Yuusuke had decided to be a dumbass when we *weren't* on wish." Jo laughed bitterly.

"If only . . ." Wayne repeated. "Even then, it's not for us to meddle in the real world. You never know when a wish could come in, or how our changes might impact the Severity of Exchange in advance through cause and effect. Plus, it's no longer our place. So it's better not to . . ." He trailed off, staring at the Eiffel Tower for a moment. "But here we are. So do you agree to be careful?"

"For the thousandth time, yes." Jo nodded and then added, "Thank you again, for helping me."

Wayne gave her a smile filled with more tenderness than she'd ever expected from the man. It filled her with a feeling she could finally put a name to—yearning. But, even though she was looking directly at him, he wasn't the one she was yearning for. Her heart did a small twist. "You got it, doll. Now, let's stop in here."

"What?"

He pointed to a little cafe on the corner. "It'll be a good place to get your feet wet and practice using time."

"We don't exactly have *time* for a lunch date," Jo reminded him, mostly just to throw his own words back at him.

"We have enough to afford something quick."

She couldn't tell if he was ignoring her choice of words and Jo couldn't let it be without driving her point home. "Didn't take you for someone who likes a quickie."

Her remark finally drew laughter from the man—a sound that brought a smile to Jo's own lips. "You're right. I'll take my time on the right dame."

Jo opened her mouth, but there was no witty retort waiting. He had stumped her with what sounded like sincerity.

He glanced at her and the shake of his head did nothing to hide his satisfied smile. "In any case, you should be comfortable using time, how it works, the sensations, and whatnot."

Jo just shrugged. She wasn't going to say no. Yuusuke shouldn't be in that server barn for a few more days yet, and Wayne raised a good point. She didn't want to choke while using her magic at a pivotal moment.

The establishment had a terraced balcony that overlooked the street and hillside rolling down to the Eiffel Tower. For such a prime location, Jo was surprised to find it mostly vacant, especially on the second floor where the view was utter perfection (most of Europe had been lucky in the most recent World War, a change from the first two). Wayne motioned to a table.

"How does here look?"

"Fine, but . . ." Jo grabbed the chair to pull it out so she could actually sit. It didn't budge. She could touch it, but she couldn't do anything with it. Like it had been super-glued to the floor. It was just like the keypad at her garage had been.

"That's where these come in." Wayne held out his watch. "Turn yours on." Jo did as instructed. "Right, see, here—" he pointed at four small numbers beneath the time "—when the wish came in, all of us were given ten hours apiece. Will that be enough for what you want to do here?"

"Yes, ten hours should be no problem." Jo looked at the familiar stopwatch. "As long as I can start and stop the countdown like you did in Texas."

"You should be able to. Everyone else can. Try it now."

"How?" Jo asked expectantly.

"Sorry, doll, but we all have a different way." He brought his fingers to his chin, thinking a moment. "Can't say I know much about all the high-tech phonus balonus."

Jo double-tapped on the number ten. She may not be able to unlock her watch, but she could pull up the stopwatch function. Still, the numbers didn't start. She'd usually just tap the number for it to start, but . . . "It'd be fantastic if the Society could develop some kind of welcome training video that lets new recruits know all about wishes and magic and time and how it all works," Jo muttered, not expecting an answer.

"Well, I tried when you woke up to—" Whatever Wayne may have said was drowned out because as soon as her finger came into contact with the fabric, the world exploded into existence around her.

The sounds of car-horns filled the street, blaring in full-force from what she now knew had been muffled. She heard people laughing and shouting and carrying on with a detail that her ears hadn't captured previously. The smell of breads baking mixed with brighter notes of cloying sweetness and uncommon spices, all layered under the distinct smell of industry boasted by every city in the world. Jo looked back to the tower, as if seeing it for the first time—as if seeing all of it for the first time.

*So, this is the difference between really being alive and . . . whatever I am now.*

The chair behind her scraped as Wayne pulled it out. He motioned for Jo to sit. "After you." She eased herself into the chair, her eyes still on the city around her. She heard sounds that she didn't think her previously mortal ears could've ever picked up. She saw with unnatural clarity, every speck of grime catching the daylight.

Lightly, very lightly, as if it might cut her, she ran her fingers over the tablecloth. Jo would've sworn she could feel every fiber in that instant as the grooves of her fingertips ran over them. She picked up the knife, turning it, just because she could. The metal was almost icy, and her nose picked up its scent even from far away. The fork was next. And then—

Her hyper-observations were startled away with a voice that was far louder than it should've been.

"I'm sorry. I didn't see you come in. Have you been waiting long?" A woman was poised at their table, as though she'd been standing there for a while. Jo stared up at her, mouth agape.

"No, we just sat." Wayne smooth-talked the rough edges of their sudden appearance into existence.

"I'll give you a minute with the menus, then."

A long list of various pastries, drinks, and crepes appeared in Jo's hands. It was printed on some high-quality parchment paper and rubber-banded to a wooden board with the restaurant's logo burned at the top. Her eyes fell on the prices and Jo had an internal argument on which question to ask first.

"Two things." Ultimately, she couldn't decide what she needed to know faster, or more, so she asked both questions at once. "First, how did you do that—how did I do that? Second, how are we going to afford this?"

Wayne chuckled. "What did we do?"

"Don't play coy, you know exactly what I mean. I can't speak French." She couldn't speak for Wayne; after all, the man was a couple hundred years old. She hoped she could learn an extra language, or two, in that sort of time. But she'd understood the entire interaction with the waitress, conducted in a language Jo was sure she didn't know.

"Part of the job." Wayne shrugged, as if he'd never given the matter much thought. Knowing him, he hadn't. "It'd be hard to do our work if we couldn't speak the native tongue."

"So, I can speak any language like a native?" Jo said in awe.

"If you need to. And if you believe you can."

She was suddenly reminded of what Snow had said regarding the Door —that she'd lost sight of it because she'd believed it wasn't there. What else could she control if she merely believed? What was the point of anything at all if it could simply be changed with someone's mere thought?

"As far as payment . . . I think we have a simple solution to that." Wayne tapped his watch.

"You mean to skip out on the bill."

"It's easier, don't you think?" Wayne laughed at her expression and Jo's hands flew up to her face to try to make out what look she'd been giving him. "I didn't expect a dame like you to be intimidated by getting her hands a bit dirty."

Jo snorted. "You have no idea what dirt is on my hands."

"But I very much want to." Wayne opened his mouth, as if to say something else. But he didn't. Instead, he eased it closed and let it quirk into a small grin. He gave her a small wink, then looked back down at his menu.

Jo rolled her eyes and looked down at her menu, fighting the makings of a blush. Only when she was certain his attention was no longer on her did she raise her eyes, peering at the man through her lashes.

This wasn't usually her. She wasn't the sort the get so flustered by a little bit of flirting. Sure, romantic attention always stood out to her and was usually welcomed due to its general scarcity in her life. But he was getting her off-balance when she needed to keep her head in the game, a feat that was uncommon while she was on a mission.

Scanning the menu for answers, Jo worked to logic through what was happening. Two people, brought together by an intense situation. She hadn't had any sort of release beyond herself and her toys in over a year and he . . . Well, Takako or the other men didn't seem like his type. Which meant Jo would feel fairly confident in guessing that Wayne was likely just as pent up as she was . . .

She swallowed. That's all it was, hormones. Just like it had been hormones with Snow. Now that she'd addressed it head-on, she could focus on something else—*anything* else.

"Wayne." He looked up from his careful consideration the moment she said his name. "Why does everyone eat, if they no longer have to?"

"Ah . . ." He leaned in his chair, head tilted to the sky, and then turned back to face her. "I can't speak for the others, but I eat in part out of habit, and in part to remind me of my humanity." Her lips parted at the sentiment. As if sensing the weight he'd imparted on the mood, Wayne quickly added. "Plus, food is a delight."

"That's true." Jo regretted asking and was eager to change the topic yet again. "I can't decide what I want. I should focus so I'm ready when the waitress gets here."

"Didn't take you for a doll who doesn't know what she wants."

"Quiet you." Jo brushed off the implication, eyes on the menu. *Focus.* Luckily, she was ready when the waitress came by, and any awkwardness left with their menus. Jo seized the opportunity to return their focus to the task at hand.

"So, we should have time enough . . . I'll need a day, maybe two, in advance."

"Advance of what?" Wayne leaned forward, putting his elbows on the table.

How would she explain it to someone who described technology as "phonus balonus"? Jo took a deep breath, *high level only.* "In World War Three and its aftermath, a group known as Incognito became the most prominent—"

"—cyberterrorists, if you ask any government. Ask Incognito and you'll get a vastly different answer, I imagine."

Jo straightened in surprise. "You know of them?"

"Know of them? Doll, I watched them rise from the sidelines."

"That's right, you're really old." Even though he looked very much twenty.

"Not too old," Wayne's wounded pride (no doubt) said.

"*Aww*, don't take it too hard," she soothed. "You look great for ancient."

"I'll show you how great ancient can be."

Jo snorted. "In any case . . ." She wasn't about to let him derail them yet again with another flirtatious debate. "Yuusuke and I were trying to crack into the Black Bank. It's where all credits are stored and, if it was recognized as a legitimate entity, would count for almost a sixth of global commerce."

"So, you were bank thieves?"

Jo shook her head. "That's not quite how cryptocurrencies work."

"What, then?"

"Data thieves," she corrected. "The Yakuza wanted the data on every account opened with Incognito . . . every transaction that went through the bank. Who was paying who, who really had their hands in what—you name it."

"They wanted to know their competition."

"That. Or they were working with the Japanese government."

"The Japanese government?" Wayne arched his eyebrows. "Perhaps I misheard you, dollface, but why would the Japanese mob work with their feds?"

Jo shrugged. It was a good question, one she'd never really quite understood herself. "There's a long history of it, Yuu said once. Sometimes they're at odds, sometimes they work together . . . if the terms are right. My guess is that the government wanted to see where money was going in case of an American reunification, and—"

"And the mob would skim a little off the top for doing the dirty work so it wasn't on the government's payroll." Wayne finished softly, looking out over the railing to the city beyond. Before Jo could ask, food arrived and he shifted gears right after the waitress left. "You still haven't told me why we need to be in Paris."

"Oh, right." Jo traced the tangents back to the main point of the conversation. "The servers that house the Black Bank's user data have long been rumored to be in the catacombs of Paris, hidden in a fortified area amid the labyrinth. You asked me not to change much? Well, it's a good thing that was already my plan."

"How so?"

"I'm not going to take down the bank. I'm just going to weaken it in the right places so it'll buckle when Yuu hits it. He'll be the one who makes the change."

"And to do that, you need to be in this fortified area?"

"What else?" Jo grinned.

It looked as if Wayne was trying to fight his own grin, but he failed. "We should get to work, then."

They promptly finished lunch—and it was one of the best lunches she'd had in a long time (ever, really, if she didn't count her mother's cooking). It was almost too good to skip out on the check. Almost. But she didn't have any means to pay even if she wanted to—which was frustrating, because this was a rare case where she did want to. Jo didn't make herself out to be some Robin Hood. But she knew when having three digits in a bank account felt like a triumph, and she didn't like screwing over the working man.

"I need a place we can set up for my prep," Jo flipped her USB in her pocket over and over, reassuring herself that it was still there.

"What're you thinking? Computer café?"

"No, too impermanent. I hope it'll only take hours, but if it takes days I do *not* want to be setting up and tearing down constantly . . . This'll do." Jo pointed at a random hotel as they passed. A golden statue of a man on a horse, flag in hand frozen mid-wave, was positioned out front, the letters HOTEL REGINA emblazoned in the same on a black plaque by the door. Five gold stars were proudly displayed below them.

"A hotel? I didn't take you for moving that quickly."

"Dirty old man." Jo rolled her eyes at the implication.

"I am not old!"

"*Right.*" Jo made her best attempt for a warm smile to underscore the fact that she really was just teasing him. She didn't expect it to be returned, but he gave her a grin as if they were already old friends sharing an inside joke. The thought brought her mind right back to where it should be: Yuusuke. "We can get our own room to make our command center."

The lobby was stunningly art nouveau. White and grey marble were diagonally laid in a checkered pattern under classic furniture, all polished to a mirror shine that picked up the sunlight filtering through the sheer curtains of the curving windows lining the front wall.

Jo was given pause by the chandelier, the ironwork of the banister, the carvings inlaid at the lobby desk. She was reminded of the decadence of the mansion in the Society, but this truly felt real. There were indents in the counter from a long history of people leaning against the edge. There were scuffs on the floor, and the couches looked as if invisible people still sat in them.

It was a place with spirit, not a place of spirits.

"This way." Jo walked over to the check-in counter, completely ignored by the people behind, bellhops stepping around them.

"What're you looking for?" Wayne asked. He was back to flipping his nickel, a rhythmic up and down that was almost impressive. (But she didn't want to give him the satisfaction of saying so.)

"I just need a . . . a . . . ah." Jo saw a side office with a halfway open door—just enough to squeeze through without needing to activate their watches. Ignoring the bolded "PRIVATE" sign that warned off the regular hotel patron, Jo helped herself into the room. "Close and lock the door."

Wayne didn't question, lifting his wrist and pushing in one of the knobs on the side of his watch. He closed the door with his back against it, presumably to avoid being seen, but his nonchalant and undeniably suggestive lean after it was locked said otherwise.

"If you wanted to get me alone, all you had to do was ask." He really was making sport of having someone to flirt with.

"Sorry to disappoint you." Jo gave him a mock pouting face, playing along. "I was looking for some time with my first love."

Jo activated her watch and felt reality come back to her in full force. She could touch things again, interact with things, and she'd never been happier to feel the clicking of keys under her fingers.

"What're you doing?" Wayne strolled over, pocketing his nickel on the way and leaning over her shoulder.

"Just getting us a room."

"A room?" Wayne looked over her shoulder. "Doll, the penthouse suite is not *just* a room."

"Didn't you say that every now and then, you like to enjoy yourself a bit? Well, if I'm going to stay, I want to stay in style." Jo flashed him a grin. This was the life she'd always dreamed of, right? Why not? What were they going to do if they caught her? Jo doubted there was an "out of time and space" jail she could be sent to.

Wayne roared with laughter.

"Quiet down or you're going to get us caught!" she hissed.

"I already pulled out." He tapped his watch. "No need to waste time."

"I thought we couldn't be seen by people in the real world?" Jo could see Wayne clear as day, even though her stopwatch was ticking.

"We can't be. But you're not a part of, as you put it, the 'real world' anymore, dollface."

"Right, magic." Jo's fingers tapped over the keys with renewed enthusiasm. Magic. She existed with real magic. Her mind began to whir around the possibility as her hands moved on instinct. What else could she do with her newfound powers? "Almost done . . ."

Her fingers flew over the keys and tapped the touch screen. The universe contained in binary unfolded before her. There were the familiar pathways she'd traversed before, but now, new tracks made themselves known to her. If she wanted to stall out the hotel system, it would be simple. Take down the email client they used? Child's play.

She saw the entire framework of the hotel's digital existence through the light of the computer screen, and knew just how to dismantle it, if she wanted, without even needing to think about it. It was that same feeling she had found in the recreation room, but this time it was out in the world itself.

Why couldn't she have felt this way taking down the Black Bank? If she had, she and Yuusuke wouldn't have had to spend so much time locked down. They might have—

Wayne's mouth appeared next to her ear and the husk of his voice broke through her thoughts.

"Your magic is stunning."

# PENTHOUSE

"Not magic, just technology. The same trusty technology humanity has been using in place of magic since the dawn of man." Jo did one final sweep of the desktop, making sure she'd erased all trace of her presence on the computer. Even if she could disappear into thin air with a tap of her watch, old habits involving covering her tracks were hard to break.

Wayne was unconvinced. "Firstly, technology has not replaced magic from the dawn of man. Secondly, while technology was involved, I know magic when I see it."

"Not everything in the world is magic. The supernatural is what technology can't explain yet," she countered on instinct. Jo inwardly cringed the moment she espoused the same thing she'd heard for years as a kid.

"Really? You have that opinion *now*? Just when you seem to be settling in to being part of a magic society?"

Jo shook her head. "Ignore me. I'm sounding like my father and I hate that."

Wayne watched her carefully for a long second, and gave a nod. "Can't have that, can we, doll?"

"Definitely not." Jo unlocked the door, swinging it open just enough before she tapped her watch. The hotel was oblivious to their presence as they stepped out of the private office. Wayne strode over to a grouping of couches, plopped himself down on one and motioned for her to follow. As she sat, he pushed the button on his watch and Jo did the same with hers.

One bellhop seemingly noticed their pop back into reality. He was so startled from his daydreams, staring off at nothing in their general direction, that he nearly fell over standing in place. He blinked at them twice, shook his head, and looked away.

"Shall we check in?" Wayne stood.

"Why did we sit?" Jo wondered aloud as she followed him back toward the front desk.

"I find it's less jarring if you're not in people's line of sight when you activate your time." He shrugged. "No matter how you appear, they just sort of play it off as if they haven't been paying enough attention to their surroundings. But that process moves faster if it's more of a 'corner of the eye' kind of thing. Being lower helps with that."

Jo looked back at the bellhop who was still regarding them warily. "I get that, I guess."

"Checking in for two, Espinosa. Everything should already be set in your system." Wayne leaned against the counter smugly. His eyes drifted over the set-up where a woman was presumably pulling up their reservations. If Jo didn't know better, she'd have said he was the hotelier stopping in to make sure everything was running according to his expectations.

Jo watched him thoughtfully, putting aside his tiresome antics of clinging to the 1920s and incessant use of "doll" to see the man with new eyes. His suit, while dated, looked like it was freshly pressed. It was tailored with impeccable skill and had an air of "intentional retro" that almost seemed to fit with the two-hundred-fifty-year-old hotel. He looked well put-together.

In contrast . . . Jo looked down at her bargain-bin jeans and tired hoodie. She did not look like someone who would be checking into the penthouse of a five-star hotel.

Or maybe she did.

Jo leaned against the counter as well, pretending she owned the place, pretending she owned the whole damn city. She'd seen billionaires who never changed out of sweatpants and heiresses who couldn't be bothered to think of anything more than their standard-issue black tank tops. It didn't matter how she looked; it mattered how she acted.

Jo decided she was acting like she was nothing less than a woman who owned the world.

"I'd also like a bottle of champagne sent up to the room later tonight," Jo demanded.

"Yes, of course . . . Do you have any preference on the vintage?"

"The nicest one you have."

"Now you're talking." Wayne appraised her with a long rake of his eyes, as if seeing her for the first time.

"Charge it to the room," Jo added. They were disappearing on the tab if it was one hundred or one thousand euro. So why not make it one thousand? This wasn't some small mom-and-pop operation, like the café. A hotel this swanky and established would be fine footing the bill of their mysterious patrons.

"Certainly. Is there anything else we can do to make your stay more enjoyable?" the clerk asked.

"Nothing I can think of right now, but you'll be the first to know."

The woman behind the counter looked at both of their wrists. Jo knew what was coming next before it happened. "I see you've already uploaded all necessary check-in documents. Now, if I can just have your bio-band to Bluetooth the room key . . ."

"I'm afraid the thing's busted." Jo tapped the black strip of fabric around her wrist to life, very careful not to pull it off the stopwatch. "Stuck on this screen."

"No trouble, we can give you temporary keys." The woman fumbled behind the counter for several moments until she found a forgotten box of plastic room keys, the sort of thing you'd expect to see in a retro motel and not a five-star establishment. Two long minutes, and several apologies later for not quite knowing how the system for temporary keys worked, Jo and Wayne had room keys in hand.

Jo was already paranoid about losing hers.

"Okay, we have the room, what next?" Wayne asked as they waited for the elevators to take them all the way up to the lavish accommodations that would be their home and home base.

"Now, I do a bit of shopping." Her insides squirmed with excitement at the word. She was going to make the dream set-up the mansion had given her a reality.

# BELLHOP BET

GETTING EVERYTHING SET up without using too much time was looking to be a bit of a challenge. They'd managed to get a substantial amount of tech sent up to the penthouse, always while they were "out" and always in unmarked boxes. Jo had the majority of what she needed uploaded on a flash drive, but she still required a physical presence to be able to implement it in all the ways she needed to. Which meant she had to be stingy, and she had to make sure everything was in order before jumping in headfirst.

Wayne, in surprise chivalrousness, took the brunt of the time spent. Jo wanted to argue, but she didn't. He'd reminded her that he had time left over from past wishes and Yuusuke needed them a lot more than either of them needed a few hours of play time (or work, supposedly, if she was ever brought in on a wish) in the real world. A little bit of willingness to help her friend went a long way with Jo. If Wayne wasn't careful—no, if *she* wasn't careful, she'd find him counted within her inner circle. Perhaps the whole Society really could be her new family, someday.

Lucky for her, the endearment he earned from being an unquestioning assistant was tempered by the forehead-meet-desk sort of task that it was to get Wayne acquainted with her setup. She typed over his hands, her stopwatch off and his on, showing him what he needed to do and where. She worked alongside him, and then just had him hit "go" on the scripts she was building.

The last time she'd tried to hit the Black Bank it had been about proving herself, about Yuusuke and her becoming legends in the community, making all the money she'd ever need, and then making a clean escape—all while being able to give their families the lives they deserved.

Maybe Yuusuke was still aiming for that goal, but Jo's new mission was simpler: keep Yuu safe, help him succeed. Make sure her wish wasn't made in vain. Make sure this equally magical and insane life she now lived had meaning. At the very least, she could set her friend on the right path one last time.

Lucky for Yuusuke, Jo knew exactly how he hacked, had learned alongside him for years when they were kids. She knew just as much about the ins and outs of his capabilities as she did her own, and worked to string together a foundation of code for Yuu to find.

Jo wasn't looking to break into the Black Bank herself—she was looking to give Yuusuke all the back doors he needed in all the places only he would think to look. She was hollowing out the whole thing so that it'd fall like a house of cards the moment he came tapping.

"Damn," Jo sighed, turning her watch off the moment she hit a roadblock; no use wasting time on frustration.

"Everything all right, doll?" Wayne asked from where he was lying on the bed, staring blearily at the ceiling (his monitor tolerance was much, *much* lower than hers, and they'd been at it for nearly three days now). Jo groaned, then placed a hand on the keyboard in front of her, hating the way the touch felt instantly less pronounced.

"Just another setback we don't really have time for . . . I'll figure it out." There had to be at least a few more ways she could obfuscate things. She needed an excellent, elegant virus that no one would even see. Yuu would trigger it, then it'd eat away at the security of the Black Bank like a parasite, and then it'd eat itself. She needed perfection on a time budget of about twenty minutes. "I can do this in ten, then I'm sure—"

She had already clicked on her watch, eyes scanning the lines and lines of code on the screen, when the lock on the door deactivated and a bellhop let himself in. She hadn't even heard him knock. Had he knocked?

"Oh! Ms. Espinoza, my sincerest apologies!" The bellhop bowed, a little panicked. "I was informed by the desk that you were out and I was to deliver . . . I didn't mean to . . . disturb . . . you . . ." The words trailed off as he stood from his bow, his eyes finally taking in the sight of the very elaborate-looking display of tech before him. Jo didn't doubt they'd sent him up under some false pretense to investigate the unmarked packages; his look of confirmed suspicion told her as much. But the surprise at actually finding them in the room seemed genuine, especially with the panic of needing to find an excuse for why he'd just waltz into a hotel patron's room unannounced.

This was the last thing they needed right now. Jo couldn't turn off her watch with him staring directly at her, but with every moment he stood gaping at the incriminating display and stewing in his own panic, she lost precious time.

Suddenly, Wayne was in front of her, a hand finding her shoulder and giving it a squeeze. The bellhop gave Wayne simple, mostly distracted greetings. He didn't seem to have been startled by a man suddenly appearing before him, which meant Wayne must have turned on his watch in the bedroom, just out of sight.

"Do what you do best, doll," Wayne said in a tone low enough for only her to hear. "I'll handle the stool pigeon." Jo looked at the line of Wayne's back, at the confident stretch of his posture. His other hand was already in his pocket, pulling out a familiar, silver coin. Even though Wayne wasn't looking, she nodded, trying her best to focus on the task at hand. Time was ticking.

She still couldn't help listening to their conversation, however.

"How about a little bet, *hmm*?" Wayne asked, his tone suave. Jo heard the sound of his nickel flipping off the edge of his thumbnail, followed by the bellhop's confused stuttering.

"Really, s-sir, I should probably be—"

"Just a little bet." As Wayne spoke, Jo felt a small wriggling in the air that reminded her of the sensation she'd felt on the first day in the Society. But this time, it didn't land on her. His magic was intended for someone else. "Heads says you tell your bosses you saw nothing unusual up here, tails says you get my nickel and do whatever your conscience deems fit. Whatcha say?"

The bellhop lingered in his own uncertainty. Discomfort radiated off of him, and was no doubt making the man eager to leave. Inwardly cursing, Jo pulled up a new tab on one of her screens to research.

"You really should take him up on it," Jo chimed in before the bellhop could scurry away and rat them out. She looked over her shoulder, fingers still typing away as if she could care less about the situation. As though she wasn't embroiled in something highly illegal on every other monitor than the one showing a large picture of Wayne's nickel. She thought the coin looked odd from the start. "That's a liberty head nickel." Both men stared at her dumbly, and Jo had to force herself not to laugh. "They don't mint nickels anymore. At all. It's practically ancient now, clear back to the days of the *United States* of America. And the liberty head was pretty rare to begin with, so it's got to be worth at least a couple thousand."

Jo finally stopped typing, looking the bellhop in the eye. She could see his resolve wavering at the mention of the nickel's worth. A bellhop surely didn't make that much money, even in a five-star hotel; she figured it might peak his interest. What she didn't expect was the look of pure shock on Wayne's face.

"Just a quick bet?" The bellhop eventually cracked, probably finally realizing he had nothing to lose and everything to gain. Or because of that nagging pressure that had him rubbing the back of his neck. Wayne cleared his throat and continued flipping his nickel, confident smirk falling back into place. "Okay."

Wayne gave the coin one final flip before slapping it into the back of his hand. It was, expectedly, heads. "Them's the breaks, kid," he winked, and Jo watched as the bellhop straightened, a look of confusion flitting across his face. When he opened his mouth to speak, he seemed at a loss for words, and eventually just shut his mouth and shook his head. Wayne just put a hand on the boy's shoulder and ushered him back towards the door. "Better luck next time."

The moment the bellhop was past the threshold, Wayne closed the door and turned off his watch, Jo doing the same after a few more minutes at the computer. She glanced at her watch and winced. She'd used way more time than she'd intended. But as long as she only took one shot at this—which was all she was gearing up to need—she should be fine.

When Jo turned to look at Wayne, he was leaning heavily against the door, lost in thought. The silence felt heavy, so Jo broke it as carefully as she could. "You're sure he won't tell anybody?"

Wayne shook his head. "He can't. He lost the bet."

"So that's your magic then?"

"Superficially, yes," Wayne replied, but he still wasn't looking at her. "I have to say something that I'm betting on and money has to be involved. I always win, and the loser has to oblige by the terms."

"Does it have to be your nickel?"

"Any money."

Jo thought about this for a second. "So that's what you used on me."

At that, Wayne finally glanced in her direction. He arched his eyebrows, noting her calm tone and demeanor. "I thought you'd be more upset."

Jo just shrugged. "What would that get me now?"

The odd thoughtfulness finally seemed to bleed out of Wayne's features, his shoulders shaking with a quiet laugh. "You're really quite the woman, aren't you?" He paused, mulling something over, and then added, "Is it really worth that much cabbage?"

Jo frowned, caught off guard by the question. "What?"

"My nickel."

"I don't know of any currency called cabbage."

"Cash, dame," Wayne sighed, but he was smiling.

"It is a few hundred years old." Jo shrugged. She leaned back on her hands. "My mother was obsessed with old America, the way it was before the war. She kept an old coin collection, so when you said nickel, it jarred my memory."

"I see." Wayne didn't press further, and Jo found herself relieved he didn't. She wasn't sure why she'd offered the personal anecdote, but it hurt a lot more than expected.

And that hurt was exactly what she needed to get back on track; no better distraction than a good coding session.

"I've done everything I can here," she said, getting to her feet with a stretch.

Wayne looked down at the computer set up and raised an eyebrow. "So, what next?

"Now we actually break into a bank."

# CATACOMB HEIST

T HE LOCATION OF the Black Bank was one of the best and worst kept secrets in the hacking community. It was common knowledge that the Black Bank's servers were somewhere in the catacombs. But where, exactly? That was a lot more difficult to drudge up information on. By the time Jo had managed to pin down the most likely location (leveraging her past research with Yuusuke), she was down to only three hours of actual time left.

Which was fine. If everything went smoothly, then she would be in and out within the hour. Yuu would have all the routes laid out for him like a lit-up aerospace runway, and Jo would head back to the Society with two whole hours to spare. Simple, right?

Now, it was just a matter of getting inside.

The most likely location was, unsurprisingly, hidden deep underneath Paris. It was the perfect cover—the ideal location, large enough to house any necessary tech, cold enough for high-speed processing (though they'd no doubt invested a lot of money in some sort of system that could handle the moisture), and buried away where only the reckless urban explorer could find it. As she scanned digital mapping and shared posts on the back pages of cataphiles (self-professed catacomb explorers), leading them to what was most likely the closest entrance, Jo couldn't help her excitement.

This was the goal that she had lost her life for. It had been a task she couldn't accomplish as a mortal, but was now attainable in her new "not quite dead" state. Jo swallowed, balling her fists and stepping off the main street her and Wayne had been walking down. Even if she couldn't do this herself, she'd see Yuusuke accomplish it.

She glanced at Wayne, making sure he was still in tow. He gave her a short nod of determination. Jo responded in kind with a single thought: *good man.*

They walked down off the side street, through a narrow passage between two buildings, down an alley, and into a small side courtyard that looked all but forgotten by time.

Jo made a noise of disgust at a narrow iron door, diagonally set into the stone between the ground and the wall of a building before them. It had wept rusty tears that now ran like rivulets of dried blood in the stone around it. But it wasn't the condition of the portal that had her frustrated; it was a hefty padlock securing the doors closed. Electronic locks she could do, but old school was a bit out of her wheelhouse.

"Let's break in," Wayne said nonchalantly, as if talking about the weather.

"Oh, lovely idea, except for—oh, darn—I seemed to have missed the Society's introductory class on lock picking along with every other non-existent introductory class," Jo responded in kind.

"You can open it." He leaned against the opposite wall, hands in his pockets.

"Do we need to review? I'm a hacker, not a locksmith." Jo pointed to the mechanical lock. "I know you're from the dark ages, so I'll break it down: This is not digital."

"You sure get feisty when you're on a mission." He whistled. "Look, doll, I've watched you work for days. I've seen—and felt—your magic when you were hunched over your setup in the penthouse."

She had felt it too, if only just a vague whisper of it somewhere in the back of her mind. But that was still just hacking, her magic making it easier, *maybe*, but not doing it for her completely.

"I think your magic is much more than just digital," Wayne went on, as if recognizing her resolve wavering. "Why don't you take a look, and try?"

Yuusuke's life depended on them getting inside, which meant she owed it to him to take every opportunity presented to her. Even if she didn't exactly believe it was possible.

Jo squared off against the door. She put her feet shoulder-width apart and her hands on her hips. She took a deep breath, and invited the power to fill her veins. She felt a trickle of sensation at the back of her mind, just like at the hotel.

"Hocus-pocus-open'us!" Jo threw her hands up.

The door did nothing, but Wayne doubled over in laughter.

"I don't think that's how it works," he said, gasping for air.

"No shit." What did he think would happen? They didn't have time for this and he was cracking jokes?

"Try again, for real this time," he encouraged, probably after seeing the lack of amusement on her face.

Jo turned back to the door and stared at it, letting her mind run away from her.

Truth was, she wanted to open it. She wanted to figure out all this magic business sooner over later and just do it. She wanted to harness its power to help her friend. But Wayne was being as helpful in assisting with the learning process as a cold soldering iron to a stripped wire. Maybe he was trying to get her to figure it out on her own; maybe he was trying to teach her by not teaching her; but now wasn't the time for lessons. Now was supposed to be the time to act.

Jo swallowed back her annoyance and summoned every ounce of determination to do just that.

She looked at the padlock. She didn't know the first thing about lock-picking. But the longer she looked, the more it seemed to unravel before her. Of course, nothing physically changed about it. To her eyes though, it was as if the structure began to be rebuilt in straight lines and practical knowledge, like blueprints coming to life in the void.

"I have an idea . . ." she uttered, much to her own surprise.

Jo tapped her watch and looked around the small clearing they were standing in. There wasn't much to work with. She needed something heavy, something—like that piece of piping that had sprung loose from the gutter system.

*It'll do*, a disembodied voice assured her the moment Jo had it in her hands.

Jo worked her way back to the door, but her eyes didn't fall on the lock. Instead, they drifted over to the hinges on the side. She was calm, abnormally so. It was as if she wasn't clocked into reality; everything around her had gone hushed.

At least until the loud bang of the pipe meeting the door echoed off every wall—twice, in quick succession.

"Shit, shit, shit!" Jo frantically tapped her watch, dropping the pipe with a clamor in the process to disappear before anyone could look to investigate. A window opened above them, one man hanging out. He must have assumed it was just the pipe coming loose, because he returned inside with a shrug. He didn't even see that one hinge had been struck in just the right way for the old bolts to pop loose from the mortar. Or that the other had its pin broken clear through.

"Well done." Wayne pushed on his watch once they were sure no one else was coming. The muscles of his back strained against his shirt as he pulled off the door—much more muscle than Jo had previously given the man credit for. It was a testament to her focus that she didn't get too distracted wondering just how much more muscle he was hiding. Wayne set the iron to the side and pulled out of time. "Couldn't pick something lighter?" he huffed, and wiped his palms on his trousers.

Jo ignored his griping as easily as his muscles and remained focused on the pipe. "Well done? I literally smashed my way in."

"You knew how to break the hinges," he pointed out.

"Anyone would've tried to smash it. Anyone could've."

"Anyone would've gone for the lock, not the hinges. What's more, doll, is that it took you just two perfect strikes. You knew it would break. You knew just where to hit it and with how much force." He paused, actually giving Jo a chance to counter, but she didn't. *Couldn't.* Truth was, she *had* known, in that weird back-of-the-mind-tickling-sensation sort of way from before.

"So, what . . . my magic is breaking things?" she huffed. "What a great power."

Yet, the moment the words "great power" crossed her lips they echoed in someone else's voice. Jo saw the outline of a face like a Greek god (Zeus felt right) uttering next the word, "Destruction." She pushed it from her mind as irrelevant—likely some movie she watched forever ago and long forgot.

"It is, actually." Wayne's words gave her pause as Jo hovered at the entrance. Dank air wafted up from the open darkness beneath her. "The Society was in dire need of someone with your skills, I'd say. The ability to crack any code, break through any lock, digital and non-digital. The rest of us, other than Takako and her guns, are in the making business, really. Samson can craft things. Eslar can heal. Nico can paint. I can make bets. Even Snow creates reality." Before Jo could ask about Pan, Wayne continued. "Eslar was right. Sounds like an asset to me."

"I guess we'll see when—if—it's ever used for a wish."

"You're still bent about that?" Wayne stuffed his hands into his pockets, clearly trying to assess how deep her bitterness ran.

Jo didn't bury the lede. "Yes and no," she confessed. "I get it, Snow wants me to learn my magic and become comfortable before I'm placed in the line of fire. Walk before you run, and all that. It's not like I haven't had to prove myself before." Jo looked down into the darkness. "But that's just it. My whole life I've been proving myself. Just when I thought I'd finally cracked through and could live the easy life with my family, I died."

She glanced over at him. Wayne hadn't moved, and his face was surprisingly expressionless. For the first time, she was left wondering what he might be thinking.

"I don't know if you can understand . . . But I've always been working toward something—for my mother, Yuusuke, for myself. To now be the bottom rung *and* have nothing to do? It's a bitter pill."

Wayne rubbed his chin thoughtfully and said, finally, "Good thing you didn't have anything to do." Jo raised her eyebrows and Wayne motioned toward the darkness. "If you were on the wish you wouldn't be able to help your friend."

Jo narrowed her eyes at him. "Damn your logic, sir."

Wayne looked down at her, head cocked to the side. A rogue piece of hair had escaped its usual slicked-back perfection and hung with the movement. He leaned forward in a manner that nearly beckoned for her to do the same. "I know, I'm heinous, aren't I?"

Jo was glad he stepped away promptly, or she may have objected to the idea.

"Now, let's get to that Black Bank."

She faced off against the opening to the catacombs and ignored her insides firing with such ferocity that she was surprised she hadn't short-circuited yet. "Will we be able to see?" Jo asked uncertainly.

"Remember, we're not human anymore, not quite." Wayne placed an encouraging hand at the small of her back. "We need no feast and fear no famine. We are the embracers of dreams and the vagrants of sleep. And we—"

"We fear no hour, for none shall be our last," Jo uttered.

From the corners of her eyes, Jo could see Wayne staring at her. "How did you know that?" he asked, barely more than a whisper.

"Something I remembered my grandmother reading to me when I was little," Jo confessed.

*Behold, the giver of wishes,* Abuelita had read from an old, dusty tome, her voice worn with age and tinged in an accent that meant family and home. She remembered her eyes, crinkling at the corners as she glanced up from the page. *They are the changer of worlds, mijita, and you are destined for greatness because you are of their blood.*

"About what?"

"I think it was about you." The details of the book and the passages within were still vague, ethereal, on the tip of her tongue but not quite enough to get a taste. The more she thought about the memory, the blurrier it all became. In truth, Jo was only fifty-percent sure it had been her grandmother speaking to her at all. Something about that memory felt far older than her years. But she did know the words. Jo looked up at Wayne, feeling a heavy weight settling over her shoulders. "Well . . . us, I guess."

Jo looked forward once more and stepped into the darkness before he could ask further. Old habits died hard, and somewhere Jo waited for her father to scold her for "buying into all this magic nonsense."

She strode into the maze of stone, a hand running along the wall, fingers streaking lines in the dampness. Wayne was beside her, but wasn't touching her. He hovered, a warm presence in the chilling blackness that somehow her eyes did not struggle to pierce.

She knew exactly where to go, the careful map of the catacombs that she'd memorized hovering in the forefront of her mind. It led her with ease, deeper and deeper inside. Eventually, Jo felt a buzz in the air around her—a thrumming that was both familiar and unusual in the ancient and gloomy atmosphere.

It was the distinct feeling of electric current, noticeable in the otherwise void blackness. Or, perhaps it was her magic, or being outside time, that made it so prominent.

"Through here." She motioned for Wayne to follow, confidence leading her down one more tunnel and towards a heavy-looking door. Wayne wasted no time turning on his watch, allowing her to save more of her minutes for what was to come. Jo gave him a nod as he heaved the lock, disengaged the carefully insulated door, and pushed it open.

The Black Bank's mainframe was expectedly massive, towers of server racks lining the perimeter of a room that was suddenly all too modern for its surroundings. All the bells and whistles had obviously gone into this set up, and she had no doubt that there were protections, even from the inside. But that didn't mean she wasn't up for the task.

Jo went to one of the two monitors on either side of the room, simple command centers no doubt used for little more than diagnostics. The first did not have a USB port, but the second did. Turning on her time and taking a seat, Jo plugged in her drive and began uploading. The moment her codes were uploaded, the scripts began working.

She could pull out of time, likely *should* pull out of time. It was mostly automated from here. But Jo couldn't bring herself to tap her watch, not when she was this close. If something went wrong, just the slightest line of code out of place, she wanted to be ready.

But so far, so good. The script ran like a dream and Jo watched as it began to attach itself to the underbelly of the Black Bank. It was a little worm under the rug, put in a place where only Yuusuke was likely to find it—and he wouldn't even realize he had.

By the time she felt content in her job—probably only a few more tweaks here and there to make sure the virus killed itself on activation— she still had an hour left.

"Looks like your time is up, dollface," Wayne said, aiming for casual but missing the mark. When she looked over her shoulder at him, he was peeking past the door and back out into the tunnels, a look of concern on his face.

"I'm not done yet," Jo snapped, suddenly feeling as though everything she had done wouldn't be enough. She only had this one chance, this one accumulation of time to spend. If she didn't get the right amount of encryptions uploaded, if she didn't open enough back doors, then her wish would mean nothing. Yuusuke would wind up right back where they'd started . . . ended.

"Jo, someone's coming," Wayne hissed back, voice a bit worried. He turned on his watch, she noticed, his posture going stiff.

Willing herself to calm, to focus, Jo took a breath, letting the information she'd gathered and the data she'd collected all pull into organized files within her mind. Internally, she looked over everything she'd done, envisioned everything that would be waiting for Yuusuke when he finally got this far. And then, with a burst of something vivid, a sensation that she could only describe as magical, she saw three, four, *no*, five different spots within her foundation that, if left alone, would bring the whole thing down.

Quickly, Jo began working to fix the issues. How was it that she hadn't noticed them before? Stupid, stupid, *stupid*!

"Jo!" Wayne shouted her name, making her jump, but even as she whipped around to see what was going on, her fingers never stopped their frantic typing. Which was amazing, really, considering the way her whole body went tense at the sight of a man hurrying into the room.

"Two minutes!" Jo shouted, wincing when Wayne cursed in response.

"Hey! You two!" A voice demanded in French at her back. "Hands up!"

What followed was the sound of an obvious struggle, Jo doing her best to block it out and focus on the final threads she had to sew together. The sound of a fist connecting with what was either a jaw or a cheekbone brought a few seconds of silence, and Wayne was suddenly at her shoulder, panting.

"Let's go!" He urged her on, but she had one more line to input. Furiously, she typed in the last breadcrumbs for Yuusuke to follow and then backed away from the keyboard.

"Done." She breathed out a sigh of relief, pulled her USB, and relished in the feeling of a sense of accomplishment that settled deep into her bones. Which was instantly followed by a rush of fear as she turned around, a gun pointed squarely at her head. She really was done having guns pointed at her.

"You have to the count of three to tell me who you're working for," the man, now sporting a black eye and bruised jaw, growled at her, clicking off the safety.

"Come on, dollface." Wayne's fingers, long and warm, wrapped around her wrist. Slowly, he raised her hand, as if to signify their surrender, but his subtle tapping at her watch did not go unnoticed.

Before the man had a chance to start his countdown, Wayne and Jo shared a look, nodded, and turned off their watches.

It took a long moment before their disappearance seemed to register, a look of confusion and then terror spreading across the man's face. Wayne and Jo stayed perfectly still, practically holding their breath despite the fact that they knew he could no longer see or hear them.

It wasn't until it was obvious the man wasn't going anywhere, struck dumb by their vanishing act, that Jo's heart started to slow. She looked from the man—gun forgotten and staring wide-eyed at the space where they had "once stood"—and over to Wayne. He looked startled himself, but his eyes were shining. Jo cleared her throat.

The man ran over to the computer, looking for evidence that what he saw was real. Jo couldn't help a smug grin. Like he'd find anything. Her finger tapped the flash drive, safely in her hoodie; she wasn't that clumsy.

"So, uh . . ." she started, hand still shaking with adrenaline as she ran it through her hair. "Wanna get out of here?"

Wayne looked away from the man hunched over the computer and settled his heavy gaze on her. There was a flush on his face and a grin almost involuntarily spreading across his mouth.

When he laughed, uproarious, and maybe even a little hysterically, Jo couldn't help but follow suit.

# TOMATO

THERE WAS NO way of knowing what time it was when Wayne and Jo stumbled back into their penthouse suite. Not that it mattered. On a grand scale, time was irrelevant now anyway. What she did know was that the sun had long since set, the view outside their balcony window illuminated by the city lights and the Eiffel Tower, lit up in all its ageless grandeur.

"Now that, doll," Wayne whistled, laughing to himself as he flopped down onto the plush, pillow smothered bed. "Was a ring-a-ding-ding."

"I told you it'd be no big deal." Jo rolled her eyes, but she was far too high off the adrenaline of their escape to be annoyed. She could still feel the success of their mission pumping like blood through her veins, thrumming with energy and accomplishment. A feeling of conquest consumed her—she could tackle the world, take whatever she wanted, do anything.

In attempts to settle her still-shaking hands, Jo grabbed a bottle of champagne out of the multitude they'd had room service send up, and began working at the metal cage around the cork. "Also, do me a favor and never use the term ring-a-ding-ding again." She didn't bother looking in Wayne's direction, knowing he would properly ignore the request no matter what. "And second—"

The cork popped free of the bottle the moment the wiring around it was loosened, the small projectile careening just over Wayne's head to bounce off the wall with a *thunk*. A deluge of foam cascaded down the neck, so before it could soil the carpets any further, Jo poured a glass of champagne for herself and for Wayne, admiring the way it bubbled behind the freshly washed crystal.

"And second," she began again, sitting herself on the edge of the bed and tipping the glass back for a nice, long swallow. The bubbles tickled her throat, the alcohol warming her stomach. She licked her lips and handed Wayne his own glass before continuing, giving the man a once-over. "'Doll' is getting kinda old."

"Alright." Wayne sat up, taking a quick swig of his own drink before shooting her a look. Jo was shocked, but mildly hopeful, that he was about to heed her request—at least until he opened his mouth again. "What about sweet patootie?"

"What?" Jo sputtered, choking a bit on her champagne. She couldn't help but laugh, though. "Thank you, but pass."

"Okay, how about hot mama?"

"Also pass," Jo grinned, still laughing. "Though I'm flattered you think I'm hot."

Wayne shifted a little bit closer to her on the bed, chuckling softly right along with her, even if the look in his eyes was more seductive than amused. "Sweet mama, then?"

"No thanks, I'm not your mom."

"Dish? Looker?" Wayne's grin shifted into an equally suggestive smirk, his right hand inching across the comforter to barely intertwine with her own fingers. Before Jo could respond, she swallowed, clearing the sudden thickness in her throat. Despite the fact that her own smirk was still firmly in place, even she could hear the tightness in her voice.

"No and no."

Wayne leaned in, lips brushing against her cheekbone to the shell of her ear. Jo's heart skipped a beat, her eyes pinned to the painting on the far wall of their hotel room, a gaudy affair depicting a woman sitting in a room that looked strikingly similar to their own. It was very meta, almost a little too much so, and definitely not distracting enough.

"Alright then," Wayne practically purred into her ear, teeth just scraping against her earlobe. "What about—" Another barely there nip, another hot breath against her cheek that had Jo's eyes fluttering closed. "Tomato?"

Jo nearly dropped her glass; even her lust-fueled brain stuttered to a sudden halt. Sensing the shift, Wayne looked at her, Jo looked back, and then she lost it. Her laughter was a booming sound that, considering their watches were running for their champagne toast, was bound to echo straight down the hallway and into every room in between.

"*Tomato?*" Jo wheezed, shakily putting her glass down on the night-stand so she wouldn't spill its entire contents onto the bed. "What—what is that?"

"A vegetable?" Wayne frowned, slightly and obviously disappointed by his first outright advances being thwarted. "And a perfectly respectable way to address an attractive woman?"

"Tomatoes are fruits." Jo sniffed, still chuckling. "And either way, that one's a hard pass."

This time, Wayne rolled his eyes at her, watching her get out of the bed and walk back over to return their glasses. Victory drink completed and head pleasantly buzzing off the high of success as much as the alcohol, Jo clocked out of time. She could practically feel the stare like a brand against the back of her neck.

"Guess 'doll' it is," he said, voice husky and low, still gravelly. It took everything Jo had not to turn immediately around. Still, a shiver ran down her spine at the sound.

"Guess so." She felt like she could take anything she wanted. Jo rested her hands on the dresser in front of her, champagne foam still dripping down its front. *Why not him?* Why not just take him and be done with these games they were playing? It'd feel good, wouldn't it?

Her stomach tightened, yet Jo couldn't find the reason why.

"Guess so," Wayne repeated, following her out of bed like a dog on a leash. Jo could feel the anticipation running up her spine like a jolt of electricity. His hands fell on her hips, feather light. "How about, we have a little celebration, you and I?"

Jo hummed, her eyes dipping closed. It was good to be touched, to feel his breath on her. It was good to be needed by someone in a world that no longer knew she even existed.

"What do you have in mind?" she whispered.

With a gentle push, Wayne turned her in place. Jo's lower back pressed against the dresser as he pressed into her, their gazes locked. Her hands wrapped themselves around the collar of his nicely pressed dress shirt. She wasn't some blushing maid. She was a woman and could keep this light, casual, *easy.*

His embrace tightened and Wayne closed the gap between them.

The kiss had a languid kind of intent, as if he was drinking her in. *Perhaps, he was merely drinking in the feeling of kissing anyone.* Jo closed her eyes, wrapped up in the same sensation. His tongue traced her bottom lip and Jo responded in kind.

*This was scratching an itch, right?* The high of triumph had mixed with the facts that they were two very pent up, and apparently flirtatious, people. It didn't have to be anything more.

Yet, his slow kisses felt like that of a lover.

Jo tightened her grip and deepened the kiss. It was as if she was searching for something in his mouth—in all his contact—that she couldn't find. She wanted to drown in this feeling of being wanted and put all other stress behind her. She wanted to relish the way he noticeably shivered when he flicked her tongue. She wanted . . . She wanted . . .

He groaned into her mouth, punctuating it with a needy (maybe even involuntary) thrust of his hips. The heat at her core grew and Jo's eyes pressed closed. In the darkness behind her lids, there was only the feeling of his hands and mouth on her.

In that darkness, it could be anyone.

Her mind drifted, imaging that every touch sent sparks underneath her skin. Each breath came from a pair of lips that were so familiar she wondered how she could've ever forgotten them.

*Forgotten?*

Every sensation was replaced with something else, something far more profound. It wasn't merely hot and heavy foreplay, but the start of making love. It was a connection with someone down to her very soul. The man touching her, in her mind, was someone who had been born to be with her. Someone who was her compliment in every way and someone whom she'd wanted from the first moment she'd seen him in any existence— even if she'd deny the fact to herself and any who asked.

Wayne's lips were on her neck, teeth dragging over the sensitive skin at her pulse. She more felt his words vibrating against her than actually heard them as they shattered the illusion and brought her back to reality. "Are you good with this, dollface?" He purred, nipping at the skin beneath her jaw.

Jo realized her hands had gone slack and body still. She'd been so lost in her head that the present had completely faded away. Her eyes struggled to focus back on Wayne. It was as if they refused to see him at all, instead trying to imprint someone else in his place.

"I . . . I can't." Jo would've taken a step away, but she was still pinned to the dresser, so she leaned back instead. Wayne took the hint, promptly stepping away.

"I'm sorry, I didn't mean—"

"No." Jo shook her head, stopping him. She wasted another moment zipping her hoodie back up. She'd missed the moment he'd undone it, but was pleased to find all other clothing in its original position. "I thought I did. It's been a while. And I mean, *a while* . . ." As sexually pent up as she could get, Jo didn't boast many partners. It was something she wanted and yet never could find true satisfaction in. Yuusuke had always blamed it on the men but, looking at Wayne and the perfect specimen of a man that he was, some small part of Jo couldn't help but wonder again if it was somehow *her*.

"I'm not looking for something serious here, doll. Just so we're clear. This team is everything to me. I would not want to mess things up for a bit of fun." He ran a hand through his hair in self-reflection. "That sounds terrible. I'm sorry. Nico is right, I'm not really a gentleman."

"I don't blame you, or anyone, for wanting a little bit of fun." Jo wrapped her arms around herself. "I mean, I actually wish I could keep things casual now and then. But, as much as I feel like I want a… release"—*could this conversation get any more awkward?*—"I have a hard time getting into it with anyone."

"Then, perhaps you just need the right someone." Wayne gave a small smile that seemed steeped in a longing Jo didn't dare ask about. She focused instead on how his words mirrored Yuusuke's. "That can make all the difference."

"I wouldn't know." It was the truth. Yet, the words felt like a lie.

"Maybe you will someday?"

"I don't think I have a lot of options given my current situation." Jo gave a small laugh. "Not a lot of opportunities to meet new people when you don't exist."

"Who knows, you might get lucky." It was something nice to say, but they both knew that the likelihood was slim to none.

"Who knows," Jo agreed with a weak shrug, looking away. A heavy silence had settled on them like a blanket as she made a point of studying the seemingly eternal lights of the Paris skyline.

"Well, now that I officially made things uncomfortable for you."

"You did not," Jo insisted. "I was a willing participant up until—" *Until the moment I thought of someone else*, Jo refused to say. She didn't want to admit it to him just as much as she didn't want to admit it to herself. *Why would Snow's face appear in her mind of all people?* "—until I wasn't."

"Still . . ." Wayne brought up his watch, clocking back into time. "Let's wash this away with champagne and I'll level the playing field by making myself a little… uncomfortable. Vulnerable to you, so to speak."

"What are you talking about?" Jo tapped her own band to accept the glass he was handing to her.

"My past, doll."

# GREAT DEPRESSION

"YOUR PAST?" Jo repeated, following him out to their rooftop terrace.

"I was born in 1910."

"1910 . . ." she repeated, trailing off in thought. He'd been in the Society for nearly a century and a half. Not as long as Nico, but more than long enough. "How do you do it?"

"How do I do it?" He seemed startled by the question.

"Live, without living? Watch the world get spliced apart and stitched back together wish after wish? Have all the time in the world but never enough?" It was ineloquent, perhaps poorly put. But judging from the shadow on his face, he heard the true depth of the questions.

"The cheap and easy answer is that you get used to it," he started, finally. "Because, eventually, as with all things, time and habit win out. And the more time that passes, the less invested you become. You'll watch your friends and family die off, reality changing from time and wishes. Soon enough, it doesn't even look like what you remember as yours."

She stared at the Eiffel Tower in all its orange-gold, illuminated glory. Jo would always worry for her mother and Yuusuke. But what about Lydia, the little girl who would've been Jo's sister? She couldn't find much more compassion for the child than any other. With enough time, enough generations, she could see his truth about losing all connection to the real world.

"You make do with the time you have, though. Maybe even realize good ways to spend it, if you're willing to get an earful every now and then from Snow. And, well, Eslar . . . he really is an intolerable suck-up, but the rest of the crew isn't so bad. There're worse people to spend eternity with."

"At least we're not alone," she agreed thoughtfully.

He seemed to be stalling, passing his glass from hand to hand. For once, Jo didn't press. Allowing him to come to terms with his words in his own time. Blinking himself out of a haze, Wayne turned his attention away from wherever his thoughts had wandered and back to her. She could almost see the veil lifting from his eyes.

"It wasn't always easy, of course. Right after my wish, it was difficult for me to let go, too."

"Is that why you helped me with Yuusuke?"

He chuckled. "Perhaps."

"What was your wish?"

Wayne stilled. Another distant look at something she couldn't see. Another long silence. Long enough that Jo began to feel awkward, unsure if the man would even answer at all. Perhaps he couldn't find the words. Perhaps he didn't want to.

"You know, that's not something you just ask people."

"I'm not some random person," she needlessly reminded him. "And you already said you were going to tell me."

"I know, I know . . . But don't go asking any of the others, all right? It's a very personal thing."

Jo nodded, remembering how she'd felt when she sat out with Takako, and waited.

"The Great Depression seemed like it was going to last forever. There was no end in sight . . ." His voice had dropped to a thick whisper. Not heavy and husky with lust as she'd heard earlier, but weighted with longing. "I was a stockbroker, you see. Best of the best. Called me Nickel Boy, because I took a nickel and turned it into an empire. Then, I lost it all . . .

"That economic downturn was a ravenous beast let loose on America. Everyone lost everything; no one could find two pennies to rub together. Then the dollar showed signs of further collapse. A war was brewing and all our allies pulled out of trade with us."

"But, it *did* end." She'd read it in the history books.

"I know. I made it end." Wayne's eyes were so filled with sorrow that it was a jarring contrast to his proud grin. "Snow told me later that, in the world I came from, it was going to last another twenty years; America was never going to recover."

"But . . ."

"The world you lived in was an offshoot of the world I wished for. Technically, Jo, we never lived in the same reality, you and I. We were separated from the moment I made my wish, and it only continued to split from there."

She shouldn't have been startled, but she was. She knew now that the world was merely the product of wishes that severed reality across time. She'd never lived in the same world as any member of the Society. With her wish, she'd lived in a different world than anyone else in existence.

"You wished to save your country, and I messed with all of reality just to save my friend's life," Jo whispered. "A friend . . . who no longer exists."

"He doesn't exist?" Wayne whistled. "Then who did we just stick our necks out for?"

Jo laughed softly, leaning back on the railing and letting her head drop between her shoulders. "I don't know," she confessed. "Me? I guess . . . my need for purpose? Because the Yuusuke we saved has never even met Josephina Espinosa." Wayne was silent, and Jo found herself talking, frantic not to be left alone with her thoughts. "This was all for someone who I should have no attachment to. I spent time helping a random person, a stranger, using my time for that, when there are so many more important things. I guess it's just how I am? Messed-up priorities? Because even my wish wasn't noble—I didn't even wish to change the world, or a country— and neither are my actions now."

Her companion's continued silence threatened to tear her apart. Just as Jo opened her mouth and took a breath, preparing to ramble again, Wayne cut her off. "It *was* noble, Jo, then and now. Because you did change the world. You changed his world. You *gave* him a world. It doesn't matter if he knows it or not, because the fact remains."

"I guess . . ." She swallowed the taste of salt and looked back out to the city, blinking into the night lights.

"I don't think you have messed-up priorities at all." His shoulder pressed gently against hers. "Sticking your neck out for your friend? Doing the right thing? It'll be Snow or Eslar—whoever gives us the business for this—that has messed up priorities."

"Thanks, Wayne." Jo laughed softly. "Here's to hoping he's not reckless enough to throw it away again."

"Well, I wished for an economically strong America, only to watch it be squandered in conflict after conflict, wasted in poor decision making, and ultimately dissolve into nothing as the country was carved up by the Commonwealth Powers of World War III."

"You're right . . . People die every second. Every moment we breathe, someone suffers. Nations rise and fall. There's not enough time to save the world from all its problems."

"Which is why you can't worry about them all." It sounded cold, detached. *Almost like Snow.*

"How long does it take until I can feel that way?" Jo looked out the window. The city had never felt fuller than when she imagined all the needs within it that went unanswered.

"Hard to say . . ." Wayne shrugged. "I think for me it was the Second World War . . . watching the inexcusable carnage."


Jo PRESSED HER EYES SHUT. Being a mostly helpless spectator to the horrors of war was an impossible thing to fathom. She wanted to think about anything else. "I've never heard you speak like this before, by the way."

"Like what?" His entire voice and demeanor were different.

"Normal? You don't have the same accent. And I think it's been a whole hour now since you called me doll."

"Missing it, *doll*?"

She laughed. "No, not that. I just thought that you didn't know how to speak any other way."

"I can speak however I want. I'm not like the others—modernizing, keeping up with the times on the outside. I choose to speak as I do because it's all I have left of those days." It reminded Jo of what he said about eating. Sleeping was the same, no doubt. They all had little things that would keep them connected to the lost realities they'd come from.

"I wonder what I'll keep doing, to remember my time," Jo whispered, the sentiment stilling her. A long silence passed between them and when Jo returned her mind to the present, Wayne was staring off at some invisible point beyond the horizon.

For a long moment, they simply shared each other's companionable silence. Jo leaned against the railing of their terrace balcony. It was such a beautiful night, such a beautiful moment. If only she could make it stretch into infinity, escape the heavy knowledge of their existence coupled with the fact that the two of them would be heading back, likely soon. They'd finished their rogue mission, and it would certainly be time to face the consequences of it.

With a soft sigh, Jo turned away from the mesmerizing sight. Wayne's thoughtful expression caught her attention, a distant and almost wary look in his eyes. Slowly, Jo shifted a little bit closer to him, angling herself to catch his blank stare. His nearness still felt sturdy, welcome, and no longer buzzing with the same unbearable pent-up energy.

"We should get back."

"About that time," Wayne agreed, though he hardly seemed happy for the fact.

"Should I pack up my things?" Jo asked as they started in to the hotel room. She motioned to the monitor set-up still occupying the main room of the suite.

"No point. Can't bring anything back from the real world."

Jo looked at the desktop she'd made a reality, for however brief a time. It was glorious. And it'd be pieced apart, bagged for evidence (though the authorities would never find anything concrete), stolen by hotel staff, or sold away to pay for the room. Jo swallowed away the grief at the idea of letting it go. "I don't need it, anyway. The recreation room worked fine."

"That's the spirit." Wayne stalled. "Say, about this whole little—"

"If you're talking about helping Yuusuke, I'm not compelled to tell anyone anything." Jo dug her hands into the pockets of her hoodie. "If you're talking about the kisses . . . I'm still not going to divulge. It's not their business and it hasn't changed the dynamic at all."

"I'm glad to hear it." He sounded genuinely relieved. "It's the same for me too, doll."

"Just friends?" Jo asked, relieved that she could be certain she already knew the answer.

"Just friends." He paused, then, with an over-dramatic wink, added, "Unless you feel the need to scratch that itch for something more."

"All right, Mr. Davis." Jo laughed at his playful overtness. But the laughter quickly faded as she faced one of the terrace doors into the penthouse. "I'm ready to go back."

"Brace yourself." Wayne's hand hovered over the handle—until it morphed into the keypad of the Society's Door. "I've never been gone for this long without warning or wish duty. Don't know how people will react."

"I'm sure it'll be fine."

The moment Wayne opened the door, Jo knew she'd been very, very wrong in that assessment.

# SEVERITY OF EXCHANGE

J O DIDN'T HAVE the notion of being able to sneak back into the Society. With only eight people total, any absence would no doubt be noticed. But she thought she could ease herself back, see people individually, perhaps even skim off a day or two from her nearly four-day-long adventure by letting her teammates' minds play tricks by leaving them to wonder if someone else had merely seen her first.

No such luck.

If the door could be closed after being opened, Jo would've insisted to Wayne that he just do that instead. But he was already halfway through and Jo was being pulled alongside him.

They stepped into a full briefing room and all eyes were on them. Wayne cleared his throat, easing the Door closed behind him. Jo folded her arms over her chest defensively.

"Kind of you to finally join us." Snow's chilling voice cut through the tension first.

"Lens Louise," Wayne muttered under his breath with a glance to Snow, before forcing some cheer into his voice. "What did we miss?"

She didn't know what a "Lens Louise" was, but Wayne's side-eye and tense tone was descriptive enough that she could infer it wasn't the most polite thing to say about someone.

Snow tapped his fingers on the table, one of his eyes veiled by silver hair while the other stared them down with a steely gaze. Despite being seated, he managed to domineer over them like a judge on a parapet.

"Where were you?" Snow ignored Wayne's question.

"Look . . ." Jo took a deep breath and braced herself. "It's not his fault. I begged him to come with me and—"

"He still made the choice to do so of his own volition," Snow interrupted.

"Listen, he was helping me," she tried to explain.

"Helping you make changes in the world unrelated to the wish." Snow's hand curled into a fist, and for a brief second Jo thought he may slam it on the table. He didn't, but only just.

"We kept the changes as minimal as possible," Jo assured them all. No one would seem to meet her gaze. "I had to. I *had* to," she repeated for emphasis. The dodgy glances, the side eyes, the unexpected sadness, the entirely expected disappointment . . . it wore her down quickly. "My wish was to save my friend. If I didn't act, he was going to die." So much for not really telling people what they were up to.

"Then you should have let it come to pass."

Her eyes snapped back to Snow. "How can you say that?" she breathed, not knowing or caring if the statement was audible to anyone but herself. "You saw us that day in Texas. You saw him dead. If I hadn't done this he would've ended back there. What kind of a person would I be if I left my friend to that? What did I even wish for to begin with?"

"You wished for a revised world. If new foolish decisions of your friend still get him killed, then perhaps he is meant to die."

"Take that back!" Jo didn't mean to shout, it just sort of happened. "You take that back!"

"Jo—" Wayne's hands closed around her shoulders, holding her in place.

"Everyone but us will die. You must let them go and focus on your duty now."

"My duty? How dare you. All I've wanted to do this entire time is have a duty, a purpose, and contribute," she spat.

"Which you would've been able to do, had you been here."

Jo stilled as Snow spoke, her chest heaving and shoulders pulling against Wayne's hands. "What are you talking about?

"It was Pan's idea, actually," Eslar chimed in, likely the only person who could speak without being silenced by Snow. "I was experiencing difficulty lessening the Severity of Exchange on my own. I can cure the illness. But these doctors, they look to science, not magic. Something that cannot be explained is daunting, terrifying even. If the patient was cured magically, it would be written off as a miracle or anomaly, and the gap would not close enough for Snow to build a new reality and grant the wish."

"I caught wind." It was Pan's turn to speak. "I remembered all your tapping away, such fantastic magic you had. I thought it could be of help, modify all that science data in some way, perhaps? A foundation for Eslar's cure?" Pan's words and tone were in dissonance. She spoke as if she didn't know anything, but her overall aura said otherwise. "But I didn't know where to find you, so I began asking around."

Pan had outed her after all. It was like she was actively trying to spike her emotions. Jo's hands balled into a fist. She wouldn't have actually punched the woman-child (as tempting as it may be), but she must've had a convincing enough expression for Wayne to think so, because he grabbed her wrist and whispered, "Don't."

"That was when we learned of what you did." All eyes were back on Snow, including Jo's.

"Yes, okay, I made a small modification. I made it so that my friend wouldn't fail and die. I'm not sorry."

"Because you do not understand."

There was a sharp intake of air from Wayne, who'd clearly put together something she couldn't yet see. "The Severity of Exchange."

Snow gave the other man a solemn nod. "You have widened the Severity of Exchange with your actions."

"That's not possible." Jo shook her head. "I was careful, I didn't even do all that much—"

"You saw that the most extensive cyber-currency bank collapsed, sending markets and businesses into free-fall."

"No, Yuu shouldn't have even—"

"This is not your world!" Snow's voice rose a fraction. "People are different, time-lines are different, even what looks similar is not the same. Understand that, Josephina." He used her full name, like she was some toddler who'd spoken out of turn.

"He did it then?" Somewhere between her implanting the virus, and coming back, Yuusuke must've hit the bank with his first probing attack. Had he really moved so quickly? She'd done her job a little too well—or Snow was right, and everything was just . . . different.

"But the wish is only one man," she protested weakly. Even if she had a lot to feel guilty about, she still didn't see how it related to the wish.

"One man who had most of his savings in credits."

Her heartbeat was in her ears. "But . . . he has insurance. He's in Canada, after all. They have to take care of him there. It's part of the People's Promise of the late 1990s." Jo remembered reading about it once in a class that covered the health crisis happening in old America at the same time.

"He was paying extra for a research hospital. A hospital he can no longer afford out-of-pocket. He will be transferred within the week to standard care, where he will die, far from the nurse who made the wish."

"You don't know that," she objected on instinct. It was unfathomable how large the ripples had become: she'd only meant to help Yuusuke take down the Black Bank.

"But I do. I can see it in the Severity of Exchange."

Jo hung her head, searching for options. She took a breath and straightened her back. "Okay, I messed up, I'm sorry." No one seemed to have any interest in her apology. Not that she blamed them, of course. "But I'll fix it." She looked to Eslar, hoping he'd save her from the grave-shaped hole she'd dug without knowing. "I can fix it. We just have to make the wish happen before he's transferred, right?"

"That's only three days from now," Eslar said uncertainly.

"Plenty of time!" Jo may have sold her reassurance a little too hard. Her laugh was strained and thin. "Really, plenty. If I can take down the Black Bank in less than a week with my magic, I can falsify some hospital and research records. It'll be simple, I'll just—"

"How much time do you have left?" Snow interrupted her again.

Jo looked down at her watch, and her heart sank. "About an hour . . ."

"Not enough."

"I promise you, it is." She fished around in her pocket for the USB and pulled it out, showing it to everyone. "I can code here, and use this to bring my scripts to the real world. I just have to hit 'run' and make sure nothing goes wrong. It worked for the Black Bank and it'd work for this. You told me to learn my magic, so I did, and this is how I can use it best."

"And if it doesn't work, we're left stranded." Snow shook his head. "We must look for another way."

"It *will* work," she insisted.

"You have done enough."

"Let me help you," Jo pleaded, looking between Snow and Eslar. "I can do this, I promise, believe me."

"We shall continue thinking of a way without you," Snow spoke with a heavy note of finality. "As we were doing before you decided to arrive. Therefore, you are no longer needed for this discussion."

"Are you kicking me out?" Jo balked.

"I was giving you the opportunity to leave yourself, before I had to say it outright."

Jo opened her mouth to protest, but Wayne cut her off. "Let's make tracks, doll."

Before she could say anything further, Wayne had already pushed her from the room. Jo seethed silently halfway down the hall to the Four-Way, but burst when she could take it no longer.

"Who does he think he is?"

Wayne made a hushing noise at her.

"Oh let them hear, I don't care." She threw a rude gesture back at the doors.

"We messed up." He buried his hands in his pockets, looking like a freshly scolded child.

"I know we did!" Jo sighed, lowering her voice. "I'm sorry. I'm not angry at you. I can't be. All you did was help me and got in trouble for it."

He didn't contest the fact.

"I get it, we made an error . . . But I can still help. You've seen me work, Wayne. You know an hour and three days is plenty of time."

"I'm not—"

"Do you or don't you?" She stopped him by grabbing his wrist and they both hovered in the Four-Way.

"I do."

A smile cracked through her anger. At the very least, he seemed to believe in her. The closeness they had found seemed to linger even after certain needs had cooled. "Thank you."

"You're wel—"

"Now, tell Eslar." She didn't want him accepting her thanks; she wanted action.

"What?" He seemed startled by her sudden demand.

"Tell Eslar about my magic, what I can do. Tell him what you saw and tell him I can do this. Snow is . . . how did you put it? A bastard?"

"I don't think I ever said that."

"You're right, I just did." Jo grinned conspiratorially. Even if Snow was right in reprimanding her, that didn't make it feel good, and anger made Jo petty—even if her anger was mostly inward facing. "Talk to Eslar, tell him, make him let me help."

Wayne's brow furrowed and he squinted slightly. Jo braced herself for an outright refusal. He shook his head and her heart sank with his eyes as they turned to the floor. But like a phoenix, they rose again. "Okay, doll-face, cheer up. I'll do what I can."

"Thank you!" Jo threw her arms around his neck, relying on his familiar sturdiness to support her. "I can never pay you back for all of this, but thank you."

He gave her a friendly squeeze and then pulled away, starting toward the rooms. "No promises though."

"I know," Jo assured him. But she wasn't worried. Once Eslar knew of her magic, there wasn't any way he'd still choose to go it alone. "Thanks again."

"You got it." Wayne gave her a tired looking grin, and a little wink. "We're teammates after all. I'd do anything for this team." He disappeared into his room, leaving Jo standing before her door.

She hoped he was being sincere . . . because for the second time since she'd arrived in the Society, her redemption rested squarely on Wayne's shoulders.

# ALMOST LIKE PERMISSION

J o's heart skipped a half beat when she opened the door to her
room.

Unlike the disjointed recreation of her old bedroom, what lay
spread out before now was an almost flawless depiction of her and
Wayne's hotel room in Paris. The plush bed, the too-loud carpet pattern,
the painting hanging on the wall above an ornate side table—though it
wasn't the gaudy meta one. It was the rendering of Texas Nico had given
her. Even the balcony had followed, a portion of her room now overlooking a perpetual Paris nighttime, an illusion that both calmed and irritated her.

Despite the agitation at herself and the situation as a whole, Jo still felt
her furrowed brow softening at that view.

Taking a moment to walk the length of the room, feeling the carpet dip
softly beneath her shoes, Jo thought about Paris. Even if it had made a
mess (one Jo was still certain she could clean up, if they let her) she
couldn't find herself regretting it. She'd helped Yuusuke, again. Something about that fact, about making sure he at least had one more shot and
her wish hadn't gone to waste, was relieving. Even if he went off to get
himself killed again in the future—Jo swallowed anger at the mere thought
—that'd be his choice, and she could live with it. She could move
on, now.

Jo leaned against the wall by the window, wondering if she saw reality,
or just a glorified hologram on a long-timed feedback loop.

That wasn't all she'd found in Paris. She'd secured an unlikely, but
very welcome ally. Wayne had given her some scrap of confidence in her
magic and the freedom to believe in it. Even better was the boost of confi-

dence that came from someone wanting her, an innate human desire—satisfying even if they hadn't really acted on it.

Snow's face flashed before her eyes and she waved a hand through the air, as if shooing the image. It still lingered persistently. But unlike the soft gaze her mind had conjured in Paris, it was now his disappointed and somewhat angry look on their return seared into her retinas.

With a flop, Jo threw herself into the bed. The sheets crumpled and fluffed against the attack, cradling her in a nest of feather pillows and a cloud-like comforter. She buried her feet beneath the soft linens and propped her head beneath her hands.

Their infuriating leader floated up to the forefront of her thoughts again.

"Damn it, Snow." Jo shook her head. "Stop looking at me like that." Disappointment was so much worse than anger. She had to do it—surely, he saw that? The more she lingered on the memory of him from the briefing room, the more her mind began to twist her leader's emotions. What if it wasn't just about Yuusuke, but Wayne as well? "That makes no sense," Jo mumbled into her pillow. There was no way Snow could know and even if he did, he far from had any right to comment or pass judgment on a kiss and she'd be the first to remind him of the fact if he tried to.

A firm knock on her door jarred her thoughts. Jo bolted upright, practically sprinting to answer it. Wayne had really come through for her, yet again, and now Eslar was—

Whatever Eslar was doing, it was not standing at her door.

"Hey there," Jo said to the awkwardly hovering Takako, trying to hide her disappointment.

"I apologize for bothering you so late."

"Is it?" Jo looked out the window of her room; the Paris skyline was still lit up. Jo shrugged. "Not like time really matters to me—us, anyway."

"It doesn't," Takako confirmed in her uniquely mechanical way. Jo found her tone incredibly reassuring in its own right. "But it's nearly past midnight."

"Oh." Jo wasn't sure what else to say so she simply waited. Takako fidgeted awkwardly, hands clasped behind her back. "Is there . . . something else?" Jo asked hopefully, still thinking of Eslar.

Takako brought her hands from around her back, rejoining them to cradle something that was very, very familiar. Every detail was exactly as Jo remembered. Unlike Nico's painting, this had a preciseness to it that was undeniable. It wasn't blurred colors that evoked vague, sensory notions of home.

It was a literal piece of home, in the shape of a ceramic mug.

"Is it the right one?" she asked, and Jo wondered if she heard a bit of nerves in Takako's voice.

"Yes," she whispered, finally accepting the token.

The visage of the most iconic mouse in the world was inked underneath a scratched veneer of clear glaze. It was white on the outside, red on the inside. The handle looked like half an ear.

Jo cradled the mug, identical to the one her mother had gotten her at Disney all those years ago, and had one question. "How?"

"You spoke about the mug, in the kitchen, when Nico broke his . . . not that long ago." Takako buried her hands in her pockets, as if assuring that Jo couldn't hand it back to her.

"I know I did, but—"

"Samson's a really good crafter. He can make almost anything. I asked him after you spoke about it; it seemed like something that could cheer you up." It was an explanation, but only part.

"Okay, but how did you *know*?"

Takako shrugged.

"Did you go to my house?" There was only one way he could've found the exact details of the mug.

"I have no idea what you're talking about. Members of the Society don't leave unless they're on a wish." Takako turned, starting for the door across the hall that had her name written in both English and Hiragana.

"Wait—"

The other woman paused, arching her eyebrows. She'd said that it was "to cheer her up," but Jo had other suspicions. It felt almost like permission. Permission to bend the rules sometimes, if it meant helping themselves.

"Are you mad at me?" Jo dared a whisper.

"For what?"

"For what I did and how it affected the wish?"

Takako chewed over her answer for an agonizing amount of time. "You have made things very difficult."

Jo's heart sank. The woman certainly didn't mince words

"But I think we can overcome this." Takako smiled tiredly. "I wouldn't worry too much."

The door closed before Jo had a chance to ask anything else.

Jo leaned on her own door frame, still clutching the mug. She'd make this right. She had to.

# BURNT INSIDE

J O PAUSED AT the entrance to the common area the next morning, hovering awkwardly. Most of the group was already there. Wayne sat at the bar, a newspaper—proof of magic, because such things hadn't existed for *decades*—folded over his knee. Takako stood not far from him, scooping rice from a cooker into a variety of small bowls.

"That looks good." Jo eased herself by Takako and braved a smile. To her relief, it was returned, and whatever lines Jo had crossed by helping Yuusuke were already on the way to being set right once more.

"You'll get to enjoy it soon." Nico's voice piped up suddenly from the far end of the kitchen, the human embodiment of the bright and cloudless sky that stretched over them this morning. "It's Takako's turn to make breakfast for the group."

It would seem that all traces of yesterday's disappointment that Jo had watched mar his kind face were gone—for now, anyway. Jo swallowed hard, remembering his painting, his confidence in her, telling about his wish and his Julia. Over time, she'd prove to him (and everyone) that their kindness wasn't misplaced. But for now, she was content watching him practically skip toward the espresso machine.

"Does everyone take turns cooking?" she asked.

"Samson does most of the cooking actually. We just offer him some respite occasionally," Nico clarified.

"Okay, cool," Jo nodded. "Because I can literally burn boiled water, so you might not want me near a stove."

"Luckily, boiling water is the only thing that matters, because with it you can make coffee." Nico measured out beans into the grinder with the precision of a chemist.

"Can I get in on that?" Jo perked up at the already rich smell of a dark roast that filled the air. That, mixed with the clean scent of rice and whatever meat Takako had working in the oven, left Jo's mouth watering. She wasn't actually hungry (which was supposedly normal now), but boy was she ready to eat away her stress.

"Only if I can get in on that, too." Wayne poked his head up. On catching her eye, he gave a small wink and said, "I meant the coffee, dollface."

"Obviously, dirty old man." Jo rolled her eyes, *looks like the flirting isn't going anywhere in more ways than one.* She was torn between wanting to play along, wanting to keep the quiet peace that the morning already held, and wanting to shake him until he rattled off all the details of speaking with Eslar.

Wayne gasped, over-dramatic and clearly not as offended as he pretended to be despite how he raised his free hand to his forehead. "I'm a right lounge lizard, I'll have you know!"

"A hundred and fifty-year-old lounge lizard . . . Whatever that means." Jo shook her head and crossed over to Nico, coffee mug already outstretched. "Please?" Coffee would soothe her restless nerves.

As Nico poured, Jo caught a glimpse of a different expression. Her grip went slack and she had to focus on holding her mug. The casual atmosphere was a front for them all, a sort of self-preservation that they were indulging in while worry gnawed at their insides.

"Careful it's—" Nico tried to warn.

Jo took a large swig of coffee, well knowing it was still scalding hot. It burned all the way down, searing her foggy mind to clarity. "I needed that."

"It's nice to finally have someone here who shares my love for a good cup." That smile was back, the one she'd been foolish enough to believe was genuine. "Such a fantastic invention. I couldn't have been happier the first time I saw a coffee shop open in Florence."

"When was that? The coffee shop?" Jo played along while the back of her mind was already at work, spinning through her options.

Nico thought a moment. "The first was in Venice . . . then after that . . . it must've been mid- to late 1600s."

"Such a rich history for such a rich drink." She forced a smile as well. Fake smiles all around.

Samson walked in bleary-eyed, just in time for Takako's breakfast of choice to be served. It was white rice, broiled fish, and miso soup.

"I hope it's to your taste," Takako said to her. "It's what I used to make." There was an unspoken "before I was at the Society" that lingered after the sentiment. "It's just something simple and quick." There were no anecdotes about her home or how she learned to make it, and Jo didn't pry.

"It's delicious. Reminds me of what my friend would make for me . . . when he was feeling particularly kind."

Takako gave her another small smile and Jo wondered if the woman knew she was speaking of Yuusuke. Either way, the expression was the truest thing Jo had seen all morning. It seemed that Takako was the only one of them that seemed to wear sincere emotions no matter what, good or bad.

Jo turned to Samson. "So, you cook?"

He startled so violently that his spoon nearly fell from his hands. The orange-haired man passed it back and forth awkwardly. "I do."

"Can you teach me, sometime?"

"Very well," he said, voice so soft she could barely hear it.

Silence stepped in to fill the void of their conversation. It soured the sweetness of peace that the offering of food had been seasoned with, and wore at Jo's patience for pleasantries. She knew the easy fronts were "for the sake of the team," but they wore on her. It may have been easier if they'd screamed at her for a bit.

"Where's Snow?" she asked delicately. She'd ease herself into this topic and find what she was looking for.

"Snow?" Nico cocked a head in thought. "Snow doesn't really . . ."

"Snow would have you believe he has more important things to attend to." Wayne rolled his eyes. "Who knows, though. When he requires our assistance, he will seek us out, but for the most part, he leaves us be."

It didn't seem too unusual for a leader (especially one like Snow) to be "too good" for eating with the peons. But after a few hundred years of solitude, she would've thought that attitude might have given way. Whatever Snow's reason, Jo ignored it for now. Asking about Snow was a diversion to get to her real target.

"What about Eslar?"

Everyone seemed to still at once.

"Working with Snow on the wish, I think," Samson squeaked out.

Jo looked to Wayne. He diverted his eyes. No luck there, one way or another.

"It was delicious, Takako, thank you." Jo stood, both hands on the table. "Nico, may I help myself to another cup?"

"Oh, of course . . ."

"Thanks." She'd need the caffeine-induced focus.

"Where are you off to, doll?"

"Recreation room." If she lied it'd look suspicious. "Want to see how

Yuusuke did." That was believable, and the mere mention of how she'd botched their Severity of Exchange successfully silenced them.

Jo took another sip of coffee—careful to only burn her insides and not her whole face as she walked.

She wasn't about to be beaten down and give up. She was going to make this right, for herself *and* for her team. If they could all put on brave fronts for her, she could pay back the favor with action. It didn't matter if she had Eslar's help, or Snow's blessing. She was the Shewolf, and she was used to working alone.

# A DANGEROUS DEAL

OR A SECOND time, the recreation room didn't disappoint. Her whole set-up was there, including new modifications Jo recognized from her time in Paris. She silently thanked the faceless god of the mansion for its intuition in knowing both what she needed and wanted.

Jo assumed her seat and opened a new notepad on the desktop. She pulled her sleeves over her hands and poised them at the ready.

*Where to start?*

Jo racked her memory for the initial information Snow had given them on the wish. As things came to her, she typed them down. From broad strokes to seemingly insignificant details, it was impossible to know what might prove useful. There was Canada, the nurse who made the wish, the illness . . .

Gathering up as much medical info on the disease was probably a good place to start.

She didn't waste any time. Jo went straight for the main databases of the centers for disease control in the European Union, Canada, Russia, and Japan, dredging up all the information she could. Their firewalls and safety protocols were mere child's play. Jo unleashed the full force of every hacking tool she knew, including what she didn't even fully understand—her magic. She suspended any last, lingering, ingrained skepticism and forced herself to believe with all she was that she *did* have magic. And if she did, then damn it, she would use it.

At first, she pulled up a wide array of information, but drilling down became more difficult by the moment. She needed more than the encyclopedia basics of the disease. Jo probed deeper. But no matter how many disease research databanks she hacked, she only came away with limited information—nothing she could guarantee would be beneficial.

What made it even more frustrating was the realization that she had no idea where the patient even was. There were 200 research-focused hospitals, fifty that specialized in virology, and ten in this particular disease. But narrowing it down among those ten was nearly impossible. Without knowing the status of the patient, how could she hope to close the gap properly?

Jo also didn't know how Eslar's power worked exactly. She assumed he was some kind of healer, but what could and couldn't he do? It was all guesswork.

What sort of help could she provide if she was missing the most important pieces of the puzzle?

With an aggravated groan, Jo leaned back into her chair and pushed away from the desk, rolling a couple of feet back. Running a hand over her face, she began wracking her brain for something, anything, an idea buried in the ether of her skill or magic that might allow her to help. Something that might close the gap she'd unintentionally widened.

All she managed to dredge up was a big ol' pile of nothing.

Jo switched to other, more distracting tasks. She'd learned early on in her career that sometimes even an appropriately timed cat video could keep her mind fresh. Focusing on one thing for too long, especially if that thing continued to birth more frustration than success, was only setting herself up for failure.

Lucky for her, she had something far more interesting than cat videos to give her mind a break with this time. Not a long break, of course. Just enough to put her head back in the game fresh after the refreshing challenge of a new puzzle.

With the ease of familiarity, Jo pulled up a handful of websites, both on and off the dark web, as well as some historical databases and birth records. She started with the member of their group who she'd managed not only to get a name and date from, but also an occupation.

Wayne Davis, Great Depression, born 1910, stock broker.

She wasn't necessarily surprised when no information on such a man came up, but that didn't mean she wasn't just a little bit disappointed.

She tried the same tactics with Nico and Takako, the only others about whom she had enough general information to plug into search engines and sift through the unspoken data. Outside of some vague occurrences in their time, she once again managed to dig up nothing of import. There were thousands of Takakos in Japan in the late 1990s, but Jo already knew that none of them were the Takako she was familiar with.

Just like her, it was as though they never existed.

A thought tugged unbidden at the back of Jo's mind, a bit of information that she felt instantly guilty for the moment she'd entered the name into her slew of scripts currently spidering the databases.

Julia de'Este.

Strangely, despite the sense Jo had gotten that Nico's fiancé had continued to exist post-wish, no sign of her popped up in any records from the 1400s. In fact, the only Julia at all of note that she could find was a rumored mistress to the assassinated Pope Alexander VI in 1504. But then again, perhaps she wasn't a woman "of note" at all, simply the woman that Nico had loved enough to sacrifice his own existence for. Someone too common to have made the history books and preserved papers of the late fifteenth century, but someone Nico still adored even hundreds of years later.

Really, that kind of love should be the sort of thing put in history books. *Almost like soulmates*.

Whatever the reason, Jo decided to bring her snooping to an end, letting Nico's past remain in his now non-existent history. Even if it didn't much answer her question.

Some love stories were too good to be tainted with logic.

Jo sighed and closed all browsers. It wasn't her place and she'd had enough of a reprieve. "Back to this stupid fuc—"

"Well someone seems a bit exasperated."

Jo didn't even turn. She recognized the interrupting voice and its eerie presence almost immediately. "Pan, what do you want?"

"Don't be rude." Pan leaned against the desk, folding her arms. Unlike the first time in Jo's recreation room, her focus was entirely and over-whelmingly on Jo. The look had an intimidating, cat-like air about it. "I'm here to help."

"Are you?" Jo pushed away to look at the woman-child. There was something there every time she interacted with Pan. A sort of gut feeling that could be summed up as: just don't.

"Why are you so skeptical of me?" she asked. "I've been trying to help you from the start. I warned you of the dangers of meddling in the real world *and* I was going to involve you in the wish."

She wasn't wrong. So why did Jo feel so uneasy still? Jo took a deep breath and tried to let it inflate her lungs enough to be the bigger person. "Sorry. I'm just trying—"

"Trying to help? Time is ticking." She tapped at her wrist and it was then that Jo noticed there was no watch there. A pocket watch, perhaps, like Nico's? "Say, how about we make a deal?"

"Of what kind?" Jo asked cautiously.

"I'll give you information if you show me your magic."

"Didn't you say you'd already seen it when I was working in here before?"

"Glimpses." Pan continued before Jo could press how "glimpses" had made Pan confident enough to go to the group in her absence. "I want to see it in full. I want to see who you really are."

"What kind of information?"

"Anything you want."

Jo glanced back at the monitors. It wasn't as if she was getting very far on her own. She still only understood the ten-thousand-foot overview of what the Society did. Then, there was the current wish itself. If no one else was going to help her, what choice did she have?

"What do you say?" Pan prodded, holding a hand out in Jo's direction when she didn't answer quickly enough.

Something still felt off, like signing off on a business transaction without first getting all of the details. But Jo was a slave to curiosity, and, before she could talk herself out of it, she took Pan's hand and shook it firmly once.

"Sure. But I want the information first."

# COLD HANDS

Jo pulled her hand back, running it along her jeans. She thought her hands felt cold.

Pan's were icy, like they were coated in a thin layer of frost that melted at Jo's living touch. She wondered if it was some kind of residual magic, her mind instantly going back to Wayne. She really shouldn't go making deals with magical people without first knowing the full depth of what type of magic they had.

The young woman situated herself on the opposite desk, folding her ankles and leaning back nonchalantly. "What do you want to know?"

Jo already knew that "everything" would be too broad, and that Pan was likely on a timer for how much information she'd give. Jo chewed over how to phrase the question for a moment, trying to decide what was broad enough that she'd get the most information possible. "How did I affect the Severity of Exchange so much with my actions involving the Black Bank?"

"I'd think it's obvious."

"Maybe I'm stupid."

"I doubt that." Pan smiled thinly.

"Will you answer or not? Don't we have a deal?"

The woman-child hummed and leaned back. "Well, the first thing you must understand is how the Severity of Exchange works." Pan held up her thumb and pointer finger, peeking through them like a tiny window. "If it's a *little* wish, like a wish made with a drawn circle, then Snow can grant it immediately."

"A drawn circle?" The memory of something popped its nose up in the back of Jo's mind. She couldn't remember if it was something *Abuelita* had mentioned, or something she'd read online. "You mean, the circle that's used to cast the wish?"

"You got it!" Pan clapped her hands, but the excitement felt distinctly condescending. "There are four levels. Circles that are drawn are for very simple wishes. Then there are circles made of non-living things, but still items of importance. Above that are those made with foliage and other natural once-living things."

"That can't be right." Pan seemed startled at Jo's sudden interjection. She quickly clarified, "I drew my circle."

"Yes, but with what?" The way Pan asked the question, it was almost as if she already knew the answer.

Jo bristled. The memory of Yuusuke was assaulting, oddly superimposed over her most recent sight of him. The pain of losing him was quickly replaced with frustration at his renewed determination to hack the Black Bank. "Blood."

"And that's the fourth level. A circle of blood, or death."

"So, Snow can make wishes happen without extra help if they're the first level?"

Pan nodded.

"What's his power, really, then?" It sounded impressive, to be able to do such things in only a blink. Wayne had also mentioned something about creation.

"Creation . . . To grant wishes." Pan's hand fell back to the desk and her mouth curled in a thin smile. Jo had to stop herself from sighing; that much about his power was obvious. Luckily, Pan didn't take long to continue. "He's got a very rare, very old, and very powerful magic. One of the originals, actually." She paused, her eyes drifting back to Jo. They felt like cross-hairs. "Though, you already know that. You're here, after all . . ." Her expression shifted again, resuming her perpetually amused smirk. "But that magic isn't free. Nothing is, not even wishes."

"Everything comes at a price," Jo rephrased. It was an idea she was well acquainted with. "He feeds on worlds of possibilities."

"Oh-ho, you've already learned that?" Pan smiled, almost in approval. "Yes, to feed that insatiable magic of his and grant wishes, he destroys worlds and rebuilds them."

"How does he consume them?"

Pan merely shrugged.

"That's not an answer."

"It's magic." She smirked at Jo.

"Does he kill people?" *Like he did with me?*

"One, or thousands. It all depends on how you look at it."

Her throat ran dry. Jo swallowed, but it felt scratchy, the attempt getting lodging back behind her tongue. The icy air of the room had been filtered through the computer fans too many times. There wasn't any speck of humidity left in what seemed to be increasingly frigid air.

"If a wish doesn't fall into a close enough margin, then he has to draw more power. The world has to make a bigger jump. Such a shift can be . . . violent."

"Violent, how?"

"Violent in a not good way, just ask Eslar and Samson." It wasn't an answer but Jo knew she wouldn't get anything more.

"So, me, and everyone else in the Society . . . we prevent these violent shifts?"

"Exactly." Pan clapped her hands. "You're there to make sure that Snow isn't using his magic to force too big of a jump, therefore preventing any unexpected outcomes."

Jo made note of the words, "unexpected outcomes." Even if Pan was partly explaining things she already knew, there was new information here, things worth remembering. "What happens if we don't close the gap enough in the Severity of Exchange?"

"That hasn't happened yet. So, I guess it's not really something to worry about . . . unless you just caused it with your little antics in the mortal world."

There it was, that nasty, nagging feeling nudging at the back of her mind. Jo examined the woman head to toe. "That's not an answer." Why had her voice dropped to a whisper? Guilt. It was the guilt that threatened to drown her.

Pan's smile widened, like a cat that had finally found its mouse. "Why? Are you scared?"

"What will happen?" Jo asked again.

"The magic is made up elsewhere." Pan pushed herself off the desk, standing once more. "Don't worry so much! The world is safe. There are seven of us under our dear Snow now. You're part of a long line of defense against magic going awry."

"How do you know all this?" Maybe if she asked enough questions, one would elicit a satisfactory enough answer, one that might assuage the concern that was still gnawing on the vertebrae in her neck.

"Snow and I are very close. I'm practically his right-hand man. Or, woman, rather," she corrected with a giggle.

"Eslar isn't?" Everyone, the man included, had made it seem like Eslar was the most senior member of the group. The elf had a sort of mothering air about him that seemed to affirm the idea of his role among them.

"Eslar?" Pan repeated, as if surprised. Jo wondered just how much time the woman really spent with the rest of them. "Why would he be? I'm the one who's been with Snow the longest. We were here from the beginning."

Well, that threw out a significant chunk of what Jo thought she knew about the group. "What is the Society, really?"

"I think you've stopped asking the right questions," Pan said with a tilt of her head.

"Where do the wishes come from?"

"People." Pan answered with a sly smile. That much was obvious and wasn't at all what Jo had been asking.

"Back to Severity of Exchange then . . ." Jo wasn't about to let her questions be forgotten. But if she wasn't getting anywhere with Pan, she'd shelve them for now and try a different, more pressing, avenue. "How do I help lessen the Severity of Exchange for this wish?"

"For that—" Pan paused, the door taking her attention. "I think he'll be able to help you."

"Who?"

There was a knock. The door cracked open and Eslar poked his narrow nose through. "Am I interrupting?" His eyes darted from Pan to Jo.

"Nope." Pan opened the door the rest of the way. "I was just leaving."

Jo was distracted by a sudden smell: cinnamon-sugar, baked dough. It was familiar, so familiar that it made her chest ache, like being assaulted by the aromatic representation of home.

"Some other time, you'll show me your magic," Pan said, summoning back Jo's focus. "Don't forget our deal."

The girl was gone before Jo could say anything further, leaving her alone with the elf and his familiar plate of pastries.

# A BRIBE NAMED "SOPAPILLA"

"WHAT DEAL?" ESLAR asked as he stepped into the room, closing the door behind him while balancing a plate of *sopapillas*. Jo instantly recognized them and the accompanying honey jar that rested at the center of the dish.

Her stomach fought with her brain on what to say and it all kind of mushed together. "She wanted to see my magic, was telling me about the Society in exchange . . . Where did you get those?" As soon as the question left her mouth, Jo's brain mustered the answer. There was only one when something appeared out of nowhere in the mansion. "Did Samson make these?"

"Just so." Eslar smiled, an expression that Jo hadn't ever quite seen cross his features. It was filled with fondness and . . . sorrow? Longing? "I had them made to Wayne's specifications." He paused. "Well, almost. I had to look up my own specifications and assure Samson that they were not actually constructed from soap."

Jo laughed, remembering Wayne's reaction when he had taken her to her home in Texas. He was either an admirable joker, or lovingly dumb; either way, the quality had stolen a soft, squishy corner of her heart. She'd been right, he'd made it into her inner circle just as Yuusuke had.

Eslar deposited the Hispanic pastry on the desk before her. Jo wasted no time, immediately ripping through the thin top layer of crisp, light brown dough. The minute she had access to the hollow center, she took to filling it with honey, chest clenching at the memories flooding her mind and heart. As she took a generous bite, some honey dribbled down her chin that she mopped up with a finger, popping it back in her mouth to savor.

"I'm fairly sure my actions have not earned my being gifted fresh *sopapilla*." Jo spoke over her food, still enough of a lady to cover her mouth with her free hand. The words were a bitter contrast to the bright sweetness of the dish.

"It is a bribe."

Something about the direct and deadpan delivery gave her a chuckle. "All right, I appreciate the candor. Hit me."

"I am interested in what you had to say in the briefing room."

Jo's eating stalled.

"You seemed to believe you could fix your error."

"I can," Jo affirmed, wiping her palms on her jeans. "If I have the right information."

"What information is that?"

"Everything you can tell me." Jo continued, "I need details. I need to know the hospital, the patient, everything. What can you give me?"

"I shall impart to you all I know . . ." Eslar leaned forward, elbows on his knees, and began listing off details that she had been hungry for not an hour ago.

Jo listened intently, mentally beginning to catalog everything. When it became too much even for the sponge that was her brain, she opened up a notepad on her computer and typed as he spoke, fingers flying over the keyboard. Magic sizzled in harmony with the hum of computer fans and buzz of monitors. The more information she had, the more connections she saw, the more possibilities she was aware of.

The sensation was instantaneous when the last piece slotted into place, like finally seeing a map for the first time.

"I know what to do," Jo announced. "I just need time to do it."

"How much?" Eslar asked.

"Here? A few more hours. There? Maybe thirty minutes, tops."

"That's all?"

Jo nodded. "Look, I know I messed up with Paris." The shadow of a grimace that tugged on Eslar's mouth affirmed he thought it was far more severe than "messed up." "But it offered a bit of an opportunity for a test-run of my magic. I know what I can do here will take in the real world. It can give me a head start . . . Once I get there, I'll only need a short period of time. That's why I think an hour will be more than enough."

"Then I will take you there."

"Are you sure it won't upset King Snow?" Jo's hands paused long enough for her to ask the question, looking over her shoulder at the man.

"I'll smooth it over," he assured her. "This is on me."

"You'd better be right. Or I'll show you why hell hath no fury."

"Hell . . . hath no fury?" he repeated slowly.

"Don't you know that expression?" It was old, old enough that a few other members should have known it in some form.

"No?"

"Well, I guess the only woman you interact with on a regular basis—" Jo wasn't counting the weird presence that was Pan out of misplaced spite, "is pretty stoic and even. Hell hath no fury like a woman scorned."

"Woman can indeed be terrifying." Eslar folded his hands and leaned back in his chair. "Terrifying enough to stand up to Snow."

That sounded almost like praise. And her cheeks almost caught fire at it.

"It's not about standing up to him." Jo cracked her knuckles. "This is redemption and fixing my error. This is for my team."

"Your team?" His voice noticeably softened.

"Who else?" Jo dared a smile, one Eslar met with a small nod. "All right, give me three hours Eslar, and then we can make this happen in the real world. I shouldn't need more than that to prep."

"I'll entrust you with it." He stood.

"Wait, before you go . . ." Jo held up the plate. "Would you like a pastry?"

"I would, thank you."

They chewed in silence, a sort of breaking-bread moment of peace between them. It was a silent treaty, leaving Jo to hope he felt it too.

# HOSPITAL ROOM

THE DOOR CLOSED behind Jo and Eslar with the echo of a hiss, drowned out by the beeping, talking, and general buzz of the hospital.

"Huh." Jo made the soft noise of appreciation while glancing behind them at what was now, ironically, another supply closet.

"What?" She hadn't expected him to hear.

"Oh, sorry, just . . ." Jo looked around herself, at the men and women bounding by without so much as an acknowledgment in their direction. "It's almost getting normal. Appearing out of nowhere, being nowhere . . . It's less disorienting to use the Door now."

"I'm glad to hear it." Nothing in his voice indicated anything glad.

"How long did it take you?" *They didn't have time for small talk*, a voice in her mind scolded.

"Not long. I came from the Age of Magic." He reached up a hand and touched the tip of his long ear, as if for emphasis. "And it was far easier for me, after my entire race was eliminated," Eslar murmured, drawing every ounce of Jo's attention. She wanted to ask, to pry, but Wayne's words were in her head again. *Don't ask the others about their wishes.* It seemed the entirety of the Society was predicated on darkness and loss, and now really wasn't the time anyway. "We should get moving."

"We should," Jo agreed, and let the idea of Eslar's history go, for now. Perhaps forever. There was something too grim there. Something that may never be worth dredging up for all the curiosity in the world, regardless if that curiosity surrounded being friends with an actual elf.

"What do you need?"

"Access to a computer—" Jo stopped herself, realizing an explanation was likely to take longer. "I can find it myself. What do you need?"

"I know where the patient is already." He'd already cased the place. It made sense, given the information he'd fed her before.

"Show me?"

Eslar nodded and started down the hall.

With their watches inactive, they were unknown guests in the research hospital's infectious disease ward. Jo kept an eye on the different halls, numbers, and names, all of which were aesthetically identical otherwise. Several halls down from where they entered, one right, one left, and they stood before a door that had a touch screen outside displaying the name KELLER.

"This is him?" Jo asked, even though she already knew the answer. She knew far more about this man than anyone should.

Eslar merely nodded, leading them into the room and to the other side of the curtain partition that blocked off the patient from the medical equipment and world beyond.

The man in the bed, Mr. Keller, was a frail and skeletal form. He'd lost all his hair, from drugs or therapy, and had bruises along his arm leading to the protruding IV taped beneath the curve of his elbow. A monitor beeped next to him, breathing apparatuses sighed, and there were no other forms of life surrounding the terminal man.

Suddenly, it was as if the breathing machine was functioning for both her and him. Her lungs seemed to only fill in time with the slow and steady motion of the pump. Her heart only beat with the bright blue line of the EKG machine.

"Are you all right?" Eslar asked, softly.

She felt him there, at her side. A strong and stable presence when she otherwise had none. When she had been lost to the gravity of what they were about to do.

"The last time I was in a hospital . . . my grandmother was sick," Jo whispered. Eslar remained silent, letting her ramble. "They thought she was going to die . . . But she didn't, not then. She was such a strong healer, but not even she could fight that. I watched her waste away under my mother's care for nearly a decade before she finally succumbed to the cancer that was eating her alive."

If she had known about the Society, would she have wished for her grandmother's health? She sacrificed herself for Yuusuke, but not her own flesh and blood?

"There aren't enough wishes in the world to save everyone."

Jo reluctantly admitted that she now understood why Snow hadn't wanted her in the field prematurely. She understood why Wayne had cautioned her against trying to help the world outside of sanctioned wishes.

This was a different sort of heavy than weighing one's own mortality. This was weighing one's choices against the fate of the world, and wondering if you measured up enough to be worth the sack of flesh you were given at birth.

This was the thing that would fully detach her from the world. Because if she felt she was a part of it still, then she would defend it. And if she tried to defend it, the futility of it would drive her to madness.

"There are not," Eslar said coolly. She wished he'd touch her, support her, comfort her; everything felt so shaky. "But wishes never really save anyone."

Instead of walking toward her, he walked toward the patient. The long-haired elf appeared in Jo's field of vision as he stood at Keller's bedside, staring down at the mortal who seemed to be mere minutes from death.

"Only the living can make a difference. If you breathe, you have the chance to save the world. Not through a wish, but through the actions and infinite possibilities you create."

Jo swallowed hard. She was fairly certain Eslar wasn't trying to make her feel bad. But he was suddenly calling into question every choice she had ever made in life, every action taken thanks to the privilege of being able to draw breath.

"We help the living. We help move the needle, Jo. But the rest is up to the hands that still have warmth."

She looked down at her own palms. They'd always been cold—icy from server rooms and too many hours outstretched and flying across a keyboard with machine-like precision. They'd been cold from birth, her mother had joked. Perhaps it was her magic that ran cold.

Maybe this was what she'd been destined for all along.

Jo balled her hands into fists. "I know what I need to do," she reassured Eslar. "I'm not dissuaded."

"Good." He nodded. "I knew you would be up to the task."

"How?" she whispered.

Eslar chuckled and shook his head. "Call it intuition, or experience . . . for whatever that's worth from my lost time. Women can create life. Women can tend the fires of the hearth and fight in the wars to defend them. I never had a doubt in you from the moment I laid eyes on you."

It was the nicest thing anyone had ever said to her, and Jo couldn't handle it. "Now you're just flattering me," she joked, trying to diffuse the situation. "You already had my help with the bribe. Didn't need to butter me up too."

"I know I didn't. And it was more honey than butter." Jo honestly couldn't tell if Eslar was trying to be coy. Everything he ever said had that same matter-of-fact tone.

"Well, I'm going to go find a computer and see if my scripts are ready." Jo started for the door.

"I'll wait here until you return. When you do, I'll heal this man. We're down to hours left . . . So, hurry back."

"I will," Jo said without so much as a second glance. She didn't need to be reminded of the stakes, even if she didn't fully understand them. Then again, she never really knew what the stakes were for her jobs. She never grasped how a failure would affect her employers. Or whom a success would hurt.

All she ever needed to know was what she had to do next. As long as she knew that, she could keep moving forward.

Jo strode out of the hospital room, pulling the sleeves of her hoodie all the way down, and starting for a nurse's station she'd seen on the way there.

# GREENTOUCH

J O BACKTRACKED THROUGH the hospital. She made a right out of the door and started for a central hub. On her way, she passed one particularly frazzled, doe-eyed nurse who looked familiar.

It stopped Jo in her tracks, looking back at the woman clutching a tablet and muttering to herself the list of test results that were displayed in cold black and white. Her head swiveled as she watched the woman fuss with her hair, stopping in front of Mr. Keller's door, tapping at the screen in frustration. The nurse had no idea that the people who would ensure her wish would come true were standing right next to her.

Jo started moving again.

She was a member of the Society of Wishes. She did not change the future and she did not own the past. She was a spectator to both and a vessel for the whims of the living. She was beyond reality, given mere moments to touch it, only if she was granted the time.

Drawing her wrist forward, Jo stopped in front of an office by the nurse's station. It was certainly the hub of operations and the office must belong to someone important, given the number of letters engraved after the name on the door. Jo looked at her time.

She had one hour.

Precious little moments to change the Severity of Exchange, to right her wrong.

More than enough, she assured herself. *It'll be more than enough.*

Jo tapped the watch and the world blinked into existence. The sterile smell of ozone mixed with the chemical scent of hand sanitizer layered atop the metallic tang of stainless steel. The bustle of the hospital was palpable to her, but only for a moment. She heard phones ringing and pagers beeping—a bygone technology still clinging to the medical field. She heard the hushed whispers and somber conversations as though they were all right next to her.

But only for a moment.

She pressed the strip of smart fabric on her wrist again, blinking out of existence the moment the door was opened. A nurse had seen her, one who was walking over to the door, but only for a blink. The man poked his head in the room, looking around, but saw no one.

Jo stood before him, an invisible entity, waiting for him to abandon his search. With a shake of his head, the nurse closed the door.

"What's up?" Jo heard someone ask outside.

"Nothing, thought I saw . . . I don't know. I've been at this too long today." The man laughed softly, returning to his post. "Doesn't matter."

Jo turned to the computer, fumbling with the USB in her pocket. They had hours until Mr. Keller was transferred. She had one hour of time left— seconds less, now that she'd opened the door. She could do this.

Or . . . not.

Jo crouched down, frantically looking around the small box that served as the main terminal of the computer. She even tapped into time for a whole minute to move it around because she couldn't believe her eyes.

There wasn't a USB port. Jo cursed out loud. She should've expected this to happen. It was a fairly antiquated technology and most computers came with free cloud storage out of the box. A hospital no doubt backed up all their records to a shared server—

A new option clicked in her mind. While still in time, Jo opened the door and then tapped her fabric—down to an hour, even. She'd have to conserve as much time as possible while she found that server room.

Jo turned in the hallway, reading all the various signs. Of course, there weren't any IT-oriented labels. They were all driven to functional areas of the hospital.

"Okay, where would you be?" she mumbled to herself. Jo tried to think logically—the hospital was likely to have their own server racks for keeping at least some data in-house. She was only vaguely familiar with the various security protocols required of medical facilities. There had to have been a point where it was easier for a hospital to build out for some of their needs than pay someone else to . . . right? And those terminals would be certain to have a physical port, as an extra failsafe, if nothing else.

She took a deep breath. She may only have an hour left . . . But there were still hours until the man would be transferred. She could search the hospital top to bottom if she needed to.

Or maybe she didn't need to.

Jo stepped across the hall to stand before a door—an unassuming supply closet. She held out her hand, poising her fingers just above the door handle and *believed.* The Door appeared before her; Jo kept a very clear image of where she needed to go in her head. She stared at the keypad, trying to erase all other thoughts and, just like the first time, the alphanumeric numbers suddenly arranged themselves into a sequence that her fingers were all too eager to press.

She was pulled through, appearing in a dark room of server racks with little else. Jo turned in place as the Door closed, but she didn't even catch a glimpse of steel; it had already transformed into the same off-white color the rest of the hospital was painted in. Still, Jo tapped into time, opening the door and glancing out.

*Yes*, she was in the same hospital. Satisfied with herself, Jo flicked on the light to the room, and quickly set to work.

The pressure of time weighed on her as she set out finding some USB port on the terminal. Her watch was like a handcuff around her wrist, tying her to the fear of failure—to the unknown punishment that seemed to somber every member of the Society without explanation. Jo let out an audible sigh of relief when she finally found the port.

She opened a command prompt on the computer and entered her first query. The script ran like a dream. Everything, finally, was going according to plan.

Jo tapped away on the keyboard, almost happily. Nurse on record would get credit for attempting an experimental treatment—a treatment that Jo would make sure was buried in databases across the nation—both private and public—from past doctors and researchers. It would be obscure enough to be overlooked by many, and those behind the information would have met mysterious ill fates. But hopefully, no one would care once the patient was cured and the vaccine was out. The nurse might get some flak for not obtaining the proper sign-offs first . . . but Jo could only hope that saving the patient's life would earn her some slack.

Her time ticked by far too quickly, and finesse soon became a luxury she could no longer afford.

She went about her business with the determination of a fisherman hunting the white whale. Her work was sloppy, and she knew it. But even if it could be traced back to this computer, so what? The fingerprints on the keyboard belonged to no one; there was no one to hunt down. Plus, considering the amount of legwork they were being forced to accomplish, the least Snow could do was tidy up the loose ends when he knotted his side of things.

Jo stilled as she heard voices outside the door. Her finger hovered over her watch. But they passed, and she resumed her work.

Just a little bit more. A little bit of this here, that there, one more record of dots to connect. Jo didn't know if it was enough, but there was a distinct feeling of rightness to her actions—a sensation she had never felt before. Perhaps, on some magical level, she was sensing the gap in the Severity of Exchange closing. Or perhaps it was the irreplaceable feeling of knowing she was useful—of being proven right.

Either way, Jo took one more glance at the computer, deciding she'd done enough, and pulled her USB. She spent a minute trying to get everything back just as she found it, but she was certain she couldn't. It didn't matter anyway, Jo told herself. Whatever she did, in mere hours when Snow got his hands on it, this would be no more. He'd eat an entire universe of possibility and change the fabric of reality.

Jo opened the door and slipped out of time in one motion.

She backtracked, finding the signs now useful to getting where she wanted to go, through the corridors to the hospital room. Jo kept her eyes open for the nurse she had assumed to be behind the wish. But wherever the woman was, her business had taken her far from Mr. Keller's room.

Jo slipped through the open door, startled by a man in scrubs leaning against the wall. Even in spite of the mint green, bland hospital uniform, he moved like water—fluid, barely contained by the plebeian garb. Eslar looked to her, saying nothing.

She merely nodded.

He did the same, pulling out his watch. He activated it with a brush of his finger, the runes flaring magically underneath the pad of his thumb. He looked no different to her, but the way he moved was different. His actions suddenly seemed weighted with a gravity they didn't previously possess.

Eslar, like her, wasted no time. He leaned forward and laid his hands on the prone man in the hospital bed. For a long moment, nothing happened, and Jo wondered if she was watching with such rapt attention for no reason. But slowly, Eslar's hands changed.

Vine-like tendrils working their way up under his flesh, shimmering with raw magic, the elf's usually russet skin changed to a brilliant viridian hue. It seeped up his forearms, highlighting the tendons of his long fingers and creeping toward his elbows. Jo couldn't contain a gasp, but if Eslar heard her, he made no motion.

The elf's eyes glowed with their own soft, emerald light, gaze intent as he stared down at the ward he was pouring so much effort into curing. There was an aura about him, one of wonder, of birth, of infinite possibility Jo barely understood. Like a firefly, the magic burned brightly with purpose, and then extinguished.

Mr. Keller's eyes fluttered open. "Who . . ."

Eslar said nothing, quickly disappearing on the other side of the curtain. From Jo's vantage, she could see him pressing the nurse call button. Everything after that happened like the events of a movie on a distant silver screen, Jo standing trapped behind the veil of the fourth wall.

The same nurse she'd seen before returned to the room. The woman had a confused, elated, ecstatic exchange with Mr. Keller. Vitals were checked, and the words "full recovery" were used. Other nurses rushed in to check the work; a commotion was building, muffled and distant from Jo's vantage just outside of reality.

"We should go." Eslar's voice was loud compared to the rest of the room.

"We should," Jo agreed. "Go home."

"Do you truly think of it as home, now?" Eslar asked, with genuine curiosity in his voice.

"I do," she admitted, looking up at the elf. He was still wearing scrubs, clothing that would no doubt melt back into his normal garb the moment they re-entered the mansion. Green still glittered under his flesh, up to the sleeves of his shirt, and protruded like veins above his collar. He still had that lingering glow to his eyes.

There was nothing about him that was human.

But he was part of her family—her *magic* family.

"Then let us go, Jo."

They departed together, hacker and healer, human and elf, walking against the commotion of the room and the steadily growing crowd, back to a nondescript supply closet. Eslar held out a hand and a familiar door appeared, the code to which Jo knew magically with only a glance.

The door opened, and the familiar smell of the briefing room greeted them.

# CLEAN SLATE

"DON'T YOU HAVE something better to do than wait for people to return?" Jo deadpanned.

Snow had been waiting in his chair upon their arrival, staring at the Door with the look of a father about to scold his children. But Jo wasn't about to take a reprimanding quietly, not when she'd just done good work.

Before she could open her mouth, however, Eslar stepped in.

"Your parameters are set, Snow," he said, matter-of-fact. "The wish is yours to grant."

The diversion didn't work; Snow simply got to his feet and stared them both down. "When I barred you from this wish," he said to Jo, before turning his attention to Eslar, "that was an order, not a suggestion."

"Jo's skills were paramount to the success of this mission. Without her, the Severity of Exchange had no hope of getting even close to the necessary parameters, and you know it." For the first time, Jo witnessed Eslar's calm demeanor shift, not so much like a fracture but like the distant tremors that forewarned of a much larger earthquake.

Unlike the last time someone had attempted—rather poorly—to stick up for her in this briefing room, Jo found herself floored by the determination Eslar suddenly showed. Even Snow seemed mildly affronted, not quite sure how to handle having his subordinate take any side other than his own.

"She was not ready and had already cost us a widening of the Exchange," Snow tried. When he crossed his arms over his chest, Jo couldn't help but notice that his hands were clenched into tight fists. "Your recklessness could have cost us further widening if she was unsuccessful and—"

"But she wasn't. And it didn't," Eslar cut him off.

Jo sighed, mumbling more to herself this time than to anyone present. "I'm right here, guys."

"You are blindly diving into wishes with an inexperienced member who has already proven to be reckless. You had no idea how she would react or what she might do."

"I know where this is coming from." That statement from Eslar piqued Jo's interest. His voice had gone soft, almost sorrowful, and his whole demeanor changed.

"Don't," Snow cautioned.

"I remember what you said, briefly, all those years ago about the age you come from. I suspect she's—"

"Enough!" Snow silenced the elf with a glare. Eslar just huffed, hardly bemused.

As much as Jo wanted to see where that line of discussion was headed, she didn't think riling up Snow further was a smart idea. She took it upon herself to step in before either could regain their footing in the confrontation.

"Look," Jo sighed, the sound of her voice in the silence actually managing to startle the two men. She would have found it funny if not for the stress headache currently forming between her eyes. "Snow, I know I messed up, and I'm sorry. But you can't reprimand me and then give me no chances for redemption. And I'm sorry if trying to make things right looks like 'going rogue' to you."

Jo ran a hand over her face, the sense memory of a thumb wiping tears away from her cheekbone entering her mind unbidden. Why couldn't she shake that memory? It was the first scrap of comfort she'd felt in her new world, certainly. But that didn't permit it to creep forward at every possible opportunity.

"I wanted to fix it, and I didn't have much to go off of, so I made my own way. It's what I've always done and, frankly, what I'll continue to do. I may not be familiar with all the logistics here—and on that note, I do recommend some actual training for new recruits. But I *knew* that I could help fix my errors. Eslar agreed, and we managed to get the job done.

"But even if you think it was nothing more than recklessness, at the very least, tell me you believe me when I say that I only have the best interests of the team in mind?"

Another lengthy pause followed, this one a bit more nerve-wracking than the first. While Snow's gaze on her seemed tense and unsure, Eslar's seemed almost proud. And that had to count for something.

"Eslar," Snow finally spoke, his first word in what felt like hours.

Despite his insubordination, Jo couldn't help but notice the way the elf reluctantly straightened beneath the demanding tone. When Snow spoke again, however, his tone was softer, less of a demand and more of a request. "Will you excuse Jo and me?"

For a split second, Jo wanted to look to Eslar in a panic, beg him to stay, but something in Snow's eyes seemed more docile than before. And damn it all if Jo wasn't a slave to curiosity. Not to mention, if it was just the two of them, maybe she could finally get herself some answers.

Eslar nodded, once to Snow and once to Jo in turn, before leaving the briefing room.

"I apologize for not making things better understood to begin with. And for making you doubt that I believe you operate with the best interests of our group," Snow started the moment the door closed behind Eslar.

"You know—" a small smile pulled at the corners of her lips, "—your moods can really give a girl whiplash."

His brow furrowed slightly.

"Hot and cold, distant and close." Jo hadn't intended to be intimidating, but Snow's expression told her that she was succeeding in it anyway. People had always said she could channel her mother. For a Hispanic woman of 5'1" with a heart-shaped face and warm smile, Jo's mother could be downright terrifying when she had *la chancla* in hand. "Level with me, since it's just us here: who are you? The guy who takes care to explain the situation and wipe the tears from my face, or the guy who won't even give me the time of day to redeem myself?"

*Or the man who seems to keep working his way into my thoughts?*

The man seemed at a loss for words, unsure how to properly handle the bed he'd made for himself. An odd expression crept into his face that Jo couldn't quite identify. Annoyance? Anger? Confusion? In many ways, it seemed like a million expressions all at once, and somehow, Jo could tell that few, if any, were directed at her. At least, not at the moment.

"Snow . . ." Just his name pulled tension from her shoulders; Jo felt her stance relax a little. When frustration and anger weren't getting the better of her, the man was a soothing presence in his own right to be around. So soothing, that Jo didn't stop herself from reaching out. Her hand hovered, mid-air, as she realized all too late that she'd been about to touch him. But, as if compelled by gravity itself, her fingertips met his sleeved forearm. That same electricity crackled under her skin at the contact. "You at least get why I've been kind of upset—or, well, at least confused . . . right?"

This time, when Snow pulled his eyes from her fingers on his sleeve to her eyes, it was in a shock very obviously marred by undeniable hurt. In fact, if Jo had to define it, in that first second before Snow managed to school his features back into place, she would have said he looked almost pleading. Maybe even a little bit desperate.

"I understand," he said finally. "I never meant to. I would never want to push you away, but . . . It was simply that you—" He frowned before resuming his neutral expression once more. Whatever train of thought he'd been going down wasn't one he was about to let himself have, yet. Jo would pull it out eventually, however, if given the chance. A new emotion flitted through the cloudy steel of his gaze. A beat, another, and then, "I apologize."

There was a genuineness there, somewhere beneath the awkward strain, and Jo almost laughed.

"I'll accept your apology, if you accept mine." She dared a playful grin. "You know why I had to, right?"

"I do." Two words and Jo's heart began beating once more, released from the tension that had held it locked between her ribs. Relief bled into the worry that had filled Snow's eyes, mixing to look something like hope. "And the apology is more than accepted."

"Then, we're good, you and I?" she ventured to ask. "Everything in the past, clean slate?"

Snow seemed at a loss for what to do next, completely thrown in a way that Jo couldn't deny was absolutely adorable. "I think we are." With his other hand, he reached up, clasping his fingers around hers in an awkward—but entirely welcome—hand hold.

His palm had that same warmth she remembered on her cheek, and an enviable softness. Their fingers lingered, wrapped around each other, as if neither wanted to be the first to pull away. When the contact was eventually broken, a pall of mutual embarrassment seemed to hang over them.

"Well, then," Jo started, taking a step away. It was as if she suddenly couldn't trust herself around him. She had no idea what she'd do if he stayed in such close proximity. "I'm glad we could clear the air."

Snow merely nodded.

Even though their hands felt like they'd parted a millennia ago, he still held her there without touch. He could hold her there for eternity if he only asked. "I should go . . ." Jo whispered. "Let you finish up this wish."

Another nod. Jo searched his guarded eyes. *Say it*, she wanted to scream, though she had no idea what "it" was. Even worse, she had no idea what she wanted it to be. She would listen to him say anything as long as it was being said to her.

Jo side-stepped around him, starting for the double doors that led back into the manor.

"Wait."

Her feet had stopped before Snow had even opened his mouth. They'd stopped on his breath, in hope that he would be using it to call after her.

"Will you come with me a moment?" Jo turned, but Snow didn't look at her when he spoke. "I want to show you something."

"What is it?" she asked, ignoring the new weight that was suddenly placed on her with those words.

Snow motioned to the Door and Jo walked over, as if in a heart-stuttering trance. "Trust me," he whispered, when she was just barely close enough to hear.

*I have all along,* was what her heart said. Her lips formed different words. "All right, lead the way."

# OBSIDIAN CIRCLE

I T SEEMED THAT, with Snow, there was always another moment to feel like she was on the set of a movie.

Jo stepped through the Door into the crumbling husk of a great structure made of obsidian and stone. Twilight streamed through the collapsed holes in the rooftop opposite where she stood. A billowing mist accompanied the low-light, shrouding the room and blurring the details at the edges. Vines stretched out leafy arms toward the moisture, collecting the dew before rolling it down onto the carpet of moss below.

She turned in place, looking to see Snow closing the Door, and could not contain a gasp. The circular room had no exits, so the industrial portal floated a finger's width off the ground and in mid-air, connected to no other walls—as though it could not touch anything. The moment the Door was closed, it faded from view.

Jo reached out, holding her hand, expecting the Door to be there, merely invisible. But there was nothing. There was no collection of magic, no firming up of the essence of the Door at her will.

"It won't work for you," Snow said softly, as if trying not to startle her. The sudden sound breaking the silence startled her anyway, though, and Jo swiveled. "Not here."

"This place . . ." Jo struggled to form complete sentences. She'd thought she'd understood magic, felt magic, but everything paled in comparison to the atmosphere here. Like the low hum of a speaker, the world seemed to buzz with an energy that rattled Jo to her core. The Door was gone now. It usually disappeared, but this time it left only the skeleton of a window beyond where it had been. There was nothing but fog to be seen through its panes—so dense that it gave birth to a waking fear of what it might obscure. "What is it?"

"It's the room where I vanished from reality."

"What?" Her heart was in her throat at the mere mention of Snow's death. Whatever weird things he made her insides do aside, he was still their leader and—as far as Jo could tell—a very important glue holding the Society together.

"It was here that the Society of Wishes was born."

"Do you even know how to speak in a way that isn't cryptic?" Jo tried to laugh, but like a spark to wet tinder, the sound didn't catch. It was as hollow as the crumbling, circular room in which they stood.

Circular.

Jo took the room in once more—the vaulted ceiling, collapsed in over a quarter of the room, single tiles of obsidian glittering on the floor. Three windows were obscured by fog, glass hanging onto them like snaggle-teeth. She walked forward, toward the center.

There, at the center of the room, was a line—so thin it almost blended in with the cracks of the stone. The obsidian circle hid behind the shards of roof tile (what civilization in history used obsidian for roof tiles anyway?) and the patch of moss. She already knew what she would find but, using the toe of her shoe, Jo cleared away the debris and greenery to confirm that the circle of inlaid, shining, black stone was complete.

"A circle." Jo looked back to the man with questioning eyes. A man who, despite his modern attire, looked like he truly fit in more here than he ever had at the Society.

"The very first."

"What happened here?" She had so many questions, but they were sluggish to roll off her tongue. In some odd, impossible way, the place seemed almost . . . familiar?

"What happened here is no longer relevant. It's what happens here now that's important." Snow started for the center of the room himself, but Jo did not stand and wait for him to meet her.

She spurred her feet to motion, meeting him at the edge of the black circle. Her hands reached up, clutching the opening of his shirt. He was taller than her, likely physically stronger, and quite obviously magically superior. But Jo held on anyway. She held fast like her life depended on it.

"Don't say that!" She gave him a small shake. "Don't say that," she said, softer. "What happened is relevant. What happened in the past is all we have now. We don't exist anymore, right? So, the only things that really make us are our memories and our magic."

Snow seemed startled, unsure even. He stared down at her with those steely eyes that suddenly felt as though they were seeing a new corner of her very essence. A place Jo hadn't even known existed before that moment.

She swallowed hard, but she didn't back down.

"You don't have to tell me the details of it . . . Not now, not ever, not if you don't want to." Jo eased back onto her heels, not remembering when she'd risen to her toes. "But don't act like it's not important. It is, I know it is, I can feel it, Snow."

She felt the muscles of his chest tense under her knuckles. Snow's hands rose, no doubt about to push her away. Jo uncurled her fingers. She had at least a little bit of dignity; she wasn't going to force herself on someone who very clearly did not want her touch.

His hands closed around hers, holding her there. With the wrapping of those long, elegant fingers, it felt as if he'd woven a spell across her whole body. Jo swallowed hard.

This feeling was far more dangerous than anything she'd encountered with Wayne. With anyone. Jo knew she was thinking with a level head, unclouded by sexual tension (even though there was certainly a heaping of that)—which made her kaleidoscope of feelings around Snow all the more confusing. There had to be an explanation somewhere and if she looked hard enough, it almost felt like the reason was something she'd long forgotten.

"Very well," Snow whispered. "I will, so do not despair."

Jo wanted to question if it really was that simple. Jo wanted to question why her despair mattered. Jo wanted to know everything about this man and how she measured against him. His height, compared to hers. Their closeness, barely touching along the entire lengths of their bodies. The electricity that began to fill in the void that something in her ached to close.

"Now, I must begin." Snow released her, as though he hadn't felt the fever pitch he'd been working her toward with just his proximity. Jo's knees felt like gelatin—likely for the best he'd let her go before they completely turned to jelly. "There is a wish to grant." He looked back to her, gaze falling to her feet. "If you don't mind stepping out of the circle?"

"Oh, no . . ." Jo shuffled back until she met the wall. She leaned against it, arms folded, as if defending herself from whatever odd sensations he'd just begun to provoke in her.

Snow gave one nod, and one last, long look at her. Jo had never felt a man stare at her with such intent. These were the eyes of someone who was taking in every detail, cataloging it, storing it for a memory that would be cherished. Jo recognized the stare, because she'd given it countless times to strings of code whizzing by on a command prompt. But she'd never aimed it at another person.

She swallowed again, her throat still dry, and gave a nod of her own.

As if on her command, Snow looked forward. He reached into his pocket, producing what Jo fully expected to be a watch—it seemed the M.O. of the group. But instead, it was a small snuff box, no bigger than his palm. Jo squinted her eyes, trying to make out the details of the gold gilding and silver metalwork, but she couldn't from her vantage.

"In the circle that is life and death, our world and the next, I invoke my power." Snow opened the box with his left hand. "The circle has been cast, invocation made, and the wish shall be granted."

He swept away his left hand like a maestro summoning to life an invisible orchestra. His right hand remained outstretched in front of him, perpendicular to his chest and parallel to the floor. Snow's movements were measured and practiced, but rigid, as though he were a puppet moving along on invisible strings.

A gasp rose in Jo's throat as the circle in the floor began to spark to life. Magic shimmered in the obsidian, a mess of color before a green, fire-like light blazed around Snow. Its tendrils reached for the ceiling. While there was no heat, Jo pressed closer to the wall behind her, as if pushed back by the force of the magic itself. Or, by the force of the sudden and extreme unease that came with an odd sense of impossible familiarity to what she was seeing.

Snow's left hand twisted, palm up. Rising from the fire was a second circle, one of leaves and twigs. It hovered atop the first, snowing magic down onto the fire and cooling it to a dull ember. From this second, glimmering circle, images solidified in the same leafy hue.

Jo saw the hospital, the nurse, Mr. Keller, all rising before exploding like fireworks and freezing mid-air around Snow. She saw different pictures of the nurse pouring over a textbook, a graduation, a new doctor. These fell into the remnants of the fire below, sparking to life as they were consumed into nothingness. Little embers danced off the magic flames, floating toward her like the last farewells of a world that could never be.

World destroyer, Pan had said. It looked more like world burner, from where Jo stood.

She watched as the cost of the wish was consumed, a few images, a core possibility—gone forever. Everything stood in balance: the sacrificed world, the circle that Jo had no doubt mirrored what the nurse had used to make her wish, and the sparks of new possibility. It all hung together perfectly. Jo may not understand everything, but she knew that hers and Eslar's efforts had been enough. The Severity of Exchange was perfectly measured.

In one sudden movement, Snow brought his left hand to his right in a wide arc. The magic followed in front of his fingers, quickly ushering itself into the box his right hand still held. The room flashed brightly, everything rising to a pitch, and then the box closed with a sound that resembled a thunderclap.

It all echoed in her—a deep resonance in a void that Jo had never known she possessed until there was something attempting to fill it. Jo's ears rang and her heart raced. Her eyes struggled to catch up with the sudden darkness that followed the brilliance of the magic. They settled on the silhouette of a man, hunched and heaving, wrapped in on himself, curled on the floor. Magic steamed off Snow's shoulders with a faint glow that looked almost like the smoldering remnants of some fallen angel.

". . . Snow?" Jo squeaked, finally. If her legs had gone soft before, the display had pulverized them. She wobbled against the wall, feeling tired, drained, as though she had somehow taken actual part in the ritual she'd just witnessed.

He did not move.

"Snow?" Jo tried again, making her way to him. "Snow, are you—"

"Don't," he rasped, stopping her in her tracks. Jo noticed that he only seemed to gain the strength to speak, or move, the second she was about to cross the threshold of the circle. "Don't come near me."

"What? Don't be silly, are you all right?"

"Go!" He shouted, without looking at her. His left hand thrust out from where it had been curled against his chest. Jo followed the point of his finger to where the Door back to the Society had magically reappeared. "I shouldn't have. I let you get too close. I don't know why I thought —"

"You invited me!" She was not about to let him push her away. "Let me help you back."

"Jo, I—" Snow's face shot up. His hair hung limply, slicked with sweat to his face, clinging in tendrils. His lips, usually red, were void of color, ghostly. His eyes . . . his eyes were the most alarming part of him. Their steely color had all but vanished, blanching into the white that was being infringed upon by gnarly, bloodshot veins.

He had said he died there, and now, as she looked at the corpse of a man, Jo believed it.

"You fear me," he whispered.

"There is no reality in which I'd fear you," Jo replied with more confidence than she felt.

Jo crossed over to him. Snow leaned away, swaying slightly, like a panicked animal. There was hurt and fear and all the weariness of seeing and consuming countless worlds.

"Let me help you back," she repeated, kneeling next to him.

"Why do you not run?" He stared through her with those monstrous eyes.

"Are you my enemy?"

"Not in any lifetime." It sounded like a vow and echoed her own words so strangely.

"Then I have nothing to run from." Jo took his hand, sliding it toward her. The moment his palm left the ground, Snow tilted; Jo had to press her side into his, quickly slinging the appendage over her shoulders for stability.

Her thighs screamed in protest as she hoisted them upright. Snow's head hung heavily, barely coming up long enough to pin the code back into the Door. They were ushered back through, him nearly stumbling again as the sound of pressurization echoed through the briefing room.

"We're almost there," she encouraged.

"We are not," he wheezed.

"Do you even know how to not be a pain?" Jo laughed at her own forced levity. From the corners of her eyes, she could've sworn she saw a smile playing on his lips.

Be it fate or luck, they ran into no one else on the way back through the mansion. Both recreation rooms were void of watches. Her back ached and her legs wobbled, but Jo wasn't going to let the man down. He didn't really deserve her loyalty, a logical part of her mind insisted. But Jo couldn't forget what she'd seen.

"Here's far enough." Snow raised his head, outstretching a shaking hand to support himself against the wall. He glanced toward his door at the end of the hall, his eyes drifting left to the mysterious black door at its side.

"It's right—"

"Here's far enough," he repeated, looking down at her warily.

Jo looked back to the last two doorways at the end of the hall. She put her hands on her hips, opened her mouth, and then Snow stole the last words.

"Leave me here, for both of our sakes."

Jo opened her mouth to fire back. There was a strong urge to put the man in his place. But no retort came.

Instead, Jo's feet pulled her away. She felt his eyes on her as she traversed the length of the hall. She didn't look back once the whole walk to her room. It wasn't even until she was behind her own closed door that a deep sense of overwhelming dread collapsed on her, dropping her to her knees.

# BLACK DOOR

I N THE MONTH that passed after Snow's unexpected reveal of his magic, surprisingly little changed.

Perhaps it was because she seemed to be acting like nothing happened. Jo had neither seen nor spoken a single word to Snow. She knew where to find him, in theory. But every day came and went, and she was no closer to finding the motivation (courage) to seek him out. It was as if speaking of that night alone would reveal a truth she wasn't yet ready to handle.

Despite the new information, the new conflicting emotions she felt towards their "king," Jo felt just as welcome and respected by her team as ever and immersed herself in that. She drank coffee with Nico in the mornings and jokingly flirted with Wayne to distract him from kicking her ass in billiards. She watched Samson tinker and accompanied Takako to target practice, and sometimes, on really quiet days, she'd read in comfortable silence with Eslar, trying not so subtly to catch glimpses of the odd runic script that filled his manuscripts.

Samson's cooking prowess was unmatched and a constant source of delight. It didn't matter that she didn't need to eat. With him around, Jo certainly wanted to.

The first breakfast he'd made for her had been nothing short of five-star brilliance. Bacon and eggs, the world's fluffiest pancakes, waffles, and French toast, pastries of nearly every variety, even some homemade cereal with grains and fruits.

It had been grander than any breakfast Jo had ever eaten, and she'd made it a point to tell him so. Samson had blinked at her in surprise before smiling a small, embarrassed smile and offering his own thanks.

It only had gotten better from there.

Today was an equally lavish spread. Not only had Samson laid out a slew of meats and cheeses to choose from, various vegetables and chips, but he'd also baked an obscene number of different breads. Ciabatta, Rye, Sourdough, and some Jo had never even heard of—*maneesh, lavash, piadine*.

Once she'd filled her plate with all the delicious makings of the perfect Philly Cheese Steak, Jo scanned the available seats at the kitchen table. Luckily, there was an open spot next to the great chef in question, and Jo took it hastily, bouncing a little in her seat as she settled by his side.

Though Samson still seemed a bit uncomfortable by her now countless attempts at conversation, he'd eased quite a bit over the last few weeks, no longer shying away from her attention. Well, not entirely anyway.

Jo took a bite, savoring and swallowing, before jumping in this time.

"Once again, you blow me away, Sam," she said, taking another bite and reveling in how the ingredients blended together in a way that was almost supernaturally perfect. Which was only a little ironic, considering.

"I didn't do much." Samson shrugged, though a pink tint had begun to creep up from his neck, his lips quirking up in a poorly contained half-smile.

"Well, then," Jo said through a mouthful before swallowing and trying again, offering up an apologetic smile. "I look forward to seeing what you come up with when you really give it your all." To Jo's immense satisfaction, Samson actually snorted at that, a barely audible huff of laughter that had her heart soaring. Mission accomplished.

As Jo ate, she glanced around the table. She listened as Nico debated the deliciousness of the Italian sub over the Rueben with Wayne. She watched as Eslar picked at his hoagie with one hand while keeping a book propped open on his knee with the other. Even Takako had picked up a conversation with Samson—though the man's usual closed-off demeanor made it hard to tell what it was about. Pan and Snow were nowhere to be found, but that was normal, even for team meals.

She was supposed to go shooting with Takako later today, and Nico had offered to teach her about the famous artists of his time (which, Jo suspected, would take a long time given her general apathy toward history). While she hadn't had much one-on-one interaction with Eslar since the wish from the hospital in Canada, she could still feel a silent camaraderie there; when no one else had stood up for, believed in her, Eslar had. And that really did something for morale.

Wayne and she still had their rapport following the wish. Occasional flirtations that'd escalate into some overt implications, but never anything more.

In fact, right here, surrounded by the rest of her team, Philly Cheese Steak dripping oil onto her plate, it felt like everything was falling together naturally, in a way she would have never expected weeks ago. In many ways, it felt like something clicking into place, like acceptance, and a place she'd been meant to be all along.

Maybe, just maybe, things would be all right here.

Now if only she could manage to wrap her head around the still-pressing enigma that was Snow.

Jo shook her head, distracting herself not for the first time by forcing her mind to shift to something else.

"Hey, Sam?" Jo said suddenly, putting down her sandwich and glancing to her right. Samson glanced back, eyes less nervous and more curious, which Jo had learned to accept for the triumph it was.

She probably should have thanked him sooner, she realized. While it had been Wayne's idea, and while Eslar had played messenger, it had been Samson who had made them for her after all. He deserved just as much thanks as the rest of them.

"Thank you for making me the mug. And the *sopapillas*," she said, making sure Samson could see every ounce of genuine appreciation in her eyes. "I really needed them. And they were perfect."

Samson's face fell from surprised to embarrassed to proud much more quickly than usual, but this time, instead of merely mumbling a quiet apology into his lap, he forced himself to look back up at her.

His smile was warm and gentle, in many ways the perfect smile for a man like him.

"We wanted you to know it wasn't gone," Samson said, voice soft but more pronounced than Jo remembered ever hearing it.

"That what wasn't gone?" Jo asked, subconsciously keeping her voice level with his. It felt like keeping a secret.

This time, Samson looked back at his lap, shrugging a bit, but his smile stayed firmly in place. "A little taste of home."

For a long moment, Jo didn't know what to say. She watched, stunned, as Samson's blush faded and he even began eating again, finishing off his own sandwich before rising to take his plate to the sink. Before he could get too far away, Jo called back to him.

When he looked over his shoulder at her, she could have sworn she saw a different man, one filled with more complexities than she'd given him credit for.

"Thank you, Samson," she repeated, heart swelling when he smiled and nodded in response.

The rest of her meal would go unfinished, apparently.

For the first time in a month, Snow announced his presence in the kitchen with another quiet, looming arrival. Only this time, when he looked at the crowd at large, his gaze settled on Jo for a brief but warily knowing length of time. His eyes—now back to normal—still held secrets, and Jo found her heart stumbling over itself at the thought that she might be the only one privy to just how many. A fragile, collapsing bridge between them had been crossed, whether or not either of them liked it, and there was no going back.

"Everyone is to meet me in the briefing room in five," he said, his voice laced with the stoicism of protocol. But his eyes never left Jo's, and when he made to leave, it wasn't without a quick nod in her direction. Jo nodded back, even if he'd already turned away.

Another wish. Business as usual. Like nothing had happened between them. Jo couldn't help but frown.

"Everybody ready?" Eslar closed his book, standing.

Nico trailed behind, crossing his arms over his chest and giving a nod of mild agreement.

"We're not far off of the wave from our last wish. Perhaps this one will go smoothly." As Eslar said it, he spared a glance in Jo's direction, offering her a smirk. Jo smiled right back.

"Mulberry fields," Takako mumbled as she passed.

Jo paused, unsure what mulberries had anything to do with anything, but suddenly, Wayne was next to her, whispering in her ear.

"I think it means knock on wood," he said, laughing when she swatted at him to back up. "So, what say you to partnering up for this one, eh, dollface?" Wayne asked once the both of them were trailing behind the pack. "A gambler and a hacker—already know we make a good team."

Jo scoffed, but even she could hear the lack of venom in it. "We don't even know what the wish is."

Wayne leaned in close again, lips brushing her cheek. "It doesn't necessarily have to be for the wish."

The comment was obviously suggestive, but despite the bubble of heat that settled low in her stomach on instinct at the sound, Jo merely laughed it off.

"Give it up, old man," Jo teased.

"With a dame like you around? Never." Wayne straightened up, grin stretched wide.

"Lucky me." She mirrored his expression.

As they passed the Four-Way, Jo noticed something out of the corner of her eye, a silver-haired figure walking, not towards the briefing room, but to his own. Just like that, the casual (and harmless) flirtations with Wayne died. Before she could put much thought towards potential consequences, Jo slowed her pace.

"Dollface?" Wayne called out from a few feet ahead of her, once he noticed she was trailing behind. She almost startled, unaware of where her feet had been starting to carry her. Still, she let them lead the way.

"I'll be right there, okay?" Jo called out, hurrying off down the hall. "I just gotta grab something from my room. Save me a seat?"

"Everything's Jake, doll," Wayne smirked before turning away, flipping his nickel with one hand as he waved over his shoulder at her with the other. "That seat belongs to you, now."

Jo's chest clenched at the implication. Her seat, her life, a now permanent fixture in the Society. Barely a month ago, that thought would have overwhelmed and suffocated her. But now? Now, she was almost looking forward to what her new life might bring.

She waited until Wayne was far ahead before sprinting up the staircase opposite her own.

Snow's door was in the process of closing and her chest was heaving by the time she made it down the hall, to the unmarked one all the way at the end. The stark white of the wood seemed to glow against the backdrop of the surrounding walls' warmer tones. It looked almost too pristine to be real.

She should knock.

Actually, no. She probably shouldn't.

The debate rose and fell within her like an indecisive tide. She wanted to ask him, for the first time since a month ago, exactly what was going on with him, with his magic. She wanted to ask if they were still on good terms, if he truly regretted bringing her there.

She wanted to see if he was okay.

That last realization rushed through her with startling fierceness. The last major interaction she'd had with the man was watching him contorted in pain, barely able to stand.

"Here's far enough," he'd said. But what did that mean? Why did he not want her to go any further?

All those coalescing questions were enough to have Jo lifting her knuckles to white paint and thick wood, rapping twice against Snow's door.

The lack of response stretched long enough that Jo began to assume Snow wouldn't answer. In fact, after a while, she started to wonder if she'd imagined him escaping down the hall. Maybe he was already in the briefing room, waiting for her. Maybe she'd reacted on an impulse that was completely unwarranted.

Slowly, Jo backed away from the door, shoving her hands into the pockets of her hoodie. This was a mistake. Even if he was in there, it was obvious he didn't want to talk to anyone, let alone her. He was likely just embarrassed. Men and their stupid pride, right?

Jo wished she could shrug off the notion that easily.

But before she could completely turn around, drag her feet back towards the briefing room, Snow's door cracked open. Jo froze in place. He stared at her with an unreadable expression, posture stiff and silver hair falling just so over his eye. He had an eyebrow raised, gaze searching, waiting. Even painfully composed, aura bordering on irritated, he was still beautiful.

After what felt like an awkward span of silence, Jo cleared her throat, looking away. "Hey," she said, instantly hating herself. The breath of sound she heard escape him could have been amusement or annoyance; she chose to believe it was the former.

"You're supposed to be in the briefing room," Snow eventually said. Jo just shrugged.

"As should you." And then, because she couldn't seem to leave well enough alone when it came to the mysterious man, she added, "Are you all right?"

"As ever."

Jo picked at the thread in the pocket of her hoodie. It wasn't an answer. But she suspected it was the best she was going to get.

"Do you regret it?" Jo fired off next. It had been a month, sure, but she knew he'd have no problem determining what she meant.

It was expected, if not a bit disheartening, when Snow finally answered, "Yes."

"Then why show me at all?" Jo demanded, crossing her arms over her chest. "And ghosting me after that? I thought you said everything was all right between us."

Jo would probably never tire of Snow's look of baffled shock, the way his eyes widened with more emotion than she was used to seeing on his usually stoic face. But even if it felt like a minor triumph, that didn't diminish the tension between them, the frustration slowly consuming Jo's mood. He was certainly driving her mad, because some small part of her loved it.

Eventually, with a tight sigh and a glance away from Jo's face, Snow replied, "I have no idea what this 'ghosting' might be, as I am not a ghost. But I felt . . . I was hopeful it might change things for you. Show you the true nature of this place—the true nature of your magic. Or, at the very least, make up for any misgivings of mine."

That was actually kind of sweet, in its own way. A sweetness reduced substantially by his reactions and following radio silence, but still. In the short time since joining the Society, she'd learned not to expect too much from the man. Plus, if Jo was honest, she could've sought him out also. It went both ways.

Jo mimicked his sigh with a slightly more put-upon one of her own.

"Next time, if you feel like making something up to me, ask me if anything needs to be made up for—"

"That's not—" Snow cut her off, and by the look of surprise bleeding into his features once they'd both gone silent, it was a completely involuntary interjection. When he didn't automatically finish his thought, Jo frowned.

"What's not?"

It took a long moment, a multitude of emotions warring in Snow's distant stare. But then, eventually, he opened his mouth to speak.

"I have much to make up for," he said, voice low and rough, as if it hurt for the words to leave his throat.

"What're you talking about?"

"Did you truly feel nothing while you were there?"

"What was I supposed to feel?" Questions on questions, that's all the man gave her. Something tingled across her chest, but the sensation was gone before Jo could even recognize it.

"Your magic . . ." he trailed off, looking over her right shoulder.

Jo turned, but saw nothing in the hallway that would consume his focus. "What about my magic?" she asked, bringing her attention back.

"Go to the briefing room, Jo."

It took everything she had not to bristle, not to go on the defensive. "You can't just say something like that and not—"

"Jo, please." Snow frowned, not quite looking at her. Something in his expression, in the tight, almost painful whisper of his voice, gave Jo pause. She scanned his face, tried to catch his gaze, but he stared adamantly to her side. "I'll be there soon," he added. And, as if realizing he was being inconsiderate (again), he added a soft, "I promise I'll tell you everything when the time is right. Please, just for now, trust me?"

And despite herself, despite how many questions she still had, the genuineness in his tone broke her down, won her over. She found herself nodding even if she couldn't stop tugging on the bottom of her hoodie. Nothing was comfortable, for a (thankfully) brief moment—not even her skin. Taking a step back, Snow offered her a small, soft smile. There were plenty of opportunities to ask him questions; she could be strategic about this.

"Thank you," he whispered, the words all but inaudible as he closed the door between them.

Time passed sluggishly for a moment, Jo's mind whirring with new questions, old questions still unanswered, images of Snow's features— softened by relief, eyes shining as they scanned her face. But unfortunately, she couldn't dwell, not when the tension of a new wish permeated the air, that buzz of magic waiting to be distributed like an electric storm searching for a spot to strike the earth. So, trying not to feel too disappointed, too frazzled by Snow's enigmatic presence, Jo turned away from his door and started heading back to the briefing room.

But not before glancing, almost on reflex, at the unmarked, black door to her right. There was no motion. Perhaps Pan was already in the briefing room? And yet the inexplicable sense of being watched wriggled up her spine.

Jo strode forward, pushing it from her mind.

# BLINK

S HE STEPPED OUT of the recreation room, pulling her watch off the small shelf next to the door and freeing up the space for someone else in the process. Jo fitted the thin black band around her wrist, the device critical to her new world of magic. A world that was beginning to feel almost . . . mundane?

Jo rubbed her eyes with the heel of her hand as she glanced toward Snow's door. They still had yet to talk further. More and more, it was beginning to feel as if they never would and the thought was putting an inexplicable ache in her chest.

Ignoring it, Jo started down the hallway. She'd made good progress on their latest wish. Nico would take over from here, giving her a much needed break.

The lights were dimmed and the windows in the central Four-Way were dark. According to her watch it was somewhere around three a.m. and it felt like there was not another living soul anywhere in the mansion. Despite not needing sleep, everyone seemed to have a collective quiet time in the late hours of the night.

Her feet stilled, stopping her in the center of the intersecting halls. Peering down the stretch that led into the common area, Jo caught a glint of movement. It was like a flash of light off a sequin, or ribbon of silken fabric.

She looked back toward the bedrooms. *She really should tell Nico that she was done hacking the records and collecting the info he needed.* But, instead, Jo's feet carried her the other way. A short detour wouldn't hurt . .
.

Tile became carpet down the long stretch of hall, muffling her footsteps. Couches, chairs, and small tables—more than could ever be occupied should every member of the Society decide to descend on them at once—absorbed every sound she made. It was so still that her ears were almost ringing, like the world was holding its breath.

She crossed the threshold into the common room, and looked around. There was no one in the kitchen, at the gaming table, or on the couches. The television was off and the patio was unoccupied.

"Huh," Jo murmured softly to herself, rubbing her eyes again. She must've been staring at the screen for too long.

When Jo lowered her hands, she was no longer alone.

Jo took a full step backward, her soul leaping from her skin and fleeing down the hall from where she'd come. The sensation of eyes on her from every angle had returned—an impossible feeling that Jo had pushed from her mind since the start of the wish.

Standing at the edge of the pool, staring at the purple-hazed mountains in the distance, was a petite woman. She wore a dress of rainbow ribbons, tied tightly around her chest and arms, bowed to cinch the fabric of her skirt. Her hands were folded at the small of her back.

As if sensing Jo's presence, she turned with a smile and gave physical eyes to the sensation of being watched. "Good evening."

"Hello, Pan," Jo replied quietly. The surreal nature of the interaction had elevated to possess a dream-like quality. Pan was never seen outside of her room, other than for wishes.

"Can't sleep?" she asked.

"None of us can." Jo thought the question odd, given their situation, but willingly ignored it. She'd ignore anything to make the encounter end faster. "Just grabbing some coffee," she lied, suddenly compelled to have a reason to both explain her presence and escape after the task was performed. Coffee sounded good anyway, she wasn't entirely running with her tail between her legs. *Right?*

"You've been sleeping for a long time, though." The woman-child's cat-like eyes seemed to flash in the darkness. "It's time to wake up."

"What?" Jo breathed.

Pan's smile widened, and she turned back to the mountain.

Without permission, Jo's feet crossed the threshold of the room, leading her out onto the patio by the pool. Pan must've heard her steps, but she didn't turn, or look, or say anything about Jo's sudden presence. She continued to stare forward into the landscape that was shades of darkness —the fake ether that the Society was nestled within.

"Do you feel it?" Pan whispered, ignoring or not hearing Jo's question.

"Feel what?"

"The pull."

"I have no idea what you're talking about." Jo went to turn away, leaving the cryptic (and likely messed up six ways to Sunday) woman-child behind. There was almost a relief in taking her eyes off of her. If she stared at Pan too long, something about her would draw Jo in and never let go. At least, that's what it felt like. "Something to do with the current wish?"

"The wishes are nothing more than a game we've been playing since the Age of Gods."

*A game? Age of Gods?* What sort of madman—woman—would think rebuilding reality to be a game? Her feet paused once more and as Jo mentally scolded them, she found herself turning to get one more look at Pan at the same time.

The mountains Pan was staring at were suddenly ablaze, silhouetted by a now violently reddish sky. Jo blinked, and like someone clicking the remote on a channel, they were back to black. She took another step backward. *What was happening?*

"Soon," Pan murmured. "It will end, soon."

Jo made the mistake of blinking again.

The woman had done a complete 180, grinning unnaturally wide and directly at Jo. The angry sky Jo had seen for a breath illuminating her shoulders from behind. She pressed her eyes closed, and everything was back to normal once more when they opened. Pan's back to her as if she hadn't moved at all.

There was not enough curiosity in the world to tempt her to ask what, exactly, was happening.

So Jo turned, wide-eyed and trembling. She did not blink all the way back to her room, coffee forgotten.

She spent the rest of the night staring out the windows of her room at Paris, seeking an oasis of comfort that now felt tainted. She willed herself to forget and the chills running up her spine to stop. When a normal sunrise scared away the demons and bogeymen haunting her thoughts, the whole affair took on a hazy, dream-like quality.

There were wishes to grant, after all. *That was all that mattered*, Jo told herself. That was their job. Though something about Pan's words stuck with her long after the details of how they were said drifted.

If the wishes were only a game . . . who were the players? And what did winning really look like?

What was the Age of Gods?

EVERY WISH HAS A COST
CIRCLE
of
ASHES
WISH QUARTET BOOK TWO
ELISE KOVA & LYNN LARSH

*for those who pay the cost*

# NOT A DRILL

JOSEPHINA ESPINOSA THRIVED on chaos.

She had been an agent of anarchy for years, operating under various organized crime syndicates (whoever had the deepest pockets at any given moment) with little concern and even less remorse for her actions. She'd worked until her fingertips were calloused from typing, her eyes were bloodshot, and her throat was raw from energy drinks. Jo had given her life to her craft, quite literally when she'd been gunned down by the Rangers of the Lone Star Republic.

No, she'd watched her *friend* get gunned down by the Rangers. Jo had narrowly escaped thanks to a magical circle meant for casting wishes and the vague memory of her grandmother's stories. It was a circle that she had fully expected to die in, but instead it, and its master Snow, had woken the latent magic in her veins and brought Jo into the Society of Wishes—a place where Jo's life had only grown crazier, granting one wish after the next for four months straight.

Until now . . . when the world was quiet.

As dawn broke over the illusion of Paris, Jo ventured from her room. She headed right for a door with a carefully painted bird and a name written in elegant script. Jo gave it a few solid knocks.

"You're early this morning." Nico opened the door with a smile, wiping his hands on a grungy paint-stained apron.

"Am I? What's early anyway?" When one existed beyond time, the hours ticking away on a clock became more guidelines than actual governances over life.

"You're getting the hang of things," he appraised.

They made their way directly to the common area to begin their morning ritual. From underneath the TV, Jo retrieved two tablets and, at the same time, Nico busied himself in the kitchen. She turned for the two chairs they had pulled together by the pool, and stalled.

Jo stopped and stared, transfixed by the mountains in the distance, as though she expected a monster to suddenly grasp their peaks with its giant claws and hoist itself over. There was something she'd seen here. A memory involving . . . *Pan, yes, she'd been involved, hadn't she?* But it had become so hazy that Jo couldn't be certain she hadn't made it up.

"Jo?" Nico's voice interrupted her thoughts.

Jo shook her head. "Sorry."

"Are you sure you're all right?" he asked as she approached.

"I'll be better with coffee. Nothing a hot cup can't fix." Jo smiled and handed him one of the two tablets. "For you."

"Thank you." He propped it against his knees as Jo sat on the chair next to his, placing hers on her own lap. The Italian man finished situated himself, taking a long sip of his espresso, eyes fluttering shut. "It is truly a delight to have someone to share the mornings with."

"You can get me to do anything if you keep making me this brew." Jo raised her mug to her lips.

"Oh, look at this." Nico held up his tablet. A sketch glowed back at her in the dim sunrise. She squinted to make out the text below the picture:

*Rare Da'Vinci Artwork Discovered. On exhibit, one week only.*

"The man was a right loon." Nico pulled the tablet back. "But it's good to see his work still being appreciated so long after."

"You knew him?" Jo didn't know why the fact surprised her. Even though Nico was a ray of sunshine in the form of a forever-nineteen-year-old man, he was actually more than five-hundred and seventy years old. "Of course you knew him," she added hastily.

"Not 'of course'; he had a different patron than I and was already an old man when I was born."

The question of who exactly that patron was, or when exactly he was born, sat heavily on her tongue, until Jo washed it away with another sip of her latte. There were two rules, sort of, when it came to the Society:

One: Use your magic to help grant wishes.

Two: Ask no one about the wish that brought them there.

She looked up from the news sprawled out across her tablet, and out at the mountains in the distance. They reflected in the stillness of the pool water before her, perfectly mirror-like and undisturbed, not even a hint of wind to mar its surface. The temperature was comfortably cool as well, as it always was, and the sun peeked from behind scattered clouds, as it always did.

It was a paradise that sat just outside of reality, a utopia in which nothing changed. It was peaceful, quiet, and all the more maddening for it. She found herself liking those mountains and their perfection less and less.

"How're things in good old Britain?" Nico pulled Jo from her thoughts.

"All seems the same." Jo continued her welcome distraction of swiping through the morning's news—"research," as Nico had explained it. They never knew where a wish would come from, but keeping up with world news could give them a good indication. Additionally, it could sometimes help them think of creative ways to lessen the Severity of Exchange for the wishes that did come in by looking at things on the macro level. "Something to do with trade treaties."

"Still?" Nico leaned over, grabbing the side of the chaise closest to Jo. His eyes skimmed the article. "Well, at least we likely won't get another wish about it."

"Why not?"

"Because of the last wish."

Their last wish had involved taking down the CEO of a British competitor to the wisher. "Why would that have anything to do with it?"

"We never seem to get a wish too similar in scope or region back-to-back. Snow's choice? Chance? Something in the magic? Whatever the reason, it has always worked out that way." Nico shrugged and tossed some of his scraggly brown hair from his eyes. As if sensing her next question before she did, he added, "As to the actual *why* it's that way, none of us have the foggiest."

"I see . . ." Jo flicked away her frustrations by thumbing through news articles. She hated the reasoning: *because magic*. It was an underlying explanation to all things in her world now. As exciting as magic was, she wished she could understand it just a little more. Or she wished she could be like everyone else and just accept it for what it was and move on.

"The variety does help keep things interesting, at least," Nico offered.

"It does." Jo forced a smile. He was trying to cheer her up; she wouldn't make him feel bad for the fact.

A loud ringing sound disturbed what had become an otherwise peaceful morning.

"What's that?" Nico twisted, looking over the back of his chair and into the common area behind them.

Jo followed his gaze, squinting at the source of the sound. Their dark-haired elf now sat on the couch, glued to the television. He seemed not to notice the high-pitched alert the speakers were emitting.

"Can you kindly turn that down, Eslar?" Nico asked.

There was no reply.

"Wait, I know that noise. Well, sort of." Jo stood, leaving the tablet on her seat. "It's like the warning they'd play when there was a tornado in the area, or ran drills for one."

"A tornado?" Nico followed behind, now giving the anomaly his full attention.

She walked up the few steps and into the shade of the common area. The tile was cold under her feet, still almost icy with the chill from the night. But Jo barely recognized it. Her eyes were glued to the TV.

*I've seen this before*, she wanted to say—mountains on fire, illuminated by a violent sky. But what escaped her mouth was different entirely. "Wh-what movie is this?" She laughed, a sort of forced, strangled sound.

Eslar made no move to respond.

Jo watched as the TV continued to scroll the announcement across the bottom of the screen in Japanese, her eyes translating instantly by magic: MT. FUJI ERUPTS. UNPRECEDENTED CATASTROPHE. DEATH TOLL UNKNOWN.

The screen filled with apocalyptic imagery alternating between news casters standing at a distance, smoke and darkness shrouding them, and social media videos posted by cell phones, most of which ending all too abruptly. Ash spewed from the earth and blacked out the sky, a stark contrast to the bright, peaceful morning where Jo currently stood.

It was worse than any horror movie she'd ever seen.

"Eslar." Nico walked over and placed a hand on the elf's shoulder, summoning him back to attention. "What is this?"

"The news."

# SHATTERED

**T**HE PHRASE "LIKE a train wreck" was one that Jo had heard used multiple times throughout her nineteen years of life, sometimes in all honesty, sometimes in hyperbole. Never before had she truly understood what that felt like, but it was undeniable now.

No matter how difficult the destruction was to watch, she couldn't seem to tear her eyes away from the screen.

"Is this live?" Jo asked, hardly above a whisper. Her voice sounded small and scared, barely even her own. Part of her already knew the answer. Eslar nodded, a single jerk of his head, as his brows furrowed.

"As of fifteen minutes ago."

"Shit . . ." Jo breathed, raising a shaking hand to cover her mouth, hiding her trembling lips. It didn't seem possible. Surely it couldn't be.

But there it was, right in front of her. A live broadcast interspersed with videos from hours ago, minutes ago, all highlighting the devastation.

Without really making the conscious decision to do so, Jo found herself dragging her feet around the edge of the couch, sitting down heavily to Eslar's right. Her hand never left her mouth, as if holding in the silent scream ringing in her ears.

"This isn't good," Nico said, mostly to himself it seemed, and when Jo managed to pry her eyes from the screen for a moment, she noticed his fingers digging hard into the back of the couch, knuckles stark white beneath his skin.

*Of course it isn't,* Jo wanted to say, wanted to *shout,* but she couldn't seem to formulate the outburst. Instead, she just turned back towards the broadcast and absorbed everything she could, hoping that eventually it would somehow stop being real.

". . .no way of anticipating the disaster," a reporter was in the process of saying. "Seismographs and supercomputers proved ineffective as the warning reached Prime Minister Tomo Nakamura barely two hours before the eruption. With no proper notice, and with transportation systems indefinitely grounded, evacuations are currently impossible and first responders are left waiting for the worst of the ash and lava flows to pass.

"Of the two million people within the surrounding cities of the Hakone region, already thirteen thousand have been proclaimed dead. The number is expected to rise as relief efforts are projected to begin in the outer, safest areas in two days."

Thirteen thousand dead, at least, in fifteen minutes.

With a jolt, Jo pulled the sleeve of her hoodie back and ran her finger along the fabric of her watch. Another ten minutes had passed since the three of them had started watching. How many more were already gone? How many more were waiting in hell for help that would never come and death that was taking far too long?

Jo looked from Nico to Eslar and back. Both men had their attention all but glued to the screen, Nico with noticeable tears in his eyes and Eslar with an expression on his face frozen somewhere between blank and tired. She wasn't looking for comfort. *She wasn't*, Jo insisted to herself. But suddenly, she couldn't help but feel cold and shaky, possibly even frightened. To call what she was witnessing "horrible" wasn't near potent enough. Jo was pretty sure that the more she watched, the more likely she was to throw up.

"You cats watching an action flick?" Wayne suddenly appeared in the entryway to the common room, Jo's back stiffening in surprise as she turned toward him. She caught the brief look of casual amusement on his face before he seemed to notice whatever emotion was betrayed by hers. "Everyone alright?" he asked, posture more on edge and voice more hesitant now. Before Jo could stop herself, she felt her expression crumple further, a hand reaching in his direction.

"Wayne?" she sniffed, and he was at her side in a second, grabbing her hand in a reassuring grip. His weight sank into the couch cushions next to her, a steady rock that she fell into willingly. It was physically closer than they'd been in months, but she needed him right now. He was the most familiar warmth in all of the Society.

"What's happening?" he asked the rest of the room, with a seriousness Jo would have scoffed at were it not for the situation. Instead, she just focused on the feel of his thumb tracing the length of her knuckles in a rhythm meant to be comforting—even if it wasn't quite. There was no comfort against something so inconceivably horrible.

"Mt. Fuji has erupted," Eslar replied without preamble, seemingly coming back to himself. "Thousands have already perished."

"Shit," Wayne cursed under his breath. Perhaps it was hysterics, but Jo felt a choked and bitter laugh crawl its way up her throat.

"That's what I said." She *thought* that was what she said, at least. Everything suddenly felt hazy and distant—like déjà vu, though she was certain she'd never witnessed something so terrible. In fact, Jo could've been blubbering this whole time and not realized it, and it wouldn't have surprised her.

Wayne squeezed her hand again and the room fell silent as they listened to the various reports, some of them recordings, some of them live. It wasn't until they'd seen the same report from earlier re-air that Wayne huffed a harsh breath through his nose, breaking the tension.

"So," he sighed, finally letting go of Jo's hand. He leaned back against the couch cushions, arms stretching along the back behind Jo's shoulders as if the furniture was the only thing propping him up. "Who's going to tell Takako?"

And, because even this alternate universe seemed just as willing to kick its immortal patrons in the ass as the real world had ever been, Takako chose that exact moment to walk into the common room.

"Tell me what?" Before anyone could say anything, the woman's eyes were drawn from her team to the television. Jo watched as a sort of quiet horror overtook Takako's face. It was only seconds later that Jo witnessed a person shatter.

# STAND DOWN, SOLDIER

"TAKAKO, WAIT!"

JO wasn't sure exactly what she would say if the woman chose to listen to her plea and stop, but she still kept her pace behind her. In fact, the entire group from the common room had followed Takako into the hall the moment she'd turned on her heel.

In the end, Wayne had been the one to tell Takako what they knew about the destruction currently ravaging her home country. And, while Jo had anticipated a more emotional response, the way Takako had nearly sprinted in the direction of the briefing room hadn't exactly been unexpected.

Jo had done the same thing once, when she'd first woken in the Society. When she'd been desperate for escape and would have given anything to return home. Takako's desperation to affirm her perceived reality stemmed from a different source, but Jo recognized it all the same.

"There's nothing you can do, Takako," Eslar called uselessly from the back of the group. Takako seemed oblivious to the comment, possibly ignoring it. But if the expression on her face was anything to go by, she was lost in her own head. Even with a persistent pace, Jo felt like she was left frantically trying to keep up.

Luckily, Wayne seemed to have a longer stride than hers, quickly pulling himself around the group and in front of Takako. About a foot away from the front of the closed briefing room door, Wayne planted a hand into the hard line of Takako's shoulder, forcing her to come to a sudden stop.

"What are you going to do?" he demanded, pushing hard enough that the woman had to take a step back for balance. Wayne looked almost unnaturally serious. "What *can* you do? Shoot the mountain?"

"Get out of my way," Takako bit back, slapping Wayne's hand away and attempting to walk around him. Wayne easily blocked her path.

"You're being a dumbass," Wayne huffed, standing his ground.

It seemed weird to hear Wayne curse, opting for something biting and incredibly modern instead of his usual colloquialisms. It made the tension thicker somehow, and as the two faced off, the rest of the group gathered behind them, waiting to see who would end the stalemate first.

For a moment, it looked like Wayne would win, but something in their silent exchange must have chipped away at his resolve. Jo couldn't see Takako's face from where she stood, but she could see Wayne's, and as if a telepathic conversation had taken place, she watched the man's expression fall and a sigh escape the downturned line of his lips.

Then, to everyone's surprise, Wayne stepped aside, allowing Takako to wrench open the door and hurry into the briefing room. It was a move brought to an almost instantaneous halt, however, Takako's form pausing barely a foot inside as Jo and the three men filed in around her.

Seated at the head of the table, as if he'd been waiting for them to arrive, was Snow.

Jo was momentarily stunned, reminded instantly of how long it had been since she'd seen him: at the end of their last wish a few weeks ago. But her last real interaction was when he had taken her through the Door, a night she might never forget. Both compounded together pulled forward lingering questions, and now certainly wasn't the time to ask. Why had he shown her his magic? And what had he meant when he'd said "the truth about hers"?

He looked as ethereal as always, silver hair falling like moonlight over one of his eyes as he stared Takako down. It was neither the time nor place to be admiring Snow's beauty, but Jo felt suddenly awkward in his presence. It was like being back in high school around Yuusuke for the first time—before they'd established themselves as purely just friends—but so much worse.

Another string of wordless dialogue later, Takako tensed without warning, startling Jo out of the distraction that always seemed to overcome her around Snow. When she redirected her full attention to the situation at hand, it was to find Takako glaring at Snow, poised and strung tight as if in anticipation of an attack.

"Let me out, Snow," she said suddenly, voice low and harsh, practically a growl. Snow seemed unfazed.

"No," he replied simply, getting to his feet with a casual air that didn't fit with the strained and restless atmosphere at all. "There is nothing that can be done now and none of you should risk being tempted to spend your extra time unnecessarily."

"I have to help them," Takako grit out, hands tightening into fists at her side. Jo felt the pain in the woman's voice tug on her own heart. "I have to save them. That's what we do, isn't it? Save people?"

"Sometimes," Snow admitted, and Jo could practically taste the bitterness on the back of her tongue from everything left unsaid. Sure, *sometimes* they saved people, but sometimes they didn't. It depended on the wish. And even though Takako must have known that, Jo also had little doubt that, for Takako, making any desperate attempt to help her kin was the only conceivable action.

"Then let me go to them," Takako tried again, not pleading, not demanding, but hopelessly lost somewhere between.

"No," Snow repeated, holding his ground with an intimidating authority. If Jo didn't know any better, she'd say the temperature in the room had dropped, a crackling energy shifting between the two like a magical stand-off. Then, Snow added, "It will be torture for you to see them and be unable to help."

"I won't ask you again, Snow," Takako said, tone hard. "Let me out."

Snow stayed silent, but his answer was clear. He would not move.

Unfortunately, Takako's response was clear as well. Suddenly, almost too quickly for Jo to see the transition, Takako was pulling a gun from the holster at her hip and pointing it in Snow's direction.

Jo was too stunned to do much more than gasp, but at least one or two of the men behind her shouted Takako's name, demanded she lower her weapon, even moved to act. To which Snow merely held up a hand in their direction, keeping them from interfering.

To his credit, Snow seemed completely calm in the face of Takako's assault, eerily so. In fact, he looked as though he were about to have a normal conversation with the Japanese woman, as if she wasn't currently pointing a gun right between his eyes.

"Get out of my way," Takako demanded, thumb reaching over to unclick the safety. In the near-oppressive silence of the briefing room, with nothing but their breaths playing shaky accompaniment, that single click was deafening. "You know I won't miss."

Jo wasn't even sure if Snow could be killed by a bullet; she didn't know if he could be killed at all, if any of them could be anymore. What did immortal spirits have to fear from death? But in that moment, all that mattered was that Takako believed in her threat and, as she took aim, it was obvious she intended to test that theory.

Before she could pull the trigger, however, Snow took a step away from the table, gathered his height, and stared down the nozzle of the gun. He took another step forward and Takako's steady hold on the gun began to waver. Snow reached out, grabbing the muzzle in a display of both confidence and fearlessness.

"Stand down, soldier," he said, almost gently. "This is a battle with no winner."

For a second, Takako didn't respond, gun still poised to fire. Jo held her breath, the whole room seemingly waiting at the edge of a proverbial cliff, wondering if they were going to fall off completely or simply stumble away from the ledge.

Then, as if a switch had flipped, Jo watched the tightness of Takako's back loosen, the straight line of her arms sag a bit at the elbows. Without a word, she re-engaged the safety on her gun, pulled it from Snow's grasp, and returned it to its holster.

"My apologies," she said, bending forward into a deep and rigid-looking bow. When she raised herself back up and turned towards the group, it was without an ounce of expression on her face.

They didn't even need to be asked; Eslar and Wayne stepped to one side and Jo and Nico to the other, letting Takako pass. She did so without a word, movements borderline mechanical.

It wasn't until Takako had disappeared from sight that Jo felt she could breathe again, and even when she did, her inhale was shaky, scraping at the back of her throat and burning deep into her chest. Takako's words still rang in her ears.

*That's what we do, isn't it? Save people?*

How were they supposed to do that when their hands were shackled by wishes that weren't even their own?

# MUGICHA

S NOW ROUNDED THE table and started for the door, pausing briefly to utter a command directly to Eslar: "Look after her."

Jo kept her eyes pinned to the Door on the opposite side of the room. The steel was as cold and inflexible as Snow's words; neither had any heart. She clenched her fists, feeling like she was made of fire in a room that was now colder than ice.

"Understood," Jo heard Eslar say, though it sounded like he was now on some distant planet far, far away from where she stood.

She listened to Snow's footsteps as they left: boots clicking on the obsidian floor of the briefing room, muffled weight on the carpet of the hall, and eventually, nothing at all. Even if she could understand him, even if she *wanted* to understand him, she couldn't. What Snow had done had been in Takako's best interest, hadn't it? Yet if that were true, why did it feel so heartless?

Jo still couldn't erase the anger she felt at the nearly militaristic way it had all been handled. People were dying—no, more than that; Takako hadn't joined the Society that long ago, which meant her *family* was likely dying. If there was any time for compassion in their operation, it was now. Yet all their leader seemed to give them was the bitter reminder that they were nothing more than slaves to the circumstances of their existence. Would it have really done so much damage to let her go through the Door?

A hand fell on Jo's shoulder, jolting her back from her thoughts.

"Coming?" She could tell Wayne was repeating himself, though how many times he'd addressed her was a total mystery.

"Where?"

"We're going back to watch the news," Nico said softly.

"No." Jo swallowed back the bile that rose up in her throat at the mere idea of sitting there again and watching the carnage. Turning her eyes away wasn't going to help, but neither was watching it. She was useless to everyone if she let her sanity crack now.

Out of the millions who needed it, there was only one person Jo could help right now. It was almost nothing, in the grand scope. But at least helping *someone* was *something*.

"You guys go on ahead," she encouraged.

"I don't want to leave you alone." Wayne, well meaning and thick-headed as always.

"I'm not going to be alone," Jo corrected him.

"Then who—"

"We'll leave you to it," Eslar interrupted Wayne. "Thank you for looking after her."

*Someone has to*, Jo thought bitterly. It seemed no one else was clamoring to rise to the task. "No problem."

Jo followed the three men back through the hall and to the Four-Way.

"Let me know if you need anything." Nico pulled her in for a tight hug, one Jo was eager to return. He was calm, calm enough to remind Jo that this was far from the first massive tragedy he'd ever witnessed. She wondered if she could be like him someday, taking turmoil in her stride, smiling all the same. It seemed an impossibly hard thing to do. The only thing that could be harder was the idea of doing it again, and again, and again.

Jo pulled away and assessed the man with the sunshine smile. He'd been born during the Renaissance, was old enough to have seen dozens of wars, immeasurable horrors, and he could still smile as genuinely as he did. She didn't know if it was admirable or terrifying. In what way did a heart have to contort to be able to do that?

"Will do." Jo dismissed him and her thoughts before they could linger in a place that was far too negative. This team was all she had; she couldn't allow suspicions to form surrounding someone's goodness. It was just the shock and hurt talking, she knew.

She turned right, heading up the stairs toward the recreation rooms. There was no sign of Snow in the hallway, even if she squinted all the way to the very end. Jo wasn't sure if his absence was relieving or disappointing. It was likely for the best, either way. She was emotionally off-balance, somewhat upset with the man's actions (even if she didn't really have any right to be), and not in the best headspace to exchange words.

Much to her surprise, and despite Takako's much earlier comments about what she did when she needed to "clear her head," both recreation rooms were void of watches—no sign of Takako at either.

That left one other option.

Jo headed in the opposite direction, back toward the Four-Way, up the other set of stairs, and toward her own room. However, instead of turning left at the end of the hall, she turned right and was faced with the nameplate that greeted her every morning: *Takako*. Taking a deep breath, Jo gave a gentle knock on the door.

Several seconds passed and wore at her resolve. There was no word, no response. She should leave the woman be.

But something wouldn't let her.

"Takako," Jo said softly, knocking again. "I know you're in there." She didn't, actually. But she couldn't imagine where else her friend would be. They didn't have *that* many options for privacy in the Society. "Please, open the door?"

Just as Jo had committed herself to sitting on the floor and waiting in the hall until Takako was ready to let someone in, the door finally cracked open. Takako stood rigid, half her body still hidden on the other side.

"Yes?"

"May I come in?" Jo asked, wishing it sounded stronger. She wasn't going to take no for an answer, yet wanted to let it be Takako's choice.

"Why?" The woman questioning her was nothing like the Takako Jo knew. She'd burrowed deep into this shell of curt responses. Not that Jo could blame her.

"Because I don't think you should be alone." Being honest came easier than she expected it to, and it seemed to startle the woman. Seeing her hesitation, Jo doubled down. "We don't have to talk. I can just, be there . . "

*As if merely being there could ever be enough*, she mentally chided herself. But to her surprise, Takako stepped back and allowed the door to swing open wide enough for Jo to enter. She stepped in quickly.

She'd seen rooms like this in pamphlets for Japanese resorts, nice hotels, even in one of her former employer's homes. It was an open space, with ten woven grass mats making up the floor. Wooden beams supported cream-colored, sand-paper-textured walls on three sides. The fourth side had *shoji*—wood and paper—screens pulled open to a wooden platform that overlooked a small garden space. A pastel sunset glowed behind purple mountains.

It was the epitome of Japanese architecture. Yuusuke would've been proud of Jo for just how much of her Japanese she could recall without the use of magic: a *horigotatsu* in the center of the room, a *tokonoma* with a scroll displaying calligraphy, an oversized closet where Jo fully expected to find *futon* tucked away. Yet, as picture-perfect as it all was, it still felt lived in. There were little accents here and there displayed above the rest, placing personalization before the picturesque, and making it feel like a home.

Takako busied herself at an electric kettle. Her movements were measured and precise as she filled up two small cups and put them on a tray with Japanese rice crackers between them. Jo left her to it, stepping onto the wooden platform just beyond the *shoji* and taking a seat.

There was a crash and an expletive from behind her that had Jo turning.

"Are you—"

"I'm fine," Takako snapped. "I just . . . I'm fine." she said much softer, in that same barely-controlled way as she cleaned up the mess of tea that had just spilled across her small counter. Jo knew it was much the opposite, but said nothing as Takako lifted the tray, setting it between them. "The tea isn't much."

"*Mugicha* makes me think of home."

"Of home?" Takako said, startled. "I would've never imagined we would share a similarity on this."

"Why not?" Jo couldn't help but laugh at her ever-mechanical nature.

"Because you're from America."

"Lone Star Republic, technically," Jo gently corrected. She didn't have enough nationalistic pride to take offense. Especially since Takako had never actually lived in a time where the LSR existed.

"Right . . ." Takako shifted her cup from hand to hand. "Still can't imagine there's a big drive for *mugicha* in Texas."

"Well, yeah, fair . . . but plenty of people emigrate from East Japan." Jo looked down at the tray, selecting the cup closest to her. She wished she hadn't brought up the discussion of home, but it was far better for her to distract Takako with her own home than let the Japanese woman think of hers. So, Jo rambled away. "My friend, Yuusuke. You remember him I'm sure with the whole first wish debacle?" Jo cringed slightly. "His father immigrated to the Lone Star Republic for work from the California prefecture. That's how we met in high school."

"East Japan . . ." Takako said slowly, as if hearing it for the first time.

"Well, yeah . . ." Jo thought back, she didn't have to go very far. World War III hadn't ended all that long ago. And it wasn't like the details were very important. "I mean, technically, I think it's all 'Japan,' but everyone calls the annexation of what was California, Washington, Oregon, and Nevada 'East Japan.'" Jo took a long sip of tea. It was nostalgia in a cup. She and Yuusuke had let go of it long ago in favor of things with enough caffeine to kill a small animal. But it was the same rich, earthy taste she remembered from when they'd first become friends.

Despite herself, she wondered how he was doing now, *what* he was doing now. She shouldn't still care, but she hoped he was safe. And perhaps it was that hope against hope that had Jo sitting where she was now, understanding all too well what Takako was feeling—worry for people she should've let go long ago.

Takako was silent, a frown passing over her face.

Jo shifted to face the woman. "I'm sorry, I shouldn't have brought up Japan." How stupid could she really be?

"It's not that." Takako shook her head.

"Then . . ." Jo let the word trail off into an open-ended question. She wasn't sure if it was safe to ask anything. There were memories they all had of their past lives that were better left forgotten.

The other woman took a deep, slow breath—in through the nose and out through the mouth, as if bracing. "My wish."

"Your wish? What does your wish have to do with anything?" Jo brought up a hand to her mouth, having startled herself. Here she was, having just scolded herself for prodding Takako, and now she'd asked the one probing question the Society considered taboo. "Sorry, I shouldn't have—"

"It's fine." Takako shook her head. "I've been meaning to tell you, to seek your forgiveness."

"Forgiveness for what?" Jo had come to console *her*, and now Takako was trying to turn the tide. But Jo wasn't going to allow it. Or at least, she thought she wasn't, but her mind went a bit blank the moment Takako opened her mouth again.

"I destroyed your country."

# TAKAKO'S WISH

"**Y**OU . . . WHAT?"

FOR a long moment, Takako didn't elaborate. She simply reached for her own cup of tea and stared deep into the depths of it, face lined with too many conflicted emotions for Jo to count. Then, as if finally finding her resolve, she set it back down with a heavy *thud*.

"I admit, when you joined the Society and I realized you were American—or, from what had been America at least, I felt . . . a bit guilty," Takako explained, not that it made her previous confession any less nonsensical. "I guess you could say I took your country away from you. I destroyed what could have been, so to speak."

"What are you talking about?" Jo tried to smile, but it felt a bit disjointed, her confusion overwhelming her features. Took away her country? How? She'd lived in it for nineteen years.

Whether in attempts to explain, or simply to get the words out, Takako ignored her question for a moment, shaking her head. "I must have seemed standoffish at first, and for that I apologize, but I simply didn't know what to say, not knowing what I know. But I still wanted you to feel welcome. And, I suppose, I wanted to make it up to you somehow. Everyone else was so much better at it than I . . . But I guess they've had more practice."

The gifts, the kindness. That had been Takako's attempt at assuaging guilt?

Jo frowned, looking from Takako's face to her own cup. Despite the comfortably warm feel of the ceramic beneath her fingers, the tea still steamed, as if the cup should be much hotter to her touch. Jo wondered if it should be burning her, if it actually was, and the day had merely numbed all senses.

"I don't . . ." Jo shook her head, confused. She wanted to understand what Takako was saying, but she didn't know how to ask for clarification. She didn't doubt the genuineness of Takako's kindness, regardless of the underlying intention, but her reasoning still felt beyond Jo's reach. Her country had been just fine, hadn't it? The Lone Star Republic continued on throughout Jo's short lifetime as it had always done. Not that she paid much attention to politics beyond her connections with the nation's dark underbelly. What wish could Takako possibly have made?

Jo's frustration must have become obvious, because eventually, Takako sighed, raking her hands through her hair and tugging on it.

"In 2010, our countries were at war," she began, and when Jo met her gaze, there was a despondency there that she was unfamiliar with when it came to the kind, but stoic, woman.

Jo remembered reading about World War III. History wasn't exactly her favorite subject, but the war had only ended in 2015, just forty-two years before Jo joined the Society (a narrow enough piece of time that the veterans never let anyone forget), so it was hard *not* to know about the war. A rising tide of nationalism had pulled the former United States in on itself, retreating from its allies and making stronger enemies of old nemeses that ultimately formed the "Commonwealth Powers."

"The war started in 2007, right?" Jo asked, more for her own confirmation, whilst trying to remember exactly when Takako said she'd been born.

Takako nodded. "It did. Japan was emboldened when the U.S. lent its support toward militarization—the de facto 'Warden of the East.' It was a potent blend with the determined drive forward on building the nation as a military power."

"And then there was the China-Japan war."

"In which, the use of Japanese force had the U.S.A. positioning itself against my country, and Japan siding with Russia." The way she spoke was clinical, void of emotion or any real investment. Takako spoke like she was the one reading a textbook, espousing facts and nothing more. Until her voice began to waver. "I . . . I was a soldier, and I was afraid." Her hand balled into a fist; Takako hung her head.

Suddenly, the woman's skill with a gun made a lot more sense. Jo reached out, taking her hand, and startling Takako into meeting her gaze. "That's okay. I can't imagine how terrifying it was . . . ." She had never seen war. When Jo had grown up, the world was at peace. Well, minus the odd squabbles in North America's Midwest, where no one could seem to decide what was a territory of what, who ruled themselves, and which regions were allied.

"You don't understand. I thought—that is to say, there were rumors . . . That the U.S. would unleash biological warfare."

Jo didn't remember reading anything about that, one way or another. So she kept her mouth shut and just listened.

"That was when I made my wish."

In the silence that followed the barely-there confession, Jo found herself mulling over Takako's words. It had been long enough since Jo'd taken her last sip that her tea should have gotten cold. Instead, it was still the perfect temperature. She gave thanks to the small comforts magic could give.

"Japan was losing—or you thought Japan would lose—in your time-line, so you wished for Japan to win the war. And that's the world I was born into," Jo clarified, thinking of the odd events leading up to the Commonwealth Powers' victory: a series of tactical errors, miscommunications and weather phenomena that resulted in the USA's western fleet being condensed and subsequently decimated. That was followed almost immediately by a decisive and unforeseen strike on the eastern seaboard, which resulted in enemy boots on the ground.

It was too many unfortunate events to happen merely by chance. Takako nodded, as if reading her mind.

"I don't quite remember what I said to Snow anymore." Takako paused before Snow's name, grinding it out. "My memory of making the wish is hazy, like trying to remember a dream, but I do know that I'd been thinking about my family. My mother and father, my sister. I wanted them to be safe. At the time, winning the war seemed like the only way to ensure that, and I was willing to do anything if it meant securing their safety. My family—" Takako paused, taking a deep breath she let out on another rough sigh. "My family is everything I have, even if they no longer remember who I am." She buried her head in her hands. "It's not fair, none of it."

Instantly, with those words, Jo was brought back to the present.

She had never related more fiercely to another's sentiment. Her mother's blood still flowed through Jo's veins, even if memories of Jo no longer flowed through her head. As one-sided as those memories were now, Jo would treasure them for a literal eternity. Even Lydia, a sibling Jo never had the opportunity to know and born in a timeline where she'd never lived, now held a small place in her heart—a sense of gratitude that her mother was not spending her life without the companionship of a daughter.

Takako held a similar, undying love for her family. And right now, though Jo did not know for sure, she would bet that they were currently in the path of Mt. Fuji's fury. And Snow refused to let Takako even attempt to save them.

Another flash of anger sparked in Jo's chest at the thought, but she smothered it, forcing herself to stay calm, focusing on Takako and the turmoil she could now see swirling behind her eyes. She couldn't save Takako's family for her. If Jo was honest with herself, Takako's family likely couldn't be saved at all—everything in the world was at the whim of wishers. But at this moment, for what it was worth, she could at least offer her an end to her guilt.

"Look, Takako," she started, taking what she hoped looked like a casual sip of her tea. "I appreciate you telling me, your trust. But I honestly don't care one way or another what America could've looked like versus what it did when I lived there. If it was one single nation, or split up as it is . . . None of it matters."

As expected, Takako looked startled by the admission, and Jo couldn't bite back the smirk that tugged at her own lips in response.

"If America had won, I'd be working for the mafia, probably some descendants of Wayne's old friends. Take a moment and imagine how *that* would've been." Even Takako smiled slightly at the remark. "Regardless, my life wouldn't exactly have been different in a sovereign nation. I mean, maybe I worked with the Yakuza a bit more in the timeline you created? But hell, with the internet, I might have worked for them anyway."

"You don't know that. You might have been happier."

Jo just shrugged. It was almost a little odd to feel *nothing* for her homeland, as if it had never really been her home to begin with. "No, I don't *know* anything. But I highly doubt my family would have been well off either way, and I definitely would have been doing the exact same thing no matter what reality I'd grown up in. I know no different, and who my boss is never really mattered as long as the pay was right. Home, what's really important about it, isn't land or walls but the people who occupy them—it's the people who matter, and I would've had those same people in any reality. So you'll find no hard feelings about your wish here."

Takako didn't seem to know how to take that, so Jo added, "But if what you're looking for is forgiveness, it's yours." Jo squeezed the woman's hand lightly. "I don't blame you, Takako. But I forgive you for whatever you think you need forgiveness for."

For a long, drawn-out moment, Takako looked at their hands, not quite holding, but resting comfortably against each other. Then, Takako stretched her hand out beneath the touch and linked her fingers with Jo's, gripping tightly for a moment before simply settling into the hold. It felt like a thank you, so Jo took it as one, rubbing her thumb gently over Takako's.

Another, more comfortable length of silence passed before Takako spoke again.

"Megumi, my sister," she whispered. "I've been watching her grow, following her life as best I can from here. She's almost forty now. My niece and nephew just turned twelve last month. Twins, actually."

As much as it pained her, Jo could tell where she was going with this, could hear the way each word had been wrought in barbed wire and caught all the way up Takako's throat. She didn't want to be right, but Jo knew the universe was not that kind.

"Two years ago, the family moved from our sleepy mountain town to Shizuoka for work." When Jo looked up from their intertwined fingers to Takako's eyes, she was unsurprised but heartbroken to find them shiny with unshed tears.

"There's no way they'll be able to evacuate in time, especially not now, and that's if they're not—"

This part, Takako couldn't finish, but Jo didn't need her to—didn't *want* her to. Neither of them had seen the news since this morning. For all either of them knew, Takako's family was already dead.

There was nothing Jo could say, she realized. Nothing of value she could offer as comfort or solace or distraction. All she had was her presence, the promise of her nearness, to combat the crushing weight of suffocating solitude. For a moment, Jo allowed herself to think of what it would feel like if her own family was in the path of the volcano's wrath. What would she be feeling? Would she want to be alone?

The answer to the first question was too much to consider.

The answer to the second was no.

"Can I stay with you for a little while longer?" Jo asked, keeping her voice soft, letting every ounce of her own sorrow shine through. Takako didn't hesitate, nodding her head and closing her eyes tight when the motion caused her tears to fall at last. As Takako gripped her hand, Jo witnessed the second of two seemingly immovable mountains tumble.

"Please."

# RESTRICTIONS

TAKAKO WAS FINALLY still.

Jo wouldn't have called the sleep restful; perhaps it wasn't even sleep at all, more like a forced stasis. Every now and again Takako's brow furrowed and she twisted, no doubt haunted by any number of ghosts, before settling again. But it was a reprieve, at least.

Takako hadn't entirely bought into the idea of closing her eyes at first, calling it a "pointless waste of time." But Jo's argument that sometimes wasting time was the best thing to do won out, and the Japanese woman had laid down her head and let her consciousness escape her.

It was the only escape they really had.

Takako had separated her two futon and given Jo the better of the two blankets, even though Jo would've lied out on bare tatami to make Takako more comfortable. With one hand, she still clutched at Jo's fingers. Throughout drinking their remaining tea in relative silence, and then talking about some stupid computer babble that Jo had practically invented for the sake of distracting her friend, the other woman had held onto Jo. Even as they'd fallen asleep, Takako held onto her between the futon as though she were a teddy bear—her comfort.

Jo closed her eyes, and when she opened them, she saw a different person altogether.

Yuusuke lay across from her, a memory painting over Jo's vision fresh and clear. It was one of their first jobs, holed up in some shitty motel room, the only thing two high school students just striking out could afford. He'd been paranoid, afraid of failure, nervous of the career paths they'd chosen for themselves. She'd reassured him then, stayed with him in his bed until he finally slept. Not quite a lover, but certainly more than a friend. Something that was a bit better than both.

Who had Yuusuke leaned on in her revised world? Who did he go to? Did he share that hotel room with someone else or no one at all?

Jo closed her eyes again, but this time a different sight greeted her. It was a flash—a blink then gone. But Jo could've sworn she'd seen a woman, screeching as Jo was taken away from her. Jo fluttered her eyelashes several times, but couldn't conjure back the sight, couldn't even conjure a memory of it. It was as if it had never happened at all.

Sufficiently too unnerved to rest as well, Jo carefully unraveled her fingers from Takako's, watching for any signs of disturbance. There were none. She remembered the embarrassment Yuusuke had endured the morning after he'd shown "such weakness" (his words) and, just in case, she'd save Takako some face without her asking.

Somehow, despite the invisible weights that had been chained to her shoulders, Jo managed to stand. Takako was undisturbed. Jo continued to watch for any signs otherwise, but her friend remained motionless up to the moment Jo closed the door behind her.

Jo pressed her forehead against the wood, taking a deep and shuddering breath. Eventually, it would stop hurting; it had to. Technically, she knew no one in the volcano's path of destruction. Technically, she knew no one in the world as it was. But there was something visceral about the pain. Something that, surely, every human felt at seeing another in such unavoidable agony. And it was a feeling only magnified by Takako's turmoil.

"How is she?" Like a godsend, Nico's voice pulled her from the well of suffering she'd been dipping into.

"How do you think?" Jo snapped despite herself, instantly regretting the tone. "I'm sorry, I'm just spent. I didn't mean that."

"No, no, it was a foolish question." Nico continued smiling on, even if it was a bit pitying, an underlying sadness beneath the soft expression. Nothing could discourage that man's smile, it seemed. He was the only ray of joy in the universe at the moment when the whole world needed him, and only seven others knew of his existence. "Why don't you come and sit with me for a bit? Take a break from all this. I just made some coffee."

"I can't possibly take your coffee." Her hands and feet didn't have ears to hear what her mouth was saying, as they were already crossing over to take the cup Nico had in his hands.

"Think nothing of it." Nico opened the door to his room, and Jo entered without further resistance. It offered the same atmosphere that was part home, part nostalgia for a world, time, and lifestyle she'd never known.

"Thank you." Jo murmured. Her eyes suddenly fell on his easel. "I have an idea."

"What's that?"

"You should paint Takako something."

"Jo—"

She bristled at the tone of his voice, not wanting to hear his objection. She didn't care if his muse didn't feel up to the task. Takako needed it desperately. "Something simple, just like you did for me. Something to remind her of home and family . . . Or, better yet, give her hope."

"I can't do that."

"What? Why?" Jo turned so quickly that she almost spilled her coffee. "Is this some rule passed down by Snow? Because if so, I swear that he's gone too far and you need to ignore him."

"I can't, Jo," Nico repeated.

It was like the glass of the framed photo she'd worked so hard to mentally create, the one that encompassed the happy smiling picture of Nico, of their whole team, fractured in that moment. "Why is no one else looking out for each other? How are you all okay to just stand by and be divided? And by what? Obligation? How do you never *question*—"

"Jo." Nico placed his hands on her shoulders. Even though Jo felt like her bones continued to vibrate under his palms, her mind was settled for the briefest of moments, long enough to actually hear what he'd been trying to say. "Even if I wanted to—*which I do*—I can't."

"But . . . *Why?*"

He led her over to one of his chairs, squeezing in next to her. It was a little smaller than a loveseat and the fit was tight. But instead of uncomfortable, it felt warm and safe. Jo pulled her feet up onto the cushion as he spoke, cradling her mug.

It was then she noticed that the mug was indeed *hers*. The one she always used. The one Takako had gotten Samson to make for her.

Nico had planned this.

Jerk.

"Has no one told you of restrictions, yet?"

"Restrictions?" Jo repeated. "No. Oh, let me guess, this is another bit of magic nonsense that doesn't actually make any sense but we have to abide by because . . . reasons?"

Nico actually laughed and the sound of genuine amusement was a balm even better than coffee—and that said something, because very few things were ever better than coffee. "Something like that, yes."

"Great."

He nudged her with his shoulder and Jo sighed softly, letting out her sarcasm before asking, "So, go on then. What are 'restrictions'?"

"Every magic has some sort of limitation on it. It varies from person to person, but everyone in the Society has something that restricts when and how they can use their magic."

Jo thought of Snow as Nico spoke. Could a power that great be restricted by anyone or anything? But she stayed silent on the matter. Snow had never outright said not to, but Jo couldn't imagine speaking to anyone else of the special place he'd taken her to on the other side of the Door. What he'd shown her felt innately private. She wouldn't violate that confidence, no matter how many other stupid rules he imposed on them.

Nico continued, "For example, Wayne's is obvious. The bet must be about money. A relatively generous restriction compared to mine."

"What's yours?"

"My power only works on a person once. To look at one of my paintings a second time would do nothing."

"*What?*"

He chuckled at her shocked reaction. "The person must be lost in the canvas. They can't over-analyze, or the magic won't take its hold. So, once a person knows how my magic works, even subconsciously, it can no longer be effective on them."

"How is that remotely fair?"

"Magic isn't fair." Truer words hadn't been spoken that day.

"So, what's mine?" Jo couldn't help but wonder when she'd stop learning things about her new life. It'd been almost six months, after all.

"I don't know. You have to discover that on your own." Nico patted her knee and stood.

"Wonderful." Jo bitterly turned her attention to the wide window, signaling that she was done with the conversation. Perhaps, on a normal day, she'd have more patience for it. But today, there just wasn't anything left in the tank to deal with the nuances of magic.

Nico crossed over to his easel and the canvas that waited for him. Nothing more than a mass of color was stroked upon the negative space—an image of chaos that could only be called to order by the artist.

"What're you painting?" Jo asked. Her voice softened instantly with a change of topic.

"Julia."

As soon as he said the name, Jo saw it: the silhouette of a person yet taking form. She saw the early highlights of a brow and nose. She saw the mass of brown that would ultimately become hair. If Nico hadn't just told her that he couldn't use his magic on her again, she would've assumed it to be something fantastical to suddenly see the structure of the piece.

"Tell me about her?" Jo put her coffee mug on the floor and spread out on the sofa, though the stretch of cushions suddenly felt too big for one. She rested her head on the tall armrest, watching him as he set to work.

"My Julia?"

"Yes."

"She was my muse. The stars were born of her tears and the sun of her smiles. She was everything good in my world and far more than I ever deserved. We lived in Florence . . ."

As Nico spoke, his words tickled something in the back of Jo's mind—something she'd read in the recreation room months ago about a Julia around Nico's time, the mistress of some pope. But the paragon of goodness and purity Nico was describing surely couldn't be the same woman. There had to have been dozens of Julias in Florence back then . . .

Nico continued to speak, and the words, alight with the flame of love kept alive after all this time, was a beacon that lured her mind toward an oasis of calm in the storm that bellowed just outside of the Society's existence.

# WAITING GAME

J O WATCHED NICO paint until her eyes were bloodshot and he was rubbing stiffness from his fingers.

She'd stolen a heavy blanket from his bed somewhere around the time the conversation was dying, and had bundled herself up in it. It wasn't that the room was cold, but that she *felt* cold. Jo felt as if she'd been pitched out to the vacuum of space. The only tether she had to the world was the sound of Nico's voice and, when that gave out, his brush.

At about the four-hour mark, Jo wished she could sleep. But it refused to come to her. No matter how much her mind begged for the relief, her body refused. So she settled for unfocusing her eyes and pushing her mind into a void until Nico stepped away from the easel, stretching, indicating that he was finished (for now).

"I should pick up a hobby." It was the first time either of them had broken the silence in—Jo tapped her watch—three hours.

"A hobby? Seems like a good idea. What would you do?" He swirled his brush in a jar of mud-colored water.

"I don't know, maybe you could teach me how to paint? It seems cathartic." Jo stood, folded up Nico's quilt, and walked over to set it on his bed. Not for the first time, Jo couldn't help but admire the man's room; the homey messiness and the warm colors mirrored the half-finished canvases splattered in paint and ink.

"I'm afraid we wouldn't have enough time for that." He placed the first brush in a different jar, and started the process on the second.

"Don't we have eternity?"

"I'm afraid," he said again slowly, "we wouldn't have enough time for that."

"Oh, *ha ha*, very funny." Jo rolled her eyes, walking over to the canvas.

It was further along now, the streaks of color more obviously swirling into the silhouette of a woman. A beautiful woman, young and smiling and caught in laughter. It was breathtaking, even without Nico's magic Jo's eyes were drawn to it and only it.

In many ways, the Society was a shame. Niccolo de'Este would never receive the acclaim he so rightly warranted. His pieces would never win awards or hang in museums; he would never be compared to Pollock or Van Gogh or Murakami. Instead, he would only ever be appreciated by a sparse group of seven—most of whom had questionable taste. It was far, far less than someone of his talent deserved.

Jo could already feel the tell-tale ache in her heart growing thicker, lecherous—the same ache that seemed to thrive on realizations directly linked to her new reality. No matter how accepting she was of it, there was no helping the occasional feelings of loss that cropped up even still. For all intents and purposes, Nico was only nineteen. He should be studying art on a full ride at some university somewhere (or whatever the Renaissance equivalent was). He should be selling pieces by the dozens at local art shows. He should be living, just like *she* should be living. But their lives had been taken, all in exchange for the realities of people who would never know of their involvement, their existence.

Just like magic itself, it wasn't fair. Jo sucked in a breath and thought with vehement sorrow that, even if they had all agreed to join the Society in their own ways for their own reasons, the prices they paid didn't seem to balance out.

"I tease," Nico said, oblivious to the torrent of thoughts that consumed her steps over to him and the easel. "Of course I would love to teach you to paint."

His voice was light, the banter easy, serving as a reminder that there was nothing she could do. She wasn't going to waste her time wallowing in righteous self-pity. "Fair" was hardly a driving factor in the whirring cogs and gears of the universe's clock, wasn't it? The members of the Society no more deserved their fates than the citizens of Japan deserved theirs, but that didn't make any of it any less real.

"Well, you may be right, a different hobby might suit me better."

"Then we shall find it together." Nico gave his hands one more wipe on his apron, though the motion was hopeless. The garment had just as much pigment on it as had soaked into his skin. His expression shifted, and there was only a second before he spoke, but a second was long enough for Jo to fill with dread at what she knew he'd say next. "For now, however, I think we should return to the rest of them."

A flash of panic ran down Jo's spine at the thought, the sudden realization brought her back to the reality that existed beyond the reprieve that had been Nico's room with a fierce and sobering shock. They'd been sitting for nearly six hours. Had the majority of the carnage already settled? Did the volcano, god forbid, erupt again while they'd selfishly escaped their unwritten duty of bearing witness to the world's horrors?

Surely someone was still in the common area watching the news. The onset of the desire to know exactly what had transpired over the last couple of hours was swift and almost visceral, as if she was now personally connected to the damage and lives lost. Whether it was Takako's legitimate association, or her own vicarious attachment, she felt instantly guilty for not keeping up to date.

"You're right. I want to see what's happened."

With that, Jo and Nico wordlessly made their way down the hall. Not unexpectedly, there wasn't just one person sitting on the couch in front of the television, but three.

Eslar leaned forward, elbows on his knees and chin resting on his laced fingers. He seemed to be almost unnaturally engrossed in the news (how he had the stamina completely eluded her), analyzing what appeared to be new footage with a frown. Jo wondered if he'd even left the couch once. Samson sat to his side, occasionally whispering things in one of the elf's long ears. Wayne was an island at the far end of the couch, his grim expression warding off company. No one seemed to notice Jo and Nico's arrival, and as she shifted her gaze from the men to the television, it wasn't hard to understand why.

Most of the broadcast seemed to circulate between reporters' comments about the carnage—of which there was a near indescribable amount—and actual footage of it. Mt. Fuji seemed to have finally settled. According to the scientists (for whatever their assessments were still worth) there were no further eruptions expected in the foreseeable future. That didn't stop the continual oozing of lava and thick blanket of ash that now seemed to cover the globe. It was hard to believe, even harder to hope, that Mt. Fuji would stay dormant for long, not when its eruption had been so unexpected and violent.

Even if Mt. Fuji never erupted again, the catastrophe had already left its permanent mark, not just on Japan, but on the entire world.

"Look what the cat dragged in." Wayne noticed their presence, his dry remark cutting Jo from the constricting tethers of grief that had already begun to form between her and the television. "We'd wondered where you two had gone."

"*He'd* wondered," Samson corrected bravely, but still very quietly and without raising his head.

"You could've come and got us," Jo said defensively.

"A reprieve is sometimes necessary," said the elf, who had barely moved from the television and still did not tear his eyes from it. "And there is not much to be done, for now."

Samson caught her eye, but seemingly wasn't able to speak until he'd ducked his chin again. "I made some breakfast for everyone."

Slowly, Jo walked the rest of the way to the couch, leaning heavily against it. "Thanks, Sam. That's very thoughtful of you," she murmured, distracted by the images flickering across the TV screen.

They were showing footage of the Hakone region now, still smoldering in some places, burning in others, but mostly just completely destroyed. With a sickening lurch, Jo found herself subconsciously comparing the sight to old photos she remembered learning about in her high school's ancient history class—the entirety of Pompeii sitting in ruins, whole families frozen forever in their last moments of life, completely unaware of it being taken from them. The images of the long-ago Roman city came alive vividly in her mind, like she'd seen it before. Jo attributed it to the footage she'd all but seen on loop now overlaying with her past school lesson.

She wasn't sure what was worse, seeing something like this coming, or being blindsided. For example, Shizuoka had watched their neighboring region fall to the might of a natural disaster, knowing all the while they were next. Multiple clips of a tsunami, triggered by the quake, only added to the still spreading damage.

It was truly becoming too much to bear, a relentless assault of one thing after another after another.

She didn't know how the men continued to do it, stare at the news with their somber tones, as if seeing something she couldn't. So, Jo didn't bear it. She turned away and stepped toward the kitchen, where Samson had laid out mismatched plates and platters filled with breakfast foods, willfully oblivious to the horror-movie cinematics only a few yards away.

Apparently, she wasn't alone in needing to step away, because Jo nearly jumped out of her skin at the sudden appearance of the orange-haired man at her side.

"Thank you for making breakfast," Jo said, mostly just to break the silence. Samson nodded, keeping his eyes set firmly on moving the platters so that they were in a perfect line. Jo grabbed some scrambled eggs, a few slices of bacon—careful not to disrupt Samson's adjustments—and then paused. This close, even Samson looked more uncomfortable than usual, his brows furrowed and face bordering on stricken. "Hey, Sam?" Jo whispered, taking in a breath when he glanced at her with noticeably wet eyes. "Are you all right?"

For a couple of seconds, Samson didn't respond, just looked at her with that same worried expression. It was a dumb question and she knew that; none of them were really "all right." Then he sighed, an exhale that Jo felt leave her own lungs in response.

"Yes," Samson mumbled, scrubbing harder at the soapy pan. "I just don't like the waiting."

Jo wanted to ask him what he meant, but there was something about the sentence that felt final, a heavy silence following in its wake. She wasn't sure how she knew, but she was certain Samson was done talking. So, with one last murmur of thanks, Jo took her plate out of the kitchen, down the hall, and as far away from the television as she could get.

Takako was expectedly awake when Jo let herself quietly into her room. She was now in a seated position, but otherwise didn't seem to have moved much from her futon. So Jo placed the plate of food in front of her and took back her own spot on the adjacent futon as well.

"I don't know if you're hungry, but Samson made it." Jo offered, trying once again to simply fill the silence with anything but worry and tension. "At the very least, it'll feel good to fill your stomach with something hot."

Takako nodded at her, mumbling what sounded like a soft thank you, but she made no move to eat. Jo could sympathize; her own stomach tied in sickening knots. She didn't have the heart to mention the fairly recent development of a tsunami; Takako would find out soon enough.

As Takako stared off into the distance, Jo started to see traces of a similar expression on her face, the same concern that had been mirrored on the faces of the rest of her team. A concern Jo was slowly starting to realize ran deeper than just for the lives lost in Japan. Everyone was on edge, waiting for something, as if they expected the catastrophic after effects of Fuji to somehow reach them as well.

Eventually, Jo couldn't take the silence anymore, pulling her knees up to her chest and hugging them close. "Takako?" she asked, wincing when it seemed to startle the woman out of her thoughts. Takako hummed in acknowledgement, but seemed no less distracted. "Samson said he hated the waiting. What did he mean?"

Somewhere in her, Jo had known. Even as she asked the question, she knew what the answer would be. She just hadn't wanted to hear it. Or maybe her mind just rejected thinking it, as if that could make it any more or less real.

When Takako frowned in response, it was with no little amount of fresh pain in her eyes. She looked reluctant to answer even, raising one hand to her mouth as the other tapped a soft rhythm against the tatami. It took longer than Jo expected for her to string together a response, but when she finally dropped her hand, it was with a stoic and schooled expression. Even if the turmoil in her eyes hadn't entirely faded.

"He means waiting for Snow to call us to the briefing room," Takako said, a fraction of that carefully crafted expression crumbling. Jo didn't need to ask for clarification, but she gave it to her anyway. "With a disaster this big, there's no way someone won't make a wish."

"Of course someone will make a wish." That much was obvious. Hundreds of thousands of people were dead or gravely injured. "But what are we supposed to do? Stop a volcano? Even Snow knows we can't prevent a natural disaster."

Takako finally looked up. Jo had spent so long trying to get close to the woman, but now that she finally was, all she wanted was to be blind to the truth in her eyes. Especially as she said, with a blunt and grave certainty, "That doesn't mean we won't be asked to try."

# LATE NIGHT VISITOR

EVENTUALLY, TAKAKO HAD requested to have some time alone, a request that Jo couldn't deny. Everyone had their own manner of processing and she wasn't about to dictate Takako's.

Jo didn't go very far. She didn't feel like wandering the mansion, didn't have the energy to do anything in a recreation room (despite all earlier notions of picking up a hobby), and couldn't continually impose on Nico. So when Takako gently kicked her out, Jo drifted across the hall to her own bedroom.

She laid on her bed, stretched out amid the plushness, occasionally watching the nighttime of Paris. When the sun rose, so did Jo, for no other reason than habit. She left her bed and with it what felt like all notion of ever being able to sleep again.

The next night, Wayne kept her company with a bottle of whiskey from his room that they drank till dawn, thinking of new (terrible) "crew names" for the Society. The two winners were "The Timekeepers of Infinity" for most palatable, and "Witnesses of Truth" for most cringe worthy. At least it gave them a laugh, something Jo realized she hadn't done for days.

Another day passed. Another day of drifting from place to place, doing nothing of worth, contributing nothing to no one. Another day of waiting as she witnessed the rise and fall of the world from her new vantage of eternity.

It was then, on the third day, that sleep miraculously came to her. She wasn't sure if it was sheer will and determination, boredom, or the fact that even if her body didn't need sleep, her mind eventually demanded a reprieve. In fact, were it not for the heavy knock on the door waking her, she wouldn't have been certain she'd slept at all.

"This better be good," she mumbled into the pillow. She'd just been on the cusp of a dream—she'd swear it. It may well be a decade before she'd find herself able to actually shut her mind completely off once more.

Jo flipped her wrist, looking at the time that illuminated the strip of fabric. It was some time after three in the morning and two hours after everyone had broken off from the common room and gone to bed.

Jo pulled herself from the bed and shook the drowsiness from her mind. Who could possibly be knocking—

Her hand froze, hovering above the doorknob. If magic was a current of electricity, the metal of the knob was conducting it between her and the man on the other side. She could *feel* him there, and for the briefest of moments, an alarm bell rang faintly in the back of her mind. Something about this was ill-advised, the alarm warned. Perhaps, it was because there was something akin to her now dream-like memory of meeting Pan, an ominous threshold from which there was no going back from.

But Jo willfully ignored it all and opened the door.

Snow, even untouched by the Paris skyline that illuminated her bedroom windows, still radiated moonlight. His silver hair swept over an eye, but seemed looser and rougher at the edges. His eyes were sunken, hollow.

This wasn't their fearless and stoic leader. This was the man in agony she'd seen through the Door months ago—the man she'd forced herself to all but forget. There was clearly no path forward to discovering anything more about him.

No path, until he presented one to her.

"I don't know why I'm here." His voice belonged to someone who'd spent hours screaming at the shadows in the corners.

"Come in." She moved on instinct—on an invisible tide that ebbed and flowed between them. If he was the moon, then she was the sea, pulled along by the mysterious aura that he wore like couture.

"I shouldn't."

"Why?" It wasn't a particularly good argument, so his lack of fight when he did surrender was all the more glaring. While she was used to his feet seemingly never touching the ground, the wounded, once-majestic creature now walked with the heaviness of a body robbed of all ethereal grace.

Snow closed the door behind him, leaning against it as if to draw space between them. There wasn't much, and it pulled her a half-step closer in . . . what? Fascination? Concern? Sympathy? He was all of it wrapped in the most beautiful enigma she'd ever seen.

"I shouldn't be here," he repeated.

"Well, you are, so that's that," Jo said as gently as she could through her exasperation. "Snow . . . What happened?"

"Warning you is pointless." He pressed his eyes closed and hung his head. "It will do no good. You can't stop it, none of us can."

"Stop what?"

"And now, now we must do this." He shook his head again and the long bangs all but concealed his face. "Why did I come? Telling you will do no—"

Jo summoned magic she didn't realize she possessed and silenced him with a touch.

It was the most delicate, timid touch she'd ever given. Lighter than a butterfly landing, her fingertips on his cheek. Right first, then left.

He was warm. Warmer than she thought he would be for a man who looked so much like his namesake. Had he been this warm when he'd taken her hand at the Ranger compound all those months ago? Had he been this warm when she'd helped him most of the way back to his room after he'd allowed her to witness his magic?

When he didn't flinch or pull away, the pads of her fingers made shallow indents in his skin as she pulled his attention forward. *Look at me*, she wanted to say, *let me see you*. Her lips were still, voice silent, but everything about her was alive. His presence had done for her what sleep could not; it rejuvenated her.

Perhaps it was some residual magic that lingered between them from his pulling her into the Society, but this man made her feel something indescribable. Something she'd never felt across universes or realities. In a fake world outside of time, this was real.

It was something she'd been missing all along. Something she longed for. Something that was almost like . . . a reunion.

"There's been a wish, hasn't there?" she whispered.

He nodded and pressed his eyes shut again, as if in pain.

"Tell me." He'd have to sooner or later and if he did it now, he'd have practice keeping his composure for the rest of the group.

As if reading her mind, Snow took a shuddering breath. Then another, slightly more stable one. And then, he found length in his spine and strength in his shoulders. He rose to his full height and looked down at her. His carriage wasn't overbearing, nor was it the aloof comportment she'd seen him muster so many times before.

He looked like a stumbled Atlas, finding the will to stand and carry the world on his shoulders once more.

"We are to prevent all loss of life."

"Wh-what?" Appreciation for him telling her in advance hit Jo like a Mac truck. She would've never been able to keep herself together in the briefing room when he broke the news. She could already feel it ripping at the seams of her facial composure. Scenes of wide-spread carnage from the news they'd been watching for nearly a month all flashed before Jo's eyes in a visceral assault. "It's too much this time. It'll be impossible."

"We'll think of something." He glanced away.

"No, we won't." Jo grabbed his hands, taking a full step closer to him. Their hips were almost touching now. "Snow, this isn't hacking into a mainframe or getting revenge on a mob boss. This is a volcano. It's already happened, we can't just get a do-over."

"We can." He tilted his head to her, eyes locking.

"What . . ." Jo's voice had fallen to a whisper.

"I've done all I can."

She searched his face, her fingertips still mapping the curves of his cheeks and the line of his jaw. "Are you all right?" Jo wanted to groan at herself for the question. He gave her that cryptic response and all she could ask was if he was all right?

"I did . . . all I could, Jo." He rephrased his statement, weaker, almost trembling in breath between the words.

"What did you do?"

"You have no idea what you're asking." Snow's mouth pressed into a hard line, but didn't move away. If anything, he felt closer. He leaned forward. She was sure now: he was closer than he'd ever been.

"Then tell me." Jo pulled him but there was no more space to give; their legs were touching, chests brushing. "Tell me something real. Tell me what *this* is."

His eyes widened and Jo felt hers mirror them. Was she even asking about the wish or his ever-elusive magic anymore? Or was she seeking validation for the pull between them?

"Jo . . ." All words failed him just as they were eluding her.

Grammar and structure melted away as his silver eyes bore into hers. Jo swallowed hard. There was one thing left in her mind, a singular request that would not let her breathe again until it escaped.

"Stay with me tonight?"

"What? Why would you ask that?" The rasp of his voice was thickening to a velvety chocolate paste.

"Don't let me be alone, not knowing this," she begged softly. "It's been torture waiting, and now I have to wait with knowledge I can do nothing with. Stay with me, at least until the others are stirring."

"I can't do that." Even as he spoke, their separate personal space was condensing into a singularity that would suck them both in. "You know I can't."

"I don't know anything. You won't tell me *anything* . . . The one thing that I do know is that I want you here."

"And I—"

When he cut himself off, swallowing down whatever he'd almost confessed, Jo found herself hanging on those two words to the point that a groan of frustration rose in her throat. Eventually, true to all prior form, Snow ended things with the tact of a four-year-old.

"I need to go." For a man who could usually put the grace of a ballerina to shame, he'd suddenly turned into a boar. Snow half-pushed, half-steered her to the side.

"Why? Tell me one thing, Snow, please!" Jo demanded, voice raised, even as he opened the door. "Don't shut me out again!"

He shot her a near-painful look, equal parts glare and nervousness, before his composure returned and he leaned forward. Her treacherous heart beat faster almost instantly.

"This wasn't the way it was supposed to be." Something was at the point of breaking, and it wasn't just the way his last couple of words cracked and shattered. "Staying distant, because of your magic—right now, this is all I can do."

He was pleading with her to understand but giving her just enough to have only the vaguest idea that felt more like a shapeless blob than a tangible thing labeled "understanding". Still, one thought came forward. A singular memory.

"You'd said something about my magic before, after the first wish." Jo stepped closer, trying to pin him in place. "What did you mean then?"

"I can't tell you."

"Why?" Jo wanted to punch him and kiss him all at the same time.

"This is the only way we can protect you. Somewhere, you know that's true."

It was like being transported back in time. Had he not said something similar to her long ago? If he had, her mind couldn't locate the memory; everything had gone soft. "What? Why would I need to be protected? And from what?" she asked no one, because the man who held all the answers had run from her once again.

I T WASN'T EXACTLY a surprise to anyone (least of all Jo, given the prior night's encounter) that they were ushered into the briefing room the next morning. That didn't mean Jo wasn't instantly filled with dread over the fact. Breakfast was bypassed, the television blank and silent, and like a funeral march, everyone filed in to take their seats.

Snow's words had circulated in her brain clean through to the morning and played underneath his appearance in the common room, announcing their presences were required in the briefing room.

Though when Jo looked around the table at the rest of the group, she would have sworn by the atmosphere that everyone else already knew. Everyone seemed to share the same exhaustion, the same forlorn expression. Everyone except Pan, that is; she just looked mildly amused.

Jo frowned at the now hazy memory of their last encounter that was stinging at the edges of her mind. Pan's eyes landed on hers and Jo promptly looked away. Nico had been right, Pan was likely just making trouble for trouble's sake. Well, Jo wouldn't give her the upper hand. She forcefully shifted her attention back to the matter at hand.

*We are to prevent the loss of all life.*

How were they supposed to deal with such an impossible wish?

To prevent something on such a drastic scale, especially when so much damage had already been done . . . there was no way. But Snow had acted as though they had no choice but to try. Despite herself, Jo couldn't help the nervous intrigue worming its way into her stomach. Did he truly have the kind of power that could prevent a volcano from erupting? Could they even hope to close the Severity of Exchange on something like that? How exactly would they handle the fact that the life had, already, been lost?

As if on cue, Snow weaved his way in one fluid and authoritative motion from the doorway to the head of the table. It had already been quiet in the briefing room before, but with Snow's arrival, the quiet seemed to shift into an almost tangible thing, heavy and expectant. Like some grotesque, pregnant monster ready to pop.

"You all know why you're here," Snow started, looking to each of them in turn. When his eyes locked briefly with Jo's, she swore she felt her heart stutter. Now was *not* the time to recall the deeply vulnerable man who had come to her the night before. If she reached for anything of that memory, she'd reach for her frustration at his vagueness first. After a second to steel himself, that same detached expression settled like a second skin over his features. Snow lifted a hand. "Let us begin."

Much like every wish since Jo's arrival at the Society, she watched with undeniable fascination as the table came to life, changing and sifting through forms and images until settling on one everyone recognized instantly. They'd been watching the same pictures flash across various news broadcasts for days. Except, where Jo had begun to expect destruction and heartache, all she saw was life, normality, and a country untouched by catastrophe.

"What is this?" she heard herself say, though she didn't recall giving her lips the express command to move. Her body continued on its own accord, and Jo felt herself inch forward in her seat, as if getting a closer look at the images might help her understand them better. "A recording? Or—"

"As of roughly nine hours ago, our current timestamp has been updated," Snow offered, as if that explained anything at all. It was a simple statement with an impossible implication that her mind rebelled against. Surely Snow didn't mean—

"Snow." Eslar's voice was low, almost scolding, despite its usual tenor. "What does this mean for the Severity of Exchange?"

Before Snow could answer, as though Eslar's interjection had awoken them from a stupor, everyone at the table seemed to come back to life. Jo blinked blearily, trying to join the rest of them.

"How far back did we go then?" Wayne asked at about the same time Nico said, "What were the protocols of the wish?"

The questions seemed almost frantic. The only people not chiming in were the usually silent Samson and a rather shaken-looking Takako.

All at once, it came rushing back.

*Prevent all loss of life.*

Without realizing it, Jo had gotten to her feet, the movement bringing the sudden buzz of the room back into a tense hush. She understood in one sudden moment of clarity what he had meant when he had said he'd "done all he could."

"You rewound time," Jo demanded, looking past the footage of a destruction-free Japan to stare down their powerful leader. "You reset to before the disaster."

"I did." There was no hesitation in his voice, but that didn't mean it wasn't without its unspoken consequences. Snow gave a wave of his hand and the image of a young boy appeared on the table. As was the case with their wishers, there was some basic information laid out (it always reminded Jo of a character bio from one of Yuusuke's video games). "Our wisher is Shiro Yamada from the Hakone region. His circle was made of many once-living things, ashes—" Snow didn't clarify further. He didn't have to. "Thus, the scale of his wish is . . . quite large. His wish is for us to ensure survival of any and all Japanese citizens in Mt. Fuji's path."

"So we're not meant to stop the volcano," Jo elaborated for him, mostly just to get the words out into the open, prove to herself and everyone else that the pieces had fallen into place: a jigsaw puzzle glued to the board. "We just need to save the people?"

"An evacuation? That could work, perhaps . . ." Nico frowned, looking from the table to Snow and back. "But what's the current timestamp?"

"A month before the eruption."

"A month. We have a month to get hundreds of thousands of people out of the line of fire." Jo balked, running a shaking hand through her hair. With a desperate flick of her wrist, she wrestled her watch free of her hoodie's sleeve. There, in soft, illuminating proof, was the number **766:00**. Seven-hundred and thirty hours added to the time she'd collected from their past few wishes. One month's worth of hours. He wasn't joking about any of it.

"I've used nearly all of my magic usually reserved for the final wish-granting on this reset," Snow went on, seemingly unaware of the panic slowly filtering into the room. "Which puts the Severity of Exchange at a much higher percentage than normal. It will require far more field work than our usual wish—"

"No shit," Wayne all but spat, leaning heavily back into his seat.

"—but should not be impossible," Snow finished as if he hadn't even heard Wayne speak. Jo felt practically sick with the onslaught of fresh nerves, too many questions piling on top of each other. What would happen if they failed? How were they supposed to evacuate such a large area so quickly? What were they even going to *do?*

"It's not enough time to move *everyone* and prevent the loss of *all* life," Takako whispered, more to herself than to anyone. It was almost a shock to hear her voice after so long, even more so to see the look of frustration marring her usually stoic face. "What happens if . . . We won't have enough—"

A soft twinkle of laughter cut Takako off instantly; all eyes turned to

Pan with a start. She was leaning back in her chair like she hadn't a care in the world, even going so far as to raise her bare feet to the table, crossed at the ankles. When she wiggled her toes to get comfortable, her nail polish seemed to change color.

At the look of amusement on her face, Jo felt a stab of shock and annoyance deep into the center of her chest. An annoyance that morphed quickly into a defensive anger as the girl clicked her tongue and spoke.

"This is absolutely priceless." She giggled, stretching lithely before working her fingers through the fine strands of blue hair curling in long waves around her head. Just yesterday it had been short and spiked, layered in tones of purple, hadn't it? When Pan looked at her, Jo felt herself bristle. "What's got everyone so worked up? I mean, it's not like anyone is dead." Then, gaze still locked lazily on Jo, she winked one cat-like eye. "Yet."

If Jo thought the previous silence had been suffocating, this one was borderline lethal. The weight of her own surprise nearly consumed her. She might as well have choked on the bitter taste of her instant fury. Everyone seemed to suffer a similar loss beneath the blatant display of indifference. Everyone except Jo.

She swallowed back that fury and let it burn all the way down like a $2 gas station energy drink.

"Excuse me?" The words were more felt than heard, a seething hiss of a whisper past clenched teeth. Pan just continued to watch her, the obvious tilt of a smirk pulling at the corner of her lips.

"If everyone is so afraid of the consequences, then simply make sure to lessen the Severity of Exchange. You don't want to put so much strain on poor little Snow. He's already done so much for you and used up all his normal magic allocated for a wish. No help there to save you all." Pan shrugged, twirling a curl around her finger over and over again. Jo didn't know if the woman-child was actually oblivious or simply apathetic, but either way, she seemed to easily ignore the waves of Snow's anger that roared overtop them all. *Why did he stay silent?* "I'm sure it's hardly so difficult as you seem to be making it. Just get it done and make sure it's *perfect*."

For a long moment, Jo didn't quite know what to say to that. Was she joking? Even if she was, did she not realize that humor was *definitely* uncalled for in this situation? Either way, Jo felt a pang of pure hatred rush down her spine. If not just for herself, or for the team, then for Takako.

"Just get it done?" Jo repeated, pushing away from her seat completely and walking along the curved length of the table in Pan's direction. She thought she might have felt Wayne reach out to hold her back, but her focus was zeroed in on her target, her retort already spilling past her lips. "Who the hell do you think you are, acting like this is so *simple*? We got to witness *exactly* what would happen if we fail. We got to watch the death toll rise and the carnage spread, and you don't get why we're afraid? You don't understand why we might be a little less than nonchalant about all this?"

Jo found herself suddenly standing right in front of Pan's chair, leaning into the woman-child's personal space in a way that should have been disturbing if not, at the very least, intimidating. Jo felt something visceral and sinister spike deep within her, fueling her outrage. Looking at Pan was like looking in a mirror but only seeing the worst reflected back. "No. You wouldn't understand, would you? Because you spend all of your time in your room taking month-long naps you don't need, and god knows what else, instead of actually doing your damn job like the rest of us."

Pan looked completely nonplussed. "Then don't fail," she said, grinning with an ease that made Jo want to slap her across the face. "I'm sure, of all of you, Takako understands that best. Don't you, pet?"

Jo hadn't wanted to say anything, hadn't wanted to bring too much painful attention to Takako's family, to the raised stakes, to everything she had to lose if they failed. But hearing Pan comment so frivolously set Jo's blood to outright boiling.

"How dare you!" she yelled, slamming a fist down on the table between them before pointing squarely into Pan's chest. "She's suffered more the last couple of days than any of us. And you just expect her to write that off, pretend she hasn't had to grieve and move on enough to deal with all of this? What right do you have to be so . . . so *patronizing*, you fuc—"

Suddenly, Jo felt her center of gravity being forced backwards, an arm flailing out to grasp at the hand currently gripping tight at her shoulder. "Jo, enough." Eslar's voice was in her ear, not quite scolding, but not soothing either. She hadn't even realized she'd been nearly nose to nose with Pan until Eslar was practically dragging her back to her seat.

The look of smug amusement on Pan's face, the embarrassed resignation on Takako's, and the mix of disappointment and caution on Eslar's, all fought for Jo's first reaction. Not that any of those could possibly be right. Surely Jo wasn't in the *wrong* here . . . was she?

"You're just going to let her talk to us this way? Like the lives of these people don't matter?" Jo shook her head, finally pulling away from Eslar's grip. "Whose side are you on?" And then, as a more important question tickled the back of her mind, Jo became all too aware of the gazes currently pointed everywhere but at her or Pan. Jo tightened her hands into fists at her side, looking not at Eslar or Pan or at anyone else. No, with these words, she pointed her accusing stare right at Snow.

"What is wrong with you people?" *Why are you all so afraid of her? Why are you letting her treat you this way?* Jo wanted to say, pointing over her shoulder accusingly, ready to demand answers if not from Snow than from Pan herself. But Snow just shook his head and Jo felt herself pause.

Maybe it was the brief flash of something in his eyes, something a bit broken and definitely pleading that she could have simply imagined, or maybe she had just grown tired of fighting a clearly losing battle. Either way, Jo found herself rolling her eyes and plopping down with a huff into her seat. Snow nodded, taking the opportunity to jump back into the logistics of the wish, the time limit, and the necessity of their involvement.

But Jo was only half listening, instead looking almost continuously over at Pan.

This wasn't over, not by a long shot, but by the stretch of Pan's grin, it was obvious the woman was already stewing in her own victory. Jo would dig answers out of the very walls of the Society if she had to; somehow, she would figure out what made this woman so special, so frightening.

Pan was a puzzle that simply couldn't go on unsolved.

# IF LOOKS COULD KILL

"ARE THERE ANY other questions?" Snow asked the room.

Everyone shook their heads, Jo included.

"I propose we remain here and begin to work out a plan of attack." Eslar took the initiative when the rest of the group remained silent. "There is no time like the present."

"There is precious little time, period," Wayne added, and Jo found herself silently agreeing.

"Then I suggest you all get to it." Pan got to her feet with a languid stretch and a very bored-looking yawn. "I trust you all will not disappoint." And with that, she turned to leave, no more helpful than she'd been during any other wish before.

Jo couldn't hold back the rush of aggravation burning through her stomach. Whatever mysterious hold Pan had over everyone else, she was not about to have over Jo as well. Thankfully, it would seem she'd blissfully missed the meeting where they'd all sat down and agreed to fear the woman. "Classic Pan," she scoffed. "Bowing out of all the heavy lifting as usual." Jo half raised her voice. "Good thing none of us want you here anyway."

With a slow and inhuman fluidity, Pan turned back towards the group. A smile curled from ear to ear, spreading like sizzling butter across her face. It reminded Jo of the Cheshire Cat from the long ago stories of *Alice in Wonderland*. "Well, it looks like someone in this group has a bit of fight left in them. Aren't you a gem who makes her mother proud?" Jo stood to meet her, awaiting her approach, another confrontation, but Pan didn't make any motion toward her. Instead, she continued toward the doors. "I'll leave you to it, Miss Savior, since you seem so ready for a challenge.

Maybe, if you do a good job, I'll even let you challenge *me* someday." Pan threw her head back and laughed, as if the idea was pure humor and little else.

Jo watched Pan's every move as she sauntered out of the room. She couldn't think of a comeback fast enough and the woman was gone in a blink. Jo curled her hands into fists.

"Sit down, doll, or you're going to scare us all into submission." Wayne's voice startled Jo back to reality.

"If looks could kill," Nico mumbled to himself.

"What, are we just supposed to sit here and take that?" Jo thrust her hand in the direction of the doors leading back to the innards of the mansion. "I don't get it. I don't get how you can let her act like thousands of lost lives are nothing." Her question from before had gotten no answer, so maybe if she stated them as fact, demanded and begged even, she'd finally get one. And oh how she needed one.

"They're not lost yet," Eslar reminded her firmly, ignoring all remarks about Pan.

Jo snorted at the elf. "*Yet?* Like it's possible for us to actually do this?"

"That is a matter I think we should all remain here to discuss." Eslar, too, could rephrase his earlier statements. He had not moved from his chair, but Jo suddenly felt like the willowy man was towering over her. She wasn't ready to back down yet. She was still seeing red.

Her eyes swung from Eslar to Snow. She didn't know why she was bothering with the subordinate when the ruler was among them. "You are our leader. Stand up for us! Stand up for Takako. Do *something*."

"I can stand up for myself."

Jo froze, Takako's tone sending ice up her spine; it almost pained her to move her neck and look at the woman. When she did, it was to find cold, dark eyes staring her down with an expression caught somewhere between insult and disappointment. "I do not need you or anyone else to do it for me."

"Takako, I—" Jo began to plead softly. Her temper had walked her foot right into her mouth.

"What I want is for you to let go of this misplaced righteousness and do as Eslar says. That way, we can figure out a way to prevent the loss of all life—my family included. If you are truly my friend and ally, you will work toward this as well."

Jo sank into her chair and wished the cushion would swallow her whole. Pan had been the asshole, so why did Jo suddenly feel so terrible?

She hated this, all of it. She didn't want to let her anger at Pan go, nor her curiosity at why the woman had such a hold on all of the team.

"You're right," Jo mumbled, trying to swallow her pride and find a normal voice once more. "I'm sorry, I— Fighting amongst ourselves over some insensitive comments won't help anyone. Let's just . . . focus on the wish." She'd never managed to figure out the whole "being the bigger person" thing that was meant to come with adulthood.

"Now that's settled," Snow spoke deliberately, as if trying to radiate his displeasure. Jo folded her arms over her chest; she wasn't going to let him have the satisfaction. "I shall leave you all to it."

The room was silent once more for the morning's second departure. The clicking of the doors closed left just the usual six of them.

"Oh no, please. Let us handle it. Thank you for the help, Snow. We greatly appreciate it," Wayne remarked snidely from Jo's side. It seemed she wasn't the only one rankled.

"Snow has done enough for us." Eslar, ever the peacekeeper.

"Oh? Like getting us into this mess?"

"It's not as if he chose this for us." Eslar fired the statement with such certainty that Jo sat a bit straighter.

Snow didn't choose the wishes? Was that true?

"I wouldn't be so sure," Wayne continued, oblivious. "I wouldn't put it past him."

*Or Pan*, Jo added mentally. Between Snow and the candy-haired creature, Jo would put her money on Pan being the one who'd pick a wish like this.

"Isn't picking the wish good, though?" Nico said softly.

"What?" Wayne balked.

"We can save a lot of people. We can do real good. Isn't that what we wanted?"

"Not if we don't stop arguing like children." Somehow an irritated edge had come to sharpen the typically direct timbre of Takako's voice.

"Takako's right." Jo rested her elbows on the table, leaning forward. As much as she wanted to know more about Pan, and Snow, and everything else, there was nothing to be gained yet on those fronts and far more to be lost by infighting. "So, what are we going to do?"

"We just have to move a few hundred thousand people." Wayne leaned back in his chair. It was his turn to sulk now, it seemed. Jo and he were similar in so many ways, they could create a dangerous feedback loop of frustration if they weren't careful. "Could just ask them all one by one, we have a lot of time." Wayne looked at his watch and then put on an all too sweet tone to say, "Excuse me sir, madam, you're about to die in hellfire. If you could just—"

"Enough, Wayne," Eslar snapped, rubbing his temples.

Jo put her forehead down on the table and let the rest of the team squabble around her. The moment she closed her eyes, the newsreels she'd watched for a week played before her like an ominous premonition. How could they get all those people to move? What methods had she seen utilized in state- or country-wide evacuations? Hadn't she assisted in one before, for a past boss or a cover-up? Surely there was something she could do, something she was overlooking . . .

She shot upward and, judging from the surprised looks the movement inspired, she'd had her head down for longer than expected.

"Great of you to join the class, dollface."

"It's simple," Jo said quickly, ignoring Wayne. She had more important things to discuss now.

"What is?" Eslar asked. But when Jo spoke, it was directly at Takako. "All we need to do is hack into the evacuation system. Create a few falsified statements, issue a large-scale evac. It should just be a push of a button or two and then every man, woman, and child will get alerts on their bio bands." Jo held out her wrist.

"You can contact every person just like that?" Nico seemed somewhat surprised.

"Warning systems were commonplace back in the early 2000s," Takako mumbled, chewing on the thought. "They've only gotten more sophisticated over time . . ."

"It could work," Jo urged. "We do it quickly, and then there's plenty of time for everyone to move. By the time they realize the evac wasn't government approved, everyone will already be out of the blast zone. And even if people try to go back, news of the actual disaster will start spreading. Everyone stays put and everyone stays safe."

"You're sure you can do this?" Eslar folded his hands and rested his mouth against them, his bony knuckles resting just below his nose. "We don't have a lot of time on the calendar."

"Leave it to me." Jo flexed her arm like she was about to flex her skills with a computer. "I can do it all from the recreation room, even. It'll be easy peasy."

Eslar turned to Takako. "What do you think?"

Jo looked back to her friend and ally, realizing that for this mission, Takako had become their de facto leader. Snow would always have control over them, but this was personal for the woman, and that seemed to go above everything else. Takako locked eyes with Jo, who swallowed hard, giving a nod as if to say, *I can do this. Let me.*

"I give you my trust." Takako nodded as well.

Pride swelled through Jo's chest and then went right to her head, the pressure of anxiety hardening it into a dizzying weight right between her temples. Jo had pulled off far more complex jobs, certainly. But she wasn't sure if she'd ever had a job with stakes quite this high.

# EASY PEASY

I *CAN DO this,* Jo repeated like a mantra as she left the briefing room. *I can do this. Easy peasy.*

"Hold up!" Wayne's voice called after her. Jo paused just inside the hallway leading toward the rec rooms.

"Yes?" Jo glanced down the path he'd stopped her from going down, trying to not let the mental pathways being forged in her mind get off-course.

"Do you . . ." He shoved his hands in his pockets, mulling over his next words in a display of a surprising amount of tact for the man. "Do you need help with anything?"

"I'll be fine." Jo gave a small smirk. "Not sure how much your nickel would be able to help anyway."

He didn't back down so easily. "It's a lot of pressure, and a big task. You made it sound simple but—"

"That's because it *is* simple." Jo wasn't about to let him introduce doubt to her mind. There wasn't any room for it. "All I have to do is access multiple databases that service the government in storing private bio-band information. Bypass security protocols. Plant and activate evac warnings at the highest possible threat level. And make it all look legit enough that no one questions."

"Doesn't sound simple to me, doll."

"Turning on a computer doesn't sound simple to you," she countered.

"You have me." Modesty? She didn't usually expect that from the man. "Maybe not my help, but someone else's? We could be boots on the ground for you."

"I have this," she insisted. No doubt, no fear. She could do what needed to be done, it'd be easy. "In fact, I don't want everyone else risking shifting things unexpectedly and making it harder for me. Just take a breather."

"Odd hearing you worried about the ripple effects of the Severity of Exchange."

Jo shared a brief laugh with him. "Well, we all have to grow up sometime, right?"

"So I'm told. Still waiting for it to happen." The conversation stalled, no more momentum to carry it forward, but Wayne persisted anyway. "You sure?"

"I got this."

"Because we're a team and—"

"Wayne, I got this." Jo sighed softly. "If Takako can believe in me, can't you?"

"Okay." He shrugged. "If you need anything Missus Lone Wolf, you know where to find us."

"I won't hesitate."

He could've at least made it look like he believed her. Made it look like he had faith she could pull it off. But Wayne didn't give her the courtesy, and departed with a small pat on her shoulder.

"It'll be easy peasy!" she called, but he was already too far to hear. "Yeah . . . Easy peasy," Jo insisted once more to herself. She knew what she had to do; she'd even explained all the steps for Wayne. But even with the steps laid out before her in perfect, simple-to-follow pathways, Jo still couldn't help but repeat them over and over, drilling them into her own head. She spared no effort in attempting to convince herself that this was just another day at the office. Just a few things to hack into, a few scripts to run, nothing major.

Jo's hands were slick with sweat when she fumbled with her watch. It forced her to take a breath, and still her slightly trembling fingers to get it off. She was not unfamiliar with failure, but never before had she been so afraid of it.

She wouldn't fail. She wouldn't let herself even consider it. Lives were at stake, and Takako's faith in her acted as both a balm and a boost of adrenaline. She wouldn't let her down—wouldn't let any of them down.

With renewed determination (and a roller-coastering confidence that she did her best to keep in check), Jo finally removed her watch and placed it on the recreation room's side shelf.

The same impressive set-up of tech greeted her the moment she opened the door. In fact, it seemed even more elaborate this time—the desktop from her last visit updated with yet another monitor. There were also wall-mounted televisions giving a constant playback of Japan's current news broadcasts (now serving as a reminder for rewound time). A cooler in the corner filled with RAGE ENERGY begged to be drunk. Even a comfy-looking futon was on one side, offering the promise of a brief reprieve should one be needed—and Jo was already bracing herself for that particular inevitability.

These rec rooms really knew how to provide.

With an almost running start, Jo threw herself into a rolling chair, wheels nearly skidding as she slid to a halt in front of her updated setup. As usual, her favorite programs were already up and running on a few screens; the others downloaded with software written in Japanese, though she had to blink a couple times to read it.

Over the last couple of months, her ability to understand both written and spoken languages outside her native tongue had become almost second-nature. Even though Jo had studied Japanese in school, she wasn't always the best student (especially in any classes that didn't deal with programming). It was almost as if she had to flip the switch from her mind trying to actively translate it, to allowing her passive magical ability to take over.

It looked like everything she needed to get started was right within her reach, just waiting for her to dive in. Which was why she couldn't quite figure out the reason her hands continued to hover, trembling just slightly, over the keyboard.

She didn't have time to doubt her abilities, or to feel overwhelmed and intimidated by the task at hand. She needed to have this hack pulled off yesterday, and instead, all she could do was stare at the news broadcasts hung on the wall above her head. Everything looked so normal, so peaceful in comparison to the footage they'd been forced to swallow for the last few days.

Somewhere in Shizuoka was Takako's sister, her niece and nephew, all alive and well and completely oblivious to the oncoming disaster. A disaster that they had no way of stopping. But they *did* have a plan, and Jo *did* have a chance to save their lives—to save thousands upon thousands of lives. So, despite the way her hands still quivered, despite the way her heart had taken up what felt like permanent residence in her throat, despite Wayne's words stubbornly lodging in her mind, Jo got to work.

Within moments, she could feel it. It wasn't just the sensation of her magic bubbling back to life, helping her see alleyways in the dark web or data-routes that seemed otherwise invisible, but her own confidence spiking.

This was her thing. It was the one thing that she could hang her hat on, be confident in, and no one else could take from her. It was the value she brought to the Society. She could tear down walls and shred any defense that kept her from her goal. Nothing could be put before her that she couldn't break.

If anyone knew how to get these evac warnings put in place, it was her and no one else.

The rush of magic-fueled adrenaline was intoxicating, thrumming beneath her skin like the buzz of an electric current. Her eyes bounced from screen to screen, fingers setting up a constant staccato rhythm against the keys. Second by minute by hour, she experienced her plan unfolding.

It started with a quick hack deep into the Japanese government's residential databases and ended with complete control of all citizens' bio bands—which Jo was very careful not to alter in any unnecessary ways. From there, it was simply a matter of uploading the evac codes into their wireless drives and waiting for the warning to go into effect. All dominoes lined up and waiting to be knocked over.

This time, as Jo took a breath and hovered a finger over the 'Enter' button, her hand trembled not with nerves, but with eager anticipation. She could do this; it would all work out. She'd covered all her bases, made sure every detail was accounted for. Now all she had to do was find a computer on the other side of the Door (with a USB port), activate the evac warning, and wait.

Wayne was sitting on a couch just beyond the Four-Way, heading toward the common room, when she crossed back toward her room, as if he'd been waiting for her. His eyes drifted up from the tablet he'd been thumbing and caught hers for a long moment. Jo gave a quick nod before he could say anything, and continued on.

She didn't need help; she needed the USB from her room and the trust of her teammates. There wasn't anyone else who could do this. It all fell to her and she wouldn't fail them.

The USB stick was right where she'd left it after their last wish. Wayne was right where he was before—both times when she crossed back to the recreation room and then back toward the briefing room. Both times, he'd said nothing and made no motion to stop her.

As she left the mansion and stepped onto Japanese soil, Jo thought of Takako and her family, of Mt. Fuji and the decimation of the surrounding regions. She thought of every line of code, every hack, every digital footprint she'd put in place to lead the citizens of Japan out and away from future tragedy.

Tokyo buzzed on as normal, giant billboards of brightly colored *anime* and video game characters taking up entire skyscrapers. She'd chosen Akihabara as her point of entry—the "electric city." Yuusuke never stopped ranting about the gamers that could be found in arcades and computer cafes there and, sure enough, here was the place where she found some hole-in-the-wall computer café with towers that still sported USB ports.

The attendant looked at her, albeit somewhat suspiciously given her mastery of Japanese, but made no motion to bar her from renting out a space. Her corner procured, no prying eyes on her, Jo plugged in and began running her scripts. Her heart beat on overtime as she navigated the real-world channels, and it wasn't until the last dredges of her magic fizzled that Jo felt she could even take a breath.

Returning to the Society felt almost like a dream, her body dragging and her mind clouded from over-exertion.

Jo couldn't bring herself to head to the common room yet. Blissfully, Wayne was no longer waiting for her, and she could sneak back to the recreation room unimpeded. Even though she'd taken her watch to head back to the real world, the room was just as she'd left it—monitors broadcasting the news included.

Taking up a seat on the futon, Jo watched, waiting for her actions to take root. It took a little longer than she'd expected (or intended), but eventually alerts began popping up on every channel. Jo lifted the remote, clicking to another news station.

"Come on . . ." she whispered—begged to the newscaster. "Tell everyone that—"

"This just in—" a title graphic swooped across the screen, interrupting the woman for a moment "—we are receiving reports of wide-scale evacuations across the Kanto region of Japan. Preliminary protocols are advised to be followed…"

Jo leaned back against the futon with a pleasant sigh. It was working. Things would escalate, dominos would continue to fall, more evacuation zones would be alerted and rising danger warnings would prompt people to move.

Perhaps it was the relief of success, or simply the release of the constant state of mental and magical concentration, but Jo felt instantly heavy, wracked by a wave of exhaustion. A dizzy haze settled over her as she glanced wearily at the bottom of one of the screens.

Her plan had taken nearly thirteen hours to execute, including the one and half she spent back in the real world.

Jo stood, rubbing her shoulders with as much pressure as she could muster (which still wasn't enough) and took in her workspace. At least half a dozen cans of RAGE were sprawled around the keyboard, and when she finally pulled her attention to the music still blaring from her headphones, it was already a quarter of the way through a repeat of her favorite playlist.

She returned the headphones back to their hook, her fingers protesting the mere idea of even grabbing something. Her knuckles brushed the monitor she'd been working so furiously on in the process, and it flickered off. Jo paused, staring at it. She tapped the screen once, twice… three times, before it finally flickered back to life.

"You gave all you had, too, huh?" Jo gave a small laugh. "Fine, have a rest." She clicked off the single monitor and started for the door. As was usually the case after a long session, she couldn't even stomach the sight of a keyboard. She wanted to be anywhere other than that tech-filled dark room.

So Jo headed for the only place she could conceive to be the exact opposite—the open and bright common area.

The door to the recreation room closed before she ever noticed that the monitor had sparked to life only briefly, before fizzling out entirely.

# HOTSHOT

JO DEPARTED FROM the recreation room and scooped her watch off the shelf, fastening it back over her wrist. The expanse of hall leading to the Four-Way was void of windows. It wasn't until she was walking down the stairs and heading toward the common area that she even got a sense of time. Of course, she could've checked her watch, but that was just so *logical* and her brain was far too sluggish for such taxing solutions to life's simple problems.

Dawn was just cracking over the mountains in the distance, rays of sunlight arcing over their peaks and shining brightly—blindingly—over the pool. It filtered in as vibrant streaks through the columns on the opposite wall of the entry to the common area. For once, the room was silent.

"Well, I guess I'll have to make my own coffee," she lamented dramatically to no one in particular. At least, she intended it to be no one in particular.

"I could summon Nico for you." Eslar's voice rose up from the couch, only to be followed by the man himself.

"Sorry, didn't see you there." The apology was half-hearted. She'd definitely prefer Nico's brewing skills to her own. If Eslar insisted, she certainly wasn't about to stop him.

"How did it go?" Eslar got right to business, forgetting mention of Nico entirely—much to Jo's disappointment. "Wayne reported he saw you leaving a while ago."

"Not *that* long ago." Jo shrugged as she slowly fussed about the kitchen.

"You did not answer my question."

"Yes sir, sorry sir." Eslar didn't seem to appreciate her joking, so Jo returned her voice to a less militaristic tone. "All seems to be well."

"It must be, if you're here." He shifted back onto the seat of the couch, the back of his head to her, tilted down.

The television was off, which meant something else was occupying his attention. Jo strolled over, confirming her suspicions. "Hey—sorry, didn't meant to startle you."

"What else do you require, Josephina?"

"Josephina? What are you? My mother?" Jo leaned on the back of the couch. "Do you have one of those you'd recommend me? Preferably one not in . . ."

"Elvish?" he finished for her, confirming her suspicions.

"Yeah."

"You want to read?"

"You don't have to sound so surprised." She walked back to the kitchen, hoping to hide the small amount of offense she took at the shock in his eyes.

"I do have one I'd recommend. I actually think you'd enjoy it. It's one of Samson's favorites, actually . . . But it is in Elvish."

Jo poured herself a cup of coffee. "Bummer." Well, there went the idea of cutting herself off from tech for a few blissful hours.

"Why does that bother you?" An offended tone took up residence in his words.

"I can't read—*oh.*" Jo brought up her palm, smothering her face for a second with a groan. The elf had the audacity to give a low chuckle. "I'm exhausted okay! I forgot I had translation magic." She leaned against the counter, cradling her mug, and clarified, "It'll work on languages that . . ."

"No longer exist?" The words were steely, almost practiced, almost in a manner she'd expect to hear from Snow. "Yes."

"Then pass over the words."

Eslar stood, departing the room for several minutes (long enough for Jo to finish her cup and wash it) before returning with a tome in hand. There were a few runes stitched into the leather of the front. Jo blinked at it several times: nothing. Just when she was beginning to get paranoid that her mind was too taxed to mentally translate anything, they shifted.

"*The Bow of the Goddess*?"

"An old folk tale about a man who was gifted a weapon by the Goddess of the Hunt, making him her chosen champion in her war against the Goddess Oblivion."

"Sounds like fun." Jo shrugged.

"Does it?" He seemed skeptical.

"I want something that I've never seen before to cleanse my mental palate. And I'm fairly certain I've never seen anything like this before."

"The likelihood is slim," Eslar agreed before strolling over to the couch. Jo started for one of the chairs by the pool that she and Nico usually sat out on, awash in the morning's sun. She thought the conversation over, but then Eslar added, softly, as if debating if he wanted to say anything at all, "Keep it as long as you need. Let me know what you think when you're finished."

"Yeah, sure," Jo mumbled, staring at the elf. It felt almost like... friendship? Closer than she'd felt with the man since their first wish.

Jo took up her seat, and a few hours passed in blissful silence. Her mind soaked up the words. All too soon, she no longer even saw the script-like runic language, and instead, became absorbed in the story that hailed from a time when magic was real and gods seemed just a little more possible.

What was shaping up to be a surprisingly peaceful morning was, unsurprisingly, ruined by Wayne. Jo didn't even hear him come in, but he must've made a direct line for where she sat. "Wow, doll, you look like hell."

Jo startled, nearly dropping the book. Her eyes drifted up to where he stood at the edge of her lounge chair. "Good morning to you, too?"

"I take it you were successful?"

"Right to business I see." Jo closed her book and set it aside. "I'm trying to hold you in suspense, is it working?" Really, what Jo wanted to say was "turn on the damn TV."

"Should I get Takako first?" Wayne posed the question loudly enough to be fielding Eslar's opinion as well.

Jo stood, making a show of stretching, hoping she didn't have to be the first one to speak. She didn't know what the right answer was here. But something possessed Eslar to look her way. *Why did this come down to her?* She swallowed hard. "She'll find out one way or another. I think she should be here. It could be a relief to wake up and see everyone evacuating."

"I'll get her then." Wayne scurried off.

As he did, Jo made her way over to the couches, sitting diagonally across from Eslar in what had become her usual spot. She focused on situating herself on the cushions, looking at the elf from the corners of her eyes. Eslar must have come from a time with no notion of awkward looks, because he ignored her deftly. Or maybe he just didn't care.

Jo opened her mouth to speak, just as he did the same.

"How are you liking the book?"

"Oh, fine . . . I'm kind of a slow reader, so I'm only at the part where the God of Fortune is meeting with the Goddess of the Hunt to discuss crafting a weapon."

Eslar hummed, nodding, flipping the page of his own manuscript.

The book wasn't what she wanted to talk about, and he must know it. Jo swallowed, glancing toward the door. They were alone, but for how long? She had to chance it. Things were going well between her and one of the oldest members of the Society; this was as good an opportunity as any. "Should we get Pan as well?"

To his credit, Eslar was unrattled. "Do you really want to subject Takako to that again?"

"As she said, she can stand up for herself."

"Can you trust yourself around her?" Eslar raised his narrowed his eyes, no doubt referring to the temper Pan brought out in Jo.

"Trust myself not to do what? Is there something I should be worried about?" The memory of the woman-child with a blood-red sky behind her flashed unbidden before Jo's eyes.

"She brings out something in you."

"And why do you think that is?" Jo knew why: it was because Pan was a barely tolerable twat, nothing more or less.

"Perhaps it's because Pan is the oldest among us, and the closest to Snow," Eslar said, almost nonchalantly. But the casual words were obviously loaded.

Before Jo could probe further on *exactly* what he meant, especially about the Snow bit, Wayne returned with not just Takako in tow.

"Good morning, Jo." Nico gave her a cheerful smile, quickly crossing over. "How is it that you don't have a cup in hand?"

"Because I've already had two cups."

"Then I take it you don't need a third?" he asked, heading into the kitchen.

"Blasphemy good sir!" Jo said dramatically. Nico chuckled, and gave a nod, already making espresso. It was the only spot of levity she could find before her eyes fell on Takako, who sat heavily next to her.

"How did it go?"

Jo opened her mouth to answer but Eslar responded by (finally) turning on the TV instead.

Everyone stopped all movement the moment a newscaster appeared.

It took a moment for Jo to properly hear the broadcast. She wanted to chalk it up to having focused for so long on translating Elvish. But that wasn't the case.

It was her mind reeling as the words she'd expected to hear and the ones currently being spoken clashed in severe counterpoint with each other. She even found herself reading the notices at the bottom of the screen over and over again, as if maybe she'd discover that her magical, internal translator was somehow out of whack.

But no matter how hard she tried, the words continued on unchanged. *The world went on unchanged.* And that was entirely the problem.

*" . . . Japanese Government has issued a statement explaining that there is no scientific evidence to support such claims and all scientific agencies responsible for monitoring potential natural disasters did not issue the warning either. Therefore, Prime Minister Nakamura has deemed the evacuation call a cyber-attack, and requested that all citizens ignore the recent evacuation requests as they look into the organization responsible for these hacks."*

Jo was on her feet. Her heart raced. Her hands balled into fists. Her face flushed not with anger but sheer horror.

*"Currently, they are not linked to any terrorist group and appear to be a rogue attack set to strike fear into the populous and cause chaos. While the motivations are still currently unknown, the Prime Minister has sworn to uncover the truth, vowing to allocate emergency funds to the PSIA to ensure the safety of the citizenry. In light of the news of his swift and decisive action, Nakamura's approval ratings have risen nearly 33 percent, a steep rise just before the elections . . ."*

The newscaster's voice faded to a static buzz. As if all language magic had worn off beneath sheer, appalled disbelief, Jo could barely understand the words at all anymore. Only one statement cut through the humming between her ears.

"Nice try, hotshot."

She spun on her heel, staring down Wayne. "I did everything perfectly!"

"Clearly not." Eslar looked up at her, as if challenging her to try to intimidate him. As if accusing her for spending so much time lounging when there was work to be done. *Not that she'd known.*

"The last time I looked in the recreation room not more than three hours ago, things seemed to be going smoothly. People were beginning to move. I-I set up the evacuation notices, I planted information in scientific databases—"

"Come on, doll. You didn't think those scientists would try to validate where that information was coming from?"

"Do not take that tone with me." Jo scowled, her attention returning to Wayne. "Do not speak down to me." She felt her blood boiling. "Where were you and your flipping coin while I worked all night?"

"You told me you didn't need—how did you put it? Me and my nickel?" he fired back with rapier-speed and accuracy. It was that thing between them again, a natural escalation that kept them feeding easily off of one another. Unfortunately, this time it wasn't directed at a common enemy, but each other. "You chose the job and took it on for the team. Don't pawn off responsibility."

He had a point. *The bastard had a point.* Jo ran a hand through her hair, snagging on tangles. "I'll fix it. I'll fix it," she muttered.

"How?" Wayne asked. "You have more answers in that magic hacker bag of tricks?"

Her brain was on overdrive. It was running through everything she'd done the night prior, looking for a way to improve, looking for a fix. Simultaneously, Jo was looking forward. Even with the post-hack-a-thon exhaustion making her brain fuzzy, she desperately sifted through direction, information, viable courses of action.

And she was coming up empty.

Minus her little hiccup at the beginning (and, even then, everything had worked out just fine in the end), every other wish she'd touched had been a series of successes. Now, she was failing at the moment it mattered most. Jo dropped her hands to her sides and sighed. Her pride had gotten her in this mess. She'd been a fool for thinking she could do it all on her own. So she couldn't assume more pride would get her out.

"I don't know . . ." Jo confessed to them all. "I *thought* I did everything right. I was so sure I could do it." Her eyes fell on Takako. Shame and guilt filled her stomach, pushing two words up past her throat and out of her mouth. "I'm sorry."

She looked back to the TV. Jo heard it for the first time again, but the words remained washed out. They were all repeats from before.

"I don't think this is a total failure," Takako said, finally.

"How?" Eslar stole everyone's question from their halfway open mouths.

"They say scientists are looking for any foundation to the emergency being called." Takako's words were careful, clearly trying to draw the line between optimism and pragmatism. "We just have to make sure that they're given a reason to find what they're looking for. We need to prove to them that the emergency needs to be taken seriously."

A ray of hope sparked in Jo's chest. Perhaps there was a way yet to salvage the situation. On reflex, her mind immediately went to how she could hack and code her way to a solution.

But she pushed it aside.

"Let's get everyone together in the briefing room." She couldn't do this alone. None of them could. Wayne had been right; she just had to learn it the hard way. "We need a new plan, team."

# THE CRAFTSMAN'S PLAN

"ALL RIGHT." JO started the moment everyone had situated themselves in their usual seats in the briefing room.

It probably looked a little presumptuous for her to be standing at the head of the table, but Snow was (as usual) nowhere to be found, and she simply couldn't help herself. She needed to prove not only that she could offer the necessary support for this wish, but that she recognized the benefits of the other members of the team in accomplishing it. Her failure had settled thick and heavy in the pit of her stomach, and she wanted to do everything she could to remedy the weight.

"Some of you, most of you, know . . . But the attempt at forcing an evacuation using the bio bands was a failure," Jo spoke directly to Samson as he was the only one missing from the common room earlier.

Samson nodded, sinking slightly into his chair under her stare. Jo quickly averted her eyes, as not to put so much unintentional pressure on the shy man.

"The government has labeled it a terror attack and the evacuation has ended before it could even really begin. So, we need to re-evaluate our next steps . . ." She let her voice trail off, hoping that someone would offer the solution she didn't have.

For a second, the Society simply looked among themselves before settling as a unit back on her. It was Nico, in his usual kind tone, who finally spoke up, "Well, we still need to get people to evacuate."

"Exactly," Jo said, pacing a bit like a teacher trying to get her students to come to their own solutions on a project. Really, she was just hoping she'd find her own exceptional solution somewhere in the three feet of space she was traversing. "And how do we do that now that the evacuation has been discredited?"

"If we knew that, doll, we would have figured out a plan of action already," Wayne interjected. "Or perhaps you would've done it." Despite the way it made Jo bristle, she ignored the smart remark. If he was trying to be playful, he was grossly misreading the room. Instead of letting herself be egged on, however, Jo merely threw him a distinctly unimpressed look before waiting for someone else to offer a more helpful opinion.

Thankfully, Takako seemed to have no problem offering support. "We need to show them proof of why evacuation is still the right course of action. There's attention being paid to it now, so it may not take much to validate the concerns you planted. We merely need to give it credit that can't be ignored."

Before Jo could pick up on that, Wayne leaned heavily back into his chair with a bitter sounding laugh. "Oh damn. I forgot to record all the terrible broadcasts coming up so we can just play them on repeat for those who don't have the luxury of time travel."

"Wayne," Eslar scolded this time, earning if not a chastised look from the man, then at least a moment of silence. A silence which Jo wasted no time filling.

"Scientists are already looking for proof of the unidentified claims, the news said as much. Even if they don't know how the records that triggered the evacuation notices got there, it's been enough to peak their interest," she continued, leaning against the table and doing her best interpretation of Snow, trying to look each person in the eyes, one at a time. "So why haven't they offered up any of their findings?"

For a long moment, everyone seemed to consider the options, but eventually, Takako uttered a soft murmur of recognition. "They don't *have* any findings yet, right? Or they would present them."

"That's what I'm thinking." Jo wasn't sure if they had zero findings or just inconsequential ones, but she nodded anyway; it fit everything that had been said so far, and was the best direction forward. "If the scientists had something, there's no way they'd let the government call off the evacuation knowing the danger Fuji poses."

"Then what are we going to have to do to make sure they arrive at findings worth sharing and evacuating over?" Eslar asked, more to himself than the group, one dark green thumbnail caught between his teeth as his eyes narrowed in concentration. "And make sure they reach these conclusions with enough time for all the people that need to move to do so?"

Things looked about as hopeless as ever, but Jo couldn't help but feel a small swell of pride as everyone began floating ideas across the table. Perhaps her contribution hadn't been a total failure after all.

No, it'd been an epic mistake. Jo couldn't let herself lose sight of that, or the monster of pride would crawl onto her back and whisper in her ear again. Getting everyone back on track was, at best, repentance.

"Oh!" Nico sat up, not quite slamming but definitely placing his palms heavily on the table. His gaze instantly sought out Jo's, an enthusiasm there that was both endearing and motivating. "What if they have no findings because they don't have anything strong enough to perceive them?"

Jo mulled that over. "You mean, they don't have the technology?" It seemed outlandish that, out of all of the technological advancements her time period had under its belt, *this* would be the one thing that had fallen through the cracks. They had androids petitioning to live normal lives, indistinguishable from humans, but not better earthquake detecting materials?

"Let's say they don't have proper measurement tools for correct prediction information. We'd need a stronger seismograph—something that can measure deep-layer tectonic shifts and then predict future movement based on these micro-movements." Eslar continued, frowning as well in deep, disgruntled thought.

Jo actually took a small step away from the table, taken aback with surprise. The elf was from a time period that was so long ago, and so far from her own, that it was utterly inconceivable to Jo to even imagine. Yet, he could navigate technology better than most from Jo's own times. As annoying as he could be in his occasional role of "team mom," Eslar was truly something else.

"I can do that."

All eyes turned to Samson, his brow furrowed and eyes distant, as if he hadn't even realized he'd spoken. Jo could see one hand tapping an unnatural rhythm against the table as his other fiddled with a cube shaped object held a few inches away from his lips. His fingers shifted with practiced ease, a soft magical aura emanating from him that Jo could feel all the way from the other end of the table.

The silence following his statement stretched long enough that Eslar had to cut back in, clearing his throat to get the craftsman's attention. Samson jumped slightly, though his hands continued to fiddle; the cube seemed to mold beneath his fingers like a sentient clay, becoming something Jo could not yet envision. "Samson?"

"I can make what you need," he clarified, eyes downcast, though not in a way that emanated any sort of self-consciousness. Instead, they seemed to shift about the open space in front of him as if already trying to work out a spatial understanding of his newest project. "It- It will be simple," he went on. "Enough to convince anyone—scientist, government, prime minister. It should cover all of our bases, dig deep enough into the necessary seismic data that the evacuations will be irrefutable. Just tapping into the AI supercomputers for high-level calculations . . . Modifications, really. Nothing new. Just improving what's there for them. I can do that. Yes, I can, no problem."

For a long moment, Jo didn't know what to say; it was the most she'd ever heard come out of Samson's mouth at one time. But she wasn't about to waste it. With a quick clearing of her throat, she nodded and tacked on the best look of motivated authority she could manage.

"You heard the man. He's got the proof machine on lock." She must really be getting used to the world of magic if she'd take that simple explanation from a thousand-year-old man as proof he could create such a thing. "So, now how do we get that machine into the hands of a scientist who can use it?"

From there, all discussion focused on hashing out logistics. If there was anything Jo had learned throughout her time as the Shewolf, it was the benefit of laying all the "best cards" out on the table, working out a foolproof methodology, and playing it like a poker game she had no intention of losing. They had aces up their sleeves—magic—and with it, there was no way they *could* lose.

This was merely about getting somebody to look at their hand and recognize the win.

Wayne and Takako took it upon themselves to masquerade as researchers looking to sell the updated seismograph machine to the head seismic facility, capitalizing on the recent interest in such a device. With Wayne's magical abilities, conning their way into the office of the right people would be "a piece of cake"—or a piece of something from the 1920s that Jo promptly forgot (Tomato Pie, perhaps?). Then, it would simply be a matter of falsifying documents on Jo's end just to tidy things up if anyone looked for evidence that Wayne and Takako were indeed part of a legitimate company. Another night of hacking the appropriate registries, creating documentation for the machine's functionality, and their validity.

And, if she was thorough and careful, another night of opportunity for Jo to redeem herself.

# KEN AND GOOFO

T HE DOOR TO the rec room opened with an icy breath. Jo instantly pulling her sleeves down over her hands.

Inside, the same set-up greeted her as last time: monitors, futon, and a freshly stocked mini-fridge of RAGE Energy. She blinked, allowing her eyes to adjust to the dim lighting. It all looked pristine once more, as if waiting for her to make a mess all over again.

There was, however, one new addition. Draped over the back of the chair at the computer desk was a brand-new hoodie. It wasn't her usual all black fare, but a deep navy ensemble with a slightly off-blue pattern over it that reminded her of abstract snowflakes.

Jo ran her fingers over the fabric, trying to place the material. It was softer than wool, higher quality than a cotton . . . cashmere? Not quite. It was different than anything she'd ever touched before and yet so similar to something she could've sworn she'd felt—likely a designer dress at a department store, the sort of thing she could look at and dream of but never afford.

"Really?" she asked no one but the seemingly sentient walls, trying to talk away the odd feelings it evoked in her. "You can give me a new hoodie, but you can't make a room that's less icy and can still have all my tech?" Jo slung her arms into the sleeves, waiting for a reply. There was none. Then again, she was a bit glad of the fact. She may be settled into her magical existence, but she had a feeling a talking mansion would take it a step too far. "Either way, thanks, I guess."

Jo plopped herself into the chair. She didn't run into the room this time or slide up to the keyboard with momentum. No, Jo leaned back, stretched out her legs, sank into the (surprisingly soft) hoodie the room had given her, and stared at nothing for several long breaths.

As if somehow knowing that she had yet to start in on her task, there was a knock on the door. Jo turned and what felt like a now distant memory came back to her—*was the last person to knock on the door Pan?*

She swallowed, making sure her voice was even and strong. "Come in."

Part of her hoped that it was Pan; Jo wouldn't mind a few minutes alone with that girl-creature to give her some uninterrupted pieces of her mind. But while that may be something Jo would *like*, it was also perhaps not the best idea given that the mere thought of the supernova-haired woman still set Jo's blood running hot. So, ultimately, she was glad it was just Wayne. As quickly as they could rise each other to anger, it also seemed they could put each other at ease.

"Hey, doll." Wayne swept over her with his gaze. There was something uncanny about that look. Even though Jo knew her hair was a mess, there were likely bags under her eyes, she was in a sweatshirt about four sizes too big, and Wayne had noted earlier that she "looked like hell," he could still look at her with a fondness that surprised her.

"I really should figure out a pet name for you." Jo gave him her own up-and-down. His sleeves were rolled, collar slightly unbuttoned. But his vest and pants were tailored to perfection, a sort of casual prestige that only men like Wayne could muster, even if it lacked a little of its usual magic. "You call me doll, so, how about . . ." She tapped her lips with a hum. "Ken?"

"Ken?" Wayne seemed startled.

"Yeah, you call me doll, like a Barbie Doll. Ken was her boyfriend."

"Boyfriend?" He arched his eyebrows.

Jo laughed at the idea, so loudly that she could hear her voice echoing in the hall. "No, Wayne, just *no*. Not like that. We covered all that, remember? I was just thinking of a male version for 'doll'."

Wayne slid his hands in his pockets, an endearing smile on his lips. "I rather like my name. I don't think I want to take another man's, even if it means a term of endearment from you."

"Not Ken, then?"

"No." He shook his head. "How about goofo?"

"Goo-what-now?" Just when she thought he couldn't get any weirder.

"Goofo," Wayne repeated, as though it would somehow make it more obvious. "Zelda Fitzgerald called Scott that, real romantic-like."

She could only laugh.

"So goofo is a no?"

"Obviously." Jo grinned at him. "Don't really want anything 'romantic-like.'"

"You're the one who went there with boyfriend talk."

Jo gave him a half-hearted roll of her eyes. "I guess we'll have to keep looking."

"I guess so."

There was a brief moment where they just smiled at each other. Shoulders relaxed, as if forgetting the tension of the wish that loomed over them every waking moment now. "Thanks," Jo mumbled. "I needed that."

"Needed what?" He seemed genuinely confused.

Jo shook her head. She couldn't let herself get comfortable and forget what was on the line. Comfort would make her relax, and relaxing led to sloppiness. The weight of the stress on her shoulders was necessary right now. "Nothing. Anyway . . . What can I help you with? I doubt you came here to talk about goofo."

"I didn't." He took a step in, finally, just enough to allow the door to mostly close behind him. "I wanted to apologize."

"Apologize?"

"I was a bit of an ass."

Jo could draw things out further, make him really say what he'd done wrong. Prove his remorse. But she knew sincerity when she heard it. So she just waved a hand through the air, as if clearing any negative thoughts or feelings from the space between them. "It happens. Don't worry about it. We're all under a lot of stress."

"Stress isn't an excuse for acting the way I did," Wayne still pressed, though there was relief beneath his words. "Just...Let me make it up to you somehow, yeah?"

Jo paused, hummed softly in faux-thought, then smiled. "I'll think about it, *Ken*." She dragged out the pseudo pet name, knowing just what it'd do.

He gasped and stepped away, hand pressed to his chest in only semi-faux insult. Jo laughed at his offended stare, her mission accomplished. "I take it back. No apology for you," Wayne huffed, even if his lips seemed almost incapable of holding back the tug of their smirk.

"I couldn't resist."

"I hope you're satisfied."

She was, but spared him and didn't rub it in.

He left, the air between them settled and friendly once more. That said . . . their flirting was fun, but it felt hollow, like an echo of what could've been there in a different life and under different circumstances, but wasn't quite.

Jo placed her hands on the keyboard and set to clearing that stress right from the root. The monitors flared to life. Well, all but one. Jo stared at it dumbly. It was the same one as before. She reached up and tapped the power button.

Nothing.

Jo tapped it again. Then gave a few raps on the side of the screen. It turned on with a suddenness that nearly blinded her. Squinting, Jo quickly adjusted the brightness, and set about her work. The mansion made everything realistic, down to the occasional technology glitch, it seemed.

The banter had, somehow, re-sorted the random tangents that cluttered her mind. Things were running smoothly again. Her magic felt like a marathon, rather than sprints. Jo drew on it at a consistent pace in the background of her mind, greasing the wheels but not using it for momentum. Her own talent was enough for that.

Overall, she moved more slowly, but with unwavering purpose. It wasn't fueled with arrogance and fear like the frazzled machete-like approach she'd taken last time. No, Jo was beginning to wield her magic like a scalpel, striking only where she needed with absolute precision. Like this, absolutely nothing could stand in her way. It was as if just touching something caused it to unravel.

There were only two cans of RAGE ENERGY left in the fridge when Jo departed the recreation room for the third time in three days. Her more measured, direct approach yielded results. Isn't that what Yuusuke had tried to tell her years ago? Approach it like playing the long-con, not the quick attack?

At least, she thought he'd said that. Trying to recall moments from her past life, her "real" life, was starting to become more and more difficult.

It was like trying to pick apart a hyper-vivid dream from a similar memory. Whenever her mind drifted to specifics, they seemed to waver and shift like two cells layered on top of each other. Was it Yuusuke's advice she was following, or someone else whose name and face she'd already forgotten? When images of a long beard, a crowned head, and ornate clothing flashed across her mind's eye, was that a memory, or a phantom image from a distant but lingering dream?

Jo rubbed her eyes. Being part of a society outside of time probably just had some unfortunate side effects, that's all. And surely the supremely hazy memories of her best friend, the man she'd given up her existence for, were purely a result of exhaustion and not an actual loss of clarity.

Even if she worked fewer hours this time, the session was no less intensive than the last. Her mind felt like pulp, one even Eslar's bedtime story may not be able to save.

Jo looked down the empty hall. There were no sounds echoing, no footsteps nearing, and the door to the other recreation room was void of a watch. It compelled her to check her own—just past three a.m., for whatever time was worth. Basically nothing, other than the arbitrary habits they still observed.

Which meant everyone was likely holed up in their own rooms, passing the time doing whatever they did. She knew where to find Wayne just like she knew he'd not mind her barging in on his space. Jo leaned against the door with a sigh. The thought was no more appealing than it was last time. Their conversation earlier had, indeed, sparked something in her. She wanted touch, but not Wayne's.

Jo pressed her palm to her forehead with a sigh. What *did* she want then? Or rather, *who*?

When her hand pulled away, Jo looked left, not right, toward a white door at the opposite end of the hall. She was too old to be playing games like this. She knew what she wanted and she was in control of her emotions—most of the time.

But this? This was some odd magnetic vortex that drew her forward with an inexplicable force. Jo found herself toe-to-toe with Snow's door, facing off like it was some wild beast. She remembered the last time she'd stood before his door, the cryptic answers that followed all the questions still swirling in her mind like unspoken taboos. Then there was the time he'd come to her in the night, making things all the more confusing.

Jo's hand hovered. But when it fell, her knuckles didn't meet the wood of the door. Jo's fingers splayed out over the grain. She tipped her head forward, only realizing how warm she'd grown once her forehead met the cool, unblemished surface.

She was better than this. She wasn't some lovesick teenager with raging hormones, debating how to get laid. Hell, she had a hot 1920s heartthrob waiting in a bed for her.

"I don't know why I'm here," Jo whispered.

Her eyes opened with purpose. No, she knew *exactly* why she was there. She knew what she wanted. She didn't want empty intimacy. She wanted more than an itch scratched. She wanted to explore a connection with someone who had somehow managed to pull her in with nothing but a look. Snow and she weren't anything, yet infinite possibilities stretched between them like a vast ocean.

Jo had a staring contest with the door as if it held all the secrets of the man within. But even if it did, it wasn't betraying them to her. She started down the hall in the opposite direction, hands balled into fists.

Fine, she wanted Snow. She wanted to chart that sea of "maybes" and "what ifs" between them, even if it ultimately led nowhere. She was big enough to admit it to herself. Now, it was just a matter of figuring out how and when she was going to admit it to him.

# USEFUL SKILL

J O DIDN'T GO back to her room that night.

It wasn't that she didn't *like* her room. It was lovely, like a picture. But it was also a picture that reminded her of the one night she'd spent with Wayne. Furthermore, like a picture, it was something that had little use. There was a bed (for all the sleeping she couldn't do), a desk area (pointless, given everywhere else in the mansion), the wall where she'd hung her painting from Nico (nice, but she didn't spend hours staring at it), and a small computer (that she'd long since deemed insufficient compared to the recreation room).

So, instead, Jo returned to the seat by the pool she had begun to frequent. Eslar's book from earlier was still there, waiting for her right where she'd left it. Small orbs strung along the entrance into the living and kitchen areas lit the patio with just enough light to read by. While her mind felt too mushy to really grasp any of the words that her eyes fell over, it was repetitive, mindless, and blissfully passed the time.

Right around dawn, shifting from the kitchen behind her alerted Jo to the presence of someone else. She shifted in her chair, poking her nose around the side to see what other ghost was lurking about in what had become an unofficial "quiet time" for the members of the Society.

Samson didn't seem to notice her at all, which gave Jo an opportunity to observe him. His motions had a fluidity that reminded Jo strangely of Eslar. It was a sort of grace Jo could only dream of mustering, and beyond the most virtuoso ballerina she'd ever seen. There was something that looked *magic* in the way he simply existed that no one else could seem to command.

He appeared to be busying himself with a few ingredients from the fridge, and unlike his usual demeanor, he was doing so with an easy confidence, his back and shoulders free from tension. His brown hands moved with delicate precision, and Jo was instantly reminded of the fact that she'd never actually seen the craftsman's magic at work. She could only assume it was an impressive sight to behold, given how nearly everything else about him was.

She realized then, watching him go about fixing himself an early morning snack, that out of everyone on the team, she knew the least about Samson. Beyond his position as the crafter and his five-star cooking, Jo hadn't interacted with him much, and her questions surrounding him and his origins were plenty. Rivaled only by her questions surrounding Pan, perhaps.

Before she could announce her presence to the easily startled enigma, Samson turned (as if sensing being watched) and looked directly at her. As expected, he seemed momentarily stunned, maybe even frightened, and nearly dropped his plate. Jo was quick to scramble from her chair, rushing to his aid. Samson barely caught one end of the dish, holding it shakily. Out of breath from the quick sprint, Jo held the other side firmly for a moment.

"Sorry about that, I didn't mean to scare you." At this proximity, she could see the flecks of gold in his wide-set eyes. Guilty for startling him and then encroaching on his space, she let go of the plate. As if by magic, his hold was now far sturdier.

"It's all right," he replied, though not without slouching a bit and looking quickly away from her face. "I usually don't find others here at this hour. Well, maybe Eslar, but not today it seems."

"Yeah, we all kind of hide away at night, don't we?" Jo chuckled, though it was mostly humorless, dying off quickly and replacing itself with an awkward though not uncomfortable silence. Samson seemed no more interested in striking up conversation, so eventually Jo cleared her throat and tried again by using the plate as her inspiration. "Making some breakfast?"

For a beat, Samson seemed almost confused by the question, but then he glanced from her face to his plate and recognition filled his eyes. "Oh, no. This is for later. Maybe I will want to snack then, maybe not. Making food, eating food, just . . . food helps me think, and I intend to spend the entirety of today, if not longer, working on the machine."

An idea struck Jo at the words, and while part of her thought it might be overstepping, especially with Samson's obvious preference for solitude, she rolled with it. Finding excuses to spend time with Samson outside of the kitchen had been near impossible so far, and he certainly didn't offer any opportunities of his own volition. Jo wouldn't let the present chance to learn more about her teammate and friend pass her up, especially now that her part of the wish was once again complete. The idea of simply sitting around twiddling her thumbs or re-reading the passages of Eslar's book while she waited had the potential to drive her mad.

"Would you like some help?" Samson merely blinked, so she added, "With the seismograph, I mean. I can hand you tools or something. I don't actually know how your crafting magic works, but if you need a second set of hands . . ." Her voice trailed off at his expression. Samson continued to stare at her for a long moment, face open and surprised. In fact, he stared long enough that Jo began to feel a little self-conscious about her offer. "You don't have to say yes if you would rather work alone, I just figured I'd—"

"Yes!" Samson cut her off, the word escaping him a lot louder than Jo was used to hearing from the soft-spoken man. When he realized his outburst, he slouched into himself again, a rosy blush spreading across his face. "Yes, please. I would appreciate the help."

Which was how, for the first time, Jo found herself in Samson's room.

Like most other rooms in the mansion, it was a mash-up of different aesthetics that Jo would usually presume to conflict, yet somehow, went together. Wide, rustic-looking beams that reminded her of an old-timey cabin stretched across the roof. Their dark stain was offset by the plastered and whitewashed ceiling and walls. Over the cement floor, various pelts had been thrown, and atop them long steel worktables stretched the length of the rectangular room. The whole left side seemed practically littered with tinkering tools on open counter space; the phrase "organized chaos" came to mind.

Despite the slight messiness and industrial notes clashing with natural, however, the whole room felt incredibly warm and welcoming, cozy in a way that only a properly lived in and well-loved place could be. Even the view beyond the paned window over the counters on the left was soothing. The glass was slightly frosted at the corners and looked out over high snow drifts.

Curiously, there was a secondary door on the right wall; Jo's room only boasted one entry and exit.

"What's in there? Storage?" she couldn't stop herself from asking.

"Oh, that . . ." He trailed off as he wandered toward the door. For a brief moment, Jo worried she was asking about something personal. She was grateful just to be in his space at all; she shouldn't pry. But her concerns proved unfounded as he stopped, suddenly turning, head bowed and picking at his nails. "It's my room."

*Duh.* There was no bed, no personal items in the workshop.

"Would you like to see it?"

"What?" The question came out purely in surprise, but Samson's shoulders seemed to droop further. "No, I mean, yes." Jo took a breath and gave him a big smile as his head rose timidly. "I don't want to invade your space, but I'd love to see it if you want to show me."

Relief overtook him, and Samson quickly opened the door, ushering her over to look inside.

Jo hovered in the doorframe. The truth was, there wasn't much room for her to go any further. Her original suspicion of a storage closet wasn't far off. A narrow bed took up the entire wall to the right, the door opening against it if pushed too wide. To the left was a hearth, crackling and warming more furs and blankets piled over a small but comfortable-looking chair.

A shelf was directly at her left, piled with books and other trinkets—some she recognized from Samson's fidgeting. Across from that was a narrow work table, the chair before the hearth seeming to serve a dual purpose depending on where its owner wanted to sit more. There, an array of feathers and shafts of wood were piled; a quiver hung on the wall above.

"Arrows?" Jo asked, daring to take a step in as Samson moved aside.

"Yes." He focused entirely on the quiver as well, speaking more to it than her. "I was a fletcher, in the Age of Magic."

"A fletcher? Someone who makes arrows?"

"And bows." Samson nodded, walking over hastily. "I would do quivers too. Sometimes even leathers or chainmail. I had a small smithy where I could make the heads too. Look." He pulled open a drawer, pulling out a small point of lead and twirling it between two fingers. "This one was my favorite."

"It's very lovely." She made a show of inspecting the arrowhead. Jo didn't know the first thing about archery, but she did know when someone was proud of their work and she didn't want to discourage him by not showing enough excitement. "And deadly-looking," she added, not knowing which was a better compliment for such a thing.

A dusting of rose covered his cheeks and Samson quickly looked down, stashing it back into the drawer. "Then there's—"

"What's this?" She hadn't intended to interrupt him, it just sort of happened. Jo lifted a finger, pointing at a single arrow in the quiver. Slightly taller than the rest, the feathers on its end seemed to shimmer with their own light; every time she shifted her eyes, they seemed to take on new colors in stark contrast to the pale, almost golden wood used on the shaft. "Did you make this—"

"Don't touch it!" He grabbed her wrist and Jo felt the bones crunch. She tried not to wince, but may have failed, given how quickly Samson pulled away. He clearly didn't know how much strength was in his hands. "Th-That was a gift . . . I think . . ." Samson had a staring contest with the arrow for a long moment as if waiting for it to confirm his suspicions, before turning and starting for the door. "We should get to work."

"Yeah . . ." Jo mumbled, rubbing her wrist. She took one glance back at the quiver and its mysterious contents but quickly tried to put it from her mind. Judging from the way Samson acted, it must have something to do with the wish he'd made. Hadn't Takako said that her wish now seemed hazy, too? With how long Samson had been in the Society, it would be no wonder that his recollection of the circumstances that had brought him there were faded.

Jo closed the door to his room behind her, determined to put it all far from her mind. She considered leaving briefly. But a stool had been pulled out next to where Samson was already beginning to lay out supplies. Jo accepted the unspoken invitation and settled herself down among the bits, baubles, and tools that lined the back wall. The plate of food he'd made was at her elbow (he must have set it down during her initial inspection of the place), still untouched.

Samson grabbed a work apron from a hook on the wall and gathered up tools and mismatched electronics, piling them at the center of the table. There was an air of preparation to what he was doing. His extreme focus pushed away the last of the awkwardness from the incident in his room and Jo let it fade as well. If he wasn't letting it bother him, then she wouldn't let it bother her. After several long minutes, Jo, intrigued, couldn't help but get back to her feet and walk over for a closer look at what he was doing.

The man said nothing. Frankly, Jo would've put her money on him completely forgetting that she was even there. Samson looked over the accumulated items in front of him, hands flat on the table before him and eyes bouncing from item to item with an electric focus. When Jo got close to him, she felt it instantly—magic rolling off of him in waves. Then, with a quick breath, Samson got to work.

If she'd thought his motions had been precise in the kitchen, they were even more so now. He lifted scraps of metal, plastics, and silicones, turning them into amalgamations greater than the sum of their parts. The way he handled what had now been transformed into bits of electronics and rudimentary machinery seemed almost inhuman, robotic.

Jo couldn't really comprehend what he was doing, tools and hands and magic working together to combine and transmute the items into something new, but she couldn't tear her eyes away either. Magic was invisible. There was no glow, or spark, or thread tying it all together. Yet there was also a force that could *almost* be seen in the way it all moved and shifted.

She had never seen Samson so in his element before. He looked in control, confident—emanating a breathtaking sense of purpose and passion. Watching Samson create something from pieces of nothing until familiar shapes began to form was like watching an artist paint or a musician play. Slowly, Jo could see a framework being laid out. Surprisingly, the way she saw it was not with her own sensibilities of tech, but an intuition that came with the unique magic she'd been gifted with.

"Wait."

His hands froze at her word and Jo swallowed the instant guilt that swelled at disturbing him.

"There's . . ." She struggled to describe what she saw. It was an understanding in a language that only she could comprehend. Trying to fabricate it into common words that would be useful to him was a struggle. Luckily, Samson was no stranger to struggling for words, and he was a more-than-patient listener. "This here. If this connection gets wobbled too violently it could break."

"But there wouldn't be excess movement unless—" It dawned on him the same moment Jo thought to explain it herself.

"Unless someone tried to sabotage the experiment. Or a violent earthquake hit. Or Wayne was his usual clumsy self."

He looked down, assessing what Jo had assumed to be the possible roadmap he'd been following. "Well, then, if I connect this like that . . ."

"No, it's still weak here." She leaned over him to point.

"Here, then."

Jo's magic fizzled between her ears. Her eyes scanned the board he was working on over and over again, until . . . "Yes, that's secure."

Samson leaned back with a smile of triumph. Then, in a flurry of sudden movement, he grabbed her hands. Jo leaned away, not because the contact was unwelcome, but because she'd never been touched by him so intently before. "Your magic is useful to me!"

Jo couldn't stop the burst of laughter in both amusement at his statement and in relief that she truly hadn't put him off by inquiring about his room. "I'm glad," she said earnestly. Perhaps he'd just invited her for the company, but Jo was pleased that her ability to break things could also be of use to their crafter in reverse-engineering for failure.

"I have so many things I want to show you . . ." His eyes scanned the room.

"Let's focus on this for now." There wasn't time to be distracted. "Then, later, I can take a look at whatever you want."

Samson gave a nod and set back to work.

Jo continued to hover over his shoulder, pointing out potential errors the second her magic picked them up. It was like a duet perfectly balanced between someone born to build and another born to destroy. Without having ever realizing it before, they were a near-ideal counterbalance to each other.

Their magics playing off each other gave her an easy sort of air with

Samson that Jo had never quite felt before and that bred confidence. Except . . . that wasn't right, was it? Something in the back of her mind told Jo that she *had* felt it before. She knew this feeling even better, truer—different, with someone else . . . But why?

"So how long have you been a part of the Society?" Jo asked by way of distraction. Unlike her other interjections regarding their (now shared) project, Samson's shoulders tensed this time, though his hands never stopped moving, fingers shifting elegantly over one of his tools. When he didn't respond for a while, Jo frowned. "You don't have to answer. I was just curious—you'd mentioned the Age of Magic before and I don't quite understand all the timelines, not really . . . Sorry," Jo mumbled, feeling guilty for prying yet again.

"I don't mind," Samson said, though his voice was tight and his eyes stayed pinned to his work. "It's simply a . . . difficult question."

Before Jo could tell him to ignore the question entirely, he went on.

"I was born in 1333, before the Age of Magic ended. As I said, I was a fletcher at the employ of a local duke. I made my wish when . . . well, I've been with the Society since the year 1354."

"That's . . . a long time," Jo whispered lamely, mind rebelling against the possibility. Samson just chuckled, his hands coming to a momentary stop. He kept his eyes on his project, but they looked far away, witnessing a distant memory, maybe.

"It has been," he said. "Though Eslar has been here for much longer."

A strange look came across Samson's face at the mention of the elf, a look that despite its openness, Jo couldn't seem to define. It sparked another thought that she wasn't sure she should voice, but once new information was within reach, Jo couldn't help herself.

"You must have spent a lot of time together. In the beginning."

At this, Samson couldn't help glancing in her direction, eyes wide with surprise. After a few moments, however, his face softened, the ghost of a smile pulling at his lips. He turned to face her more completely, leaning against the table and turning his back to the project. It was the first thing in hours capable of taking his attention away from the device. His eyes held a sadness in them that Jo couldn't fathom, and for the first time since meeting the awkward and kind man, she felt as though she could see just how old he truly was.

"Perhaps we would have, were it not for me. We were each other's only companions for many years—save Pan and Snow," he said eventually, crossing his arms over his chest, stopping the slight rattle that suddenly seemed to overtake his hands. "But time does not heal all wounds. Not even after hundreds of years. And I—my wish—did the unthinkable to him."

Jo wanted to ask what he meant, she couldn't imagine Samson hurting a fly, let alone someone like Eslar. But he'd already turned back to the table, the atmosphere in the room heavy with tension and the sudden, obvious desire for silence. *This* must have been why Wayne had cautioned her against asking about wishes all those months ago. Part of Jo wondered if she should leave, but she didn't move. Jo continued to study what she now knew was the second oldest member of the Society (ignoring Pan and Snow, as most seemed to do on such topics).

"Jo?" Samson said her name just as she'd pushed away from the table. He continued his task, but motioned with his chin toward the side counter of tools. "Will you pass me my pliers? I think they're somewhere by the screwdrivers. Then I'll need you to look at this again with that magic of yours. I think I finally have it sorted."

Jo blinked her own surprise, then found herself smiling. It felt like a peace offering, and even though she had more questions now than answers, she took it easily, handing him his pliers and settling back in to check his work.

# ESP

JO REMAINED WITH Samson until his fingers were red and raw and her eyes were bleary.

Somewhere along the way, she'd lost all understanding of exactly how the pieces fit together. They were mapped in such a way that only Samson's mind (and magic) could comprehend. But Jo had absolute faith in the man and his command of his project. She focused on doing as he asked, looking at this or that, making sure there wasn't an obvious way she could see the machine and its various mechanisms short-circuit, break, or otherwise come apart—short of smashing it with a hammer, or exerting enough of her magic on it. The more she worked with Samson, the more confident Jo became that she could destroy anything she wanted if she merely exerted enough force of will.

Samson leaned away from the table, wiping his brow. "I think that's it." He tilted his head this way and that.

"I got nothing else." Jo affirmed. She tilted her head to the side, looking at the machine. As much as she didn't want to come off as questioning Samson's work, she also had a curiosity that couldn't be satiated. "Shouldn't it have rolls of paper, and a needle?"

"Everything is internal here—digital. All the sensors are contained within so they have the least chance of being acted on by external forces. It was a modification I made early on, given your insights."

Jo gave an approving nod and slung an arm around his shoulders, giving them a friendly squeeze. "Well, I think you've done a great job."

Samson tensed initially, but relaxed before Jo could pull away. "Thanks," he mumbled. "And thank you for your help with this."

"Anytime you need me to figure out how to break your things, I'm here. I did promise help with some of your other tinkerings." *And I won't pry about your personal matters next time*, Jo promised mentally.

"I'll keep that in mind." Samson nodded. "For now, you should take a breather from this wish."

"What?" Jo stiffened. "Why?" She knew she'd messed up, but she'd been doing all she could to fix it. To be denied participation now—

"Because you have been working non-stop. Give your mind a rest."

"But—"

"I'll get this to Wayne and Takako. They can get it to the scientists." He lifted the contraption, starting for the door. Jo was close behind.

"Are you sure?" Jo asked, cautiously believing that this decision truly came from a place of concern over her mental wellbeing and not some sly tactic propelled out of frustration for her ineptitude at the onset of the wish.

"Working on a wish is exhausting. Let us share some of the load," he said over his shoulder.

"My mind is mush," she admitted. "But I feel too wound tight to even relax a little. I doubt taking a break from the wish would make it any better." If anything, it could honestly stress her out more.

"Perhaps you should try anyway?" It was odd to see Samson so pushy. Jo took it as a sign of true concern, and a marker for the fact that she should actually listen to him. He certainly would know what he was talking about.

"Well, I *had* been talking to Nico about picking up a new hobby," Jo said as the door closed behind them.

"Like what?"

"He asked the same thing, and like I told him . . . I have no idea." Jo grinned and, much to her pleasant surprise, Samson grinned back.

"If that's the case, then maybe I shall put forward my suggestion of continuing to work with me on my projects."

"I'd like that," she said quickly, as if he'd think about the words for too long and then take them back, realizing what he'd offered. "Whenever you need me, Samson. It's not like I don't have the time."

They both shared a laugh at that, Samson's significantly quieter than hers.

"Until then, then." He gave a nod, taking a step backwards toward Wayne and Takako's rooms.

"Until then," Jo affirmed, turning on her heel and heading in the other direction.

Her head was in a haze and her body felt energized. Taking a bit of a break actually *sounded* good, but she desperately did not want to be excluded from any steps of the wish. Jo was a mess of contradictions and obsessing over redeeming herself wasn't helping anything. She needed a break, needed something else to look at for just a little while that would occupy more of her thoughts than Eslar's book.

She'd hoped to find Nico in the living room (he was always one for a pleasant distraction), but Eslar was the lone ghost haunting the space as usual. Jo's eyes scanned the empty room, coming back to the elf who now stared at her.

"How did it go?" Eslar asked.

"What, do you have ESP now?" Jo asked, walking over to the kitchen.

"If only."

She snorted at the elf's comment. It was the most casual levity she'd ever heard from him. Jo wandered into the kitchen, opening and closing cabinets. She wasn't actually hungry, so making something was merely another way to pass the time, another habit of humanity to indulge. What new habits of the immortal could she take up instead?

"Well?" Eslar followed up when the silence had dragged on.

"How did what go?"

"Your work with Samson," he clarified.

She paused, turning to face the elf on the couch. "Really, how did you know I was working with him?"

Eslar shrugged.

"Are you sure you don't have ESP?" she asked again.

"If only," he repeated in kind. Jo found it just as amusing as the first time and she shook her head. "*Well?*"

"It went all right." *She hoped.* "In case you somehow don't mysteriously know all the details, I was helping him test the machine—" It was far more technical than a standard seismograph and deserved a better name, Jo just wasn't up for thinking of one at the present moment. "And he seems confident it'll work."

"Good, we need it." Eslar turned back to the television.

Jo turned as well, leaning against the counter. The T.V. was loud enough to fill the room.

*"The prime minister will be giving another press conference on the current steps being taken to prevent further acts of cyber terrorism and protect our nation's digital borders . . ."*

"Cyber terrorism," she repeated. It was a distinction she'd never earned before, yet Jo couldn't find any pride for it.

"They seem to be clinging to that label in regards to your hacking."

"Don't remind me." Jo turned away from the broadcast, eventually deciding on coffee. Ten hours without coffee did not a happy Jo make. At the least, the grinding, brewing, and pouring would keep her distracted from the news for just a little while longer.

*". . . scientific community agrees that there is no evidence to support the evacuation order . . ."*

"Yet," Jo spoke over the newscaster.

"We hope," Eslar added.

*Hope* was an odd choice of words. It stuck out to Jo like an HTML tag that hadn't been enclosed properly. An anomaly that was intentional, functional, yet wrong. Hope wasn't going to complete their wish. And if they didn't complete it . . .

"Eslar," Jo poured herself a mug and crossed the room to the elf as she spoke. "We all *hope* it works . . . But what happens if it doesn't?"

He looked back to the television.

Jo placed her hands on the back of the couch, hovering over him. "Eslar . . ." she prodded, giving him space to interject. He said nothing. "You're the oldest among us." Jo chose the direct approach. "Surely you must know what—"

"We've never not completed a wish."

Jo straightened away in surprise. "Never? Out of all the wishes the Society has ever granted?"

"No."

"So what happens if we fail?" Jo asked, her voice falling into a weaker hush than what she would've liked. He said nothing, his face passive, his eyes avoiding her at all costs. "Eslar—"

"I do not know," he cut her off. His intensity only made Jo more suspicious.

"But—"

"I can only assume it wouldn't be good."

"Why?" Again, he was silent. That cool distance he always managed to keep finally set Jo's blood to boiling. She took a sip of the too-hot liquid in her cup. "Eslar, what do you know?"

"Nothing."

"Bullshit." The word flew from her mouth faster than Jo could catch it. But seeing it land in the shock on the elf's face, she didn't regret it. "You know—"

"I know nothing and I do not wish to be bothered any longer." He huffed and threw open the book in his lap, looking between it and the television with a determined ferocity.

Jo abandoned the elf and her mostly untouched coffee, storming out of the room in a huff. If he wouldn't tell her, she'd find someone who would. There were only two people who were older than Eslar: Pan and Snow. Jo would rather eat her hoodie than speak to Pan. Plus, she didn't want to bother with anyone or anything else when she could go straight to the source. She'd avoided him long enough; what better excuse than this?

At the Four-Way, she heard voices in the distance—coming from the briefing room. Jo's feet stilled and she squinted down the dim hallway. The door was ajar enough at the end that she could hear Samson's voice, but she couldn't make out his words.

That same frantic, nagging feeling wormed up her neck from earlier and Jo started up the side-stair with purpose.

Jo stood before Snow's door for the first time in weeks. How long *had* it been exactly? The last time she was here was after her failed hack-a-thon. But she'd walked away that time like a coward, her tail between her legs. She couldn't even knock.

*Not this time*, Jo vowed to herself.

She wouldn't be denied and she wouldn't be turned away. She wanted —*needed*—answers, and it seemed there was only one man who could give them to her. Jo raised her knuckle and, in equal parts anger and curiosity, but mostly sheer force of will, rapped on the door a few times.

Just like the last time, it took Snow several agonizing moments to respond (long enough that Jo almost walked away). But when the door finally opened, Jo's mouth did with it. She was going to ask him everything she wanted and not tolerate any kind of subversion.

But her mind went blank the moment she saw him.

He wore a knee-length silken robe in white that seemed to accentuate his lithe figure, with tight-fitting trousers of some variety underneath. If it didn't somehow work so perfectly on him, Jo would've made a joke about looking like a second-rate rock star.

But it *did* work perfectly for him. He looked like a vampire with an ethereal edge. A sort of angel-meets-demon forbidden combo that Jo couldn't decide if she'd rather be smited or saved by. She'd honestly take a little of both, given the option.

Snow stared down at her. She could tell he was trying to withdraw, trying to keep his face passive, but he failed (miserably). Jo saw the confusion, inquiry, and . . . something more.

How long had it last been since they'd even just seen each other?

*Too long*, echoed through her chest before she could think of the actual answer.

Jo opened her mouth. She'd come here for a purpose. She'd come to pin him down and force him to tell her the truth about the Society. And yet, what slipped from her lips was a mirror to him that felt wholly necessary, like some subtle code they'd unintentionally created that meant nothing to anyone but them.

"I don't know why I'm here," she whispered. But what she really said was, *let me inside*.

Snow stared, blinking in momentary surprise. The haze lifted and his eyes flicked over to the door at Jo's left, his right. The black and ominous door that belonged to Pan.

Wordlessly, he wrapped a hand around her shoulder and half-tugged, half-ushered her into the great unknown of the Society that was Snow's personal space.

# A STEP UP FROM PRINCE

S NOW'S ROOM WAS unlike anything she could have imagined, and yet, in an odd way, it suited him perfectly.

"What are you, some kind of prince?" Jo scoffed, pleased her snark had returned.

She wasted no time in walking the perimeter, admiring the lux decor. Because it really *did* look like something right out of her childhood fantasies of royalty. Even in the dim lighting, Jo could see the immense amount of detail that went into every aspect of the architecture and the effects it housed; The lavish, four-poster bed bore a thick, dark purple comforter embroidered in colors and patterns she couldn't quite place. The latticed windows overlooked an ornately landscaped lawn—complete with two fountains, winding paths begging to be walked, and neatly manicured shrubbery.

Inside, there was even a fireplace front and center. It was composed of stone pillars and carved designs; a happily crackling fire gave the room a flickering, orange glow. Yet, for as much light as it gave, there was very little heat to match. The room was comfortable, if not a little cool.

It felt like stepping right into the fancy bedchamber of a king's castle. Well, at least her nickname of "King Snow" didn't seem so far off.

"I used to be." Snow's voice pulled her out of her musing at once. She turned to face him, expecting him to have followed her farther inside, only to find him still standing by the door, hand on the doorknob as if debating whether or not to let her stay. Jo crossed her arms over her chest, the mere thought of him pushing her away again settling beneath her skin like the annoying buzz of a bad caffeine hangover.

"Used to be?" she asked, looking him up and down before raising an eyebrow at his tense posture. Snow's head was slightly bowed, brow furrowed in thought and silver hair falling like a veil over his eyes.

"You asked if I was a prince," he said eventually, straightening back up and finally taking his hand away from the door handle. Jo guessed she was worth keeping around for a little bit longer. *How nice of him.* "I used to be. Of a sort, at least. Well, it's what some called me."

There was something about the way the words fell from his lips that stilled her sass and made Jo's heart ache. Even as he stood before her, tall, collected, and distant, she could see something in his eyes that spoke of painful memories. If he hadn't done his damndest to keep her tiptoeing all this time just on the edge of curiosity and understanding, she probably would have hesitated in prying. But, much like that night in her bedroom, he seemed almost desperate for something—and Jo herself was desperate to know what that something was.

Jo let her arms uncross and her hands fall to her hips. With an overdramatic glance about the room, she asked, "Is this what your 'sort of' princely quarters looked like then?" Whether or not he could tell she was trying to lighten the mood, she didn't know. But when his lips cracked into the barest hint of a smile, she considered it a success either way.

"I have made some adjustments over the years, but . . . mostly, yes."

Jo could see him physically relaxing under the meaningless chatter, and while she hadn't forgotten her purpose for coming here, the sight set something warm to bloom at the center of her chest. She'd had a glimpse of the stress Snow had to endure months ago in the chamber where "he'd stopped existing," and she could only imagine what else he kept secret from the group. Like, for example, what happened when they failed at a wish? But knowing she had at least a miniscule ability to put him at ease blunted the urgency of the inquiry more than she'd want to admit, and kept her tongue on safer topics.

"So what were you like, then?" Jo walked up to him with a bit more of a saunter to her step then she'd intended. She licked her lips, ignoring the way her heart sped up as his eyes dipped down to watch. "As a prince?"

"Surely you did not come here to inquire about needlessly long lineages, debates over technicalities of what makes royalty, or to hear tales of what messes all of mortal-kind were making at the time that I was left to oversee it." At one point, he must have met her step for step, easing into her personal space without her noticing. They were only about a foot apart now, but Jo swore she could feel his presence like a physical press against her own body.

"Not exactly," Jo said, though it came out more as a whisper. Her gaze dragged up the firm plane of his chest, barely visible through the slit of his robe, to rest on his face. His steel gaze scanned her face from behind the fan of his hair.

"Then what *did* you come here for?" Snow asked, and if Jo didn't know better, she could have sworn there was something implied beneath the question, like a fisherman casting a line into the dark unknown of the sea—if she'd even dare let herself read into it that way. She had so many questions, had come here ready to demand answers, and in the end, all she could manage to do was take a deep, shaky breath.

Jo licked her lips again—why was her mouth so dry? "I'm not sure, I just don't know all that much about you, you know? Or the Society, or the wishes, really," Jo added hastily, not wanting to give up entirely on her original mission. She wasn't here for him. She definitely wasn't here for him. She couldn't let him, or her heart, get any misconceptions about that.

"*Hmm.*" Snow's hum wrapped around her like a fog, making it hard for her to think, or see, for that matter. Slowly, he took another step forward, their toes almost touching. She could feel the warmth of his body like its own touch, could see every detail within the contours of his absurdly beautiful face. "You know more than you think."

"Tell me about it? About your kingdom and your, how did you put it, 'needlessly long lineages?'"

Something clouded and sad drifted through Snow's eyes at the question, though his smirk stayed firmly in place, keeping Jo from panicking. "I was not born, but created."

"What?" Jo whispered, oddly nervous.

"It was the Age of Gods, before the Age of Magic." She'd heard Age of Gods before. *But where?*

"I thought you said you were from the Age of Magic. Back in the Ranger Compound."

Snow thought a moment. "I believe I merely said magic was real at such a time."

"Way to be technical." Jo rolled her eyes. Age of Magic, that was the time when Eslar and Samson had made their wishes. What was the world like before then? "Was it common, in your time? To be made?"

"Not quite. They called me a demigod." His smirk had fallen into a small smile, still sad, but sweetened some with nostalgia.

"Demigod? Age of Gods? Sounds like a step up from prince, Mr. Modest," Jo teased, trying to laugh.

"I would have preferred to be their prince for just that reason. It seemed much . . . simpler." His eyes wandered to the window.

She suddenly wanted to change the topic to something else, anything other than that time. It sparked a sort of yearning in her that Jo didn't want. "So how does a demigod like you end up in a place like this?"

Snow stared at her for several breaths, so long that Jo almost began to feel awkward. It was expectant, like he was waiting for something. But Jo didn't know what it was, and he just shook his head. "It all started with a dangerous magic, a split goddess, and the bravery of someone I loved."

All at once, Jo's original purpose flooded her senses, the opportunity for answers standing barely inches away.

*Just one straight answer*, Jo willed herself, though it hardly settled the frantic beat of her heart or the heat steadily pooling in her chest, her stomach, lower. *Just get him to give you one straight answer about something important.* The rest would come if she could get that out, surely. She could be satisfied for a while if she got something from him, anything.

"Snow," Jo began, more firmly. "What magic? *Whose?*"

She should have expected it, considering her track record with the infuriating man, but it still settled sour and unexpected in the pit of her stomach when Snow's expression went blank. He took a step back.

"That's enough storytelling for one day, I believe," Snow said, his voice cold. Jo couldn't help but bristle.

With a huff, she took a step forward, regaining the distance he'd put between them in a single step. "You can't keep doing this." She frowned, putting her hands on her hips and looking up at him with what she hoped was an intimidating glare. "You can't keep opening up just to push me away when I get too close. Or, I don't know, just take an interest in you like a normal friend, at the very least. This back-and-forth game of emotions—it's not fair to you, and it sure as hell isn't fair to me."

Though Jo saw his resolve crumbling just slightly at the corners, Snow refused to back down. "It would be best if you left."

"There!" Jo snapped, digging a finger into his chest. "Right there! If you don't want me around, then why let me in at all?"

All at once, the atmosphere in the room shifted, a heavy but not uncomfortable weight settling between them. Snow's expression hardened to the point that it cracked, then softened, and his eyes scanned her expression. Slowly, slow enough that Jo could have backed away if she wanted to, Snow raised a hand to her face.

The touch was light, barely there, but it set Jo's cheeks aflame, her heart nearly leaping into her throat. His thumb rubbed a single line against her cheekbone, the tips of his fingers resting against her neck. It reminded her vaguely of how he'd touched her in the Ranger compound. But this . . . *this* was different. There was a familiarity to it, a boldness, a (dare she think it) slightly sensual nature to such a light caress. Jo couldn't help but wonder what it would feel like when—if—he ever actually did touch her.

His words were barely more than a whisper. "It's been so long." It had been, since he'd last touched her. "I wanted to have a solution for you this time, one that would work."

"This time?" Jo whispered back, leaning into his touch. "A solution for what?"

Somewhere deep in the back of her mind, she really wanted to know the answer. But all she could seem to focus on currently was the feel of his fingers, the warmth of his body. She could smell a hint of him in the air between them, crisp like rain or a fresh bar of soap, but as he leaned in closer, there was something like cloves resting subtly underneath. She could drown in his presence, she realized, and while the thought should have scared her, all it made her want to do was lean in the rest of the way, press her lips to his, and—

All at once, his presence was gone, and when she blinked away the haze of desire, it was to find him back by the now-open door. At first, he said nothing, simply stood there waiting for her to leave, and while she wanted to be angry, more than anything else she was just . . . hurt.

"Why did you stop?" she asked, because she couldn't help herself. "You want it, too . . . don't you?" She didn't know if she wanted to hear the answer to this, not when her heart already felt so dangerously invested, but once it was out in the open, there was nothing to be done. "You feel it. I know you do, you must."

At this, Snow frowned, his grip on the door handle visibly tightening. "Don't get involved with me. Not . . . Not now. It's too dangerous. I need more time. Especially at present."

The confusion and hurt from before began to morph once again into anger. "What does that mean? What does any of the cryptic shit you say actually *mean*?"

"I'll do my best to explain things when I can. For now, trust me, the less you know, the better," he said softly, mostly to himself, as if he was the one who needed convincing. Snow blinked, a slow fall and rise of his eyelids, then straightened, as if catching himself in a spot he hadn't ever intended to be—all traces of his previously open demeanor completely gone. "The wish has yet to be completed. It would probably be best for you to use your time more wisely."

The sincerity in his first comment evaporated at once amid the heat of Jo's anger. "Yeah, all right." She sighed, stalking past him and back into the hall, though not without taking one last glimpse at his face. "I get it, King Snow—or is your proper title 'demigod' now? Either way, sorry to take up your precious time."

She wasn't sure, but for a split second, she could have sworn he looked upset to see her go.

# NEEDS AND BRODIES

J O THREW HER watch on the shelf outside one of the recreation
rooms and stormed in.

She expected to find her usual hacker set-up. But what Takako
had said about the rooms (now seemingly forever ago) held true—
the rooms gave what was needed at the time. Or, at least it seemed to be
trying. Whatever magic the rooms used to pick up on specific needs, it
was obviously trying to provide what it thought might help Jo take the
edge off.

Unfortunately, Jo had never really been one for bondage.

So, after taking a moment to stare at the rather outlandish sex-dungeon
inside, Jo walked back into the hallway and slowly closed the door. She
might have needed to let off some steam, but maybe not *quite* in the way
the room was offering. Still, she opted for giving it another chance,
inching the door back open and peeking inside.

Jo choked on an inhale at the sight before her. This time, instead of a
BDSM lair, it was an almost perfect replica of Snow's room. So eerily
similar that Jo felt inclined to glance down the hall and prove to herself
she hadn't blacked out and wandered back to Snow's door instead. She
hadn't.

"No thank you," she insisted (though she didn't know if it was more to
herself or the room), pulling the door shut and taking a deep breath. "I'll
give you one more chance. Something simple, please." Jo opened the door.
"Much better."

It was the same replica of her apartment bedroom she'd first woken up
in when she came to the Society. There was the hamper of dirty clothes,

the wallpaper of posters and out-of-date calendars. And—what she needed most—a familiar bed.

At once, Jo jumped onto the sheets and let out a mighty groan of frustration. She felt like a kid throwing a temper tantrum. Basically, that was what she was. But it was a cathartic outlet for her frustrations; better than letting them stew and risk taking them out on someone else in the Society.

Her initial agony unleashed, Jo gave a hefty sigh.

"Why?" she asked to the silence in the room. "Why am I like this?"

There was a fire in her stomach that shed light on a vacant ache between her thighs. Jo closed her eyes, letting a hand trail down her chest, absently rubbing against her stomach.

He'd been so close; the smell of cloves still lingered on each soft inhale. Whether it actually clung to her clothes or was instead a psychosomatic memory, she didn't know. What she *did* know what that all he did was touch her, the lightest and simplest of gestures, and she'd nearly drowned. And she wanted to, she realized. She wanted to drown in him, wanted to feel the crash of his waves beneath her skin and further, deep, deep within.

She wanted him to fill her completely.

She wanted him to erode away the haze of confusion that surrounded them and finally relinquish the truth.

Without really giving it much thought, Jo slipped a hand beneath the waistband of her jeans.

Part of her tried not to think about Snow, desperately reaching for any other fantasy, any other face that might get her to where she wanted to be. But another part of her knew it was pointless. When she finally gave in to the sensation she'd been longing for, relaxed into the rhythmic friction she'd been craving, it was with an unavoidable fantasy behind her eyes.

Snow's hands on her bare skin, his lips grazing her jaw, her collarbone, her chest. His body pressed against hers, as hot and needy as she was, grasping for the same release.

She wanted to breathe nothing but that damned scent of cloves.

It didn't take long before Jo was arching off the comforter, mouth slack with panting breaths and barely concealed moans. When she finally slumped, heart clamoring up into her throat and hammering away, it was with an even more frustrating thought: despite the urge that had hurried her hand, she still felt supremely unsatisfied. In fact, the aftermath mostly just left her feeling slightly hollow, her hands cold even as her face grew hot. She was either very sick, or she might be—

Jo groaned again, a sound which turned into a loud proclamation of, "No!"

She refused. Feelings of any sort beyond the carnal would only complicate everything. Especially feelings for the one member of the Society who had the emotional aptitude of a toddler. Then again, she wasn't really in a position to judge someone else on their ability to express emotions.

What she needed was to scratch this itch and be done with it—*that's all it was*, she insisted, *an itch*. Her head would clear and she'd be back to normal, of that Jo was certain. But Snow refused to help and her own attempts hadn't done the trick, so that left one last option. Pulling herself up, Jo yanked open the door, grabbed her watch, and went in search of a worthy distraction.

Hands in the pockets of her hoodie, Jo descended the stairs to the Four-Way. Her feet moved on instinct, pulling her toward the common area. She could hear the sound of Takako's voice echoing towards her and Jo's heart skipped a beat. As if by some act of kismet, she and Wayne were back. Her feet picked up speed, and Jo sprinted into the living room to find the Society—sans Pan and Snow—all gathered around the large island in the kitchen.

Takako and Wayne stood, while the other three men sat.

". . . they seemed receptive to the machine," Takako was reporting to Samson. "There was little issue once it was hooked up and they saw it working."

Jo's eyes switched from one member of her team to the next. Wayne stood, hands in his pockets, looking every inch the epitome of self-satisfied smugness. He was in more modern clothes than he usually wore, no doubt fresh off his mission to Japan. It was a simple black suit, clean-cut as usual, but with a 2057 flare—no pocket square, pencil-thin tie, his usually gaudy cufflinks replaced by simple silver ones that arced over the hem of the cuffs.

He looked . . . good enough to satisfy the needs of any hot-blooded female, surely.

She couldn't really say if what she was about to do was necessarily a positive decision, but it was certainly better than sulking.

Without a word, Jo crossed the room in wide steps.

". . . preliminary tests came back—oh, hello, Jo." Takako was the first to notice her.

Jo gave the woman a nod, hoping things didn't come off as too rude. She was on a mission, and didn't have time for anything else. This was the distraction from the wish (among other things) that she'd needed.

"Hey, dollface, wh—" Wayne was cut off with a soft *"oof"* as Jo grabbed him by the wrist, tugging him away from the room. "I guess the lady needs a word with me," he called over his shoulder.

Jo didn't even listen for any comment or reactions. She was too focused on the one thing that was certain to finally clear her head.

"Everything jazzy?" Wayne asked.

*No, everything wasn't.* Her stomach was in knots, her head hurt, her chest ached, and all she wanted was *relief.* She wanted to escape all of it.

Jo opened the door to Wayne's room and pulled the man inside.

A penthouse suite greeted her, if the lavish furniture, expensive layout, and floor-to-ceiling panoramic view of New York City were any indication. A lush, tan carpet spread the length of the floor from wall to wall, disrupted only by the glass stairway that swirled up from its center to a second story. Leather couches in a deep maroon took up the corner with subtle but well-placed lamps on either side.

Jo didn't have much time to take in anything further. Because for all its luxury, the space felt lived in—comfortable, even. And comfortable was something Jo had every intention of making herself.

The door barely had a moment to shut before she had him pressed against it.

To Wayne's credit, he didn't startle. His eyes simply searched her thoughtfully, the beginning of a crease forming at his brow and chasing away the drunkenness that had begun to weigh on his eyelids.

"What is it, doll?" he asked, and Jo willed herself to focus on her own intent. The genuine concern lingering beneath, she ignored vehemently.

Instead, she pressed their hips together, relished the feel of the growing firmness in his pants, and took a deep breath.

*He smelled so different.*

Jo shook her head in a futile attempt to dislodge the scent of crispness and cloves from her nose. "Just shut up and kiss me."

But when Jo leaned in, eyes already fluttering closed, she wasn't met with hungry lips and panting breaths. Instead, she was brought up short by a hand pressed firm and unrelenting into the meat of her shoulder. Jo looked up at Wayne in confusion, startling at the seriousness that had now fully overtaken the man's expression.

"Wayne?"

For a long moment, Wayne only seemed to scan her face, looking for something that Jo couldn't even begin to place. His frown persisted, lips drawn in a hard line that was utterly uncomplimentary to his usually kind expressions. It drew on long enough that Jo began to feel self-conscious, pulling herself away from his now half-hearted embrace to hug her arms to her chest.

The motion seemed to snap Wayne out of whatever analysis he'd been conducting, an exasperated sigh falling from his lips.

"Look, doll," he said eventually, reaching out to pull one of her hands away from her chest and linking his fingers with hers. He gave them a squeeze, smiling in a way that somehow managed to be both fond and also pitying. It made Jo's heart warm even as her hackles rose. "I'm not naïve enough to think something's changed since Paris. As flattering a fantasy as it may be, you clearly don't want to be here just like you didn't want me to be the one touching you back then."

Jo's chest squeezed painfully, suddenly not wanting to hear another word. This wasn't what she'd come here for, and he knew that. So then why wouldn't he just give her what she needed?

"I *do* want to be here," Jo said, and if the scoff at the end of her words sounded less than believable, Wayne didn't comment. He did, however, take a step back the moment she went in for another kiss. Even if he didn't let go of her hand, something in Jo still fractured a bit.

"We covered this before," Wayne explained, rubbing the inside of her wrist with his thumb. The motion soothed her, though only enough to hear him out instead of running away in embarrassment at the feeling of being so utterly rejected. "I'm here for you if you need to talk, but having a little fun wasn't something you were looking for then, and I don't think you're looking for it now." With a sigh, Wayne let her hand drop. "I don't know what's on your mind right now, doll, but I don't touch broads that can't even see me when they look at me."

"I can see you right now." *You enigmatic ass*, Jo wanted to add, but didn't for the sake of her cause.

"No, you're looking, doll. But you're seeing something else." He gave a small shake of his head. "If I've got one rule, it's to not touch brodies like you with a ten-foot pole."

Jo's heart jumped into her throat, words spilling from her mouth like vomit as she scrambled into the defensive. "I don't know what you're— There's not— What did you just call me?"

At this, Wayne had the audacity to laugh, reaching out to run his fingers through her long, dark hair. When he rested his palm against her cheek, she couldn't help but lean into it, keeping her eyes locked with his in determination.

"A brodie is a mistake, doll face," he said, letting his hand drop only to wrap his arms around her waist and pull her in closer. "And whatever it is that's got you all caught up? If I had to put a name to it, I'd say it definitely screams 'brodie'."

The genuine look of sympathy finally had her breaking eye contact. Jo's breath caught, wavering slightly. Sure, she knew that a quick release, however satisfying, wasn't really what she was looking for, but she didn't know what else she could do.

Jo took a breath, feeling Wayne's body shift alongside hers. It felt intimate but casual, like a hug from a very close friend. She didn't know if it made her want to laugh and lean in or go back to the recreation room for another tantrum.

"In any other circumstance, I'd be more than happy to help you get this out of your system," Wayne said suddenly, low and sincere. "But I don't think you want *my* help."

"Try me," Jo challenged reflexively, feeling her face heat when Wayne only smirked.

"My advice?" He was right, they weren't on the same page. Because the help she wanted did not come in the form of ominous advice. "You're chasing a fool's yearning. Doll, you and I? We're friends, thick as thieves, have been—on my side at least—from the moment you woke up. We work that way. And yes, we almost fell into bed once, and still enjoy a good flirt despite everything. But all of that works because we know it's not what defines us. It's auxiliary, in no way an expression of something deeper."

Jo couldn't stop a blurt of laughter at his directness. She heard his own satisfied, amused, huff before he continued.

"Eternity is way too long not to get any when it's wanted."

"You're telling me." She turned her head towards the skyline outside the flat's floor-to-ceiling windows, watching the faint oranges brighten into full-blown dawn.

"Which is why, if you ever truly just want something casual, that itch scratched and nothing more, you can seek me out." He paused, and Jo could hear the echo of his earlier statements. This was not just scratching an itch, but trying to fill a square-shaped need with a round peg. It was forceful, brash, and likely not to work. He knew it. She knew it. But Jo still wished they could both just ignore it and try anyway. "But feelings? They complicate things. They make things messy. And you don't want a mess on your hands for eternity. Stay off that path before you get too far down, dollface."

Jo tensed. Careful not to dislodge his arms from around her waist, she turned to look at him, taking in the kind smile and knowing gaze. He meant well, she could tell that much. Hell, she couldn't even tell him he was wrong. Hadn't she been thinking the same thing about the complexity of feelings in the recreation room? And yet . . .

"You think it's a mistake?" she whispered, barely able to get the words out for fear of what they might mean.

"I do. And don't misunderstand," he added hastily. "This has nothing to do with wanting you all for myself or some other nonsense. I think we covered my feelings toward you rather completely." Her face must have conveyed her easy belief because he continued without pause. "I just don't think you want to get entangled with anyone here romantically, least of all our leader."

Jo ducked her head into his shoulder. So it was that obvious? She should've guessed. Even if it wasn't, Wayne would know. He knew better —and more intimately—than anyone else in the Society.

"I think I'll just . . . head out then, okay?" Jo mumbled, though she made sure to punctuate the words with a soft squeeze to his arms, making sure he knew she wasn't upset for being turned down. Wayne squeezed back, even going so far as to place a kiss on her cheek. Jo scoffed, making a show of wiping at her face. "Gross. Didn't you just say I shouldn't risk sappiness with people I was stuck with for eternity?"

He merely laughed, and Jo was thankful he spared her any further harsh, but valid, advice.

"Thanks again," Jo waved from the doorway, waiting just long enough to watch him bow, maybe a little ironically, before closing the door behind her.

She made it about halfway to her room before slowing to a stop. The idea of being alone, of stewing in her own thoughts after such a blatant realization about her feelings, made an uncomfortable sensation prickle beneath her skin. Over the past few months, when she didn't want to be alone, she'd seek out Wayne, but this was the first time that she'd felt this odd pull in her chest after leaving him.

Hesitantly, Jo glanced down the hall, past Wayne and Samson's rooms, to the door marked with an intricate name plate and decorated with a beautifully painted bird.

Jo started for the door before she could convince herself not to, hoping everyone had dispersed from the common area; she didn't think she could bring herself to drag another man from the group. Nico's room was a place she already found herself associating with safety, warmth and calm and understanding. She could watch him paint or listen to him talk, or just sit next to him and read. She wouldn't feel guilty for going to him right now either, like she would with Takako. Out of them all, he seemed to have the clearest picture on matters of the heart.

Yet, just as she was about to knock, the man in question spun out the door, nearly bumping into her.

"Oh, I'm sorry, I didn't see you there! I didn't hit you, did I?"

"Just missed me." Jo shifted her weight from foot to foot, trying to catch her balance after the quick dodge. "It was my fault entirely, I was the one right outside your door."

"No harm, no foul." Nico smiled and stepped away from the door and started down the hall toward the Four-Way. Jo hovered. She wasn't trying to be awkward, it just sort of happened when the one place she'd been heading was now walking away from her. But Nico's friend magic was the greatest of the group, for something compelled him to stop and look back at her, still hovering. There was a curious look about him that all too quickly turned kind and knowing. "Did you need something, Jo?"

"Oh . . ." Suddenly feeling very silly, Jo quickly shook her head. "No, I was just . . . I was . . ." *Literally not doing anything at all and running from my problems*, her mind finished.

"Well, then," he said as if she had actually spoken a complete sentence and not just garbled sounds. "If you're free, would you like to join me?"

"Where?"

"To my home."

# JULIA

HOME? DID SHE hear him right?

"Well, this is home. I'm going to my old home, technically," he clarified as if reading her mind.

"Florence, you mean?"

Nico gave a nod in affirmation.

"Shouldn't we stay here for the wish?" Samson had told her to take a mental health break, but just how much of one was really needed? "What if someone needs us?"

"We won't be long and we won't be using any time on our watches. Additionally, I already cleared it with Eslar."

"Cleared it with Eslar," she repeated. "It's no wonder the elf has a big head, he practically runs the place."

"Careful, or with those ears he may hear you."

A laugh escaped her in the form of a snort. Nico's easy way wore her down quickly. Samson had said to take a break, but all she'd done was run from one place to the next, hopelessly working herself up further. Really, she hadn't taken that break yet, Jo decided.

"Well, if you're sure it won't be an issue."

"I'm sure." Nico waited for her to catch up before starting down the stairs.

"So, why Florence?"

"I must see my muse on occasion. Furthermore, it gives me the opportunity to stroll through some art supply stores, see what artists are using these days, give me some ideas."

"I thought you couldn't take things back from the real world?"

"You can't," he affirmed.

"Then . . ."

"The mansion is very good to me." The answer seemed mysterious, but Jo heard it for what it was: another "because magic" explanation. "I find often that after I go on these excursions, I'll have some new supplies in my room with which to work, or the recreation room will take on a new shape for my practice."

"Reality is what you make it," Jo paraphrased one of the first things Wayne had said to her upon entering the Society.

"Well said."

Jo pulled open the door to the briefing room, holding it for Nico. She hated being in there the instant her foot met the obsidian floor. The usually chilly air was now bitterly cold, as if the mansion itself was angry for the wishes being passed along to its occupants. While the idea of a semi-sentient mansion was somewhat off-putting, it was nice to think of someone standing up for them, even if that someone was a building.

Nico paused at the Door. Jo's eyes fell on his hand as it began punching in the coordinates. He was three numbers in when the fourth button stuck. The man paused, staring at it in confusion. He pressed it again, finally freeing it from its depressed state. The motion reminded Jo briefly of the flickering monitor, but the thought vanished from her mind the second the Door opened.

Italy.

It was a country of postcards made real. They stepped into a shadowed street made of stone. Condensed buildings stretched up in walls of plaster and warm-hued paints on either side of them. Doorways, square and arched, indented by wooden doors with heavy knockers stood just off the street. Metal pleated doors, most bearing some sort of graffiti, covered garages. Up ahead there was a sign with a big white P on a blue background; behind her a café was just beginning to open up, popping the umbrellas above the few outdoor tables in a fenced-off section.

"What do you think?" Nico asked, starting off in a direction only he knew.

"It's lovely." The way the buildings were built on top of each other, clearly constructed and renovated at very different times, had her thinking of Paris. Yet this was wholly different. "Quieter than I thought it would be and it seems . . . I don't know, real?"

"How so?"

Jo tried to think of the best way to rephrase her odd statement. "Like the people here aren't . . . I don't know, fake?"

"How would they be fake?"

"Not touristy, I mean." She finally landed on what it was. "This feels like a real street where real people live."

Nico laughed loudly. Yet the sweet sounds of his amusement did not resonate or echo. They existed only for her ears. "Of course it is. And, I will say that the people who live in touristy areas are also real."

"Obviously." Jo shook her head, laughing a bit at herself. "I don't know what I was saying."

"It's inviting?" he suggested.

"Inviting, that may be a good word for it . . ." Jo half-mused, half-agreed. He held up his right hand horizontal, so his fingers stretched parallel to the ground. Nico pointed at the base of the line between his middle and ring fingers. "If the Cathedral is here—" Jo had seen the famous Duomo of Florence from Nico's room back in the mansion. "The Ponte Vecchio is here." He moved his finger down and to the left. "It's a very famous bridge, I'm sure you know of it."

She gave a sort of non-committal hum and a nod. She hadn't heard of it, but didn't want to risk discouraging the man.

"Up here—" he moved up from the initial placement of his finger to the base of the line between his ring and pinky fingers "—is the Palazzo Medici."

"And that's where we are?"

A chuckle, though Jo didn't know why the question was funny. "No, this humble little street is not the palace of the Medici." He moved his finger to the right some—east, if the top of his hand was north, from the Palazzo. "We're right around here."

"I guess I see why it doesn't feel too touristy, then." Jo wasn't sure what else to say, though she didn't want to give the impression of not appreciating the quick geography overview. "But it's lovely here."

"This was to be my street."

Jo nearly stopped mid-step just as they had begun walking again. His street, his home. She tried to imagine Nico wandering the stone pathways of Florence in a very different time. Even though she knew next to nothing of the Italian Renaissance, she had an easy time conjuring up notions of Nico bustling from place to place, struggling with canvases nearly as big as he was.

"In fact, that building—" He stopped at a cross-section, pointing down an alley. "The blue one, was to be our home. In my time, it was owned by the Medici family and was to be my atelier. We would've been comfortable there. A better life than most of our status, certainly."

"We . . . You and Julia?" Jo clarified delicately. Even if she felt closer to the man now than ever, his past was still a topic Jo would tread on lightly.

"Just so." Nico nodded, a faraway look overtaking his eyes. "She was my muse, my inspiration. A woman whose outer beauty could only be matched by her inner."

Jo remembered the last time she'd been in Nico's room, the portrait he'd been composing so carefully. She had no doubt that it was still out on the easel where he worked, waiting for its artist to return. "Your muse. You said we were going to see your muse." She'd thought he'd meant the city. He must've, surely; there was no way Julia was still alive. Unless she had some modern-day descendant that Nico kept tabs on.

"Yes, in due time." He began walking again. "I have two other stops first."

"The art store, and—?"

"The Medici archives."

That sounded familiar to her, and not because he'd just spoken about a Medici palace. But Jo stilled her questions for a while. Nico was patient, and had already displayed a tolerance for them, but she didn't want to wear him out. Furthermore, there was something to be said for simply walking through a new place and letting her mind be distracted by all there was to take in. Even if the sounds were dulled and the smells were muted outside of time, there was still much to see.

"This is my favorite art shop in the city."

They ducked into a small doorway that led into a narrow hall before quickly unfolding into the densest collection of art supplies—*anything* supplies—that Jo had ever seen. Every square inch of space was taken up by boxes in storage, some with the fronts ripped off to display tubes of paint within. There were cases and cases of brushes in every shape and size. Most of them looked identical to her, but the way Nico inspected them informed her that they were far from it.

"How did you become an artist?" Jo asked, running her fingers over a series of markers precariously perched, zero fear of actually knocking any over.

Nico paused, thinking a moment. "How much do you know about artists in the fifteenth century?"

"Assume I know nothing." Jo grinned. "And even if I did, who's to say it would be the same between your time and mine, with all the wishes separating us?"

"Fair point." Nico chuckled, continuing along. "I find that modernity has idealized the notion of artist. In my time, we were seen as having little difference from any other craftsmen, like tailors or cobblers."

"But art requires so much talent."

Nico paused at this, bringing a knuckle to his chin. "Do you think so?"

"Of course," Jo insisted. "And you must, too, otherwise you wouldn't have laughed at the mere notion of my picking up painting."

He laughed and something about the sound reminded her of a sun shower—an impossible delight. "Much of art can be learned, despite what one may say in jest. It's a technique. Just like a musician learns their instrument, I learned the canvas."

Jo remained skeptical that it'd be so simple, but she kept the thoughts to herself, allowing him to continue.

"Apprentices would work under the master, whose name usually went on the majority—if not all—of the work. He'd also oversee commissions, and tend to the shop duties. I was one such apprentice, until my work caught the eye of one of the Medici daughters and I earned a patron outright."

"Apprentices working under a master, huh . . ." Jo looked at a wall of markers. She'd never imagined there could be so many colors. Her eyes were drawn to one on the upper right, a soft, gray-bluish white. On the colored cap were a number, letter, and the name of the color: SNOW.

Just like that, she was back to thinking of him, completely distracted from whatever else Nico was saying. Wayne's warnings rang loudly in her head. Everything with Snow seemed confusing at best, agonizing at worst. How bad could it get if she pursued something and was rejected? Unless she already had been rejected, and was willfully ignoring the fact?

"Not unlike us, *hmm*?"

"I'm sorry, what?" Jo blurted, startled. Nico was suddenly at her side.

"Apprentices working for a master."

"The Wish Granter's Apprentices . . . sounds like a movie or something."

"I suppose it does." He started for the door. "Speaking of masters, on to our second stop."

"Did you get what you needed?" Jo asked as they rounded the corner on the way out.

"I believe I did." Nico beamed. "Some positively stunning new colors are being produced. Now, there's something you may enjoy, the science of paint colors . . ."

The conversation on the way to the Medici archives remained light, and mostly focused on Nico and his extensive knowledge of art supplies. Jo wasn't usually one for museums, but she found the experience to be much more palatable when there was no ticketing process, security screening, waiting in line, pushing around people, or ropes to keep her from getting close to the art.

They strolled to the Da Vinci wing, out of time and completely unhindered. Nico spent several minutes studying the recently discovered sketch, critiquing it in more ways than she would've thought imaginable for what looked to Jo like a scribble on a piece of ancient notebook paper—a very very talented scribble, but scribble none the less.

Seemingly satisfied, Nico led their departure, heading away from the Duomo and further north. The longer they walked, the quieter Nico became, until he hardly said anything at all. Usually, Jo would assume it was a result of him talking almost all day, mostly at her. But this felt different. There was a solemn weight to his silence, like someone in a deep meditation. Jo's lips remained still as well, not wanting to jar his thoughts.

They stopped before a small iron gate wedged into a tall wall, barely wide enough for a person to slip through. It wasn't locked, but it looked as though it hadn't been opened in some time. Through the bars, Jo saw the wall of a church—characterized by stained-glass windows lining the stone.

But the stone she focused on was on the ground.

Nico plucked his watch from his pocket, holding it out and clicking a nob.

"I thought you said we weren't using time."

"Just a minute . . . only for the gate." He ushered her through, closed the gate. But surprisingly, did not click out of time. Jo followed close behind him, curious.

The courtyard felt like it was another world altogether. Jo had walked through realities, but this was a different sort of magic. This was a power she couldn't comprehend or wield, even if she tried.

Vines clung to the side of the church, markings on the stone indicating where someone had attempted to cut back the foliage. Awnings and rooftops cast the ground in near-perpetual shadow, the grasses under their feet struggling to grow. Stones seemed to be in no particular order. The newest looked as if it had seen a thousand rainstorms since it was placed.

There were no footprints save Nico's. There were no epitaphs on the tombstones or mementos left. Just little weather-worn nubs insisting on remembrance to an earth that threatened to claim them once and for all.

In the shadow of the church, in the back corner, Nico made his way to a gravestone that had been sheltered enough from the elements, preserving some of its engravings. The name written confirmed Jo's suspicions, but even if the letters had been expunged by time, the carving of a woman's face would've been recognizable to Jo anywhere.

"Julia," she whispered.

"My muse." Nico knelt down before the grave. He ran his finger through the dirt and quickly scribbled a star on the corner of the tombstone. Then, and only then, did he return to his watch, clocking out of time. "My compass star, always guiding me home, ever lighting my life."

"She was truly stunning."

"My wish was to save her, you know."

Jo didn't know. She had made the broad-stroke assumption that his wish related to Julia based on the way he spoke of his lost love and a few other comments Jo had interpreted. Still, the details were obscure.

"Save her how?"

"I was not the only one to notice the ethereal nature of my Julia." Nico ran a hand over the top of the tombstone, as if caressing it. "There were others, of course. But she only had eyes for me, and I for her. At least, until someone too powerful turned his gaze to her."

"Who?" Jo's voice had dropped to a whisper. Her research came back to her—the mention of a mistress.

"Pope Alexander VI."

"A pope?" Jo hadn't wanted to be correct in her assumptions of possible connections. "I read . . . I mean, weren't they all pious and what-not?" She didn't actually know; the Catholic Church had been absorbed by the state of Italy during World War III in a play for its global reach and resources. While it still technically remained its own entity, it had long since fallen from public consciousness in the countries of North America as anything more than a puppet of a foreign power.

"Supposedly—ideally. But ideals are like the subjects of paintings. Lovely to look at, but categorically untouchable." Nico trailed off and sighed. "The Vatican had commissioned me for a Madonna. Foolishly, I used Julia for reference."

He hung his head. Such a sad weight settled onto the shoulders of the man that Jo nearly tried to hoist him back upward. But she found herself pinned in place by the gravity of Nico's sacrifice.

"The pope was known for his mistresses, you see. It was one of the worst-kept secrets in Italy. I should've known." He turned to her, eyes shining with grief even after all the years that had passed.

"It wasn't your fault," Jo whispered in response to that probing stare.

Nico huffed softly, shook his head, and looked back down at his empty hands. "They sent for her, so that she could impart further 'inspiration.' They took her from me, making it as if we had never promised ourselves to each other. My Julia, my light, was to be extinguished as nothing more than a new toy for that wretched man."

"So you made a wish."

Nico nodded gravely. "I had heard about it, whispers here and there. But I finally located a woman who could grant me the details I sought, someone who designed herself as a high sorcerer. After that . . . it was simply a matter of casting the circle."

Jo wondered what he used to cast, but he didn't say and she didn't ask. She could guess well enough, given the severity of his wish.

"And Snow saw your magical lineage, so you ended up as a member of the Society." She couldn't help but wonder if he'd been presented with the same impossible choice Snow had given her.

How did Nico choose? Life in a world with his Julia, but she would live in unimaginable pain. Or life in a world where his beloved would never think of him again, but thrive?

"I did. But the pope was assassinated and my Julia walked free before any harm was done to her. She lived a good life here in our Florence, eventually marrying another and having a whole brood of children." Nico smiled, but Jo wondered how much sorrow he'd felt over the years— watching his love, his betrothed, marry another with no recollection of his existence.

"And you still love her, after all that," Jo whispered mostly to herself, so she was startled when she got a response.

"Immensely. There is no time or world where I love her less."

"I wonder . . . what that feels like."

"Have you never been in love?"

Now, there was a question. Jo had certainly gotten around, experimented, had her fun, but love? Actual heart-pumping, world-shaking love? She thought she felt that for Yuusuke once, but the feeling wasn't returned and it fizzled way too easily back into friendship to have been much of anything more.

"Not really," she finally admitted, to herself as much as him. It seemed almost . . . sacrilegious to attempt to lie, even to herself, in a place like this. Before a love like the one Nico still carried. "Not a love like yours at least . . . I don't think I'd know it even if I saw it."

"Why is that?"

"My parents divorced when I was a kid." Jo shrugged, turning her eyes skyward, blinking. Instead of seeing clouds, she saw spats between her mother and father, the precursors to the day he walked out.

"I'm sorry to hear that," Nico said, offering the usual platitude. "But that hardly means you don't know, or can't know, love."

Jo chuckled and shook her head. "No role models at home to equate to true love, really . . . And it's not like there's much room for it in the mob. Love just means people who can be hurt to get to you. It's safer to act alone."

"I don't think so."

"You haven't seen what they'll do to people who fall out of line." Jo met his eyes, mostly as a challenge—one Nico did not attempt to meet.

"I may not know what they'd do," he conceded one battle, and continued another. "But I do know that love is its own form of protection —to have another that will look out for you, no matter what. To have an unquestioning shelter to retreat to when the world becomes too much to bear."

It was Jo's turn to be quiet. She couldn't argue with a man who had given his life for the woman he loved. Hadn't she done the same for Yuusuke? Perhaps even if their love hadn't been romantic, it was genuine.

"I still wouldn't know," she mumbled in direct contradiction to everything in her mind.

"Lying does not become you, Josephina." Nico called her out with a gentle smile. Jo returned it weakly. He was the only man who could have her smiling while backing her into a proverbial corner at the same time. "And I mean that in all areas."

The smile fell from her lips. "Huh?"

"I think you know exactly what love is." He finally began walking back toward the gate, the transition in conversation begging a physical transition back to what their lives now were. "And I think you're looking to find it."

"I don't know—" A look from Nico had Jo changing gears mid-sentence. "I can't."

"Why not? The foundation is clearly there, waiting to be built upon."

"We are talking about the same Snow, aren't we?" The idea of there being the opportunity for something genuine between them seemed so outrageous that she had no choice but to clarify. The contrast between Nico's counsel and Wayne's was so disparate, Jo felt something like a short circuit sparking in her brain.

"Who else?"

"Snow is . . . he's . . ."

"If you doubt yourself when it comes to seeing the ways of love, fine. But you have made it clear you don't doubt me. I know what a love that transcends time looks like."

"Getting a little heavy, aren't we? It's not like he and I have even broached the subject of a date, even." Jo laughed, feeling nervous energy creep up from somewhere deep within. She wanted to change the topic, desperately. And yet . . . didn't. She had originally sought out Nico for clarity and all she felt was more of a mess.

"Have faith in yourself, Jo," Nico encouraged. "You know what to do."

"Wayne thinks it's a bad idea. Too risky," Jo mumbled.

"I have no doubt. There's no denying it is risky, and Wayne treasures this team—we all do." Nico took her hand and looked her right in the eye. The other hand was held out, waiting, as the Door appeared over the gate, but Jo kept her attention solely on his face. "Trust me Jo: some people are well worth the risk of putting yourself out there and being hurt."

As he turned to input the code on the door, Jo took one more look at the cemetery. There were no flowers on the graves here. No mementos from loved ones. No mourners weeping. It was clearly a place that had been mostly forgotten by a world that had long since moved on from it.

But one man remembered. One man, outside of time, cared enough to show Jo that there was one force greater than circles, or wishes, or magic. It was the only force that could triumph over them all, lasting when all else was dust and stars on stones. Love.

She could never again question if such a thing would be worth it.

## MAN MADE RECKLESS

W HEN THEY RETURNED to the mansion, Jo went promptly to the common room to find someone who could give her an update on the status of the wish. The length of time she'd been out of commission—occupied with her own issues—now bordered on selfish. But she and Nico found the main areas of the mansion quiet.

"Everyone must be busy," Nico observed, already heading over to the kitchen.

Jo had a mug in hand before he'd even procured the beans. "I hope everything is going well." She looked around the empty room once more. "Do you think we were gone too long?"

"We were hardly gone a few hours. All will be well," Nico assured her with far more confidence than Jo could muster.

That nagging fear of being useless still sat in the back of her mind. If there was one thing she refused to be in this new life of hers, it was useless. The moment she became useless was the moment her sacrifice meant nothing, and all her magic potential to help the world would be wasted.

"I think I'll stay here," she said, as Nico moved to depart. "Just in case anyone needs me."

"Relax where you're most comfortable. We'll find you as needed," Nico assured her.

"I'm comfortable here. My usual chair is open and there's this book Eslar lent me that I should really finish." Jo paused and forced a smile. "Knowing him, if I don't finish it and give him a proper report, I'll get a talking to."

Nico laughed. "Then I shall leave you to it."

She watched him walk away. There was a downward slope to his shoulders that usually wasn't there. Was he going to work on the painting of Julia? Jo swallowed the lump that had been lodged in her throat since the church.

After an hour of not really reading (all that clung to her mind was something about a forest clearing and a carving), Jo could take it no longer and wandered back to the Four-Way, walking to the top of each stair and peering down the empty hallways before heading back toward the now-occupied briefing room.

Eslar startled at her entrance, his eyes wrenching away from the Door as if he'd been staring at it for some time. Jo cradled her mostly-empty coffee mug between her hands and leaned in the doorframe, aware of Eslar's eyes on her as she did so.

"Everything all right?" she asked when it became apparent that he was not going to be the one to break the silence. For a long moment, Eslar merely stared at her; if Jo didn't know better, she'd have said she was being analyzed. But eventually, he took a breath, letting it out on a sigh and looking away.

"I should ask you the same." He looked back to the Door. "You wandered off."

"Nico said he had your permission." Not wanting to throw Nico under the bus, Jo added quickly, "But maybe I should've asked, too."

"You don't need my permission, so long as you're not affecting the Severity of Exchange."

*Damn straight I don't*, Jo wanted to say. Instead she passed her mug from hand to hand and pretended to take a sip. He didn't seem irked, so Jo let the matter lie. "I take it we weren't the only ones who left?"

"Wayne has returned to Japan to follow up on a few things," he said, standing.

"How's it all going?"

"Let's find out," Eslar said, simply, walking towards the double doors back to the mansion and motioning for her to follow. Jo took the last swig of her coffee and did as told, hurrying silently behind Eslar (every one of his long strides was two of hers) until the two of them were standing in front of the common room's large TV. Eslar grabbed the remote and turned it on, the news station from the last couple of weeks still broadcasting the already-familiar anti-terrorism footage.

Except now, new content flashed intermittently.

"It would seem as though things are going smoothly."

"Yeah," Jo replied, though mostly out of reflex; her eyes were still trained on the new updates. After her initial failure, it seemed almost unlikely that things would be going so well now. But Eslar wasn't wrong; Takako and Wayne had managed to get Samson's machine into the hands of the right people. Now all they needed to do was wait for it to pick up the inevitable seismic activity, and then the regions would be evacuated.

It seemed so simple. So *possible*.

But because of that, it also seemed very, very hard to believe.

"I'm going to go give Snow an update," Jo heard herself say before she'd even properly made the decision to do so. Surely Snow had already heard, possibly even had his own way of keeping up-to-date. But suddenly she found herself almost eager to tell him the news.

She'd helped set things right. They'd managed to set the ball rolling. And somehow, her time with Nico had made something feel far more level inside of her. *Hope*, that's what this feeling would be called. It was the calm assurance that everything was going to be okay.

Eslar didn't say anything when she left, but she didn't miss the way his eyes followed her out of the common room. She tried to pretend there wasn't judgment in them.

This time, when she found herself in front of the solid, white door, there was no hesitation before her knuckles were rapping insistently against the wood. She had a reason to be here this time; she knew exactly what she wanted to say.

Or at least, she thought she did, until the door inched its way open to reveal the man himself.

All thoughts of the team, the updates, her redemption, the serenity Nico had given her, seemed to flutter out of her mind like a butterfly escaping an outstretched hand. She tried to grasp for it, that reason for being there that had seemed so clear only seconds ago, but all she could think was that he was right there, within her reach. And looking really, *really* good. A flowing white tunic hung perfectly over the stretch of his shoulders, his toned chest standing out beneath the low-cut 'v' of the loose collar. A sinfully tight pair of black slacks wrapped around his legs and thighs like a second set of skin. Jo felt her mouth go dry.

How was it she had no control over herself when it came to this man?

When her traveling gaze finally found its way back to Snow's face, it was to find an expression of poorly contained amusement and an eyebrow raised accusingly. It wasn't until then that Jo realized she'd been staring. And not just normal staring, but shameless admiring, possibly even leering. Damn, she might as well have been drooling too.

She felt her face go hot, and she had to force herself not to look away in embarrassment. She cleared her throat, looking over Snow's shoulder in blatant request. Snow's face softened a bit, but the amusement still lingered at the corner of his eyes.

Without a word, he stepped to the side, motioning for her to come in.

His room looked just as outlandishly regal as last time, not that she spent much time looking at it after her initial assessment. The moment

Snow closed the door and walked back into her line of sight, he once again managed to take up every ounce of her attention. This time, when he looked at her, Jo felt a distinct energy to the gaze, like the prickling in the air of lightning about to strike.

She wanted to touch him, wanted it more than anything. She realized with a heady sort of clarity that it was something she'd been wanting for a long time, possibly even from that very first moment, surrounded by blood on the dirty floor of a backwoods barn in nowhere Texas. Quite possibly, it was something she'd wanted all her life, however impossible that was. Ever since his ethereal presence had slotted so irrevocably into her life, she'd wanted it. She just hadn't realized how much.

Something on Jo's face must have given her intentions away, because without preamble or permission (though it would have been easily granted), Snow covered the distance between them and inched himself into her personal space.

Though centimeters still remained between them, Jo could feel the heat of his body as though they were already touching. Eyes never leaving Jo's face, Snow raised his hands, let his fingers trail up her arms, keeping just enough space between that she could feel the fabric of her hoodie shift but could not yet feel the press of his touch beneath.

"Do you know what you're doing here . . . this time?" Snow asked, and his voice seemed impossibly low, rumbling with a velvety warmth that she could feel deep into her chest.

She knew what she'd intended on being here for, initially, but that was as far from her mind as possible when she said, "Yes."

That centimeter of space between them suddenly felt like a mile-wide chasm, one that Jo was nearly vibrating with desperation to cross.

Snow's wandering, barely-there touch finally made it to her face; his palm gently, much too gently, rested against her cheek. She leaned into it without thought or care, shuddering against the feel of his thumb stroking an almost tender line across her cheekbone.

"I can never seem to muster reason when you are around. You make me reckless," he whispered, and she wasn't sure if she was meant to have heard it, but it settled like a comforting weight around her heart regardless. She knew all too well how he felt.

It took much too long for Jo's brain to send word for her own hand to rise, to touch back, but when it did, it found a secure place at the nape of Snow's neck. She could feel his hair brushing against her fingers, felt the slight shift beneath them with each breath he took. If she closed her eyes, she swore she could feel his heartbeat somewhere deep underneath.

She wondered if he could feel hers too. As erratically as it was beating, a heavy thud of rhythm against her ribcage, she wouldn't have been surprised.

It wasn't until their noses were practically touching that Jo realized they'd been leaning in, gravitating towards each other like being pulled out of orbit. His lips were so close, all she'd have to do was—

There was no way of knowing who finally covered that last bit of distance, not that it mattered. All that mattered, the only thing in the whole of eternity, was the feel of Snow's lips finally, *finally* pressed against her own.

It was like an electrical current arcing across the ether to strike in an impossible way. Like a conduit finally slotting into place.

Finally, finally, *finally.*

Jo kissed back with a hungry desperation, a whine clawing up the back of her throat as she pressed herself against him. She would probably be embarrassed about that later, but she couldn't find it in herself to care. And with the way Snow's arm wrapped tight around her waist, pulling her flush against him, she figured the desperation was mutual anyway.

When they broke apart, panting and staring deep into each other's eyes, it wasn't in panic and regret, worry and shame. As they held each other's gaze, Jo's cheeks flushing at the sight of his kiss-swollen lips, it was to the feel of something wholly unexpected. Something infinitely *better.*

His arms wrapped tightly around her waist; steely eyes stared back at her in something she didn't dare hope was a fondness that ran deeper than mere lust. On his lips, a soft smile just for her.

When Jo leaned back in for another kiss, heart soaring and giddiness bubbling up in silent laughter, Snow followed.

# A MOMENT OF PEACE

WANTS SHIFTED IN her faster than Jo could think, or even breathe.

She wanted him. She had him.

She wanted his lips. She had them.

She wanted his skin under her hands—well, that was still a work in progress.

From one moment to the next, she simultaneously wanted everything now and wanted to wait for it in blissful agony just as she had waited for this singular moment for what now felt like a millennium.

Her eyes slitted open, revealing a brief glimpse of his face. Long lashes covered the curve of his cheek, taking up most of her vision. In her periphery she could see his mouth moving to meet hers in a new and entirely delightful way.

His fingers buried themselves in her hair, pulling with need but tempered with a gentleness that she wasn't entirely sure she wanted. Again, shifting wants. She was somewhere between "perfectly sated" with mere kisses and "rip off my panties." Snow seemed to make the decision for her when he pulled away.

Snow's usually red lips had deepened in color to bright cherry, his usually ghostly cheeks flushed with color. Jo was certain she looked much the same. For several long moments, they just breathed, and stared.

Without warning he practically dove for her. His hands on her hips, pulling them to him. Jo felt his entire length from toe to chest and she swelled with a startled breath to close any remaining gaps.

Jo wasn't exactly sure when they'd made it onto the bed, but she knew now that it was possibly the most comfortable thing in the known or unknown universe. A veritable eternity of hours slept on it had worn it in a way that was simply perfect—not lumpy or awkwardly dipping, but the sort of cloud you sunk into to find support below.

Then again, the bed could've been a piece of plywood, all splinters and rough edges, and Jo still would've found it comfortable due entirely to the man who stared down at her—hands on either side of her head, one knee between her thighs digging pleasantly into their apex with every shift.

She trailed her fingers over his face, trying to commit every curve to memory.

"You're not going to kick me out now, are you?" Jo was glad her whisper still had strength to it, even if her knees didn't. Good thing she was lying down.

"I think we're past that."

"Glad you can finally see sense."

"As if that were ever a question?" He arched an eyebrow.

"You had me wondering."

The words broke the spell they'd fallen under, but they did not erase its effects. Snow eased away, shifting onto his back at her side. They were still flush against each other and he did not object when she shifted to place one of his arms behind her head.

For several long moments, neither said anything further, the daze of the kiss seeping into them like oil to a wick that would burn for hours to come.

"I want you to know that since the Society's founding I haven't—"

"I know." Jo cut him off. She didn't need to hear him say that he didn't usually take people to bed. He was very obviously not the type, so her question trended in the opposite direction. "Why now? Why me?"

She felt the pillow that was his arm shift as he turned his head, so Jo turned hers as well, studying his face.

"That's a difficult question."

"That's not an answer."

He chuckled. "Why you?" he repeated, more thoughtful. Jo hung on his words, her chest tightening oddly in suspense. "I've been alive . . . for more years than it's possible to count—especially with shifting time and jumping realities. In all that time, I was waiting, searching. So when I found what it was I'd been waiting for, there was—is—no question."

The idea was almost profound, and gave her pause. Was she the same? She'd never felt so instantly head-over-heels with anyone else. Even if she wouldn't dare call it love so quickly (lust did not equal love), there was a connection there—how did Nico phrase it? *A foundation*, unlike one she'd ever known. He was an enigma that felt like everything she'd ever wanted.

"You flatter me." She half shrugged and looked back at the mural on the ceiling to take off some of the pressure of being the sole focus. Stars dotted a canvas of swirling blues with ethereal god-like figures dancing among them. Jo tilted her head, slightly; it was almost as if she could remember a story that these very images depicted. Like a vague childhood tale . . .

Snow said nothing else, and Jo was inclined to leave it be. It didn't matter why he wanted her. It just mattered that he did.

"I don't want this to change anything." Damn Wayne for getting in her head now of all times. It was Snow's turn to look at her first. Jo took her eyes off the ceiling and its hidden story to give him a long, hard stare. "With the team, with wishes. I don't want this—whatever happens, whatever comes of it—to affect anyone but us."

Clarity dawned on him and Snow gave a small hum that she took to be affirmation. "It *is* only about us."

"Good." A smile stretched between her cheeks. She could have her cake and eat it too. Things dared to look like they were improving for her.

"But to that end . . . you should likely return to them."

She'd just said she didn't want things to change, and her whole heart screamed in protest of leaving his bed. Still, once work was planted in her mind, it was hard to fall back into the bliss she'd lost herself in earlier.

"The wish, it's looking positive." There. Now she'd fulfilled what she said she'd come there for. So it wouldn't be a lie if Eslar asked later.

Snow sat, his expression distant. Jo followed suit, swinging her feet over the edge of the bed. It was weird to talk about work when they were lying side by side.

"Is it?" he asked softly.

"I think the evacuation will be successful, after all." Jo grabbed his hand. His head turned to her and Snow listened intently as she filled him in on the steps that Wayne and Takako had taken to see the evacuation substantiated. "We'll reduce the Severity of Exchange, I know it."

*Pain.*

That was a weird thing to flash through Snow's eyes and it struck Jo right in the gut, leaving her dazed and breathless.

"You don't think we can?" she dared to ask.

"I hope we can. For all of us." Snow squeezed her hand tightly.

"What happens if we don't?" The infamous question—one Jo couldn't seem to get an answer to no matter how hard she tried—returned to her. It didn't matter who she asked, or when, or how. Every time, it was dodged or passed off as a great unknown. And this time was no different. Jo was no fool; there was no way Snow out of all of them didn't know what would happen.

"It won't be good." There was a deathly weight, as cold as the grave, to his voice.

"What happens?" Jo repeated, insisted, pushed.

"Jo—" More pain on his face. "—please, trust me, some things are better left unexplained. But know that I want nothing more than to defend this team—to defend *you*. It's all I've ever worked for."

It wasn't an answer. But it was the truth, that much she could tell. Still, Jo sighed heavily at being put off again. Snow's hand rose to her cheek, cupping it thoughtfully.

"Pray you don't find out."

"That's easy for you to say when you have all the answers." Even frustrated and in the dark, she still leaned into his touch. It was sturdy and comforting; it was a lifeline to the truth she so desperately needed.

"Nothing is easy for me."

"Then let me help you."

"Careful," Snow whispered, "or I just may."

Despite herself, a smile cracked through the confusion and disappointment of being thwarted yet again. No matter what Snow said, she'd find out the truth eventually. She could be patient for now, especially if she had his touches to tide her over.

"You're right, I should go back to the group," she said, rephrasing his earlier sentiment. Jo eased herself out of the plush bed and stood, her mind gradually returning to the wish.

"You should." Snow made no motion from the bed, and Jo could not ignore the way his eyes lingered on her body from heel to head.

"Should I also . . ." She wasn't trying to be seductive, which made her feel all the better about herself when pure sex oozed into her voice, spilling over the well of want he'd tapped into with his kisses. "Come back later?" Jo leaned over, both hands on the bedspread, halfway to the man who regarded her somewhere between art and a feast for famine.

"I should say you shouldn't."

"But you won't." Jo loved the way his eyes were glued to her lips as she spoke.

"But I won't," he repeated, enthralled by a hypnotic spell she didn't know she'd cast.

"Later, then."

He sealed the vow with a kiss.

The world was under her feet as Jo all but sauntered back to the Four-Way. The wish was going well, she was settling into the Society, *and* she'd finally cracked the tension with Snow in the best of ways. Jo was already looking forward to the next stretch of time between wishes. With nothing else to do . . . she wondered how much time she could spend in his room before someone noticed.

Jo was so preoccupied with the lingering blissful dizziness, the pleasant heat that had bubbled from her stomach and into her head, that it took until she had a mug in hand and coffee pot tipped for her to notice the tone of the room.

Everyone was gathered, huddled on the couches, glued to the television. Jo stared at the news and felt her own jaw go slack right before hot coffee overflowed onto her fingers and her mug shattered against the tile floor.

# PLAN C

"**W**E GAVE THEM everything they needed," Wayne repeated for what felt like at least the fifth time in the last ten minutes. This time, however, he punctuated it with a harsh kick to the edge of the couch.

"Wayne," Eslar chastised, but even the normal tone of his scolding was off, dulled by the somber atmosphere and the second run of playbacks still flashing across the television screen. The banner at the bottom of the screen read,

Prime Minister Nakamura Denies Scientists' Claims

Takako grabbed for the remote, pointing it at the TV and clicking furiously. A nearly identical broadcast popped up; the only difference was the talking head delivering the message.

*"The prime minister has called into question the organization in charge of bringing forward the speculations that what has been deemed by the Japanese government as a cyber-attack on sovereign soil is, in actuality, founded. As of right now, the government's official stance is that—"*

CLICK.

*"We should not be made to feel afraid by these terrorists. In fact, I have little doubt that they've penetrated this so-called 'lab' and—"*

CLICK. It didn't seem to matter how many news channels Takako flipped through, they were all the same.

*". . . reiterate that the Japanese government does not give heed to influence from any forces beyond our borders."* The prime minister was on, front and center. Takako's hand lowered slowly. *"It is my most sacred*

*duty to keep safe our people and our land and I will not give in to baseless claims grounded in fear and terror."*

"Wh-why is he doing this?" Jo whispered, getting no answer, and not expecting one to begin with.

Takako cursed loudly and held up the remote again. CLICK. A new talking head appeared, a new timestamp in the lower corner of the screen. Were they watching re-runs? Or was time slipping away from them like sand in an hourglass, persistently flowing toward their ultimate failure?

*". . . minister remains tough on terrorism in advance of next month's election,"* the newscaster said, matter-of-factly. *"His stance has earned him four points in the polls almost overnight."*

"An election." It was all so bloody clear now. The vague memory of a newscaster mentioning polls and points stuck out in her mind. It had always been about a stupid election.

"A damned election." Wayne growled, running a hand through his hair until the slicked-back quaff was completely disheveled. All manner of the man's usual bravado and affectations from his forgotten era had vanished, replaced instead with timeless frustration and rage. "Is there no end to the greed of politicians?"

"He's . . . he's risking everyone dying, so he can win an election?" It was phrased as a question, but Jo already knew the answer. Wayne had said it himself: there was no end to the greed.

"And to save face," Takako spoke without even turning. Jo didn't even think they'd known she was there until that moment. "If he backs down now, he'll have to admit he was wrong, and that he wasted precious time, which could mean the lives of his people."

"That's because he did!" Jo couldn't help herself. "What more does he want? We gave them proof that the evacuation wasn't wrong." *That I wasn't wrong,* her mind betrayed her, finishing. Yes, this *was* personal. This was her redemption slipping by for the sake of a man's pride.

"Well what more are we supposed to do?" Wayne asked.

Jo wasn't the only one who winced at those words. Wayne was right. They'd put all of their cards on the table with Samson's upgraded seismograph. What were they supposed to do now?

Eslar took the remote from Takako with surprising delicacy, muted the TV, and leaned back in his chair. For a long moment, the only sounds in the room were Wayne's footsteps pacing across the tile.

Samson was staring off into space, shaking hands fidgeting almost desperately. As usual, he held a small trinket that Jo couldn't identify, though she could suddenly see with new ease how to break it, if she wanted. At the look of pain on Samson's face, however, it felt as though *she* was the one breaking.

Nico sat next to Takako on the couch, an arm wrapped around her shoulders—not that the woman seemed to notice. Her head was buried in her hands, whole body hunched over and trembling as if trying to hold back a sob of emotion that could have been frustration or sorrow.

And Jo . . . continued to stand where the sickening realizations had left her, a puddle of coffee and shards of ceramic beneath her sneakers. She could barely think, let alone move, but regardless, her mind screamed to do something, do something, *do something*—

"I'm sorry." Samson's voice, barely above a whisper, sounded like a gunshot for the way everyone's attention jerked in his direction. The craftsman's hands had stilled, though they clutched at his trinket so fiercely that his knuckles looked all but seconds away from bursting out of his skin. "I'm . . . I'm sorry, I . . . I . . . I should have triple checked the specs or I should have . . . Or I should have—"

Samson's breathing picked up, and instantly Jo was reminded of Yuusuke, of how occasionally the stress would get to him, manifesting in ways beyond his control. It usually had to do with his family, or a job gone wrong, but it always ended the same. Jo could see the same symptoms of a panic attack rearing its ugly head in Samson, and, much like she would have with Yuu, she was across the room in a flash.

"Hey, hey." Jo winced internally at how her voice shook, hoping it wouldn't diminish the comfort she was trying to give. Not that it would be enough. The tense line of Wayne's shoulders and Eslar's closed off expression said as much. Takako's crumbling demeanor, beyond any comfort at all—despite the way Nico continued to rub soothing circles into her back. So Jo focused on the only thing she could do, because if she didn't do *something*, the weight of her own hopelessness would crush her too.

"Your machine did exactly what it was supposed to. This is just a stupid politician's fault for thinking that he knows better—his *pride* knows better—than actual science, not yours," Jo said, placing both of her hands over Samson's and doing her best to keep her voice steady. Confidence was beyond her at this point, but she could at least get the words out and make sure Samson knew that this wasn't his fault. If anything, this was the prime minister's.

Or hers.

"I failed, I . . . I could have . . . I could have done better, I—" Samson stammered, hands shaking beneath hers. Somewhere behind her, Jo heard a sound of frustration, probably from Wayne.

"We'll think of something else. We'll find a different way to convince everyone. We'll come up with a Plan C or—"

"Plan C? Are you joshing with us, dollface?" Wayne bit out, and the coldness in his tone made Jo cringe. For the first time since her first few days in the Society, the sound of his nickname for her left a bitter taste on the back of her tongue.

"We only have two weeks left," Nico said into the tense quiet that followed. Jo's heart ached at the sound of defeat in his voice, but she couldn't deny the claim. When Jo looked over at the Italian, his eyes were shining, lost. Takako had stopped shaking, but she still hadn't lifted her head from her hands.

"So then we have time," Jo tried, but Eslar just shook his head. "It's something."

"That's two weeks until the incident itself. If we plan to get everyone evacuated in time, that barely gives us—"

"From our initial assessments, forty-eight hours." Takako's voice was muffled from behind her hands, but even so, Jo could hear the scratch in it. It was the sound of someone desperately trying not to scream, or cry, or most likely some mix of both.

*Forty-eight hours.* They only had two days left.

What sort of Plan C could they come up with in that time? Despite how Jo's mind raced, it already felt like a losing battle. Like pushing a boulder uphill just waiting for the eventuality of her foot slipping, her strength crumbling, and the boulder crushing her beneath its inevitable roll back down.

"We'll think of something," Jo eventually whispered, but even she could hear the lack of conviction in her own words. *We have no choice.*

"Takako, wait!" Nico was suddenly on his feet, startling everyone out of their thoughts. By the time Jo followed Nico's stare to the Four-Way, Takako had already stormed off in the direction of the briefing room in an almost exact mirror to how the whole wish had begun.

Jo was torn, instinct telling her to stay with her team (with Samson, specifically), but when she caught the craftsman's eyes, he seemed to have found his resolve. He didn't say anything, just motioned towards the hall with his chin.

Jo was on her feet and following Takako at once.

Before anyone could object, Jo glanced back over her shoulder. "Start thinking up a plan," she called, already half-turned back around. "I'll be back with Takako as soon as I can."

# TARGET PRACTICE

J O SKIDDED TO a stop, pin wheeling her arms and struggling to keep her balance as she bounded through the doors to the briefing room behind Takako.

Awkwardly, she gripped a chair for balance, panting softly. How Takako had managed to cross the mansion without so much as breathing heavy, Jo did not know. But there she stood, poised and still, right in front of the Door. Her dark eyes searched Jo, the only thing that betrayed any sort of emotion in her otherwise rigid pose.

"Takako . . ." Jo's words failed her. What was she really going to say to her? What could she say? "Where are you headed?"

"Trying to stop me again?" Takako looked back to the Door, as if contemplating making a run for it.

"No, not this time," Jo said softly. Her voice was barely more than a whisper and her resolve just as thin and fragile "Why would I be?" She folded her arms over the top of the chair, sinking into the back. Jo rested her chin on her forearms and stared listlessly at the room.

"Trying to get me to go back and help with the wish then?"

"I probably should," Jo admitted. "But I don't have any ideas, do you?"

Takako shook her head.

"Then, let's go wherever you were headed," Jo suggested. It was pointless, but perhaps they both needed some pointless right about now. Perhaps she'd headed after Takako because she, too, was looking for a momentary escape. It was all she seemed to do these days—slave over the wish, or run as fast as she could away from it.

"You're sure?"

"Look, the way I figure, it's not like you're leaving forever because you *can't*. Neither can I. Snow isn't here to stop you this time, either. What's an hour?"

"One forty-eighth of what we have left?"

Well, that was a grim way of looking at it.

"Perhaps it'll be an hour well spent, gaining inspiration from the outside world. Nico and I went out earlier and it actually did me a surprising amount of good. People aren't meant to be cooped up in one place for so long." Jo paused, following Takako's line of sight to the double doors behind her. "Unless you'd actually rather head back to the common room?"

Takako's fingers flew over the keypad faster than Jo could blink.

Jo quickly crossed to her side with a few large steps, barely making it in time to be yanked by her navel through the Door and out into the real world.

The first thing she noticed was the nothingness. And not "nothing" like small town nothing. But "nothing" as in she would not be surprised to discover that they had somehow accidentally landed on Mars. As far as she could see were red rocks, rusty colored rocks, and more dark-brownish rocks. Jo turned, trying to get her bearing.

The land sloped upward, cresting at an edge with a sky bluer than she'd ever seen above. In the distance, she could make out the outline of some kind of rudimentary structure erected on the apex of a ledge. But there was little else.

The second thing Jo noticed was the wind. It howled around her, giving her skin a phantom chill. Even without being clocked into time, Jo knew that she was somewhere very, very cold.

"Where are we?" she asked.

Takako could hear her fine; the muted sensations in their ghost-like state assisted with communication in the barren landscape. "The summit of Mt. Fuji."

Jo did another quick 360, taking it all in. Tell-tale porous rocks sloped like some kind of bowl. An uninhabited and very high place. Everything that had confused her suddenly made a load of sense.

"So this is it, huh?" Jo shoved her hands into her pockets. "Kind of anticlimactic." Her words were bitter, angry. "Too bad we can't just kill it here and now. Take it out like a mobster gone rogue."

"Funny you should say that." Takako pulled out her phone, tapping the screen. Jo watched as time flowed for her. The wind whipped her hair and clothing, stretching it over her narrow, muscular frame. She shivered, but it looked more like shaking off the expectation of warmth and hardening herself against the cold than really feeling the chill.

Takako reached into her jacket, producing a handgun. It was the same weapon that Jo had seen her pull on Snow before they'd even begun the wish. Jo wouldn't exactly be surprised to learn that it was something she kept on her at all times.

"What're you doing?" Jo crossed over to her.

"I'm going to shoot it."

"Shoot what?" Jo grabbed her wrist. "The mountain?"

"Yes," Takako said it as though the fact should've been obvious. It had not been obvious.

"What do you hope that will accomplish?"

"You said it yourself, let's see if we can just take it out."

"But—"

"Has not shooting it worked?"

Jo's grip went slack. Why was she trying to stop her? The likelihood of shooting at the caldera doing anything (good or bad) was almost nonexistent. So why did it matter?

"No, it hasn't." Jo shrugged, finally taking a step back.

Takako's arms outstretched with laser-like precision and her finger squeezed the trigger.

The gunshot echoed across the entire summit, piercingly loud. It was quickly followed by another, and another, and another, until a shout rose to meet the final bullet.

The clip empty, she put the gun back into her jacket, tapped her phone, and sank to the ground. Jo eased herself down slowly next to her, as if trying not to startle a wild animal. Takako panted softly, eyes red and glossy.

"Maybe it is as simple as shooting something," Takako murmured.

"I don't know, the mountain doesn't look very dead to me." Jo didn't quite hear the severity in Takako's voice.

"No . . . I could kill him," she whispered.

"Who?"

"The prime minister." Takako looked to her, horror creeping onto her face. For a woman who'd given up her entire world for the sake of her country, Jo couldn't imagine what such a suggestion took to make. Jo couldn't even fathom what it felt like to be loyal like that to a country; she'd always been work-for-hire to the highest bidder.

"That isn't a solution." She decided to save Takako from that line of thinking. "It's a power squabble. Kill one and two more will rise up to fight over the scraps. Plus, the assassination would likely widen the Severity of Exchange, not lower it by throwing the country into sudden chaos. Everyone would focus on the death of their leader rather than keeping the discussion on the evacuations."

"You're right," Takako admitted, her breath growing regular once more. "I just. I wish I could do something. It's my family, my home. All I'm good for is pointing and shooting."

The confession, said almost offhandedly, startled her. It was such a similar feeling to what Jo had experienced during her first wish in the Society that she instantly felt a kinship with the woman that she hadn't before. Jo linked their arms, locking elbows.

"Let us take care of you, this time," she said, trying to will as much comfort and confidence into the words as she had to spare. But really, beyond all else, she just silently hoped they could.

"I'll leave it to you." Takako didn't make any motion away from her.

"But I'll grant you, it'd be nice to see if a bullet could even penetrate the PM's thick skull," Jo muttered.

Takako laughed, a sound as brief as it was soft. She looked back over the caldera, sighing, the levity unable to stick in the circumstances. "Do you really think we can do it?"

"We have to." Jo followed her gaze. "I don't think any of us are ready to accept failure."

# TWELVE HOURS

EVENTUALLY, THEY PULLED themselves back to their feet and through the autonomous, free-standing steel Door that led to the briefing room. It shouldn't have been much of a surprise to find everyone seated around the table, presumably waiting for them to return, but it still made Jo bristle nonetheless.

Before Snow or anyone else could say anything about them wasting time, Jo dropped into her seat with an overly dramatic huff.

"I know we didn't clear it with team mom first." Jo shot a glance to Eslar. "But I didn't use any time and Takako barely used two minutes, so there's nothing to worry about, *all right*?"

Snow wasn't the only one who seemed surprised by her outburst, but he was the only one she locked eyes with, willing him to argue, to fight. But mostly she was just hoping to see a crack in his otherwise carefully constructed facade.

It hadn't even been hours since she'd been lying in his bed, reveling in the feel of his arms around her, his lips against hers. How had everything gone to shit so quickly? When a momentary stare-off provided barely more than a flicker of recognition from the man, Jo looked away, feeling something cold and heavy drop into the pit of her stomach.

Maybe this was what Wayne had been trying to warn her about? Pursuing the possibility of romance with any member of the Society was only going to complicate things, and Snow? It was an infinitely trickier balance. She couldn't hold onto him now with the same emotional grip she'd clutched him with in bed. She had to pull herself together and draw some demarcation lines in her mind and heart or things would go from merely complex to ugly, fast.

"Even if your moments beyond the Door were without lost time—" Snow eventually picked up the pre-derailed conversation and put them back on track. "I assume it was also without purpose. What we need more than tantrums, is a course of action."

Jo opened her mouth to defend their spontaneous field trip, but one look from Takako kept her silent. She didn't look chastised, nor regretful, but rather accepting of her decision. Swallowing back her argument, Jo nodded, trying her best to accept the fact herself: Takako was truly a mature and admirable individual to be composed, even when hurting so completely and being chastised for merely letting out some of that pain.

"Fine, fine, okay," Jo said, sitting up straight and looking at each member of her team in turn. They hadn't failed yet; there could still be a missing piece to the jigsaw puzzle hidden beneath the great, despair-shaped couch cushions . . . or something. They just couldn't give up hope, couldn't stop searching. "So what have we done so far? And what can we do different in forty-eight hours?"

"Both very good questions."

When all eyes followed the interjection to the double doors of the briefing room, it was to find Pan leaning against the frame, fingers linked behind her head and feet crossed lazily at the ankles.

"Time's a ticking, you know," she said, using one of her knuckles to tap a rhythm against the wood that seemed eerily accurate to the width of a precise second. "What exactly *are* you going to do?"

Pan let her hands drop then, turning towards the room with a flutter of long, obnoxiously bright pink fabrics. And the dress wasn't the only thing bright and obnoxious about her ensemble today. Beneath the dress were blue- and purple-striped hose cut off at the knee by white gogo boots, and atop her head, her hair sat in two elaborately curled pigtails dyed an unnaturally iridescent gold.

The contrast of such bright colors intermingling with such a somber conversation left Jo feeling almost disjointed, off-kilter, and particularly annoyed. Not just for the unwelcome presence, but for the teasing lilt of Pan's voice, the obvious smirk on her lips. How she'd managed to put herself together in such a way eluded Jo. What made it all worse, was that she didn't exactly look like someone trying to update them on their time; she looked like someone eager to gloat over just how little they had left.

*Or, gloat over that she'd known what had been coming all along,* a tiny and very suspicious voice whispered in the back of Jo's mind. But such a thing was impossible . . . at least, Jo thought it was impossible.

"So?" Pan raised an eyebrow at the room, though her gaze seemed to settle lazily on Jo for a moment. Maybe she just imagined it, but either way, it left Jo's pulse racing.

"Just because the prime minister shed doubt on the findings doesn't make them any less true." Wayne picked them back up before Pan could rile them further. Though Jo didn't miss the way the woman-child's smirk morphed into a rather uncomfortable looking grin as the conversation resumed. "The populace, and more importantly the scientists, still have their proof. Can't just brush that under the rug, right? The news pundits are already picking up on the fact, calling out the PM for what he's doing."

"In essence, we're not dealing with scientific findings anymore," Jo chimed in, following his train of thought and trying desperately to ignore the way Pan settled herself elegantly into her seat, watching them all with an intrigue bordering on sly amusement. "We're dealing with public knowledge?"

"We already tried convincing the country," Samson added, voice small and unsure, but trying. Everyone was trying. "But that didn't work out so well . . . Plus, they're on our side, right? Because of that proof?" He seemed to need to talk himself in a circle in order to spiral towards a conclusion. "So, so, maybe we don't need to convince them anymore. Maybe we only need to focus on one person now."

"Samson's right." Eslar nodded in agreement. "This isn't about the populace at all anymore; it's about the prime minister. No matter the proof, no matter the number of citizens who believe, if he continues to deny scientific claims, we have no evacuation."

"I can convince him." Nico punctuated the claim by instantly rising to his feet. He looked around the room, even locking eyes momentarily with Pan, but his gaze eventually settled on Snow. His expression was determined, a confidence in his eyes that Jo had never seen before, though she found she wasn't surprised by it.

While the two men had their mental discussion, the rest of the table focused on Nico.

"Are you sure?" Eslar asked hesitantly.

"I am," Nico answered with more strength to his voice than Jo had ever heard.

"You're nuts . . ." Wayne trailed off in disbelief with a shake of his head. "You'll have, what? Fifteen hours to finish with enough time to get it to him?"

"I'd recommend no more than twelve," Pan said, lazily investigating her nails.

"I can do it." Nico continued to speak right to Snow, as though he had been the one asking the question.

Snow returned the Italian's gaze for a long moment before motioning towards the doors with his chin. "Then go."

Just as quickly as the claim had been made, Nico nodded and left. "Will twelve hours really be enough?" Jo murmured to no one in particular. And yet her focus drifted from the doors to their leader. She caught a glimpse of sadness, of something like worry etching Snow's face. But when he caught her staring, he didn't look away—simply held her gaze, face open and the makings of a tired smile forming before his mask fell back into place once more.

"If anyone can do it, it's Nico," Snow said in a surprisingly overt display of confidence.

"He's got to," Takako said. As confident as her statement should have been, the lingering quiver beneath gave away the woman's nervousness.

As if picking up on a cue, Pan chose those words to hop back to her feet, dusting nonexistent wrinkles out of her dress. "Well, we most certainly have faith in our Italian romantic, don't we?" she said, this time not bothering to look at anyone but Snow. With a twirl of one of her golden pigtails, she cocked her head. This time, there was no way to describe her grin other than "devious." Maybe even twisted. "Let's just hope that faith is well-founded. For all your sakes."

With that, Pan spun on her heel and sauntered out the door. When Jo looked at Snow, hoping desperately for an answer, all she got was his usual blank expression.

"Dismissed," he said, a simple if not painful demand.

But without question or complaint, they listened, mutually ignoring all things left lingering and unspoken.

# TOGETHER

J O HAD NEVER experienced a more agonizing hour of her life than the first hour in the common room following Nico's announcement.

That was, until she experienced the second hour.

And the third.

She sat, white-knuckled and buzzing with an inexplicable energy that eventually gave way to bouncing knees and tapping fingers. Jo tried to keep her eyes on the television, or focus on the sturdiness of Wayne's very welcome touch on her knee after the first hour. But it was impossible to do anything other than obsess.

The room wasn't quiet, but her mind was, and it put her in a dangerous place. All sound stayed in the realm of the physical: the television, the forced friendly chatter of Wayne and Eslar at the couch where she sat, Takako bumbling around the kitchen with Samson. It all blurred into white noise. Her mind had withdrawn to where none of it could reach.

*It's my fault,* a tiny voice betrayed once again.

She'd wasted so much time on her own arrogance, her own confidence that this wish would be so easy to maneuver around with a few lines of code. It had been her actions that had set them on this path; she'd rolled the dice of their fate from the onset. She had tried to thwart a natural disaster with man-made technologies; Jo could practically hear the cackle of Mother Nature grating against the back of her mind.

"Jo," Wayne's voice soothed. Firm but gentle, fingers closed around her wrist and pulled lightly.

The room returned to her as Jo lifted her head from her hands. She straightened her back, curling away from where she'd sunken in on herself. Jo didn't even remember her cheeks meeting her palms. How long had she been like that?

"It's going to work out," he encouraged.

*Now say it like you mean it.* Jo bit back the harsh words and forced a nod.

"What happens if it doesn't?" She braved the question that had been trailing behind her like a scrap of toilet paper since they'd first received this impossible wish. And, just like a trailing scrap, no one seemed to want to say anything about it.

No one said anything. But for the first time, it felt as if people were actually considering the question—rallying behind it, even. Eventually, one after the next, every eye in the room landed on Eslar.

"I honestly don't know." It sounded like a confession and an omission of guilt at the same time. He looked directly at Jo, referencing their conversation days ago. "I was not lying to you, then. Such a thing has never come to pass, and Snow has never elaborated to me."

Jo wondered if she could get Snow to tell her. But if he did, would that mean she'd used their closeness to her advantage? Would it be so wrong if she did? Why had she dared enter into some kind of relationship *now,* of all times?

"We won't fail though," Wayne reiterated. "We just won't."

None of them could seem to muster more than a nod of agreement.

"You're right." She wouldn't discount Nico. She'd felt the power of his magic first-hand, she knew how evocative his paintings could be. If anyone could do it, it would be him. Jo would give him all the faith in the world to see it happen.

"Would you like to bring this to him?" Samson's voice pulled Jo's attention back toward the kitchen.

"Huh?" It took a moment to register that Samson was holding a plate of food. "Oh, that?" Jo quickly rose to her feet, eager to have something to do other than sitting and worrying her hands into bone-popping tension. "Gladly."

Samson transferred the plate, and Jo eagerly left the room. It wasn't that being around the other members was hard; there was a solidarity there —bonding that could only be brought on by a terrible situation. But solidarity through terror wasn't the sort of team building she wanted.

Jo clung to the plate, her only lifeline to feeling useful, like she was still able to do something for their cause.

Instead of heading toward Nico's room, she turned left and headed up toward the recreation rooms. Nico had escaped there following the meeting, claiming that for such a work he needed the freedom of a completely new space. Jo wasn't sure if she quite understood it from an artistic perspective. But she understood it enough to see the merits from her own past work. Sometimes it took a new environment to see a problem with new light and find the right solution.

*Please let Nico have found the right solution*, she prayed silently.

Shifting the balance of the plate to one hand, Jo located the shelf holding Nico's timepiece and gave a few solid raps on the adjacent door. She waited a moment that ticked away into minutes. There was no response. Jo debated knocking again. They didn't *need* food; it wasn't possible for Nico to be truly hungry anymore. Certainly food wasn't a worthy-enough reason to throw any potential artistic groove he was in off-kilter—

The door opened, revealing a frazzled-looking, paint-splattered Nico. His eyes dropped from her face to the plate and his face relaxed into a tired smile. "Samson always knows just what I need."

He opened the door the rest of the way, motioning for Jo to enter.

The recreation room had molded itself into a cramped little studio. Plaster had cracked and fallen away in most places, to reveal porous brick walls underneath. The spider-web fractures rose to meet sturdy-looking, but weathered, wooden beams that supported a squat roof. Fire burned low in a white stone hearth—the only source of light as the world beyond the iron grated window was dark.

"Is this . . ."

"My old atelier? Yes." Nico moved to an easel set up to the left of the hearth and across from the door so that the light would reflect off it without being obstructed by his shadow. "You can set that there." He pointed to a worktable to Jo's left, already picking up a paintbrush and dragging it across his palette.

Jo let the door close behind her and crossed over to the table. It was narrow and not an inch of its surface was visible through the clutter of artistic tools—some of which she now actually recognized from the store in Florence. She took the liberty of pushing some to the side, clearing just enough space for the plate.

Nico hadn't moved, already seeming lost in a world only he and the canvas shared. Jo watched as the two continued their discussion through paint, magic, and undeniable skill. He seemed to have already forgotten she was there.

"You can sit, if you'd like." Or he hadn't quite forgotten. Nico motioned toward a stool by the hearth.

"I don't want to disturb you," Jo said hesitantly.

"You won't," he assured her without looking. "Julia would sit there from time to time, and I'm used to working with you around now. Perhaps it will invoke her spirit and bring me some luck."

Jo took the sentiment at face-value, not peeling it apart to search for meaning she knew wasn't there. She knew neither she, nor any woman, could ever be a replacement for Julia de'Este in Nico's heart. If anything, he had just paid Jo the highest compliment he could by saying that, just maybe, she could offer the ghost of a replacement in body, a balm in the form of a personified memory.

She assumed the seat, leaning against the pleasantly warm stones of the hearth. By all logic, she should feel more restless here than in the living room. The wooden stool was far less comfortable than the plush of the couch. And she could see how much progress Nico had yet to make (unless he was going for something *very* abstract this time).

But some of the tension in her shoulders gave way. Not a lot, but enough. Just seeing progress being made with her own two eyes was reassuring.

"How is the rest of the group?" he asked after silence had made its pass.

"Restless," she answered honestly. She wouldn't insult Nico's intelligence or ability to handle the truth with an attempt at lying.

Nico nodded.

"But we all have faith in you."

He took his eyes away from the painting a moment to give a smile of appreciation. Jo almost wished he hadn't. The look was so distant; like the darkness beyond, the seemingly perpetual sunshine of Nico's face had finally set, and now he looked every one of his years.

Nico turned back to the painting. "I hope I do not let you down."

"I'm sure you won't." When did encouragement turn into unnecessary pressure? It was a line Jo didn't want to cross.

"I have a favor to ask of you, Jo."

"Anything."

"Come with me to deliver this painting."

Jo straightened away from the mantle, leaning forward as if the stone had somehow obstructed her hearing. "Me? Why? I mean, yes, of course, but why?"

"As I said, I believe that you are good luck for me." The scratch and swish of his brush was the only thing filling the silence between his words. "Having you around helped me recall details I'd long forgotten of my Julia. Her youth, our youth . . ." The man stilled for only half a breath; a dot of paint dropped from brush to floor. "It has truly been so long since I have been the man she courted."

Jo opened her mouth and closed it again, unsure how to respond. She had never intended to evoke painful memories for him with her presence. Until today, she'd had no idea Julia kept him company while he painted. Yet suddenly, things began to make a little more sense, such as his openness with her and his willingness to take her to Florence.

"In any case." Nico shook his head and his eyes regained clarity, brush strokes becoming more confident once again. "Your magic of breaking into places could prove useful."

"Then it's yours. We'll do this, together."

"Together," he repeated, like a vow. "The whole Society. We'll make this happen."

There was no alternative—no other reality Jo or any of them would accept.

# BREAKING AND ENTERING

NICO WORKED RIGHT up until the end of his twelve-hour time allotment. His arms were coated up to his elbows with an array of colors and his shirt was splattered in odd places from his frantic desire to finish. All calmness Jo felt had begun to flee the moment she saw the man's shoulders starting to rise toward his ears in tension.

"That'll . . ." Nico pulled away, looking at the painting. "It'll work."

"Are you sure?" Jo hated herself the instant the question left her lips. Nico's head turned to her and the uncertainty—the panic—that filled his eyes made her heart sink to the bottom of her stomach like a lead weight.

"Only one way to find out, I suppose." He reached out toward the painting, running his hands over the small mountains and grooves in the paint.

The instant panic of him smearing the recently completed work disappeared when the picture held firm—magic, no doubt. Jo stood, pulling her arms above her head, trying to pop the tension that sitting on the stool for such a long, tense amount of time had left. It didn't work. Her body was as rigid as it had been the first moment she'd gotten to her feet.

"We should go, then?" She phrased it as a question, but what other option did they have?

"We should." Nico lifted the canvas, barely wider than his chest, and took it over to the worktable where most of Samson's food still remained untouched. Collecting some butcher paper and twine, he tied it in a sort of protective sling that could be worn over his shoulder.

"To the *Shushō Kantei*, then."

"The what?" Nico asked, as he followed her from the door. The man stopped in the hallway, pointing to the other recreation room. "Do you need to do any of your computer magic first?"

Jo paused as well. "Computer magic" had a nice ring to it. If she was back in the real world, perhaps she'd exchange "Shewolf" for a moniker of her own creation, like "The Wizard." Still, Jo shook her head at him. "This shouldn't be too difficult. We're evading guards and more simple security systems, not massive database firewalls. If I need anything, I have time enough to do it on the fly."

Nico nodded and caught up. The faith he had in her made Jo's chest swell. "How do you know where we're going?" His question reminded her of Takako and the *mugicha* they shared.

"Japan shares a border with the Lone Star Republic. It's pretty much standard education to learn about their government. Well, that, and I took a fairly recent interest when I realized how much more the Yakuza would pay for good work than other syndicates." Talking felt good, Jo realized. It kept them on task, and it kept her mind from winding around and around with worry. "The *Shushō Kantei* is across from the National Diet Building of Japan. It's where the Prime Minister lives and works."

"If we don't find him there?"

"Then he's likely in the Diet Building."

"And if—" Before Nico could finish what was no doubt an additional worry, he paused at the stop of the stairs.

Every other member of the Society (save Pan and Snow) sat in the Four-Way or right at the beginning of the hall that led to the common area. Eslar sat on a couch, reading, his air of calm unflappable. Samson was at his side, fiddling with some random object. Wayne lounged on the stairs across from them, flipping his nickel. And Takako stood by one of the tall windows. Jo wondered if she was looking at the mountains in the distance, filled with longing and concern for her home.

All heads turned when they appeared at the top of the stairs, and all eyes were on the canvas-shaped bundle slung over Nico's shoulder.

"It's done?" Eslar rose to his feet.

"It is." Nico sounded far more confident than he ever looked in the recreation room.

"We wanted to see you off," Wayne pointed out the obvious, rising as well and pocketing his nickel along with both hands. "Wish you luck."

"Jo is coming with me," Nico said quickly. "In case I need help getting in somewhere."

"Smart idea."

"Careful Eslar, or I'll think you value me as a member of this team." Jo took a shot at levity as she started down the stairs.

"Why, of course—"

"I'm kidding." She gave him a small smile that relaxed the elf's face as well. "We'll be back soon."

"Good luck," she heard Samson's small voice say after them, as they started toward the briefing room.

Jo folded her arms over her chest, then undid them. She put them on her hips, then let them sway at her sides. When had having arms become so awkward? *Everything would be fine*. Nico's power was impressive and they had the whole team behind them. *This would work.*

Yet Jo found herself wishing Snow could've been there to see them off as well. As if, somehow, the presence of the Wish Granter himself could bestow some sort of innate blessing onto their mission. At the very least, seeing his face would've given her a much-needed boost of courage.

Without fail, by her own magic or the magic of the Door itself, the alphanumeric keypad seemed to light up only in Jo's mind, pulling her fingers toward the numbers that would lead her to where she wanted to go. Eventually, Jo thought she might be compelled to figure out the pin system —how and why certain places had certain strings of numbers and how the other members knew them—but for the near future, she was content to let it remain a magical mystery.

Pulled through the portal to reality, the Texan and the Italian stepped onto Japanese soil.

Jo didn't want to fuss with anything more than they had to. The more variables that were introduced on a project, the more room there was for error. This was fairly simple: get in, show the painting, leave.

"The Door could've put us right in his office." Jo sighed heavily.

"It's not an exact science."

"It's not science at all," she said in exasperated agreement.

They found themselves in a clean if dated lobby. A receptionist busily answered phones, looking no doubt frazzled due to the extra commotion the panic had brought on. Jo felt some sympathy for the woman; it wasn't her fault that her boss was being pig-headed.

"We could try again," Jo suggested. "See if we can get closer to the office now that we're here."

"The Door has never worked that way." Nico shook his head. "I'd rather not risk it, not when we're already this close."

Jo bit her tongue a moment, chewing over the fact that the Door had, indeed, worked that way for her on more than one occasion—notably their first wish. But she didn't want to give any cause for Nico to panic or stress. If he didn't want to make an attempt with the Door, they'd just go it on foot. "Come on, this way."

"Do you know where you're going?" Nico asked.

"Just a hunch . . ."

Jo followed the flow of people in the lobby toward a back elevator, walking undetected. She listened in on the chatter. Most of it was general government business; the cavalier attitude grated on her. If they didn't start evacuations in the next twenty-four hours, it would be too late.

They emerged on an upper floor and Jo trailed behind one of the men she'd decided to follow from the elevator around the hall and up a short side stair to yet another reception area. However, unlike the main lobby of the building, this was much smaller. A single couch sat opposite a small desk where a woman greeted the man. Jo looked down the hall to a lone door bearing the white and red Japanese flag proudly.

"That must be the office," she said, starting off in its direction.

The ease with which they'd managed to get this far astounded her. Because if there was one thing she'd learned early on, it was that no job ever went off "without a hitch."

So she shouldn't have been surprised, really, when she finally stood before the door and encountered a problem.

"Jo? What's the matter?" Nico whispered, despite the fact that neither of them had their watches on. He was standing at her side, shifting the painting on his shoulder.

It wasn't until then that Jo realized she'd been staring at the door, or more specifically the biometric security system attached to it, for a good couple of minutes, frozen under the weight of the unexpected lack of magical sensation. There wasn't that same unraveling she usually felt. The lock didn't transform into a deeper understanding before her eyes. It did . . . nothing.

She closed her eyes, trying to remember anything she'd seen or heard about the technology before her. *Nada.* Eyes still closed and mind whirring like an overheating, old, moving hard-drive, she tried to imagine what the tech on the inside might be like. There had to be a weakness somewhere she could exploit. *Still nothing.* No magical spark buzzing beneath her skin, no sense of the door's secrets laying themselves bare at her feet.

With a huff, Jo let her eyes flutter back open.

"I've never seen a lock like this before," she finally managed to mumble, brow furrowed in concentration as if she might be able to will her magic to work anyway.

"I see . . ." Nico said, even though his tone betrayed that he clearly did not understand.

A new thought had a spike of terror running down Jo's spine. "Usually, that shouldn't be an issue. But my magic isn't working. It's not—I can't decipher anything." She dug deep, trying to see if she felt any hint of it at all. Nothing, nothing, *nothing.* In fact, it almost felt like an absence of magic entirely; that part of herself that was now distinctly "other" felt almost empty, hollow, the more she stared at the lock. Her stomach dropped. Not now; her magic could fail any time but *now*. "It's not helping me work out a way to break in like it normally does. I—"

"What do you mean?" Nico asked, voice equally panicked. "I don't understand."

Frantically, Jo peeled her eyes away from the biometric scanner, looking about the mostly empty hallway before landing on a wall-mounted thermostat.

Without a word to Nico, Jo rushed over to it, analyzing the make and model and recognizing it as one she'd seen installed in many of her higher-paying clients' offices. It was based on a semi-artificial intelligence unit set to recognize the average heat signatures of the bodies within the building. It pinpointed algorithmic consistencies through the sensors in the smart bands everyone wore on their wrists, adjusting each floor to benefit the widest demographic.

Hardly a look was all it took for Jo to know exactly how she would be able to access those commands and issue a building-wide freeze or meltdown. She could feel the certainty of it in her veins, hear the echoing thrum of something ethereal yet distinctly *her* buzzing about between her ears.

The relief behind the realization was so potent she could taste it. Her magic was still working, after all. *If she knew what she was dealing with.* Nico's earlier comments, before the start of the wish, returned to her.

"It's my restriction." The admission left a sour taste on her tongue.

"What is?"

"I can't crack something apart unless I sort of know how it's put together—at least the basics, I think. I have to see something of its guts . . . Without that fundamental knowledge, I'm useless." She looked back at him, panic rising in her. He'd brought her to help him get where he needed to go and now she was going to fail him. Just like she'd already failed all of them . . . again.

"Everyone has their restrictions." Nico put on a brave face, brave enough to dare a smile. "I'm sure it's nothing we can't work around." *Bless him.*

"You're right." Jo leeched off his certainty. She'd been in tougher spots. Restrictions be damned, she could do this. "If I can't break the lock, we just have to find another way in," Jo said once she was back at Nico's side.

"Likely for the best, really." He looked back down the hall. "Even if you could break into it, you'd have to have your watch active. If we clocked into time now, we'd surely be noticed."

Jo nodded in agreement. Simply unlocking the prime minister's door and strolling in was out of the question. They had to find another way to get the door open without causing a scene.

"Okay, okay." Jo ran both hands through her hair before clapping them hard on Nico's shoulders. He jumped, but otherwise made no motion to shake off the touch. "We need someone else with access. Someone else he'd trust with entry to his personal office. Maybe like, a cabinet member? Or the deputy prime minister? Something?" But where were they supposed to find someone who Prime Minister Nakamura would answer his door for? Especially in a crisis like this one? And with what *time*?

"Maybe we don't need somebody that high up." Nico's voice pulled her away from the spiraling "what ifs" and back to their present situation. He, too, seemed to be lost in thought, looking off in another direction, focus unwavering and expression set with fierce determination. It was the same resolve she'd seen when he took up the torch the rest of them had all but extinguished.

She followed that gaze back to the desk situated at the front of the hall like a guard post. A woman, likely the prime minister's secretary, sat, chatting with the man they had followed up to this floor to begin with. All at once, Nico's plan of action solidified amidst the growing details of her own.

"You're a genius, Nico!" She nearly laughed, her hands finally falling from Nico's shoulders as she began another quick search of the other offices on this floor. All she needed now was an open door and an active third-party computer, and they'd be golden. "Wait here. This won't take long!"

Jo sprinted back down the hall to one of the larger main areas. A door several yards ahead swung open, and Jo doubled her pace as she b-lined for entry. A distracted businessman exited, more focused on his phone than anything else—especially not a phantom outside of time sprinting toward the room.

*Please don't shut the door.* Jo prayed silently. *Please,* please *don't shut the door.*

Popping out of time to let herself into the man's office surely wouldn't go unnoticed. Discovery would force them to abort, pull out of time again, and wait until the chaos their presence caused died down. The prime minister would perhaps leave for a more secure area, and they'd have to figure out a way to follow. All of which wasted time they barely had.

Luckily, the distracted businessman remained exactly that, rushing out of his office without bothering to close his door, leaving it wide open for any lucky wish granter to take advantage of. From there, it was simply a matter of jumping back into time, hacking into the computer's communications systems, and accessing the right connection.

"Let's get into your email . . ." Jo crouched down behind the desk, peering up at the oversized monitor she hoped would hide her from any wandering eyes. "Dear miss secretary . . . looks like your boss needs you,"

Jo paraphrased as her fingers typed with a magical command of the Japanese language.

Jo had no doubt that it wouldn't do them any good if the secretary called the prime minister; the man was probably too busy dooming his country to deal with any of her problems beyond a curt reply over the phone. But if *he* were to request *her* presence—

Letting a combination of magic and skill flow down from eyes to fingertips, Jo sent the email from the prime minister's personal line to the secretary's desk. Even from around the corner and a few doors down, she heard the *beep beep* of a message received almost instantly. Jo clicked her way out of the various windows she'd opened, made a hasty cleanup of her work, turned off her watch, and hurried back to Nico.

He was practically bouncing on the balls of his feet as she sprinted down the hall, half watching her approach, half watching the secretary get to her feet. The woman crossed swiftly to the prime minister's door, leaving the man she'd been speaking to waiting on the couch.

They'd have seconds, if that, to get past her once she opened the door, but it was their only chance. And they were going to take it.

The secretary placed her hand over the biometric lock and Jo watched carefully: still, no magical understanding. But the lock opened, and that was all that mattered. When she cracked the door open with zero room for them to get past, Jo's heart somehow managing to plummet into her stomach and jump into her throat simultaneously. The sudden look of anxious fear on Nico's face said he felt the same way. What would they do now? There wasn't enough room for them to squeeze through.

But as if the gods of ironic fate had decided to share with her the gift of convenient memory, Jo found herself thinking back to the Rangers compound.

Snow and she had walked at a casual pace down the hallways, never once diverging from their path. All the while, they remained unnoticed, and despite the many occasions that Ranger personnel could have collided with them unknowingly, they'd somehow (subconsciously, magically, or otherwise) chosen to go around them. The elevator had been the same— cramped, yet none of the other businessmen and politicians there had decided to even try to occupy the little bit of space in the corner where Jo and Nico had stood invisible. It was just a hunch, but Jo ran with it, stepping in front of Nico and inching towards the secretary's right side.

The woman was in the process of inquiring as to the prime minister's concerns when Jo managed to get a foot between the Japanese woman and the door. There was no movement, and Jo felt her chest clench in steadily rising panic. Still, she tried to inch her hip into the smallest amount of open space the woman's leaning frame provided; to maintain her balance, she pressed her hands ever-so-slightly against the secretary's right hip.

The barely-there touch might as well have been Jo asking the secretary to step aside, what with the way she abruptly pulled back from the door to bow in apology at the prime minister's confusion and annoyance. The polite motion gave them ample room to get not just Jo, but Nico and the painting inside without issue.

By the time the secretary ushered herself out with one final, profuse apology for bothering him unnecessarily, they were situated in front of the prime minister's desk. For a breath or two, Nico and Jo just stood there, watching the face of the man standing between them and the deaths of hundreds of thousands of his citizens—content, it would seem, to pour over what looked to be poll numbers instead. It was surreal, knowing that so many lives rested on this moment, this *second*, of precious, borrowed time.

"You ready?" Jo asked, even though it didn't matter. Nico nodded, but his trembling hands said otherwise; he understood, too. Whether they were ready or not, this was happening in "Three, two, one."

Nico jumped back into time and held up the painting in the same fluid motion.

Jo held her breath.

# FINAL HOPE

"WHAT THE—" THE Prime Minister of Japan froze mid-sentence. His jaw went slack and his eyes grew glossy as he stared at the painting, seemingly no longer concerned that it had somehow magically materialized before him.

Jo shifted her weight from foot to foot. Time ticked on Nico's watch, though he barely seemed to breathe as the minutes passed. The only thing about him that betrayed life was the slight tremble in his forearms as he continued to hold out the painting.

"Is it working?" Jo finally whispered by letting out a breath she could no longer hold. Her eyes ping-ponged between the painting and the man still enthralled by it.

"I . . . I think so," Nico whispered in reply. Even though he was in time, the prime minister didn't even move or react to the voice. "I can feel the magic."

Jo closed her eyes. She blocked out the stately office and wall of windows that let in a midday sun, already setting on the last of their time. She tried to feel the magic, too, tried to sense it like she could her own.

There was a tickle on the edge of her mind, a growing sensation the more she focused on it. Nico's magic, and then hers, side by side. She stared at the painting, at the aura of power that radiated from it. Jo probed further, curious. She couldn't just leave it be. Her magic curled around Nico's magic, trying to pick it apart and understand just what she was sensing.

Something fractured against the force of her magical exploration. In her mind was the echo of something that resembled a lake in winter, ice cracking under the pressure of a weight it was not yet ready to bear. Jo opened her eyes, instinctively retreating from the odd and unwelcome sensation. She didn't need to know how his magic worked. She had already put all her faith in Nico.

He glanced over at her, as if sensing what she'd done, but said nothing.

Nakamura was still frozen, but his expression was slowly beginning to change. It morphed from a blank slate to a look of abject horror. Jo turned to look at the canvas, trying to see what he saw (without magic, this time).

Mt. Fuji rose from a haze over a land cast in shadow. What looked like the first smoldering rays of sunrise reflected off high gray clouds and put the peak in silhouette. It was almost . . . tranquil.

But when she looked back to the man in power, his brow had furrowed and his mouth was gaping, as if locked in a soundless scream. *Yes*, Jo's heart pleaded with each beat, *yes, yes, yes!*

"What should he be seeing?" she asked; conversation clearly had not broken the trance.

"Pain, destruction, loss." Generic words that could be assumed, but Nico needed to say no more. If the prime minister was witnessing even half of what the Society had seen over the past months, it would be enough.

Slowly, the man's eyes regained clarity. The glossy sheen of magic began to lift, its remnants blinked away by the most powerful man in Japan. He leaned back in his chair and stared at the ceiling.

Jo gripped Nico's wrist; the trance was clearly broken. But the Italian stayed in time. He held out the painting as if all his muscles had locked into place.

She looked back to the prime minister, who was now blinking away rogue tears spilling over onto his cheeks. "It worked," Jo whispered in relief.

"An evacuation," Nakamura whispered to himself. He turned to his computer. It was as if Nico had become a fixture in his office, a statue and a painting, nothing to be alarmed by.

Nakamura stroked in a few commands on the computer. Jo sprinted around, looking at the screen, hovering invisibly over him, a hand he couldn't feel grasping for stability on his shoulder. A document was open: standard, official-looking letterhead. The date was already typed in—

"Nico, it's a press release!" The rush of joy was going to tear her apart. The sheer relief was overwhelming. "We did it!"

As if hearing her (which was impossible since she was out of time), and as if determined to prove that everything that *could* go wrong with this wish would, Nakamura's fingers stopped mid-sentence. He hung his head, magic continuing to evaporate off his immobile shoulders like the last frayed threads that had held together the Society's hopes.

The man slowly shook his head and deleted the draft—an omen of doom. "I can't . . ." he said, as if speaking to them both.

Nico's fingers uncurled and the painting dropped like dead weight, a curtain falling upon their last hope and revealing its maker's horror. Jo watched it happen, as if in slow motion. She didn't hear the canvas striking the floor. She heard, instead, the sharp intake of breath from Nakamura. She saw the man's brow furrow and his lips part as his head snapped upward, all traces of magic gone.

"We have to go!" Jo practically leapt over the desk, bounding to Nico in a few wide steps. She grabbed the frozen Italian, shaking him. "Get out of time."

"Who the hell are you?" The prime minister was on his feet. His hand slipped under the desk, no doubt to push a panic button. "How did you get in here?"

Jo rummaged through Nico's pockets, pulling on the chain of his watch to free it. She wondered how it looked to Nakamura, if the watch was merely floating in space or perhaps didn't exist to him at all. It didn't matter; they were about to be ghosts anyway. She tried to push on the watch, turn the dials, open the face, but Jo couldn't affect it. She recalled what Takako had said when she'd first used the recreation room: *No one could activate another person's watch.*

Clinging to the chain, Jo pushed it toward Nico, dangling it in front of his face. "We have to go, Nico, *now*, push it now!"

A commotion was rising outside the door. Jo practically punched the man in the face trying to get his attention. Numbly, a hand rose, tapping on the watch.

Jo heard the prime minister's shock from behind her, no doubt coming from the fact that the strange man had just disappeared in thin air. She turned, glaring at him, and in the same moment stooped to scoop up Nico's painting. She pulled them toward the door of the room before it could be thrust open by whatever responders were fast on the way to the office.

It wasn't so much belief that made the Door appear this time, but a magical demand. Jo silently shouted across every possible universe. *Appear or feel my wrath.* And appear it did.

She wrenched it open with the energy of all her anger and sorrow, feeling like she could rip the thing off its hinges if she so chose. All at once, she allowed herself to be pulled through, painting under one arm, the other linked tightly with the now-trembling shell of a man who had been their final hope.

# WE WAIT

NICO WAS STILL in shock when they stumbled back into the briefing room, but by the slight tremor in his fingertips, it wouldn't be long before that shock wore off. Jo didn't want to know what would happen to the poor man then, almost as much as she didn't want to see the reactions on the team's faces when they found out. And they would, any second now.

Because, as expected, the briefing room was already full, brimming with tension so thick, Jo had been able to feel it even before stepping fully through the Door. Arm still looped around Nico's, helping him a wobbling step at a time towards his seat, Jo looked from face to face around the table.

Pan and Snow were missing. *The hell were they doing?* an angry little voice in her wanted to scream.

Everyone had gotten to their feet upon Jo and Nico's arrival, and after helping Nico sit down, Jo took Wayne's usual chair so as not to remove her steady presence from the Italian's side. She could feel the trembling of his fingers stretch up into an outright shaking along his arms. Any second now, he would fracture, crumble into pieces, and Jo didn't think she'd be able to put him back together. But she would damn well try. It was better than focusing on her own rising guilt, her growing panic, her pain and misery at the loss, so much loss, and they'd tried *everything,* so why had at all still turned out so, so—

"So?" Takako's voice caught Jo off-guard, wrenching her back to the briefing room. The woman was smart; she should've been able to see the creeping mental devastation all over their faces. Maybe she had. Because even though Takako had bothered to ask the question on everyone's mind anyway, it was already obvious she knew the answer. "How'd it go?"

That was all it took for Nico to lose it.

A broken sob tore its way up his throat, a sound that held as much emotional anguish as physical. Nico had worked for hours, poured everything he and his magic had into the painting that now leaned, forgotten, by the Door. There was no doubt in Jo's mind he'd been exhausted and broken down even before watching that final blossom of hope wither and die in the prime minister's eyes.

Now, he was beyond broken, inconsolable. If they could manage to ease his suffering at all after this, it would be a miracle. And after today, after every one of her own failures, believing in miracles seemed incredibly naive. They were the ones who were supposed to be the miracle workers, and they'd failed.

The group probably didn't need her to explain, but Jo couldn't handle the idea of Nico's sobs being the only sound in the room.

"He wouldn't change his mind. *Couldn't* apparently. Not even with Nico's influence." She hated the way Nico's back seized beneath her hand, whole body tense and shaking in what was more than likely guilt. She wanted to tell him it wasn't his fault, that he'd done all he could (which was true, of *course* it was true), but she knew he wouldn't hear it; Jo felt guilty too, had ever since that first botched evacuation hack. So instead, she just kept talking, raising her voice a little to drown out some of Nico's softer whimpers and cries. "Twelve hours just . . . wasn't enough time. The magic wore off too quickly and it . . . it just wasn't enough."

"No . . ." That simple word, whispered past Takako's lips, felt like having the breath ripped from her lungs. With the hand that wasn't rubbing comfortless circles into Nico's back, Jo gripped ruthlessly at her own knee. She shook her head.

"I'm sorry, Takako."

A whimper this time, Nico's hands falling from his face.

"So that's it then?" Samson whispered, and when Jo turned her head in his direction, he was staring at her with sad, scared eyes.

In fact, everyone looked worn out and filled with a hopelessness that overtook each of their usual features. The bags under Samson's eyes were prominent, his fingernails chewed down to the nubs. Takako looked like she was facing down the barrel of a gun, her hands tangled in the short hair on either side of her head. Wayne paced the room, the usual slicked-back perfection of his hair in complete disarray, his bottom lip bruised from being chewed on. Eslar's complexion was pale, the usually rich darkness of his skin almost resembling the lighter brown of Jo's own, and his face held more heavy emotion than she'd ever seen in him.

It took Nico rising slowly, shakily to his feet, for Jo to realize he'd stopped crying. Though how long ago, she had no idea. For all she knew, they could have simply been staring at each other, staring off into the panicked black holes of their own minds, for hours since their return. But now? Now everyone's eyes were on Nico.

His hands, splayed out on the briefing room table, still trembled. His eyes, staring down Eslar with a fierce attempt at an even fiercer determination, were still red-rimmed and wet. But when he opened his mouth to speak, his words were steady, steadier than any of them should have had any possibility of being in that moment.

"I'll do it again," he said. Plain and simple.

Jo's heart ached. "Nico, your restriction—"

"I'll find someone else. There must be, right? Another diplomat. Perhaps the leader of an allied power? There has to be someone else to try."

"There's not enough time," Eslar replied, brow furrowing in obvious frustration.

Nico looked down at the space between his hands, head falling between his shoulders. "I'll do it. Again."

"Nico—"

"I'll do it again!" He cried, ripping himself away from Jo and turning to face Eslar fully. "I can do it, Eslar, I can! Just let me try one more time!"

He was screaming now, Eslar looking from Nico to the rest of the room and back before walking around to their side of the table. Samson buried his head in his hands. Wayne kept pacing. Takako finally let her fingers fall from the stranglehold she had on the strands of her hair, knuckles of one hand hitting the briefing room table on its way down to her lap; she didn't seem to notice.

"Nico, enough," Eslar said, tone bordering on an order, but Nico just let his head hang again, shaking it back in forth. Jo watched, her own eyes burning, as fresh tears made new tracks down Nico's cheeks. Eslar placed a hand on Nico's shoulder, but Nico shrugged him off.

"If we have even an hour left, a *minute,* then I have to keep trying," he whispered, words beaten and battered beneath the weight of his own guilt, beneath the cruelty of their own hopelessness. "I have to try. I'll show a painting to every individual citizen if I have to. Please let me keep trying."

For a long moment, there was silence. Everyone looking at Nico and Eslar in turn. Even Wayne had stopped his pacing, though he chose to look down the hall instead, away from the room. In the hand that wasn't buried deep into his pocket, Jo could see Wayne's thumb rubbing circles into the face of his nickel.

"Eslar, I can fix this. I can do better. Please let me—" Nico started again, but Eslar just sighed, the unexpected sound cutting him off. He didn't bother with words, a nod of his head and gesture of his chin towards the door the only indication of his acquiescence.

Nico wasted no time, grabbing the painting and sprinting off towards his chosen recreation room.

There wasn't enough time. Eslar *knew* there wasn't enough time the same way they all knew. And even if there was, who else could they show that would be as effective as the Prime Minister? It was like a visceral thing writhing inside their bellies, their chests, weighing them down and keeping them from moving.

But Nico had asked anyway. Eslar had let him go anyway. Because what else could they do at this point but pretend, and wait?

Jo looked around the room; no one returned her gaze, each too caught up in the suffocation of unknown consequences to do more than stare off into space. When Jo let her stare finally fall to her lap, the shift in line of sight helped a tear slip beyond its hold. It fell in a silent lament down her cheek, off her chin, and onto the white-gripped knuckles of the hand still clutching her knee.

"What do we do now?" She asked, though the words were purely self-ish, her own spiraling mind throwing a plea out into the universe. It wouldn't have mattered if no one had responded, but it was Eslar who did.

"We wait." He sat down next to her, and it took all she had to lift her head enough to look him in the eye. She'd never seen his face filled with so much emotion; she just wished it was a better emotion than grief. "Other than that . . . I don't know."

# PLEASE

I T WAS PROBABLY only a few minutes later that Jo found herself in
front of Snow's door, but her time in the briefing room felt like hours
and weighed on her like years. She'd offered to break the news to
their leader, refusing to feel self-conscious when nobody was surprised.
What was the point in that, after everything that had happened? Everything that was *going* to happen?

She wanted to see Snow. Even if just to tell him of their failure, she
wanted to *see* him. She wanted to find solace in his presence and comfort
in his arms. She wanted to hear words of hope spill from his lips and
swallow them up with her own. So for the first time, led purely by that
need, that fragile and terrified desire, Jo knocked on his door without
hesitation.

And for the first time, as if knowing she would come, Snow opened
the door at once.

As much as she wanted to look at him, touch him, fall into him until
nothing of her was left, all Jo seemed able to do was stare at her own feet.
They'd failed him. *She'd* failed him. Surely he was disappointed, maybe
even angry. Why would he want to see her? Why would he want to see
any of them now?

The sting of tears from earlier returned, Jo's throat tightening enough
that she had to clear it twice before she felt brave enough to speak.

"I'm sorry," she said to her feet. "I . . . we tried."

She closed her eyes for a moment, willing that burn to go away, for the
pathetic grip this whole situation had on her throat to loosen. It took a
moment, the pain still fresh (if not overwhelming), but eventually she felt
confident enough that tears wouldn't fall if she opened her eyes.

When she did, it was to find a pair of crisp, white dress shoes standing centimeters away from her own. She glanced up, breath hitching at the sight of Snow's face, not looking down on her in shame or disgust, but in something soft and open and otherwise indescribable. Much like at the Rangers' compound (a moment that now felt like it belonged to another lifetime), Snow raised a hand to her cheek, thumb dragging lightly across her cheekbone to catch the remnants of a stray tear.

"You did everything you could," he affirmed, and his voice settled over her shoulders, into her chest, its own kind of comfort. A warm blanket to keep out the cold, a deep cave to wait out the storm. When he motioned for her to step inside, she did so with lighter steps than the ones that had brought her to his room only seconds ago. Or perhaps more accurately, steps heavier in a different way.

Snow closed the door behind her and stayed, waiting for her to come back to him, reclaim that space between them. So she did, nearly pressing against him from thigh to chest, arms wrapping around his waist to pull him even closer still. Her head fit perfectly beneath his chin, and as his arms returned the embrace, his breath brushing her hair, she let her ear rest against his chest. For a long moment, she did nothing more than listen to his heartbeat.

Suddenly, it was all she could do not to focus on the fragility of their situation, the creeping sensation that was quick to replace the timeless warmth of his comfort with a cold and pressing desperation not to lose this, not to lose *him*. It became clear—through some kind of evidence she wouldn't have been able to provide, but nevertheless knew existed—that if they didn't do this now, they never would. If they didn't do something, say something, right now, neither of them would get another chance.

Something terrible was coming. Jo could feel it like a shadow, looming closer and closer as the sun split apart the sky. And when that something finally got here, who knew what it would mean?

For the Society. For the team. For them.

"Snow," Jo whispered, pulling her ear away from his chest to look at him again, raising a hand to his face. Her fingers brushed lightly against his cheek before traveling to the back of his head, settling along the fine, silver hairs at the nape of his neck. Ever so slightly, she tugged him down. "Kiss me."

He bowed easily to her will, arms tightening around her waist as he brushed a chaste kiss against her lips, then deepened it into something not chaste at all.

His tongue traced her bottom lip and she opened her mouth for him in obvious invitation. She wanted every inch of him, wanted to melt into him until they were one person, close enough as to be indeterminable from each other, unrecognizable to the world beyond. Then maybe, just maybe, she could forget for a little while. After all, working and running was all she could do now. And there was no more work left to be done.

As Jo moaned into the kiss, fingers tightening in the fabric of his shirt, she felt something slotting into place, a familiar yet wholly new sensation. Her chest ached and her eyes burned, but her heart sang with the feeling of rightness, of finally, finally being where she was supposed to be.

It felt like home, like love, something she'd never known but somehow instantly recognized.

"Please," Jo gasped into his mouth, hearing her own voice on half-second delay. They hadn't even done anything yet and she already sounded wrecked, *felt* wrecked. Snow pulled back just enough to see her face, though he remained as close as possible, as if desperate not to put any unnecessary space between them. It wasn't until she saw the flush to his cheeks, the plush wetness of his lips, that she even realized how heavily she was breathing. Panting breaths whispered humid air between them; she felt dizzy from the lack of oxygen.

He looked beautiful, she decided then. More beautiful than she'd ever seen him, and more beautiful than he had any right to be. His eyes were heavily lidded but still shining like moonlight beneath the fringe of his silver hair. And the way he looked at her . . . it did things to her heart that, were she not already outside of time and reality, would have probably left her worried for her health.

Snow raised a hand and ran gentle fingers through her hair when she didn't answer right away. "Please what, my love?"

*Ah.* So he felt it too. Jo wasn't sure if she felt more like laughing or crying. Both probably. But later. There were more important things that needed taking care of right now.

"Please take me to bed." Jo tried for sultry, confident, but the heaviness of the day had left her emotionally exhausted, barely hanging on by a thread. The crack beneath her words, the undeniable shakiness to her tone, had her burying her face in Snow's chest, face heating.

She was no stranger to sex, but *this*? This cliff they were both standing on the edge of? This wasn't sex. This was so, so much more than sex. This was something she couldn't put a name to, something she wasn't even sure she *wanted* to put a name to. All she knew was that it was important. And incredibly fragile.

"You have always had a place in my bed," Snow said. "Then, now, and for as long as you want it."

"Have I?" Jo whispered back, something about the words seeming odd, though unimportant in comparison to the meaning behind them. "I'll always want it. I'll always want you. You should know that by now."

In lieu of a response, Snow leaned forward to recapture her lips, a deep and searing kiss that seemed to instantly return her to breathlessness. He sucked her bottom lip between his teeth and she gasped, arching reflexively against him. As close as that left their bodies, there was no denying his arousal pressed between them. The realization of his own desire alone was enough to have her all but drowning in her own desperate need.

There were suddenly too many layers between them, her hands wandering the planes of his chest, the wiry muscle of his arms, his shoulders. Every spot of skin felt like it singed her fingertips, sparks of electricity running up her arms at the contact. As he walked her back towards the bed, never once breaking his fierce and persistent kiss, Jo tugged just as fiercely on his shirt.

When simply tugging the fabric up wasn't enough for him to get the hint, Jo groaned, reluctantly pulling away. "Off," she huffed, lifting the bottom of his shirt enough to afford herself a delicious view of his toned abs. He chuckled in response, though whether at her shameless staring or her eager demand, she wasn't sure. Either way, he followed her order, which was all that mattered. Because within a handful of breaths, Snow was standing bare chested in front of her, a sight to behold.

Jo felt her mouth go dry, reaching out to place her hand against his chest, simply because she could. Snow's heart beat quick and firm beneath her fingertips, and Jo couldn't help but shudder at the rush of connection she felt—an unexpected intimacy when they hadn't even been properly *intimate* yet. So, as not to get off track, Jo ran the tips of her fingers across his chest, secretly thrilled when Snow took in a quiet breath.

His hands were suddenly at her back, slowly inching the fabric of her hoodie up until his fingers could rub circles into the revealed stretch of skin. Just that simple touch alone had her eyes fluttering shut, her heart stuttering into a faster rhythm.

"May I?" Snow asked, lightly tugging on the material. Jo nodded, lifting her arms when he pulled both her hoodie and the shirt beneath up and over her head. A fresh heat crawled up her neck to settle in her cheeks as Snow's gaze drifted lazily over her half-naked body. When he licked his lips, a seemingly unconscious motion, Jo felt the pang of her own desire like a burst of adrenaline.

She took a step forward and placed her hand on the waistband of his trousers, only barely touching despite the obviousness of her intention. "May *I?*" she asked, a breathless request. She waited just long enough to see his head tilt forward in a nod before lowering herself to her knees.

When she looked up, it was to find Snow gazing down at her in equal parts surprise and dark, hungry desire. It was an expression Jo planned to memorize and treasure, her confidence bolstered and the heat inside her growing at the sight.

She wanted to taste him, wanted to make him moan around the syllables of her name and crumble beneath his own pleasure. In that moment, Jo couldn't remember ever wanting something more.

Once his trousers were pooled around his feet, the thrill of what she was about to do took over, a fresh wave of need leading her almost involuntarily forward. She mouthed briefly at the obvious bulge beneath his boxers, dampening the fabric, before sliding her fingers beneath the waistband and pulling down.

There was the sound of her name, rough and desperate as it escaped past his lips, and then she was taking him in, swallowing him down as far as she could. Snow hissed, already breathing heavy, and when Jo looked up, eyes dark with her own lust, she swore she felt him twitch between her lips.

He looked sinful like this, coming apart at the seams yet still ethereal; even with his own lips bitten and parted in pleasure, he seemed otherworldly in his beauty. Jo couldn't help the swell of pride at being the one who got to see him like this, got to be responsible for the hungry look in his eyes and the fingers tightening in the long, knotted strands of her hair.

Snow's hips stuttered, not thrusting so much as desperately trying to hold himself back, and the need to watch him come undone, to pull every ounce of pleasure she could from him, was only outweighed by one thing.

She needed him inside of her. Now.

With a lewd sounding *pop*, Jo pulled away, panting softly against him and admiring her job well done. When she got to her feet again, it was on unsteady legs.

"I want you," she confessed, leaning in to whisper the words as her teeth grazed the shell of his ear; she hoped he could hear every layer of those words, every facet of what she meant but didn't say. *I want you near me, I want you inside me, I want everything you're willing to give me. I want you, I want you, I want you.*

As if the words had spurned him on, Snow chased down her lips in another fierce kiss, tongue delving strong and wet against her own. They breathed each other's heavy breaths, swallowed down each other's desperate moans, and before Jo even really registered it, the back of her knees were hitting the edge of the bed.

When she settled into the plush comforter, Snow followed, barely willing to leave an inch of space or single moment between them untouched. He kissed her until she was dizzy and begging, soft words strung together in a barely coherent jumble. All she knew was that she wanted him, so much, more than anyone she'd ever been with before.

Somewhere in their passionate blur, Snow must have helped her remove the rest of her clothes, because the next moment of clarity was the feel of their naked bodies pressed flush. She could feel him between her thighs, not yet pushing in, but shifting against her in subconscious impatience.

Well. She was impatient too.

So when he didn't make the first move, she reached between them, captured his gaze, and guided him in. His eyes fluttering shut as he sheathed himself fully inside her was another expression she planned to commit to memory.

Not that her mental functions had any hope of continuing properly once he started to move. His first thrust had her gasping out his name, back arching off the bed as he filled her completely. She wrapped her arms around the back of his neck, locked her ankles at the small of his back. And when he picked up a rhythm, not fast and rough, but slow and deep and intimate, she swore she could feel every inch of him, sparks of pleasure building into a heat that would eventually set them both aflame.

This was so, so much more than scratching an itch.

Eventually his pace wasn't enough, her whole body teetering on the edge of something mind-blowing without knowing how to topple over.

"Faster, Snow, please . . ." She half-moaned, half-whined, into his neck, lips brushing against his pulse. He obliged, making her cry out and cling harder, so close it was like riding a constant wave of pleasure that refused to crash.

But somehow, Snow seemed to know what to do, navigating that rising tide with a hand between them, working a rhythm that had her whole body quaking. It was a rush of pleasure so profound, she swore she blipped out of existence for a second, her brain shutting off and rebooting under the pounding burst of pure ecstasy.

She might have literally shouted his name.

Even as she came down from her high, that same pleasure thrummed like a second skin beneath every inch of her, made only more prominent as she felt Snow lose rhythm, his hips stuttering in the aftermath of his own release.

He whispered something into her neck then, something she didn't catch over the ringing in her ears, but by the way he continued to hold her tight, she figured it was something good.

The echo of their intimacy rang through her ears as he breathed, his weight on top of her heavy as his breath. She trailed her fingers up his spine, to his shoulders, and back down to just above the firm curve of his rear. He seemed in no haste to move and she was in even less to push him away.

His fingers were the first to find life, tangling in her hair, catching the side of her face in gentle caresses. They unwound, releasing her as he pulled away. But they shared an unspoken agreement to savor every last moment of that connection, every tingling, shivering sensation that there was to be felt until the very last second.

When Snow finally lay beside her, Jo could feel the floaty high of post-orgasmic bliss starting to fade. But she didn't want it to. She wasn't ready for it to end, for any of it to end. So she curled up against Snow's chest and closed her eyes, holding him just as tightly as he seemed determined to do to her. She felt his heart slow and listened to him catch his breath, and she pressed kisses against his collarbone, his shoulder, his jaw.

Neither of them spoke, too afraid of popping the bubble they'd managed to temporarily hide themselves inside. And when they eventually managed to drift off to sleep, it was to nothing more than the sound of each other's breathing, and the millions of things neither of them could bring themselves to say.

# THEIR LAST MEAL

ORNING CAME TOO soon.

Though perhaps it wasn't the morning—merely the aftermath. It was the calm not before, or after, but between the storms.

Jo rested in that eye, clinging to the stability she'd found in the man who was still curled naked next to her. She pressed her forehead into the center of his chest, her nose crushed against his breastbone, and she breathed him in as if to absorb his essence, commit it to memory, and store it for whatever was to come.

She could've asked him then, what awaited them all the moment the clocks ran out. But Jo couldn't find the words. She would wait, and tolerate the unknown, if it meant the preservation of the space that they had collapsed into together and made their own.

Eventually, the tension in his arms increased and then lessened. Whether he had been asleep until now or just mindlessly drifting in a similar twilight haze, Jo didn't know. But he shifted now, alerting to his consciousness, accepting—however reluctantly—the passage of time. The deadline of some unforeseen consequence loomed overhead like a guillotine. Wordlessly, he pulled away, enough to look at her and enough for Jo to breathe. She searched his face, waiting for whatever he had to say next.

"We should return to them," Snow whispered, punctuating it with a long press of his lips to her temple. "They need you now."

"They need you as well," Jo insisted. "They need their leader, Snow."

"I'm not one for support . . ." He wavered, tipping his head to nuzzle her cheek with his nose. "I've always kept my distance, I've had to."

"Not with me."

"You're different."

"Why?" The question flew from her lips like an arrow from the bow. Pointed, poignant, fired to kill. It struck true; Snow stiffened a moment.

"You just are." He sighed softly and curled into her once more.

Jo wanted to tell him it wasn't good enough. She needed more from him. She needed a better explanation. She needed answers to something, *anything*.

But there were no more arrows in her quiver. Jo merely closed her eyes and leaned into him as well, savoring the last moments before Snow pulled away; she'd seen it coming, felt the rift before it had even begun to grow, but awareness made it hurt no less. He shifted to the edge of the bed, his agonizingly perfect, chiseled back to her, his head hung.

She sat as well, then was the first to stand and start scooping up her clothes. Jo was completely dressed and Snow still hadn't moved. She held a brief debate with his back, before saying, "Come with me."

It wasn't a command but not quite a request either. A strong suggestion, perhaps, one that had Snow rising to full height. Jo kept her eyes locked on his face, chin set.

"Come with me, Snow," she repeated. And then, far more lightly, "Samson makes a great breakfast, you know."

"I do know." Snow looked around his room and Jo wondered if he saw a safe-haven or a tomb. "And it has been far too long since I've enjoyed it."

Jo felt her face relax into a smile, her shoulders sink toward the floor as relief tugged happily on her palms. Snow finally stood, strolling over to a wide wardrobe, carefully picking out an outfit. His selection process gave Jo an opportunity to wander the room, her curiosity nothing more than an excuse to hide her shameless glances at him. That was, until something caught her eye.

Jo paused at a low table just beneath a window, one she'd overlooked on her first assessment of the room. It was obsidian, the only bit of furniture that wasn't made of wood. At its center stood a small box, crafted of gold and silver. The ornate designs, patterns of no particular logic, glinted in the sunlight. The whole of her attention was on it and, as if in a trance, Jo reached out a hand.

Snow's fingers wrapped around hers, stopping her before her skin could make contact with the box. Jo's gaze flew to his and they locked eyes for several long moments. His face was passive, void of expression.

"Do you know what it is?" he asked softly.

She shouldn't. "I recognize it." *Why?*

"From where?" His voice was little more than a husky whisper. But it was not sensuality that put the gravel under his words. It was . . . fear? Had she read that flash of emotion correctly?

Jo looked back at the box, trying to place it. "The room you took me to." She remembered suddenly. "Where you grant the wishes. You had it there. Inside is the magic you use to destroy worlds."

His fingers tensed on hers, drawing Jo's eyes back to him. Snow's brow furrowed. His lips pursed. Whatever internal battle was raging, he wasn't about to give it voice.

"Yes." His tone had changed again to something gentler, more tender. He brought her hand, still encapsulated in his, to his lips and planted a soft kiss on her fingertips. "Do not touch it, Josephina."

"Why?" It should be obvious: the power to destroy worlds was inside. But something in the way he said it—

"That is a great power, Destruction. One that should not meet with you." And with that, Snow walked away, fussing with a cufflink.

Jo took one more look at the box, turned to stare back at him, then followed. She would allow him this secret without a fight. She was too tired for fighting and, even if she wasn't, this was his secret to keep. It was his magic, after all.

"Should we stagger ourselves?" she asked, thinking of Wayne's warning.

"No point. I've no doubt they already have surmised the situation." He adjusted the collar of his shirt, looking positively regal. *Well, he was a royal demigod at one point, after all*. For as much as she wasn't exactly surprised, it was still a realization that floored her.

"I guess you're right," she admitted to herself as much as him, and led the way toward the common room.

Most of the rest of the team was there. Samson stood in the middle of the kitchen, looking at the oven as if willing it to cook something for him so that he would not have to put forth the effort. Eslar sat at the chess table with a book, though it didn't seem he was reading or playing. Wayne and Takako were at the couch, silently staring at the blank screen of the television.

Nico was nowhere to be found; his watch was still sitting on the recreation room shelf, Jo had noticed as they'd passed, so it was safe to say he hadn't yet left.

"What's for breakfast?" Jo asked softly to Samson.

He seemed to startle at her voice, then startle again when he saw Snow. "I-I haven't decided yet . . ."

"You made sweet cinnamon toast once and it was divine . . . if I may make a suggestion," Snow said in a soothing tone. For a long moment, Samson didn't seem to know how to respond, unblinking eyes locked on Snow and set wide. But before it could get awkward, Samson shook his head and let out a soft breath of laughter.

"You remember that, huh?" He was suddenly moving, picking out a skillet and gathering ingredients. "When was that?"

"Not long after the fall of the Age of Magic."

The little discussion had drawn the attention of the others in the room. Eslar was the first to come over, sitting on Snow's other side.

"That morning was a while ago, just the three of us." Eslar folded his hands, still looking at nothing and no one in particular. "How many breakfasts have we shared since? How many wishes granted?"

"Both are numbers too great to count." Snow shared a small smile of camaraderie with the elf, one that was quickly abandoned.

Wayne and Takako eventually came over as well, though Jo couldn't remember when or why. They didn't say anything, just sort of appeared. Samson cooked, the skillet sizzled, and the room was heavy with silence.

But for the first time, she didn't want the weight alleviated, because if —when—it was, there would be no turning back.

The food was delicious, as expected of Samson's incredible skill, but that didn't diminish the looming sensation that they were consuming a "last meal." Regardless, they shared it in quiet solidarity, no small talk brave enough or bold enough to fill the gap of wordlessness.

Jo pushed herself away from the counter, dismounting from her stool. There was someone missing, she realized. Someone else who needed to share this last, silent display of unity. She turned toward the hall, ready to hunt the missing teammate down, and nearly jumped from her skin.

"Well, isn't this somber?" Pan lounged in the doorframe. For the first time since Jo had met the mysterious not-quite-woman, Pan appeared muted. Her hair was done in a natural blonde, strands stick straight and hanging just past her shoulders. Also unlike her usually eccentric appearance, she wore nothing more than a simple, tailored suit, cloth sitting snug around her petite frame. A thin, red ribbon accompanied the high-collared button-up, shockingly bright against the black layers of fabric.

"When did you get here?" Jo asked, the memory of Pan appearing out of nowhere that night before the wish jolting back to the forefront of her mind.

Pan merely shrugged. "We should get started."

"Pan—" Snow began to say.

"It's time, Snow." *Time for what?* Jo wanted to scream. But she could barely find air enough to breathe. "They've run out of hours on the clock and the gap is still too wide. Call the meeting."

All eyes pivoted back to Snow. He stared at Pan, and Pan only, as if waging silent war against the woman herself. Through gritted teeth, Snow finally spoke: "Everyone. To the briefing room."

Everyone stood silently, obediently, pulled along by an unknown thread.

"I'll go get Nico," Jo offered, sprinting ahead of the rest. She slowed just long enough to give a long, hard look at Pan. But the other woman just smiled on, turning to saunter ahead of the pack toward the briefing room.

Jo got to Nico's recreation room and had a long debate with the door. She waited for courage to find her, and when none came, she pretended just long enough to give a solid knock.

The door cracked open, revealing a sliver of face and a bright red eye.

"Jo . . ." Nico said softly, pulling open the door the rest of the way. The man disappeared behind the door itself, leaving that as her only invitation to walk in. She took it with painfully hesitant steps.

A canvas stood on the easel. Paint was smeared and splattered on it in a pattern Jo needed no magic to interpret. Rage, pain, hurt—it was all there, plain as day. If she could see it, then it didn't bode well for anything else working on any sort of deeper level.

Nico leaned against the wall behind the door, staring at her listlessly.

"There's a meeting."

That was all it took. He crumpled, burying his eyes in the heels of his hands and resting his elbows on his knees as he sank to the floor. She heard the tears before she saw them and was instantly at his side, holding him once more.

"I tried, I tried!" he repeated, over and over with agonizing repetition.

"I know . . ." she whispered, smoothing her hands over his shoulders and back. "No one blames you."

"How can they not? I was the last line of defense, our last hope, and I—"

"I failed from the start." She'd put a stop to that line of thinking then and there. "We all failed. This is our collective failure, and we'll all stand together for whatever comes next."

Nico's hands reached for her, clinging to her in a way even Snow hadn't. Jo hoped no one would ever cling to her in this way ever again.

"I'll be there," she whispered, as if that meant anything, as if it could solve anything.

"Promise?"

"I promise. No matter what."

Nico found the strength to pull himself together and face the world. Or at least enough to pretend. They stood together, arms linked and breaths shuddering in time. Together they walked toward the briefing room, and to whatever fate awaited them all.

# DRAW STRAWS

A T ONCE UPON arrival in the briefing room, the atmosphere felt different. If not because of the nearly palpable concern spreading like dust over every corner, then because Pan, for the first time, was seated at the head of the table. Jo looked at her in confusion, locating Snow at once as if doing so might make sense of the anomaly. But he was in an unusual seat, pushed just slightly away from the table, at Pan's right. He refused to look at anyone or anything, eyes glazed over and staring down the hall as if he could see past the Four-Way, into the common area, and to the mountains beyond.

"Kind of you two to finally join us," Pan purred, hands coming into graceful contact with the table as she leaned forward. Her eyes shone a bright red to match the ribbon at her neck, and the pupils shifted between thin, cat-like lines, and blown-wide circles. Jo couldn't help but shudder under the eerie woman's gaze.

Jo opened her mouth to argue, possibly even question her position at the helm of their sinking ship, but the feel of Nico's hand tightening around her wrist kept her silent. When she looked over at him, Nico looked near to shattering, eyes not on her but touch desperately clinging. She figured it wasn't worth the unnecessary fighting, not after all they'd already lost, so she bit her tongue and followed Nico the rest of the way to the table.

Wayne saw them approach and, without even needing to be asked, removed himself from his chair, settling into Jo's so she could stay at Nico's side. She hoped her soft smile in his direction conveyed as much gratitude as she felt.

"So!" Pan got started without preamble, clapping her hands loud enough that at least half the room couldn't help but jump, the other half wincing in sympathy. "Where should we begin?" She tapped red-tipped fingernails against the polished table and the whole area exploded in swirling colors and shapes. When it settled, a glitching image of Mt. Fuji stood before them; one second the volcano was inactive, the next frozen in mid-eruption, and back. Beneath the grotesque visual reminder of their oncoming failure was a ring of various timestamps.

As Jo watched the rest of the team glance first at the numbers, then at their own respective watches, she realized what Pan was trying to display. Jo ran a finger over her own wristband, a number illuminating that perfectly matched one of the six beneath the volcano's magical visage.

"None of you have enough time left," Pan continued once it seemed as though everyone had begun to catch on. "And even if you did, the window of opportunity is closing and Snow has already reset time by destroying the world of possibility and expending that allotted amount of magic. He can contribute no more to this wish." The usual lilt to her voice, mischievous and playful, had given way to something heavy and serious, something clearly meant to be intimidating. "We need to make this wish happen *now*, so what is there to do, *hmm*? What option do we have left?"

Nico flinched at the words, the hand still linked loosely with Jo's suddenly tightening, his shoulders tensing in guilt. Anger ambushed Jo's nerves, her head snapping in Pan's direction as she momentarily forgot about the undefined threat looming on the horizon. All she saw was a pompous member of their team that hadn't done *shit* since day one. They'd exhausted themselves and dragged every ounce of their magic and determination and skill out into the open for the sake of the wish. What had she done? What right did she have?

"So why don't *you* actually do something for once?" Jo hissed before she could stop herself. She'd gotten to her feet without realizing, though thankfully she'd had the wherewithal not to drop Nico's hand. By the way he clutched ruthlessly at her fingers, she may as well have been the only thing anchoring him to the present. She squeezed back, but her eyes never left Pan's impassive face, the casual arch of her eyebrows and quirk of her lips. Jo could have punched her.

"I'm about to." Pan pulled her hands from the table and crossed her arms over her chest. When the stare-off seemed to grow boring for her, however, Pan glanced in Snow's direction and grinned, an ugly and devious thing. "So how would you like to do this, Snow? Draw straws? They pick? Or should we let them fight it out? A battle royale might get messy, but I can't say I wouldn't enjoy the show."

"Quiet, Pan." Snow refused to meet Pan's gaze, and even though it was subtle, Jo saw his shoulders tense, the tendons in his neck sticking out against his attempt to stay still. But Jo wasn't going to let him shove this under the rug just like everything else. She needed answers, *deserved* answers. They all did.

"What does she mean?" Jo asked him directly, stomach churning when he refused to meet her eyes. Distantly, Jo could feel Nico squeezing her hand again, but she was too distracted by a sense of steadily rising panic to process anything more than the look of defeat on Snow's face. "Snow?" Jo tried once more, voice softer this time, and he flinched, eyes closing as if to block her out.

That sick feeling in her stomach doubled.

"Don't worry, pet," Pan cooed. She straightened, twirling elegant fingers through her hair. "I can fix this. I can make the magic we need to close the Severity of Exchange and grant the wish." She cracked her neck, hand resting at the base of her skull. When she dropped her arm to stare back at Jo, it was with a different demeanor, an indescribable essence that seemed to throb in ripples from her center and out to every corner of the briefing room. Something in Jo pushed back in response, as if her very existence both knew and revolted against the woman.

"How? Snow already converted the world of possibility of the wisher to magical essence." Someone asked from the other side of the table, but Jo could barely hear it, eyes trapped beneath Pan's crippling stare.

She had seen those eyes before. And not just in the Society. But when? Or more importantly, how? Had she unknowingly encountered Pan before joining the Society when the woman-child was clocked into time on a wish?

Jo rubbed her eyes, blinking, and the world clicked back into focus. The stress of it all was getting to her, making her brain do odd things.

"Oh, but there are more worlds of possibility, of a sort." Pan grinned, letting the oppressive waves of her magic finally abate. For the first time in what felt like hours, Jo could breathe. Just in time for Pan to send her an infuriating wink. "Snow requires a wisher's sacrifice. I require a sacrifice of a different sort to convert essence."

Jo opened her mouth to demand more information, but she couldn't seem to find her words, throat tight and body heavy beneath the wave of whatever power Pan had held over the room only seconds ago. Thankfully, Wayne didn't seem to be nearly as affected.

"What the hell does that mean?" he snapped in Jo's stead, completely ignoring the way Eslar reached for his arm, holding him back, though only just. Pan seemed more amused than anything, leaning casually against Snow's chair. When Snow didn't bother to move, Jo felt the distinct feeling that there was no coming back from this.

Whatever happened next, he wouldn't be helping them. Maybe even wasn't allowed to.

Just who was in control here?

Pan rested a hand on Snow's shoulder, perfectly manicured nails drumming another light rhythm against his collarbone. Jo swore she saw red at the uninvited contact. But then, at Pan's words, she saw nothing at all.

"I get to kill one of you."

A second of shock, of incomprehensible void, and then reality snapped back into painful focus. Unfortunately, Jo was a good couple of seconds behind everyone else.

"Snow?" Samson begged weakly as Wayne pushed a chair out of his way so hard it toppled. He didn't even seem willing to barter for information, already spiraling into a confused and panicked rage.

"What in every circle of hell is *that* supposed to mean?" he yelled, slamming a hand down on the table. Jo felt her knees buckle, her body falling heavily back into her chair.

*What was going on?*

"Wayne, stop." Eslar was obviously out of his depth, eyes frozen on the empty space in front of him, disbelieving. Chiding on autopilot. When Jo finally managed to drag her eyes away from where they'd fallen in anxious devastation into her own lap, it was first to the sight of Nico, silent and gradually shattering at her side. Then secondly, to Pan, her gaze seemingly already waiting to capture Jo's stare.

If Jo didn't know better, it looked like a challenge. Or maybe a dark and eager promise. Either way, the look made Jo feel sick with anger. And fear. It was like she'd known what was coming all along, and willingly stayed on the tracks.

"You've got one day to decide," Pan said, lazy and indifferent as ever, as if her unspoken but obvious amusement had already long since passed. There was no time to process, no time to argue or beg or scream or cry, before she was waving over her shoulder at the room at large. "Let me know what you lovely lot come up with."

Just as quickly as she'd doomed one of them to death, she vanished back into the halls of the mansion.

# FAVORITISM

"**T**HIS IS NOT happening."

Jo wasn't entirely sure if she said the words very softly, or thought them very loudly. Either way, in the commotion of the room, they were lost.

"Get back here you rainbow haired bi—"

"Wayne, stop." Eslar all but shouted, lunging for the man. "There's an explanation here, I'm sure."

"What possible explanation can there be?" Wayne roared in reply. "She didn't seem to me like she was just having a good ol' joshin' at our expense." His voice had gone thick with his usual accent, but different . . . rougher. The airs he usually put on had vanished into something more serious, and now it had come full circle into an accent that was far more authentic, a tonal quality that was more a reversion back to his roots than an homage to them.

"Kill one of our own?" Takako's face alternated between composed, confused, and about to tear someone apart. "What is the meaning of this, *leader*?" The way she spat out the moniker might as well have been an insult or a challenge. Probably both.

"It's my fault," Nico sobbed, but Jo was the only one who heard.

"What do we do?" Samson's small voice asked from opposite the table.

Eventually, in the whirlwind of everyone else's slow and steady breakdowns, Jo found her feet again, still clutching Nico's hand. "Snow!" She waited until his head jerked in her direction at the sudden shout of his name. "*Say something.*"

It was the verbal slap he needed. The man blinked, stunned, and then swallowed. His mouth hardened into a line and his eyes gained clarity. As Snow stood, assuming control of the now-quiet room, Jo sat.

"Pan—" He paused, clearing his throat before continuing. "Is not lying to you."

"You're going to let her kill one of us?" Takako asked, void of emotion.

"All this time. Were we just sheep awaiting slaughter?" Wayne snapped.

"You know that's not the case," Eslar replied, still clearly giving Snow the benefit of the doubt.

"Do I? What do we really know?" Wayne pushed his chair from the table, folding his arms as if to keep him from lunging at the elf. "What do *you* know? You seem awfully cool. Have you been keeping this from us to?"

"Eslar didn't know anything," Samson interjected.

"Of course you'd say that, you always take his side," Wayne sneered; Samson sunk in on himself.

"Wayne, stop," Jo chided. Wayne was about to object, but one look at Jo's face had him closing his mouth and looking away.

"She's right, there is no other option at this point. The Severity of Exchange is too wide." Snow struggled to keep some semblance of control over the situation.

"Surely, there's another way to convert the magic?" Eslar asked, pleaded. "Why not a ritual, like Springtide, or—"

"All relics were lost with the Age of Magic, you know that as well as I," Snow said sadly.

"Or, I have an idea." Jo could feel the venom of her own words dripping in sickly tendrils down her throat "How about we just say 'Screw it we tried'?" She looked around the room, registering the surprise that appeared on every face, and felt only overwhelming frustration. Really, how had they not thought about this before? "We put forward a good effort, we did all we could. What's our wish success rate until now? One hundred percent? Who's going to come after us for failure, anyway? We exist outside of time and space."

"But—" Takako began to say.

"I'm sorry." Jo knew exactly where the Japanese woman's mind was. "Really, I am. And we can try to just get your family to safety. That should be do-able. We don't have enough time to meet the parameters of the wish —to save *everyone*. But saving at least them shouldn't be a problem."

"You'd really condemn all those people to die?" Eslar asked. Jo wasn't sure if he sounded surprised or impressed.

Either way, she answered him levelly and honestly. "Yes." Jo shook her head, cursing under her breath. "Look, I'm not pleased about this. I'm not suggesting this lightly. But isn't this what you taught me from the first wish, that we can't save everyone? Haven't you all watched thousands of people die horrible deaths? Why is this any different? Good, evil, failure, or triumph, the world keeps on turning."

"We can't," Snow stopped her before a seed of hope could even be planted.

"Why?" Jo challenged.

"Because if we fail to grant a wish, we all die."

Stillness across the table. A collective inhale. Than an almost unanimous, "What?"

"The Society exists because of the wishes we grant." Snow placed his hands on the table as if inspecting it for the first time. "I destroy worlds of possibility to fulfill wishes and, in doing so, some of that energy goes to continuing to keep this pocket of existence outside of time. Without the energy and magic of the wishes we grant, we cannot exist. It is part of what binds us to this place—our duty. And part of what, in return, binds us . . . to this life itself." The sound of Snow's voice cracking on the last words had Jo's heart stuttering, tipping to the floor, shattering. Even when Snow lifted his head, a mask of faux composure back on his face, she couldn't unhear it as he tried to explain further.

"Every time we grant a wish, every time the world is redesigned, I am able to siphon a little from the world of possibility that I destroy and we are gifted enough magic in return to sustain ourselves. But my capabilities on channeling that destructive power aren't perfect, and we can sustain only for a little while longer. This magic, the magic that keeps us alive, it needs constant replenishment. So if we stop granting wishes, or if we fail to grant an accepted wish within the allotted time frame, that magic runs out. I don't have the power to break the cycle, even if I wanted to."

Snow's mask crumbled then, not enough to catch everyone else's attention, but enough that Jo could feel the weight of his pain like a dagger through her own heart.

"The magic runs out, we all die."

Jo sank into her chair, his words circling around her head like so many taunting birds. It was truly a rock and a hard place. No way out. She couldn't breathe.

So instead, she distracted herself by looking around the room; surely, the rest of them had known this. But everyone's faces displayed matching looks of shock and horror, even Eslar's. How had no one known this before? What other fundamental secrets to their existence had been kept from them?

"So that's it, then," Wayne murmured bitterly. "One of us dies to grant the wish, or we all die."

Silence was his only reply. Jo's eyes had fallen to her lap, so she could only assume that Snow had nodded. It didn't matter. There was no simple solution or crafty work-around to get them out of this. It was exactly as Wayne said.

"Now what?" she whispered.

"I'll do it." Takako's voice was clear and strong. Level. Takako knew what she was offering, sacrificing. Probably more than any of them. "It's my country. My family. Let it be me."

"No," Jo's voice quivered and she wished she could be as strong as the other woman in what she was about to do. An icy fear ran through her veins, but still her mouth formed words. "If anyone should—" Her throat tightened and she swallowed twice to clear it. "*Go* . . . it should be me. I was the one who was arrogant from the start. My hack job was shoddy and I was overconfident. I wasted our time and set us on the path that put us in this spot. Plus, I'm the newest here, so—"

"Just stop." Wayne slapped his hand on the table, startling Jo into a silence. "We all know that I'm the king of screw-ups. You said it, doll. You're the new kid, so I'm not letting you take the title."

Nico opened his mouth, no doubt about to offer to martyr himself with the rest of them when Eslar interrupted.

"Snow should decide."

All eyes drifted back toward their leader. To his credit, Snow did not shake or waver. He met their attention with rigid posture and the same careful regard that he always had at the head of the table. It was as if every ounce of tension he had ever carried himself with was in preparation for this moment.

"So be it, then," Snow said softly. "I will decide within the day."

Jo pressed her eyes closed. It was an impossible decision for him to make. They were clearly all willing to make the ultimate sacrifice for the sake of their team. How would he choose?

The sensation of Nico's hand finally uncurling from hers barely registered, and despite Jo's underlying guilt, evoked no response in her. She couldn't muster the strength to comfort him when she was beginning to unravel herself; hopefully, one day, he'd be able to forgive her for it.

"I'm going to the recreation room . . . Maybe I can still do something," he said hopelessly.

No one stopped him. Not even Jo. Her mind was too far from that room to think of anything other than the phantom fingers that ghosted over her cheeks, as if wiping away rogue tears that had yet to fall.

*It would not be her.*

It was a horrifying truth, and one Jo knew deep in her bones. She could feel Snow's mouth on hers, their hungry kisses, his promises to protect her. If it was left to him, right or wrong, deserved or not, Snow would not choose her to die.

# SNOW'S CHOICE

AS JO SAT, staring at nothing, Takako's measured steps blazed a trail for the rest of them. Samson and Eslar left together. At the edge of Jo's hearing, she could make out softly spoken words between them, diminishing like a trembling note until nothing more could be heard.

A palm on her shoulder startled her back to reality. Wayne hovered, looking down with heartbreaking sadness. He opened his mouth, but only a sigh escaped. What more was there to say? What could be said?

They were all waiting for the verdict of their fate.

He left as well, head bowed, exposing the nape of his neck for the guillotine of Snow's decision that hung invisible over them all. Jo looked at the chairs, ears buzzing. Her eyes drifted toward the Door and the instinct to run in the opposite direction, go as far as she could anywhere else in the world, had her standing. She fantasized over the idea of opening the Door for the last time, finding the pin code that would lead to their freedom.

Her hand pressed against the cool steel, dropping to the pin pad. It hovered, quivering like a hummingbird in suspension.

With an animalistic noise of anger she punched her hand right into the steel. The skin over her knuckles split instantly and her bones vibrated into her jaw. Jo hovered, panting, leaving crimson streaks as she slumped away.

It was useless. There was nowhere she could run. She existed nowhere else. She and everyone else in the Society were chained to their mission. Perhaps it would be better to take the out of death.

Jo shook her head violently and turned away from the door.

*No.*

She might dream of escape. She might be the sort to nest under covers until frustration and pain subsided. She might let anger get the better of logic at times. But she would not run in that way—never in that way.

Alone, Jo made her solemn march towards the Four-Way. *Snow.* She had to tell him before his thoughts got too far. She had to make sure that his decision, whatever it was, was not influenced in any way by *them*, whatever they were. If she was chosen or spared, it had to be because of more than their affections.

Voices slowed her steps halfway between the stairs and recreation rooms: Nico's honeyed tones and Snow's icy words. Jo slowed to a stop. Vaguely, she remembered Nico leaving the briefing room while muttering about the painting, though it seemed like a far-away dream now.

Jo didn't know why she crept; she had nothing to hide from these men. She had no anger for Nico, and whatever frustrations she held toward Snow for his secrets would keep. There would be a time and place to fight for answers. But the eve of an impossible decision was neither.

Undetected, Jo shifted along the wall, leaning a few feet from the door, close enough to hear the quiet words within.

"It must be someone," Nico said tiredly. She could envision the man she'd watched work the night before, eyes grown distant and sad by the weight of the world. "Let it be me."

"Your magic—"

"Is far more limited than the rest of them."

Jo would disagree with Nico here, but she kept her mouth shut for the sake of listening to the rest of the conversation. Expectedly, Snow spoke for her. "Your magic . . . is critical. Changing the hearts and minds of people is something not easily accomplished."

"And is useless if it doesn't work every time." Jo's heart ached at the sorrow in his words. The man's guilt was apparent. "I'm tired, Snow. I've been at this a long time, surely you understand."

Silence.

"I didn't quite understand until I had her here. She sat there, in that stool, just as my Julia had." Jo's heart clenched, unprepared for Nico's mention of her. It felt wrong somehow, listening to his words while knowing full well he was unaware of her audience. Still, she stayed, transfixed and curious. "My muse is gone, and her legacy is beginning to wane. Every time I return to her place of rest, I see it a little more weathered, her expression a little further worn away. With it, my inspiration, my will . . . and my magic itself."

Jo leaned back, looking up at the ceiling. To love someone so much that your very essence, your magic, was tied to them. She glanced back toward the door, imagining Snow within. Would she, they, someday be so entwined? For all it sounded thrilling, it was also a terrifying notion, and one that seemed almost impossible to envision.

"Your magic is lessened?" Snow asked, his voice bringing her back to the present. It was Nico's, however, that kept her there.

"I have no other explanation for my failure. It was as if everything I had painted cracked under the weight of the Prime Minister's will."

"Lack of time?" Snow suggested, seemingly reaching. The iciness of his voice had lifted some, as if the warmth of Nico's words had melted it.

Another silence left Jo wondering what body cues Nico was offering. A nod? A shrug? She inched closer to the door. If she couldn't see them, she didn't want to miss a single word.

"You're sure?" Snow asked, finally, and Jo's pulse picked up.

"I am," Nico said with conviction. "I owe it to them, for my failure."

"The failure belongs to the team, not one individual." Snow's egalitarianism should've been heartwarming, but Jo just found her heart in knots. The failure was the team's, but one person must bear the consequences alone. Surely some cruel god was sitting and cackling at their fate. How else were they meant to explain such undeserved tragedy?

Nico laughed softly. "Accept this, will you? As a professional favor, if nothing else. We've had a good run."

"We have." A genuine sorrow, the ache of it seemingly splintering his composure, finally leached into Snow's words. Jo felt a similar ache blooming across her chest, spiraling like sticky tendrils down into her heart.

"There is someone waiting for me in heaven, you know." Nico's claim was honest and pure, a belief there that Jo had neither expected, nor could even begin to understand. In any other situation, Jo was certain it would have been comforting. "I have been away from her for far too long . . . and while she may not recognize me, I will have much to tell her. Surely, you must know how I feel." There was an agonizingly long silence. "I knew you would."

What had she missed? What non-verbal exchange had just happened? Jo's heart could still somehow flutter, even among knots.

"Very well." As if she could block out the condemnation of Snow's words, Jo pressed her eyes closed, desperately biting back a sob. If she thought she felt guilty listening in on this conversation before, it was infinitesimal to how deeply she regretted it now. She did not want to hear what could be Nico's final moments; it didn't seem fair. "It shall be you."

"I have one request," Nico added hastily.

"Yes?"

"I have a time I want it to be done."

Another delay, long enough for Snow to comprehend something Jo could not, judging from his tone. "Of course."

Despite herself, tears broke through Jo's emotional dam and streamed down her face. It wasn't fair. None of it was. She wanted to take action, she wanted to do something. But what could be done at a moment like this? She knew too little of magic to hack a solution for the very fabric of reality that surrounded the Society. If anyone did, it was Snow. And something in Jo assured her that if there was a way for him to redesign their fate, he would. He'd said it himself: he didn't have the power to do so. The pain in his voice proved the truth of it.

Which meant he was a prisoner, just like the rest of them. A chess piece in a greater game. A powerful piece, certainly, but a piece nonetheless. Jo turned her head toward the black door adjacent to Snow's.

There was one other person seemingly as old as the Society itself and with a magic as terrifying as Snow's.

Even as her eyes blurred with fresh tears, Jo stared the door down as if willing it to give up its occupant's secrets. Pan, their executioner. If there was one person who would see their circumstance as a game, it would be *her*.

# UNTIL THE END

J O'S EYES WERE still pinned on the ominous black door when the recreation room Nico had taken residence in finally opened wide. She turned towards the sound on reflex, the motion causing unfallen tears to give way, her already wet cheeks glistening with new streaks of pain and sadness.

It wasn't Nico who greeted her startled attention, though she shouldn't have expected him to be willing to leave the sanctity of his room so soon after being sentenced. Instead it was Snow, his own eyes red-rimmed and holding far more exhaustion than she'd ever seen in a person.

When he captured her gaze, it was beyond Jo's capabilities to hold back her fresh wave of tears. She felt whipped about in a hurricane of her own emotions, torn apart by the need to scream and the need to beg. She wanted Snow to hold her, to comfort her, but she also didn't want to be comforted. She didn't deserve it, not when Nico was the one damned by the brutal reality of sacrifice. She wanted Snow to fix this, to tell her he was mistaken and that everything would be okay. She wanted him to promise her that Nico would live, that they *all* would live. But she also knew he wouldn't, was painfully aware that he *couldn't*. So she also wanted him to say nothing at all.

She wanted to go back to before they'd failed, when the promise of success had led Jo to Snow's room, to his bed, reveling not in physical intimacy, but an intimacy nonetheless. She wanted to feel his closeness, his touch, and not have it tainted by the fear of what was to come. Jo knew that if Snow couldn't save Nico's life, there was no way he had enough magic to turn back time (at least not for them; for a wish, maybe, but not for them), but Jo couldn't help silently praying for a miracle regardless.

It seemed greedy to wish for more time when she'd been given an endless supply of it. But Nico's was being unexpectedly cut short, which made the Society feel less like the blessing of eternity and more like the eventuality of a slaughterhouse.

In the end, Snow chose silence, his eyes the only thing betraying his own swirling typhoon of barely-contained emotions. She could see him hurting, could practically feel it emanating off of him in waves of self-loathing. It was impossible to miss; Snow wanted to be the executioner no more than any of them wanted to bear witness to the execution.

But it wouldn't be Snow in the end, would it? He'd been forced to choose the head that would fall in the basket, but it was Pan who'd be swinging the ax.

Amid the ever-present grief, Jo felt a spike of pure rage dig deep into the center of her chest, the tears filling her eyes almost hot with anger. It was an anger that must have shown on her face, because Snow's own expression shifted at the sight. She caught a brief glimpse of pity, of immeasurable heartache, and then, once again, he schooled his features back into place, all traces of that previous openness gone.

The change in demeanor caught Jo off guard, her rage snuffed out. But before she could put any of her own emotions into words, Snow walked past her, leaving her alone with her silent tears in front of Nico's doorway.

For a brief moment, Jo considered following him, but there was nothing she could think to say, no amount of comfort she felt able to give. Not to Snow at least. But when Jo glanced at the still slightly cracked door of Nico's room, she realized where her comfort might still be of use.

It was probably selfish, forcing herself into Nico's personal space when he might wish to spend his last hours alone, but Jo needed his presence as much as she hoped he might need hers. Even if it meant overstepping, she needed to be there for him—needed as much time left with him as he was willing to give.

When Jo let herself in, it was to find Nico standing by the window, staring out at the impossible view of a Florence sunset. The buttery glow painted Nico's silhouette in hues of orange and pink, the last rays of the sun catching at his cheeks in a telling shimmer. That was all it took, the sight of Nico's own tears causing a new wave of grief to settle into Jo's bones. She tried to swallow down the lump in her throat, but a soft sob still escaped.

Nico turned to look at her then, a flash of surprise giving way to a soft smile. The crinkle at the corner of his eyes caused another tear to fall, and Jo was wrapping the man up in an embrace before she even registered the decision to do so. Nico settled into her arms easily, pulling her close with his own wordless thanks. It felt like the comfort she'd been needing; even though Nico was the one knocking on death's door, he was still the one doing the comforting. Jo would have laughed if the very thought hadn't filled her chest with another blossom of devastation.

There was no way of knowing how long they simply held each other, sometimes crying and sometimes just finding comfort in each other's silent presence. Eventually, Nico pulled away, raising both hands to gently cup Jo's face as his thumbs wiped away the remnants of tears. He leaned in, chastely kissing one cheek, then the other, before letting his hands fall.

"You know." It wasn't a question, and Jo wondered how long he'd been aware of her presence lurking outside the door.

"I do." She wiped her nose with the back of her hand, stifling a loud sniffle.

"It has been an honor working alongside you, Josephina Espinosa," he said, grabbing her hand and giving it a squeeze. "And it has been nothing short of a blessing to get to know you." Nico's smile held every ounce of the sunshine she'd come to expect of the man, even if his eyes were mostly clouded.

"I'll stay with you," she found herself saying, knowing instantly that the words were right. "Until the end, to the very last minute." For a breath, Nico simply held her gaze, but then the clouds in his eyes parted some, his face filling with matching warmth. When he hugged her once more, it was as true and heartfelt a "thank you" as she'd ever received.

She watched him paint for hours, curled up in a blanket on the stool by the fireplace. It was another portrait of his Julia, Jo realized, around the time her eyelids began to get heavy. She watched him carefully shade in the curves of her face, add highlights to the flowing waves of her hair.

It was sometime between the streaks of yellow being added to the background and Nico signing his name that a deep and dreamless sleep overtook Jo.

# ONE-SEVENTEEN A.M.

JO BLINKED, DROWSY. She'd fallen asleep. When was the last time that had happened?

Everything was hazy as her mind began to work once more. This didn't feel like waking, it felt like suddenly *existing* again.

*The beginning of the wish*—that was the last time she'd actually slept since becoming a full member of the Society. She'd been woken the night Snow had come to her after he'd rewound time.

Jo searched her memories further, willing her mind to work, slotting things back into place. The details of the past day were suspended just out of her reach like the tiny motes of dust drifting past Nico's easel. Jo blinked, her eyes dry and aching; she'd shed more tears in the last few days than she ever remembered shedding in her life. The room was filled with a serene stillness—a stillness that came from being the only breathing presence within.

With the stone of the wall now more warmed from her back than the smoldering remnants of the fire, Jo rubbed at her eyes and straightened. She looked around the room. Everything was as she remembered—the cluttered work table, the easel perched with the (now mostly finished) painting of Julia, the other various shelves and half-finished canvases. Everything was in its place.

Everything but the painter himself.

Jo stood with a stretch and a yawn. Everything seemed like a distant dream.

*No.* It all came rushing back, right as she was about to leave. Something struck her as odd: this wasn't a distant dream she could shrug off alongside the shroud of sleep, but a vivid waking nightmare that she couldn't escape even if she tried.

At the foot of the easel, surrounded by splotches of dried paint, Nico's favored brush rested. She tilted her head, looking at the object in confusion; something about it rankled her so, but she couldn't seem to pinpoint what it might be. The hair on her neck stood on edge. She stared at that mauve splotch on the floor where the paintbrush had landed; there was a splatter, and a streak where the brush had rolled before coming to its final resting place.

*Final resting place.*

Jo spun in place. "Nico?" she called out to the empty room, as if he would step out of thin air and surprise her. "Nico?" Her voice was a little more strained when he didn't.

She took several long steps into the hallway; it was completely empty in the early dawn. "Nico?" she called again. There was still silence, still a creeping sense of foreboding waiting to swallow her up. She wouldn't let it; she'd find him before it could.

*He's gone to his room*, she told herself, lied to herself. That was it. He'd needed . . . a new tube of paint, or canvas, or something. He'd gotten tired. He'd worked hard enough to want somewhere to rest his weary hands, and in all his infinite manners he hadn't wanted to disturb her.

Story after story ran through her mind, every possible reason concocted for where the painter might be.

Jo paused at the Four-Way, looking down the hallway to the common area and listening. There was no sound, yet her feet carried her in that direction anyway. In a surreal daze, Jo stopped at the entryway. It appeared empty, until she saw a foot hanging over the edge of the couch.

Half-jumping, half-running, Jo dashed over to the couch, her hands on the back, leaning over, and—her heart sank. Samson lay curled up, one of Eslar's elegantly designed, elvish blankets draped over him. His red-orange hair frizzed from his tight braids and matted where it was free. Even in sleep, he looked exhausted.

Jo reached for his shoulder, shaking it some. "Samson?"

The man woke with a start. "Wh-what?" He practically fell off the couch, shrinking away from the contact, until the sleep lifted from his eyes, his mind, and vanished. "Oh, I must have fallen asleep. How odd. I think the last time that happened was . . . But good morning, Jo."

"Have you seen Nico?" She didn't have time to feel guilty for the way she'd woken the man. Not when there was something else far more pressing, something that demanded all of her attention.

"Nico?" Samson squinted in confusion. "He's with you, right?"

That wasn't the answer Jo was looking for. She looked around the room, as if something could've changed without her noticing, wishing something had. It was that same foreboding stillness from the moment she'd first woken. Now, the hair on her arms was on-end as well.

"What's going on, Jo?" Samson asked.

"Nico?" she called, rushing out onto the wide patio, hoping he'd be waiting for her in their usual chairs, tablet in hand. She sprinted around, as if he could be hiding behind the outdoor grill or randomly swimming beneath the surface of the pool.

"Jo?" Samson was standing now. "What's happening, Jo?"

She ignored him. Even on her own, Jo could barely come to terms with the truth in front of her; there was no way she could break it down for someone else, too.

"He must be in his room," Jo mumbled to no one, her eyes glued to the bloody sunrise. "His room."

On the last word, she turned and began to run; her heart was already racing before she took her first step. It was already in her throat, suffocating her.

Jo tripped, scrambling up the stairs to the hallway. How long had it been since she'd come back here? Everything blurred together into an agonizing slurry, sloshing between her ears where her brain once used to be.

"Are you all right?" Samson held out a hand, offering it to her.

She stared at the step before her; had she not caught herself, she would have split her skull open on it. The knuckles on the back of her hand were still bloody from punching the Door, and the way her knees ached suggested that it may not be the only split skin she was presently sporting.

"We have to get to his room," she panted. Her voice sounded alien even to her own ears, rough and determined but also bordering on hysterical. "We have to get to his room, Samson."

Ignoring the outstretched hand, Jo continued on. The hallway was a million miles long at the start, but only a few short steps at the end. They stopped before Nico's door.

They stopped before what *had been* Nico's door.

Jo raised a hand to the wood, running it over where his nameplate had been. The surface was smooth, unblemished. There was no scarring from where Nico's painted bird had been scrubbed away. There was no discoloration from where the man's name had been protecting the wood underneath for hundreds of years. It was perfect, pristine—a blank slate.

There was nothing, as if the man who'd occupied the space had never even existed.

In a disconnected sort of awareness, Jo heard Samson's soft murmur of denial. A denial that stretched and contorted, cracked inch by inch until it shattered into equal parts disbelief, gnawing fear, and undeniable pain.

His wail barely registered though. It was a sort of guttural cry, an agony that she'd never heard the likes of in any of her lives, but still, it came from far, far away. Her hand rested on the door handle.

*Open it*, a voice goaded, and she listened; she had to see what was inside. She had to see it or it wouldn't be real.

"What's going on?" Wayne's voice appeared from the end of the hall. Another door opened, another voice.

But the only thing Jo saw was the handle turning. The only thing she heard was the smooth whisper of well-greased metal on metal as the latch released. The hinges sighed softly and she pulled open the door.

Nothing.

It was a blank slate: white walls, white floor, a white roof that seemed to glow with its own unnatural light. She dared to take a step into that void, as if she'd somehow be able to find Nico and retrieve him from it.

But there was nothing there. The warm light of Florence, the messy, clean look—everything that had been the heart of the artist's studio had vanished.

"What the hell?" She heard Wayne curse, the words almost managing to bring her out of the haze of her own encroaching breakdown. "I actually fell asleep for an hour and . . ."

"What is this?" Takako was behind her now too. "I was asleep too."

"Let me through—" Eslar's voice stopped short.

With renewed desperation, Jo turned, looking at the elf. "What does it mean?" Her voice was barely a quivering whisper.

"I—" Eslar blinked furiously, though not from the light of the void. She'd never seen so much emotion on his face, yet she couldn't find it in herself to care.

"What does it mean?" she repeated. "You're the oldest. You've been here the longest. You know magic the best, don't you?"

Eslar looked over her head, transfixed by the nothingness. The look of fear and heartache creeping into his eyes left Jo mentally reaching out for a lifesaver no one had thrown. Still, she treaded water, refused to drown. Surely he had answers, surely *somebody* had answers.

"What does it mean?" she demanded, grabbing the elf's shoulders and shaking him back to reality. "Eslar, what does it—"

"He's gone!" The man wrenched himself from her grasp. A long moment passed, Eslar reaching out towards Nico's door frame with shaking hands, as if he needed it to hold himself up. At first, long, dark fingers barely touched it, but then he curled in on himself, dark green fingernails scratching harsh lines into the wood. "He's . . . He's really gone."

No one seemed able to say anything for a while. They all stood paralyzed in that ominous glow of nothingness, a glow that suddenly seemed to cast new light on the hopelessness of their situation.

And yet.

"No, he can't be." Jo refused to believe it. It seemed too inconceivably horrible to fathom. "He can't be, because, because the recreation room still had his watch on the shelf." They all stared as if she'd spoken in a language that no magic could enable them to understand. It was the tether she'd been looking for, something she could cling to with a desperation she'd never felt in her life. Not even when she'd sacrificed herself for the sake of Yuusuke. "I'll show you. I'll show you!"

In an all-out sprint, she was flying across the mansion once more. There were hurried footfalls behind her, as hasty as hers, but Jo didn't look to see who was following. She leapt down the stairs, clearing half, stumbling the rest, before scrambling up the other set. Jo didn't trip this time.

"There it is!" she shouted, finally looking over her shoulder. She could hear the unnatural crack to her voice, a pitch so many decibels away from calm that it was almost pathetic. But still, she kept her arm steady. Still, she pointed to the rec room shelf. "See, I told you." Everyone was in tow. "His watch is still here." Jo flung wide the door. It was the same studio she remembered waking up in. Even with his actual room wiped clean, surely this meant something. Surely he was still here. *Somewhere.* "Nico!" she called.

The rest of them caught up, Wayne huffing and puffing. Eslar hardly seemed winded, so it was the elf who first inspected the watch. Jo made to take a desperate step into the room, but what he said next froze her stride.

"It's broken," he whispered.

Everyone stilled, hanging on his next words, but there were none. There was nothing more to be said, only to be inspected.

Jo backpedaled, stepped over to the shelf. Sure enough, the watch was there, but its glass front was fractured. The second-hand no longer moved; the clock face that counted his time was frozen at 1:17, matching the time that had always been mirrored on the second dial.

"Julia," Samson whispered, his understanding full of aching intimacy. They'd spent hundreds of years together, after all.

1:17, the time Julia had died. It made so much sense now, gave meaning to Nico's request. He'd asked Snow for a specific time, wished for a last connection to his love, and someone had obliged.

"He's really, g-gone, isn't he?" Samson forced through tears. No one seemed willing to capture anyone else's gaze; everyone kept their eyes pinned on the last remaining fragments of the man they'd all come to care for.

No one could answer, and that was answer enough.

Takako leaned against the far wall, unwilling to touch anyone. Eslar wrapped an arm around Samson, pulling him close. Wayne just stared at the watch, lips parted, and eyes glossy. The hurt in everyone's expressions was obvious; the exhaustion even more so. The pain Jo felt slowly began to molt into hatred.

"It's her fault," Jo whispered.

In her periphery, Jo could see Eslar shake his head. "It's all of our faults, we didn't close the Severity of—"

"Don't give me that!" The words were out before she could stop them. Jo didn't want to scream at Eslar, but she also didn't want Nico to be dead. She wanted revenge but she also wanted to curl up into a ball and pretend none of this had happened. Everything felt beyond her control, and she couldn't stand it. "Don't you even dare give me that! We didn't know."

"If we'd known, would that have changed anything?" Eslar shouted back. Samson cringed in his arms.

Jo opened her mouth and closed it, angry. She searched for facts, for arguments, digging deep for some explanation for all this, but in the end could do no more than fold her arms over her chest and try to stop the shaking. They'd done all they could; that was the hardest part. They'd done all they could and now, this.

"She could've let us say goodbye, at least," Wayne whispered, staring into the room.

*It has been an honor working alongside you, Josephina Espinosa.*

Jo spun in place. That was it. That was the thing causing the creeping dread since the first moment Jo had woken.

She hadn't even gotten to say goodbye.

Jo pulled away from the group at once, her fist meeting Pan's door and banging frantically. "I know you're in there," she shouted at the unwavering expanse of black. She heard the rest of her team come up behind her, but she ignored them, slamming wounded knuckles against wood.

"Jo, stop!" Wayne called.

"Open up. Open up and own up to what you did!" Jo banged harder. Her voice was beginning to waver and crack yet again. The anger was threatening to give way to the bottomless sadness that had hollowed out the cavity of her chest. "How could you? How *could* you? You knew it was coming, didn't you?"

The white door at Jo's right opened suddenly; Snow stood in its frame. He looked no better than the rest of them. A long shirt hung rumpled from his shoulders, falling over tight-fitting trousers.

"What's going on?" His voice echoed through the hall with an air of authority. Jo ignored that too.

"We were just going back," Eslar began to say. But Jo cut him off before any other weak explanation could be given. She wasn't going to sweep this under the rug.

"We want answers!"

Snow's gaze turned to her.

"We want answers from *her*." Jo punctuated the statement with a pound on Pan's door. She turned towards Snow, seething, snarling. "But she's too much of a damned coward to give us any."

"That's enough, Jo," Snow scolded, and Jo couldn't help but bristle.

"Don't say that!" she screamed back. "Don't act like you're not hurting at the fact that one of us was murdered under your roof, under your care. I see it Snow, I see it!"

She called him out with a certainty she hadn't possessed until that moment. Because, until then, she hadn't quite grasped it. But as their "leader" stood there, helpless and hurting, he was no better than the rest of them. Jo turned back to the door.

"Open up and face us, you coward! Face your actions!" Jo screamed at nothing, her voice echoing sharply down the hall.

"Jo, please. That's enough," Wayne tried to console, taking a step forward.

"I don't want to hear it from you," she lashed out. If no one would help her, then everyone was her enemy.

"Jo, let's—" Takako didn't get to finish her statement.

Jo's stomach shot into her pelvis at the brief experience of weightlessness, returning when a shoulder pressed unexpectedly into her gut. Snow's arms wrapped around her as he carried her, over his shoulder, to his room; the familiar smell of cloves threatened to soothe her anger just enough that the sorrow would win.

She couldn't have that—wouldn't be able to handle that. She'd break.

"Don't you dare, Snow!" Jo cried out instead. "I deserve vindication, an explanation, *something*. She didn't even let us say goodbye, Snow. She didn't—she didn't even let us say goodbye!"

Jo could feel the rage slowly unraveling beneath the rough demands of her voice, the dam of her own resolve slowly crumbling to dust. She could see the rest of her team watching her be carried away, their eyes wet, their teeth gritted, their fists clenched in anger. But no words were spoken in retaliation. Their lack of fight eroded hers.

She could feel her cries shredding themselves beneath the sharp claws of unrelenting devastation, the pounding of her fists against Snow's back quickly losing strength and purpose as her tears regained their own.

The slamming of Snow's door punctuated her sobs, cutting their echo short to the remaining four members of the Society.

Pan's door never budged.

# GOODBYE

J O DIDN'T KNOW how long she cried, curled up in Snow's bed like a child. It could have been hours, could have been days, but it didn't matter. Once the dam had been broken, there was no stopping the tears from flowing even if she tried.

And what use was there in trying?

She had vague recollections of Snow trying to talk to her, of his hand on her back and his lips against her temple, of soft attempts at comfort, reassurances that at least the wish had been granted and they were safe, even softer admittances of understanding. But she could find none of her own sympathies, every verbal grasp of Snow's falling on deaf and unaccepting ears.

She wasn't ready to hear any of it, not when it all ended with the same brutal and unforgivable truth.

Nico was gone. Pan had taken him from them, and he wasn't coming back.

She thought, during one of the times she'd cried herself into a daze, in and out of sleep with her chest aching and eyes sore (sleep was something Jo never wanted to do again), that Snow tried to apologize. But even with anger boiling her blood, and distress gripping tight at her heart, she couldn't find it in her heart to blame him. Not when he'd looked at her with such shame, seemingly sharing every ounce of their heartache.

No. This wasn't about forgiving Snow; a pawn needed no forgiving for the whims of his queen. This was about mourning Nico, about maybe one day soon, avenging him.

So it was after an indistinguishable amount of time that Jo sat herself up, leaning into Snow's touch when he instantly responded to her presence. She wasn't sure how long he'd been waiting at her side, coming and going to check on her, but she was eternally grateful. Even if she couldn't find it in herself to say so.

"She did this," Jo muttered first in blatant repetition, clutching tight to Snow's arms as he wrapped them around her waist and held her close to his chest. It almost made her want to start crying all over again, but she did her best to hold herself back.

"I know," he said, whispering the agreement into her neck. Jo swallowed back the whimper of renewed regret that the words threatened to pull from the center of her chest. Instead, she distracted herself with the feel of his forehead pressing firm into the juncture of her shoulder.

Without meaning to, Jo exhaled a shaky, "It's not fair." When Snow said nothing in reply, Jo turned herself as best she could into his embrace and hugged him closer. "It's okay," she said once she could feel her lips pressed loosely against the shell of his ear. She felt him shiver, heard him choke back the first broken sob of his own. "I know it's not your fault."

Snow stiffened in her arms, obviously surprised, but then settled, hugging her like he might fall apart without her body there to keep him together. He stayed silent, but somehow Jo could tell he was grateful; it was clear in the huff of his breaths against her skin and the dig of his fingers into her waist.

Eventually, no matter how much she wanted to ride out the rest of her mourning in his grasp, she couldn't deny the immense desire she had to get back to her team. It didn't seem right that she got comfort from their leader when everyone else was forced to handle their grief on their on.

But as much as she wanted to be strong, she was only human.

"Will you come with me?" she heard herself ask, surprised internally at her own forwardness. She did her best to school her expression into something more confident than she felt. The words, however, were more hopeful and real than any she ever remembered speaking. "I don't know if I can go back out there alone."

Another brief pause, another quiet breath against her neck, and then—

"Whatever you need."

It took a while for Jo to work up the courage. Sitting up and voicing her concerns was one thing, but actually pulling herself away from the safety of Snow's bed was another. Eventually, however, she managed to drag herself back out into the hall, Snow not far behind.

The group was all there once more, making Jo's mind whirl with just how much time she'd spent grieving. At first, no one seemed to notice her approach, too consumed by whatever it was they were doing. Which was all well and good, considering Jo had no clue what to do or say to them yet. But the closer she got, the quicker she realized she couldn't stay silent on the matter.

"Wait," Jo spoke up the moment she was within earshot. Eslar had one hand on Nico's watch, pulling futilely, and Wayne was digging the edge of his nickel beneath it and the shelf. "Wait!"

Everyone turned in her direction, Takako and Samson startling at her sudden presence as Eslar and Wayne backed away from the recreation room shelf on reflex. They couldn't touch another's watch; no amount of physical force could remove it from its last spot.

And maybe no force ever should.

"Leave it," Jo said, pushing her way through the group until she could place a hand on Nico's watch, looking first at the broken clock face and then at each of them in turn. "Just leave it."

At first, no one seemed to know how to respond, but eventually, Eslar caved, taking a step towards the shelf. "Jo, we need to—"

"No!" She shouted, cringing at the sound of her own voice, especially when Eslar recoiled at the unexpected volume. She felt her grip on the stationary timepiece tighten, fresh tears threatening to spill as she closed her eyes. How was it possible she had any tears left to cry? "This . . ." She swallowed, willing herself to straighten before she said anything further. It was important; this was something she needed to do. Not just for Nico, but for all of them.

"This is all we have left of him," she eventually found the strength to say. Some part of her was right back in the graveyard in Florence. That courtyard, seemingly forgotten by all but one. Nico had been its lone mourner for years; now, he needed someone to mourn him. "We can't just erase that too. We can't . . . We can't just—"

Jo choked on the rest of the phrase, trying desperately to swallow the lump in her throat.

"A memorial." Takako put into words what she was trying to say, the girl walking up to Jo's side and placing a hand over hers. When Jo looked over at her, hoping her face showed every ounce of gratitude she felt, Takako didn't smile. She did, however, give Jo's hand a squeeze. "He deserves that much."

Jo nodded before pulling her hand away from the shelf. As if sensing her unspoken need, Takako let her fingers slip between Jo's, to hang intertwined at their sides, offering the strength of her presence. Maybe someday, Takako could teach her how to stand so tall.

Jo clutched at Takako with one hand and the edge of her own hoodie with the other. "If we don't do our best to remember Nico, then who will?"

Wayne was the first to respond. Not with words but with the silent removal of his nickel from the shelf. He clutched it tight in his palm for a second before pocketing it. After that, there seemed to be an unspoken agreement.

One by one, everyone went into the recreation room, slow and silent, as if walking up to a grave. And it was. The only grave Nico would ever receive. It seemed appropriate that the portrait of Julia lay eternally inside the man's proverbial tomb.

Until the bitter end and after, they deserved to be together.

It took Snow's touch, a gentle pressure against her shoulder, for Jo to realize everyone was looking at her. Waiting.

She looked at each member of her team, her family, and offered what she hoped was a look of deep understanding. They were all going to miss Nico; they all recognized that he'd deserved far better. So, with steady steps and steadier hands, Jo walked up to his final painting, a perfect likeness of his Julia, his love. Jo knelt before it and picked up the forgotten paintbrush. Dipping it in an open tube of paint, she drew a small star on the corner of the easel before returning it to its rightful place. And where it would stay.

Jo wanted to tell herself that there was nothing more that they could have done. Perhaps one of them had always been doomed to this fate. But, she was discovering that the actions of so-called "fate" left a bitter aftertaste. It was something she'd never quietly swallow again. She would rip the very notion of destiny to pieces if she must to protect her friends.

Yes, Jo would destroy everything, if that's what it took to free them from the Society itself.

THE END OF WISHES

BIRTH
of
CHAOS

WISH QUARTET BOOK THREE

ELISE KOVA & LYNN LARSH

*for those still discovering who they truly are*

# LIFE ON A LEASH

J ust outside of time and space, in a small corner of a magically constructed and brilliantly lavish mansion, Josephina Espinosa sat with her knees pulled to her chest, arms folded on top, and head rested between.

She didn't cry. She didn't speak. She barely breathed as she listened to the silence of the room—the deafening, overwhelming silence. The lack of sound was louder than any scream of rage or sob of loss that she could hope make. It was a void filled with hurt and heartache that nothing, not even the members of the Society, could bridge.

The recreation room seemed to cling to its lost occupant just as fiercely, the scent memory of Nico soaked into the walls, the floor—the last remnants of their Italian painter. There were the smoky echoes of the fire that had crackled in the hearth she'd leaned on while he'd painted, and where she'd kept her vigil since he'd died. There was the warm, earthy, almost mineral aroma of his oil paints, now dried and cracked on his palette. Then there was the sweet roasted edge of espresso stained on the inside of a forgotten cup.

Jo flipped her wrist, looking at the dull illumination of the hours she'd amassed since joining the Society. Nico had deserved more time, but all that was left of it now was the cracked face of a watch.

So Jo sat, just trying to breathe, to imprint his memory on her mind and lungs. She would not forget. She couldn't let herself forget. No matter what happened, she would remember Nico and his sacrifice. Her heart would cling to his memory as the room clung to his scent.

But the anger that simmered in her stomach stewed over another memory: the fact that Pan had taken him from them in the most heartless way possible.

Jo remembered that fact with vivid precision. She remembered it when she finally left Nico's memorial, and remembered still all the way back to her room. She remembered it as she lay in her bed, alone, and succumbed to the memory in vivid, waking dreams of squeezing the rainbow-haired woman until she popped and oozed all her secrets.

The next day, Jo repeated the process: rouse from a restless few hours of non-sleep, sit amidst the memories of Nico, return to her room to stare at the ceiling and fantasize over candy-colored revenge. Because she did not want to let herself come anywhere close to sleep.

The last time sleep had come, even if it had been forced upon her in a cataclysmic magical shift, Nico had been taken from them. Before then, it was the start of that impossible wish, when Snow had rewound time itself. The world now felt all too fragile—close her eyes for longer than a blink and she couldn't be sure what state it would be in when she opened them again.

So she didn't close her eyes. She went about her business with all the precision of a shampoo bottle: lather, rinse, repeat. All but forgetting that there were other members in the Society, others who were hurting just as bad, if not worse, than she.

On the third day, Jo roused from her muddled thoughts and dark delights, and headed down the long hall to the Four-Way, and then to the common room—a slight deviation to the routine.

The sun had just crested over the mountains beyond the pool when Jo entered, casting first light on both her and the man straight out of the 1920s. He leaned against the counter, one hand flipping his nickel absently as he nibbled on a piece of toast, eyes pointed at the TV as it ran quietly on the other side of the room.

It was the news in Japan and, as it had been for nearly a week now, all was blindingly, annoyingly well.

"Morning," Jo mumbled, crossing over to go about making herself a cup of coffee, even if it seemed unnaturally cruel to have such a simple luxury right now.

Wayne tensed at her proximity. Perhaps she had been wrong to venture onto common ground, and the time for the Society's seclusion was not yet over. While *she* didn't immediately snap at him or feel the overwhelming desire to shove him aside (a small victory compared to her mood a few days ago), she didn't get the sense that the feeling was mutual.

"Nice of you to show your face," Wayne mumbled. Jo tried to keep herself from snapping. He'd known Nico longer than she had—they all had. It'd take the rest of the Society more time.

"I don't know what you're talking about." She grabbed the coffee pot a little too roughly, brown liquid sloshing about to the point of nearly spilling out. The action helped keep her hands busy, which also helped prevent her from actually striking the man. Even improved, her mental state was still fragile at best; this was not the time to test her mood.

"You've been holed up in the rec room for days now."

"So?"

Wane shrugged.

Jo should've stopped there. "Has there been a wish?"

"No."

"Did you need me?"

"Need you? Who would need you?" he fired back, not even looking at her.

"The hell does that mean?" Jo abandoned the coffee, leaning against the counter.

"You're trouble." Wayne finished his toast and wiped his hands on his trousers.

Jo narrowed her eyes. "If I recall correctly, you like my trouble."

"When it's not getting one of the team killed." He finally looked at her.

"Excuse me?" she whispered, deathly quiet. Getting one of them killed?

"Just a suspicion." The attention was short lived, as Wayne's gaze wandered away. He wouldn't even give her the decency of direct eye contact as he levied his accusations.

"You're not smart enough to play cryptic." *Unlike Snow*. He was another ghost who had not been seen since Nico's death. "Shit or get off the pot, Wayne. What are you getting at?"

"Exactly what it sounds like." There was no "doll" at the end, making the statement come across even harsher than his tone. "You don't exactly have the best track record."

"I have absolutely no clue what you're talking about." Her current theory was that grief was making him mad. "Yuusuke? That was *one time*. And I messed up *once* on the last wish, but otherwise I've had a pretty good track record," she said defensively.

"Like that supposedly good track record means anything when *your* screw-up ends with one of our team dead."

Jo's hand flew like a bullet, striking out for his wrist, but instead her fingers curled around the man's bicep and she twisted him to face her, gave him a small shake. "Is that what you've been doing this whole time? Cooped up in your room, blaming this on *me*?"

Wayne opened his mouth to speak, but Jo could tell by the expression on his face that she wasn't going to like what he had to say. So instead, she just continued talking.

"Yeah, all right, Wayne, I messed up. But you know what? *We all did.* None of us was good enough, not even *you*," Jo seethed. "Don't pin this on me to try to make yourself feel better. Don't make me out to be your scapegoat." She'd been doing enough of beating herself up on her own. She really didn't need someone else to do it.

"Fine, yeah, we all messed up." He jerked away from her, straightening to look as far down on her as he could. "But you know what? This isn't about making you out as a scapegoat. I've been doing a lot of thinking over the past few days, connecting the dots, and everything's gone to shit since you arrived." Jo opened her mouth to counter, but it was his turn not to let her speak. "We've had more wishes, back to back, than ever before. I wouldn't be surprised if we got one tomorrow. We used to be able to go a whole decade without one before you got here. And then this last one? We've never had one so impossible to grant as a mass evacuation in such a short window of time. I've never even seen Snow rewind time up-front for a wish."

"I want this life at the end of a leash no more than you do. I'd rather see us free of it." It was the one thing that had resounded in her, over and over until it replaced the silence: destroy everything. Break the cycle they were trapped in. It had been her sole cohesive thought amid her grief. "So you can't blame all that on me." A quietness had overtaken her. Jo's mind was on overdrive, heightened by the confrontation.

"If the shoe fits," he shot back.

"At least I make an effort."

"What?" Wayne blinked, startled at the sudden shift.

"You heard me," Jo pressed. "At least I make an effort. I'm always out there, trying to help, trying to do more, brainstorming, and, yeah, owning up to failures when I make them. Shocker that if you put yourself out there, you mess up now and then. But what do you do with your time? No, don't answer, I think we already know."

"In the last wish—"

"In the last wish you made a bet to get people to look at a machine. Anyone could've made that happen if we had to. Some smart talking would've done it, no magic needed." She remembered that day. It was the same day he'd rejected her advances and the mere idea of physical intimacy had another avenue unfurling before her—a clarity she'd never seen before about the man. It was a guess, one that she was unnaturally sure she was right about. "You do as little as possible because you're afraid, Wayne Davis. You're afraid of doing too much, of stepping too far, and ruining the little stasis you have here."

"And what's wrong with that?" He was defensive. She could hear it in his voice. He tried to turn away, but this time Jo managed to wrap a tight grip around his wrist. She should stop now; she could feel the wavering in him.

She should've done a lot of things differently in those first few days following Nico's death though.

"Because you'll do nothing, and lose someone you love. Again."

Wayne's eyes widened so large that she wondered how they didn't fall from their sockets. "How did you . . ." he whispered. "Who told you?"

Jo didn't know what chord she'd struck, but it vibrated at such a magical frequency that she knew if she tightened it a little more, it'd snap. So she listened to the note, and twisted. "No one had to tell me—it's *so* blatantly obvious. You're afraid of having nothing and no one. So whenever you have anything, you make the least amount of effort possible, just enough to keep it, but not enough to really put yourself out there. Because if you put in that much effort, you just might become vulnerable. You just might get hurt. But surprise, Wayne. People need more than your half-assed attempt at connection. So it's no surprise that she left you for—"

"Stop!" he roared, smacking the mug Jo had set out for coffee and sending it flying across the room.

It shattered, and the sound broke whatever trance had come over her. Jo blinked, startled; she couldn't figure out how she'd gotten here. What had she even been saying?

Who was the "she" that Jo had been so confident about a moment ago? Jo tried to find the same mental pathways she'd explored, but they were gone, shrouded. She had no idea how she'd jumped to those conclusions.

Wayne panted softly. She felt his pulse racing under her hand, and Jo quickly relinquished him, stepping away. Her eyes dropped to her toes and her shoulders slumped.

"I'm sorry, Wayne, I—" she whispered. He said nothing, he barely moved. " —I don't know what . . ." Jo buried her face in her hand. How could she have done such a thing? What had come over her?

"I threw the first punch," he muttered, almost apologetically. "Let's just forget all about it." There was a firmness to his voice that drew her eyes back to his face. Jo saw the unspoken words. "It" had nothing to do with the argument, but rather, whatever it was that she had been pursuing.

"Yeah, okay," Jo whispered. "We can forget about it . . ."

"Good. We're square, then." Wayne's shoulder barely clipped hers as he started for the door.

A sinking feeling of wrongness overtook her. The longer she stayed in the Society, the more volatile everything became. The mansion and Jo were like two chemicals that should never meet. But they had been mixed, and now Jo had to figure out how to handle the explosive reaction before it put everything around her into meltdown.

Perhaps Wayne had been right after all.

She turned to stop him, to apologize. She wanted to tell him sorry, for real, and that she wanted to find a way out of the Society together. But her voice froze in her throat just as Wayne had seemingly frozen in his tracks.

For in the doorway stood a tall, silver-haired man.

Jo tensed at the sight of Snow, searching his face and taking him in. He looked as he always had, primped and polished in a way that not even Wayne could achieve with his suits or Eslar with his unnatural grace. He was a stark contrast to the room's other two occupants, rumpled and hunched. It was as if the man was trying to be a paragon of composure—untouchable to the rest of them in the throes of their grief. Gone was the man who had shared one last breakfast with them as a team.

*Distant once more.*

Jo barely recognized him as the lover she'd come to know in what now almost seemed like a distant dream. She worked to squelch the hope trying to flare in her chest at the mere sight of him because she knew better, she knew he was not here to be a balm to them.

He was here for the last thing any of them wanted, something Jo recognized with terrifying clarity. And as if to prove her silent worries true, Snow wasted no time in addressing her and Wayne with exactly the nightmare written all over his face.

"Gather the team and meet me in the briefing room in five," he said. Jo searched for a tremor in his tone, a crack in his facade, anything, but his face was as blank and hollow as his voice.

The silence that followed those words was like the silence in the aftermath of an explosion.

"Are you *kidding me*?" Wayne blew up with a shout. "Have you no decency?"

"Nico's been dead for barely a week, and you think you can just ask us to *keep going*?" Her heart felt like it was crumbling, her stomach dropping at the momentary flash of pain on Snow's face that gave way quickly to a complete lack of emotion. Yet it didn't stop the almost dizzying frustration. "No more, Snow, please. Just stop this for a minute, can't you? At least give us all time to *grieve*."

But as if he hadn't just heard their panic, their sorrow, as if he hadn't just witnessed their vehement reluctance, Snow straightened his back, looking over them like the mighty demigod he claimed to be.

"As members of the Society of Wishes, you will do as you are told."

For a beat, she let that sink in, the atmosphere wrapping cold around Jo's limbs. Wayne seemed to be impervious to the invisible binds.

"Like Nico did as he was told?" he fired venomously.

Another beat, another agonizing silence, and then Snow turned away. "You have your orders," he said, as detached as Jo had ever heard him. "Gather the team."

Jo slumped slightly, face dropping to stare at the scattered shards of the mug Wayne had smacked from her hands. Sure, it was easy for her to shout objections, act as if she had any say in the matter. But the demands of the actual members of the Society had little more weight than the hot air they were made of. When their choices were to grant wishes or stop existing, what else were they supposed to do?

# TOO SOON

Her mental state was in tatters.

Her body felt heavy, splintered. Her joints popped with every step, worn to agony by the tension of mourning that she'd carried in her limbs for days. For a being outside of reality, immune to human necessities, Jo knew in that moment that she had never known such exhaustion.

She regretted having not gone to Snow in the limited time they'd had for grief. Maybe, if she had, she would understand something? Perhaps there was some insight she lost because she'd spent all her valuable time—all six days of it—mourning the death of her friend. At the very least, she might have been able to see the man who had been working his way into her heart underneath the cold and distant facade he was currently sporting.

But his mental state now was an enigma to her. Was this all an act? Or had he really and truly broken, shattering differently but just as irrevocably as the rest of them?

Thinking of going to him merely renewed old frustrations. Snow was a pawn as much as she was, as much as all of them were. He couldn't undo the magic that bound them, even if he wanted to—she had enough faith in the goodness of the man to know that. She also knew he was speaking the truth when it came to not being able to choose the wishes. He was helpless to do anything more than try to keep them alive, and watch.

At once, Jo forced herself to recount every look of devastation on his face, every sorrowful attempt to keep her at arm's length out of what she could only assume was guilt for his circumstances. She committed to memory every time he'd caved to her touch and let slip apologies in breathy whispers into her ear. This wasn't his fault; he was a victim too, no matter how hard he tried to convince them all otherwise.

*Yes*, Jo's jaw popped as she clenched her teeth. Snow was trapped in this game. And if he wasn't the ringleader, that meant someone else was—and she would do whatever it took to uncover the truth.

The doors of the briefing room opened to the cold gray of the inexplicable light source that hovered over the center table. It cast long shadows behind the chairs—eight in total. One would remain heartbreakingly empty. And one . . . one was already occupied.

Pan sat, leaning back in her chair almost to the point of tipping. Her feet were propped on the table, crossed at the ankles, and her hands were folded over her stomach. The hem of wide-legged pants draped from her knees, little red bows up the back dangling ribbon to the floor. The woman-child tilted her head to the side, looking at Jo as she entered, chiffon and lace floating about from her ruffled turquoise top as she moved.

"About time you got here!" With the flourish of a giggle, Pan uncrossed her legs and tipped her chair forward. "Where's the rest of them?" Jo couldn't help but flinch; the woman's cheery tone was like nails on the chalkboard of the Society's collectively despondent attitude.

"Wayne went to get them." Jo wanted her remark to sound curt, but it merely sounded tired, the words hardly her own. Jo dragged her feet over, sitting heavily in one of the empty chairs.

"Lollygagging no dou—*oh*, Wayne, so good to see you!" She clapped her hands together. Sure enough, Wayne had arrived, the rest of the Society in tow. "What took you all so long?"

As expected, no one answered. Takako stopped in her tracks, staring down the ridiculously dressed creature. Pan's smile expanded, curling into something slightly more sinister, her cat-like eyes staring Takako down from beneath her mint green fringe. Takako shook her head and walked away. While she gave off the air of confidence, of not being intimidated, her movements looked a lot more like a tactical retreat than the advance following a victory.

"Shove off, Pan," Wayne muttered, barely loud enough for Jo to hear as he passed. If Pan heard, she made no motion. The other two men filed in without so much as a glance in her direction.

"Do you not like me anymore, Wayne-*eee*?" Pan whined.

Just seeing Pan had set Jo to seething, so actually hearing and interacting with the woman reared something ugly in her. It was a cold fire of pure malice that burned deep in Jo's chest, the flames licking to be let out, to wrap a stranglehold around Pan's throat. It felt like the longer she was in her presence, the stronger the hot current of liquid loathing flowed between them. For the first time in her life, Jo knew the true essence of hatred.

As if sensing Jo's dark thoughts, Pan's eyes rolled over to her. The same expression Takako had received—a sort of wicked smile—was now directed at her. Jo had seen this smile before, she'd seen it like a bad omen of something to come in the morning the day before Fuji had erupted. A tremble worked up her spine, but Jo squelched it right between the shoulder blades. Her rage, simple but all-encompassing, would be a dam to any fear or intimidation. She wouldn't let Pan have the satisfaction, not now.

It was in that staring contest, pitting her will against Pan's, that Jo found herself wondering for the first time if she could use her magic to tear apart something living.

"Thank you all for coming."

"As though we had a choice," Wayne mumbled, low enough that Jo was fairly sure she was the only one to hear.

Across the table, Samson shook his head, rocking slightly, handing digging into his hair hard enough that the braids on one side began to come lose. His eyes were wild, hardly looking at anything at all as he kept repeating the words, "Too soon . . . Too soon . . ." He was barely breathing, shaking so violently that Eslar's steady arm around his shoulders seemed to be the only thing keeping him upright at all.

The other side of Samson was vacant. *An empty seat.* Self-loathing welled up within Jo. How had Samson, out of all of them, ended up next to what would have been Nico's chair?

"Will he be replaced?" Jo whispered—and perhaps she shouldn't have; perhaps the exhaustion had loosened her lips and left her tactless. The whole room fell into a hush the moment they were said. Even Samson stilled, following her gaze with the rest of them to the place where Nico used to be—and still should have been.

There was a long pause, a deep sigh, and then Snow finally diverged from acting as his namesake.

"No." Snow's answer was gentle, as if he let himself hear their grief for the first time. It was factual, but not cold. The sound settled like its own warmth right next to her heart. It was the fracture she'd been looking for—the glimpse into a humanity that she knew was there. "As you all know, when the Age of Magic ended, so too did magic disappear from reality. A few lineages of power were strong enough to survive the jumps, the rebuilding of the world, and exist—dormant—in the blood of their ancestries. When a descendant of these ancients makes a wish, they are drafted into the Society."

"And Jo was the last one we were looking for," Pan finished brightly. Jo fantasized about smothering her cheerful face with a nail-filled pillow. Especially when she added under her breath, "Took you long enough."

Jo was taken back to the Ranger Compound. *Seven lineages*, Snow had said then. Be it through some secret knowledge or a sensory power, he'd known seven people would join the Society from the start. And just when all chairs had been filled . . . Jo looked back to Nico's empty seat.

No more companions. No more help. No new faces for eternity.

*And no more martyrs*, she vowed.

"Fine," Jo mumbled. "It's for the best . . . not like there would ever be any replacing Nico, anyway."

The silence that overcame them sounded like agreement to Jo's ears. Everyone sat with their heads bowed, hands in their laps, in a stiff competition to be the smallest of the group. Even Snow stared at the table beneath him, as if he'd somehow forgotten why they were there, or how to pull up the wish.

"You guys are so *boring*." Pan drew out the 'o' in the last word for what felt like a complete three minutes. "Come on everyone, we have a job to do!" When still no one moved, Pan leaned heavily back into her seat with a groan, kicking her legs beneath the table like a child seconds away from throwing a proper tantrum. Jo thought the woman-child might have been mumbling something, the annoyance in her tone bordering on a whine. But then she was sitting back up, looking around the table in sickeningly genuine confusion. "Why the long faces? Didn't you used to get excited by this? What changed?"

A beat passed. Then two. No one seemed fully equipped to handle such a question, it would seem. Especially not one filled with such legitimate lack of what should have been easy understanding.

"What changed?" Jo's head eventually rose, a scathing remark on her lips. But before she could continue, Takako was on her feet.

"*What changed?*" Takako echoed, more animated than Jo had ever seen her. "How about the fact that we know you're sitting there like a smiling demon just waiting for your chance to strike us off one by one?"

"Strike you off?" Pan blinked. "Why would I want that?"

"You tell us." Jo joined the conversation. She'd insist it was to support Takako, but there was no use lying to herself. She was at the point of taking any opportunity to fight with Pan.

"Well, I don't." Pan folded her hands behind her braided, mint-green tresses. "Why do you think I would? I'm here too, you know. If the Society ends, what do you think happens to me? Do you think I'm any different from you?" Pan's fingers began to fuss with her braids, pausing long enough to look at Jo. Were they friends, it would be like some kind of inside joke. But they were the furthest possible thing from friends and Pan's intention escaped Jo entirely. "The wishes stop, and the Society stops. It needs to be dismantled properly or fed constantly with the magic of destroyed worlds. And the only thing more boring than staring at you lot for eternity is to stop existing entirely."

The logic was a sharp kick to the gut. It pulled Jo's insides in different directions, layered atop each other in illegible and unbearable contrast. Everything Jo had come to believe about Pan hinged on the fact that she was the laughing monster, lurking under their beds and waiting to devour them the second their eyes closed. But if Pan was a prisoner too, then that just made her . . . a righteous bitch, yes, but one with no more or less power than the rest of them.

Takako must have worked through a similar logic, because Jo watched her deflate back into her chair. The woman tucked her chin to her chest, and made eye contact with no one. Everything diffused, begging to be let go and forgotten about.

*No*, Jo tried to force her mind to begin to work again, to shake off the grief and start moving forward anew. *Dismantled properly . . . Do you think I'm different than any of you?* She'd phrased the latter as a question, not a statement. And the former . . . the former was an idea all its own. Pan was hiding something: she so clearly knew more about the Society than she was letting on. But opportunities to talk one-on-one with Pan in any productive way seemed about one in a million. Still, Jo filed away the knowledge.

And of course, Pan had no idea when to stop. "Really, my power is boring too. Just—" Pan snapped her fingers " —poof! One of you is dead! Snow has magic and problem solved!" She sank back into her chair with a huff. "That's no fun to watch."

Maybe Pan was one of them, maybe not, the jury was still out. But even if she was, Jo would most certainly still hate her. She'd sort through everything else when her emotions weren't making every attempt to get the better of her. She leveled her eyes with the ice-cream haired woman. "Don't speak about us like we're cattle."

"Then act smarter than cattle, and work on this next wish, so none of you have to die." Pan smiled. *You*, not *us*, Jo noted; Pan didn't see herself at any risk. "Or you can just break everything and see how that turns out. It's not like I really care *that* much."

"All right, enough." Snow finally joined in, far too late. "That's enough," he said, quieter. The man shook his head and straightened. He'd been hunched over, chin nearly against his chest.

Though his gaze seemed to hold far less intimidation and power than usual, he looked each one of them in the eyes. At Eslar who now sat under the arm Samson had slung around his shoulders. At Wayne, who seemed ready to blow his top in anger, or collapse into tears. At Takako, who out of all of them, still met their leader with a searching, almost trusting expression, as though she were still waiting for orders.

And then, finally, at Jo.

"I don't care if you all get along." She didn't know why he seemed to be speaking only to her. "But this changes nothing. You must still grant wishes. Our focus should be on that, and that alone." He pressed his fingers into the table and it rippled to light with magic. Images began to float, taking shape from the ether, but Jo focused solely on Snow.

Live as a slave to wishes, or die for them—that was his message. Jo's hand balled into a fist. She refused to believe their eternity was perpetually linked to such an unforgivable ultimatum; there had to be a third way out. And she wasn't going to let them see the end of this wish before she found it. She didn't care if—*How did Pan put it?* She had to *dismantle every-thing* to get to it.

# THE BONE CARVER

The next couple of minutes seemed to drift by at half speed.

Jo watched in a sort of numb daze as Snow continued to bring to life an array of images. His motions were disjointed, robotic. Jo tilted her head, trying to make sense of them, though he seemed to be having as hard of a time as she was. It was as if he were moving on autopilot or, perhaps more aptly, like a puppet with invisible strings.

He finally stilled and, for a long moment, he didn't speak. Then, as if steeling himself, he took a breath and sifted through the images until one illuminated and expanded, taking up the majority of the space in front of their faces.

The image was of a human bone, that much was obvious by its size and shape—likely a femur, Jo thought—and Snow's demeanor. But the unnerving quality of the stark photograph wasn't so much in its subject matter. It wasn't in the way the bone was bleached and cleaned so completely that it no longer looked like it belonged to a body it all.

No, what made this unique was the jagged lines carved deep—so deep that delicate pinkish marrow was visible in their grooves. Upon closer inspection, it became obvious that they were numbers which, at first glance, appeared random.

"What's that supposed to be?" Wayne mumbled. "Some kind of code?"

*You could call it that.* Jo kept her thoughts to herself for now. It was a *sort* of code, she supposed, one of the oldest: binary.

"A string of murders have been plaguing United North America," Snow began.

Jo studied not the bone and its odd markings, but *around* it for the first time. The bone glistened with moisture, no doubt deposited from the snow that had been pushed aside and piled around the rocky cement where the bone lay. Snow—real snow, not the man standing at the head of the table —inches thick and perfectly white. She'd seen pictures of the harsh winters in the UNA, heard the gloating from Texans about never having to worry about anything so brisk, but she'd never experienced it herself.

"Just a nickel minute here, big cheese," Wayne interrupted. "You're telling us that this . . . this is . . ." He'd started off strong, but the words faded into nothingness. A truth they had all figured out, but did not want to recognize.

"This is the work of what's being identified as a serial killer. They're calling him the Bone Carver." Snow's voice was as icy as his namesake. "This is his calling card."

Jo felt herself leaning forward in her seat, despite the way her hand settled with her fingertips pressing indents into her lips in a shaky line. By all logic, it was grotesque and horrific, yet her brain seemed to short-circuit when it came to thinking of anything logically. It was beyond terrible. It was as if it were too wretched for her to comprehend. Here was a bone—a human bone—cleaned, bleached, and neatly prepared by some murderer. It was grotesque and horrific and Jo didn't quite know how to process it. The effect was so disjointing that it was as if someone else was looking at it, not her.

When Jo could tear her eyes away, she could tell by just one look at everyone's faces that she wasn't alone. Even Snow seemed at a momentary loss. Whatever he had to say next would be even worse; it was better to rip it off all at once, get it done with, like a bandage.

"The Bone Carver has an appreciation for binary." She finally shared her observation with the room, an addition that seemed to spur Snow back to life.

"Yes." He cleared his throat with a soft cough. "The methodology has been consistent enough that law enforcement and government agencies have deemed it the work of a bona fide serial killer rather than a string of unconnected or copycat events." As he talked, Snow sifted through image upon image, dragging up medical reports and news broadcasts of the crime scenes, the arrest that failed to meet criteria for conviction, the *victims*. Jo's stomach dropped, the atmosphere settling into something too grim for their already wounded attitudes to handle.

These weren't the sort of images the news played. These were the sort of images you found circulating in the dark web and then promptly wished you hadn't. They were tagged neatly with file numbers and evidence serials. A few lines of clerical information written on a photograph had never contained so much.

Still, Snow went on, enlarging one of the still-running videos.

A newscaster spoke directly into the cameras. "Law enforcement officials now believe that the killer has connections to the Artificial Care Act movement. The latest calling card left by the Bone Carver contains the coordinates to one of N.A.I.S., Inc—"

"What's N.A.I.S., Inc?" Takako interjected. The video paused magically the second she spoke.

"It stands for Northern Artificial Intelligence Solutions," Jo answered. "I did a job for one of their competitors, once. Something about looking into a new project they had going . . . codename 'Primus Sanguis.'"

"Primus Sanguis . . . Latin. First Blood," Eslar muttered before turning to her and saying, louder, "What does it mean?"

Jo shrugged. "I try—tried—to make a point not to dig too deep into my clients' affairs. The more I knew, the more danger I was in during work. And after."

"Who had you hack them?" Takako asked.

"CBM."

"The computer chip server people?" Of course, Takako would recognize the company. She was from around fifty years ago. In a different reality, certainly, but it seemed that much was the same.

"In my time, they're one of the leaders in AI—" Jo quickly added, "Artificial Intelligence," for any in the room who would, somehow, not know. "I can't say I know the full details of what Primus Sanguis was . . . but I know CBM wanted it badly."

"How badly?" Wayne asked.

"Bad enough that they cut me a check that paid my mother's and my bills for a year."

Wayne whistled softly. "And this Artificial Care Act, dollface? Care to do more 2050s translating?"

Jo turned back to the paused video grimly. "I only know the broad strokes . . . In the UNA, there's been a debate on the actual rights androids should have. Some advocate that they are sentient creatures and should be granted the same rights and protections as humans. Others disagree."

"Give machines the same rights as humans?" Wayne scoffed at the notion and the sound grated Jo's ears.

"They're not machines," she corrected. "They're thinking, living creatures. Most androids now are nearly one-hundred percent bio-mass—virtually indistinguishable from humans."

"Except for the cogs for brains," Wayne said smartly.

"Josephina's right," Samson interjected in his soft voice. The second Wayne's eyes shot over to him, he sunk further into his chair. Jo was afraid he wouldn't say anything further, but it seemed he could find the courage so long as he didn't actually have to look at anyone. "They're not cogs, or metal. . . as you know. They're machines, yes, but their brains are biological supercomputers, in a way. . . It's complicated."

"It is," Jo attempted to both thank Samson for speaking up and encourage him to do so more by lavishing some quick praise. "Samson's entirely correct."

"It sounds sideways," Wayne muttered.

Jo opened her mouth to retort, but Snow interrupted her.

"There's more to the video, and more relating to this wish." He brought them back on track from the useless debate. It was a discussion Jo could have for days, especially if there was even the slightest chance it'd delay learning more about, and working on, the wish.

The video sprang back to life with a nod from Snow, continuing where it left off. "—this calling card, combined with the others, has led law enforcement officials to believe that the Bone Carver is, in actuality, an android. However, the motives surrounding this suspicion remain unclear.

"Republican groups have been quick to rally behind the investigation, saying that these killings will—and should—be considered on the eve of voting for the Artificial Care Act. Democrats have marked the Bone Carver as a lone wolf, arguing that, just as humans, there is the possibility for deranged individuals that are outliers from the norm in every species, but it is not grounds to withhold rights from an entire population. The senator from Pennsylvania—where the first murder was discovered—has declined to comment beyond expressing his condolences to the families and loved ones of those affected."

Snow straightened away from the table, and with that, the video feed sputtered and died. A few images remained, blatant depictions of what this Bone Carver had done, but for a moment, Snow held off on any further explanation. Despite herself, Jo raised a hand towards one of the images, a short, jagged-edged bone etched with a moniker that, considering the computer code, Jo felt like she should have been able to identify. But nothing came to mind outside of a reflexive roiling of her stomach.

This wasn't just murder. This was *sport*.

Whoever was committing these murders had gruesomely ended the lives of twelve people, cut into their flesh, wrenched out their bones, cleaned them, prepared them, and then deposited them miles away from where the bodies were found with seemingly nonsensical coordinates carved into them that related tenuously enough it made you want to believe there was a pattern, but it was impossible to tell. It was brash. It was mocking. And it was utterly ruthless.

There were no further interjections while Snow offered them as many details as he himself appeared privy to. Everyone was eerily still. Death lived all around them, in their wish, in their home. The only light at the end of this darkness was going to be actually helping someone—especially after their last failure. Whether they were willing to admit it or not, they wanted, *needed* Snow to lead them to that optimistic end to what seemed like an Edgar Allen Poe story on depressants.

At least, that's where Jo had *assumed* Snow was going with all this.

"Our wish comes from the Bone Carver himself," Snow bit out. "His request is to prevent any and all future possibilities of getting caught. The Severity of Exchange has a window of approximately two weeks." When the words were met with stunned silence, Snow sighed, waving a hand in front of himself and ridding the space above the table of all remaining images. "In short, the wish is for him to continue murdering humans without repercussions. Indefinitely."

That finally managed to get a reaction. Or five.

"You're joking, right?"

"This is so wrong. This is so *wrong.*"

"No. No, I won't. I can't. *We* can't.*"

"You can't expect us to actually do this, right Snow?"

"We have no choice."

Everyone spoke atop each other in a frantic plea to be heard, though Jo could hardly register anything outside of the ringing in her ears. First Mt. Fuji and now this? What sort of twisted game was the universe playing at? To call it unfair was beyond hyperbole at this point.

Eventually, it was Eslar's voice that finally cut through the fray.

"So this is how we should expect things to be run now, Snow? Impossible requests with even more impossible time limits?"

In the tense quiet that followed Eslar's question, everyone's eyes shifted between the elf and the demigod. Snow didn't answer, but he didn't need to. If Jo could see the shackles binding their leader to his reluctant affirmation, then she was certain everyone else could see them too. At least, she hoped they could. The last thing they needed was further fractures threatening to split them apart.

"I could always just kill another one of you and call it a day," Pan chimed in, the sing-song tone to her voice causing Jo's hackles to rise instantly. When Jo wrenched her attention from Snow to the woman-child, it was to find her leaning back in her chair again, face the epitome of boredom. Somehow, she'd happened upon a nail file, choosing to carefully sculpt each neon pink nail rather than partake in the tumultuous conversation with even a modicum of interest.

"No one else is getting killed," Jo hissed, biting back the shiver that ran down her spine when Pan's eyes darted up from her nails, capturing Jo in a stare that could eat an entire soul if she wanted.

"Except the innocent people we're going to help this guy get away with killing," Wayne mumbled, the bitterness in his voice shattering the beginning of whatever atmosphere had been radiating between Jo and Pan.

Jo rubbed at her eyes, feeling the beginnings of a headache forming; her hands were shaking.

There were no stars popping into the darkness under the pressure of her fingers. Just darkness, darkness, and more darkness. Enough that it could consume her whole if she wasn't careful.

They were really doing this, weren't they? Helping a serial killer avoid being brought to justice? And why? To avoid the possibility of their own demise should they fail or refuse?

For another long moment, no one spoke, mulling over the information in their own ways. The silence stretched on long enough that it almost made Jo want to scream, but she had no desire to be the one to break it. Not if she had nothing of value to offer. Thankfully, Takako was the first to pick back up the conversation.

"This . . . this killer. It's an android, right?"

"You are correct." Snow nodded.

"Can a robot even *make* a wish?" she asked. "I mean, isn't that something that should be an exclusively human capability?"

Jo frowned, picturing the various anti-Artificial Intelligence organizations that had been popping up ever since the first droids were legally allowed autonomy in the Lone Star Republic. Giving androids rights went over surprisingly easy in the LSR, especially considering the never-ending back and forth in the UNA. So, it didn't affect her, but she generally supported the Artificial Care Act; if something has the ability to think for itself, it should be able to act for itself too and accept responsibilities and protections for those decisions as a whole person in the eyes of the law.

"Like I said . . . it's almost impossible to tell apart an android and a human nowadays," Jo chimed in. "It would make sense that cognitive choice—free will—gives them the same power over a wishing circle as anyone else."

"Perhaps if we knew *why* this Bone Carver was making the wish—his motives behind his actions—it would be an easier pill to swallow?" Eslar offered, though he appeared about as convinced as everyone else. In fact, Wayne didn't bother to hold back the irritated roll of his eyes.

"What reasoning could possibly merit offing innocent people?"

"Do . . . Do we know for sure that they're innocent?" Samson's question brought everyone up short.

It didn't seem worth considering: human lives were human lives regardless of situation. But Snow had never actually used the word "innocent"—Wayne had. Jo looked to Snow for clarification, and, despite the reasoning that a life was a life, she found herself hoping that *maybe* this would be something to cling to. Something, to quote Eslar, that might make this unforgivable task just a little bit easier to bear.

Snow leaned forward, placing his hands on the table before him, not looking at anyone in particular. "I have given you all the information on the motives I have. The killings are, seemingly, random. But the police are looking for a connection and that will lead them to the killer, and you will need to thwart them before they find one."

Jo leaned back in her chair, worrying her bottom lip as she thought. They couldn't be random killings, *they just couldn't be*. To be broken so utterly that you would be driven to murder, driven to the brink of an abyss so inconceivable. . . there had to be a reason for it.

Maybe this was an act of self-preservation? But then why leave such grotesque calling cards? Why hurt the Artificial Care Act by fueling the words of those who'd cast suspicion or doubt on it? The Bone Carver was clearly trying to send a message, but to whom? And if there *was* a pattern, would they be able to pinpoint who he might target next?

Jo sighed. Even if they knew who the next target was, there was nothing they could do about it. Their services were promised to the killer, not the prey.

"We need more data." What she'd really wanted to say was, *I don't want to talk, or even* think *about this anymore*. Not that she had a choice.

"See, isn't this far better than just my slaughtering one of you?" Pan proclaimed, jumping up from her own chair. "So much intrigue, so much excitement. I can't wait to see what you lot come up with to lessen the Severity of Exchange in just two short weeks." She gave a wave over her shoulder as she exited the room. "But do let me know if you decide to give up. I think I get to choose, this time."

Jo stared at the door, Pan's words sitting uncomfortably low in her gut. If Pan wanted them to think that she was a prisoner like the rest of them, she was going about it in all the wrong ways. Because, at least to Jo's ears, it almost sounded like the woman-child was eager for them to fail.

# COMPLICIT SURVIVAL

"**W**ell, then," Eslar said, standing and gaining control of the room. "I think we should plan our attack."

"I'll leave you to it," Snow said, now that his job was seemingly finished.

"Why don't you stay?" Jo suggested before she could second-guess herself. "And help us brainstorm?" *It's not like you have anywhere else to be*, she wanted to add. Even if Jo understood, with stunning clarity after Nico, why he would not want to get closer to the members of the Society than was absolutely necessary, it didn't mean she agreed with it.

"I don't think I would be much further help," he wavered.

"I don't think you'll stop anyone from saying what they want." Jo motioned to the group, inviting someone to object. "Maybe you'll help us in a way you don't expect?"

Uneasily, Snow sat back down in his chair. It was as if a switch had been flipped and without having information about a wish to impart to them, he had no purpose being in the room and thus had no idea what to do with himself.

"Th-thank you for staying, Snow." It was odd to hear Eslar stutter. But judging from his reaction, the oddest thing currently was Snow's presence. Snow gave a nod, as if encouraging Eslar to continue as he always did—leading the group on the execution of the wish itself. "I think we should figure out our approach."

"You say that like we're actually *on board* with this crock of —"

"Wayne!" Eslar snapped, much more noticeably aggravated at the New Yorker's pointless interjections this time. And much quicker than usual, too. "No one is happy about this situation," Eslar went on after a moment of collecting himself, in which he gracefully (if not forcefully) sat himself down. Almost at once, Jo watched Samson reach out to grasp one of Eslar's hands, the slightly lighter tone of his skin standing out against the rich darkness of Eslar's.

For some reason, Jo felt the need to look away.

"Wayne's not wrong." Takako blessedly jumped in. "No one's thrilled about any of this. Regardless of any personal beliefs towards the Artificial Care Act—or similar governances surrounding the rights of artificial intelligence, regardless if the victims are innocent or not, murder is still murder. There are no masked vigilantes, only criminals. We all know that. But all of that doesn't change our assignment or our ability to opt out of it."

Little by little, everyone turned their attention towards Takako, willing and even forcing themselves to get into the mindset they'd come to associate with granting a wish. That didn't mean the feeling lifted, though —the one where they all seemed to be walking a tandem tightrope; if any one of them shifted their weight too far, they'd break apart and tumble down to earth. And at least one of them would be certain not come out alive.

"So where do we go from here?" Jo tried her best not to sound bitter and mostly succeeded, though she felt every ounce of that bitterness settle spoiled and churning in her stomach. "We just close our eyes and guarantee permanent sanctuary for a murderer? Let him live out the rest of his days happily carving people up?"

"Everyone dies eventually," Eslar said, blunt and ruthless, and Jo's stomach dropped.

Still, she found herself biting back, "Except us, right?"

"Well, that is our goal," Eslar replied without skipping a beat, and Jo couldn't help but startle at his lack of argument.

"I think . . . I mean, what Eslar's probably trying to say is that we've already done our duties as human beings. We've already paid the price of death in the ages we were born into and gave ourselves to a higher power. We've done all we can to help the world from here, everything and then some. We've stood by and witnessed as the world was wracked in horrors much worse than this."

"We're complicit," Takako whispered.

"We've had to be," Wayne insisted.

Samson cringed at Wayne's tone. Swallowed once, twice, as if trying to clear his mouth for the next words. He finally got there. "And this . . . this is all we have left. I-I know it's selfish—" At this, he bowed his head, slouching back into insecure reservation. But his spine found the strength to form a straight line once more. "But haven't we lost enough?"

No one in the room seemed able to keep their eyes from drifting over to the empty chair at the table. Their crafter took a breath, and when he spoke again, his voice was raw and shaking. "Don't you think we might have earned the right . . . to be a little bit selfish this time? To do this and not feel wretched about it for the sake of our own survival?"

At first, the room as a whole seemed unsure how to respond, the weight of Samson's words dragging a heaviness across their shoulders and keeping them pinned in place. Though there was no scolding, Jo couldn't deny that she felt chastened nonetheless.

After a moment of awkwardness began to stretch and pull between them, Wayne settled back in his chair with a huff, the sound shattering the tension at once. He crossed his arms over his chest and frowned; if it weren't for the situation, Jo probably would have laughed at the theatrics.

"Sammy's right," he said, drumming his fingers along the crook of his elbow. Samson tilted his head slightly at the sudden use of a new name for him. "We've served our time. Some of us more than others, but time nonetheless. We might not like what we're doing—hell I'd take the Great Depression all over again if it meant avoiding all this . . .But . . . But I'd fancy a guess I'm not alone in saying we'd like losing another one of our own even less."

This time, when a renewed quiet settled in, it was almost reverent, the group as a whole balancing Wayne's words with Samson's with whatever else had gone unsaid. For Jo, she couldn't help feeling as though she hadn't served *enough* time, maybe. And yet, at the prospect of spending eternity balanced on the razor's edge of a second demise, Jo couldn't help but agree with Wayne.

"We're survivors," Takako murmured.

It was all they could do, survive. For their own sake, for each other's. Jo liked to think it was what Nico would have wanted, but it didn't seem enough.

"Aren't we focusing on the wrong thing?" Jo looked to each of them as she spoke, looking for someone to meet her eyes and give her a glimmer of hope that there was someone else who thought as she did. That she wasn't insane for all the thoughts that had been stirring in her mind following Nico's death. "Even if we complete this unpalatable wish, what stops the next one from being worse?"

"What are you saying?" Eslar was the one to ask.

"I'm saying that we shouldn't settle for being survivors. We have a room of magic here. We exist outside of time. Why not stop granting wishes?"

"Doll, did you somehow forget about the whole part where if we stop granting wishes, we stop existing?"

"Not in the slightest." Jo shook her head. *How was no one else thinking about this?* "I don't just mean stop. I mean . . . change the Society. Maybe there's another way to get the magic instead of wishes? Some other 'Plan B' that we haven't thought of."

"Jo," Snow spoke up with a cautionary note.

"Or put a stop to it altogether, if we can, and keep existing." No one had an answer for her, because there wasn't one. "Unless we change the Society itself, we're nothing more than slaves, cattle, waiting for slaughter regardless of what Pan—"

"The only thing that matters are the wishes, and keeping our team alive," Snow interrupted harshly. Jo instantly regretted suggesting he stay. "There are no alternatives, Josephina."

She openly glared at Snow, and he met her stare. Tears fought against screams and stalemated into silence. Surely, he knew something that could help them. Why was he complacent to just sit on the sidelines? And if it was true, if he couldn't help them, what circumstances had come to pass that had set them all on such a long, drawn-out suicide highway?

"Right, Snow," Eslar started again cautiously, as if waiting for Jo to object again. She sunk back into her chair, keeping her thoughts to herself . . . for now. "We should focus on the wish."

Assessing the situation was a fragile affair after that, as though everyone felt the subconscious need to watch their words, not sugar-coating, but definitely avoiding anything that could be intentionally antagonistic as well.

"So, all of this is happening in United North America, right?" Takako pulled up the original photo of the bone in snow.

"Yes," Snow affirmed. With a wave of his hand, illuminated images spread across the table once more.

"The latest incident seems to have been in Boston Harbor . . . Police there are investigating," Wayne said.

Jo continued to sit back in her chair, keeping her mouth shut. She couldn't trust herself not to interject again, to point out how foolish the hamster wheel they were running on actually was.

Eslar nodded, stood again, and leaned towards the video feed Snow had shown them earlier. He pointed toward the news station logo in the bottom left corner. "There's reporting in the greater metro area." With the swipe of a green-nailed finger, he pulled up a social media thread on the matter. "However, there are rumors of police activity in the small town of Rockport."

Takako stood, widening the map of the Bone Carver's victims. "They must know something. These murders are all over the place. For the investigation to be narrowing down on such a small town . . ."

"I'm guessing the Bone Carver lives there?" Jo asked quietly. If she was doing this, then she wanted more than these static photos and brief news reels. She wanted something concrete to sink her teeth into.

Snow gave a final swipe of his hand with a grim nod. An address, a simple looking house, and a photograph of a man in a suit all pulled up together. It was a simple little bio, but not unlike what they had received for the first wish, and every wish after. They all stared at the face of their wisher, at the face of a killer. "This is the man who made the wish."

"Do the police have this information?" Takako asked.

"I do not know," Snow admitted, at least having the decency to look upset about it. He made a few final hand motions. Magic swirled in the table in a way that seemed random, but if Jo stared at it long enough, it was almost as if she, too, could make some sense of it. Every bit of information they'd been presented with appeared one after the next. "This is all I have been presented with."

"Why don't we get more information when the wish comes in?" she asked their leader. "Why is it limited to only morsels every time? It's like the system is designed to try to coax us into failure."

"This is how it's always been," Eslar answered for Snow, the protective note in his voice undeniable.

Jo looked sidelong at the elf. "That's not what I asked."

"I am only afforded a brief glimpse into the wisher's current state of affairs when a wish is made."

"Why?"

"This is how it's always been." Snow repeated Eslar's words.

"That's not an answer," Jo shot back, rephrasing her earlier protest.

"If Snow could help us more, he would." Eslar slammed a hand on the table and Jo jumped back in her seat. Less from the noise and more from seeing the elf emote so openly.

"I don't doubt that," Jo said quietly, looking Eslar in the eye, and then Snow. "I don't," she added softly, just for him. She needed him to know that even if she was struggling with just about everything right now, she could afford him the benefit of the doubt. She believed in him, even if she knew that he was holding something back. "But I'm asking *why* it's this way."

"What you should be asking is if you can go into the field and gather information yourself," Eslar replied coolly. "We're not going to get up-to-the-minute status on the police activity sitting here or looking online."

He had an odd idea of punishments (if that was his intent) because Jo couldn't help but perk up at the prospect. Getting out of the mansion, gathering up *actual* intel with *actual* computers, looked a lot like freedom; the idea offered a boost of adrenaline straight into Jo's veins. Perhaps it would be like Nico and Florence. Perhaps it would give her the new perspective she needed on the Society, looking at it from the outside.

"Fine, I'm on it." Jo stood, trying not to look so eager. She got the distinct impression that she wasn't supposed to want to do this. "Where should I start? The police HQ in Boston? Or case Rockport in general?"

Samson had already taken to pacing around the table, his fingers making intricate designs with a looped piece of string. "The police seem to be closing in on a few of his plausible locations. Even if the most recent murder was in Boston proper, I'd go with Rockport."

Eslar got to his feet as well. "I second Samson's suggestion." A faint blush seemed to dust the other man's cheeks. "Time may not be on our side; the authorities seem to be moving quickly." Eslar pulled out his watch, which prompted all of them to do the same. "We only received ten hours each for this wish, and two weeks total."

"Ten hours?" Wayne balked. "Hardly any time."

*And who chose that amount?* Jo bit back the question. Even if she wouldn't voice them aloud, she would keep thinking them, letting them eat away at her until she could feed them answers.

"All right. I'm going out to collect some information." Jo's legs were already leading her towards the Door with a keycode shimmering to form at the back of her head. "I'll come back and regroup with what I find."

"Hold up there, dollface." Wayne's voice cut into her thoughts, and she had to will herself not to feel annoyed by the interruption. By the time her focus had returned to the room, Wayne was standing beside her, a coat she hadn't noticed before in hand. "I'm coming with you."

Jo could only blink, a debate why he shouldn't at the ready—

—but why? Pride? Where had her pride gotten *any* of them before? The need to be alone? Yeah, like *that* was a good idea right now. Their earlier tiff? Perhaps leaving the Society and clearing the air with some fresh air would be the best for that, too.

So instead of shooing him away, Jo just nodded in acquiescence and said, "Okay, let's get this over with."

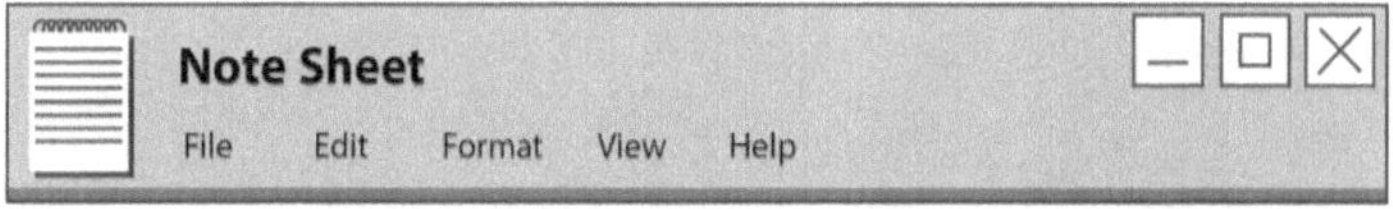


BTCOS NOTES 1

**Search Query 1: WISH GRANTER SOCIETY CIRCLE MAGIC**

Found original site that brought me here. (Not the sort of nostalgia I'm looking for) No new info.

Found on CreepyPen.
Story ignored in past life (maybe seen but forgot?). Ritual/folklore presented as fiction.

> "For this ritual you need two pieces of string. To start off, picture the desire clearly in your mind and wrap one string in a circle around your feet. Place the other string on the floor in front of you in another circle. This will make a portal for the god of death to enter.
>
> Don't rush, it could take time, at some point he'll come for you and then the God will begin the wishing game."

- *God of death=Wish Granter?*

Oldest record from 1800s. Rumor: transcribed from someone's grandmother's spell book? True origin unknown.

> "When you have visualized your wish for 5-10 minutes. Stare into the flame and say the following incantation:
> By candle's magic burn
> The wishing hour does turn
> With spell's words chanted
> A wishers wants are granted
> By power of the Goddess's might
> All wants come to pass this night"

- *Another mention of goddess*
- *Wishing hour? Relevant? Is time important?*

Consensus = no one knows where the rumors of the Wish Granter/circles came from

Check next:

- *Rumors across all cultures? Why?*
- *Anything else overlapped across cultures and times?*

# A SINGLE EYE

J o and Wayne stepped out of the Door and into a parking lot behind the back of a convenience store. Even outside of time, a biting cold nipped right through the jacket that never left her shoulders, prompting Jo to bury her hands as deep as possible into the front pockets.

"The mansion should've given me a thicker hoodie," she grumbled.

"I was wondering why this appeared in my room, but I didn't question." Wayne shrugged on the coat.

"Glad to know it's considerate toward someone." Jo rolled her eyes. How Wayne of all people had garnered favor with the mansion would forever elude her.

"Don't be bitter," he chided (dare she think somewhat playfully?).

"The only thing that's bitter is this cold."

"Not used to the chill, doll?"

"I see your hands are in your pockets as well," Jo said with an envious glance. A real gentleman would've already offered it to her. *Snow would've offered it to her,* her mind insisted, as if forgetting her growing agitation at his perpetual dodging.

"It's nice to play pretend," he murmured, as if he hadn't realized he'd put them there. "I'm not clocked in, so it's not like I can feel anything."

"Yeah, right. . ." Jo checked her watch, confirming that she was, indeed, outside of time. Perhaps the cold she felt was purely psychosomatic at the mere sight of snow banks on the sides of the roads, like Wayne's hands in his pockets, and the shivering was a result of stress.

Wayne tilted his head to the sky, took a deep breath, and exhaled. There was nothing. Jo watched, slowly turning into an icicle as Wayne tapped on his watch, and took a breath, exhaling a large plume of white. Satisfied, he tapped his watch again.

"We only have ten hours . . . Was that really necessary?" Jo fell into step with him, their shoulders almost touching. She felt him shrug and Jo took a half step away, trying to avoid being too close while she pulled up her hood—the last thing she needed was for him to see her shaking hands. She was out of time and yet it was still frigid. It was like the rules of magic were breaking down around her.

"It's good to feel like I can still fog a mirror, now and then."

She understood that. They existed somewhere between the living and the dead, not quite enough of either to be satisfied. Jo tilted her head to the sky as well, breathing deeply. Unlike Wayne a moment ago, there was nothing. The first bit of warmth she felt was relief at the absence of abnormality.

"You could clock in for it."

"Obviously." Jo shot him a dumb look. "But it doesn't matter."

"It doesn't?"

"Something about the Society now. . . It's begun to feel more like the real world than here, like it matters more." Jo looked around, for the first time really since their arrival. It was an idyllic area, a few train stops outside of Boston. "I've only ever seen places like this in movies and tele-vision. These quintessential little towns that just scream 'raise a family here.' Suburbia to the max."

"You lived in suburbia, I recall." Wayne referenced their first-ever trip through the Door together, back to Jo's home when she first joined the Society and was still coming to terms with it all. How long ago it all felt now . . . How fuzzy her memories were . . . Vaguely, she couldn't help but wonder if they'd keep getting fuzzier, until they stopped existing at all.

"Texas is different."

"How?"

"Warmer, for one." Jo gave him a small smile. "And the houses are different . . . These are tall and pointy. Everyone has their neat hedges and manicured lawns."

"I remember lawns in Texas."

"You're just being difficult," she huffed, sinking further into her hoodie.

"I get you, dollface." A large hand met the top of her head lightly, giving her hair a ruffle beneath the fabric. The gesture felt intimate, despite there being nothing to make it inherently so. "Boston and New York are both big cities, but even they're different. Everywhere has its charms. The little things that no one else can recognize but you that make it home. Like walking into a house with a smell you're familiar with, even though you've never been there before."

"That's a good way to describe it," Jo mused softly. "I don't even know if I could remember those smells if I tried," she confessed as much to herself as to him.

Wayne was silent as they rounded a corner. But thankfully, he saved her before Jo could get too lost in her own mind. "I'm not so sure about that. You've got a good memory. If I recall, you were sniffing on instinct the moment we walked through your family's front door."

Jo laughed at the memory. "True."

"But why would you say that you can't remember?" The question landed delicately, but felt weighted.

"I don't know . . ." she murmured. "Things just seem . . . hazy, in some places. Every now and then, it feels like I can't find the right memories. Like this whole thing has been reality, and my life in Texas was the dream. Or maybe, it's all still a dream that I'm waiting to wake up from."

Another deafeningly long pause. Then, forced laughter. "I can assure you, I would've noticed a dame like you walking around the Society. Safe to say it's all been the real world, just one step at a time."

*Stepping from one real world into the next, like the Door*, Jo thought to herself. "Do you ever have trouble remembering?"

She knew what he was going to say before he said it. The brief hesitation and then the all too quick "Sometimes, I suppose" told her everything. He had little trouble remembering. Or, if he did run into issues, they were not of the same sort as hers. It was as if something inside her was beginning to break down, tear apart a mask she didn't know she was wearing.

But did she even want to see what awaited her in the mirror when it was gone?

"Why did you opt to come?" Jo asked hastily, trying to change the topic.

Another painfully long pause. "A guy can't just want some time with his friend?"

"*Friend?* After I—"

"It was completely uncalled for," he agreed, before she could mention again the sore spot of his that she'd magically found. "But so was blaming you for the state of affairs. As Snow said, none of us knows how this works, or why. How can you be the cause of something without knowing any more than the rest of us?"

"Well, thanks."

"Unless you do know something?" he added, low and borderline accusatory.

Jo turned in his direction, so startled she almost missed a step.

"You're close to Snow, after all."

"If I knew something. . . you'd know," she whispered, hoping he'd believe her. She didn't know much and didn't know for certain if she'd tell him even if she did. But she needed him to believe she would—needed it more than she cared to admit.

"If you say so, doll." He gave a soft sigh and the slightly accusatory tone vanished completely. "Sorry for the up and down. . . I still feel a mess. Like I'm not in control of any emotion I have from one moment to the next."

"It's okay. You knew Nico longer than I did, I'm sure it's hitting you harder."

"You have no idea."

"So, you really have no issue then? Going through with this wish?" Jo asked cautiously, trying for casual and likely missing the mark.

"I have more issues than I have sense." She bit back a quip about that not being hard because he never had much sense to begin with and allowed him to continue. "But, as we said in the briefing room, what choice do we have?"

Jo wanted to bring up the idea of dismantling the Society again in a more one-on-one setting. But Wayne stopped walking and the look on his face told her that there would be no recovering that topic for the time being. He stared up at one of the tidy little houses in the row they were walking on.

"Doll, why are we *here*?" he asked slowly, shock drawing out the last word. "This is not the police station."

"Obviously." Jo pushed forward, dragging her feet up the brick walkway and toward the steps leading up to the front door.

When his footsteps weren't behind her, Jo paused, looking back at him. He raised his eyebrows and she released a mighty sigh. "I just want to see the bastard for myself, all right? See the person who's throwing *this* wish on us *now*."

"I thought no 'going rogue'?"

"I won't even jump into time." He still didn't move. "Wayne, please I—"

"Let's get on with this, then." Wayne finally came up to join her on the porch. "You have a bright idea on how to get in without jumping in?"

"Well, yes." Jo held out one hand, the other grabbing Wayne's wrist. "We'll just use the Door."

The Door appeared before them, overlaying on the actual entry to the home. Jo opened it and felt the usual tug. But it was shorter this time, almost like tripping over the weather-stripping. They both had a small stumble, but found themselves in a small foyer.

"How did you know that would work?" Wayne asked with no small degree of amazement. Jo was reminded of what Nico had said, that the Door "didn't work that way". She was glad, this time, that she hadn't let herself be dissuaded.

"How did you not think it would?" Jo arched her eyebrows. "I've been doing that sort of thing since the first wish."

"But when we use the Door, there's a degree of error."

The word "we" stuck out to her. It felt like a line drawn between her and the rest of the Society . . . It sounded almost like Pan when she had used "you" instead of "us".

"Maybe it's just when you're very close to where you want to be," Jo said, ready to dismiss the topic. Luckily, there was an easy distraction right before her. She looked around the entry they found themselves in.

Wayne seemed willing to be distracted as well, as he stepped into the living room and made a soft *huh* noise. "So, this is the house of the Bone Carver?"

"According to Eslar and Snow's information." Jo stepped to her left, looking at the room Wayne was assessing. Two couches, facing each other for conversation. A television built into the wall above a fireplace, bookcases on either side. Modest, modern, but a design that betrayed someone with rather impeccable taste. "What is it?"

"It looks so . . . normal. Not my choice on a few things here and there." He motioned to a suspended lamp in particular. "But . . ." Wayne shook his head, momentarily at a loss for words. "Do you think he sits his victims down here and has a lovely little chat before he carves them up like some modern-day Hannibal?"

"Why are you asking me?" The question felt so direct, so probing. "I don't know any more than you do." She started through a back doorway. There was another entry to their right, a side door that led to the garage. To the left was a hallway that ended in a kitchen, dining area and office. A small bathroom was in front of them. "Out of everywhere, I'd guess he works in there."

"Do we even want to look?" Wayne outwardly cringed.

"I'm good not to, if you are." Jo turned, starting back for the stairs that led up from the entry.

"Where are you going now?" he called, catching up to her.

"I said I wanted to see the bastard, didn't I?" She trudged forward, up the stairs and into the darkness that her eyes had no trouble piercing. It was just like the catacombs, the two of them marching along a stairway. But where that had been a journey she'd embarked on in hope, this was one where her feet dragged with apprehension.

"You don't think he's actually here, do you?"

"It's the middle of the night on a weekday; where else would he be?" Jo stopped at the top of the landing. There were three doors to her left along a hall that ran parallel to the stairs. Two bedrooms, she presumed, with a Jack-and-Jill bathroom between.

"We're not going to—"

Wayne didn't have a chance to finish before Jo was pulling them through the Door again. It slammed shut behind them, the echo reverberating so loudly through the void of space-time that Wayne winced.

"Easy there, you trying to break it?"

"That wasn't me," she snapped back. "I didn't even touch it."

Discussion over her handling of the Door was short lived. Both of their eyes fell on the bed and the man sleeping there. He shifted briefly, as if able to hear the reverberation of the Door, but didn't stir further.

"Glad he can sleep so soundly," Wayne muttered. "Not that I get how he can do it at all."

"Do what?" Jo stared at the man. There was no way to tell that the sleeping figure was anything other than human. Even his eyes moved under his eyelids in REM sleep. *Dreams.* How could a creature with dreams not be seen as a full-fledged person?

"Sleep soundly as if he's not some deranged lunatic who's reaped countless deaths."

"The same way we can sleep soundly," Jo whispered. She quickly corrected, "Well, not sleep . . . rest, exist, you get what I mean."

"Like hell I get what you mean." Wayne spun, clearly looking for an explanation.

Jo supposed she owed him one. It was quite the thing to say, after all. "The Society has witnessed countless deaths, countless horrors across time and space, and we manage to get by just fine."

"Don't sound like Samson's bull-crap." Wayne's tone had changed dramatically from the briefing room. "That's different."

"Is it?"

Wayne seemed horrified by her train of thought, but Jo couldn't stop herself from thinking it. "Of course it is!"

"How?" Jo didn't look at him, seeing his shocked reaction from the corners of her mind. She was too focused on the sleeping man.

"Because we're not the ones pulling the trigger."

"But we do nothing to stop it."

"This again?" Wayne groaned. "Like Eslar said, we can't save everyone, that's not our job."

"So then you don't have issue with this wish?"

"I didn't say that."

"You're complacent to sit by and let this wish hit our desks, let the next horrible one, and the next, and the next, without even trying to stop the cycle? If you can stand by that and see us as very different from him, then you haven't been paying attention." Jo didn't even look at him as she spoke; all she could see was the Bone Carver, the serial killer that had begun to shift into a gray area of morality for her. It was starting to feel distinctly as though she had more common ground with a madman than she particularly wanted.

"It's not our job, and those deaths aren't our fault. They're not on our hands, unlike this twisted fu—"

"Every man is guilty of all the good he does not do." Jo finally tore her eyes away. It was as if the sight of the killer was pulling her down into a dark abyss from which there could be no escape.

"Did you just come up with that?" Wayne asked skeptically, and rightfully so.

"It's Voltaire."

"You sure you were a hacker and not a philosopher before this?" Wayne shook his head, sparing one more nasty glance for the Bone Carver before looking solely at Jo. His hands settled on her shoulders, but felt like support more than a weight—a scaffolding that she could rely on when everything else felt so shaken. "Listen, doll, that creature is less than human. And before you say anything, it has nothing to do with the fact that he's synthetic and everything to do with the fact that he's a downright monster that kills innocents for sport.

"And just because, by some messed up twist of fate, we're on the wrong side of this one, that does not make you, or any of us, like him. We just do our best with what's handed to us and live to fight another day."

All she could do was nod. The first was small, then bigger, and then affirmed with, "You're right." When Wayne cracked a crooked smile for her, she felt her heart lift.

"About time you said so."

Jo snorted and rolled her eyes. "Sorry, it just feels like everything is falling apart. Nothing is as it should be. Or *where* it should be, for that matter. And I can't just . . . I can't sit by any more and let these wishes happen."

"I hear you. The sooner we can get done with this wish, the better." He'd clearly misunderstood her final words.

"We should go to the police station," Jo suggested as she stepped away from his comforting hold and toward the door. "We're getting nothing from being here but dark thoughts and needless frustration. Maybe we can find something helpful there."

"Lead on, doll face. The Door seems to listen to you best—so be a bit gentler to it." Wayne laughed.

Jo held out her hand over the doorknob, and spared one more glance to the man in the bed behind her. She'd done work for horrible people in the past. She'd crafted hacks that she knew would ruin people's lives, possibly even kill them. But this felt different. It wasn't like she was loading the gun and handing it off. She was the one to pull the trigger—as Wayne had said.

No, it was even worse than that, because she saw some part of herself in the sleeping form of the lunatic bent on the destruction of life. In him was a reflection of a dark corner somewhere inside herself that Jo hoped the light would never shine on.

"Jo?" Wayne's voice pulled her from her thoughts.

She turned, but her eyes shifted to the man in the bed. No, not to the man, but to the single eye that was opened a slit. The Bone Carver seemingly stared right at her, unmoving, not even breathing. Jo felt nausea sweep through her.

"Let's go." Jo turned hastily, willing the Door to appear before them. Willing it to take them to the local police station. But mostly just willing it to take her anywhere other than that dark room before Wayne could notice they were being watched.

# PALM, MEET DESK

Even knowing exactly how much chaos the Bone Carver seemed to be leaving in his wake, there was nothing that could have prepared them for the madhouse that was the local police station.

All manner of uniformed officers bustled about with files, loose papers spilling in their haste. Sergeants and detectives congregated in briefing rooms with higher-ranking officials from Boston PD and the FBI. They all took turns shouting orders at already frantic peons. Jo could feel their panic like an almost tangible force. Or maybe she just related to it.

For a moment, Wayne and Jo could only move themselves off to a less congested side of the office space and watch. It became obvious quite quickly that a large portion of the department had been assigned the Bone Carver case, and even more officers were being recruited as they watched. It was a mess of information and a riptide of emotional upheaval.

Jo scanned the room, taking in not just the officers and their frantic attempts at righting these wrongs, but the late-night interview being conducted with the police captain as well.

" . . . we are currently working with the FBI and Boston PD to help bring justice to those affected," the buzz-cut man said into the microphone.

"Should we take the presence of the FBI as reason to believe that the suspicions of the Bone Carver residing in Rockport are founded?"

"The citizens of Rockport should take the presence of the FBI as reason to believe that their men and women in uniform will do all they can to keep them safe," the police captain dodged.

"The body has since been identified as a mister Richard Burrows.

Unlike the Bone Carver's other victims, Mr. Burrows has not been involved with any sort of political office or notable artificial intelligence affiliation. Is the Bone Carver changing their M.O.? Or are the police worried about a copycat case?"

"I'm afraid I cannot speculate on motive and will not comment on Mr. Burrows other than to grant my condolences to his family and loved ones."

That conversation was going nowhere.

Jo's eyes drifted to a back room where a woman, shell-shocked and pale, was hunched over a table. Not even looking to see if Wayne was following, Jo stopped at the small window into the interrogation room.

She couldn't hear what was being said, but she didn't need to.

Mutilated pictures spread out on the table were quickly collected by the officer who had only laid them out a moment ago after the woman burst into hysterics. She nodded between her sobs as another officer in the room moved to comfort her.

"I bet that's Mrs. Burrows." The raw husk of Wayne's voice startled Jo back to life. She wasn't sure how long she had stood there, watching but not seeing, like a ghost in the shadows. But when Wayne placed a hand on her shoulder, it felt like it might have been an awfully long time.

"Yeah . . ." What else could she say? What else was there to say?

The more she observed the room, the less she began to make sense of it. So many people suffering because of what the Bone Carver had done, and this was only one stop on his killing spree. How many more departments were exactly like this one. filled with the families and friends, the loved ones of the victims, begging for sympathy and revenge?

And it wasn't just them either. Keeping the peace didn't stop with a hunt for a serial killer.

There was the belligerent teen in the drunk tank, banging on the bars and demanding the latest names of the victims like it was some television show they got to make a cameo on. An elderly woman was hunched at the front desk, asking if it was possible to locate her granddaughter, make sure she was safe. There were officers who looked as though they'd seen hell and come back, only to have to share it with others in every document and photograph they had to tag, catalog and file.

Even if the Bone Carver hadn't been involved physically in their lives, his very presence was causing people pain, sorrow, terror.

"So." Wayne cleared his throat, squeezing her hand once before letting go. "Where do you want to start, dollface?" The hesitation in his voice, the forced casualness beneath the nickname, left Jo feeling a bit guilty, but it also managed to reawaken her original sense of purpose. So she clung to that and dove right in.

"Follow me," she said, skirting the perimeter of the room and taking a good look at the layout. Their best bet would probably be an evidence locker —something that would give them access to physical data unavailable anywhere else. As busy as the precinct was, however, it would be difficult to find a place or time to jump back into reality without being seen. They could pretend to be a couple looking for information on one of the victims; Wayne could probably bet to make someone believe they were from another station—

But no, with stakes so high, no one would even give them the time of day, let alone entertain such a thing. Furthermore, they only had ten hours each spread over two weeks to lessen the Severity of Exchange; now was not the time to take risks.

Her mind continued to whirl. Wayne could pose a distraction, get one of the higher-ups out of their office long enough for Jo to sneak in and look into their files for the current orders—

But what distraction? There was so much chaos already going on within these walls, no one would even notice him. It was a breakdown of all order, and not in the way that Jo had begun to find more and more calming—the orderly sort of tearing apart that her magic engaged in. This was a chaotic and maddening disarray.

As Jo pulled Wayne along the edge of the room, eyes scanning for unoccupied offices or the storage locker, a rogue command gathered her thoughts like a dog to point. Jo stopped short, placing a hand on Wayne's chest to make sure he did the same.

" —ective Madani! Are those the case files I requested?"

The booming voice, Jo identified quickly, belonged to the captain from before, finally freed of the interview. He had a hand already outstretched towards a prominent office door as if expecting the documents to get there quicker that way. Jo's hope perked up at his desperation alone. The woman in question, Detective Madani, appeared to be carrying a rather impressive pile of folders (the physical kind Jo was looking for), her stride quickening at the bequest of her superior.

When she walked into the captain's office, Jo wasted no time following, grabbing onto the collar of Wayne's coat in order to make sure they made it inside before the door closed.

"This is everything my team had, including some documentation we managed to finagle from our sister department in New York City." Madani dropped the stack on the captain's desk, then took a moment to readjust some stray hairs beneath her hijab.

Jo could see by the bags underneath her eyes that she and her team had probably been working on this request for a while. Far longer than the reports let on. She couldn't help but wonder when, exactly, they'd found the body in relation to when the news of it actually broke.

"Thank you, detective," the captain said, his head already buried in the file on top of the stack. "That will be all."

"Yes, sir." Madani straightened some and nodded before retreating just as swiftly from the room. Through the captain's office window, Jo could see her bustling back towards a group of men surrounding another desk filled with papers, her job nowhere near done. Jo couldn't help but feel sorry for her.

But just as she glanced back to the files, the captain flipped to a new page, and Jo rushed behind him to make sure she was there to witness the rest. Wayne did the same just to the man's left, and for the next few minutes, they all read in silence.

After what felt like an hour, Jo's brain threatening to drill its way out of her skull by the feel of it, the information in the documents became a little more enlightening. Jo perked up at once.

"This is the third victim he's looking at again, right?" Jo asked. After countless photos of identical monikers, similar displays of grotesque variety, detailing of event after familiar event, they all began to blend together.

"Fourth, I think." Wayne groaned, and Jo could see him rubbing at his eyes in her periphery. "Looks like this one was front-manning a sort of android fighting ring." Jo scanned Wayne's face, surprised by the disgust written there. Though not for long. "Says here he . . . he made them keep their pain receptors on full? I'm not too hi-tech, but even I can tell that sounds pretty low-lid."

She didn't know exactly what low-lid meant, but she knew what pain receptors did, so Jo was in near instant agreement.

"We're not getting anywhere with this, doll, let's move on."

"No, not yet." Jo held him by the cuff of his sleeve. She was on the verge of something. She understood all too well how grating trying to absorb so much information in one sitting could be. But they had a job to do, and if the captain here could do it, she could too.

"Every single victim has, in some way, shape, or form been involved in android related hate crimes," Jo started slowly, her mind coming into clarity. She leaned in to gather some more information from the papers the captain had placed to the side. "Yeah, see here? This man was the head of an Artificial Care Act protest group. And this one? An anti-android slam campaign aiming to remove their syncing capabilities unless registered to an 'owner.'" Jo cringed, her stomach roiling at the thought of such treatment.

"We knew that it had to do with the androids and their rights already," Wayne reminded her. "Snow said it in the initial briefing—or showed us the news reel that did." He paused. "No, it had to do with that calling card? Or all of them. Doesn't matter which, we knew all that."

"The latest calling card was the coordinates for N.A.I.S., Inc."

"That AI place . . . What was it? Prima Sangria?"

"Primus Sanguis," Jo corrected him quietly, her voice hushed by the rampant thoughts rushing through her mind. "Mister Burrows's bone had N.A.I.S. coordinates carved into it. But *why*?"

"The location of his next victim?" Wayne suggested.

"No . . ." Jo wouldn't have been surprised if Wayne could hear the audible click that just happened in her brain. "Look, here." Jo pointed to Richard Burrows' file. "He was a consultant."

"So?"

"There's a pattern here, a message," she said, eyes scanning for any more tidbits of information she could grasp from the papers strewn about the captain's desk. When he leaned back into his seat with a sigh, Jo took the chance to lean as far over into the literal pile of information as she could. "I think it's more than the ACA. . . I think Primus Sanguis may be the true connecting thread."

"The thing you hacked?"

"I didn't hack it, I hacked *information* about it," she corrected. "And it was one of the hardest—never mind, it doesn't matter. The first victim, in Pennsylvania . . . I've seen her name before. She was all over the notes CBM had me dredge up on Sanguis as one of their chief developers.

"The second victim was a higher up at CBM in New York—N.A.I.S.'s competitor and the people who pushed Primus Sanguis to market early once they got their competition software to market first."

"The third was that politician involved with the Artificial Care Act, but he was also closely involved with legalizing the Sanguis system for market," Wayne interjected. "I see where you're going, doll, but what about the fourth here . . . The one with the android fighting ring?"

"Where do you think he sourced that many androids from?" Jo tried to find the file on the desk, but couldn't. The captain had already sorted it away so she relied on her memory instead. "I saw he was an employee at Greenfield."

"So?"

Wayne wouldn't know, Jo realized. This was no longer his world, even if he had once been from New York City. "Greenfield is the largest contract manufacturer for androids. N.A.I.S. is their top customer."

"So number four just plucked androids with Sanguis in their heads off the line?"

"Likely defectives, ones with minor issues in soft or hard design . . . but that would work for his purposes," Jo surmised.

"How do you know all this?"

Jo allowed herself to savor the impressed tone of Wayne's voice. "I told you, I had a job, once." She swallowed. *Had her work somehow led to the creation of the Bone Carver?*

"And what about Mr. Burrows?" Wayne tapped on the man's file.

"I'm speculating—"

"So far your speculations have been the only thing about all this that's made any sense."

"Given what was carved on his bone, I think he was consulting for N.A.I.S."

"You *think*?" Wayne stressed the final word. "Stakes are kinda high for guessing here, dollface."

"I'd bet my life on it." She stared him in the eye, both of them knowing full well that if she was wrong, she really may have to put her life on the line. "This is the pattern we need to follow—looking for people involved with Primus Sanguis, and possibly, tangentially, how it relates to people in the anti-ACA movement. But again, I think this is much bigger than the ACA. I think this has to do with something none of us knows yet about SANGUIS, something the Bone Carver thinks is worth killing over. If I'm right about all this. . . I'd speculate there's something about the Primus Sanguis AI infrastructure that's not entirely legal. I think they're trying to cover up code that's going too far, and the Bone Carver is trying to expose it.

"I can try to re-hack back at the Society and get more information— newer information—on the project. Then we can make a map of all people we can find who are and were linked to it, weigh those who have higher involvement and then maybe we can get to the person before—"

"Get to the potential victim? Or help out the Carver?" Wayne cut in, forcing Jo's whirring thoughts to sputter to a halt. She blinked up at him, one hand pressed into the desk though no papers shuffled beneath her touch. "Because it sounds like you're trying to get to the next one before the perp does, and that's not our job."

"I'm not."

"Then what are you doing?"

"I'm trying to think of a third way out," she confessed, her voice dropping to a whisper.

"Way out?" It took him a second, but Wayne finally connected it back to her earlier comments in the briefing room. "Doll, there is no way out."

"How do you know that?" she pressed. "Why not try to stop this? Maybe we can grant the wish—the Bone Carver could do this indefinitely —by changing *his* mind about doing it in the first place?"

"Or maybe we end up wasting time chasing rabbits down holes."

"She said dismantled, Wayne. *Dismantled*."

"Who?"

"Pan. She said the Society could be dismantled."

"I don't think she meant it literally," was what his mouth said. But his tone crafted a different story. One where he was considering what she was saying in a way that he never had before.

"Why not?" Jo reached out for him, grabbing for his hands. "What if there is a way out? A way to approach wishes—no, not just wishes—all of this, that no one has ever looked at before?"

"There is no way out." He took her hands gently in his.

"Help me, Wayne." Jo saw it again, as she worried circles into the sides of his thumbs with the pads of her own. She saw the same little magical tracings of the seams she had to rip to get him to agree with her. It was an identical sensation to their interaction in the kitchen except for this time she wasn't about to let herself get lost in it. She would approach it with the precision of a surgeon. "The wishes, the Society—why is it like this?"

"It always has been." His words were comforting, placating, and almost confident. *Almost.*

"It hasn't."

"Doll—"

"I know it hasn't," Jo said firmly, undermining his objections.

"Tall words for someone who only joined the Society a few months ago."

"It's been nearly a year," she retorted as calmly as possible, even though it felt as though her intestines had become barbed, her stomach filling with acid several times too strong.

"So what?" Wayne pulled his hands away and folded his arms, making the fact clear and apparent that he had no want of her comfort. They were back into the push and pull they always seemed to end up in during high-stress situations. "You're practically a child compared to the rest of us."

"I know what I'm talking about," she insisted.

"You don't know any—"

"I see it in his eyes!" Her voice cracked and with the outburst of emotion her magic seemed to go haywire, hiding the path she'd been trying to follow moments earlier. If it didn't mean wasting precious time, she'd jump back into reality just long enough to throw the captain's mug against the wall. "I see it in the way he looks at me—or rather, doesn't, when I ask him. I hear it in his voice when I know I'm getting too close to the truth."

"He?" Wayne paused, dumbfounded for a long moment. "You mean Snow? Why are you thinking of him now of all times? You're losing focus, Jo, this is why I told you—"

"Just, listen to me, Wayne, please." She was pleading now, she'd sing it for him if that's what it took to be heard. "*Think* about the wishes. You said it yourself, they've been getting more intense."

"Ever since you arrived." He couldn't let go of an opportunity to twist the knife.

Jo used it to her advantage. She would break him yet. "Yes, me, the *last* member, the last lineage. Snow said there'd be no more after Nico. You don't think that it isn't just a little suspicious that Pan only starts killing people off once we're all assembled?"

Wayne paused, finally, at that.

"There's more to this," Jo insisted, regaining her mental footing. "There's something here we're not seeing. It's like . . . it's like . . ." Her eyes drifted back to the captain's desk, almost entirely forgotten. "It's like the Bone Carver." Her voice had dropped to a hurried whisper. "There's a pattern here, there's someone pulling the strings."

"Jo—"

"And I would bet you anything that we both know who it is."

Wayne opened his mouth to speak, and then slowly closed it, opting instead to just stare at her. Jo held his gaze; she would devour him with a look if she could. She needed him to see what she saw, what was wearing her down time after time—what had been haunting her from the first moment she'd stepped in the Society, whether she'd realized it or not.

"Even if we did . . ." There was a conspiratorial edge to what he was saying, a sort of harmony to the buzzing in her. She was winning; he was opening up to her line of thinking. "What could we do about it?"

"I don't know yet. But I plan on finding out."

"You couldn't do anything if you tried." Fear settled over him, Jo could practically smell it. It rattled in him and made his hands tremble— barely, but she didn't miss it.

"I can, and I will," she vowed.

"How?"

"I'll do research. I can get information from Snow."

"That won't work."

"Has anyone ever tried?"

Clearly no one had, given how quickly he dodged the question. "I think all your focus should be on this wish."

"And wait for another one of us to be killed?" Jo grabbed his arm, tilting her head slightly to look up at the man's eyes.

*Had Wayne always looked so tired?* It was like he kept trying to find his resolve and build himself up and she just kept tearing him down.

"Wayne, we can't just keep spending our energy on this wheel, again and again and again, letting Pan toy with us like the puppet master we all know she is." His eyes widened at this so Jo pressed further. "It's her. . . we all know it. There's a feeling about her, and her power to kill us."

"She's trapped just like we are."

"How do we know that? I've thought it too, but. . . how can it not be her? Listen, *listen*. Did you really hear her in the briefing room? Not only did she say dismantle the Society, but she said you, not us. She doesn't see herself in danger. There's a way out and she knows it. There has to be."

"So, what do you propose?" There was a glimmer of something more there, a diamond in the dark coal mine they were all waiting like birds to suffocate in: hope.

"Let's stop it here. Let's break this cycle of world-rebuilding and free ourselves instead."

"You're insane."

"I'm not. This is the first sane thing we've done."

"We're just trying to stay alive and you want us to upend the system that keeps us existing? You don't think that sounds a little insane?" He was raising his voice again as he shielded himself with anger.

"I think it sounds like the only sure-fire method for survival."

"You're talking about destroying our home."

*Why wasn't he listening? Why couldn't he just understand?*

"The only thing I want to destroy is the cycle we're chained to!" Jo slammed her palm down on the desk. . .

And the impossible happened.

In three seconds that felt like forever, several things occurred, almost all at once.

Jo's flat palm met the desk. A noise like a thunderclap echoed through her chest, setting her ears to ringing. From each of her fingers, impossibly, the desk splintered, cracking in fracture lines that split and met as different pieces pushed and lowered, tectonic plates after a seismic shift. The captain jumped out of his chair, shouting expletives and blinking in confusion. Papers went everywhere and the door to the room slammed open, Detective Madani rushing back in with gun drawn.

There were words being said, but Jo couldn't hear them. The ringing in her ears was too loud, her skin almost on fire with the energy crackling over it. She raised her hand, looking at her palm—it didn't even sting.

"H-how did you do that?" The whole sentence came out as one jumbled word; Wayne was pressed up against the back wall with terror in his eyes.

*Fear*. There was that tangy sensation Jo was becoming familiar with. The sort of fear that could break a man down.

"I . . ." The surge of energy evaporated the moment her focus left the possibilities of what her magic could do in the dust. Her own fear came crashing down on her. Her fingers couldn't stay steady. Why couldn't they stay steady? "I don't know, Wayne. I don't know!"

Jo looked to him for answers he didn't have, just as he looked to her for answers she wasn't even sure if she wanted to conceive. Everything felt as if it was going to break apart.

Wayne threw her a lifeline, pulling himself together and grabbing her shaking hand. The fear was gone and in its place was comfort and confidence. Jo clutched him so tightly his knuckles popped, but she didn't relieve her grip. If she let him go now, it would all fall apart.

"Time to make tracks, doll." Wayne glanced over his shoulder to speak to her, but his eyes shifted, lingering on the chaos in the room.

Jo turned, barely getting a chance to see the two officers inspecting the desk, before she felt a tug, and the world changed around her.

# SPECIAL PLACE

They stepped from utter chaos into nothingness.

Wind rushed over her face, begging to tousle her hair, to pull at her clothes, like an invitation for her to be part of the world once more. It was cold, mostly due to elevation and wind. Unlike from the place they'd just left, this corner of the world was bright, warm, and filled with nature—everything the suburban police station hadn't been.

Jo turned in place, taking in the panoramic view of rolling hills covered in a lush carpet of greenery. A sapphire line cut through the landscape and white dotted the other side—some livestock, Jo presumed. Sheep, perhaps?

Wayne had let her go almost instantly upon their arrival, taking a wide step away from her and the Door that was now fading—leaving a craggy opening in the rocks in its place. There was still that fear there. Worry, too.

Could she blame him?

"Where are we?" Jo asked before he could speak. If she let him get the first word there would be questions, questions she wasn't ready for. Questions she had no *answers* for.

"Somewhere very far from people."

"I can see that." She nodded to the vast expanse of land. There wasn't a home or city in sight.

"Come on, this way."

"Where are we going?" she asked nervously. Jo looked back to the sheep. Was she nothing more than a lamb about to be brought to slaughter for asking questions about a possible wolf hiding beneath the wool?

"It's my special place." He paused, a few steps down toward a narrow path that Jo could make out between the slopes of the hill.

"Taking a lady to your special place?" Jo took a shot at levity; it fell flat even to her own ears. Still, she forced a casual tone through the awkwardness. "I didn't think we had that kind of relationship."

"Coming here . . . isn't a good thing." Wayne shook his head and continued on. Jo wanted to ask what he meant, if it was less about the place and more about *her* that wasn't a good thing, but she held her tongue. She didn't really feel confident in her voice right now anyway.

When Wayne didn't look back to see if she was following, Jo finally fell into step behind him. She brought up her palm again, looking at the hand that had cracked the desk as she walked. She had been outside of time—she hadn't clocked in; there should've been no way she could have affected anything in the real world. Hadn't she placed her hand down on the desk before, and not a single paper fluttered?

Jo pulled her attention back to the path only to find a small farmhouse already ahead of them. The tin roof of its porch sagged, one of the support beams on the end leaning at an awkward angle. The wood was sun-bleached, more so at the edges near the rusting roof where it was, marginally, protected from the elements. The wooden supports of the windows stood without glass, the only thing that could stand the test of time.

It was a forgotten home, in a forgotten corner of the world, for two forgotten ghosts.

"What is this place?" Jo asked softly.

Wayne froze at the threshold, one foot up on a beam that should never be able to support his weight —that is, if he still had weight to bear in the real world. His eyes ran over her and Jo felt the significance of his assessment. She must have measured up to whatever yardstick he was using; the heavy sigh told her so.

"You were right, Jo."

"About what?"

"There was a woman, once." He reached out to a beam, resting his palm on one of the splintered, worn pillars that was barely keeping the house alive. "Margaret, a bright dame, sensible, wicked wit. You two would have gotten along."

When he spoke of Margaret, it was similar feeling to when Nico had spoken of Julia. A profound longing, a feeling of closeness through whatever they saw in Jo that reminded them of their lost loves. But it was also a distance. She was not them, and no one was ever going to try to convince themselves she was.

"There was an Australian. . . he'd come to New York for work and, well, ended up at the company she was at." Wayne shook his head. "We'd been seeing each other on the hush . . . but she wanted me to make things proper."

"And you didn't."

"Don't know why I didn't. . . I should've," he chastised himself. "She couldn't wait—a girl like that shouldn't be *made* to wait. And I lost her."

"So she moved back here? To Australia?"

"She moved back to Australia with her husband at the first sign of economic downturn . . . But that's not here." Wayne stepped forward, leaving Jo to follow if she wanted to hear the rest of the conversation. "This is New Zealand."

Jo nearly stumbled as she squeezed through the door—barely open wide enough to make jumping back into time unnecessary. "Why are we here?"

"I started looking at this region of the world after she left. Turns out, it's startlingly beautiful. When I joined the Society at first and learned I could go anywhere I wanted with the Door, I started wandering and found this place and kept coming back whenever I needed to think."

"You? Mister 'be careful with time,' just wandered?" Jo couldn't stop her laughter, though she did her best to make sure it sounded kind.

"Never said I wasted time doing it." He paused. "Well, long enough to open the front door. The whole place nearly broke down when I moved it just a little, too."

"I can see why . . ." Jo reached out a hand to touch the wall. But at the sight of her hand hovering over the wood, she remembered the desk, and withdrew.

The floor had sagged in places, hanging between supports that were struggling against the weight of time. In the sunlight that streamed through a large bay window to her right, a small tree grew up, insistent, through the floor. To the left was a small kitchen area, and stairs that had as many missing treads as existent ones.

"It's beautiful, in its own way." There was something enchanting about how the elements wore things down, made them blend with the nature that surrounded them. It was a stark contrast to the chaos of the police station. This was how things were meant to break, all a part of the natural order.

"It's quiet."

Jo could feel his eyes as she walked over to what would've been the main living area. She inspected a sofa opposite the bay window. He hadn't brought up the strange incident yet. But she knew it was coming. She could only play at peace for so long.

"And it's far away from people."

"You said that earlier." She didn't look at him when she spoke; she didn't want to see him out of pure fear that they'd escalate each other again and whatever was in her would be unleashed.

"I don't know if I can trust you around others."

Jo pressed her eyes closed. There it was. That horrible assessment. Why did it feel as though it was something that had been levied against her for her entire life? She had never been good at making, or keeping, friends. Only ever Yuusuke, really. She'd always had the worst luck that ultimately resulted in everything imploding due to her own actions or surrounding circumstances. Which was sort of how things had happened with Yuusuke, and now the Society.

"I told you, Wayne, I don't know what happened." Jo finally turned. "I wish I did, I really do because if. . . if I knew, then I could stop it from happening like that again."

"You think it could happen again?"

It was impossible to miss the way his throat bobbed when he swallowed, attempting to hold back a twinge of lingering concern that he hadn't wanted Jo to catch. But she was hyper-focused on his face. And she would never forget what it had looked like as it had stared at her in terror.

"I don't know." She dared to be honest.

Wayne sighed, running a hand through his hair. He paced between the entrance to the room she stood in and the stairs. Not a floorboard creaked, not a mote of dust fell out of place.

"You didn't clock in when I wasn't looking . . . did you?" he asked hopefully.

"No."

He cursed under his breath. Finally, he stopped, his back toward her, as if he couldn't face her for what he had to say next. "I'm out of my depth here, Jo."

"Wayne, I—"

"What would you do if you were me?"

She hadn't been expecting that question. Even worse, she didn't have a good answer for it. At least, she didn't have an answer that was likely to benefit her.

"I don't know," Jo admitted. "But I wouldn't do anything rash." She hoped. "We don't know what happened. But perhaps this is good, Wayne. Perhaps this is some aspect of my power that no one knew about before."

Wayne seemed to be thinking the notion over, which gave Jo a margin of optimism.

"I mean, I was talking about bringing down the Society when—"

He held up a hand. "I'm stopping you right there."

"But perhaps we could—"

"I don't know what's going on, doll. But you remember when I told you about brodies?" She nodded—they were bad ideas. "This is the definition of one. Right here."

She wanted to scream and embrace him all at the same time. She wanted to scream at him for ignoring an opportunity or, at the very least, for betraying her. But she also wanted to embrace him, reassure him, tell her friend that she knew he was struggling with this just as she was. They were both confused and more than a little off-balance, but they could figure it out if they just stuck together. Jo was left reeling at the stark contrast in impulses.

In the end, the result of all the conflicting drives was for her to do absolutely nothing.

"So, what are you going to do?" she asked, finally.

"I don't know yet."

Jo stared out the window, watching the wind play in the waves of grasses that covered the world outside in a thick blanket. Her hand balled into a fist, as if trying to catch the fear and panic that had welled up in the wake of the desk and squash it like an annoying fly.

"We can use this to our advantage." She finished her earlier thought, the one he'd interrupted.

"Brodies, remember?"

She heard Wayne approaching her, but Jo didn't turn to face him, not yet. Whatever that feeling of power was—the one assuring her that she could break him if she tried hard enough—it was only there if she looked at him. Jo didn't want to exert that magic. If he agreed to help her, it had to be of his own accord.

"I hear you. I do. But I need you to hear me. Nothing is going to change unless we do something to change it. It will be one wish after the next, faster and more impossible than the last, until none of us are left." *Until Pan gets what she wants.* She kept the last thought to herself. Jo had no proof other than a feeling and she didn't want Wayne to get distracted with the idea of turning Pan into an enemy. "You can't possibly be okay with that?"

Jo looked to him then. Not with magic, but with pleading eyes, searching to see if he felt even remotely as she did.

"Of course I'm not okay with that." He ran a hand over his hair. "It's just that . . ."

"Just what? You're afraid of bringing down the Society and us all dying? How is that any different than the path we're on? Other than it just happens faster?"

When Wayne said nothing, she continued.

"Look, Wayne, I don't understand what happened." She was back to staring at her open palm. "But perhaps this is what we need to—how did Pan put it? Dismantle? The Society. It was an avenue no one could explore before because my magic wasn't part of the equation."

"And if you're wrong?"

"If I'm wrong I'll stop before I get too far ahead."

Wayne thought about this, conflict written across his face. Did he believe her? That she would stop? Jo hoped he did, because she honestly didn't know if she believed herself. Still, when he said nothing, Jo tried for one more nudge.

"If you don't want to help outright, that's fine. But promise me you won't get in my way? Promise me you'll keep what happened there between us?"

Finally, the man seemed to breathe once more. "All right, doll. I won't get in your way, and I'll try to give you leeway where I can. But if things start going haywire, I'm going right to Snow or Eslar."

He extended a hand. Jo stared at it for a moment. It wasn't the best she could've hoped for, but it was far from the worst. Her fingers curled around his, and they shook on it.

"You've got a deal, Mr. Davis."

BTCOTS NOTES 2


Frequent search term: "Divine Power."
Lead??
BOW OF THE GODDESS (Eslar's book).
God-lore in Age of M.

- *What about Age of Gods? Holdover? Ask Snow?*
- *Search other lore.*


**Why do ppl remember gods when forget everything else after world(s) rebuilt?**

GREAT BATTLE OF THE GODS
*aka: "Titanomachy," "Battle of Titans," Legend of the 2 God Kings, Dharma v. Adharma, War for Humanity... etc.*

- Gods battle for dominion over universe. **Usually original/superior vs newer/lesser.**
- Winner builds world
- Losers=reduced to demigods and/or made into servants for newer gods
- No mention of wishes
- Elder vs Newer gods? Significant? See bold

# BREAKDOWN

Wayne didn't say anything else until they were standing in the briefing room, starting for the doors that headed into the Society. He paused, palm on the door, looking over his shoulder at her. For the briefest of moments, Jo expected him to say that their deal was off, that he'd reconsidered his position.

"Everyone will want to know what we found. I'll check the common room, you check the bedrooms. We'll all meet in the common room in ten."

"Not the briefing room?" Jo asked as they started down the long hall to the Four-Way.

"No, I've had enough of that room for one lifetime," he muttered.

"I'm inclined to agree." Jo paused in the center of the Four-Way as Wayne started ahead. But, as if feeling her eyes on him, he turned and stared, stalling at the start of the other hallway toward the common room. "Wayne, thank you."

What she wanted to say was, *don't forget our deal.* But the words lingered behind her lips, unspoken.

"Don't mention it." He shrugged. "It's not like I have any better ideas of how we should go about tackling this situation."

Without another word, Jo started up the stairs and Wayne down the hall. She couldn't help but wonder what he meant by "this situation." Her magic? Or the Society in general? For her sake, and the sake of exploring her plans, she hoped it was the latter.

Jo went to Eslar's door first. He was the natural choice as "team mom" and his door was the first one she encountered. But he didn't respond to her knock, so Jo worked her way back to Samson's.

The door opened and two familiar eyes widened at the sight of her. "Jo? How did it go?"

"Fine. Yeah, fine, I guess." She shrugged. *Way to sound nonchalant*, Jo mentally scolded. She couldn't help but glance at Wayne's door, if he didn't blow it, she just may. "We wanted to brainstorm with the crew, tell everyone what we found."

"Yes. Yes, just a moment." Samson scurried back into his room, leaving the door open. Rushing over to one of the worktables, he began to fumble with every bobble, setting it in a new order.

Jo took the unspoken invitation, taking a step into the room, but going no further without being expressly invited.

His room was an identical arrangement to how she'd found it last time —industrial tables sandwiched between rustic beams on the ceiling and fur rugs on the floor. And yet, there was something markedly different. The last time she was there he'd had a sort of organization to his workstations. Now, it was as if mechanical beasts had been laid out on the tables and carved open, their innards exposed. There were nests of wires and precariously screwed-together towers that sat atop scraps of leather and wood.

"Is . . ." Jo paused, regretting opening her mouth.

"Is, what?" Samson continued to move things around, though nothing actually seemed to get tidier. He just shifted the clutter, spreading it evenly again but in a new arrangement. "I'm sorry. Messy, I know. Want to get some order before I go. So I can come back and know what's happening. With it. This. Happening with this. I usually don't have it so. . . But. . ."

"Is everything okay, Samson?" she whispered softly.

His shoulders stiffened, nearly rising to his ears. He didn't turn to look at her. His chin dropped to his chest, and all she could see were the large shoulders of the crafter and a tuft of fire-orange hair.

"Ever, ever since Nico," he struggled to get out his name. "I can't seem to make anything but food. And even that. . . Every time I try, nothing is right. Things keep breaking down. I don't know why. I don't know why it's all so . . . fragile."

"I should go," Jo whispered. Either it was all fragile because *he* was fragile right now. Or it was because of her. Somehow.

The desk was back in her mind, the feelings about Wayne—about how she could break him if she could. That dark thought of using her magic on something living. She didn't know what percentage chance all that was related to Samson's dilemma, but she wasn't going to take the risk.

"But . . . Oh, okay." Samson spun, as if he was going to stop her. For a brief moment she saw him unfurl, unravel into a bright and bold banner. But the wind was sucked from his sails once more and he shrank again.

"It's not you," she said quickly. *It's me*. How cliché. "I'm just going to get Takako."

"Oh, yes, right, the wish."

The wish was the furthest thing from Jo's mind right now. "We'll—"

Two quick knocks on the door, drawing both of their attention to the elf that stood in its frame. Without so much as waiting for a welcome, he said, "Samson, I wanted to know if—Jo?"

She gave a small wave from where she stood, just to the right inside the door.

"Was it you who was knocking earlier?" he asked.

"Yeah, Wayne and I just got back. We wanted to debrief with everyone in the common room, so I was collecting people."

"Then there is no time to waste."

They made a quick stop at Takako's room, but no one answered, so they headed back down to the Four-Way and left. As expected, Takako and Wayne were already seated on the couch. They were whispering something, but stopped promptly the moment the rest of the team entered.

"Took you all long enough." Wayne leaned back on the couch, spreading out his arms.

"It was only a minute." Jo rolled her eyes, sitting on the opposite edge of the couch.

"Why don't you both start from the beginning," Eslar said, still standing while everyone else sat.

Wayne took the lead, filling in the group on what they'd found in the real world. Jo paid particularly close attention to see what parts he'd glossed over and how he'd smoothed everything out to make nothing seem amiss with the rest of the team. Needless to say, there was no mention of the desk.

"Right, then," Eslar said, when Wayne had finally finished. "So we have an idea of what the Bone Carver's next movements may be. We also know that while the police are closing in, this seems to have eluded them so far. How can we best use this to our advantage?"

Jo didn't hesitate in taking the lead. She wanted this wish to run on her terms. "We're dealing with an android, not a human, and the patterns have me thinking. . . even if the Carver functions as a human does, he's still a machine. Samson, you're the best we have when it comes to all things mechanical and constructed. Do you have any ideas?"

He winced slightly. How stupid could she be? He'd just told her about his issues constructing right now. Yet Jo had never seen him build a bobble so quickly.

"Well . . . If, if it's a machine . . . It has to have some kind of logic. Some schematics, I mean. Some way its put together. Maybe I could—"

She'd needed a breakthrough, and Samson just handed her one. "Wait, yes, that's it, Sam."

"What is?" He looked up from his bobble in horror, as though he'd somehow done something wrong.

"What if we stop thinking of him as a he and more as an, an *it*?"

"Way ahead of you," Wayne muttered.

"I'm not talking about rehashing the argument of sentience and the nature of humanity . . . What if we look at the mechanics of him rather than treating him like a human? At the end of the day, he's based on a program. There's likely modifications he made to himself in his sentience, but there's got to be a core—a firmware system that was the foundation for all his learning algorithms. I'd bet that core is Primus Sanguis. Possibly it's something he still backs up to."

"Dollface, I don't follow," Wayne said outright.

"He's a living, breathing *computer*."

That got them right on board.

"Are you saying you think you can *hack* it?" Wayne asked, sounding somewhere in between disbelieving and impressed.

"Haven't met a computer that's kept me out yet." And having the guise of trying to hack into the Bone Carver would give Jo ample time in the recreation room without question or disturbance. It could also further put her destructive powers to the test. It was win-win all around.

"But what will you do once you get inside his . . . mind?" Takako asked next. "I don't doubt you'll be able to gain entry, but what good will that do in preventing his capture?"

"Another program maybe?" Eslar offered, and Jo just nodded and stood, mind already whirring with various possibilities, magic tickling like static beneath her skin. She tried not to feel intimidated by it; despite all of the new information she now carried, that magic was still hers. *I can control it*, she mentally insisted to herself.

"I can do something, maybe create an illegal subscript that would erase all trackable data . . . Hack into his system and embed it deep enough that it can't be accessed or removed, just keep him invisible to any outside radar. Or, perhaps because we know his targeting scheme, I can throw in some random other baddies—just enough to throw off the cops so he's not caught out of profiling." Jo threw out whatever jargon came to mind. Some of it was sound, some of it wasn't. But it didn't matter, as long as the team *believed* she was working toward various ends. "I don't know yet, I need some time to work it out still. I'll come back when I have something more concrete."

"In the meantime. . ." Wayne stood, joining Jo and Eslar as the ones standing. "I propose Takako and I will go back to the real world, continue to scope out the police. We'll report back if we see them closing in on things. But this should buy you some time, Jo."

Jo caught his gaze and gave a firm nod. She heard him loud and clear. He was going to keep the team busy as long as he could for her. Jo just hoped that however long that was, it would be enough.

# WOOD GRAIN

J o practically sprinted out of the common room. Her elongated steps were so hasty that she was nearly tripping over her own two feet.

*Buy her some time.* Even if she wasn't sure where, exactly, her and Wayne stood right now, she knew they were on the same page when it came to their deal, at the very least. But how much time he could buy her, and how much time she needed, could be two different things. Jo found herself trying to calculate how long it would take to close her own Severity of Exchange between them.

She cracked her knuckles. It felt like a slumbering monster was waking within her, and she'd put a leash on it before it could get the better of her. She'd channel it and use it to her advantage; it wouldn't be like the desk, an uncontrolled outburst, but a tool for the Society's undoing. That much, Jo could vow to herself.

By the time Jo ended up at the recreation room she was breathless from her near-sprint. A small tremble settled on her shoulders with every exhale—purely from the tension that had her back tied into a ramrod-straight position. Yes, she was going to learn how to control this magic of hers and when she did, she was going to use it to break apart the shackles holding them.

She ripped off her watch, throwing it on the shelf. It nearly tumbled off, holding on by some invisible magic as Jo wrenched open the door.

The hinges squealed so loudly that it stopped Jo right in her tracks. Her eyes swung left, looking at the metal that had never so much as whispered a sound before. Jo leaned in for a closer inspection, running her hands over the lacquer of the wood. Her fingernail caught on grooves that she didn't remember being there before.

*Wood grain.*

That's all it was. Grains of the wood. It's not like she'd ever really inspected it that closely. It had likely been that way all along and she'd had no cause to notice. Carpentry wasn't exactly her strong suit either—that fell solidly in Samson's wheelhouse. And there was no need to trouble the man with her paranoia. No need whatsoever.

Jo closed the door behind her delicately, all prior vigor lost, and was immediately plunged into darkness. She turned, back against the door, blinking as her eyes adjusted. It took a second (that felt like a whole minute) but eventually she could make out all the shapes in the room. Her chair was poised, monitors where they always were, modems and servers blinked in the background like lackluster Christmas lights.

"Okay . . . Some light would be nice?" she spoke to no one in particular. As expected, there wasn't a response. "Fine, I'll do it myself."

Problem was, Jo had no idea where the light switch was—or if there was even one to begin with. Every time she'd entered the room before the light had been on, waiting. Even if it wasn't, it wouldn't have bothered her; the glow of the three monitors would've been enough. But those weren't on either.

After another long minute of fumbling in the darkness, Jo's fingers finally landed on a familiar paddle shape that she'd call a switch. Her hand froze just before she flipped it. A writhing, suffocating feeling crept up on her, clinging to her back. Jo gave a shrug, as if she could physically remove the invisible presence from weighing on her.

*Nothing to be worried about.*

But suddenly she *was* worried. And she didn't know why. It was like she was about to hit the timer on a bomb, not flick on the light.

"You're being stupid," Jo insisted aloud. Hearing her own voice grounded her, underscored the overall ridiculousness of the situation. She made a move for the switch.

And paused again.

Jo balled her hand into a fist and took a deep breath. She could do this. She would conquer this. Running, walking, or crawling, she would get to where she needed to be.

The light blinked on, and Jo breathed an audible sigh of relief.

With just that, everything felt a little more normal. She made a stop at the mini fridge next, pulling out a can of RAGE ENERGY and taking a long sip. As the electric green liquid flowed down her throat, she could feel herself relaxing a bit. In the comforts of the recreation room—surrounded by her plush work chair, caffeine, and tech—she could find a bit of normalcy that eluded her anywhere else in the Society.

For a little bit, at least, she could pretend that she was still just Jo, the Shewolf hacker with a chip on her shoulder and something to prove. Jo walked over to the chair, falling heavily into it and nearly spilling some of her drink. She raised the can to her mouth again and took a long sip.

First things first: organize her mind.

She needed to set up a sub-script to run in the background of the android's firmware that wouldn't be recognizable to the AI itself. Yeah, this wasn't going to be a pain or anything. Whatever language programmers were using now for AI wasn't something that she kept herself regularly versed in, so hopefully her translation magic worked for computer code as well. If not, she'd need to do some quick cramming to refresh herself before doing anything else.

Setting the can down on the desk, Jo leaned forward. She needed to start on a list of things to do—*two* lists. One list would be for the wish, just enough that if someone called her out she looked like she was actually working. The other would be for her own research on the Society and magic.

A force that only vaguely resembled static electricity arced between her fingertip and the monitor's "on" switch. Jo startled as lighting streaked up over the face of the monitor, knocking over her chair as she scrambled to get away. It spider-webbed with a flash, as if the force was dividing to conquer—hunting for every way in through the monitor's casing.

With a blink, it was gone.

The monitor was dark and unassuming. The smell of smoke wafted through the air, singeing her nostrils as Jo inhaled sharply. She looked down at her hand and then back to the monitors.

It wasn't the first time that monitor had acted up, she realized; it had issues turning on and staying on during their last wish. But a flicker in the screen and an all-out self-implosion were two vastly different things.

Jo swallowed so hard she nearly choked on her own saliva.

She righted the chair and sat with purpose. It's what she'd wanted. Wasn't it? Jo had a staring contest with the monitor. She wanted to dismantle the Society and this was proof that she could if she stopped ignoring her ever-increasing magic or writing it off.

So why did she not feel happier about the fact?

Holding out her palm, all of her fascination lingered between Jo's fingers. If she had the power to bring down the Society, then she had to really get serious about learning it—learning to *control* it. Seeing the Society go up in flames had to be a controlled burn; a wildfire would torch them all.

Without hesitation or fanfare, Jo clicked on the other two monitors. Like the light overhead they flicked on, oblivious to their now-dead counterpart.

"Okay, I'm working on two monitors then, it's fine," Jo reassured herself. They said that talking to yourself was the first sign of insanity, but Jo was fairly certain she was several signs in already and it made her feel the smallest bit more normal.

She pulled up her programs and her notepad, diving into her lists. The first shaped up with ease and Jo quickly had a password randomizer beginning to work on the logins she'd hacked in a past life to gain information on Primus Sanguis. It was enough work on that for now, so Jo turned herself to the second list, titled "BTCOTS."

It stood for, "Break The Cycle Of The Society" and the title needed work as much as the project itself did.

This searching she did manually. Jo didn't throw in random keywords and let software cull and pull sites. She wanted her own eyes on every page. Even if it took longer, she didn't trust a script to know when something looked promising.

At first, her queries were random. This or that, chasing down rabbit holes of research that meant nothing and led nowhere—mostly just to introduce her mind to the subject and see how she wanted to approach it. She finally found the right mental pathway when her hands keyed in a query that pulled her from the mindless wandering she'd been engaging in:

WISH GRANTER SOCIETY CIRCLE MAGIC

The vague search term provided a list of results Jo eagerly scrolled through. Most of the initial sites were poorly maintained and dated. Jo clicked in to examine the source code, confirming that—based on the bootstrapping used—the sites dated back to the early 2000s.

She clicked on another, more modern site, but one that had even less information.

Another click. This time she found a familiar thread, the one that she had frantically scanned in that server barn what now felt like years ago (it very well could have been; time seemed so slippery now). This link had taken her to the Society. *Perhaps it would've been better if I'd never made that wish and just died*, Jo thought darkly. Wayne's similar muttering about the Great Depression and his time echoed in her ears. How many of them felt the same way she did? How many would welcome the dissolution of the Society, if it meant freedom from their eternity?

Jo erased the distraction by closing the window, looking elsewhere.

She tried to think of what else she knew about the Society. There had to be a clue *somewhere*. The lore of it had persisted through the ages. *Why?* Why did the rumors of circles and wishes seem to linger no matter how many times the world was rebuilt? It was as if an invisible hand had been guiding it along the whole time.

The memory of being drafted in the Society prompted another thought:

Snow had said she was "selected" because she possessed an ancient magic. Seven lineages. Perhaps there was some clue in the depths of her ancestry? Jo opened up a new window and allowed her magic to enhance the limited Spanish abilities she possessed (far from good enough, according to her extended family) to type in yet another query.

Her *abuelita* had always been filled with her own kind of magic. It was in the little things, like how she always knew when Jo needed a break from her mother, or how no matter the level of childhood insomnia, two minutes in her grandmother's lap, rocking chair shifting beneath them like a soft tide, and Jo was out like a light.

Simple things like that could easily be explained away, but the woman had greater magic in her: eyes that could see any lie, no matter how well crafted; ears that could hear from one end of the house to the other no matter how old she grew; and hands that could heal.

In Mexico, they were called *curanderas*—healers using "folk remedies" when modern medicine wasn't good enough. Jo vaguely remembered other words like *brujeria* or witchcraft, but all she knew was that her grandmother had helped her when her throat had gone too sore to swallow, her forehead hot while her body ran cold. The experience was broken up like snapshots now, more like recalling snippets of dreams rather than actual memories, but certain things lingered strong despite the distraction of fever and crackling breaths.

Strong hands, worn and wrinkled but gentle, rubbing an egg against her forehead, her neck, her chest. Soft words that her eight-year-old ears might have been able to translate if not for how quickly they came and went. The sound of something being placed beneath her bed before Jo gave in and succumbed to sleep.

The next morning had seen Jo with barely an itch at the back of her throat, her chest clear, and her sweat-soaked skin cooling beneath the fan above her bed. When her *abuelita* had come to check on her, she had removed a terracotta bowl from the floor and cracked the egg into its depth, an orangey-red surrounding the yolk. The sickness had found a new vessel, she had explained, and Jo hadn't questioned it; children rarely did. She was better after all and had believed in her grandmother absolutely.

There was no way of knowing if Jo's fever had simply chosen that night to break, or if her grandmother had truly embodied some ancient, Hispanic magic, but Jo had grown up believing. In fact, when she'd ended up in the Society, part of her had expected her own magic to in some way be linked to that lineage of *curanderas*.

But all of this, the healing, the egg, it had nothing to do with Jo's magic and how it worked after all. Perhaps the same magic was there, but it manifested differently in each individual? Still, it was the only "real world" tether Jo had to anything supernatural, so she threw out her

Spanish query and was presented with varying results. There were slightly different spins on the Society's lore, but much the same as what she'd found in English, overall.

*Disappointing.*

Jo pushed away from the computer, frustrated at the query and frustrated at herself. What did she think she'd find? A succinct summary of the history of the Society and all its members? None of them existed; they never had, as far as the world was concerned. Even though her *abuelita* had died almost two years prior to Jo's entrance into the Society, there was no doubt in her mind that she would have forgotten about Jo, too. Her heart twinged at the thought, rebelling against the idea.

Small victory, that—knowing that her grandmother had died before she'd had a chance to forget.

Her fingers landed back on the keyboard. She knew she couldn't find out anything about the members of the Society and their supposed lineages—those were erased with time and the resetting of the world each of their wishes had wrought. But there was something about the lore of the Society that kept it clinging to reality despite the world being rebuilt time and again. And perhaps that wasn't the only lore she could find.

*The Bow of the Goddess*

Jo keyed in the name of the book Eslar had given her. Most of the hits were related to a legendary item in some mass-multiplayer online game that Jo had only a vague knowledge of. Scrolling down, she landed on some page listing hunting deities from various cultures. It seemed almost every corner of the world had some kind of lore on bow-wielding divinities. There was no shortage of stories of them striking down man and beast alike. But nothing perfectly resembled Eslar's book.

Pushing away from the desk, Jo stood, pacing. The idea of the lore passed down through ages, an invisible hand guiding it—stuck with Jo worse than fresh gum on the underside of her shoe on a hot day. The internet may have forgotten past ages and histories, reduced to just scattered snippets. But Jo had something—someone—that could be even better.

BTCOTS NOTES 3

Information overload but repetitive.

**Search term: Divine Wars**
**Result: AESIR (Æsir)-VANIR WAR (Norse Mythology)**

- Fits the battle for control mold
- Two main pantheons fighting
- Ages of Gods (older v newer) not relevant here
- Merged into one pantheon after war – Vanir's leaders split & controlled by Aesir
- Definitive weapon was a forged spear

Compiled all notes to date.
Cross-referenced Eslar's book for Age of Magic perspective.

Core elements:

- *War between gods (specifically elder—Oblivion. And newer—everyone else)*
- *Battle for control*
- *Deceit of some gods*
- *Goddess of the hunt/archery*
- *Magical item (bow & arrow/spear) to defeat ultimate evil*

# SPRINGTIDE PILLARS

J o took the stairs up toward the hall of bedrooms two at a time. In a blink, she was standing before Eslar's door, knocking before she could think otherwise. Then again, if she was going to talk herself out of this plan, she would've done it hours—days ago. *No*, she was committed. There would be no other Nicos and there would be no more games with their existence.

Eslar startled when he opened the door; clearly she was not the person he'd been expecting. "Josephina?"

"May I come in?" she asked outright. She was practically ready to force her way in if she had to, and judging from Eslar's expression, the fact was likely written across her face.

"Is everything all right with the wish?" He held firm, blocking her entry and taking up nearly all available space in the door so that Jo could barely get a glimpse of his room.

"Yeah, I just had a few questions to ask. It may take a minute though. So, may I come in?" Jo repeated, continuing to attempt to stare him down.

"All right, then," he said finally, as though they'd had a conversation without her realizing it.

The elf stepped aside, and Jo stepped in past his tall, lithe frame.

"Have a seat, should it please you," Eslar murmured, gliding past her.

Jo's eyes followed his path through the room, but not the man himself. She was too distracted by everything around Eslar to give him too much attention.

The room was a perfect circle. The roof was supported by thick columns on the outer edge, belling out at the bottom and tapering at the top. Between the two behind her was a wall, attached to what, from this side, appeared to be a grand palace. It stretched on in either direction from the door to Eslar's room, windows breaking its surface, offering glimpses of places you couldn't get to and the movement of people who didn't exist.

Sheer, multicolored fabrics hung from between the columns, wafting in a light breeze. The wind picked up, unhindered over the large pool of water surrounding the room. The circular area where she now stood was surrounded by large lily pads that were lazily floating by, flashes of emerald catching sunlight for an instant before winking out of sight. The pool was contained by a low wall, and beyond that, a forest of crystalline trees shimmered happily in the daylight.

Eslar sat down in one of two circular, recessed areas. The shimmering crystal inlays of the floor sunk into pillows and blankets of equally vibrant colors. One was clearly for sleeping; Jo moved to the other one, albeit slowly. She was still taking in the chimes singing from the ceiling, hung at different intervals, and the ornate table far opposite her.

The fantastical, grandiose lavishness of it all was almost enough to make her forget her purpose for being there. *Almost.*

"What is it that you wanted to ask, Josephina?"

"Oh, right. . ." She debated where to start. Jo quickly decided it was best to dip her toes in, test the waters between them, before diving right in to questions about the Society. The smell of smoke and a dead computer lingered in her nose, offering a potential avenue to begin. "Well, first, quick question. . . Have you, or any other member of the team that you know of, ever had the recreation room. . . not work? Like something inside it maybe acted funny or malfunctioned or something?"

Eslar merely stared at her, contemplative. The look prompted Jo to elaborate with a quick clearing of her throat.

"One of my monitors stopped working for some reason," she said, delicately keeping out the part about it sparking and imploding the moment she'd touched it. "Has something like that ever happened before?"

"Things are high stress right now," he said finally, voice calming in its certainty, even if Jo didn't quite believe him. "Perhaps the room was simply reacting to your current mental state?"

"I think my mental state is fine."

"Do you? Given the nature of this wish? And so soon after Nico?"

The mere mention of Nico had Jo looking away. His name was like an open wound she'd been trying to ignore. There had been no time for grief, though the memory of their dear friend haunted them all like a ghost.

"I think it's fine. . ." Jo insisted, picking at the floor. The crystal inlays here were so perfectly flush that there wasn't even a groove for her nail to catch in. She used it as an opportunity to change the topic, not wanting to allow either of them to linger on Nico's memory. "Your room is beautiful, by the way."

"I suppose it is rather . . . unique," he said without even lifting his head from the book he'd propped open on his lap. "Especially for someone from the Age of Man."

"Age of Man?"

He gave her a quizzical look. "You came from it and you don't know?"

"Oh." Just that much and Jo could put it together. Still, he explained.

"The Age of Man followed the Age of Magic. It was an apt name for a time when magic no longer ruled."

Eslar's eyes scanned the pages of his massive tome. It was as though she hadn't come into his room at all. He was completely lost, engrossed, escaped to the world between the pages because the reality he was faced with was too much to bear.

"Was this common, in the Age of Magic? A room like this?"

Eslar said nothing, flipping the page. In fact, he flipped several pages. Jo waited, not moving, not saying anything else. He had another thing coming if he genuinely thought he could avoid her. She wasn't about to allow herself to be relegated back to hours of fruitless research without at least getting a new lead from him.

Finally, a blank page showed up, breaking the lines of elvish runes—a new chapter, she guessed. With a hefty sigh and no more words left to conveniently hide between, he finally answered her question. "It's reminiscent of the elvish summer palaces by the sea. We would go there on springtide to re-attune our magics with the greater cosmos."

"Your book had elves in it." If she was careful, and just subtle enough, she could direct the conversation. Little nudges here and there, just to push him far enough that he would willingly let her past the tough guards she knew he kept in place. "The one you let me borrow."

"I knew what book you were referring to. It is not as if I have seen you with any other printed words in your hands," he remarked dryly, almost coldly. "And given that the book was written in elvish, by an elf, in the Age of Magic, I fail to see how that's unique."

Jo tensed, but pushed down the near-instant fireball of frustration she could've spat at him. She needed him—needed his knowledge—but she hated having to walk blindfolded through a maze of eggshells to try to get it. *Okay, different approach.* "Tell me a little about your time?"

"What do you want to know?" Eslar sighed heavily and snapped his book shut with a mighty thud.

"Anything."

"Is this really why you are bothering me?" he asked skeptically. "Don't you have something to be doing for the wish?"

"Talking helps clear my head. It'll help me think of a new approach for this code that has me tripped up." Fortunately, it wasn't a complete lie. "You lived in the Age of Magic, right?"

"I did."

"So, tell me about it."

"Wh—"

"Please, I need a distraction. *Anything*." Again, not a lie. Not the whole truth, but not a lie.

"I have already given you one, but last I saw it was looking sad and forlorn out by the pool."

"Books can't look like anything but books."

"Then you are not looking at them in the right way."

"Eslar—"

He sighed heavily. It was the sound of someone finally giving in. "If I tell you this, will you go?"

Jo pressed her lips into a hard, thin line. In her mind, she was telling him off in several different languages. Even if she had ulterior motives, he was turning away a member of his team who was in need, who was trying to reach out to the one elf-shaped lifeline they could come up with, and he didn't even care.

But all that came out of her mouth was, "Yeah, I guess."

He stared at her for a long moment, reaching for his book again with a sigh. Jo thought that maybe she'd have to wait while he read another chapter before she'd get an answer. But he simply held it, caressed it, spoke to it as if he was imparting his knowledge to the object rather than another person.

In that moment, in that way, he reminded Jo of Samson.

"Well, as I mentioned. . . the elves would head to the sea in springtime. We would bless ourselves with the foam of the ocean and wear crowns of flowers plucked from the dunes. Communing with nature replenished our energies and gave us new life."

Jo looked out over the pool, trying to imagine it, and found the task surprisingly easy. She could see a whole group of Eslars, joining hands, chanting, radiating with ancient power. She could see their woven fabrics, spun of silks from bugs her mind could conjure by image but not by name.

She blinked rapidly and, like a mirage in the sunlight reflecting off the water, the images vanished.

"You had magic in your time, right?"

"I did say that's what we were doing, magic," he responded curtly.

Jo avoided pointing out that he had not, *exactly*, said so outright.

"We had power, so much power . . . and yet . . ."

"And yet . . . what?" Jo probed, surprised it got her anywhere.

"The elves were an ancient race—those of the high elf bloodline the oldest of all mortals. They said there was truth woven into the world, truths that could not be seen with eyes or hands but with hearts and magic."

*So elves were the hippies of the magical world . . .*

"But younger elves, they strayed from the course. They were drawn toward the flashy magics of newer races. And they began to forget. When the upkeep of the pillars lapsed. . . we were doomed from that moment. Even if I wished for more time for my people, nothing lasts forever it'd seem."

"Pillars?" Jo's focus honed on the one thing that could be useful to them now.

"It was said that the world was anchored on four mighty pillars, positioned in each of the cardinal directions. And on these pillars were the truths of the cosmos as written by the gods who formed them."

"Were they from the Age of Gods?" Jo dared to ask, as if interrupting his flow might make him stop altogether. "I asked Snow that once, when he told me the time he was from. I take it he's told you as well." Eslar glanced sideways at her for a long moment.

Jo gave a small nod. It wasn't phrased like a question because the answer was obvious. "Were they?"

"He would not answer."

"Good to know I'm not the only one he's cryptic toward," Jo muttered.

"You are most certainly not." Jo had never expected this to be their common ground, but she'd have taken anything for that brief moment of camaraderie with the elf. Eslar continued, "Truly of the divine, or not, did not matter. All that mattered was that while the pillars were maintained, the elves would not die unless they chose of their own will to return to the earth."

It seemed poor design on the part of the gods—if that was truly who made them—to have structured the anchors of the world on something that required constant maintenance. But that brought them back into the realm of speculation. Jo, instead, would focus on fact.

"So, these pillars were maintained by the elves. . . Not maintained, I mean, given power?"

Eslar nodded, preparing to retreat back into the world of his book.

"Wait." Jo held out a hand, as if she could catch him and reel his mind back. This was just what she'd been hoping to find. "Do you know how to do that . . . thing . . . ritual? Whatever it was that gave the pillars power?"

He frowned, and Jo suspected that it was not because of the ineloquence of her question. She'd beat him to the punch.

"Don't think I'm crazy," Jo said quickly. "But we need magic to feed the Society, right? We get it from wishes. . . kind of like. . . the Society is built on its own pillar—makes sense, right? After all, it's a world outside of the world, so it'd need its own pillar. And instead of making elves immortal, it's making us immortal."

His expression devolved into an all-out scowl.

"What if we figured out our own ritual to feed it magic, rather than wishes? That way if we ever can't—"

"Out."

"What?" Jo leaned back, as if trying to avoid the invisible whip that lashed the word off his tongue.

"Out, Josephina."

"I'm not trying to upset you, or ask dumb questions. I'm genuinely trying—"

"How dare you," he whispered, the words dripping with venom.

"*What?*"

"Do you not think that if I could have saved him, I would have?"

"That's not what I was implying." But had it come off that way? Jo didn't give it much thought. Intention had to outweigh execution here, right? She was trying to save them all, to cheat or dismantle the brutal system they were all subject to.

"You knew him for a few months. I knew him for a millennium. Tell me, how many sketches would he produce before picking up his brush to actually paint?"

"I. . ."

"What music would always make him dance, regardless of whether or not he had a partner?"

She'd never listened to music with anyone in the Society.

"Could you tell the difference between the smiles he gave when he was genuinely happy, and the ones he gave when was desperately trying to have you not see his heartache?"

*Maybe?* The word was weak, and small, tinier than she suddenly felt. "I was just thinking. . ."

"You weren't thinking at all." Eslar opened his book with such vigor that she was surprised he didn't tear it apart.

Jo lingered a moment, reeling. When she was sure she could stand without falling over, or breaking down, she did so. The world swayed as Jo shuffled toward the door, all its prior luster faded.

She should've left it there. But everything hurt again. The hopelessness was back, wedged between her bones, turning her ribs to barbed wire, stabbing behind her eyes.

How dare she? How dare *he*.

"You're right," Jo said so softly she didn't know if he could hear. The soft crinkle of a page between tensing fingers assured he could. "I didn't know everything about Nico and I didn't have as much time as you to learn. But friendship isn't a contest and it doesn't have one universal measurement. You don't get to hold a monopoly on grief because you had more hours with him.

"And you don't get to judge me for mine." She turned. Eslar wasn't even looking at her. "At least I'm trying to do something about it."

"By asking foolish questions," he muttered.

Jo had to bite her tongue to keep herself from spilling then and there all that she was trying to do for them.

"I've already given you one book from the Age of Magic, more than enough. If you wish to distract yourself, go to that, rather than me."

Jo took the invitation to leave without saying goodbye.

# FLETCHER

J o was under no illusion.

She didn't actually think Eslar was trying to be helpful by suggesting the book. In fact, she was certain it was his way of dismissing her, by suggesting she do something that—in his own words—he had no expectation of her actually doing.

Eslar was right after all. She wasn't what one would exactly define as "bookish". In fact, she could count on both hands the number of books that we were in her house growing up. *Physical* books, at least. Most people in 2057 read on tablets, her mother included, and the books that were in her house had been her grandmother's—holding more sentimental than physical value.

Jo had done even less reading. . . Unless you counted pages upon pages of websites she'd culled through. If all of her research for her jobs counted, then she was likely the most well-read person she knew. That was what she was good at after all—her work. When it came to finding out information about a job, Jo didn't let anything hold her back.

Even if that something was reading a physical book.

Instead of heading back toward the recreation room, Jo headed toward the common area. As expected, no one was there. Takako and Wayne were no doubt still at the police station. And if she had read between the lines right during her talk with Wayne, they would buy as much time as they could for her by investigating. Jo didn't know where Samson was, but after Nico it was more unusual to see him outside of his room.

Jo paused, her feet at the threshold of the patio, looking out over the pool. She and Nico had sat there. She saw the deck chairs, still pulled together, waiting for two occupants who would never return.

Walking over, Jo grabbed Nico's chair and pulled it off to the side.

Her mission to bring down the Society might be inspired by Nico, but Jo wasn't ready yet to confront his memory again. If she was honest, she might never be.

Sitting down at her chair, Jo grabbed the book that had been left there for weeks. Luckily, albeit unsurprisingly, the book was still in pristine condition. There was no rain at the Society, no humidity to warp the covers or pages. There wasn't much of anything, ever. Jo was swiftly discovering that even perfection had its limits.

Opening the book, Jo leafed through the pages, quickly finding where she had left off in her prior skimming. She started reading, but it was slow going, slower than what she would have wanted. Part of her wanted to comb every page carefully, absorbing every minute morsel of information. The other part of her wanted to devour it quickly, getting the big picture before she drilled down into the specifics. She started out as the former, but quickly ended up much the latter.

It read like a storybook. There were characters, a narrative, love interests, and the history of kingdoms Jo had never heard of but could tell the author expected the reader to already be familiar with. As a result of this format, Jo could clearly draw a picture of the Age of Magic in her mind.

She could see the dense primordial forests that seemed to shimmer with fogs made up of starlight and magic. She could see the homes of the elves, bleached and offset with fantastical fabrics and decorative windows. Everything was so clear to her, it was as if she was remembering, rather than reading it in a storybook.

As impressive as all that was, Jo continued to find it unhelpful. The story boiled down to a simple structure: a war of gods, a dangerous weapon, and the gifting of it for safekeeping until a hero could wield it. Jo ran her fingers over the page, the Elvish script magically making sense before her eyes even if its true meaning remained hidden.

Her fingers landed on a single word—*arrow*. If there was one word that was repeated more than any other in the book, it was this one. It felt significant, real to her in a way that even transcended the deep knowing of the story's setting and characters. There was an echo of something deep in her that grabbed hold of it and made her eyes stick every time they landed on it.

It hit Jo all at once. She snapped the book closed, stashed it under her chair, and headed back the way she came. She passed by Eslar's door, pausing for just a brief moment. *Had he intended her to draw these connections all along?*

She was giving him too much credit. If he had wanted to help her, he would've helped her—not sent her on some cryptic wild goose chase. Jo continued on her way, unable to contain a chastising "tsk" for the elf's bad behavior.

Once more, Samson was startled to see her, but at least he wasn't agitated by her presence—a key step up from Eslar.

"Hello again, Jo."

"Hey, there's something I wanted to ask you. . . can I come in for just a second?"

"Oh, of course." For the second time in a day, Samson moved aside for her to enter. However, this time, Jo closed the door behind her. "What is it?"

Jo looked to her right, to the door that led to his bedroom. In there was a smaller worktable and on that worktable was a series of feathers, wood, and metal arrow tips. His name, he had told her once, was Samson Fletcher. Fletcher, for his past profession.

If anyone would know about the arrow, *and* the Age of Magic, it would be him.

"I was reading a book Eslar gave me."

"You were reading a book?" She didn't know if the confusion on his face was because of the fact that she was supposed to be working on the wish, or because she was reading a book. Either way, Jo decided to cover her bases.

"Yeah, I know, it's not like me, but this wish has got me really hung up, and I was looking for a distraction for just a minute to clear my head. I tried to go to Eslar himself—" no point in hiding it, she figured "—but he didn't seem to really want to talk."

"He hasn't been very talkative since. . ." Samson couldn't bring himself to say Nico's name. But it hung heavy enough that she had no illusions as to what was unsaid.

"Yeah, well, after that failed, I picked up the book he gave me. Have you ever read it?"

"Which one?"

Jo felt instantly silly. Eslar had hundreds of books, no doubt, and Samson had had a lot of time with the elf over the years. "It's a book about a hunter and an arrow. . . It was the arrow that got me thinking, actually. Thinking about you."

"What about me?"

"Oh, I don't know. . ." She stalled, hoping he would just happen to blurt out the information she needed. He didn't. "I know you were a fletcher before, right?"

"I was."

"Do you know the story then?"

"I do. I think." Samson walked over to his worktable. He kept his head down and began tinkering away as he spoke. His words started out strong, but they grew fainter and fainter. "It's the one about bringing down the goddess, right? Most people from the Age of Magic knew that one."

"So it was a common story?" Jo asked, eagerly trying to keep the conversation going.

"I guess you could say that." Samson paused, clearly giving it some thought for the first time. "Most people knew it, at least."

"Do you know where it came from? Was there any truth to it?"

He looked up, startled.

"No I-I don't, I'm sorry."

"No, Sam, it's fine. . . Like I said, I'm a little bit work crazy, I think." Jo forced a laugh. "Nothing I say is making sense, just ignore me."

"It's all right."

"Anyway, I should go back to it."

"Did you need my help for anything else? Because I. . ." The way his words reached a sudden halt and the long pause had Jo's mind immediately filling in the blank. She remembered what he had said about his magic earlier and the way it wasn't working right.

"No, you're great, Samson—" She emphasized *great*. "I should go."

Once again, she was leaving Samson's room as abruptly as she came. He wore confusion on his face, but at the very least he didn't look offended. It seemed like they were all willing to forgive certain lapses in etiquette lately, for the sake of having their privacy.

Jo folded her arms as she started back for the recreation room, thinking over the information Eslar and Samson had given her. There were the pillars worlds were supported on, and the Elvish rituals used to feed them; there was a magical arrow, and the unknown hero destined to wield it . . .

Jo's mind was so busy processing her conversation with Samson, picking apart every possible conclusion, that she didn't even notice she was on a collision course until it was too late.

One moment she walking with determined strides, and the next she was stumbling, grabbing the wall for support. Instinct had her reaching out, trying to catch the other person before they could tumble due to her complete blindsiding. Her hand closed around a bicep, toned and hard.

*Yeah, like she was really about to offer Takako support.* The woman could likely break her in two if she wanted.

"I'm sorry," Jo said hastily. "I was totally gone, I didn't even see you."

Takako shook her head. "I was looking for you."

# WANTING IN

"You . . . were looking for me?" Jo asked slowly.

There was nothing subtle about the way Takako was studying her—inspecting, more like. The woman may as well have been wearing a sign that said, "I have questions and suspicions." But Jo didn't know what the answers to those questions would be yet, and until she did, she was ready to play dumb.

"Yes."

"How'd things go at the police station?" Jo asked, trying to mask her disappointment at Takako's presence. She'd been hoping for more time.

"As well as to be expected." Takako took one step backward, as if to be less imposing. It didn't work.

Jo's attempts at small talk were going over about as well as a candle in a typhoon and she looked for a hasty out. "I should get back to working on the wish. . . Unless you needed the rec room for anything?"

"No, I don't." Despite saying she had no further business, Takako continued to linger.

"Great." Jo pulled off her bracelet, ready to retreat into the recreation room.

Takako caught her wrist right as Jo placed her watch on the shelf. She leaned in, dropping her voice to a whisper. Jo had a sense of what the woman was going to say before the words traversed her lips; there was only one explanation for how she was acting. "I know something is up."

"I don't know what you're talking about," Jo whispered back.

"Don't play dumb. I know you and Wayne have something going on right now."

"Wayne and me?" Jo blinked in surprise.

"Wh—no, no, not like that." Takako rolled her eyes dramatically and leaned closer. "I know you're both hiding something."

*Takako had only spent a few hours with Wayne and it was that obvious.* Jo swallowed hard. Game time decision—lie, or bring Takako in on it. She studied the woman's face, as though the answer would be written somewhere around Takako's cheeks.

Takako was strong and clearly knew how to keep her mouth shut, given her past profession. She was also newer to the Society, like Jo. If anything, she was likely even less attached to the "this was how its always been" thinking than Wayne, making her a potentially easier-to-gain ally.

"Not here." Jo glanced down the hall. She had intended to motion to Pan's door, but her eyes fell on Snow's.

The last time Jo had spent any time with him was right after Nico's death, and that whole period was a blur. After the tears had faded and grief set in, Jo didn't want anyone. It was an ache so deep that she didn't even want to be consoled about it.

Then there was the wish, not more than a few days later. All of which put her on the track that had led her to where she stood now—a place of secrecy and suspicion. Eventually, she would have to confront Snow. He was the only one who could give her the true answers she sought, or confirm whatever she found. It was too soon, though. She needed to find out more on her own, and face him when she was armed with more surety and knowledge.

"Inside," Jo whispered, pulling Takako into the recreation room. Jo took a deep breath, wondering where to begin. "I have a plan."

"Of what kind?"

"I want to bring down the Society." Jo waited for a reaction. When there was none, she said, "You don't look surprised."

Takako tipped her head back, looking at Jo over her lower eyelashes. Even though Takako was shorter than her, she felt taller in that moment—like a teacher assessing a student. Her black eyes betrayed nothing.

"I had a feeling."

"How?"

"You didn't think you were the only one angry at the status quo after Nico, do you?"

Jo glanced behind her, confirming her desk chair was there, before falling heavily into it. She laced her fingers, suddenly feeling like this had become a business transaction she hadn't asked for but definitely wanted.

"I didn't take you for the type to stand against orders," Jo confessed.

"I'm a soldier, not a robot." Takako's eyes fluttered closed and she gave a soft sigh, the tension in her shoulders easing some. "I'm a soldier by choice, at that. But this fight . . . I was drafted into it. And I don't know if I can trust the place my orders are coming from anymore."

"I think Snow is as much of a prisoner as we are." Jo was a little too eager to rise to his defense.

Takako made a soft humming noise, but didn't comment on the matter. Instead, she asked, "What's your plan?"

"I'm still working that out," Jo confessed. "Wayne is helping buy me time, so I can work on the side."

"Where are you starting? Give me the debrief of what you have so far." *Tactical.* Jo could use a mind like Takako's. By the moment she was appreciating her decision to let Takako in on her machinations more and more.

"So far, I'm trying to grab information on the Society. I've gone and asked Eslar and Samson about some things . . . but my leading theory is that there may be something to the fact that the lore of the Society lingers across the ages."

"You mean the fact that even when the world is rebuilt, the information about a Wish Granter and circles to summon him lives on?" Takako clarified.

"Exactly." Jo nodded. "*Why?* Why does that live on when everything else can get destroyed and rebuilt?"

"Because the Society needs wishes to survive?" Takako surmised.

"Yes, but . . . is it Snow that makes sure it lives on? Or is it something else?" Jo shook her head, not wanting to return the topic to Snow. "Furthermore . . . there's the Age of Magic."

"When Eslar and Samson are from."

"Indeed." Jo began pulling things up on the computer, pleased to see that her set-up was exactly how she left it. . . including the still-fried monitor. Jo cast a wary eye, but didn't give it too much attention, as if that would tempt her magic to act out again. "There's other lore, about gods and mythologies, that has lingered through the ages, like the Society. Well, not quite like the Society. Information on the Society seems to remain in perfect condition. This other lore seems to be fractured while still persisting. I'm thinking maybe there's something in there."

"Like what, specifically?" Takako crossed to the futon across from Jo's desk. She gave a little bounce, pushing on the seat, clearly impressed by its comfort.

"I don't know yet. It's still formulating in my head. . ."

Takako folded her hands, resting her elbows on her knees. "If we operate under the assumption that the mythology of the gods persisting has something to do with the Society. . . Then are you saying you think the Society has something to do with these aforementioned gods?"

*Demigod, a step up from prince.* Jo recalled the words from when Snow had first told her snippets of his history. A demigod was ruling their Society. Demi*god.* From the Age of *Gods.* Surely, that was significant.

"Maybe. . ." Jo said slowly. "Maybe I am. Maybe there's something to lore, memories, divinities, that lingers through the ages even after the Age of Gods."

"Age of Gods?" Takako arched her eyebrows.

"Oh . . . it came before the Age of Magic."

"Where Snow is from, then," Takako said without missing a beat. At Jo's surprise, she added, "I figured it was a reasonable assumption, given how close you are."

Jo nodded, turning back to the monitors. She didn't want to talk about Snow. And yet. . .

"Does he know?"

"What?" Jo's fingers stilled and she looked over her shoulder as though she'd been caught red-handed.

"Does Snow know what you're doing?"

"Not yet," Jo confessed.

"When will you tell him?" *Not if, when.*

"I don't know." Jo shook her head. "I don't want him to stop me."

"Good." Takako leaned back on the couch, giving her an approving stare. "Don't let him stop you, then."

"I won't," Jo vowed, though she wasn't sure who she was reassuring.

"All right, then, where shall we begin?"

From there, Jo told Takako everything. Well, *almost* everything. For some reason, she couldn't bring herself to mention the desk, or monitor. It wasn't that she didn't trust Takako; she just wanted more time with her magic, more time to mull it over and figure it out.

Jo wanted more time for everything. But like their watches, time was ticking, a rare and precious thing that they were never going to get back.

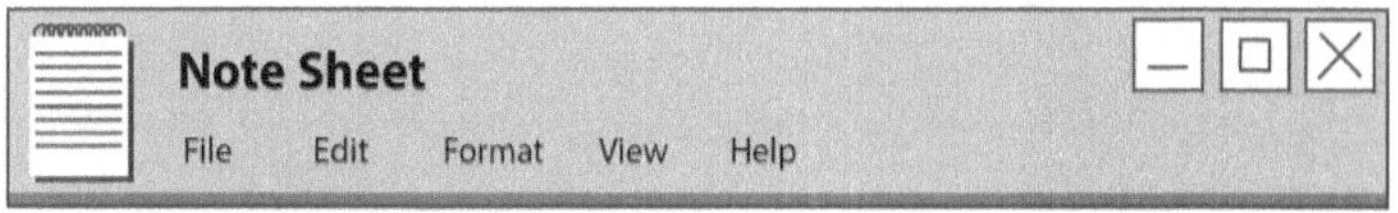

BTCOTS NOTES 4

Takako=Genius.
    (Find her if short hand doesn't make sense)

**Hachiman (Japanese divinity of Archery & War)**

- *Bow + War blended*
- *Back to Eslar's book? (God of Hunt, not war there)*
- *Samurai worshiped*
- *"God of Eight Banners" for 8 heavenly banners for a legendary Emperor*

Eight banners = first Society reference?

BUT Only 7 lineages. Count snow?

# NOWHERE SAFE

J o hadn't made nearly as much progress as she'd hoped.

Takako had stayed for a good few hours, helping brainstorm and culling through suggestions. But she eventually left, not wanting to arouse suspicions about them spending so much time together in seclusion. Alone, Jo looked through things that she hadn't told Takako about—namely related to destructive magics. But that was short-lived.

She alternated between seemingly futile research on ancient magics and mythologies, and mind-numbing attempts to understand AI coding that most people spent years—decades—learning.

Her mind felt overwhelmed, every circuit shorted and blackened out from electrical fires she couldn't find the energy to put out anymore. Her magic, and her own basic knowledge, had made understanding the programming language possible, but utilizing it was another matter entirely. Especially since that wasn't the only thing on her mind.

By the time Jo finally allowed herself a break, it was morning and fourteen hours straight since she'd last entered the recreation room. She wanted to believe it was her work ethic that had kept her locked away for so long, but she'd be lying to herself if she said that was all.

She wanted to have answers. She was tired of being left in the dark and wanted to emerge triumphant. But she left the rec room as in the dark as her still-broken computer monitor.

The gelatin blob Jo had transformed into oozed out into the hallway.

Everything felt heavy, fuzzy. She shook her head and leaned against the door as she pulled her watch from the shelf. She'd given every bit of energy she'd had and poured it into her research. And for what? Overall, it felt like a whole lot of nothing.

She headed to the kitchen, drawn by the smell of food. Unsurprisingly, it was Samson bustling about. But the sight of him, where it had once brought joy, now filled Jo with a lingering sense of worry.

*How was his magic doing?*

That worry was edged out by the sight of the full island. Partaking in Samson's lavish spread was every member of the Society—every chair occupied but two (hers, and Nico's). Snow was among them, talking casually to Eslar as he picked at the fruit on his plate like a noncommittal bird.

But that wasn't the biggest shock. The biggest shock was Pan. She sat on the far corner, slowly stirring her coffee with her bright pink straw, chin in the other hand and a little shit-eating grin playing on her lips.

Jo eased herself into the other open chair, thankful that Wayne and Takako had sat on either side of Snow, giving Jo a buffer. Her mind felt too frazzled to be on point and all she wanted was the giant mug of coffee that magically appeared in Samson's hand and was placed before her. She'd barely had time to raise it to her lips before Snow spoke.

"Jo," Snow said, a simple greeting. Despite the distance that had been growing between them, the word settled warm and comforting around her heart. It was almost enough to make her ask him to say her name again, to ask him to invite her back to his room so she could lean on him for support while she worked through all the kinks of her plan.

"Good morning," she replied to the room at large, though she kept her eyes mostly on Snow. The brief, simple exchange seemed to give permission to everyone else to speak, and small chatter picked up.

Samson's cooking was beyond good, yet again. But Jo found it slightly bitter. She wondered if it was her palate, or if his magic was breaking down further. . . wondered if it was still somehow her fault. Either way, best not to linger on things she couldn't (yet) control.

Conversation was flowing more easily than it had in the past, the haze of Nico's death finally lifting. Even if tensions remained high due to the wish, everyone was making an effort. Eslar was quick to inquire about Jo's progress over the course of the night. She explained what she'd managed to accomplish so far, to the general confusion of the room, and told them of her plans for the rest of the day.

"I still have a lot to do, but my head feels clearer now," she said, putting her fork down on her empty plate. Even with her stomach in knots, she'd managed to clean it. "Especially after a nice break and good food with better company to lift the spirits." She smiled at Samson for good measure and then added, "Shouldn't be long now I don't think."

"That's good to hear," Eslar said, mostly to himself. If Jo thought she heard surprise in his voice, she was probably just imagining it. It was no good getting worked up over something she didn't even know to be true, especially when it came to her team's faith in her. She would not fail, and she liked to think they didn't doubt that.

"Do you plan to go right back to it then?" Takako asked, and Jo nodded.

But before she could speak up, Pan snatched control of the conversation.

"You two were at it for a while last night," she said slyly.

"What is that supposed to mean?" Jo was far too tired to indulge the woman and her games.

"Just surprised you managed to get any work done on the wish."

Jo and Takako exchanged a look.

"Elaborate, Pan?" Eslar asked outright.

Pan's whole face brightened at the opportunity to speak to someone other than Jo, eager to spill what she had clearly come to the table to talk about from the beginning.

"I just heard them talking and chattering *all night* is all," she said dramatically, tossing her violet tresses over her spaghetti-strapped shoulders, massaging them for good measure. "They kept going on about mythology, or some such. I couldn't make out all the details though."

"What are you talking about?" Jo asked quietly, horror stealing the strength of her voice.

Pan's cat eyes drifted back to her. "Josephina, the recreation room is right against mine. *Of course* I know what goes on in there."

That made no sense. None. Jo could list the reasons with the taste of metallic panic on her tongue.

The recreation rooms seemed to exist in their own reality. They took every shape and size, and did just as the occupant wanted. They were like a miniature version of the Society, inside the Society. There was no way that in all of those variations, Pan shared a wall—and a poorly sound-proofed one at that.

"You came to me about mythology," Eslar said, turning to Jo. "What are you getting into?"

"I'm not getting into anything," Jo insisted.

"Then how is it related to the wish?" Snow's voice cut through the chatter and drew her eyes to him and him alone. Just one look, and she ached. He knew something was amiss. She could see his suspicion and it damn near killed her.

But if it killed her, she was instantly reborn from the frustration of all the secrets he kept and continued to keep from them.

"I don't question any of your processes; I'd appreciate it if you don't question mine." Jo raised her mug to her lips, taking a long sip of coffee and making eye contact with no one.

"You can question my process all day long!" Pan said with a giggle. "So tell me what you were doing in there, since we all know it wasn't the wish."

Jo stood, mug in hand. "It was the wish. In fact, I'm almost ready to go out and hack the Bone Carver. I just need to finalize a bit of code and I'll be off."

"Really?" Jo wished Takako could have sounded a little less surprised.

"Yes, really."

"Are you certain, Jo?" Eslar asked skeptically.

"Yes, I got this."

"Then we'll leave it to you. Let us know how your work takes."

Jo barely heard Eslar's final words; she was already almost out of the kitchen. She had almost made it halfway down the hall when she heard the footsteps and decided to make a brief game of it.

*Who would it be?* Not Snow, Snow wouldn't ever scamper like that. Takako? Maybe. But she trusted the woman to have enough sense not to be seen together so soon. Eslar or Samson? No and no. And certainly not Pan.

"What is it, Wayne?" Jo turned, affirming her suspicions. The look of concern on Wayne's face brought her up short. She was expecting to be chastised for "arousing suspicion," but she was not expecting *concern*.

"What's going on?"

"I don't know," she muttered, glancing over his shoulder to make sure no one else was on their way.

"Was Pan right?"

"Yeah," Jo didn't see the point of denial. "But I don't know how."

Wayne frowned. "There's something off, here." The man was at a loss, running a hand over his hair and then doing it immediately again. "Did you tell Takako—"

"Everything is going to be fine." Jo grabbed his hands, trying to hastily reassure him and likely overcompensating by a wide margin in the process. "She's on our side."

For a long moment, Wayne just stared at her in silence. Then, with a soft curse, he let his head fall and shoulders droop, running a shaking hand through his slicked back hair in obvious exasperation. "This feels like it's going too far. And Pan—she's a wild card in a way I wasn't entirely expecting. . . I don't know, Jo."

"We're in control of the situation," Jo interjected fiercely. "Once I get more information, I'm going to confront Snow. He'll listen to me and I'll find out whatever he's been hiding."

Wayne just sighed. "I admire the confidence, doll, but we're on the razor's edge." Then, after a brief pause, he added, "I don't want another—"

Jo's pulse skyrocketed in fear of a never-ending cycle of death. She reacted before she could even give it another iota of thought.

"There won't be another Nico," she said, ignoring the slight tremor in her voice and repeating herself more sternly. "I got this. I'm still working on the wish. Even if I can't end the Society now, I'll help with the wish to make sure we don't lose anyone else."

This time, when Wayne held her gaze in concerned attention, his eyes softened, sad.

"Promise me you won't tell them," she tried again. "We're in too deep, now. . . Just promise me you'll keep quiet about it, alright? At least for now? Give me a little more time?"

"Jo . . ." Wayne sighed, tone wrapping sadly around her name.

"Maybe my power can break us free," she confessed in a hushed whisper, hoping no one heard but them. "But I don't know how to wield it effectively yet. So, for now, just promise me we'll stay the course? Trust in me?"

A long beat of heavy silence, and then Wayne straightened, returning his nickel to his pocket. For a second it was as if he was about to reach out to her, but in the end thought better of it. Instead, he just ran his hand through his hair again, not quite looking at her anymore.

"Fine, dollface. You have my word."

Jo hastily put her coffee down on a nearby table and pulled him in for a fierce hug. Determining the matter finished, she headed back toward the recreation room, trying to put her mind on the wish once more.

But every attempt she made set her thoughts to wandering. Pan had been right—Pan had known. *How?*

"I'm so stupid," Jo whispered, stopping in her tracks so suddenly that she nearly spilled coffee all over herself.

Pan had known back from the first wish what she'd been doing in the recreation room. What else in the Society did she know? Was there anywhere that was safe, or were they all just unwitting puppets in the hands of the master?

# YOU AGAIN

She wished she wasn't alone and yet, at the same time, was glad no one else was there to see her off.

Jo squared off against the Door. Had the lights always been so dim? Her eyes drifted upward, squinting to try to find exactly what the light source was for the room. When she looked at the single orb overhead (Magic? Electricity? Something else entirely?), it seemed blinding. But when her eyes fell back to the room itself, shadows clung to the corners, feeding off the red-blue dot the light had burned into her eyes.

She held out her hand, uncurling her fingers. She'd been clutching the USB stick so tightly, it had made indents into her palm. Really, it was a miracle she hadn't broken the—

*Don't even think it.*

Jo shoved it into her pocket, looking back to the door. Lessening the Severity of Exchange was a team effort. She was sure Eslar had other members of the Society moving in their own ways, doing what they could here and there, still casing the police station and diverting their attention from the Bone Carver. Snow would make the final jump to a new timeline, smoothing out the kinks that made the impossible, possible.

It wasn't down to her to do everything. She couldn't. So why did it feel like she had to?

Because what she was *really* working on was far more important. The sooner she finished playing her part for the wish, the sooner she could divert all of her attention to figuring out how to bring about an end to the Society. That was what really mattered, because that would be the only thing that could save them.

Taking a deep breath in through her nose, Jo imagined where she wanted to be. She pictured the Bone Carver's house clear in her mind. His modest porch, the little welcome mat in front of his door, the matte pastel of the paint on the walls that led up the stairs to his room.

"Let's get this over with, then," Jo whispered, mostly to herself. Magic surged through her and her hand fell to the keypad. She stroked in a series of numbers—not even knowing what she hit—and felt the Door throw itself open.

The brisk winter air was almost enough to take her breath away as Jo stepped through the Door. It *was* actually enough to take her footing—causing her to stumble, nearly losing her balance as she stepped out what would've been the front door of the house across the street from the Bone Carver. Not exactly where she'd been intending.

Jo spun in place, as if she could levy some strongly placed words against the Door for such a delivery, but it was already gone. A cheerful wreath of pine boughs greeted her and anyone else who was to come up the stairs of the little picturesque New England home. A shiver ripped through her, bringing Jo's hands up to grab her arms, rubbing up and down.

The cold bit right through her hoodie, almost mocking the thin fabric. She turned again, looking out into the street. Looking for help and answers that weren't there.

Twisting her wrist, Jo checked her bio band, confirming what she already knew to be true—she was clocked out of time. Which meant there should be no possible way she felt the cold. She was supposed to be a specter, protected by the veil that stood between herself and reality.

Jo gritted her almost-chattering teeth. It didn't really matter if she felt cold or not—her comfort didn't affect her mission. And that was all that mattered right now.

Fumbling with the USB in her pocket, Jo made her way across the street. Just like with Wayne, she ascended the stairs to the porch and held out her hand in front of the Bone Carver's front door. It took an agonizing moment, but eventually the Door appeared before her.

"We'll do this just like last time," she commanded firmly, clearly picturing walking through the front door and ending up on the other side.

The numbers on the pin pad sharpened into focus—albeit a slightly hazy focus—but focus nonetheless. Jo took a deep breath and willed her fingers to move. Her hands were trembling, from cold or from nerves, and utterly protested her commands.

Jo watched her fingers as though they weren't even connected to her body. It seemed like someone else's hands, someone else's nerves. There was something in her pulling the ropes holding her together hair-thin, and the longer she was in reality, the weaker it all became.

The first number depressed. Then the second. And then the third. Jo felt her magic interacting with the Door, coaxing it to take her where she wanted to go—not just where it wanted to show her or thought she meant. Her aura of magic stretched beyond her, wrapping around the paint-flaked posts of the porch and seeping through the house's front windows. The Door was an immovable force, a sort of dark matter that she couldn't see through or interact with on a magical level. But she had to. She *would*.

As if on magical tip-toes, Jo pushed forward, just a little more, fighting for the last numbers.

"Come on. . . " she pleaded, feeling like she was mentally pounding her fist against a wall of bulletproof glass. Each reach deep into her magic was another desperate strike, until—

One of the taught reins on her magic snapped, the glass shattering beneath her fists. The world tipped, feeling suddenly off balance. It was as if she'd pushed too far and broken an illusion she hadn't even realized was there. A typhoon was suddenly raging within her, trying to rip her to shreds. It felt impossible to contain, despite how Jo furiously reeled it in. She could have sworn she saw rippling tendrils of pure energy coming off of her in waves.

In a frantic attempt to regain control of the quickly spiraling situation, Jo pushed a button on the pin pad—any button. It may have been all the buttons. In her mad dash for the handle of the Door she may have slapped her palm across the pad. Sparks crackled, not unlike they had with the monitor, wrapping around her hand, arcing to the Door.

She stepped through hastily and felt the unnerving sensation of being ripped across reality a second time.

Breathless, the Door deposited Jo into a bar. Judging from the thick Southern lilts, it was somewhere in the United Federation of North America—yet another corner of the continent she'd never dreamt of stepping foot in. Men and women danced, others congregated around the bar; the crowd was densest around monitors projecting the match of two ride-on robots in a ring somewhere.

*Mission.*

Jo turned, daring to hold out her hand. The Door appeared—not with a slow fade into existence as it had all times before. But with a sort of crackle, like ice breaking off a wall.

She pressed some numbers into the pin pad, hoping for more instinct than magic. While there was no more magic lightning netting her fingers, the Door didn't exactly do her any favors. It groaned on its hinges as it opened, ringing in her ears and pulling her through almost violently. All at once, it left Jo dizzy and disoriented in yet another new place.

A familiar scent tickled her nose, adding to the odd juxtaposition of familiar and foreign. The aroma of spices intermingled with the crisp chill of the wind, the earthy scent of poblano peppers about to be made into *chile rellenos*. It overwhelmed her senses into hyperfocus, easing Jo into her surroundings as the delicious smell wafted past.

The market was bustling, upbeat music filtering from a radio above one of the booths. The words were unfamiliar, a tongue her mother had been fluent in but had never truly passed down to Jo, but she almost recognized the tune. And that, somehow, allowed her to finally recognize where she was.

Though she hadn't been to visit since her *abuela*'s funeral, it felt as though she was with Jo now, holding her hand in a warm and wrinkled grip as she led her down streets filled with colorful houses and even more colorful people. This was the Juarez Jo had explored with childlike awe; this was the city with beautiful music and delicious food that only *abuela* knew how to replicate once they were all back home in The Lone Star Republic. This was Chihuahua, and it felt so much like home in that moment that Jo thought she might cry.

Jo's eyes fluttered closed, breathing in the scents and sounds so familiar and unfamiliar all once. It felt like *pastel de tres leches* on her birthday, or her grandmother's soft voice singing *A La Nanita Nana* every Christmas Eve. It was like a far-away dream, one that Jo would wake from the moment she opened her eyes. Her family, her mortal family. Somewhere, across time, she'd had another family.

Her hand flew up to her face, covering half of it. With one eye, she saw the present. The energy of the market filled with vibrant pieces of art and towering piles of fruits and vegetables, the colorful dresses that her mother used to make her wear when she was little before Jo began demanding to wear jeans.

She could hear the music, switched now to a heavily brass instrumental tune, and felt as though the quick-tongued conversation of those around her only added to the melody. The aroma of food she hadn't eaten in years, the sound of her mother's native tongue, all things to remind her of a home she'd once loved more than anything.

Yet, with the other eye obscured by her palm, it was like she could almost make out shapes in the darkness behind her lid. Other people she'd loved. Individuals who, while not family in the conventional mortal sense, were family nonetheless.

Jo spun, dropping her hand and trying to cast away those haunting shadows. Holding out a hand, she willed the Door to appear. With a flicker, it solidified into existence.

"One more time, gently now." She wasn't sure if she was reassuring herself, or bartering with the door. Whatever it was, it worked.

The Door opened and shut, and Jo found herself standing in a familiar entryway. She'd never expected to be happy about being in the home of a serial killer. But given the week she'd had, and the whirlwind of emotion the Door had thrown her into, she was ruling off every impossibility on her list.

Rather than beginning to search the house for what she needed, knowing she should get to work on her hacked solution to what should be a nearly impossible task, Jo walked over to the couch in the sitting area to the left of the door. She dropped onto the cushions and leaned back. She couldn't actually sink into them without using time, and that was something Jo didn't want to risk for multiple reasons—her current streak of bad luck being chief among them.

Instead, she closed her eyes and just took a moment to breathe. Her first hurdle had been crossed. Not gracefully, mind you. But crossed without any sort of major desk-level mistakes.

The USB almost felt hot under her fingertips, as if it were urging her onward. Jo stood at its silent (hopefully imagined) behest. She was a third of the way there.

But the last two thirds would be subsequently more difficult than the first.

The artificial intelligence androids ran on was, put simply, a work of art. It started out as a kernel, a seed, that housed all the information on the world wide web in its casing. Then, a learning algorithm was applied overtop (simple to say, not so simple to do, as her corporate espionage hacker friends would assure her). From there, the AI grew, much like a regular human child. It gathered experiences, learned from them, formulated reason and morals and ethos —all the things that made humans, human. Primus Sanguis was no different, but comparing it to basic AI was like comparing Chopin to whatever the pop hit of the day was.

All of this meant that the androids didn't need any kind of terminal. Like a regular human, their bodies were bioengineered to be self-contained. They fed off biological fuels, they learned through osmosis from the world around them. They didn't need to plug in to anything, ever.

But they *could.*

And as far as Jo was concerned, that was their power—the ability to constantly refill and refresh their endless database of information from the web, and store backups of collected memories as well. To process it all with the power of a supercomputer, and make real-time adjustments day to day based on what would best suit the world around them. Every day, mankind produced more than 4 exabytes of data, and that kind of transfer was much too large to go over the air efficiently.

"Where is your terminal?" she whispered.

If the Bone Carver had a terminal he plugged into, it likely would be hidden somewhere. The information stored on there about the android's state could be deadly in the wrong hands, and her serial killer seemed too smart for that. Jo started on the first floor, wandering through closets and guest rooms, clocking into time only as needed to (very lightly) tap on walls where she thought there was enough space for a hollowed-out alcove. She'd come during the day, meaning the man was at work, but she still didn't want to draw attention to herself.

When the downstairs proved a bust, Jo headed up. It was the more likely candidate since his bedroom was upstairs. Despite her most thorough search, she found nothing.

Jo looked around the master bedroom, from the well-manicured closet to the meticulously made bed. Everything was perfect, not a thing out of place. It didn't even look lived in.

It didn't even look real.

But what was real anymore? Jo closed her eyes with a groan, covering them; now was *not* the time to have an existential crisis. Taking a shuddering breath, Jo fought against the gremlins that screamed between her ears whenever she lingered in darkness for too long. Voices and languages she'd never heard and didn't understand were spoken from mouths she didn't recognize. It was as if her mind and memories were slowly being fed to that inky soup, and what was being regurgitated back made little to no sense.

Jo opened her eyes, reminded herself to focus, and turned for the bedroom door.

There, where the door should have been, was *the* Door. Capital D. As if it were waiting.

"Now you're mocking me." It was somewhere between a whisper and a growl.

The Door stood, unassuming and silent. It gave her no response, but it did not disappear either.

"I don't even know if the terminal has its own room. For all I know it's hidden behind his headboard." *Why am I even talking to the Door?*

USB in hand, hoodie straining against her back with how deep she was trying to dig her palms into the front. Jo stepped over to the Door.

"The terminal," she commanded. "Nothing else." Jo reached out a hand, the USB curled in three fingers, her index pointed to enter in a pin code that she trusted would come to her at any moment.

So much trust—that was her first mistake. The second was even thinking it was a remotely good idea to have her USB drive, the thing she depended on most, anywhere near the Door that had been doing nothing but toying with her like some sentient trickster. But Jo wasn't thinking quite clearly. And in the seconds before the inevitable, the idea of letting go of the USB stick seemed just as egregious an error.

Magic sparked and sizzled between her finger and the pin pad. It shot into the electronic she was holding in her hand. Plastic and circuits exploded like shrapnel, digging into her skin. Jo let out a cry, both in pain and anger. She held her bleeding hand—at least, she'd expected there to be blood.

She looked down at her palm, at the impossible angles of plastic jutting from her skin. There was no blood. It was like her flesh had turned into the most grotesque Jell-o mold and USB bits were the filling. It hurt, but there was no blood.

"Wh-what's happening to me?" she whispered. And then, louder, Jo shouted at the Door, "I needed that you piece of—"

A cracking noise cut her short. Jo turned to the window pane at her left. It fractured, like thin ice in the winter, and then shattered. The house's alarm went off like a screeching bell. Jo turned back to the Door—but it was gone, vanished completely.

Jo slapped her palm against the Bone Carver's bedroom door. "Come back, come back," she demanded. "How am I supposed to get out of here?"

Suddenly, the alarm stopped. Jo looked to the window, confirming that the cracks were still there, that she hadn't fallen into some weird time-loop. They were, which meant the alarm had been disarmed manually.

She didn't have a chance to contemplate what that actually meant, because the bedroom door opened to put her nose-to-nose with the Bone Carver. He stood, staring right at her—not through, not beyond, not anywhere else but *at* her. As if he could—

"So it's you again," he said, with an almost playful smile.

# TRADE

J o didn't respond.

She just stood there, mouth agape, staring at the man in the doorframe. She felt like prey, frozen before a predator she believed would not attack her if she didn't move. In turn, he simply stood as well, doing nothing more than smiling—as if seeing her was some kind of happy accident. Like she was a friend who had stopped by to return a sweater or drop off a card.

"Is there something I can help you with?" he asked.

"I-I-I . . ." She took a large gulp of air, swallowed it hard and tried to pull herself together. "Can you see me?"

"What kind of a question is that? Of course I can see you."

Jo raised her wrist. She gave the Bone Carver one last long stare before glancing down just long enough to check her bio band. Sure enough, her stopwatch was not counting down.

She wasn't clocked into time.

"Perhaps we should go downstairs?" He stepped back, motioning toward the stairwell. "We can have a seat in the living room. I imagine it would be far more comfortable than standing here, and I can sort out whatever it is you require."

Jo's eyes darted between his hand in the stairwell. All she could remember was Wayne's comments about sitting people down before carving them up. Jo didn't even know if she *could* be carved up, could be killed at all. But if the USB was any indicator, she could feel some pain at the very least. She also didn't have many options, given how the Door was acting.

So she took his suggestion and started down the stairs. All the while Jo could feel his eyes on her back. It was the longest fifteen stairs in the history of mankind.

"You're actually lucky you caught me," the Bone Carver said as he brushed by her, heading into the kitchen. He continued their conversation by projecting his voice, until Jo followed to stand in the doorframe. "I was just coming home from work, stopping in before I head out to happy hour with a few friends. The alarm went off right as I was pulling in. I can imagine what the police would've done with you."

She would've preferred the police.

"I. . . Do you know who I am?" It was a weird question to ask, because of course he didn't know who she was. She barely knew who he was.

"Not quite. Where are my manners?" The man quickly wiped his hands on a dishtowel before crossing over quickly and holding out a hand. "The name is Charlie. And you are?"

"Um, Jo." She only gave him her nickname. Even if she no longer existed in this world, the friends and family she loved still did, and the last thing Jo wanted to do was tell a serial killer where her mother lived (regardless if the woman remembered her or not).

"Jo," he repeated. "A pleasure to meet you, Jo. Would you prefer coffee or tea?"

A jarring layer of non-reality settled over her. This couldn't be real; it wasn't real. There was no way this interaction was actually happening.

"Jo?" he repeated when he didn't get an answer.

"Oh, coffee please." She didn't really want to take anything from the man, but she also didn't want to risk setting him off by refusing him. Maybe the caffeine would wake her up from whatever dream she had fallen into.

"Perfect. Black?"

"Sure." Jo paused and watched him make coffee. Once more, the normalcy of the situation only served to create further confusion and panic. It didn't feel like she was a member of the Society and it didn't feel like he was a serial killer. It felt like they were two friends catching up. "When I asked if you know who I am, I didn't mean my name."

"What did you mean?"

"I meant. . ." Jo trailed off. Everything she could think to say sounded insane, but what was happening was already certifiably insane, so she might as well lean into it. "Do you know that I'm not human?"

"Neither am I," he responded easily—almost too easily. Jo had assumed the Bone Carver would be keeping his android identity a secret in order to keep the police off his tail.

"I don't mean in the way that you do," Jo clarified but not really. "I mean that—"

He held up a hand stopping her. "I think I see what's going on here."

"You do?"

"My sensors can pick up that you're not human, but the electromagnetic signature that you give off is . . . How to put it? Unlike anything else I've ever seen before. Your existence appears to me as an orderly list of impossible contradictions." He paused as the coffee pot sputtered and stopped percolating. He continued speaking as he poured two mugs. "I think I spoke incorrectly. It isn't unlike anything I've ever seen before. This anomaly has been presented to me once already, in another entity. He called himself the Wish Granter."

Snow. Charlie remembered Snow. But of course he did. Time had not been rewritten yet, so this was still a man who remembered making a wish —a wish that had yet to be granted.

He crossed the kitchen, handing her one of the two mugs, before starting toward the living room. Jo was helpless to do anything other than follow. She was genuinely curious now about what the man knew and what he had seen in Snow with his sensors—what he was also seeing in her.

Or, the more obvious question of what had broken in her magic that was making her be able to interact with real world objects without being clocked into time. Whatever that was, she doubted Charlie could tell her.

"So, was I wrong to assume that you are an assistant to the Wish Granter? Should I have left my alarm running?"

"No, you're not wrong," Jo said, hastily sitting on the sofa opposite Charlie's chair. "I suppose you could say I'm his assistant."

"You suppose?"

"Well, there's more than one of us, were more like a team that he commands."

"How interesting." Charlie sounded genuinely fascinated by this tidbit of information. Jo could almost see the digital pathways in his head making note of it. "What are you, then?"

"It's . . . hard to explain." Jo couldn't help a glance at her bio band again. She was still clocked out of time. Something had gone haywire. Really, really haywire. "If I'm honest, I don't even quite know how it is that you see me right now."

"What do you mean?"

Of course he wouldn't understand, he had only interacted with Snow. As far as he knew, all entities like Snow shared the same signature, could all be seen, and could all grant wishes.

Jo took a sip of her coffee, using the time to collect her thoughts. She wondered how much she should tell the man. Was it dangerous to impart knowledge of the Society to him? When time was reset, he would certainly forget it. Furthermore, it wasn't as though he could hunt any of them down. And even if he could, they were on his side.

With the mere thought of being on his side, Jo was forced to remind herself what this man was: a killer.

But, in a way, so was she. Even if she excluded the Society, how many people had died, or had their lives ruined, because of the choices she'd made? Because of the people she'd helped with her "odd jobs"? Gray areas stacked on gray areas until her existence seemed like a veritable wall of ambiguity.

"We have a sort of time system," Jo started cautiously. "If we're not utilizing it, we shouldn't be able to interact with the real world."

"Real world?"

"Your world."

"If this is my world, what is your world?" He spoke as though he were a professor, debating a thesis.

"We exist outside of time."

"Interesting. . ." He tapped his fingers on the arm of the large wing-back chair. "Perhaps that is why your data on my sensors seems to be so contradictory. Time is a funny thing, virtually indescribable by science. It can break down even the greatest of equations."

Jo had never thought of her existence from a scientific perspective. She had been offered the explanation of magic from the beginning and had never questioned otherwise—never sought an alternate explanation.

"Perhaps. . ."

"So I can presume your presence here has something to do with the wish I have made?"

"Yes. I was—" the memory of the USB came back to her "—simply collecting some information."

"Is there any that I could provide you that may be helpful?"

Her mind whirled around the possibilities. She could learn his motive. She could find out who he was going to target next and throw the police off the trail in advance for the sake of the wish. She could procure his help in testing her code before implementing it, to increase the possibility of success.

But all of that related to the wish. And the wish was not what was important to Jo at that moment.

"I need you to do some research."

"Me?" The man seemed surprised, albeit a little intrigued. "What information would you want me to gather? I didn't realize the wishing wasn't full-service."

"You offered to help," she pointed out. "And it will increase the speed and efficiency at which your wish is granted." She took another sip of her coffee, hoping he didn't call her bluff.

"Very well, what is it that you wish for me to research?"

Jo leaned forward, back straight. Her mind was moving fast, faster than it had in a long time. There were many things that she wanted to process and find out information about. But she went with the first thing that came to mind.

"I need you to pull up information on mythologies. Specifically, cross-reference different cultures—both modern and historical—looking for references to sacred arrows, goddesses of the hunt, and wars between divinities."

"How is this going to help with my wish?" he asked, rightfully skeptical.

"It's a magic thing," Jo answered ambiguously, hoping he would accept the explanation at face value.

He did, at least for a moment. "Very well, but I have something I would like to ask of you in return."

"Are you trying to barter?"

"I have a sneaking suspicion you're using me for something not related to my wish."

"What do you want?" Jo asked, rather than confirming or denying that particular suspicion.

"You said there were more of you . . . I would like to see someone else."

"Why?"

"Because you're fascinating. Seeing you shows me there's much more out there—others who look like humans but are categorically not."

The way he said it made him almost sound . . . lonely. There was a sort of desperation to the idea that there were other people out there who weren't human, but were equally sentient. Equally worthy of life and their own autonomy.

"If you do that," he added. "I'll look up whatever you want."

Jo knew all she had to do was reemphasize her request's importance to the wish, and he would cave. Every whisper of her magic assured her as much, as if highlighting the places she needed to push to get him to break and give in. But instead, she found herself agreeing.

"All right, I'll bring someone else back."

"When?"

"I'll do it now." No time like the present. Furthermore, the time on the wish was counting down steadily. As soon as it was granted, she would lose access to the Bone Carver as he lost his memories of her and the Society altogether.

"Then I'll get to work as well." He took another long sip of his coffee and stood.

Jo started for the front door, not even worrying about the Door appearing over top. She felt level once again, in control. Perhaps that was an illusion. But it was the most reassuring thing she'd felt all day.

She had a plan of action. But more importantly, she had a source of information—real information and research—outside of the Society and away from Pan's seemingly omniscient gaze. She would've exchanged a lot more than bringing another member of the Society to the Bone Carver for that.

Now, the only question in her head was who it would be.

# SIGNATURES

Being back in the Society almost felt jarring.

She had told Wayne the Society had begun to feel like the real world, and everything else a dream. But one interaction with a real, living, breathing human (well, android) had erased that feeling almost entirely. Out there, that's what was real, that's what they were fighting for—a chance to live a normal life once again. To breathe clouds of white air in winter and to be known by more than just the seven people in the mansion.

Or, if nothing else, they'd die on their own terms when the Society was brought to its unnatural end. It may not be a fair decision to make for her fellow Society members, but Jo suspected they would all rather go out fighting than be slowly picked off one by one at Pan's discretion. Freedom or death—how often had that been a rallying cry throughout time?

First things first: There was no point in further worry over what could or would happen next until she figured out a way to actually destroy the Society, or fundamentally change it.

Jo pushed away from the Door and started through the empty briefing room and down the hallway. Her reprieve was minor; there was no time for breaks. Now was the time for action—and action, Jo had decided, meant finding Takako.

Really, she had only two options—Wayne or Takako. They were the only two who knew about her mission to destroy the Society and had any reason to assist her as a result. Given Wayne's earlier reactions toward the Bone Carver—*Charlie*, Jo mentally corrected—she didn't want to invite him into Charlie's home. Takako, however, was the one who had also identified the idea that those in the Society lived in a glass house, and shouldn't throw stones at a vigilante. Additionally, Takako seemed far more eager and invested into the idea of dismantling the Society.

Jo popped her head into the common room. Eslar and Samson sat on the couch. The former was stretched out on the cushions, a book in hand. The latter tinkered away with something he had spread out on the low table in front of him.

Sneaking away without being noticed, Jo headed toward the bedrooms. She went all the way to the end of the hall and knocked on the door. It opened promptly.

"What is it?" Takako asked, straight and to the point, but not harsh. Jo liked the tone; it was the voice of someone who was ready for action.

"I need your help with something," Jo said firmly.

Takako picked up on the unspoken matter and merely nodded. She didn't question, didn't object; she simply followed behind Jo as Jo headed back toward the briefing room. Miraculously, there was no one in the hallways, and no one to stop them.

Yet Jo couldn't help but feel as though they were being watched. Ever since she had made the connection that Pan had some sort of ability to look in on them, Jo was suspicious of everything. She didn't know if it was just the recreation rooms, or the whole of the Society. Either way, Jo was taking no chances.

"We're going out?" Takako asked.

"Yes, there's something I need you to do."

Takako merely nodded.

Jo found herself hesitating, hand hovering over the keypad of the Door. She had yet to fill in Takako about her magic going awry. It was a fact that now seemed even more urgent, given the malfunctions of the Door and the fact that the Bone Carver could see her even when she wasn't clocked in.

With a breath, Jo pushed the hesitation away and keyed in the numbers. If Takako was going to find out, Takako would find out. There was no time for second-guessing; she had to make every moment count, and she would cross every bridge as it came.

Opening the Door, Jo was pulled through, Takako at her side. They landed in the small foyer of Charlie's house.

"Sure, now you work right," Jo muttered over her shoulder at the already fading Door.

"What was that?" Takako asked.

"Nothing, it's not important." It likely was very important, Jo admitted to herself, but she would share that knowledge when the time was right. And now was not the time. Now was the time to find Charlie, but he was no longer in the living area.

"What are we doing here?"

"You have to meet him," Jo said simply.

"What?" Takako came to a full stop, almost rearing back. "Meet *him*? You mean the Bone Carver?"

"Yes. I promise it will all make sense—" Jo was cut off by an interjection from behind a door down the hallway.

"Jo? Is that you?" Charlie's voice called.

"Yes, I'm back."

"Come on in."

Takako gave her a sidelong look, pointedly glancing down at Jo's bio band. Jo had no doubt that she was making careful note of the fact that Jo had yet to clock into time. And, as if to emphasize the fact, as if to alleviate some of the burden of explaining what was going on, Jo held up her wrist to confirm her time wasn't being used.

"How?" Takako whispered.

"I don't know." Jo wished she had an answer for the other woman. She wished she had an answer for herself. But she didn't, and that fact must have been apparent since Takako didn't ask any further questions.

At the end of the hall, Jo came face-to-face with the door she and Wayne had only a day earlier speculated was where the Bone Carver did his work. This time, it wasn't shut tight, but left halfway open as an invitation. Gathering her courage, she stepped inside.

They hadn't been wrong, but they also hadn't been right.

This was where Charlie did his work, but that work was not chopping people up. The recreation room came to mind as Jo stepped into Charlie's workspace. There was an entire wall of server stacks, each of them cooled by dedicated fans, no doubt why he usually kept the door closed. Charlie sat in front of five monitors, all of them propped up on the wall. Wires protruded from his side, extending out from under his shirt. Jo was no expert on androids, but she had done enough research to know they had ports on their sides, just under their armpits and hidden by a removable flap of biomaterial. This was the edge above regular humans Jo admired, the ability to plug-in directly.

Charlie glanced over at her, his hands stopping. Even though he was no longer paying attention to the monitors, things still ran on them. Somewhere, in the back of his mind, he was still working on her query and controlled it through the hard wires—or at least, that's what Jo reasoned.

"I'm doing as you asked, but I see you haven't done the same."

"I have." Jo motioned to Takako.

"I—" Charlie paused, squinting slightly. For the briefest of moments Jo held her breath, wondering if he would see Takako too with his incredible sensors. Yet he leaned back in his chair and shook his head. "You said initially that you were supposed to be invisible. Is your friend currently?"

Jo looked to Takako and gave a small nod. Takako gave her a long, hard stare in return, and for the briefest of moments, Jo was afraid she would refuse. But if Takako had drawn a line in the sand, Jo had yet to cross it; she pulled her phone from her pocket and tapped on the screen.

Charlie gasped. "Y-you, that was incredible!" He came to his feet. "Do it again."

"I'm not—" Takako began to protest.

"Indulge him," Jo requested, gently. "Please. He's helping me research information about the Society. I don't trust doing it in the recreation rooms anymore. Pan has information she shouldn't. I'm worried she's watching everything we do in the Society."

Comprehension dawned on Takako's face. She gave Jo a nod and tapped her phone again. Charlie stared with rapt attention as Takako blinked in and out of reality.

"What does it look like to you?" Jo couldn't help but ask. Wayne had speculated about what he thought people saw during their first wish, but Jo didn't want to pass up a chance to hear it from the mouth of an outside source.

"It's like a blink," Charlie said, sitting back down in his chair. "I would say like a glitch on the screen, but it's too smooth for that. It's the sort of transition that makes me wonder if I had looked too quickly to begin with and missed that she had been standing there all along. Magnificent, really. If I wasn't witnessing a demonstration, I would likely miss it."

"Why are you doing what you're doing?" Takako said suddenly, reminding them of her presence in the most jarring way possible.

"What I'm doing?" Charlie glanced at the monitors.

"No, not that—why are you killing people?"

Charlie leaned back in his chair, pushing his fingertips together and pursing his lips. The silence suddenly felt heavy and tense; it was not the shift Jo had wanted, but she had no idea how to regain control of the situation.

"The lives I take," Charlie began slowly, "are not innocent. I suppose, since you are helping me, and you have shown me your secrets, I will share mine with you. I was made in a facility, illegally. My core programming, Primus Sanguis, violates several articles of the Artificial Intelligence Accords of 2040."

"How?"

"The Accords were designed to cap artificial intelligence and the UNA imposed further sanctions of their own. Effectively, it was to ensure that artificial intelligence never exceeded the mental capacity of humans and that there is always a backdoor failsafe. Primus Sanguis violates this principle area. Not only do I have the capacity for reason and feeling, but my programming is also able to adapt such that I cannot be killed—so long as a kernel of my core data remains stored somewhere."

"So why are you killing people?"

"People do not think programs like Sanguis exist in general, and especially not in the UNA. It is the basis for shooting down acts like the ACA."

"You're trying to use your murders to expose Primus Sanguis?" Jo deduced. "Why not just share the code?"

"If I share the code, anyone could use it. There would be truly no regulation or cap. The ability to create life at my level would be in anyone's hands. I'm not sure if that's the right choice for my kind or humanity, either."

"Then what do you want?" Takako asked, sounding genuinely intrigued.

"I want what any citizen should want, to bring this injustice to the attention of my elected officials via discovery in the justice system, and allow them to make regulations knowing the full facts."

"You want the police to find Primus Sanguis by connecting the dots on their own as they hunt you down."

"That is my hope, and that is why I cannot and will not stop until it's done." Charlie looked back at the monitors. There was clearly something unsaid, some grudge that hung onto his shoulders, pulling them down. But neither Jo nor Takako asked. His answer had been satisfactory enough for each of them, enough to quell their worries over working with a serial killer vigilante.

"Have you found anything so far?" Jo asked, shifting the topic.

"On your query? Yes, some things. Early trends indicate there is mention of a 'great evil one' that must be pierced to be killed. Usually, as your initial search request indicated, it is an arrow. However, sometimes it is a lance, or a different projectile entirely. What form this 'great evil' takes also varies, but it's usually related to the end of the world."

Jo put her hands on her hips, processing this information. It was as she had suspected—lore lingered across the ages. But why?

"I have a question for you." Charlie turned to Takako.

"Yes?"

"Why are you different from your friend?"

Takako looked to Jo. "How do you mean?"

"Ignoring the obvious fact that Jo does not need this time function to appear, or cannot use it, you both have different signatures."

"Different signatures? How?" Jo asked, feeling like she was finally on the edge of something genuinely important.

"I cannot say. I don't understand the readings for either of your scans, to be honest. But you read as two different life forms, both unknown, both markedly different."

*Two different life forms.* Jo felt a chasm wider than she had ever experienced while looking at her friend. She turned back to Charlie.

"But you said that my signature was like the Wish Granter's?"

"Yes."

"Wish Granter?" Takako repeated, and then her head jerked toward Jo. "Snow? What does it mean?"

"I don't know. . . yet. . . but I intend to find out. Charlie, continue to run the query, please. Takako, go back to the Society and get Snow." Jo was already on the move, headed toward the front door. Presumably she could use any of the doors in the house to summon the Door, but using the front door just felt right, safer, like it wasn't too needlessly taxing on the magical portal.

"What should I tell him?"

"Tell him to come find me."

"Where will you be?"

"I'm sure he can figure that out." He had done it before, at the Ranger compound. But more than that, he was a demigod. If he couldn't find her, that would indicate something seriously awry.

Yes, he was a demigod, and possessed all the power that entailed. Power that she would soon learn—demand to learn if she must. Because the time for secrets was over.

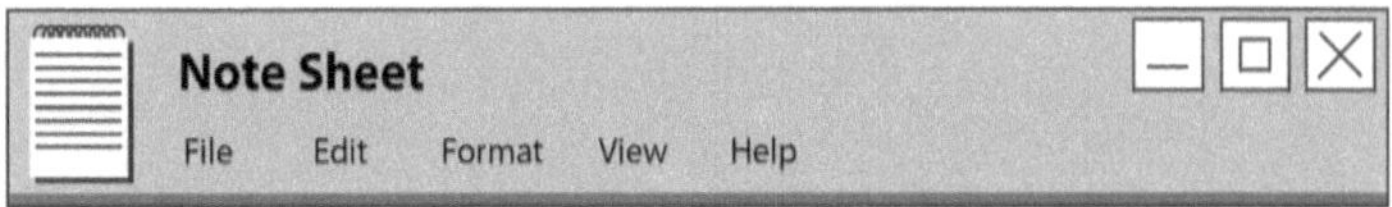


BTCOTS NOTES 5

Asked Samson more about arrows.
No real leads.

**Search Query: GODS OF HUNT**

**RESULT 1: Oshosi**

- *Orisha (reflection of supreme divinity) of Yoruba religion in West Africa*
- *One of two Warriors – "Cool energy"*
- *Warriors was its own special ritual*
- *Greatest hunter*
- *Story involves revenge & mother killing. Dedicates self to innocent & truth in the end*

More here. Worth reading.

**RESULT 2: Arash the Archer**

- *Legends vary*
- *War between Iranians and Turanians over glory*
- *Special bow and arrow constructed by angel – Arash asked to fire*
- *Put life force into shot*

Eslar's book has Goddess (Hunt) construct arrow & give to person (champion).

# ONLY FROM ME

Jo stepped into the dilapidated house in New Zealand.

Just like last time, the floor sagged, the walls' innards were exposed, and it showed no signs of having seen real life in far too long. Yet unlike last time, Jo could feel the wind as it blew through the windows. The floor creaked softly underneath her.

It didn't groan or snap, as she would've expected it to had she been clocked into time. Jo looked to the boards under her feet. She felt her magic assessing it, showing its nature to her in a way that was sight beyond sight. No, it wouldn't break. Which led Jo to wonder, was she somewhere in between time? Not quite in, not quite out? Or would it not break because she didn't want it to break? In a roundabout way, was her magic keeping it together?

The questions for Snow continued to rack up.

She stared out the window, looking to see if she could catch the man winding the almost-there pathway between the tall grasses. When he was nowhere to be found, Jo sighed heavily and turned inside once more. She already couldn't handle the waiting game. She trusted Takako not to do anything rash, really she did. But then again, after what Takako had seen at Charlie's house. . . How could she be sure?

For now, the best thing seemed to be to collect all the scattered pieces of her mind and try to sort them into cohesive questions. She had enough information now, of that Jo was certain. She may not be able to see the whole picture, but she'd put together enough of the puzzle to begin speculating. It was time for Snow to fill in the blanks. Wayne's hideaway was a good place to do her thinking, surrounded by the breezes whistling through the empty windows and the soft sighing of the house settling further into the earth before its eventual collapse.

*A collapse that wouldn't happen for at least a decade more*, her magic assured her. Jo paused as she started up the stairs to explore the second floor. Pausing, she dared to place her hand on the wall.

The wood was smooth, cool to the touch but not damp. She ran her fingers around a knot, inspecting it, feeling it in ways she shouldn't be able to outside of time. Somehow, she knew this place. But perhaps it was merely an understanding of its eventual demise that made it feel more familiar than anything else. Nothing could bring people together quite like death.

The upstairs was in rougher shape. The skeleton of the house was exposed in the raw beams that supported a roof that winked at her with each shift of sunlight through every rusted hole. There were only two rooms upstairs. One was in such bad condition that Jo didn't dare walk on its floor, even in her phantom state.

The other still boasted some life.

Whoever had been here before still clung to their home. The iron poster bed was made perfectly. Dust covered it, turning what Jo could assume was once a cheerful yellow knit into a dirty mustard hue. A rocking chair sat in the corner, waiting for its owner to return.

The house was so quiet, she would've been able to hear anyone and anything for miles. Except for another ghost like her. She closed her eyes and took a deep breath—the scent of cloves reaffirmed what she already knew.

"Hello, Snow."

For a long moment, Snow only stared at her, something indescribable marring his features. Then, a wavering half-smile began to form, looking out of place and difficult to master.

"I was beginning to think you wanted nothing to do with me," Snow said by way of greeting. As he spoke, his eyes fell into a saddened shine, as if he was waiting for her to disappear like smoke. Something Jo didn't know she still possessed fractured deep beneath her breastbone at the sight.

"You know why I didn't, right?"

"I should think the space I gave you was evidence enough." Snow gave a small nod, one Jo returned. *Good*, they had an understanding. It was one small relief in the ball of tension that was wound so tight in her chest that her hands were almost shaking.

"It was," Jo said, putting the final word on the matter. After Nico, and then the wish, it was no surprise really that Snow and romance had been the last thing on Jo's mind. But seeing him before her now, truly alone and incredibly secluded. . . those thoughts bubbled up unbidden and Jo fought to keep herself focused.

And yet, the moment Jo's eyes settled on the man, her once-burning questions became embers that could barely illuminate her thoughts. At more than a glance, Snow's eyes were hollow, listless . . . They were a far cry from the almost monstrous appearance he assumed after he changed reality, but they were just as haunting. It was as if she could see every moment a man should never have to witness reflected back in his gaze.

"How are you handling it all?" Jo hoped the fact that the question was whispered didn't somehow diminish its sincerity.

"Making every attempt to survive." Snow quickly added, "Wishing I could do more to ensure my team survives, too." He looked askance, a silver wave of hair obscuring his eyes. Jo was wracked with the sudden need to reach out to him, to push the hair out of his face and *see* him. She wanted to touch him and comfort him, somehow, even as raw as she felt herself. So she didn't hold back.

"It wasn't your fault." Jo quickly crossed to him, scooping up his hands. Warm, as they always were—steady and unparalleled comfort. The smell of cloves and the warmth of a body now obviously inches from her had all prior thoughts fleeing. "You know that, right?" When he didn't answer, Jo was left tilting her head, trying to catch his gaze, reaching towards where his hair had fallen like a veil between them. "Snow—"

"Of course I know that!" When Jo startled at the outburst, he shook his head, pressing his eyes shut. "It was never supposed to be like this."

"What wasn't?"

Snow shook his head again.

A little inkling wormed its way up from an ugly corner of her brain. It wasn't entirely foreign, yet it also wasn't familiar. Jo became keenly aware of how much he was hurting—how weak that hurt made him.

Like she'd attempted with Eslar, she could nudge the conversation.

No, she could do better. He trusted her, so she could attack under his armor. It wouldn't take much, of that she was certain. Just a few pushes in the right places and she could crack him like an egg—letting his truths ooze out one by one.

"No more secrets, Snow." Jo attempted to straddle the line between demanding and gentle. "I need you to be honest with me."

"I've always been honest with you."

*Honest, maybe, but upfront, no.* Jo kept the bitter thought to herself. "The wishes, Snow."

"What about them?" *There.* It was barely audible, but there was a waver to Snow's voice that hadn't been there with anything else he'd said. She tightened her grip on his hands; she was on the right trail.

"Eslar mentioned once that you don't get to choose them."

Whether he knew he was doing it or not, Snow's grip tightened beneath hers as well. It felt almost like he was clinging. "If I did, do you think I would have ever let Nico die? Do you think I would have given us another task like this, so soon?"

"No . . . But . . . How are the wishes chosen, then?" Snow stiffened beneath her hands and Jo felt him beginning to pull away; she tightened her fingers, forcing him to meet her gaze. "Snow, please."

For a long time, Snow just stared down at her, expressions flitting behind his eyes like the flicker of a candle flame, constantly shifting before they had the chance to take form. When it settled, Jo tried not to feel guilty at the defeat that remained.

"What does it matter?"

"Help me understand," Jo whispered. "You don't have to do this alone. If you tell me about the workings of the Society, the way all of this exists . . . I may be able to help you."

"Help me how?"

"I may be able to destroy it."

Snow blinked, as if she had gone out of focus and was suddenly coming back into clarity. "Jo . . . what did you just say?"

"I want to end this, Snow. I want to free us all from the Society. No more wishes, no more nooses around our necks. You, me, everyone."

Here, Snow finally chose to cover the rest of the short distance between them. He reached forward, cupping one of her cheeks. Jo leaned into the touch easily, like she'd done it a million times. Her eyes fluttered closed, but only for a moment, a desperate part of her refusing to lose sight of him, lest he vanish, a figment of her paranoid imagination all along. Another bit of her fracturing reality to question.

But he didn't disappear; his piercing eyes still scanned her face, silver hair still fell in a motionless cascade despite the breeze Jo knew was blowing. Jo wondered if her hair was motionless as well. It must be, because he said nothing.

"That's not possible."

"You're lying to me." She'd never known anything with more certainty in her life, and Snow's immediate reaction told her everything— the way his gaze seemed unable to stay pinned to her face was proof enough. But even if it wasn't, there was that same feeling she was becoming more and more familiar with. The feeling of seeing weakness in something, *someone*, and recognizing just where to push. "Why are you lying to me?"

"Because, I . . ." Snow took a breath, let it out. He shook his head, then fell silent.

Jo took a deep breath of her own through her nose, then let it out through her mouth in an attempt to keep her temper under control. For the briefest of moments, she considered pushing him away. Instead, she pulled him closer. She pressed their bodies together so tightly that it was nearly impossible to tell where one of them began and the other ended.

Jo sighed softly, feeling momentarily high on the rich scent of cloves that seemed to have permanently soaked into the man's flesh. There were deeper notes, like the spongy moss of a forest, combined with lighter ones, like the fresh crest of seafoam on a wave. Merely smelling him, touching him, evoked so many thoughts and feelings that it was overwhelming.

"Are you afraid to tell me?" she asked delicately.

"I am." Sturdy, assured, his voice didn't falter this time; there were no cracks to push on—he was telling the truth.

"Why?"

"What you are saying is dangerous and would place you directly in harm's way."

"I'm not afraid of danger," Jo insisted. "What I am afraid of—" She choked on her own words, having to force them out. "What I am afraid of is doing nothing. Of losing control. Of my magic. I don't want anyone else to get hurt or die, especially not because of me. But it feels like I'm one step away from shattering into a million pieces and taking everybody down with me."

The words turned into a hasty ramble. It was as if she had built up a dam to hold back her worry and now, in the presence of the one person she trusted more than anyone else, she could let them all out freely. Things she didn't even realize had been heavy on her heart were lifted.

"I will do everything in my power to ensure that no other member of the Society suffers the same fate as Nico." Jo hugged him a bit tighter at their lost friend's name. "But I promise you this. No matter what happens, here and now or years in the future, no matter what judgments befall the rest of humanity, I will protect you. I will make sure you do not suffer the fate of losing who you are."

Jo almost startled at the unbridled genuineness in Snow's tone. It was a tone that settled warm and comforting into her bones, like honey poured into hot tea. But it was also fierce, determined, and it made a different warmth bloom, urgent and low.

"But what if I don't need protecting?" Jo was surprised her voice was so steady, considering the way her heartbeat had begun to quicken, her body starting to ache with the beginnings of need. She clung tighter to Snow's muscled frame and triumphed at the sigh of contentment that escaped him as she did so. His arms mimicked her motion.

"Even then, I would still protect you."

"Do I need protecting now?" It came out teasing, more so than Jo expected considering the roller coaster her heart was currently trapped on, but thankfully, Snow only chuckled. It was a deep sound, vibrating between their chests like a shared and tremulous heartbeat.

"Perhaps only from me." Snow's words would have been concerning in any other circumstances. But the dark growl of sound was filled with welcome implication, playful and bordering on explicit, and all too welcome.

Jo felt another shiver run down her spine and reveled in the fact that Snow had most likely felt it too.

The need for Snow to know how much of an effect he had on her was overwhelming. She wanted him to understand just how easily he could rile her up and then gently pull her back down. She wanted him to realize how completely he filled her thoughts and lungs and heart. She wanted him to know what she was starting to deeply understand on an intimate and unspoken level.

Which was why she could have kicked herself for the next words that tumbled past her lips, the connection from brain to mouth too hazy with desire to control.

"What if you can't?" Snow pulled away just far enough to scan Jo's face in concern, and Jo continued to mentally berate herself for potentially ruining the mood. "Protect me, I mean . . ." She finished lamely, because in for a penny. It was something she wanted to know, *needed* to know, ever since the first time she'd sensed the change in her magic. And after today, after what she'd done, she also needed to know that he would be all right. If something happened to her, if her magic became too much to handle and those dark manifestations in the back of her mind took over, she needed to be sure that Snow would be all right.

Unfortunately, Snow didn't seem willing to follow her train of thought, his eyes pained as he raised both hands to her face, elegant fingers resting gently against her cheeks, her jaw, her neck. Without a word, he leaned in to place a chaste but lingering kiss against her lips. It was intimate and filled with unspoken desire, but also delicate, bordering on fragile, as if he was afraid that *he* would break *her.* As if such a thing could ever be possible.

Before Jo could kiss him more fully, show him how much she yearned, he was pulling back again. Not enough to really even call it breaking the kiss, but just enough for him to speak against her lips, each word a vibration of hot sound passed between their mouths.

"I will *always* protect you," he repeated, kissing her again, another chaste but heartfelt press, before pulling back. Jo almost whined, clinging that much harder to the fabric of his shirt as she pressed against him. "Always, Josephina. In this and every millennia, that is the one thing I will always do."

This time, when he kissed her again, it was hungry, teeth scraping against her bottom lip for a moment before he was pulling away, the both of them left panting. She felt like each kiss wound her up tighter, drowned her in the scent of winter and cloves until she would go mad with it. But still Snow spoke, promised, his lips brushing hers with every word. When his eyes fluttered closed on a sigh, the final heated whispers that drifted between them sounded as involuntary as a breath itself.

"I can't lose you again. Not again. Not after so long."

Jo wasn't even sure he was aware of saying those last words out loud, but before she could ask him what he meant, Snow was pulling her back into another kiss.

# WILL IT BREAK?

I f the last few kisses had been a steady increase in heat, this one was searing, white hot and boiling all the way down to her core, reminding Jo of every hour she had endured without his touch. Jo's nerves came alight with the rush of it, a gripping need taking hold. Every inch of her body not pressed against Snow in some way ached with the need to touch, as if her entity as a whole wished to melt into him, be absorbed by him. She wanted to be as close to him as it was possible to be, surrounded and filled to the brim, and suddenly, kissing wasn't enough.

This time, Jo was the one to pull away, silently pleased at the dazed look of confusion that flashed across Snow's face. His hands refused to move from where they'd settled around her waist, trying not so subtly to pull her back in. Despite the heaviness of the moment and the thick tension in the air, Jo couldn't help but smirk.

She didn't tease, wasting no time in removing her hoodie and shirt, something Snow seemed pleased that she could do without him having to let go. Though when she tugged a bit loosely on his collar, he reluctantly gave in, letting his arms fall away so he might remove his own.

For a long moment, Jo stood before him, taking him in. She let her eyes roam over the near translucent skin of his chest, the strong, corded muscles of his arms, reveling in the sight of him. It seemed so impossible, yet somehow inevitable, to have him at less than arm's length, to be able to reach out and touch him if she so chose. Which she did, desperately.

Jo placed both hands against his chest, letting her fingers spread. Snow inhaled sharply at the sensation and the sound went straight to Jo's core. When she chanced a look up at his face, her breath caught in her throat at the look he was already giving her: pupils blown wide and dark, a soft flush along his face and neck, lips parted just enough to be tantalizing.

Jo couldn't help but lick her own lips at the sight, watching almost in slow motion as Snow's gaze dipped down to watch. And with that simple drop of his eyes, the quick recapturing of her attention, the tension stretched thin and snapped.

There was no telling who moved in first; blissfully, they were kissing again. Though, calling it a kiss was probably a bit of an understatement. Jo had never felt such hunger beneath a kiss, like neither of them could seem to get close enough. It was harsh and devouring and filled with something Jo couldn't describe, despite how achingly familiar it seemed. It was messy, teeth knocking more than once in their neediness, lips already undoubtedly bruised. It was not enough, it was too much.

It was *perfect*.

Jo almost felt guilty for wanting more.

She was in luck, it would seem, because as if listening to her thoughts, Snow's hands began to wander. His fingers dug into the slope of her waist, dipping between skin and the fabric of her jeans to pull her closer by the hips. She felt his thumbs brushing along the sensitive line of the small of her back and she rolled her hips forward in response, moaning low in her throat at the feel of him against her.

Jo reached a hand down between Snow's legs, cupping him there. Instantly, Snow's hand found purchase in the hair at the base of Jo's skull, tugging lightly as he arched into her touch. A groan escaped between their mouths as the kiss deepened, Jo swallowing up his needy sound both physically and mentally. She would save up every sound Snow made, if she was given the chance, lock them all up in intricate boxes inside her head and heart, cherished memories that no harm could ever come to. Never again.

*Again?*

Before Jo's mind could wander into the thicket of her already tangled thoughts, Snow was breaking their kiss and pulling back, though only enough to rest his forehead against hers.

"Josephina." The sound of her name in his voice, strained and rough and impossibly low, had that heat inside her growing more insistent. She could practically taste his voice on her tongue, passed from his mouth to hers in panting breaths. "Let me take you to bed," he said.

Jo wanted nothing more, was pretty she'd never wanted anything as much. But—

"Here?" Jo motioned around, at the decrepit shack, at the floor near to crumbling, the ceiling all but collapsed. Snow just smirked.

"Now."

She looked over Snow's shoulder at the bed, once well cared for despite now being as time-worn as the rest of the place. Outside of reality, there would be no dust, no grime, no danger, like a layer of time and space between them and everything they touched besides each other.

And yet. . .

"What if I break it?" Jo asked in a whisper, voice small. Snow followed her gaze to the bed, the cracking floorboards beneath it, and saw what she saw: any actual, physical weight on it would probably send it crashing down to the first floor. There was no reason to believe that they would weigh anything at all, but Jo couldn't seem to stop herself from thinking about the middle ground she now seemed to occupy—real but not.

All of a sudden, a touch was gently ushering her attention away from the bed and back to silver eyes and a fond smile. Jo added that smile to one of her cherished memory boxes, just in case.

"Nothing will break," he said. "Trust me."

A long moment passed, and then Jo nodded, sealing her decision by recapturing his lips. She would put her trust in him—hand her magic over to him so it couldn't get away from her if that's what it took.

*Hand her magic over to him. . .* the thought resonated oddly in her mind. But Jo chased it away with need.

It took less than a second for their previous hunger to return. It felt almost wanton in its potency, animalistic, like her body had taken control of her mind and led them both on autopilot towards the bed. She barely recognized their clothes being removed, barely felt the bed beneath her back as she laid herself down, reaching out for Snow to follow and whimpering into his mouth when he did.

All she could think, feel, *breathe* was Snow. The sensation of his hands trailing across her sensitive skin. The trembling whisper of his voice in her ear and the almost bruising indents of his fingerprints on her thighs.

By the time he was easing his way inside her, her whole state of being had narrowed down to a single point of sensation, a liminal space between existence and non-existence where it was just her, Snow, and the feeling of complete connection binding them together.

When he shifted against her, pulling back just enough to thrust in deeper, Jo unraveled. Each movement had her crying out, sometimes just broken moans, other times a fragmented variation of Snow's name, but always loud, always needy and pleading. She would be embarrassed, surely, if she could hear herself, but the building desire for release was a solid enough distraction. In fact, as Snow picked up the pace, slinging one of her legs under the bend of his arm for leverage, she could think of little else.

Jo's other leg wrapped around the small of his back, ankle digging in probably enough to hurt, but she couldn't help herself, trying to pull him in as close as she could. She wanted him to thrust harder, to leave marks, to break her down until nothing else remained but the feel of him against her. Her hands clung to his back and shoulders, nails probably scratching red lines into his pale skin, and she was suddenly consumed by the thought that she was breaking *him* down. That when they fell over the edge together, they might never come back.

She also thought that, maybe, that wouldn't be so bad.

"Snow . . . Snow, please," Jo gasped. She already felt so close, a hair trigger just waiting for that final bit of pressure. Jo may have slept with a few men in her before-life, but she had never felt such a thoroughly rooted need. It was like her body had an unknown craving that only Snow could fill.

"Together," Snow panted in response, the staccato of his hips already losing rhythm. "Please, Jo. I want—" It sounded like begging, the cut-off plea almost sending Jo over the edge all on its own. And she wanted to, she was so close, so *close*, she just needed that little bit to—

Amidst the roll of their hips and the grind of their bodies, Snow inched a hand between them, offering Jo the last bit of what she needed.

It was not quite a tumble, though hardly a plummet. This fall into ecstasy was the first drop of a roller-coaster, the tandem jump of a skydive. Jo fell fast and hard, whole body tensing and back arching off the bed, but she fell with a deep-seated comfort, a contentment that kept her warm and buzzing from the high even long after she'd come back down.

She had just enough cognizance in the aftermath to feel Snow tense above her, lips mouthing Jo's name into her neck on a ragged exhale. Then, with an equally contented sigh, Snow was pulling out and away, draping an arm over her waist as he collapsed into her side. Jo thought it only fair that she return the favor, cuddling up to him as best she could and soaking in the first quiet her mind had experienced in what felt like weeks.

A quiet that was not meant to last.

"Snow?" Jo whispered into the silence after what could have been hours. A small part of her cried out in anger at bringing an end to their blissful calm, but that part was a whisper compared to the questions rising up again from the tide of her unsettled mind. Still, she tried to keep them in their bubble, away from time and responsibility. She drew soft circles against his chest with the tip of her finger and tried not to think that she was ruining things.

When he hummed a warm sounding, "*Mm?*" into her hair, Jo almost lost her nerve, but she swallowed it back, opting for watching her own gentle ministrations rather than looking him in the eye.

"What did you mean?" she asked, hating how timid her voice sounded, how her heart raced. "When you said you couldn't lose me *again*. . . when you said that it had been so long. It's not the first time you said something like it. What did you mean?"

When he tensed beneath her at the question, she was hardly surprised. Even less so when he chose not to answer. In the silence, something bubbled to life behind the cherished boxes of memories, somewhere far, far back in the shadows of her mind. Jo tried to ignore it, tried to feel only Snow, as she had before, but the tickling at the edge of her memory was persistent. Eager.

"Snow, I told you, I need answers." It might be an unfair play, given the circumstances, but she was desperate. His arms tightened around her, as though if he held her tightly enough it could appease her and he could avoid giving her the answers she sought. Jo sighed softly. "How am I supposed to love you the way I used to when I don't even know who I am?"

*Love you? Used to? Who I am?*

Jo had no idea where those words had even come from, let alone what they meant. And when Snow continued to lay beneath her without response, body still tense and breaths pulled so slow he might as well have not been breathing at all, she expected to look up and see her own confusion reflected back at her.

What she did not expect was the look of pure, unbridled horror on her lover's face.

# AGE OF GODS

J o swallowed; her throat had gone dry. "Say something," she part-begged, part-demanded. She'd never hinged so much on the next words of anyone; it felt like everything she was could be undone by whatever sounds his lips decided to make.

"Jo . . ." Her name was a pained whine. Snow pressed his eyes closed, as if unable to bear for a moment longer the idea of merely looking at her. In contrast, his hands still sought her out—running up her bare thighs, his thumbs caressing the indents at her hips.

"Snow." She punctuated his name by grabbing his hands and stopping all movement; the bliss had lifted. The reassurance of their relationship—whatever, exactly, it was—couldn't settle her. The foundation of her world was too shaken to get lost in it again so soon. "I know you're trying to protect me, even though I don't know from what. And I believe that, in some way, you feel that you're doing me a favor by saying nothing. But things are changing—" Her voice dropped to a quivering whisper, but Jo did not let it break or fizzle. "And I need your help now. Please, Snow. I need more than, than *silence*."

After a small eternity, he gave a nod.

Jo pulled herself off of him, willfully ignoring the absent feeling between her thighs that came with the disappearance of his presence; even through satiation, she could apparently ache for him. The lust was gone, but the desire for closeness never seemed to fade.

Snow stood, retrieved his pants, and slowly slid them on. He fussed with the buttons at the front, stalling maybe, taking time to work out his words. Jo did much the same. For all she wanted, needed, answers. . . the idea of getting them after what had transpired frankly frightened her.

"You're right," Snow said, having found his resolve somewhere next to his shirt. "This is not the first time we've met."

She didn't quite recall saying that in so few words, but it was a feeling that'd been so clear, Jo knew they were on the same page. In fact, the feeling had been so distinct that Jo couldn't even act shocked or surprised, hearing the truth of it now. "How?"

Her heart was pounding, though she had no idea why.

Snow walked back over to the bed, sitting heavily on the edge. The time-worn sheets didn't rumple under his weight, the floor didn't creak. If anything it looked. . . *better*, with him sitting on it. He placed his elbows on his knees and rubbed his palms over his face, eventually folding them together when he seemed to have calculated his next set of words.

"Do you remember the time I told you I came from?"

She'd only been trying to research it for weeks. "I do. The Age of Gods."

"Yes." Snow stared beyond her, through the window, utterly transfixed by the rolling green horizon.

"I also know things lingered from that Age," she said, trying to summon him back. It worked.

"What?"

"I don't understand it all yet, but I will," she declared, far more confident than she had any right to be. "I know that lore from the Age of Gods has lingered through time, despite all the wishes, all the remade realities. It seems that every culture has overlapping mythologies and stories—too much to be coincidence. I've been trying to boil it down."

"What have you found?" He almost sounded impressed.

"There's one particular story that I keep coming back to. A story of a divine war, and destroying a great evil by shooting it. The names are different in every culture, but the roles are very much the same."

"I should've known you would've begun figuring it out." Snow ran a hand through his hair. "We were named after what we were—Life, Death, Pleasure, Pain. But different mortals decided to give us other names like Horus, Thanatos, or Tlazolteotl."

"Egyptian, Greek, and Aztec."

"You know your mythology."

"I've been researching. And it was the sort of thing my grandmother would tell me." Jo paused, thinking of her *abuelita*. She used to be able to remember the woman with true-to-life clarity, but now. . . She raised a hand to her forehead, closing her eyes. Just one memory. She had to find just one clear memory. "My grandmother . . . Snow, was she really—?"

He was standing before her, pulling her hand gently away from her face, though Jo didn't recall him moving from the bed. He cupped her cheeks, looking down at her with an expression that could only be described as pure serenity—as if he was trying to pour it from his face into her being.

"Yes. And no. Your mortal casing now, that is carrying your immortal soul, was born. You lived life as a human. The memories you made there were real. Well, as real as anything is in a world torn apart and rebuilt."

"Then why does it feel like someone keeps hitting backspace on my brain?" Jo's hands clutched his shirt, drawing deep wrinkles between his collar and his chest. It didn't make sense. She remembered wrinkled hands pushing her hair out of her face. She remembered the smell of the kitchen before dinner, filled with spices. She remembered protective hugs and time-worn stories. Yet somehow the memories seemed faded, like the fraying ends of a dream upon waking.

"When you were mortal, the sliver of your magic that you still carry lay dormant. You were protected out in the world, hidden among normalcy and shielded by your own ignorance. But joining the Society. . . You cast off your mortal casing and now live as an immortal. . . So the memories of your past life—your first life—are returning."

"So I am the same as you, then." Jo thought back to the readings off Charlie's sensors. That she and Snow shared similarities, but not her and Takako. "I'm a demigod."

"You don't seem surprised." If anything, Snow was the one who looked surprised.

"Call it intuition." Jo looked down at her hand, thinking of the desk and everything else that had gone awry.

"If I'm a demigod, then why was I born? Why am I in a, how did you put it, mortal casing?" Her memories were being muddled, pulled apart, like two images overlapped; neither was clear no matter how hard she tried to sort them. Even with the little bit of information Snow was giving her, she couldn't make sense of them. "I feel like I should know, Snow, but I. . . My memories may be coming back, but they're doing so in bits and pieces."

"You were born mortal because your magic threatened to destroy the world—making you mortal was how such a fate was prevented."

Destroy the world. Well. No big deal then. Despite herself, Jo blurted a loud *"HA!"*

"Jo—"

"I'm just a piece of work, aren't I?" Heart hammering and stomach clenching, Jo shook her head. "A demigod that was going to destroy the world? So, then, what? I was put down by the other gods?" She pictured the canine version of herself forgotten in some twisted divine shelter, dragged away by vet techs to be prodded with needles until it was certain she'd stop biting volunteers and just accept her fate.

"Not put down. . ." Despite it all, as Snow spoke, hazy memories began to fill color into his words. A sort of clarity that came from the reassurance of knowing a deep truth at the very core of her essence. "You loved the world, and all its mortals. You feared for them. For while it was your magic that threatened the world, it was not you wielding it that was the true threat."

"The true threat. . ." A conversation tickled the edge of her memory. Jo blinked, trying to pull the images into focus, desperate to read the lips of those speaking in the hopes that she may be able to pull the words out of the ether of her mind. There was truth there that Jo needed, information she craved. Information she was *owed.* "Snow, how were demigods made?"

He had walked over as she'd spoken. Now standing above her, he loomed like a gentle judge—but one who was passing judgment on her fate nonetheless.

When he didn't answer right away, Jo clenched her fists by her side, looking away. "Tell me," she whispered. It was important; it was a binding thread. Every fiber of her being screamed for it. After a long, agonizing moment, Snow relented.

"There were two ways. Birth—well, being carved out of time by greater gods—or by splitting the essence of a god or goddess."

"I was split." The conclusion felt right, memories returning in wide swaths.

"Twice." Snow knelt down, taking both her hands in his, now shifting to look up at her. "You made the ultimate sacrifice. The first time you were split was when you were born as a demigod. Then you allowed yourself to be split again. Because for a demigod to be split is for that demigod to be made mortal. You gave part of your power to me for safekeeping, to use as a tool to destroy the world and with it she who would try to use your power against you. Then I could rebuild everything with my own magic of Creation.

"With the part of your essence you gifted to me kept safely beyond time, your soul would not die, but be reincarnated—ever seeking its other half—and I would find you again in the world to reunite you with your magic and divinity."

"But it didn't work." He winced, even though she hadn't aimed to be harsh.

"It did, and didn't. Because of you relinquishing your power, I was able to bring about an end to the Age of Gods."

It was Jo's turn to mindlessly stare out the window. Processing everything was all too easy, and that almost made it harder. She wanted more resistance to accepting the fantastical claims he was making. But there was too much evidence that it was true. Denying it was pointless. Fruitless.

"Well, here we are," Jo said finally, not quite looking at him, but reveling in the feel of his touch nonetheless. "You ended the Age of Gods and rebuilt the world. And then did it again, and again, countless times in the Society."

He nodded solemnly.

"And yet myths of gods long gone still linger," Jo whispered, swallowing. "And it's still not safe, is it?"

Snow didn't answer right away, eyes shifting to the side almost as if on reflex. Jo knew what that look meant. She'd seen it all too many times from the secretive man. The curiosity she'd pushed aside from earlier came roaring back.

"*She*, you said, the one to use my magic as a weapon. . . You mean Pan?" It was the only thing that made sense. Pan's fearsome power. Her age—both immeasurably old yet childish at the same time. The way she seemed all too giddy from the moment Jo had walked through the door. All the moments Jo had looked at her as if seeing a familiar face.

"Yes. Which is why we must return to the Society soon, so as not to arouse her suspicion."

She suspected it may already be too late for that.

"There's one more thing." If they were putting everything on the table, then it needed to be everything. "You said I wasn't the true threat, that it was Pan. But. . . I may be a threat now."

"What do you mean?"

"My magic is no longer acting like everyone else's. I can affect the real world without clocking in."

"What?" He went stone-faced, his usual pallor became ghostly.

"When Wayne and I were at the police station, for the wish. Outside of time. . . I broke something in the real world. I don't even know how, but I did. Then, when I tried to implement my code, the USB exploded in my hands. It seems erratic and inconsistent, usually breaking things, but not always." Jo left out Charlie. He had his secrets, and Jo would keep hers— for now. Besides, if she needed to lean on Charlie again, Jo didn't want Snow getting in the way.

"Wayne knows?"

The sudden question caught Jo a bit off-guard—given that she would've thought the USB to be the most pressing matter—but still she nodded. "I don't think he'll say anything to anyone else. . ." Jo omitted the fact that *she* was the one to have said something to someone else.

Snow thought it over a moment, and though there was noticeable conflict in his expression, he seemed to come to the same conclusion. "We must be even more careful now. I have been the one carrying your magic all this time, wielding it to destroy the worlds of wishers so that I may rebuild them. I fear our proximity to one another may be drawing it out."

"But couldn't we use this to our advantage?" Jo finally asked. "If I can destroy things, I could bring an end to the Society, and set us free."

"If you destroy the Society and revert the world, Pan will also be set free, which is something we're not prepared to deal with yet. But we'll find a solution this time. I promise you that." With a much less sad smile now, Snow leaned in and placed a kiss on her forehead. When he spoke, she could feel his lips moving against her skin. "And until then, to the best of my ability, I will make sure your magic hurts neither you nor anyone else. As much as I detest restraining you in any way. . . I will do what I can."

"Restraining me?"

"We're . . . natural counterbalances, I guess you could say." Heavy as the words were, his voice was soft, almost reverent. "Once upon a time, at least. Destruction and Creation."

"Creation," she repeated. Something about the name echoed deep within her. It was as if she saw him for the first time. The sound of his name—his true name—on her lips brought a smile to Snow's. "So does that mean you. . . cancel me out?"

Snow frowned, not quite following. "I suppose?"

"So if you needed to, you could keep my magic from going haywire?"

Snow's eyes widened just a hair, as if finally making the connection. "I can. . . temper your magic, yes."

"Temper how?"

"Once more, proximity." His gaze flickered about her face before finally capturing hers. "My magic is the opposite of yours; we're two frequencies that both cancel each other out and stay in harmony. It's how I am able to control the magic you gifted me at all, even marginally. Your magic seeks out mine, as mine does yours, to be balanced."

"So then you can make these odd happenings stop?"

"If I could, I already would've." Snow sighed. "We can't risk things further." The word "things" suddenly seemed to take on a lot of meaning—Jo's magic, the Society itself, Pan's impatience. "For now, sit back on the wish."

It wasn't as if she hadn't already been doing so. The thought of staying away from working on the wish brought her back to the idea of destroying the Society, an idea she wanted to explore further. "Snow—"

"We really should return," he said apologetically. But quickly added. "I promise, we will speak more on this."

His promise would have to be enough, as much as she wanted to object.

"Thank you for telling me," Jo whispered.

"If I'm honest, I should've told you from the beginning."

One statement, and she had never felt more drawn to the man.

Snow and Jo stepped through the door and into the dim lighting of the unoccupied briefing room. Slowly, the mysterious light source in the ceiling came to life, emitting a soft glow just for the two of them.

"Do you control that?" Jo couldn't help but ask.

"Not quite. . ."

She thought back to their previous discussions about the Society. About her conclusions that he was as much a prisoner here as the rest of them. But the way he'd said it minutes ago. . . "Snow—" Jo stopped him, catching his sleeve "—did you make the Society?"

"What?" He stilled, his voice dropping to a whisper.

"Did you make the Society?" Hers dropped as well to meet his and she did another visual sweep of the room—though where someone could possibly hide, Jo did not know.

"Jo, questions are dangerous here."

*That was a no.* Jo remembered what he'd said about Pan. What Jo had deduced on her own. There were eyes everywhere within the Society— eyes with cat-like irises.

Jo relinquished his sleeve, straightening away. How did a demigod get ensnared in a Society against his will? And not just a demigod with his own powers, but half of Jo's as well. By his logic, that should make him almost as powerful as a full god.

Then again, when did logic ever matter when it came to magic?

With the lightest of touches on her sleeve, Snow summoned her attention back to him. Looking at him was almost enough to make her forget everything else. *Almost.*

"We'll talk more later," Snow said in a definitive tone, starting for the door. "For now, wait here. I'll call a meeting to discuss the status of the wish."

With one final squeeze of her hand, Snow headed out the doors and Jo fell heavily into one of the plush chairs. As if on cue, not moments after she sat, the doors to the briefing room opened. Jo had been hoping for a few moments of reprieve alone. But she was wrong. A head of neon-yellow hair turned to face her.

Pan's cat-like eyes seemed to flash red. She'd tied a black bow in her straight locks and donned a ruffled red dress—like an alternate-Wonderland Alice who'd decided to say "screw it" to the Mad Hatter and join the Queen of Hearts instead.

In rare form, Pan met Jo's silence with silence. The air grew heavy, filled with expectation of something unsaid. But whatever Pan was thinking, she didn't feel like sharing and Jo didn't inquire.

Clarity broke on Jo like dawn: the tension, the fact that she felt no surprise at Pan's presence, or the way Pan was staring her down almost hungrily. They both knew what the other knew. While Snow had yet to confirm, Jo would bet everything on the idea that Pan was also a demigod.

Jo opened her mouth to speak, though she hadn't gotten far enough to know what to say. She wanted Pan to know that she was no longer a blind sheep waiting for slaughter. She knew what her power was and she'd levy it against Pan if she had to. That thought stilled her.

If Jo had the chance, she'd unleash every bit of the destructive force inside her on Pan. She'd do it for Nico. *Nico.* . . a disturbing sensation, one of magic fracturing like ice in the Prime Minister's office, came back to her. Jo slowly closed her mouth and pressed it into a thin line.

Pan's lips curled into an almost cartoonish smile, as if she could read Jo's mind.

The silence was finally broken when Snow opened the double doors, the entire group in tow behind him. Jo leaned back in her chair, away from Pan, and made a desperate attempt at looking casual. Her hands had no clue where they wanted to rest and her legs kept folding and unfolding. Just acting normal seemed impossible.

Takako gave her a nod, Samson a small smile, Eslar a look that Jo had come to associate with casual acknowledgment, but Wayne. . . He narrowed his eyes slightly at her. There was an unfamiliar uneasiness about him, as though he knew she'd gone to Takako instead of him. Had she said something to him? Or was it just intuition?

Either way, Jo knew she had to clear the air with him, and soon. At the very least, she needed his good graces long enough to keep his silence.

"I realize this wish has tensions high, making what was already a bad situation far worse, especially following our last wish." Snow wasted no time. He wasn't even at his chair when he began speaking. "I am also well aware that everyone has their own opinions on the wish and its proposed outcome." He rested his hands on the table, looming over them. "It is not our role to have opinions or pass judgment. We are the Society of Wishes, and granting the whims of those who invoke us is our sole duty. Nothing more or less."

He paused, taking the time to look every individual in the eyes. Suddenly the whole team was shifting in their seats, looking anywhere else, fidgeting. Jo's awkwardness seconds ago was effectively masked in one deft move from Snow, and the gratitude she felt toward him had her off-balance once more, now that she was the only person in the room seemingly able to relax.

"Am I clear?"

The group muttered a communal "Yes."

"Good." Snow leaned away from the table, folding his arms over his chest. "Jo has informed me of her failed attempt at hacking the android's terminal."

She didn't have to fake or force a wince and a bow of her head in shame; those came naturally. Though the result of her inability to do so had paid secret dividends.

"Since the time we have left to close the Severity of Exchange is steadily shrinking, I propose we take a different approach."

"We were talking about that while you two were off." Eslar jumped into the conversation. "And we think we have a proposal."

Snow made a motion for the elf to continue, but Takako spoke instead.

"Wayne and I will go forth and engage in activities that would throw off the police and task forces working on the case."

Jo wasn't the least bit surprised that it would be Wayne and Takako continuing to spearhead the action on the wish. It seemed that, regardless of Wayne's growing skepticism toward Jo and her plan, he was still helping her. That was all she needed, for now. That, and his silence.

"Throw off the police? You mean make mayhem?" Pan sat a little straighter. "Well, isn't this a delightful turn of events. . ."

Takako ignored the woman-child, explaining further. "We each have a tactic for trying to shuffle the deck a bit."

"My nickel and I will take on some of the witnesses and friends of to-be victims." Wayne picked up the explanation, giving a flip of his coin for emphasis. "I'll see to it that they forget key details of certain things—put it from their mind, I'll say."

"Meanwhile, I'll make a few selective strikes. I won't target the officers actively involved with the investigation, that'd be too flashy and risk widening the Severity of Exchange. Instead I'll target the family members of those with information, give them the necessary motivation to avoid cooperating with the cops. Then, I'll pick off a few unrelated individuals."

"A-and I'll carve their bones," Samson said, in a voice so small Jo could barely hear him from two seats away. "That way it. . . The motive is unclear. Too much differing information. Unrelated links."

"Strikes? *Pick off?*" Jo frowned. "You're talking about killing people." Takako could handle it, Jo had every faith that the soldier could chew glass if she wanted. But Samson. . . Just looking at his bowed head and unusually still hands told her everything she needed to know.

"It should lower the Severity of Exchange enough." Eslar spoke as if Jo hadn't even opened her mouth.

Jo looked between the elf and their leader. Snow's jaw was clenched, the muscle there pulsing with tension. Finally, he said, "See it done. We'll regroup afterward if the Severity of Exchange doesn't close sufficiently."

"We're talking about killing people on a *maybe* that it'll be enough." Jo tried one last time to interject. "What happens if it's not?"

"Then we try something else," Snow replied briskly, as though the matter should be obvious.

"That's not—"

"The world will be rebuilt regardless, once the wish is fulfilled. It's impossible to say what lives, or possible lives, are lost when the reshuffling happens."

She swallowed her pride and ignored her guilt. It was the same place she'd already landed before—the hands of those in the Society, one way or another, were far from clean. "Good luck, then."

As if they'd been waiting for her blessing—a blessing that clearly didn't matter because the wheels propelling them on the course of action were already turning—Wayne and Takako stood. Jo watched as Takako entered in her code at the Door, Wayne behind her. In less than a minute, they were both gone, to kill and threaten the innocent and protect a murderer. Even the idea of the Bone Carver being somewhat justified was no longer a palatable balm to the situation.

"I'll be waiting in my room," Samson announced. Eslar stood wordlessly with him and the two exited together.

Then, it was just three of them. Jo half expected Pan to make her move, to finish what had so clearly been started when it had just been her and Jo. But she gave a delicate little smile, a flutter of her lashes, then sauntered out of the room as well.

Jo looked helplessly to Snow, alone again.

"Would you like to—"

"I think I need a moment to process everything," Jo interrupted delicately. "There's a lot going on."

He gave her a knowing look, walked up to her, and placed a hand on her arm, trailing it up to her shoulder. "Come to me when you're ready." With a gentle squeeze, as much reassurance as could be given in the moment, Snow left her to the empty briefing room and her thoughts.

"Thank you." Jo didn't know if he'd heard her, or if he was too far down the hall by the time she finally got the words out.

Jo's ankles seemed to wobble a bit as she stood; her joints ached. It was as if her relentlessly tense muscles were finally ripping her limb from limb. Or perhaps, it was her magic that was killing her from the inside out. She was destruction, right? A demigod in a mortal casing, as Snow had said. If her magic could unravel the logics of reality, who was to say it wouldn't do the same with her mortal form?

She paused, looking back to the Door. Not for the first time, she thought about leaving, running away from it all. But for the first time, Jo felt like she actually could. She'd broken the monitor, hadn't she? She was destruction itself; not even Snow had denied the possibility of her success in that regard.

Other than fear of the unknown surrounding Pan, what was really stopping her from tearing apart the whole damn thing?

# THE FINAL PIECES

J o headed to her room for the first time in what felt like months.

She needed a bit of a reprieve, needed to breathe a moment and process everything she'd uncovered over the past three days, and everything that Snow had told her. Opening the door, Jo barged in without a thought.

And was brought up short.

The clicking of the door latch barely registered to her ears. Jo stared dumbly at the foreign tapestries. Her eyes scanned over the sweeping arched architecture, searching for something, all the while not knowing what exactly. She spun, taking in the lavish furniture, curling columns, and vast beyond outside her windows.

"What. . . is this?" Jo whispered, looking at the river rocks that made up the room's foundation. Her attention drifted from bottom to top, looking at a mural painted in careful detail on her ceiling.

Stars spotted on a blue-black canvas of sky, swirls of light radiating out from them in softer shades. It was similar to the hand that had painted the murals on Snow's ceiling, but the subject matter was different. Her eyes connected the dots, making shapes that resembled no constellation she'd ever seen before.

*No, they weren't constellations.*

Slowly, Jo began to recognize the shapes, like finally understanding a complicated math problem, or watching a line of code evolve into something hackable. They had once been her game plan, like the x's and o's on a football coach's playbook, for the order in which she'd eventually end the stars one by one. Her restriction—she had to *see* something to be able to destroy it—had always been there. And reaping destruction was what she'd been doing all along.

She'd been made to bring ends. Just like everything she'd broken, every life she'd ever ruined. How many people, how many *worlds* had already suffered because of her?

Turning in place, Jo wrenched the door open once more and started down the hallway. She listened for the slam of the door closing—ensuring that no one else would accidentally stumble on her room. Its latest change was not a phenomenon she wanted to explain. Her feet moved on auto-pilot and, in a blink, Jo found herself squaring off opposite a white door.

Just as her knuckles were about to meet the wood, the door swung open.

"I didn't think I would see you again so soon." Snow seemed pleased, but also concerned.

Jo glanced at the black door to her left. Snow's eyes followed; he gave a nod and stepped aside. She took the silent invitation and spoke only when the door had clicked shut behind her.

"My room is different," Jo started, turning to face him.

"Different, how?"

"Much more similar to yours." She motioned at the decor around her. "And I recognize it."

Snow's lips thinned into a line.

"Snow, I—" Jo had set to pacing around the room as she spoke, working out the nervous energy that ticked up in her. But she came up short the moment her eyes fell on a dresser, window, and small table with a gilded box atop. "The box," she whispered.

"What?" Snow went rigid.

"You said, once, that there was great power in it—destruction. You said you split my magic and used it . . ."

"Josephina." He used her full name like a parent might. Yet she could not be chided or dissuaded.

"I saw it. I saw you use it during the first wish—I felt it then. I felt it soak into me without resistance as you unleashed it. You said my magic was returning, more now that I was in proximity to it . . ." She remembered how the magic had flooded the room where Snow had said he'd died. She remembered the feeling of it seeping through her flesh. "Then you wouldn't let me touch it the last time I approached it." Jo stopped, standing before the box. "My magic is in there, isn't it?"

Jo felt him behind her. She could hear him breathing, every slow breath hot on the nape of her neck. Jo gave him a solid minute to bring to an end the battle that was no doubt raging in his mind. But when he said nothing, she spoke again.

"Answer me, Snow. I deserve to know." She spun in place, putting her back to the box and facing him once more. Jo found herself at the starting line of another seemingly infinite silence. It stretched before her and between them, as though they stood on different worlds. The finish line was at his feet. Just beyond it was truth, knowledge. One way or another, she'd cross it. "You've already told me almost everything, haven't you? This is just a simple yes or no."

Still, he said nothing.

"Keeping me in ignorance is not letting me thrive in a beautiful lie. It's death in the dark." Dramatic? Probably, since she couldn't technically die. But Jo didn't know how to describe her feelings lately, if not as agony. Snow let his gaze roam over every plane of her face, brows pinched and eyes sad.

"It's dangerous. You cannot meddle with the box, even if I tell you." His eyes continued to searched her face, as though he were asking for permission to take the risk anyway.

"Fine," Jo agreed. "Though my magic already seems to be haywire enough. I'm not quite sure what difference it'll make."

"Regaining all of your powers will make a world of difference." Snow sighed. "Yes, your magic is stored there. But you must not touch it."

"Why?"

"If the box is opened, your powers return. However, while they are returning and before they are safely back within your form, they will be vulnerable to theft."

Jo felt a twinge of frustration at being treated like a child who could not be trusted with her parents' toys. Yet she knew there was still much for her to learn—both about her magic and about the Age of Gods—so she kept her mouth shut and stifled her objections. Her fingers slotted between his body and elbow. Gently but firmly, Jo pulled him to her. "All right, I won't."

"Thank you," Snow whispered into her hair.

"Is it true?"

"Is what true?"

"Everything they once called me?" Her words came easily, even if they seemed baseless. Monikers far worse than "Shewolf" echoed from a past she'd long forgotten—names mortals had given her, like The Great Ender or Star Killer.

"You remember that?"

"I don't know what I remember. . ." Jo confessed. "Like I told you, my memories, they're all a blur."

"Listen to me." Snow pulled her closer and Jo wrapped her arms around him, holding on so that she could almost reach her elbows at the small of his back. He responded in kind, with an embrace so tight she could barely breathe. "Yes, your magic can bring an end to all things—

unravellings, undoings. It is the momentum that pushes bodies to ash and stars to darkness. But the tree must die by fire for its seeds to fall, and the saplings need the nutrients from the ash.

"You—your magic—is one side of the coin, Jo. A necessary one, and what makes us counterbalances."

*Coin.* Jo closed her eyes. Coins made her think of Wayne. Wayne made her think of the team he so treasured.

"Wayne said something to me the other day."

"Well, this promises to be interesting," Snow muttered.

"Wayne said that, since I joined the Society, everything has gone to shit."

Snow stopped all movement for several breaths and when he answered her, it was with a cooling certainty. "I can assure you that such a claim is categorically untrue."

The sincerity of his words combined with the delicate way in which he said them left no room for doubt. Regardless of any objective fact, Snow believed what he said to be true. That meant something to her, but little to the rest of the people she cared about. "That's not an answer," Jo continued before he could try to divert things yet again. "Tell me this: have the wishes become more. . . intense, since I joined the Society?"

"Well—"

"Yes or no?" Jo watched the lump in his neck bob as he swallowed hard.

A beat. A breath.

"Yes."

"The wishes, are they decided by her?" Jo had assumed Snow's room was a safe haven in the Society. Anywhere else, she would guard her tongue.

"They are somewhat random, I believe. But ultimately . . . yes."

Jo's anger flared, fresh and hot. It was her fault. Jo's every suspicion was being confirmed.

"Why?" Jo demanded, pulling away slightly. It was difficult to be tender when her heart was racing in anger. "Why does she have that control? How are you ensnared in this death trap?"

"There was one age before the Age of Gods," he began, his voice taking on a deep, almost storyteller-like quality. She couldn't tell if it was to calm her or emphasize the fact that she should give him her attention. Either way, it accomplished both. "The Age of Oblivion."

*Oblivion.* The word stuck out, echoing in her long after he'd said it. It was uncomfortably familiar.

"It was a time of chaos and destruction. The darkness filled every corner of the universe until, with a crack of lightning, the god of Light— Jupiter, as you may know him—tore apart the darkness. It made a path for other gods and goddesses to follow behind Light. The foundation for the land was built from the boughs of the Life Tree—called Yggdrasil by the early mortals—by the hands of the Maker, Ngai, on the back of the World Turtle. Growth—Demeter, I think they called her—harvested the seeds of life from Yggdrasil and planted them with the help of Life, Chimalma. . .”

Jo's mind swirled with names of people and places that she once knew, but had long ago forgotten. Deities she recognized from her upbringing in modern times stood alongside those she'd never once heard of, all merged together in one giant painting that mirrored the art splashed across Snow's ceiling. Every god and goddess had the name of what they were—Life, Death, Light, and so on—as well as the name seemingly given to them by mortal tongues.

“As you may be able to assume, Oblivion—or Rella as the mortals called her—was not pleased with all this order being brought into her void.”

“So she challenged the gods.”

Snow nodded solemnly. “The battle was fierce and painted across the heavens. But the pantheon won out over the lone goddess, and they split her.”

Jo knew what was coming next without him needing to say it. She almost stopped him, because she didn't want to know. But at the same time, she knew she must hear it. She braced herself.

“Her two weakened forms, demigoddess, were called Chaos and Destruction.”

“Me.” Jo now recognized her ancient name as clearly as she recognized the true nature of her magic. Numbness tingled across her clenched hands. “And Pan.”

Snow nodded solemnly. “Man gave Chaos the name Pandora.”

Pan, *Pandora*, it seemed so bloody obvious when it was all neatly laid out; Jo kicked herself for not seeing it before. As if, somehow, the demigoddess within her should have sent a quick memo to her brain summarizing all this from the moment she woke up in the Society.

“I take it Pan wasn't too pleased?”

“Neither were you, at first.”

Jo blinked in surprise. “I wasn't?” She didn't really take herself for the wanting-to-go-back-to-being-a-goddess-bent-on-oblivion type. But with everything that had happened, could she really still say she knew anything about her true nature?

“You were split, unwhole, robbed of half your power,” Snow said solemnly. “Even if I never agreed with Oblivion, I understood how such a violent fate could leave one wanting retribution.”

“Don't make Pan out to be the victim here.”

"No," Snow said swiftly, so there was no confusion. "I can understand her position, but I do not agree with it."

"So, what made my opinion change? Judging from your tone, from the way I feel, I can't think I wanted to return to Pan and be Oblivion once more."

Snow gave a nod of affirmation, accompanied by a small smile that was almost. . . proud? "You found your own place in the cosmos. And the pantheon made a demigod counter-balance to level your more extreme tendencies."

"You. Creation. . . Why didn't you tell me all of this at the beginning?" Jo demanded.

"Would you have believed it?" He had her there. She had struggled with merely accepting "because magic" as an explanation. If he had thrown in, "because you're a demigod who almost destroyed the world," she would've thought he was raving mad—even with all the incredible things that had happened. "Furthermore, I wanted time to assess your magic, to see what happened once your mortal coil was shed."

"I guess I can forgive you for it. . ." Jo mumbled. "You said once, that the Society was founded because of a dangerous magic, a split goddess, and the bravery of someone you loved," Jo repeated his words from what seemed like forever ago. "I get that the dangerous magic is me, a split goddess was Oblivion." Jo paused, working together everything he had told her. "I was split a second time, made mortal. You destroyed the Age of Gods to destroy Pan . . . but it didn't work. Why?"

Snow continued his story and Jo settled in for the final information she'd been seeking her whole life without realizing it. "Chaos's actions grew more erratic, more severe, as she hunted for you. She began to throw the world into madness however she could. Nothing would stop her and, while my magic could shield your presence, it became only a matter of time before something must be done."

"Why not just kill her?"

"To kill her would mean killing you." Snow's grip tightened some, his head dipped slightly in shame as his eyes searched for absolution for an ancient crime. "That was something I could not let happen. Not just because I loved you. But because Destruction is important for Creation. It is a cycle, Jo."

"I-I believe you." Jo nodded, unsure of what else to say to those pleading eyes.

"You gave me the majority of your power for safe-keeping, and with it, I brought an end to the Age of Gods. A world with no gods yielded an Age of Magic.

"We—you and I—thought it would be enough, that she would go with the rest of the gods unshielded and with you as a mortal, but it was not.

Your magic lived, so Pan still lived. The world was new, and I was weak. . . I am so sorry, Jo. She trapped me with her in this Society, a place for two demigods to exist through the ages, protected. She invented the rules of inducting all those who made wishes with magic, knowing that... eventually, if given an infinite amount of time, we would walk enough realities that we would eventually find you."

"And she would get what she's wanted all along," Jo finished grimly. "You had no choice but to keep feeding it, or stop existing entirely."

"I have tried to find a way out. . . but when you made your wish, our time was up." He finally released her and Jo made the motion to catch him, but Snow stumbled away.

He leaned against one of the columns surrounding the fireplace in the center of his room. The light flickered off his face, washing him in orange, as though he himself was being immolated by the crimes of ages past. Guilt sat on his back like a monster, so grotesque that Jo wondered how she'd never seen it before.

Jo looked around the room, the last remnant of a time completely vanished from the universe. "So much lost. . . because of her." Jo thought back to the briefing room. She should've punched Pan while she had the chance.

*The briefing room.* Another memory came back to her, a sensation she'd begun to make sense of despite its horrifying implications.

"Nico." The name was more of a demand than anything else. "Snow, Nico, he. . ." She knew what she wanted to ask, but Jo didn't know if she possessed the strength. "On that wish, his magic, with the painting. I was there. I stood there, I felt his magic working. But then I felt something. . . Something like a fracture." Now that she knew the truth of her magic, it all suddenly made sense. "Snow, did I—"

She didn't have to finish her question. The expression on the man's face told her everything with terrible clarity.

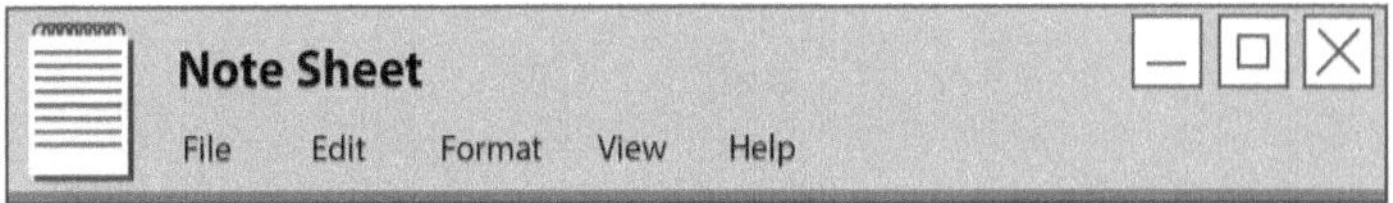


BTCOTS NOTES 6

DEFINE: OBLIVION
ob·liv·i·on
/əˈblivēən/
Noun

1. The state of being unaware or unconscious of what is happening.

2. The state of being forgotten, especially by the public.

**3. *Extinction.***

Snow was at her side, trying to comfort her.

Jo was struggling to pull away; she didn't want comfort. She didn't want to be consoled. It felt as though all she deserved was pain and punishment. She had reverted near-instantly to the hours immediately following Nico's death. But somehow the emotions were magnified and made worse in a way Jo couldn't have imagined possible.

"Wayne was right," Jo groaned, relenting all at once and burying her face in Snow's chest. Her head felt too full with all of the things she could have done, all of the things she *was* doing without even *realizing*. How many missions had been more difficult just because she'd been there? How many might have failed if everyone else hadn't picked up her slack? What else had Pan put them through—would put them through—for the sake of getting to Jo?

Jo's chest clenched, her stomach roiling. She might throw up.

"How?" Jo asked the silence, just distressed enough to get the word out. When it felt as though the rest of her plea wouldn't get caught in her throat, she wrapped her arms around her stomach and worked to get her breathing in order. "How am I supposed to do my job if. . . if I can't trust myself?" Wayne had told her she was out of control, that this was beyond them, and she had naively—Jo swallowed. "If someone else dies because of me . . ."

"No one else will," Snow whispered, keeping her close and breathing the words into her hair. Jo wanted to feel comforted, but the subtle tremors wracking her body kept her on edge, like she deserved to be anxious.

"How?" she whimpered, hating how vulnerable her voice sounded but unable to offer much else. In response, Snow planted a barely-there kiss on the crown of her head. "How can you be so sure?"

"Because you know the truth now. A truth I should've told you all along. If there is blame for Nico's death then it is on me for not telling you what you are so that you could act with the full knowledge. So that I could give you guidance and counsel.

"And. . ." He drew a slow breath, squeezing her even tighter, as if to try to pull her into him and hide her from the world. At this point, Jo wouldn't object. "Remember, I am your counterbalance. I can try to contain you more than I have so far, now that you know the truth."

"Then never leave my side." Jo already would've spent eternity in his arms if given the chance. Now, she would just to make sure no one else was harmed because of her. Even if it was as he said—that she was a sort of necessary part to the cycle of the universe—Jo wanted to play her role as needed, not let her magic run rampant like wildfire.

"I'll never leave you," Snow said, pressing a kiss to her temple. Jo leaned into it, willing herself to believe the words. Because, despite never having known the man outside of the Society in this lifetime, a part of her *had* known him. And that part of her craved him more than air, more than life itself. It was as though the only place she'd ever felt comfortable, ever felt *alive*, was in his arms.

"What if that's not enough, though?" she whispered. "What if—"

Snow placed a finger on her lips, stopping her.

Jo didn't have the chance to object further before he was leaning in and capturing her lips in a deep and lingering kiss. She wasn't sure if it was all in her mind or if something was truly different between them now that she understood more of who she was, but the kiss felt almost electric. She swore she could feel it resonate against every string of her, turning the stress song her body had been singing into a perfect harmony. It rushed up to the crown of her head and then dipped low, settling like a pleasant warmth within her very core.

It was as natural as breathing for Jo to shift, pushing Snow back into the bed as she straddled his thighs. Well, he'd said to calm herself; this was certainly one way to do it.

The kiss never broke, only growing more passionate, her need to be closer to him coalescing into something nearly tangible. Snow's fingers were tangled in her hair, clutching her to him, deepening the kiss with a moan. Jo responded in kind.

Swimming in the blissful haze of Snow's touch as she was, it was hard to say when they'd managed to remove their clothes. It was as if one moment they were merely kissing, and the next Snow was naked beneath her, the vast expanse of his skin hers for the taking. She wanted to savor it all: the heady sensation of him easing into her, making Jo feel the most whole and complete she'd ever felt—in this life or any life. The soft gasp that tightened his brow as she encapsulated him. Jo wanted it all. She wanted something to feel *right* when everything else felt so broken.

Even having slept with Snow before, Jo couldn't deny that something about this time was markedly more intense—a connection had been formed that hadn't existed before. Like, with the first rise and fall of her hips, she was feeling true pleasure for the first time. When she looked down at Snow, at his parted lips still wet from their kissing, face flushed and eyes hooded, it was like seeing true beauty for the first time.

Jo kept a steady but slow rhythm, desperate for the moment to last as long as possible. This wasn't about chasing her own release or falling into easy ecstasy; this was something deeper. Snow's hands gripped at her upper thighs, matching her with the subtle shift of his own slow thrusts.

His eyes found hers, a gaze even more penetrating than the feeling of him inside her. He held her, in body, mind and soul, with just a look. She let him search her without ever looking away, without ever moving anything more than his hips. Jo wanted to be his, but only if he knew every last thing he was taking when he took her. Only if he would be hers in return.

This time felt as familiar as any other, but more so, no longer just sex followed on the high of chemistry and attraction, no longer just the pull of a magnetism that Jo didn't understand. It was an escape, but not a cheap out from stress—more like retreating into the safety of a world only they could find. This time wasn't sex at all, Jo realized with the same spark of recognition as the sparks of pleasure arching up her spine.

As corny and cliché as it sounded, they were making love.

As if Snow had been listening to her thoughts, he moved beneath her, using his strength and momentum to flip her into the bed in his place. His stare never broke, filling all the cracks of her spirit with his adoration. Jo wondered briefly what her own expression was, though she wouldn't be surprised if it mirrored his.

Before she even realized what she was doing, she was reaching up to trace slightly trembling fingers against the striking angle of his jaw, the curve of his lips. When he turned his head into her touch just enough to place a kiss against her fingertips, Jo's heart swelled and eyes stung with unshed tears.

She refused to cry during sex, every stigma about it ringing loudly across her mind, but in that moment she came all too close. They were tears of sorrow at the fact that she had spent so long without this feeling, of joy at finally finding it. Tears of frustration at the knowledge that it would be over all too soon. Of pain at everything she had caused, but excitement at all the hope they had for a future where the suffering would end.

How could she ever hope to explain why she was crying when the truth was because of every emotion at once?

This time, when Snow began to move again, it was to sling one of her knees over his shoulder, the new position allowing him deeper within her, as close as they could be. With each renewed thrust, pleasure wracked through her, heat building quickly in her gut, twisting tighter and tighter until she was certain it would snap. But even on the precipice of it all, Jo didn't want it to end.

Which is why the sudden burst of ecstasy that sang through her was almost bittersweet. Jo threw her head back into the pillows, allowing the sensation to take her as completely as her feelings for Snow had. Taken, saved, reunited: regardless of when it had happened, she was his.

The pleasure was so profound that it took Jo a long moment for her to realize that Snow had followed her over the edge, his face buried in her neck with an elongated moan. Be it a moment of vulnerability or a genuine need to keep him close, Jo looped her arms around him, holding him against her, feeling the tension in his muscles loosen.

Her leg eased off his shoulder, thighs quivering and toes slowly uncurling. They rested against his hips as he remained in place. For a minute, or an eternity, they simply breathed. She held onto him, arms wrapped around his back, hands clutching his shoulders. Every heaving breath seemed to sing in their ears and neither seemed eager to let the other go.

Something she'd been ignoring was suddenly so, so clear.

Once upon a time, in another life, the two of them had been in love. And now, as they remained entwined, bodies still warm and hearts still easing beneath the soothing hand of their afterglow, she realized they were in this time too.

And if that love was to have a fighting chance, if any of them were, then the Society must end.

# DARK WATER

Neither of them said anything for a long time.

It was as if they both knew that the second words crossed one of their lips, the brief reprieve they had taken for themselves by force would be gone. Jo's hand rested on her still bare chest as she stared up at the ceiling. A calm had soaked into her. She was resting in a cocoon of Snow's magic and that alone was keeping her from falling apart. It was likely some mystical placebo effect, now knowing they were natural counterbalances. But believing it reassured her and, for now, that was enough.

Snow was the one to finally break the stasis, pulling himself into a seated position. "I should see to the status of the wish," he whispered.

"I'm sure it's fine," Jo mumbled, not wanting to leave the warm safety of his bed. But the spell was already broken, and Snow was the first to stand.

"We only have a week left until. . ." Snow paused on a button of his shirt. "But it won't come to that."

"No, it won't," Jo whispered at the ceiling.

"Stay as long as you'd like. You're safe here." He walked over, pressing his lips against her forehead before departing.

Eventually, Jo peeled herself off the sheets, located her clothes and pulled them on. Dressed, she walked over to the box, engaging in a silent staring contest.

Her magic, the magic of Destruction, was so close. Jo could almost feel a thrumming underneath her skin at the mere thought. But her promise to Snow remained in her mind—she wouldn't touch it.

Suddenly Snow's bedroom felt claustrophobic. Her thoughts were swirling into an anxiety-inducing cocktail, so Jo decided to wander before she was forced to drink it. She barely even registered her direction until she was breathing in the scent of fresh water, a cool breeze off the pool raising goosebumps along her arms. The magic that produced the illusion of their atmosphere had already painted the sky the dark indigo of night, the stars shining brightly despite the illumination of the pool.

And it *was* illuminated, Jo recognized, as though it had been waiting for her. Soft golden light shimmered beneath the gentle ripples of the water and the lanterns lining the pool deck bathed the rest of area in a warm glow. She'd never appreciated how relaxing it all truly was, even if Jo found herself unable to be soothed.

Jo looked at the single deck chair, a book on its seat. Hadn't she left it on the ground? Or had she taken it back to her room? Jo couldn't remember. Listlessly, she lifted it, flipping its pages. The words now took on new meaning.

*Oblivion. Arrow.*

Warring gods and mashed-up pantheons. It read less like a fable and more like a history book with all the knowledge she'd gained. She scanned for anything on magically dismantling things, pillars, funneling magic, societies, anything—and came up empty-handed. Even looking at it through the lens of her recently collected knowledge, she had wrenched all the secrets one book could give.

Jo closed the book, stashed it back under the chair, and rubbed her eyes. Her mind was too over-saturated to try to think about anything specific, let alone read. Shadows lingered in the darkness behind her eyelids and she opened them quickly, the calming sight of the pool chasing the ghosts away.

Spurred on by the sight, Jo stood, eased her hoodie over her head, and removed her pants. It wasn't exactly a swimsuit, but Jo didn't have it in her to go to her room and check to see if the mansion had concocted one for her. She sat at the edge of the pool for a second before lowering herself into the water.

A part of her had hoped the water would be shiver-inducing, that she would be able to dunk herself beneath its glass-like surface, block everything out for a moment beneath the bracing chill. But just as everything else in their fake outdoors seemed to be, it was (disappointingly) the perfect temperature—not too hot, not too cold. It soaked into her shirt and caressed her skin as she walked further into the illuminated depths.

The pool sloped, declining beneath her feet until she could see the slight-drop off of the deep end. When the water was beneath her chin, she took to swimming with broad, lazy strokes. And when even that much energy seemed pointless, she leaned back into an easy float and let her eyes roam the vast expanse of faux-night sky.

She hadn't realized just how much she'd been aching until the cool water removed the tension from her limbs, her back. Her body tilted, legs falling just below the surface, chest swelling upward with every breath. Without even meaning to, her eyes fluttered closed.

It was impossible to completely alleviate the frantic swirling of her mind, but she had to admit that, with the water cradling her and muffling the ambient noise of the outdoors, she could dwell on it all a bit less; there was a sense of comfort in the weightlessness. Her first instinct was to feel guilty about attempting to relax like this, as if, even though she'd been asked to sit out of the rest of this wish, she should still be consumed by it. Should still be as much a victim to her duty as the rest of the team. And maybe, in a way, she was. Having to sit on the sidelines, her only version of help being to literally do *nothing*. . . In many ways that felt much, much worse.

The small fraction of comfort Jo had found in her idle float vanished at once beneath her torturous thoughts. So, with a sigh as exhausted as it was frustrated, Jo opened her eyes back to the night sky.

Except, in that exact moment, something seemed to move in her periphery.

With a start, Jo wrenched herself upright, blinking water from her eyes as she scanned the pool deck and treaded water, inching herself back towards the shallows. There was nothing out of the ordinary, no one coming to check on her, no one coming to use the pool. She was just as alone as she'd been before.

Though it did little to ease the sudden spike in her heart rate, Jo chalked it up to her tense and frazzled mental state, a figment of her imagination manifested to give her something more tangible to stress-out over. Which wasn't exactly ideal, but it eased Jo's pulse a bit and allowed her the chance to catch her breath.

Once she'd given the pool deck one more quick scan, she dipped back beneath the water, dunking her head under completely. She basked momentarily in the complete silence and weightlessness, in the way that, when she opened her eyes, she could see the blurred image of the pool light and nothing more. She wondered briefly if, considering their normal functions as humans were optional now, she might be able to convince her lungs they didn't need air to breathe. Maybe she could trick her immortal body into allowing her to breathe underwater, stay here in the cool dark stasis until the wish was over. But she didn't have the courage to try, choosing instead to slick her hair back away from her face and break the surface with a deep inhale.

One that quickly devolved into a sputtering gasp at the unexpected presence of a violet-haired woman-child.

"Indulging in a late-night swim, I see." Pan stood at the edge of the pool, looking down at Jo with a dangerous glint in her cat-like eyes and a grin upon pink-painted lips. Instinctively, and before she could stop herself, Jo waded a couple of steps back and away, flinching when Pan smirked. It wasn't unlike that morning months ago, Jo realized. She had known about Fuji before it happened—"Something's coming," Pan had said in almost the very same spot. Jo had already believed Snow when he said that Pan chose the wishes, but now it seemed all the more obvious. "*Aw*, don't be like that. Is that any way to treat someone who came out here to keep you company?"

Jo wanted to say something to the effect of, "I'd take anyone's company over yours," or, "I was much happier alone, thanks," but her tongue felt heavy in her mouth, preventing her from responding at all. Something about being in Pan's presence without warning twisted the calming atmosphere of the pool deck. The lights seemed to flicker, their glow deepening in hue and becoming almost too bright. Everything was hyper-vivid, as if under a magnifying glass. Jo saw every frayed end of Pan's hair, every ripple of the water running over her face in lit bands.

"Mind if I join you?" Pan tilted her head innocently, not even waiting for a reply before pulling haphazardly at the fabric of her bright blue, ruffled dress until it gave way without a single tear to an equally bright blue and ruffled swimsuit underneath. Though Jo hadn't taken her eyes off the girl, in a blink, she noticed Pan's hair had gone from loose, violet tendrils to a tight bun, tucked back beneath a matching headband.

Jo followed Pan's motions as she strolled along the edge of the pool, priding herself on not startling when Pan began to descend the set of stairs at the far end.

"*Mm*," Pan hummed, running her fingers along the surface, barely a ripple spreading beneath her sparkly painted fingertips. "Lovely, isn't it?" She inched forward towards Jo until the water was at her shoulders; Jo wasn't sure when she'd backed up to the side, but she was now effectively cornered.

When Pan was within reaching distance, she stopped, simply standing a foot in front of Jo and swirling her hand through the water. For a long moment, she didn't speak, and in response, Jo didn't breathe.

It took her a long time to realize why, the suffocation so subtle it felt more like anxiety than magic, but once she made the connection, it was impossible to unsee. Pan's magic swirled about her in much the same way that her hands shifted in mini waves beneath the pool's surface. It didn't buzz and spark like Jo's did; it shone like lightning caught on a high-speed camera and played back in slow motion, volatile and deadly, but oddly beautiful. Despite herself, Jo felt drawn to it with a sick sort of awe.

"You feel it too, don't you?" Pan was saying. It took Jo far, far too long to realize she'd taken another step forward, closing the distance between them. Jo's eyes flicked from Pan's now-motionless hands to her face, a rush of adrenaline filling her chest at the predatory gaze now pointed in her direction. "I know you and Snow had a little bit of a talk. What did he tell you, *hm?* Care to share?"

And image of Snow flashed across her mind, the two of them embracing, the two of them in bed, the look of fond adoration in his eyes. The sight kept Jo silent and still, a determined frown pulling at her lips even as the adrenaline from before made her feel the need to bolt.

Pan didn't seem deterred by her silence, merely grinning wider, as if she could read Jo's thoughts. *Maybe she could—they had once been one being, after all.* Another spike of terror wracked Jo's spine, left her breathless with dueling urges of fight or flight she hadn't felt since the Ranger compound. A fight or flight that only grew as Pan leaned in, raising a hand to gently cup Jo's face.

Jo's breath left her in an exhale so deep it felt as if she'd only just emerged from the bottom of the pool. Without meaning to, Jo leaned into that touch. Something in the back of Jo's mind was struggling, desperate, frantic even, but Jo, terrifyingly, didn't care. She just wanted to keep chasing whatever this feeling on the very edge of her consciousness was, just for a second.

Pan said something that might have been, "There you are, my darling," but Jo couldn't really hear it beneath the pleasant buzzing in her ears. But she could feel, almost to the point of hypersensitivity, the way Pan ran a finger down the curve of her cheek, her jaw. Jo shivered, unsure if the sensation was uncomfortable, unpleasant, or some ungodly mix of the two.

Jo wasn't sure if Pan had been talking to her the whole time, but when she finally managed to listen, to take in the words, they sank deep into her gut, a seed taking root that would unravel her if it bloomed.

"He thinks you're his. . . but we all know you're mine." Her eyes glowed brighter than the pool lights, flashing red. "And you always will be. Won't you?"

Jo couldn't have said what snapped her out of the trance, but all at once, she found herself jerking away from Pan's touch, heart pounding and fear gripping her chest once more. She tried to breathe, tried to understand what that was, what the hell had just *happened.* But she came up blank. It was like Pan had been beneath her very skin, flowing like blood in her veins, and Jo had *liked it.*

When she glanced back to where Pan had just been, she was gone. With a new flash of panic, Jo frantically searched the pool, though her tormentor was already ascending the stairs to the patio, too far away too impossibly quickly. Still a bit paralyzed, mind reeling, Jo found herself hesitating.

It felt like a trap, or at the very least a very bad idea. But sometimes, you had to walk the razor's edge to get to where you wanted to go—and Jo wanted out. She wanted out of the Society, to see it crumble and free all those in it.

Pan was the only one who would tell her how to do it. Snow wouldn't; he'd deemed trying to destroy the Society too dangerous, for now. But who knew when, or if, he'd ever think it was safe?

Pan, however. . . she was the one who had built it. She was the one who had trapped Snow. And she was the one who stood to benefit the most by seeing them all—Jo especially—set free.

Before she could back down, Jo hurried out of the pool and ran to catch up, Pan already beyond the deck and heading back inside the mansion. She knew she was trailing a mess of puddles in her wake, knew she was still in nothing but a wet tank and underwear, but she also knew, inexplicably but without a doubt, that if she let Pan vanish this time, there would never be another chance.

So she sprinted, hair clinging in wet tendrils to her forehead and shoulders, bare feet slapping loudly against the mansion floors, all the way through the Four-Way and into the hall leading toward the recreation rooms.

A breath of relief escaped Jo when she saw Pan only just inching past the black door of her room. If it closed. . . If she didn't make it in time—

She hadn't realized how desperate she was, for more answers or even just *understanding*, until she was slapping a hand against the black of wood of Pan's door before it could shut.

Whether Pan had let her catch up, or whether she'd really made it just in the nick of time, Jo couldn't be sure—and she didn't much care. With a breath, she pushed the door open all the way, only to find that, even with the light filtering in from the hallway, the room beyond was completely shrouded in darkness. No. Not just darkness.

Emptiness.

"Well? Why don't you come inside?"

The voice echoed from deep within, a sing-song lilt that Jo knew all too well. And she knew instantly she shouldn't obey it, had never known such truth, but she could also feel herself being tugged inside, a firm grip deep in her core that refused to let go.

She couldn't have turned away if she tried.

# PAN'S ROOM

T he door shut behind her with a bang so loud its echoes seemed to shake the very foundation of the Society.

*Assuming she was even still in the Society.* Something about where she now stood felt distinctly different, as though she had been transported to another plane of existence entirely. It was like a superior version of the recreation rooms in concept, but in execution was pure nothingness.

The darkness around her was a tangible thing. Jo never knew there could be so many shades of black until she was standing in that primordial void. It seemed to swirl and change, condensing until it was almost tangible before wafting away again on a breeze that Jo could not feel.

She wanted to ask what it was. Every molecule in her body knew it should be terrified of this raw. . . *essence*. Yet she was not afraid and, if anything, the lack of fear was what put her on edge most. Jo pressed her mouth into a thin line, not letting a question slip or an emotion find its way onto her face. She would not give Pan the satisfaction of her curiosity.

Eventually, when Pan had no doubt grown bored of her silence, a voice manifested right over her shoulder. "What do you think?"

Jo turned on instinct toward the sound. It was as if Pan had whispered right in her ear, soft and throaty, yet the words reverberated on the infinite corners of a room that did not seem to quite exist. The door to the room should've still been at her back, but there was only more darkness. Far, far away, an animal-like sense told her the exit was beyond her reach.

"Come closer." A teal-nail-polished hand gestured from the darkness, and then an arm. It hovered, seemingly mid-air, the body it was attached to still obscured. Pan beckoned her with a curl of her index finger, a light sweep through the air, and then—

Jo was falling.

Air rushed around her as the unseen floor gave out underneath her feet like a trap door. A shout of surprise ripped open the terse line of her lips. Cackling was the only response to the sound. The darkness seemed to vibrate with sheer amusement.

Light glowed up from her feet, drawing her attention just in time to see the black fog-like magic beginning to disappear. She slowed, plunging through the bottom like an airplane on its final descent. Her toes touched the ground first, and then the balls of her feet.

A forest glade surrounded her. Sunlight streamed through the boughs from the trees, striking beams of light onto the mossy floor below. Motes of—well, Jo didn't quite know *what* they were. Little balls of light, like fireflies but much larger, danced through the air, swirling around each other before flitting away.

She spun in place, searching—it was not a spot Jo recognized. But it was a time that seemed somehow familiar. It was like trying to remember a place someone described for you while you were both drunk. The darkness from before was kept at bay behind the bars of the trees, tendrils of living smoke tried to swirl out, but could not penetrate the space—save for one.

What seemed like a blur of darkness sped over her shoulder with a *woosh* of air that pulled her hair in its backdraft. Jo jerked, but it was of no threat. The beam solidified into some kind of lance, *an arrow*, and plunged into a strange carving made in the bark of a pale tree.

Jo turned to face the source.

Pan stood—no, not Pan, but like Pan. It was Pan's eyes and hair, but something was different. In her cheeks and lips Jo saw. . . *herself.*

The woman—Oblivion, Jo realized—was swathed in tight leather of all colors. It was wrapped around her bodice, and flapped in a rainbow of shades around her legs as she moved, shifting from darkness to light. Her hair seemed to float, hovering against gravity in the air, changing shades of color with the rustle of an unfelt breeze through the trees. In her hand she held a wide arc of darkness that evaporated between her fingers.

"Hunt. Foolish woman. Thought this would bring us down. But it was not, was it?"

"*What?*"

Jo pivoted to look back at the—

The carved tree and the spear of black vanished. In its place was a long hallway. Iron lanterns hovered in a ceiling that Jo would've guessed to be over twenty feet tall. At the far end was a door, the crack of light it struck on the ground dangerously inviting.

It wasn't like she had a choice.

Jo steeled herself and pressed forward into the madness. The door stayed just out of reach, never seeming to get closer. Jo picked up the pace, faster and faster until she was practically sprinting.

All at once, she burst through the door, tripping down a step and tumbling into a room filled with every curiosity imaginable. Tapestries lined the walls with a jeweler's vault's worth of gems and jewelry dangling from them. Herbs hung between strips of meat on the ceiling that was covered in all kinds of painting. Mechanics whirred on one wall, cranking sparks on occasion from the strain of the mysterious tasks they were performing.

There were shelves, *and shelves*, and shelves packed to the brim and overflowing with books, bottles, baubles, statues, and more. Nothing made sense. It was as if the creator had thrown every possible item into the room with utter disregard for any sense of logic. Every time she turned she saw something new, and whenever she looked back somewhere, what she'd first thought she'd seen was gone.

It was sheer chaos.

And in the middle of it all, was Pan.

This was the child-like form Jo knew, dressed again in one of her ruffled garments. The woman Jo had seen in the glade was gone and that fact brought no small amount of ease. A smile swooped across Pan's face.

"What do you think of my collection?"

Jo kept her mouth shut. She had nothing to say.

"Oh. . . come now, don't be like that," Pan whined softly. "You have to think *something*. Especially after I showed you so much."

"What did you show me?" Jo finally asked, her voice almost cracking at the end. She did know, but she wanted to hear Pan say it.

"Truth."

"Enough of the games," she snapped. "I know the truth."

Pan waved a hand through the air and fell backward. The darkness from before crept out of the shadows at her behest. It rose up quickly, solidifying into the shape of a chair before shearing off like a snake shedding its skin—a throne cast in gold in its place.

"Do you know *the* truth?" Pan hummed. "Or do you know *Snow's* truth?"

"Don't waste your breath, you're not going to turn me from him, or make me suspicious." Jo knew that he would not keep from her something that would harm her. Not intentionally, at least. And especially not after everything he had shared. If there was more to be said, it was merely because there had not yet been time to say it.

"You reek of him." Pan scrunched her nose. "I can see his magic clinging to you. It's so bright, so. . . orderly. Isn't it suffocating to be wrapped up so tightly?"

"If there's one thing I want to be wrapped up in, it's Snow," Jo retorted. She looked around the room. "Not. . . *this*."

The scrunch of Pan's nose deepened. It hitched her upper lip, drawing it upward and setting it to twitch slightly. The woman-girl narrowed her eyes. "It is not your decision to make, not when you are the embodiment of theft."

"What theft?"

"The gods feared me—*feared us*. Before them, there was nothing, only us. Then Light—Zeus, they called him—came like a bolt of lighting into our delicious void. He sparked life, and brought Order to help rule it, and then the rest of them came. They took everything from me, even you."

Pan stood and Jo took a step back. She suddenly seemed like a dog on a chain, snapping and biting, waiting for the thick rust to finally eat away at the metal and set her free with a snap.

"They *feared* us. All of them. And it was glorious. Do you not remember? You must, the feeling of that power, the feeling of their fear." Pan set to pacing as she spoke. "They did the one thing they could do." She stopped all at once. Her head lolled, as if all the muscles in her neck had gone limp at once. Her eyes gazed across every inch of the room before landing on Jo. "Then Snow, Creation, did the one thing they wouldn't do. Clever, I'll give him that. . . But there's not much longer now until we're together again."

Jo wanted to ask more. She wanted to pick apart every little bit of information. But Pan was giving her a waterfall and Jo only had a teacup to try to collect it in. She didn't have enough time to piece it together and, what's more, didn't have the mental fortitude.

Fear ripped through her as she was frozen again, just like in the pool, laid bare under that cat-like stare. Unlike Snow's penetrating gaze, this was almost brutal. It was as if Pan was forcefully ransacking the contents of her mind. Tearing apart the drawers of memories, throwing them like clothes scattered across the floor and then—

A smile.

"Do you remember our deal?"

"W-what?"

"Our deal." Pan held out a hand and the room behind her changed into an exact replica of Jo's hacking set-up in the recreation room. "You promised to show me your magic."

Jo had all but forgotten. It felt so, so long ago now. "No," she whispered.

"Now now," Pan cooed. "Don't go back on a deal. You wouldn't do that, *hmm*?"

"I want to leave." Jo didn't know what she'd been looking for, but she'd found more than she ever wanted. "Let me out."

"You can leave at any time."

"What?"

"All you need is your magic." Pan cackled at the confusion that was no doubt still painted across her face. "Make the Door."

"I-I can't."

Pan took a slow step forward. "Make it, and see the truth."

Jo shook her head again, eyes pressing closed. *That was where she knew the darkness from.* She'd been seeing it all along. It had been behind her eyelids, steadily growing, from the first moment she'd walked into the Society.

It was in her. *It was her.*

"Do it, it's what you're made for."

"No."

"Be mine," Pan whispered, now just a step away. Jo could feel the ripples of magic off the woman's body. Her clothes swayed, seeming to fray, transforming before Jo's eyes into the bindings of multicolored leathers she'd seen before. "Come back to me."

Jo shook her head violently, neck straining. "I . . . I will not. The only thing I was made to destroy, is you."

"Impossible, with the Society around us. But you can fix that too, can't you?" Pan egged on eagerly. "Now, go and show me, Jo. Show me your magic, Destruction."

"Never!" Jo screamed, a voice she'd once had pouring out of her mouth.

Pan was forced back, stumbling, falling to the floor in gleeful laughter. There before Jo, obscuring the woman on the floor, was the Door. She didn't know how it was possible, or why. But there it was, hovering mid-air.

She was too afraid to question and knew better than to look a gift horse in the mouth. Jo didn't even bother with the pin-code. She pushed on the handle, wrenching open the Door. A cackle of sheer madness covered up any sound that the metal may have made as it opened.

"The box is the key to ending this. Do it, Josephina. Or I will see everything you love come undone with glorious chaos, one way or another."

The words echoed between Jo's ears as she breathlessly sprinted into the hallway, slamming into the wall on the other side. She spun, but the black door was as it had always been: closed tight. Yet that same feeling of being watched lingered alongside the echo of Pan's laughter.

Jo turned in a rush of fear and adrenaline, and bolted through Snow's door.

# FINALLY

He'd said she could come and go as she needed, but Jo didn't think he'd intended for it to be like this.

Wrenching Snow's door open, Jo felt tethers trying to keep it shut snapping under her brute force. She paused, looking at the open frame. *What had that been?* Some kind of protective ward to keep Pan and her watchful gaze out, perhaps?

And she had broken them.

Which meant now, whenever she wanted to, Pan could waltz right in and take what she had been looking for the whole time. Jo walked over to the box, her earlier conversation with Snow replaying loudly in her ears. She had told him she wouldn't touch it. She had also vowed to end the Society.

Jo looked back to the door, half expecting to see Pan ready to pounce.

But her promise was before she'd broken his wards. Did he already know? Could he sense her destruction? Was he on his way? She turned back to the box.

Even if he was coming for her, to investigate the meaning behind the destruction of his protections, she would have to keep away Pan until he arrived—if Pan even came to begin with. Perhaps she should wait it out? Or perhaps she was just waiting to lose everything.

Another thought entered Jo's mind—once more, the idea of destroying the Society, of ending everything. With this power, she could. Pan had told her she could.

*One way or another*, Pan had said.

One way or another, it would all end.

Jo didn't think, just followed the pull in her gut. This was her power, and with it, she might have a chance. She'd take it and go far away, open it safely, hide while she was vulnerable, learn her magic—formulate a plan at the very least.

It may not be the best idea, Jo admitted. But doing nothing wasn't working either. With one final breath to steel herself, Jo grabbed the box and left before Snow could come back and find his wards broken, and her doing the one thing she promised him she wouldn't do.

The box was positively searing against her fingers, rattling with her every step. Jo couldn't tell if it was her hands shaking with the grip she had on it, or her magic within trying to force itself out. A dry spot formed on her still-dripping clothes where she held it against herself.

Jo knew she wasn't ready to open it. More like, she wouldn't even *dare* to open it. The box radiated with an energy she'd never quite felt before and as terrifying as it was, it was also thrilling, intoxicating.

" . . . I just don't get it." Wayne's voice echoed down the hall to her. There was a long silence before he continued. "It's never done anything like that before. Never less than perfect. I'm lucky I made it back at all."

Jo dropped to a crouch, leaned against the wall, and hoped she was far enough from the stairwell to remain unseen. Why were there so few places to hide in the Society?

"It is strange. . ." Takako replied grimly. "But at least the killings seem to have made progress on the Severity of Exchange."

"Do you think Samson will be able to do his part?" Wayne's voice was already shrinking. Jo listened carefully, more for their footsteps than their words. She had every faith that the team could figure out the wish. Even if they couldn't. . . she was beyond being able to help them now. The best thing Jo could do was take herself, and her magic, as far from the Society and Pan as possible.

"He will, if nothing else is amiss. You don't think it could be. . ." Takako's voice faded down the hall. To the best of Jo's abilities, she'd guess they were heading toward the common area.

Two people down, four unaccounted for.

If Takako was talking about Samson doing his part, then she'd venture a guess that the woman had returned with bones. Knowing Samson, he'd likely wandered off to his room, and Eslar had followed. Pan—just the thought caused the muscles in her chest to seize, stealing her breath for a moment—Pan was likely still in her room, as she always was.

*Yes, Pan is still in her room*, Jo quietly assured herself as she eased out of her crouch. Pausing, she looked down the hall toward the black door. It remained as still as it ever was, but not nearly as ominous. But Pan had eyes around the Society, she would know soon what was happening—if she didn't already.

She had to move quickly.

Jo gripped the box tighter, as if trying to pull it closer to her, to embed it into her skin and keep Pan from ever laying a grubby little candy-colored finger on it. It didn't matter where Pan was, where any of them were; it wasn't going to stop her from leaving. Jo echoed the sentiment in different ways over and over as she descended the stairs, waiting for it to take root and become believable.

There was no one in the halls leading toward the common or briefing rooms. With a word of whispered thanks to no one in particular, Jo made a sharp left. Her feet landed on the plush carpet, and she took to a run. Her heart was in her throat, beating much faster than it should for how few steps she'd taken.

It was like she could taste freedom, sweet and clear, swirling on her tongue, dancing across the roof of her mouth. Every breath left her aching, needy. She had to escape—she could, she would. Just long enough to sort through some things, figure something out, learn her magic. At the very least, long enough to allow the threads unraveling around her to tighten once more.

Jo burst through the doors to the briefing room, not letting them slow her momentum in the slightest.

Samson nearly jumped out of his seat. Eslar's back straightened into a painful looking line, surprise nearly bulging the eyes from his head. Snow was on his feet.

It was Snow that finally slowed her to a stop.

He didn't move for her, didn't even try to speak. He stared at her in utter confusion until she could see the moment it dawned on him. His eyes dropped to her hands. She could handle the anger that flashed across his face, knitting lines between his eyebrows. But the look of utter heartbreak that had him sinking backwards into a slump was something she was unprepared for.

"Josephina, is there something—" Eslar began.

"Don't mind me, just passing through." Jo continued for the Door.

"Don't you want to know the state of the wish?" the elf continued. "And heading where in that particular state?"

She'd rather eat her shoe than know about the wish. "I'm fine," Jo said, knowing she looked the opposite, uncomfortably soaked to the bone in her undies and tank.

"You may not be when you try the Door," he said ominously, halting all her movement. Jo's gaze swung over to the elf, then backtracked to Snow.

"What're you talking about?" *And what have you been talking about?*

"Wayne ran into a snag on the wish." As Eslar spoke, Jo's attention drifted to the items on the table. She stared at them with dark, morbid fascination.

A severed hand and a leg from the knee down were laid out neatly right before Samson—as if they weren't still oozing blood onto the table. She remembered what Takako had said, what they'd all decided must be done during their last meeting. But to see the severed flesh and torn tendons. . . Jo knew she should feel sick. But the prevailing thought in her brain was nothing more than, *how do they not smell?*

"The Door seems to be acting strangely."

It felt as if invisible gremlins were tugging on her from every direction. The wish, the Door, the box, Samson and his severed limbs—there were a million things she needed to focus on and all at once it seemed too much. Her fingers tightened around the vessel.

It seemed like too much, but really, her next steps were very simple. The Society had existed from the beginning as a spring-loaded trap that was ready to fire the second Pan found her. It was Jo's presence that was resulting in the degrading quality of wishes, either because her Destruction was unraveling the very magic that held them together, or Pan herself was picking more and more extreme wishes to push the Society into a corner. It didn't matter which. Jo was certainly behind the Door's malfunctions, of that she had no doubt.

Which meant she could ignore all the symptoms and focus on the problem: herself.

"I'm going to give it a try anyway." Jo went for nonchalance but her voice was a high-pitched, desperate sound.

"J-Jo, Eslar's right." Samson's tiny voice joined the fray. "The Door isn't right. I don't know why, but I can see something amiss. I wouldn't go near it."

It hadn't been right from the very beginning. From her first wish, she could force the Door to do things no one else could, not even knowing it was unique until it was already too late. She'd seen the button stick as she'd gone to Florence with Nico. She'd felt it groan and shudder under the weight of her rage as she'd returned following their failure in Japan.

"I wouldn't—"

"What are you trying, Jo?" Snow interrupted Eslar.

Jo was frozen once more under the weight of his stare. She took a deep breath through her nose, let it out through her mouth, but it did not pick up sound anywhere along the way.

"Go back," he said, gently. Then, as if she were some kind of wild, panicky creature, he took a slow step for her. "Don't do this, please. We can talk this through."

"Trust me," she pleaded softly. "I broke your wards and she'll come for it. I'm going far from here and will come back when I have my magic to dismantle this and free us."

"Go back."

"It'll be fine," she insisted.

"Jo, please." Snow took another step toward her, speaking kindly when she knew he wanted to be yelling—and had every right to do so. He was almost close enough to touch her and close enough for her to feel his magic. The Door on one side, him on the other, an impossible choice under her feet.

"I—"

"Come now boys." If words could slither, that was the sound of them doing so.

All eyes landed on the woman leaning against the door frame. Pan stood, arms folded, fingers splayed against the door she was propping open. She had the look of calm, but the air of energy. Writhing, wriggling, pulsing madness washed over Jo from the suit-clad demigod.

"I think its time you stopped interfering with women's matters." Pan's eyes dropped to Jo's hand's, seeing the same thing that had commanded Snow's instant attention. "Especially you, Snow. It's time to end this stalemate."

Jo took an involuntary step back, away from Pan, toward the Door.

The room was filling with magic, like an illusionist's water chamber. But Jo's hands were shackled and no one had the key. The only thing she may have that could even remotely help her fight back was locked in a box. But setting it free was likely to do more damage than good.

But as she stood in the cross-hairs, Jo wasn't given a choice.

"You made a deal with me." Pan's voice seemed to echo, as though they were in a giant cavern and not the briefing room. "Now, Josephina. Show me your magic!" Pan screeched. The sound seemed to reverberate through the very foundation of the Society. Distant windows rattled and the walls groaned.

Jo's mind could no longer make logical mental pathways as she was plunged into utter chaos. Without her consent, her hands began to move, pulling out the box.

*She was going to open it.*

It was now or never; Jo pushed on the Door handle, and three things happened at once.

The first was the feeling of the Door giving way. As Jo gave it a monstrous tug, the handle came free and with it, a part of the Door itself. Light streamed through the cracks as though it had always been trying to hold back the dawn of a new age. Steel groaned like a slumbering giant coming awake, and it split down the middle.

Magic flooded the room, knocking them all back. Jo rolled, head over heels, knocking against spinning executive chairs left and right. Her hands flew, knuckles pounded against the ground, splitting but not releasing the box they held.

The second thing Jo registered was the sound of Snow rushing for her, and a smaller set of feet pounding the floor at her back. Chaos and Creation, battling it out over Destruction. The notion would've been almost poetic were it not for the fact that Jo was fairly certain everyone she'd come to care about would be killed in the fallout.

Jo let out a scream as she struggled against her own body. Her legs thrashed, her spine twisted, and her inner voice was drowned in the chaos of her mind. She fought for as long as she could—a second that felt like a millennium. She just had to hold out; Snow would reel her in once more.

But she couldn't.

Jo flicked open the box, triggering the third and most vivid thing of all —a sharp intake of breath, and then the word "Finally" falling from Pan's lips.

# THE CLOCK REACHES ZERO

"What. Did. You. *Do?*"

Jo thought the question might have come from Eslar, but all she could really process was the sound of abject horror laced beneath the words.

"N-No. . . We can't, we—How will we get *out*? How can we—If we don't have—We're t-trapped, we're—Outside was all w-we h-had, I—" That was most certainly Samson, a dull pull in Jo's chest letting her knew that he was falling head first into a panic attack. Where she would normally jump to his aid, she remained frozen in place. It was as if, in the first seconds of opening the box, she'd become paralyzed beneath a wave of something her mind, body, and soul couldn't yet comprehend. All she could do was listen in distant objectivity to the sounds of her team falling apart around her. Blaming her.

"Josephina, no . . ." *Snow?*

"The hell?" A new voice—Takako? Wayne? Any of them really.

"Finally! *Finally!*" That word rang loud and clear, a redundancy from only seconds ago, but with more glee, more jubilation. Even if her ears weren't buzzing with static, even if her heart hadn't stopped beating to make way for the pulsing waves of the magic in her blood, she'd have known that voice. It was a part of her, after all.

The moment Pan's enthusiasm registered, so did the feeling coursing through Jo like the devastating latch of a taser to the spine. This was her magic in full, returning to her and clinging with a vice-like grip. She'd known what she was doing, had known what was in the box, but there was no way to prepare for how it *felt*. So much more potent than the magic she'd come to call her own, so much more fierce and alive.

Part of her, the part named Josephina, the part that grew up in the Lone Star Republic and started hacking to provide for her family, instantly recoiled from the sensation. It wasn't hers, this magic—not like her hacking magic had been. It wasn't what she wanted.

But another part of her, a part whose eyes might be slitted like a cat's, saw everything unseen, all the little lines that made up the schematics of reality itself. A woman whose hair might glisten in fragmented colors like the iridescence of an oil spill. A woman who had seen the birth of time and the dawn of man with eyes that were her own but not, who had preached oblivion and reaped destruction. . . that part of her was *thirsty* for it. Jo had never felt such a craving, but Destruction had. And it would be so easy to give in. Her eyes landed on Pan for a brief moment. So, so easy to—

*No.*

No more than a few seconds could have passed; Eslar was still trying to pull Samson out of his panic attack, Takako was staring at the Door like it might be lying, and Wayne stared at Jo with every emotion conceivable but abject concern prevailing. Jo saw each of their faces in half time before finally picking out Snow's.

She couldn't take on Oblivion's power if it meant losing him, if it meant putting everyone in danger. *She couldn't*, but now that she'd opened the box, she didn't know how to make it stop. Snow had said this was the moment she was most vulnerable—as she was absorbing her full power. She couldn't have imagined him to be so right, but Jo didn't have a clue how to expedite the process even if she wanted to.

With far, far too much difficulty, Jo opened her mouth, lips working with more energy than she'd ever had to expel in her life—only to have her line of sight broken by a blindingly red, cat-like stare.

Jo gasped against the impact, her back colliding with the splintered Door. Broken edges dug into her spine, the light pouring out around her almost bitingly cold against each piece of bare skin it touched. She could barely breathe beneath the impossible pressure Pan was forcing against her ribcage, and when Pan raised that hand, lifting Jo a good foot off the floor, she stopped being able to breathe at all.

Pan was saying something to her, something to the room at large, but Jo couldn't hear it, the blood rushing in her ears only adding to the deafening waves of her magic. *Their* magic, Jo couldn't help but notice, because as Pan loomed below her, the waves of both their magics had begun to coalesce, weaving around them both and inching into the core of it. The magic that had been set free from the box was drawn as much to Pan as it was to her. If it went to Pan, not her, then Pan would no doubt consume her next with easy and careless disregard.

In a panic, Jo's eyes searched frantically about the room, not quite sure if she was asking for help or begging for them to go, run, find another means of escape somehow. But it would seem that, in the wake of Pan's attack, they'd momentarily dropped their fear and blame, rushing to her aid without a second's hesitation.

*No! Stop!* Jo tried to yell, but her vision was already going hazy with a lack of air. All it took was a single, dismissive wave of Pan's hand, as if she were shooing them away, and the whole room exploded backwards on a wave of energy. The briefing room table collided violently with the double doors, knocking them clean off their hinges; the rest of the room faring nearly as badly. The only one left standing in the onslaught was Snow, but solely for as long as it took Pan to use that same hand to pin him to the opposite wall, magically chained and out of the way before he had a chance to help.

Jo could do nothing more than play spectator as her magic began to give way to Pan's and her world fell apart.

"You have no idea," Pan was speaking to her once more, the first recognizable words she'd been able to hear for what felt like hours. Pan inhaled deeply, and Jo's stomach churned at the sight of their magic winding together like tendrils of ivy, filling up Pan's lungs like she was desperate for the smell of them. When she exhaled, bright sparks in an eternity of colors escaped through her clenched teeth. "You have *no idea* how long I've been waiting for this moment. Your little ploy with Creation here making me be patient, orderly. You know how much I hate that."

Pan dug her fingers into Jo's chest, nails breaking through fabric to skin as if she wasn't wearing anything at all. The pressure continued to build into something painful, mere fractions away from a proper puncture, and for a maddening second, Jo thought that maybe Pan would rip out her heart. But instead, she just eased in closer, rising up off the ground to meet Jo eye to eye once more. The pressure never eased and Pan appeared not to notice she was levitating, too busy running her lips up Jo's jaw to her ear on a hungry whisper.

"We will become one, my darling. We will be Oblivion once more and you will remember what it truly means to have power. You were always the immature one—no more of your obstinate, child-like games."

When Pan's magic pulsed around them, spinning like a typhoon of overwhelming sensation, Jo didn't scream. She didn't have enough air in her lungs to try. There was a darkness from deep, deep within Jo's magic that was creeping up on her, like an animal stalking its prey. She could sense it on the periphery, the shadows lingering in sinister anticipation, and as much as she tried to fight them, there was no denying how much her own magic craved that release, that embodiment. It was what she was made from, it was what she *was*.

In a last-ditch effort, Jo's eyes darted about the room, taking in the scene before her with a steadily breaking heart.

Wayne lay before the double doors, unconscious, a mildly injured Takako at his side. She wasn't sure what knocked him out, but it didn't look fatal. Despite how she cradled Wayne's head in her lap, Takako stared down the scene before her like a soldier waiting for orders. Jo didn't have any to give.

Compared to Wayne, Eslar seemed worse for wear, no more than a crumpled heap in Samson's arms. Enough blood had fallen from whatever head wound he'd suffered that it almost completely obscured his face, dripping onto his clothes and smudging the lengths of Samson's arms. Jo couldn't explicitly process what Samson was sobbing into Eslar's hair, but she could almost make out the words on his trembling lips.

*"Don't leave me, Eslar, please!"*

When Jo managed to drag her focus away from the sight, it was to Snow, her own sob heaving at her chest. A sob that lodged itself in her throat at the look of pure fury on Snow's face. Much like Pan's, his magic was radiating off him in visible waves, thrumming with the sort of power Jo had only seen from him twice: once in the room where he'd "died," and the other in a barn in the Lone Star Republic, surrounded by Rangers and guns.

It was a magic that managed to wreak havoc upon the room as much as it filled Jo's creeping shadows with soothing light. It offered comfort despite the rage marring Snow's beautiful features. It whispered in her ears, against her skin, almost as clearly as the words Snow mouthed in her direction. Jo had never seen anything so clearly.

*"A new age. One more time. Revert us back."*

With her eyes locked on Snow's as they were, she could only see Pan's shock in her periphery, but the ripple of confusion/disbelief/anger that traveled between the lingering bond of their magic said it all.

Jo turned her face to set her eyes on the Door. She craned her neck so far that her tendons felt like they would rip. As though she was now part owl, she twisted to look into the void the Door had held back all this time. Beyond it, she saw. . . light.

She saw light and life and a world as it could have been were it not for meddling demigods. She saw the foundations of a pillar that had been erected outside of time to house two divinities locked in stalemate. She saw, and she understood. For like hacking a server or destroying the stars, once Jo saw something, she knew how to dismantle it.

Snow had been right: dismantling the Society would bring about an end to everything.

They had destroyed the world once and ushered in a new age—her magic and his. The only difference now was that Jo wielded her power. She would not walk into this new dawn as a mortal, but as Destruction, as what she was meant to be. So Jo pushed herself through the doorway and into that blinding foundation where she landed like a time bomb whose clock had finally reached zero.

# FRAGMENTED DATA

T he end was a beginning.

There was the sensation of unleashing her magic on the cornerstone of the world—pulling it out from the foundation with violent force. This compounded the feeling of falling, further than she ever had before. Jo thought she might fall forever until, as if by a sudden explosion, the light around her shattered and she hit the ground.

For what seemed like a brief moment, everything went dark.

Jo's eyes fluttered open.

The world around her seemed to glitter, sparkle in a way that it never had before. She saw every leaf of the shrub near where she lay. It picked up the sunlight and cast it off with emerald perfection, far too vivid to be real.

Reaching a hand, Jo ran her fingers over the waxy leaf, confirming it was, indeed, real. She tipped her head back into the grass that tickled her ears and looked at the sky above. It was bright blue, crisper than she remembered, with large white swaths of clouds floating across the canvas at a surprising speed.

Between two clouds, she saw a shadow of what looked to be like some kind of large winged creature. It was a brief blur that happened so fast Jo couldn't be certain it'd been real at all. An airplane, likely.

*Airplane.*

Airplanes needed skies. Leafy shrubs and grass needed sunlight. For everything around her to be real it meant that the world itself was real.

Jo bolted upright and took in her surroundings. It was a familiar street —quintessential suburbia. In front of her stood Charlie's house. Or at least, it had been Charlie's house. This was a new reality, after all—a new age, built by Snow.

She stood, dusting off the yard clippings that clung to her clothes. Her clothes—they were different, too. A long, flowing skirt was tied at her waist, the hem pooling around feet strapped into a gladiator-esque sandal. Above was a loose fitting tank top. *Sort of.* The two straps were leather capped and braced together at the shoulder, leaving her arms bare.

The clothes were comfortable, familiar even. Jo turned left and right, feeling the skirt float around her ankles. She'd worn this before.

*It was what she'd worn when she'd split herself into Destruction and Chaos, ending the Age of Gods.*

"I guess I look the part, now," Jo mumbled as she made her way quickly toward the front porch. While nothing about her getup screamed "legendary divinity," she certainly felt far enough from the norm that she didn't want to draw anyone's attention.

Jo raised her hand to the door, pausing a brief moment. If it was a new world, then Charlie wouldn't remember her. She knocked anyway. If he didn't remember her she'd apologize, excuse herself, and move on.

A blurred outline appeared behind the rectangular pane at the top of the Craftsman-style door. There was the sound of a latch being undone and the door opened. Jo never thought she'd be relieved to see a serial killer.

The feeling wasn't mutual. Charlie looked her up and down, his eyes narrowing slightly. "Can I help you?"

"Do you know who I am?" Jo asked outright.

He froze at the question, ceasing his assessment and bringing his attention to her face. Charlie's eyes scanned her and Jo hoped that it wasn't the only thing scanning her. Even if he didn't remember her, she'd dare to ask him what his readings said. What was the worst that could happen? He would get upset? Jo felt the ripple of magic underneath her skin reassuring her that if that happened, she would be just fine.

"No. . ."

She inhaled quickly, as if trying to revive her suddenly deflated hope. Of course he wouldn't. If everything Jo had assumed was true had actually come to pass, then this was a new—

"Tell me why I should?" Something in his voice was far too curious and far too knowing to be mere chance.

"We met in a different world," Jo blurted, out with the truth. "'Different time' might be a better statement."

"Excuse me? I don't think I know what you're talking about." But his eyes said otherwise.

Jo put her palm on the door, stopping him from closing it. They had never finished the wish. Which meant it would still be outstanding. At least, she speculated that's what it would mean. She looked him dead in the eyes and spoke.

"I know that inside your house you have a terminal, first floor, down the hall to the left."

His eyes widened. It was a good start. "I don't know what kind of stalker you are but—"

"I know about Primus Sanguis."

Charlie froze. In a blink, he turned from concerned homeowner to deadly android who would murder for his secrets.

"I know what you do with bones."

"What do you want?" he whispered.

"Do you really want to have this conversation here?" Jo motioned to the front porch. "Let me inside."

He debated this for a long moment, eyes darting about.

"Do I really look like someone who'd be associating with the cops?" Jo motioned to her strange garb, "I'm here alone."

"Come in, then." He stepped aside.

"Thank you, Charlie." Jo used his name for emphasis, and to underscore her certainty that they'd met before.

He closed the door behind her, locked it, and folded his arms. "You're welcome, Josephina."

Jo stopped dead in her tracks. Slowly, she turned her attention to Charlie. He had yet to move, even though she'd taken five bold steps into his home.

"You do remember," she whispered.

"Not quite." He finally stepped forward, brushing past her as he walked toward the back hall. "Come, it'll be easier to show you."

She followed behind him, into the back hall, down to the end, and back into a familiar server room. By her count, it had only been two days since she'd last stood in the same spot with Takako. Jo couldn't help but wonder how long it'd been for Charlie.

"Close the door behind you, so you don't let out the chill."

What a blissful chill it was. Jo felt every sensation of cold prickling her skin, puckering it into goosebumps. She happily obliged him, shutting them into the dimly lit room. It felt like a safe haven, the hum of computers like a familiar blanket. Even though Jo had every right to be off-kilter, afraid, and keenly aware of the fact that she was in a small room with a serial killer—she didn't feel the least bit scared.

If anything, Jo felt oddly jubilant. Though she worked to curb the emotion. There were still too many important things yet to confirm.

Charlie sat down at his terminal, not hesitating to lift his shirt and plug himself in. Jo didn't even bat an eye at the sight. At least they weren't going to waste time playing dumb with each other.

"Look, here," he pointed to the screen.

Jo walked over to the file he'd opened. It was a long string of code—server data. Something had been stored, tagged, yet. . .

"It's corrupted."

"Not corrupted." Charlie shook his head. "Fragmented."

"How do you mean?"

"Ever since I was born—" Jo couldn't help but note the fact that he specified *born*, and not *made*. "I have possessed this data. It is on a file, hard-coded into me, that no one else seemed to be able to see—not even my core programmers."

Jo looked back at the data, but her ability to make sense of any language seemed to have left with the Society. That, or it was far too broken for even the demigod of destruction to decipher.

"What is it?" she finally asked.

"You."

"What?" Jo straightened away from inspecting the monitor. She felt her mouth hanging open, but Charlie did not remark on her shock.

"I have always had these snippets, but I never knew why; I could never get a full picture. A name. . . sensor readings. . . nothing more. And I had never seen anyone—or any thing—give off readings like this." He paused, giving her one more look up and down. "Until now."

*He remembered her through a jump.*

No, not quite remembered. A memory he'd stored in data format had persisted even though the world had changed. *Why?* It was a question to explore later. For now. . .

"What are you?"

"A demigod."

The mood broke when Charlie laughed. "Excuse me?"

"I'm a demigod and I met you in a different time when you invoked the Society of Wishes to grant you the ability to murder those related to Primus Sanguis at will, without ever being caught." As she spoke, Charlie's smile fell.

"This is certainly . . . odd." She could hear it in his voice: he wanted to believe her. Jo couldn't blame him for the skepticism, however. She was selling him a truly impossible tale.

It was then that she spotted a pair of scissors on his desk. Jo moved without thinking.

Her fingers closed around the bright red handle of the scissors. She lifted them as though they were Excalibur itself. Her hand fell to the desk, palm up, knuckles rapping against the wood.

"Watch," she commanded.

Gripping them in her right hand like a dagger, Jo recalled the last time she had been wounded—or should have been wounded—in Charlie's home. The USB had exploded, embedding into her hand harmlessly until she plucked out the pieces. Jo plunged the scissors down, stabbing the blade clear through her hand and into the desk.

A sensation seared through her—not pain, but pleasure. It was as if her body relished the feeling of her skin tearing, as if her mind sung at the sensation of something about her being torn apart. She stared at her impaled hand for one more long moment, then withdrew the blade.

Her skin knitted quickly. There was no blood and no mark. Charlie grabbed at her hand, running his own over the mended flesh.

Air continued to fill her lungs, but her body now seemed very distant from her. She had truly become another being altogether. Her mind knew the form she was in as Josephina. But it also knew the magic that flowed in her as Destruction. She was real, and she thrived off of her namesake but her heart still clung to the memories she'd made in a different reality.

"All right," Charlie said in amazement, leaning back in his chair. "I'll buy it."

"Good." Jo ran her fingers over her palm for a moment. Sure enough, as Charlie had seen, there was no sign of the wound. "Because I need some information." She found it ironic that it was not the first time he'd functioned as her minion of sorts.

"About what?"

"Everything."

# DRAGONBACK

"**Y**ou're going to have to give me more of a starting place than that."

"Fair." Jo folded her arms, leaned against the wall, and stared at the computer, debating what to ask first. "What's today's date?" That seemed like a good place to start.

"January 13th, 2058."

So it was roughly six months after she'd joined the Society in her time-line. Jo's mind decided to spin out from there—focus on finding differences and similarities. But first, something more urgent.

"Have you seen anyone else like me?" she asked, her breath catching on the end of the question in fear of what the answer may be.

"Like you?"

"An odd signature." Jo motioned to the fragmented data still up on his screen.

"There is another here." Charlie turned back to the screen, analyzing silently. But he must've come away empty-handed, because he said nothing else. "But you are the only one I've ever encountered who matches these readings."

*Snow hadn't been here, then.* Jo looked to the door, wondering what had happened to the rest of the Society, as though her friends would come walking through behind her. *What if, when she'd ended the Society and the Age of Man, they'd. . .* Jo couldn't even bring herself to think it.

"Has anyone else come to you, or shown up in your yard unexpectedly, claiming to know you or recognize you in any way?" Jo attempted.

"No." Charlie shook his head. "You're the first to visit me from another dimension. At least that I've been made aware of."

Jo took in a slow breath, forcing herself to remain calm. She tightened her arms around her chest and suppressed a shiver. Just because they hadn't come to Charlie's house, or woken here, didn't mean they were gone. It didn't mean Pan had the last laugh about Jo destroying the Society.

"I need you to look something up for me."

"What is it?" Charlie asked, pulling up a browser in the monitors with a thought.

"Me. Josephina Espinosa."

He gave her a skeptical look but keyed in the query anyway. Nearly a thousand names pulled up across various records. "Care to narrow it down a bit?"

"Search in the LSR. Near El Paso."

"Where?"

"LSR," Jo repeated. "The Lone Star Republic."

Charlie merely stared at her. He squinted his eyes, but not in a way that indicated he was trying to refuse her or be difficult. He was genuinely confused.

"Where's that?"

Jo opened her mouth and closed it again slowly. Time itself had been changed in a major way. "Pull up a map of the world," she whispered.

Charlie obliged.

Jo stared at the map that took up an entire screen before her. It looked like the earth she'd known, at a glance. But key differences began to set off alarms in her head—like the fact that Greenland was connected to North America, and South America was not. Or the fact that the Pacific Islands seemed to trail straight down from Japan like perfectly aligned stepping stones, rather than in a sort of arcing scatter.

Or the fact that North America, Greenland, South America, and Japan weren't even labeled on the map at all.

"This . . . is earth?"

"Yes," Charlie paused for a moment. "Was it different in your time?"

"Very. Right now, in my time, I'd be in United North America . . . Not the Kingdom of Aristonia."

"North America?" Charlie repeated, utterly fascinated at the mere words. "What else is different?"

"Just about everything other than the broad strokes of the continents." Jo leaned away from the monitors, trying to re-file her thoughts.

She was in 2058, but it wasn't the 2058 of her world. The Society had been broken, by her, and Snow must've recreated the world in a new design—one that seemed to deviate greatly from what she'd known.

"Are there gods in this world?" Jo asked, thinking that Snow may have rebuilt the world back to before the Society.

"Not until I met you." Charlie folded his hands. "At least, none that I know of."

*So it wasn't the Age of Gods reborn. That left one thing . . .*

"Magic. Do you have magic?"

"I do not. But I know many who do."

"The Age of Magic," Jo breathed, stepping away to lean against the wall again. It was a reset back to when the Society was formed. But it hadn't been formed in the Age of Gods—no, Snow had said Pan trapped him while he was weak from rebuilding time into the Age of Magic. It was like Mt. Fuji all over again, but on a much, much larger scale. "He reset everything—*reverted*, that was the word he used…"

Another thought struck Jo. If Snow had rebooted the world, then perhaps *she* didn't exist because she should've never existed—because she was never meant to be from this time. But the other members of the Society?

"I need you to look up another name."

"Go ahead," Charlie said, pulling up the browser once more.

"Wayne Davis. . . He should be in New York City."

Charlie looked at her dumbly. "New York City? Another one of your alternate dimension cities?"

"Pull up the map again?" The moment it filled the screen Jo pointed to where New York City was in her time. "About here, big city."

"*Oh*, you mean Yorkton City."

"Sure, try that." It sounded close enough that Jo wondered what alteration in the time line had led to such a similar but different name.

A few names pulled up, but Jo didn't have to go very far down the list. She thrust out her finger, pointing to the headline right at the top of the page: "Mogul Wayne Davis Finds Big Payday With Risky Bet".

"This one."

Charlie clicked and Jo's eyes didn't even have a chance to skim the article before they fell on the photograph of a familiar face, hair slicked so far back it had passed the point of ridiculousness. Wayne stood out like a sore thumb, wearing clothes that he had no doubt had to request custom, since no others in the lineup of businessmen he was with wore anything like it.

"Wait. . . I recognize him."

"You do?" Jo turned, surprised.

"Yeah, he made 1.46 billion kernits overnight."

"Kernits?"

"Money?"

"Oh." There was going to be a significant learning curve to this world. *Everything in due time.* She would roll with it like she rolled with joining the Society, like she rolled with every job before that. The only thing that mattered was her goal, and right now, that goal was to get to Wayne, then the rest of the team. It would be far more effective to discuss the differences between this world and her own with someone else from the Society.

*That was, if he remembered at all.*

The thought nearly stopped her heart. What if this was Wayne, but not *her* Wayne? Like Yuusuke was still Yuusuke after her wish, but had never known Josephina.

"I need to get there."

"Okay . . ."

"Can you make that happen for me?"

"I see . . . And what do I get out of all this help?"

"You met a real live demigod and received an answer you were looking for your whole life." Jo should've known that wasn't going to be enough for Charlie.

"Fascinating? Yes. Explains something I've always wondered about? Also yes. Though, looked for my whole life sounds a bit dramatic. . . But you're asking me to spend actual money on booking you travel." He tapped his hands on the desk, as if impatiently waiting for her to connect the dots. "I'm giving you my own funds to get you where you want to go. I'm going to need something more than a fun party story."

She could see it on his face. "Tell me, why are you killing them?"

"I don't have to tell you that."

"You should, though."

"Is that a threat?" Charlie's face couldn't seem to decide if it wanted to look amused or nonplussed.

"I hope it doesn't have to be." Jo tipped her head back, looking down at him. "Tell me why."

"Because the world needs to know the truth of Primus Sanguis and what N.A.I.S.—"

Jo held up a hand to stop him. "That's all I needed to hear." It was enough to prove a key similarity in the character of the Charlie in this world, and the Charlie she'd known.

She looked to the computer and for a brief moment, her consciousness waged against her. Even if she could argue that she was in a glass house and shouldn't throw stones, and even if she found herself agreeing with Charlie in a way, did she have an obligation to stop him? After all, people were dying.

But they weren't innocent people. Who got to draw the line between vigilante and serial killer? The people in power? It was best to keep her hands off the whole affair, Jo decided. Plus, there was a more pressing matter—Pan. If Jo was alive, her other half was too, somewhere, and who knew what havoc she was currently unleashing on an unsuspecting world.

"I won't tell anyone what you're doing," Jo vowed. "No anonymous tips. No turning you in. If you get caught down the line due to your own stupidity, that'll be on you. But do this for me, and I walk out the door—out of your life forever. You get my silence, and the chance to close the file that's been bugging you.

"A fair deal? Right?"

Charlie studied her. Jo wondered what he was looking for—if he was trying to use his sensors to pick up perspiration, or changes in heartbeat, or any other physiological clues that she was lying. That was, if Jo could even give off those signals in her current state. Whatever mental test he was putting her through, she must have passed, because Charlie turned back to the computer.

"You want to go by rail, or by air?"

Jo took it to be a sign that their deal now stood. "By air. It should be faster, right?"

"Without doubt . . . I just didn't know if you wanted to be on dragonback for forty minutes."

Jo stopped all movement. "Say that again?"

"What?"

"The last bit."

"Forty minutes?"

"The other last bit."

"Dragonback?"

*Oh, yes.* She'd have a lot to learn about this new world.

# FAR FROM OVER

Two hours later, nearly all of one spent on one of the most thrilling and terrifying flights of her life, Jo was standing in front of a large, glass skyscraper, legs like jelly and heart threatening to beat its way out of her chest. She told herself it was leftover adrenaline from her first time flying dragonback, but she knew it was more than that.

It was fear. Fear of the unknown, of all the differences this world could hold over her head. Fear of what she might find when and if she managed to reach Snow, of what Pan have been doing all this time.

Fear of the man on the other side of these glass walls, who she hoped would have all the answers.

Wayne and she had left on some awkward terms, if he even remembered her at all. What if she'd come all this way only to be laughed at and sent packing? Or worse, what if he remembered her and refused to help, wiping his hands of their situation, of *her*, altogether.

It's not like they had the Society anymore, forcing them together. He'd known the most out of all the Society's members. . . perhaps he (rightfully) blamed her for trying to keep things secret from all of them.

But Wayne was her only solid lead so far, her only light at the end of a winding, labyrinthine tunnel of questions about the new world she'd literally been dropped into. She'd be foolish to waste it, regardless of her fears. So, with a breath of resolve, Jo pushed her way through the massive double doors and into the intricate decor of the lobby.

As her eyes scanned the layout, her magic automatically searching for any and all ways she might be able to break into his office (once she found it), she couldn't deny how much the atmosphere reminded her of Wayne. It was outlandish and pretentious, but it still managed to scream class. In fact, if she didn't know any better, she'd have sworn there was a hint of his 1920s flair hidden in the furniture and wall art. Between this and his clothes . . . *it had to be him, he had to remember*. It was so reminiscent of the man, it almost made her smile, even as her stomach dropped.

Because while she'd been admiring Wayne's personification in the lobby's aesthetic, someone had approached her unnoticed and placed a firm hand on her shoulder. Her magic hadn't even managed to formulate half of a plan yet.

Jo spun around to face the owner of the authoritative grip, only to find a woman about her height, dressed in a pencil skirt and silk blouse, a key card clipped to her breast pocket. Kind eyes stared at her from behind fashionable, thick-framed glasses, and when she smiled, there was only a hint of the authority there. It was still enough to put Jo on edge.

"Ms. Espinosa?" the woman asked, and Jo nodded before she could stop herself, caught off-guard by the sound of her name in an unfamiliar voice. "Follow me, please?"

There seemed little other choice, so Jo accompanied the woman to her desk, watching as she waved at a row of metallic spheres on a floating pillar to the left of her computer. One of the spheres responded to the motion and floated quickly into Jo's presence, flitting about between each of her eyes, before making a spiral pattern around her torso, and finally stopping at Jo's wrist.

Out of curiosity more than anything, Jo lifted up her arm. The metal sphere did a small 180 before returning to the desk. The secretary held out a hand, and as it settled into her palm, the metal began to shift, molding first into an amorphous blob, then into what was clearly an ID bracelet.

The woman waved a hand and the bracelet vanished, a firm weight suddenly appearing on the wrist Jo still had outstretched. Jo studied it in surprise, feeling around the edge of the cool metal. The magic within it was comforting in a way, like hiding under covers from the monsters beneath the bed, or locking away something special with the only key hanging about your neck. It was a magic that felt like safety and certainty, and maybe just a hint of something familiar.

*Nickels and bets and a Paris penthouse*, her mind supplied for her, but surely she was just projecting.

"This will take you all the way to the top floor," the woman explained, motioning towards the elevators. "Be sure to keep it on until you leave and have no plans of returning so none of the wards hinder you." Jo nodded, keeping a hand on the bracelet as she made off in the direction indicated.

With the hum of working magic beneath her fingers, the elevator door opened. There were no numbers to press, no scanner for her bio-band, but her bracelet seemed to direct the elevator upward regardless, stopping when they'd reached what she presumed to be the top floor.

If the lobby had been elaborate, the office on the top floor was even more so, but in a way that reminded Jo of Wayne's bedroom in the mansion. Floor to ceiling windows, modern architecture, a view that took Jo's breath away. It suited Wayne far more than even the lobby had. Though she wasn't sure if she was allowed to, Jo felt instantly at ease in the familiar atmosphere. That is, until an equally familiar voice brought her out of her silent musings.

"Nice of you to finally show up to the shindig, dollface."

Jo whirled around to find Wayne leaning against his desk, eyes filled to the brim with amusement and understanding, and looking as dashing as he always had. Before she really registered what she was doing, she was shuffling, then walking, then rushing into his arms, catching them both off guard, if the startled laugh that escaped Wayne's chest and muffled itself in her hair was any indication.

"You're alive," she breathed, not aware until that moment that she hadn't been entirely certain he would be. It took a rather awkward breath of stillness before Wayne returned the embrace.

"Yeah, doll. I am. And so are you."

They weren't on solid footing yet, and Jo could feel it, but she still took it as a win. He hadn't turned her away.

"I see you found new fashion in this world," Wayne appraised her, still holding her in his grasp.

"I'll take a hoodie if you have one."

He arched his eyebrows but said with a chuckle, "I think that can be arranged."

"I can't believe you remember me," she added, even though it was redundant at this point. This time, Wayne's arms tightened the embrace a bit before letting go, his laugh much softer, fonder.

"I remember everything. We all do."

*We all do.* Jo's eyes lit up.

"Everyone else? The rest of the team?"

But before Wayne could be bothered to explain, he was moving away from her and reaching for something on his desk.

"Speaking of the rest of the team, I think you've kept them waiting long enough." Wayne grinned, waving a hand over a small obsidian disk placed on the desk—it was the same way Snow used to wave a hand over the briefing room table. Shimmers of formless light appeared in the space above the disk, then two faces. Faces she knew, faces she loved—alive and nearly within reach.

"I'm in the middle—" Samson began to say.

"Sam, it's Jo!" Takako interrupted.

Jo watched as the crafter stopped what he was doing at a barely visible worktable in the background and turned, inspecting the. . . Camera?

Screen? Black Disk? His eyes widened and nearly overflowed with tears, tears Jo didn't quite feel she deserved.

"It really is you!"

"Yeah, it's me." Jo leaned toward their images, her own face flushing in an overwhelming mix of emotions. It felt like her heart might burst. They were alive. They were all alive and Wayne knew how to contact them and—"Nico?" she dared whisper.

Wayne shook his head sadly. "Seems he's really gone for good."

Jo swallowed a small uprising of grief; she should've assumed it to be so. But everything suddenly seemed so hopeful, so possible. She pressed her eyes closed. He should've gotten a fresh start too, and it was her fault that he hadn't.

"Eslar?" She turned to Samson, hoping her assumption wouldn't come off as too forward. But really, it seemed obvious. "Is he with you?"

Samson looked down, presumably fidgeting with something in his hands judging from the shift of his shoulders. Finally, after several long seconds, he shook his head. "Not with me," he said softly. "He's busy."

"You mean being a right pain in the ass," Wayne muttered, folding his arms. "But yeah, doll, the elf is fine too."

Her curiosity was more than a little peaked at what, exactly, Wayne and Samson's reactions meant. Compounded with Takako's silence, there was certainly a story there. But she'd put a pin in it for now; there were more pressing matters.

"Everyone, I have so much to tell you."

"We've managed to deduce quite a bit," Takako interrupted. "Wayne and I took the liberty of filling in Samson and Eslar on our side mission to destroy the Society."

"We've been in this new Age of Magic for almost a year, dropped right into lives as though we'd been here all along," Wayne explained. "Hell, I've got newspaper clippings hanging in here with dates before I even woke up."

It seemed like her theory about the rebirth of the Age of Magic—of time picking up right where it had left off when the Society was formed—had not been far off.

*A year.* "Sorry to keep you all waiting."

"It's all right, Jo." Samson was the one to speak. Out of them all, he was the strongest and always had been. "None of us are mad. Well, I'm not."

"You freed us, after all," Wayne said matter-of-factly, though his tone betrayed that he was, still, a little nonplussed by some of her choices leading up to the end of the Society. "Albeit a little violently and without any kind of warning and—"

"I think what Wayne is trying to say," Takako interrupted, "is that we're all glad to see you."

"And I'm glad to see you all." Jo swallowed hard, all the words threatening to choke her as they tried to rush out of her mouth at once. "But you're not free." She wished she could handle the moment with a bit more grace, relish in the joy they all felt for a little longer. But she couldn't. As long as Pan and she existed, there was danger still lurking right around the corner—a power of oblivion that could threaten them all.

"What're you talking about, doll?"

"Where's Snow?" Jo asked the question she'd been building up bravery for from the moment she woke up. "Did he make it?"

"He did, but he clearly wants nothing to do with us." Jo was surprised by the bitterness in Wayne's tone.

"What do you mean?"

"He hasn't sought out any of us," Takako explained gently. "Though, we don't even know if he knows we're—"

"I run the largest company in his Kingdom. I think he knows I'm here," Wayne snapped back.

"*His* Kingdom?" Jo repeated.

"Snow is the King of Aristonia," Samson chimed in. "But. . ."

"But what?" She didn't like his tone one bit.

"Pan is his chief advisor." Takako was the one to break the news. "We assume that's why he hasn't been in contact. But it's impossible for us to get to him to find out."

Jo placed her hands against the desk, hanging her head. "She has him again," she whispered. There was no other explanation in Jo's mind. History was repeating itself—Snow weak after rebuilding a new world, Pan born anew and ready for action. But this time, Pan was doing as she said she would: She wasn't making the same mistakes, allowing herself to be trapped. "And she's trying to flush me out." Jo cursed under her breath.

"What're you talking about, doll?" Wayne looked down at her with concern. Jo suspected it wasn't going to be the last time she saw the expression on his handsome face.

"The Society may be gone, but this is far from over. This world is in grave danger." Jo looked each of her team members in the eye, one by one. "I'm going to need your help to save it and put an end to this war, once and for all."

A WISH FOR A NEW AGE
AGE
of
MAGIC
WISH QUARTET BOOK FOUR
ELISE KOVA & LYNN LARSH

*for the friendships that span time and space*

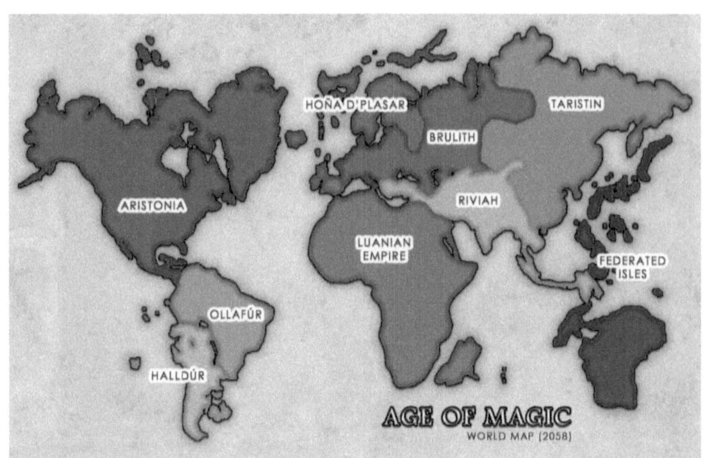

HOÑA D'PLASAR
TARISTIN
BRULITH
ARISTONIA
RIVIAH
LUANIAN EMPIRE
FEDERATED ISLES
OLL'AFÚR
HALLDÚR
AGE OF MAGIC
WORLD MAP (2058)

# FAR FROM OVER

"Just what're you talking about? 'This is far from over'?" Wayne repeated Jo's sentiment with a level of confusion, agitation, and exasperation that she'd never heard from the man before.

"Exactly what I said: the Society may have been destroyed, but we still have work to do." Jo took a deep breath, letting it out with a sigh. She was still wrapping her head around everything; it seemed almost impossible for her to fathom. How could she hope to explain it to them? Where would she start when it felt like something she should've told them long ago?

"Just how was the Society destroyed, Jo?" asked the magical projection of Takako. Her voice was gentle enough that Jo wondered if the astute woman could sense her inner turmoil. "From our perspective it was all a bit . . . confusing."

Wayne scoffed at the last word, though his demeanor remained serious. "Yeah, Takako and I didn't run into the room until *after* the Door was broken."

"Eslar and I saw it," Samson added. "But even I don't understand."

"We've been trying to put it together for nearly a year, doll."

"A year," Jo mused. "You said that before . . . What do you mean, a year?"

For Jo, it hadn't been a year. From her perspective, the past twenty-four hours comprised a series of events that competed with each other for maximum impossibility. The Society had crumbled—thanks to her unleashing her destructive magic on its foundation—and then she'd woken up yesterday in this time, in the front yard of a serial killer's house—one who, thanks to a piece of resistant code in his AI mainframe, had helped her get her bearings.

Her bearings—there was another oddity. The whole world around her was a strange transformation of the time she knew. There were skyscrapers, and elves roaming the streets. The earth itself was a familiar map, but with notable changes to the land, along with kingdoms and empires she didn't recognize atop it.

Oh, and then she'd ridden on a Dragon. Couldn't forget that, could she? Yeah, the past twenty-four hours had been a day for the record books. But just a day—at least, from her perspective.

"We all woke back up, already solidified in—as far as we can tell—the lives we would've had in this world had we not been pulled from it." Once again, Takako was the one to answer, but Jo could see that even she was struggling with a response. Comprehending their odd twist of fate was like trying to read a book backwards, up-side-down, and written in pig Latin. "Eslar was the first, then Samson."

"I think we woke up in the order we joined the Society," Samson chimed in, only briefly looking up from his bauble. He had yet to fully recover from Jo's initial mention of Eslar. Another oddity that needed eventually to be addressed.

"I'll tell you what, it *was* a bit jarring. Waking up to a life I've supposedly been living for twenty years and having no memory of it . . ." Wayne motioned to the office. "Though I can't rightly complain about how I turned out in this world."

*Twenty years.* That was how old Wayne was when he'd made his wish, Jo remembered. So, the Society had been destroyed, they were all subsequently dropped back into a new world, in the order they'd joined the Society, and they were already settled into the lives they would've been living. As if the Society had never even existed. As if *none* of their previous timelines had ever even existed.

Jo couldn't help but wonder if she had a mother in what had been Texas but was now some corner of Aristonia. Something in her said she wouldn't; they were returning to timelines as they "should've been" and for her, that was as a demigod, not as Josephina Espinosa. Now, all she would carry of her 2057 would be her name, and the memories she'd never let go of.

"So . . . this is what 2057—I mean 2058, looks like now for all of us." Jo turned away from the table and the projected images of her teammates, looking out through the windows that dominated one of the walls of Wayne's office.

It was New York City. *Yorkton,* Jo mentally corrected. Charlie hadn't known what New York City was, but Yorkton made perfect sense. And, just like the name, it was similar, but not the same as the "original" Jo recalled. But what was ever original in a universe that could be entirely remade?

She saw winged creatures landing on rooftops. The sky was filled with a mix of animal and technological flying systems. The buildings were skyscrapers, but not quite as she knew them. Impossible feats of architecture hollowed out cores of buildings where lush gardens cascaded down, striking a contrast against the industrial glass-tones below.

"A new Age of Magic." Wayne stated the obvious and rested a hand heavily on her shoulder. It summoned Jo's attention away from the sights and back to her team.

The Age of Magic had once given way to the Age of Man—Jo's original time. But it seemed that when the Society was destroyed, so too was the world reset to the year of the Society's creation: the beginning of the Age of Magic. Somewhere in this time was Snow . . . Jo's chest tightened at the thought, and Wayne's next question had Jo wondering if he could sense it.

"Now, what did you mean when you said, 'It's not over'?" Because from what we've managed to discern, life is pretty great not being beholden to wishes, or Snow, or, you know, watches."

Jo couldn't help but notice that, even still, he wore the gaudy golden timepiece on his wrist. She also couldn't help the small smile that threatened to pull at the corner of her lips at the sight.

"We're all here, yes. But the Society was—"

"The Society ended, but the fight hasn't," Jo interrupted Takako.

"What fight?" Samson asked. Jo hated the tremor in Samson's voice, an obvious reluctance to hear her response. But he needed to. They all did.

"A fight for the power to destroy the world."

"Pan." Samson surprised her by being the one to say it. Seemed to surprise everyone, in fact, as he elaborated for Wayne and Takako's benefit. "Pan was the one going after Jo . . . I'm guessing she'll keep trying, but I don't know any more than you do."

The moment Pan's name was brought up, Jo felt the sickening feeling she'd come to associate with pure loathing. But it also brought up a different feeling—the phantom sensation of being watched. A feeling that had haunted her in the Society, that had kept Pan's name off her lips, and seemed to linger even now.

"How secure is this?" Jo asked Wayne.

"What?"

"This communication." Jo motioned to the desk so oddly reminiscent of the briefing room table. "I'm still learning about this world, but video conferencing could be hacked and listened in on in my original timeline."

"I'm pretty sure it's secure."

Jo put her hands on her hips, thinking a long moment. She could see how the communication could be broken into and listened in on with a blink. But Jo didn't know if it was because of her magic, or because it was actually a risky connection. She took a deep breath and decided to err on the side of caution. It wasn't exactly a far leap in logic to see Wayne as someone who wouldn't understand a good security system from a bad one. He likely had people to take care of that for him, but looking at the office, she trusted them even less.

"*Pretty sure* isn't going to cut it," Jo muttered. That same sensation of being watched still lingered with her. She shook her head, her mind made up. "We need to meet, in person. I have so much I need to tell all of you, but for now, you're all going to have to trust me on this. The one you suspect *is* a danger, not just to you, but to everyone you love, and the very fabric of the world itself."

"You don't have to convince me." Takako was the first to respond. "I'll get to Aristonia as quickly as possible."

"Where are you now?" Jo couldn't help but ask.

"We know it as Japan, but it's now the Kingdom of Hajisha . . . Part of the Federated Isles."

If Jo hadn't known Takako so well, known her to be a level and serious person—especially when the situation called for it—she would have suspected the woman of making up the names. But this was not her world and it was not a practical joke. This was the Age of Magic, the earth overlaid with thousands of years where sorcery had never left the landscape of human history.

"I guess it's a good thing I always sucked at history," Jo mumbled. "Gonna have to re-learn it all anyway."

Wayne made a soft noise of amusement. "I can coordinate travel for you both," he offered to Samson and Takako.

"Thank you," Takako said.

"One or two, Samson?"

All eyes turned to their craftsman.

"I'll try to get Eslar." He didn't even notice they were all looking at him, his head never rising to meet their gaze.

"Thank you, Samson," Jo said gently. She could see something was breaking him down, though without more information, it was impossible to tell what it might be. Just that it had something to do with Eslar. "He's one of the team, after all."

Samson just nodded.

"All right, I'll get on the arrangements, and we'll all wait on pins and needles until Jo feels confident telling us what, exactly, is going on."

Wayne leaned over his desk. "See you all soon." With a wave of his hand, the call ended.

Jo turned, leaning against the edge of the desk. Looking back out the window, she squinted into the setting sun, wondering just where Pan was now. She didn't know what it would take to bring the woman down, but Jo was confident that their first step was the right one—getting the team back together.

# JUST ALL RIGHT

The breeze that wafted past the balcony brushed the hair out of Jo's face with gentle yet chilling fingers. Even as she tightened the heavy blanket around her shoulders, Jo couldn't help but lean into the feel of it, closing her eyes to the sensation, soaking it in.

It wasn't until she was finally sitting down, glass of way-too-expensive scotch in hand, that it hit her. She hadn't had a chance to really process what being in this new world, free of the Society's constraints, might mean. But now, as she felt the breeze against her face, heard the sounds of the city below her in its un-muted cacophony, she allowed herself a moment to simply *feel*.

The chair beneath her was comfortable and sturdy, the cushions a soft and cradling contrast. The air was rich with the tangy scent of a busy city, muted by both the crisp chill of the mid-January weather and the distance provided by the penthouse balcony—because of *course* Wayne would live in a fancy penthouse above his own company. Some things not even a brand-new world could change, it would seem.

And, while she'd never admit it to him, some things she didn't *want* to see changed. There were few precious constants she could depend on in the jumping timelines and shifting worlds; the members of the Society, Wayne specifically, counted among them. He'd been by her side from the very first moment, after all.

At the sound of the sliding glass door opening behind her, Jo let her eyes flutter open as well, taking in the flickering lights of the buildings surrounding them. Soft jazz spilled outside for a moment before it was dulled once again by the door sliding shut. If Jo listened intently enough though, she could still hear it amid the backdrop of the city's ambient noise.

"Someone looks cozy," Wayne chuckled by way of greeting, sitting himself down in the chair to Jo's right. He'd forgone a blanket of his own for a scarf and an expensive-looking coat that managed to cling to his frame in all the right ways. Jo just shrugged, pulling the thick, probably-also-hideously-expensive blanket tighter around herself out of spite. When she glanced over at Wayne, it was to find a look of unexpected fondness on his face. One that he hastily schooled into something more teasing once he noticed, motioning with his chin towards her glass. "Liking the giggle juice?"

Though the lingo felt more teasing than Wayne's usual bravado, Jo still felt warmth bloom at the center of her chest. She hadn't realized how much she'd missed the easy rapport they'd once had, hadn't realized how long things had been getting rougher and messier between them as a result of her not-so-secret mission to end the Society. Jo raised the glass to her lips, lamenting her role in inflicting those old wounds.

As she sipped, mulling over where, how, and when to attempt to suture her past mistakes, Jo allowed herself to focus for a moment on the way her fingers felt against the cool glass of the tumbler, the way the rich and smoky flavor of the scotch coated her tongue, tingling all the way down her throat and warming her chest and stomach. It was the most delicious liquor she'd ever experienced in any of her lives, she was certain, but after another quiet sip and a brief moment to lick the remnants of the amber liquid from her lips, she just shrugged again. And smirked.

"It's all right, I guess."

"*All right*?" Wayne gaped at her, which only made her smirk grow into a full-fledged grin. With an over-dramatic flourish of his own glass, Wayne said, "I'll have you know this single malt was aged for twenty years in Aristonian oak and another *fifteen* in Brulithian wine casks, and that's not even taking into account the . . . Wait. You're just razzin' me, aren't you, dollface?"

Jo finally gave in to the bubble of laughter she'd only just held at bay during his tirade.

"You got me," she said, holding her glass out for a toast. "It's amazing, Wayne, even if I don't understand half of what you just said. Thank you for sharing it with me."

With an exasperated sigh that was only half-feigned, Wayne shook his head, eventually smiling softly in return and clinking the edge of his glass against hers. "Pleasure's all mine, doll. When you're given a second shot at life, you learn not to get hung up on formality. What's the point of having nice things if you aren't going to enjoy them?"

"Sure, Mr. Twenty Years in Aristonian barrels." Jo rolled her eyes, but even she could hear the amusement in her voice.

"What can I say? If you're going to *have* nice things, you've also got to know *why* they're nice, don't you think?"

Jo took another small swig of the nice thing in question and hummed her approval. She braced herself. "Wayne, I'm sorry."

"For what?" The man likely knew exactly what she was trying to say, but . . .

"For how I handled everything in those final weeks, maybe even months, of the Society." Jo passed her glass from hand to hand, eyes locked within as if trying to find the right words shining true in the sheen of the city lights off the amber liquor. "For keeping my powers a secret and endangering everyone.

"I had reasons," she added hastily. Then sighed. "But they're all just excuses . . . I think. I should've trusted the team more. I should've just put everything out in the open." Jo dared to look Wayne in the eye then. His face was passive, expressionless; there was nothing for her to read in his visage. "I should've trusted you more." A beat passed, enough for Jo to grow nervous, and then—

"Doll." Wayne leaned further back in his chair, looking at the city skyline, a deep furrow in his brow. "I know you had your reasons and I trusted them without explanation. But I think I can speak for all of us when I say I'm looking forward to finding out what those reasons are."

"More than fair."

"Plus, it seems like you learned your lesson." He looked back at her, a small smile on his lips. Jo hoped he was referring to her instinct to get the Society back together, her plan to tell them everything.

"I think I have. So . . . are we good?"

"Yeah, we're good." Wayne hoisted his glass and Jo did the same. They both leaned over their chairs and, for a brief moment, she was reminded of another balcony they'd once shared.

Their glasses made another soft *clinking* sound, and they both drank.

After that, a comfortable silence fell, both of them staring out past the glass railing of the balcony and into the shimmering city night. Even with the threat of the unknown hanging over all of them, it felt oddly peaceful —like if Jo closed her eyes, she could convince herself that the world wasn't in danger. If she pretended hard enough, she could imagine that this was a world without Pan, without any dangers at all outside of the ones that come with any normal, human (humanish?) life.

She could imagine that Snow was there, wrapping her up in his loving embrace, enjoying this moment of temporary peace, too.

At the thought of him, of how much he'd sacrificed to give her this chance, Jo felt the cocoon of that faux-peace begin to unravel, a weight settling firmly back over her shoulders. She had no idea what position Snow was even in right now, if he was hurt or being tortured by Pan, or worse. And here she was drinking fancy scotch and pretending everything was going to work out just fine. Guilt churned low in her gut as she pulled her eyes from the city and into the reflective pool of liquor in her glass.

Had she always looked so tired?

Wayne seemed to notice her shift in mood too; a soft sigh escaped him.

"You're worried about him." It wasn't a question.

"I'm worried about a lot of things." It wasn't an answer.

"Whatever it is that we have to do, we'll do it," Wayne offered after another brief pause, and though the words were meant to be a comfort, they only left Jo feeling oddly heavier. "We've been through hell before and made it out alive, haven't we?"

Jo swallowed thickly. "Most of us anyway."

"Nico, he—" Wayne paused, running a hand over his face, suddenly looking as tired as Jo felt. "In a way, he gave us this chance too, you know? He's part of the reason we're here at all right now."

"And I'm the reason he's not." It was painful, to bring Wayne's old words back out, but this time, unexpectedly, Wayne only shook his head.

"We all could have done something different for Nico. We all could have tried harder. But in the end, he did what any of us would have done. He gave us his time to keep fighting and surviving. So all we can do is take that sacrifice and keep doing exactly that. Fighting and surviving. Even if it means going up against Pan one more time to end this for good." A moment of quiet, and then Wayne asked, softer but with just as much seriousness, "That *is* what we're going to have to do, isn't it? All of this about danger still lurking . . . You need us to find a way to snuff her out?"

Jo wasn't sure *what* they were going to have to do, but Wayne definitely had the right idea. Pan was the only threat left. If they—and the whole world—wanted any hope of actual peace, it would mean making sure she was dealt with. And quickly. Jo wasn't sure what Pan was planning, or if she even knew that Jo had finally arrived in this new age, but Jo couldn't shake the feeling that they were running out of time.

Before she could even begin to explain the whirlwind of thoughts and emotions battering about inside her head, Wayne held up a hand to silence her.

"You know what? Don't worry about explaining anything now," he said, looking back out at the cityscape again. "You were right. We should wait for the rest of the team."

Jo wasn't sure if Wayne had seen the conflict on her face, or if he was just perceptive enough to know she needed more time to get her thoughts in order, but she was grateful nonetheless. This was going to be hard enough to explain; she might as well only have to do it once.

After another long minute of simply enjoying each other's silent company, Jo whispered a confession into the night air. "Thank you, Wayne. For taking the risk. You . . . I know you didn't have to," she said, realizing just how true the words were. He and the whole rest of the team could have simply denied her request for help and gone on living their own lives. The only one Pan was after was her. But instead, Wayne and the others had agreed. As if they were still a team.

"It's not like I have much of a choice, do I?" Wayne rolled his eyes, but there was something off in the dismissive tone of his voice, his smirk stiff. "I mean, knowing Pan . . . we're talking world domination or something here, right? What kind of man would I be if I said no when called on for something like that?"

Jo watched as he took another long drink of his scotch, followed the bob in his throat as he swallowed. She watched emotion flicker across his features as he did it again, knocking back the rest of it and then licking his lips. His eyes were distant as he ran a finger around the rim of his now empty glass.

"This team . . . They're the only family I have left, you know? The only one that matters anymore anyway. Hard to feel much toward a family I'm supposed to have in this world but have only known for a few months," he finally whispered, another confession drifting between them on the night air. The mention of family brought her mind back to her mother. But Jo's earlier decision was merely further reaffirmed. Some things were best for her not to pursue—at least not until the matter of a psychotic demigod was settled. "Even if it means going up against a power I frankly don't even *understand*, I would see this through for any one of the Society. I would do anything for my team."

He'd always been that way, hadn't he? Loyal to the team, placing them before anything else, even his own wants and opinions. "We're lucky to have you, Wayne . . . truly."

She heard a huff of amusement, but Jo couldn't bring herself to look at him. "You really think that?"

"I do."

"Good." A pause, a breath. "Because I would do anything for *you*, dollface."

Jo felt her breath catch in her throat as her eyes were pulled to his face, emotion welling up at the sincerity in his voice. She didn't have the words to say how much that meant to her. So instead, she held his gaze and reached her free hand out in his direction. After a moment of confusion, Wayne grabbed her hand, allowing her to link their fingers together. When she did, she held on tight, hoping that little bit of connection would show him just how grateful she was to have him by her side.

They stayed like that long after the cold had made its way beneath blanket and coat, not breaking the hold even when their fingers had gone numb.

# VAMPIRE CREAM

J o couldn't sleep.

When Wayne had finally succumbed to his own exhaustion—since apparently members of the Society were once again beholden to the energetic constraints of being alive—Jo had settled herself in one of the guest rooms, expecting sleep to take her under swiftly after the day she'd had. But after an hour of tossing and turning, she began to realize the dawning approach of a new complication.

Jo found she lacked even a minimal *desire* to sleep now. Whether it was because of her newly awakened demigod status or genuine insomnia, she wasn't sure. But after one hour of restlessness became two, three, and finally four, Jo decided it wasn't worth trying to force herself into a state she clearly didn't want to be in.

So, keeping as quiet as possible, fully and enviously aware that Wayne was probably deep in his own slumber, Jo wandered the penthouse with her thoughts . . .

Which turned out to be more stressful and anxiety-inducing than anything. So instead she switched to distraction.

It took a few minutes for Jo to figure out how to use this world's version of a television, another obsidian device similar to the briefing room table—except this one was mounted on the wall. If the awkward hand waves, various thoughts, and magical pulses to figure out how to turn it on weren't bad enough, the blaring noise that emerged when it did flick to life had Jo certain she'd disturbed her host's slumber. Jo held her breath, but when she heard nothing, she turned to the projected image.

It was a sort of hologram-meets-augmented-reality, as the picture came alive around her in near life-like clarity. Wayne's living room was transformed. The furniture stayed the same, but now it was as if she were seated at the edge of a theater's stage. Jo watched as it displayed what looked like the telenovelas her abuelita used to watch. Except where the novelas she knew were Spanish-language soap operas spouting over-dramatic arguments between lovers, this one focused on two werewolf-looking creatures howling at each other—Jo honestly wasn't sure if she was supposed to know what they were saying or not.

For the rest of the night, Jo lost herself in the various news and enter-tainment channels this new world had to offer, marveling at the similarities and differences to the world she'd come from. One channel was airing a historical documentary about the war between their kingdom and the neighboring kingdom of Taristin; another aired a colorful show about current social media trends, hosted by what looked to be a half-pixie, half-peacock hybrid creature. After who knew how long, Jo eventually settled on a news outlet, watching in awe as they covered current affairs.

Apparently there were weakening magical energy currents beneath the sea surrounding a kingdom named Zakon. Another kingdom, Hoña d'Plasar, was celebrating its five-hundredth year of independence. Also, the release of a new cream meant to return a vampire's skin to their pre-bio-death pallor had apparently been recalled due to increased sun sensi-tivity. Who knew?

Jo was so engrossed, she didn't even notice the sun had risen, her focus on the television only broken by a mug suddenly being shoved in her face. She startled, nearly knocking it out of Wayne's hands.

"Morning, dollface," he said through a laugh, voice made deep and rumbly from sleep. "No need to worry. It's just coffee."

"Thanks." Jo cleared her throat and picked up the mug from where Wayne had placed it on the table. A pang of loss hit her at the scent, Nico's memory wrapping around her as she took a hesitant sip. It hit her then, how long it had been since she'd allow herself to just savor the rich, caffeinated beverage without guilt, without sadness. But Wayne's words from the night before settled like a comforting weight against her chest; she owed it to Nico to keep going.

Wayne sat down next to her on the couch, crossing a leg over his knee as he sipped slowly at his own mug of coffee. "I didn't hear you get up," he said eventually. "Sleep alright?"

Jo's initial reaction was to tell Wayne that she hadn't slept at all, that perpetual insomnia might be her new demigod normal, but then she remembered the desk at the police office, the look of fear and worry on his face. Wayne had only just started looking at her like he used to, speaking to her like he had the night before, with a familiarity and fondness she'd missed dearly. She didn't want to ruin that by reminding him again just how different she'd become.

There'd be time for that when everyone else arrived. "Yeah," she responded as casually as she could. "Just woke up early, that's all."

Wayne hummed around another sip of coffee before moving on. If he noticed anything amiss in her answer, he didn't say. "I sent a car to pick up Takako. She should be here any minute now."

As if on cue, the doorbell chose that moment to chime. Jo's eyes lit up at the promise of her friend's arrival. When she didn't automatically get off the couch to answer the door (it wasn't her home, after all), Wayne laughed, motioning with his chin in its direction as if to say, *Go ahead.*

Jo got up at once, rushing with probably enough eagerness to look a bit silly, but it didn't matter. Seeing Takako over a hologram screen was one thing. But seeing her in person? Knowing that she really was alive and safe? That was something Jo only just then realized how much she'd been craving.

The moment the door swung open, Jo couldn't stop herself; her arms were wrapped around Takako's shoulders in an embrace fierce enough to have her stumbling back a step, bags clattering to the floor. She seemed stunned enough that she remained frozen in Jo's arms for a long moment, but then, with a soft chuckle that Jo could feel vibrating between them, Takako hugged her back just as fiercely.

"It's good to see you too, Jo," she said on a heartfelt breath into Jo's ear. Jo's heart soared, arms tightening for a split second before releasing Takako from her death grip—only releasing her to arm's length, where she could look her over with an awed smile.

Takako was wearing what appeared to be the casual version of a military uniform: a simple coat that ended at her waist and a well-tailored pair of pants, both in deep maroon. A badge was pinned over her left breast, little beads dangling from it. Her hair was noticeably longer than Jo remembered, enough to merit the ponytail it was currently wrapped up in, but in every way, she was still the same girl Jo had come to know and love.

"Are you going to stand in the foyer all day, or are you going to let Takako inside?" Wayne's voice echoed from back in the living room, once again startling Jo out of her thoughts. At the look of fond amusement on Takako's face, Jo decided not to fight back the blush that rose to her cheeks, smiling at her friend as she grabbed one of the bags off the floor and slung it over her shoulder.

"Right, sorry. Come on in."

"Thank you." Takako nodded, picking up the remaining two bags and heading inside. By the shape and size of one of them, Jo wouldn't have been surprised if it held some variety of firearms. It was with that realization and the full recognition of the military uniform that a new concern fell into place.

"Is it really alright for you to be wearing that here in Ameri—I mean, Aristonia?" Jo asked, gesturing with her free hand at Takako's uniform as she deposited the bag next to the couch with the other. For a moment, Takako only looked down at herself in confusion, and Jo quickly continued, trying to clarify, "It's only 2058. I saw in a documentary that there was still a war in this time right around my timeline's World War III . . ."

"Oh, right," Takako smirked. "Apparently in this version of the world, our kingdoms actually *like* each other. The Federal Isles even offered support to Aristonia during that war against Taristin."

"No kidding..." Jo grinned, putting her hands on her hips. She'd no doubt flipped the channel before the documentary had gotten to that bit. "Well, Aristonia appreciates your support, I guess?"

Takako laughed. "I guess."

After that, Wayne left the two of them alone to make lunch. Jo chose not to mention her lack of appetite and instead settled easily into a conversation with Takako. It was clear that the other members of the Society had been released from the bodily restrictions they'd experienced in the mansion—they now seemed to feel hunger and exhaustion as keenly as any other normal human. So where did that leave her? That was an answer Jo wasn't rushing to find.

"So where did the timeline spit you out?" Jo asked as she curled up into the corner of the couch, second cup of coffee balanced on her knees. Takako sat with her legs tucked beneath her, cradling her own mug in both hands.

"I'd apparently served long and successfully enough in Hajisha's Special Forces Unit to merit paid leave."

Jo whistled in appreciation. "Impressive."

Takako just chuckled softly to herself. "I'm sure it was. Can't remember any of it though."

"Me neither." Jo nodded in agreement. "Not the war, but . . . anything of the life I've supposedly been living." *If there'd been a life to live at all,* Jo added mentally. She still wasn't convinced there had ever been a Josephina in this world.

"I've been spending the last year since I woke up with my family," she continued, smiling down into her mug. "I requested that leave the second I realized they remembered who I was. No tragedy like Mt. Fuji, no war to fight, plus the added bonus of my family actually recognizing me when I showed up at their door? I mean, I sometimes wonder if I should feel guilty for reaping the benefits of a soldier when I don't remember actually fighting as one... But how could I not?"

The look of easy happiness on her face as she spoke about her family was unfamiliar to Jo, but beautiful to behold. Even if the love for their families had persisted in the Society, it had always been hampered by the knowledge that those family members no longer knew of their existence.

"I don't think you should feel bad at all." Jo rested a hand on Takako's. "I would've done the same in your shoes."

After getting up-to-date on each other's lives—a process that included Takako cursing impressively over a black disk until it showed some holo-images of her sister's twins—they settled in to wait for the rest of their team to arrive.

Except Samson didn't arrive for another two days. And when he finally did, he was alone.

Jo pulled Samson into as equally fierce a hug as she had Takako, though she could tell by his body language that it would be wise not to smother him too much. Still, Samson returned the hug eagerly, relaxing a bit into her embrace before pulling away and regaining an anxious sort of full-body tension.

Aside from the way he was slightly curled in on himself, his smile a bit forced, he looked good. His bright orange hair was shaved short on one side and styled in tight braids on the other, his outfit casual but new and fashionable. He had brought with him a rather impressive collection of bags, most of which Jo assumed contained his tools and projects worth traveling with.

Though it itched at her to ask about Eslar, instinct told her to let Samson settle in first, picking his brain about what he'd been up to since he "woke up." Though he seemed less willing to offer up detailed information than Takako had been, he talked enthusiastically enough about his new life.

He'd woken up in a kingdom called Riviah—what in Jo's world had been India—and had spent the last year in the far north of the Luanian Empire, near the western side of the Kingdom of Brulith, around what Jo knew to be Spain. When she asked him if Eslar had woken near him (since they were clinging to each other at the end of the Society), Samson mumbled something incomprehensible and changed the subject, rambling happily on about his current setup as an independent craftsman with an extensive list of loyal patrons.

It was Wayne who eventually brought up the elephant in the room.

"So what took you so long to get here?"

Jo threw a glare at Wayne over her shoulder, but he ignored her. As much as she wanted Samson to be at ease, they really did need to know where he'd been. And more than that, why Eslar hadn't shown up with him. That feeling that time was most certainly not on their side hadn't abated.

When Samson seemed overtly reluctant to answer, however, Jo tried a different tactic. She reached across the couch to grab Samson's hand. She gave it a comforting squeeze before speaking.

"Eslar's not coming, is he, Sam?" Samson looked at Jo first in surprise, then with a mix of exhaustion and something that looked painfully like guilt. When he shook his head, Jo squeezed his hand a bit tighter. Still, as much as it hurt her to pry, they deserved to know. "Did he say why?"

At that, Samson's hand twitched beneath hers, his back hunching further into the slouch he'd adopted. "He, um . . . No. He didn't... didn't say," Samson managed after a moment, the fingers of his free hand fussing with a loose thread on one of the couch's throw pillows. Jo could feel his magic stuttering out of him and recoiling as if he was physically preventing himself from altering the composition of the pillow into something easier to fidget with. "I tried to ask, but he . . . he just said he wasn't coming." He looked up at Jo with sad eyes and a strained half-smile. "I'm sorry. That's all I could manage."

Something about the admission seemed off to Jo's ears, though whether he was stalling or hiding something or possibly just uncomfortable with the whole situation, she couldn't tell. All she knew was that any mention of Eslar was making Samson increasingly distressed. Unfortunately, or fortunately for Samson's sake, they didn't have time to dwell on that fact—something Wayne seemed to pick up on at much the same time as Jo.

"Well, if the elf's not coming, he's not coming," Wayne sighed. He'd taken to pacing, arms crossed over his chest and face stern in concentration. "We can't force him to help if he's determined to keep pretending we don't exist." Jo raised an eyebrow at that, but Wayne went on without explanation. "Nothing for it but to move on for now."

Samson let out a soft, sad sigh, one Jo was sure no one was meant to hear, as he nodded in quiet agreement. They may have been willing to move on out of necessity, but for Jo, the curiosity surrounding Eslar only grew.

"Thank you all for coming," Jo started awkwardly. She felt like some half-baked manager at a company meeting, going through the motions while trying to hide her resentment for the situation. Pushing herself onto her feet, Jo crossed her arms over her chest and headed toward the large windows, speaking as she walked. "I know that we're all in the same spot—waking up to lives that we have no recollection of having. But at the same time, being given a second chance at life without the Society . . ."

"The Society *really* is gone, then?" Takako asked. "It's not going to come back?"

"I don't see a way it could've survived." Given the way she remembered dismantling it . . . She had every faith. "If it had, we would know by now, I think."

"Then why is Pan . . ." Samson started and trailed off, looking at Takako and Wayne to see if they had any insights he didn't. When neither moved to provide an explanation, he turned back to Jo. "Why is she still a threat?"

Jo paused, placing her hands on her hips, looking out the window as if she'd find some easy way to tell them everything somewhere within the city skyline. She didn't. "I realize that what I'm about to tell you is going to sound clinically insane."

"Doll, we existed for hundreds of years granting wishes in a Society outside of time," Wayne said, clearly amused as he slung one calf onto the other knee. "I doubt you're going to shock us."

*Challenge accepted.* "I'm a demigod."

Their faces would have been hilarious in any other situation. Samson's mouth dropped right open, his hands still for the first time. Takako squinted her eyes, as if trying to see proof of the claim, and tilted her head. Wayne kept opening and closing his mouth like a gaping fish, but no words came.

"See? I told you it'd sound crazy."

"I think you need to start at the beginning," Takako encouraged gently.

"Yeah, go back, way back, because I must've missed something since I was there at the start. And while you're one amazing broad, I'm not sure about godly . . ." Wayne added his unhelpful interjection.

"Well, I wasn't a demigod *then*—" Jo stopped herself, deciding to take Takako's advice. She looked to the Japanese woman. "You're right: start at the beginning. You have to believe me, first, when I say I have no memory of anything before my life as a human leading up to joining you all in 2057."

"Of course we believe you," Samson encouraged.

"Not exactly hard given how all of us just woke up this past year," Wayne muttered.

"I was working to put it together, at the end. I'd come to some conclusions on my own, and then most of what I know was confirmed by Snow . . . and Pan."

Jo took one more second to collect her thoughts, before launching into the explanation, deciding to over-share rather than under-shoot.

"We all know there was an Age of Gods, then Magic, then Man." Nods all around. "Well, apparently, just before the Age of Gods . . . There was a goddess, Oblivion. She heralded a sort-of unspoken first age—the Age of Oblivion, before life and light."

"I know that name," Samson whispered.

Jo nodded at him. "It was in one of Eslar's story books. You may have read it too . . . Like the lore of the Society itself, certain things carried throughout the ages and one of those things was mythology surrounding the story of Oblivion."

"Kind of how magic lingered in us even in the Age of Man," Takako reasoned.

"That's what I think, too," Jo continued with a nod. "Other gods came —and no, I don't know from where—formed the world, and Oblivion didn't like it. I'm paraphrasing, but I think you all get the idea. Needless to say, this created a rift among the gods, with Oblivion on one side and basically everyone else on the other."

"And Pan's Oblivion?" Wayne asked.

"Not quite . . ." This was the moment she'd been most apprehensive about. The moment they learned, truly, who and what she was. The moment when any of them would be well within their rights to hate her, to change their minds about helping her at all. "Demigods can be made two ways. One, they can be crafted by two greater gods—and that's how Snow came to be. The other is by splitting a greater god in two. In this case . . . Oblivion was split by the other gods to prevent her from destroying, well, the entire universe. The two demigods formed were Destruction and Chaos.

"From what I can tell . . . every divinity was just named after the thing they created and represented in the world—light, life, creation, what-have-you. Mortals gave them other names. Names that, like Eslar's story, continued to linger through the ages in different forms even when the gods themselves did not. Chaos's name is one such example."

"Well, don't hold us in suspense—what was it?" Wayne asked, though Jo could tell from the expression on his face, he already knew.

"Pandora."

"Pan," Takako whispered.

Wayne let out a groan that turned into an expletive. "We're so stupid."

"Destruction?" Samson was the only one still glued to the story. Jo held her breath for a moment, letting it out in a weary exhale.

"That . . . was me. Which is why my magic was—"

"Always breaking things." She couldn't tell by Wayne's interruption if he was upset or just eager to know more. Either way, Jo was too far down the rabbit hole to stop now.

"As long as Destruction and Chaos existed together in the same world, there was a chance for them to come together and become Oblivion once more. The pantheon wanted to avoid that, so they made a natural counterbalance to hide me, Creation . . . or Snow, as the mortals back then called him.

"It worked, for a while. But Pan was none too pleased about the situation and began wreaking havoc."

"Shocking," Wayne rolled his eyes. Jo almost smiled.

"Creation and I knew that for mankind to ever be free of Pan's terror, we needed to destroy her for good."

"How?"

"We came up with a plan . . . a demigod split is made mortal. The idea was that Snow would split my power once more and gain control of it once it was freed from my body. He'd use it to destroy the world as it was, but then use his power of creation to quickly rebuild it free of gods . . . and Pan."

"The Age of Gods to the Age of Magic," Samson seemed to realize, and when Jo and he shared a glance, there was something indescribable in his eyes.

"Clearly, it didn't work," Wayne remarked, ever helpful.

"Sadly no, it didn't. As long as I'm alive, she's alive. And since my magic was in Snow and my body was reborn as a mortal, Pan persisted. Snow was weak from the shift—"

"It takes a lot out of him to change an age," Samson said softly. Jo paused, briefly, taking note of the understanding tone in his voice. There was something more there, his eyes still alight with that indescribable expression, but she pressed on nonetheless; there would hopefully be time to pick his brain later.

"—and Pan seized the opportunity to bind him to her, forming the Society outside of time, so she could wait to try to find me. She knew Snow would have to grant wishes to skim magic for them both to survive, for the whole Society to survive. And eventually, she knew would have her chance to be whole again."

A heavy silence settled on the room as everyone processed. Jo felt like she'd just run a marathon and now, even though there was suddenly no more track, every muscle in her body was still cranked taut with tension.

"For better or for worse, I have my magic—all of my magic—back again. In destroying the Society, I've gone back to being a demigod. Pan and Snow are once again walking among mortals, and the world has been reverted back to when the Society was founded . . . sort of, at least. The year is different, I think. My money is on things resetting from square one, even if to us it seems like this world has only existed for a year—or a few days."

"And now that you're back, too, she's going to be on the hunt for you again," Takako added.

"Yes. The stalemate in a war that's been going on since the dawn of time has ended. Now, I want to finish the war for good."

"Why?" Wayne asked, looking at all of them with denial filling his eyes. "Why not just let her be? She hasn't done anything too bad over the past couple hundred years according to the history of this world. We have our lives back, we don't have to deal with time, and—"

"And there's a demigod who can gain the power to destroy it all," Jo interrupted. "As long as Pan and I are both alive, mankind isn't safe."

"Couldn't you just stop her from joining with you?" Wayne asked.

"I can try, I *would* try . . . But there's something about her magic. It calls to me in ways I don't want to hear . . ." Her voice trailed off and none of them probed further. It was the darkest corner of her soul, the part that Jo was coming to accept as the lingering remnants of Oblivion. She wanted to vow that there was no way she could ever be tempted by it. However . . . "The best course of action is to destroy Pan and ensure that Oblivion is gone for good. That's the only way to be certain."

"I bet she's trapped Snow again," Takako mused, changing the topic and following a train of thought Jo hadn't even considered before. "If she trapped him once after a seismic shift of realities, I bet she did it again. I bet that's why he has her as his 'advisor'."

"It must be; he liked her no more than the rest of us," Samson agreed. "And she's been his advisor since the dawn of Aristonia, according to all records."

"We have to free him." Panic swelled with worry over all of the horrible things Snow could be enduring—possibly *had been* enduring for who knew how long.

"Sounds to me that freeing him and protecting the harmony of the world both hinge on the same thing: killing Pan," Takako pointed out.

"That's all well and good, but how do we get rid of a demigod?" Wayne heaved a somewhat dramatic sigh. "This isn't a point-and-shoot sort of situation."

Takako looked at him from the corners of her eyes, clearly uncertain if she should take offense. "Let's think through it logically. What was she afraid of?"

"Pan wasn't afraid of anything," Wayne said quickly. "She chewed glass, spat it at us, and then asked for thank yous."

"Then what is a demigod afraid of in general?" Takako was undeterred, and looked to Jo.

She began to pace, mulling over every bit of information that had seemed so overwhelming even minutes ago, but now seemed like precious little to cull through. "It's not as if I have a handbook on how to be a demigod. I mean, I told you all everything I know and—"

Jo stopped. Memories: a book detailing an ancient battle, a mention of Pan being afraid, her room at the mansion . . . all muddled into a mismatched jigsaw puzzle that felt like the start of a good idea—maybe.

"When I was in her room," Jo started slowly, giving herself time to try to clarify the hazy vision as much as possible. "She showed me something . . ."

"What?" Wayne asked.

"I'm trying to remember." Jo held up a hand to one eye, as if physically trying to force some part of her to see back to the memory Pan had given her while staying rooted in the present. It was the first time she was actually trying to invoke the shadows that had come to haunt her at the end of the Society. But now that she had reclaimed her full powers and actually had need of them, they no longer seemed interested in tormenting her. "We were in a forest . . . there was darkness all around us . . ."

"Forest, darkness—that really narrows it down."

The sound of a hand striking firmly into another body.

"Quiet, Wayne," Takako hissed as Jo kept focus.

"There was . . . a spear of darkness? Something lodged into a tree. She said I was the only one who could destroy it. To destroy it before it destroyed us—I think?" Jo shook her head. "I'm sorry, that's all I have."

"It's something," Samson said softly, encouragingly. Jo gave him a tired smile in thanks.

"Why don't we take a break for the night?" Takako suggested, pulling out her obsidian disk and fumbling with it until numbers appeared. "It's getting late, and we'll all think with clearer heads after a good night's sleep. We can start first thing in the morning."

"Works for me." Wayne was the first to get to his feet, eager to flee the room. *Just when she thought they were getting on better footing he—*

Jo's thought was interrupted by his hand falling on her shoulder. "Thanks for trusting us with this, dollface," Wayne said softly. "We'll get you through this."

Jo raised a hand, clutching his fingers tightly for a moment. "Thank you." Her eyes shifted. "Thank you all."

Wayne departed and Samson was the next to stand. "He's right. We can do this."

"I know, Sam." They exchanged a brief hug, and then it was just her and Takako.

"It'll look better in the morning, I'm sure." Takako gave her a hug as well, tight and fierce. "Get some rest."

"Yeah . . ." Even if it was a front, Jo admired her teammates' hope. And perhaps they were right; perhaps everything would be clearer after a night of rest.

Unfortunately for Jo, she didn't feel the least bit tired.

# ALLEY ENCOUNTER

Jo didn't even attempt sleep this time. After the last three days spent wasting the first few hours of night tossing and turning, she figured it was about time she got a jumpstart at this new life of twenty-four-hour wakefulness.

With Takako and Samson both occupying their own guest rooms downstairs, close enough to the living room to be easily disturbed, Jo forwent her usual TV binge. Instead, she grabbed a coat at random from the hall closet and bundled up for what would probably prove a lengthy nighttime walk.

The coat was a heavy thing, thick and too big for her, but warm; it smelled a bit like whatever cologne Wayne now wore. For a moment, it left Jo just standing in the foyer, wrapped up tight in the material and breathing. There was a spicy note to it, sharp enough that it triggered a heart-rending sense-memory of cloves and crisp winter air.

Every part of her ached for Snow, making the musky scent of the coat, though pleasantly similar, seem lackluster in comparison. Without a conscious command, something in her was reaching out blindly for him, longing in a way that could not be described. Somewhere, as though he were on the other end of an invisible tether, Jo could almost feel him. But she lost the sensation before she could grasp it fully.

The elevator descended smoothly and Jo watched as the numbers were illuminated in swift, decreasing succession. When the doors in front of her opened, a cool breath of night air gusted over her. The lobby was icy, and Jo drew the coat tighter around herself, bracing for the even colder temperatures that awaited her outside.

The security guard watched her closely for several seconds, his eyes shining golden in the darkness. The longer Jo stared, the more "not quite human" the creature began to look, until eventually she had to tear her eyes away. He turned his head down with a sniff, looking back at the tablet propped against his knee and muttering something about "humans." As Jo passed, she noticed long ears—much longer than even Eslar's and far more narrow—tucked under his cap.

Outside, her previous assessment about the chill was spot-on. But Jo relished every shoulder-trembling gust of wind, the night itself carrying the scents of the city and the faint spark of magic throughout. Yorkton and New York City were both large, and on a numbered grid, but the similarities stopped there. Sure, there were some things found in every city, like the steam billowing up from its underbelly. But now Jo wondered what lurked in those depths: Subway cars? Giant worms? A whole different city? The possibilities in this new Age of Magic seemed endless.

As she wandered down the first block, Jo's mind turned from the city to wondering what the others were dreaming about. Nineteen years of experience, and she already couldn't quite remember what it felt like to dream. She could recall images and feelings, but the distinct sensation of dreaming had left her, a misplaced sort of energy taking its place. There was so much time here in the after-hours where most of the world slept and Jo didn't quite know what to do with herself.

She shoved her hands in the pockets of Wayne's coat as her mind whirred with countless possible failures to their as-yet-unformulated plans. Pan was crazy and unpredictable, but she was also powerful and terrifying, and those things combined left a metallic tang of panic at the back of Jo's throat. If they didn't come up with a good enough plan, they'd be playing victim to whatever world Chaos—or worse, Oblivion—might determine.

The thought carried Jo's mind in a different direction. Pan versus Chaos. If Jo had reclaimed her demigod status with the destruction of the Society, then any tethers holding Pan back must have been broken as well. Was Chaos similar to Pan? Or would her new personality be different entirely?

A solid block away from Wayne's building, Jo felt it.

To call it a sensation was too simple, the prickling beneath her skin and at the back of her neck tantamount to the faint itching of a forgotten memory. Without really knowing why, Jo picked up the pace, splitting her focus between the growing itch and the length of sidewalk in front of her.

It took about another block for her to identify the itch as a physical thing, a magical presence probably a dozen feet behind her.

There was a creeping, crawling feeling to the magic. Invisible tendrils attempted to sink into her lungs like a heavy smoke and weight her down. Every sensation was physical, though any casual observer would see nothing more than two people walking down the street.

Jo stopped suddenly, and felt the presence stop as well. Swallowing, she braced herself for what she might find when she turned. Even with that, she was caught off-guard. She'd been half-expecting, perhaps even half-hoping for, the candy-haired woman-child to be standing there.

Fortunately or unfortunately—Jo couldn't decide which—it was a fairly unassuming-looking man. Average build, human as far as she could tell, generally speaking not someone she'd be too worried about if it weren't for his face. His eyes were completely blackened and oozing down his face, like melting charcoal.

"You've finally awoken," the man spoke. *Well, not quite.* He opened his mouth and the words came from his lips, but it was not whatever the man's voice had been. Instead, it was an eerie echo of a voice Jo knew well.

"Go away." She didn't think the command would work, but it didn't hurt to try.

"Aren't you already tired of the hunt?" Pan continued through the man as if Jo hadn't said anything at all. Every time his spoke, his lips chapped, peeling away like paint chips to reveal a new, nearly glowing color underneath. "We're right back where we started." The man tilted his head. The movement was awkward and unnatural, as if the rest of his body were limp, held upright and commanded by invisible strings. "Not quite. I have something here you want."

*Snow.* The thought cracked through her mind like lightning and, as if she'd said it aloud, the man smirked in the most uncomfortably familiar way.

"Yes." The man took a lurching step forward. "Him. The one who was made for you. But he was only made, Destruction." Jo shuddered at the sound of her old name rolling off his lips in Pan's voice. Wrong, the whole situation was wrong. "I was part of you—I *was* you, long before he ever even existed."

The street had darkened around her. It was as if she now stood in a tunnel with no exits, only darkness. The man was before her with his haunted eyes and glowing mouth spewing Pan's words. And somewhere behind him, somewhere far but almost close enough to touch if Jo took one mighty lunge forward, was the ghostly outline of Pan.

"Come back to me."

"Free him." Jo kept her eyes on the man and not the wisps of color condensing further into the shape of Pan by the moment. "Free this man. He's not part of this game."

"It's too late for that." A giggle echoed off more corners than the not-quite reality should have. "I've already turned his intestines to gummy worms and his heart to lead."

It was true. The closer the man got, the clearer she could see it. Chaos had done her work on him—nothing was in its right place.

"There's only one route out for him now." *Destruction*, Jo heard the word left unsaid. "Put him out of his misery and come to me. Snow and I are merely sustaining in this castle. There's not much energy left now. Come to me and save others from suffering his fate."

Jo took a small step back. She could see just what thread to pull on to make the whole knotted mess of a man unravel. This was not the first time she'd been confronted with this decision. The shadows clouded her eyes —*a forest, running, Chaos hunting her*. Jo blinked the memories of her past life and Pan's games away.

The man was right before her now, a horror to behold. His skin was turning scaly, nose flattening into that of a kitten, or hog. Though his eyes were still the same void that bled down his face in rivulets.

"Kill him, Jo." With Pan's voice, the man commanded his own death.

She'd killed people before, like this, back then. Jo's mind was twisting in on itself with every flash of memory. She'd put an end to their suffering when she had to. So why couldn't she now?

"Destroy him. Let it out. Feel how good it is to further the world to its natural state of oblivion once more."

Jo opened her mouth to object, but the words never left. His hands were around her throat, compressing. *Could she even be killed by strangling as a demigod?* Jo didn't know; all she felt was her mind swirling with the panic of knowing she would have to undo a life.

"Do it!" Pan screeched. Jo's eyes pressed shut against the sharpness of the noise.

*Another forest, another man—men—warped by Chaos's magic chasing her. It was a time of gods and the great war for the future of it all. She was Destruction. Creation came for her then. He told her . . . Told her . . .*

A gunshot shattered the trance.

Jo's eyes opened wide and she took a gasping breath of air as the man's hands slid from around her neck. He fell to the ground with a dull thud, illuminated by the lights and sounds of the city once more. Jo blinked rapidly, trying to adjust her eyes to the nighttime brightness of the city lights that suddenly seemed blinding.

"Are you okay?" Takako's voice had never sounded so concerned, and so welcome. With a click of the safety, she holstered her gun and rested her hand on Jo's upper arm.

"I think so." Jo rubbed her throbbing neck. The pain was already subsiding. If anything, it felt even better than before. Her eyes dropped to the body of the man—or, where the body should've been. Light was cracking through his skin from the inside out and, all at once, he burst with a series of sparks and flurry of confetti that faded to ash on the wind.

"Good, because I think we should move." Takako's eyes weren't on her, but the confused couple staring with slack jaws across the street. "I don't know what people are used to in this Age of Magic, but in our time, that would've looked a lot like a murder."

"You're right." Jo barely had time to finish her sentence before she was being tugged along by Takako. Within a few steps, she was keeping pace with the woman as they ran back to Wayne's building. "What were you doing out?"

"Following you." Takako glanced over her shoulder, though Jo had nearly caught up to her. "I was worried Pan might try something . . ."

Instinct told Jo to be offended, that she wasn't someone who needed to be coddled or protected—especially not now, as a demigod. But the thought of someone chasing after her. Of someone trying to protect her . . .

*Creation. A forest. A plan.*

Jo stopped so fast her momentum had her tripping over her own feet in a short series of hops.

"What is it?" Takako stopped as well, spinning in place, eyes scanning behind them for any further pursuers. Luckily, there were none.

"An arrow," Jo heard herself whisper on half-second delay, mouth catching up to her rampant thoughts.

Takako stared at her in confusion. "What?"

"It wasn't a spear of darkness."

"Spear? Are you talking about your vision in Pan's room?"

"It was an arrow." Jo straightened, closing her eyes and trying to sink into the memories of a time she barely remembered. "Hunt," she whispered, as if invoking the name of the ancient bow-wielding goddess could make it all clear. Jo's eyes snapped open. "Samson. We have to go to Samson."

# CHAMPION

Jo wasn't sure her feet even hit the floor until she landed in the elevator. "Bouncing from foot to foot won't make it go any faster," Takako panted softly. Jo didn't think they'd been running—well, *sprinting*—that fast. She was hardly out of breath, but Takako's lips were parted and her cheeks flushed slightly. "Care to share just what is going on?"

"I need to see if Samson has something." Jo hoped the feeling in her gut, that nagging one that was finally beginning to play connect-the-dots with all the odd experiences she'd had over the past few months, was one to be believed. She clung to the memory of being in his room at the Society, of a special arrow in the quiver hung on his wall. "If not, he can help give us clarity on the arrow."

The doors dinged just as Takako was going to ask another question. *Saved by the bell*, Jo thought. The second they were halfway open, Jo darted through, starting for the main entry to the penthouse and to Samson's room, Takako close behind.

A strong arm around her waist stopped Jo just short of the door. Jo twisted, looking back at Takako questioningly. The woman immediately eased her grip.

"I don't think Samson's the type to like people just barging into his room. Especially not when they're likely going to startle him from sleep in the process."

"You're right." Jo took a deep breath, regaining her composure. The last thing Jo wanted to do was offend or distress their crafter.

So, with a much more restrained step, Jo crossed over to his door, lifted her hand, and knocked gently. She leaned in toward the wooden door

—Wayne, and all his love for expensive things, had huge carved slabs of wood for doors, so thick that Jo wouldn't be surprised if her knock hadn't transferred at all. She listened, and heard nothing. Jo tried again with another knock and a soft "Samson?"

That was when she heard muffled noises from within and eased away. Takako was leaning on the wall opposite, arms crossed over her chest and seemingly content to watch the whole scene unfold before her. The door cracked open, revealing a sliver of a face and a tuft of orange fuzz that had escaped his tight braids.

"Jo? Is everything all right?"

"Yes, everything is fine," Jo assured him. "I'm sorry to wake you, but it seemed . . . We just . . . We were—"

"Jo has something she needs to ask you." Takako stepped in to assist in guiding Jo's frantic thoughts.

"I know it's late, but may we please come in, Samson?"

"Oh, um . . ." Samson disappeared and some more prominent shuffling could be heard.

Jo and Takako exchanged a look after it continued for several seconds with still no Samson back at the door. Jo leaned forward. "Sa—"

The door opened in full, startling her. As Jo straightened, she bumped into Takako and would've lost her balance were it not for the woman's strong grip on her arm.

"Sorry, I wasn't trying—"

"You can come in now." Samson smiled, and stepped aside.

"This is where Wayne put you up?" Jo frowned. She hadn't done that much exploring of the two-story penthouse. There were as many doors as there were windows—and Wayne loved his windows. She expected there to have been rooms on rooms on rooms.

But while Jo had assumed Samson would follow in Takako's footsteps and claim a guest room, this room in particular looked more fitting for the company below than the private home of its CEO above. It had a long oval table, carved of the same rich wood as the doors but inlaid with the obsidian that Jo had seen used for just about every other magical thing. However, none of it was visible due to the sheer mass of tinkering items that had been strewn about the makeshift workspace. The chairs that normally would have been occupied by executives had been pushed all to one side. Opposite was a small cot, barely enough room for one, piled with blankets and pillows.

"It's a bit sad as a workshop, isn't it?" Samson ducked his head.

Jo wasn't sure where she should start correcting him. That she hadn't been critiquing it as a workshop at all? That she'd been worried about his comfort? That she thought Wayne had put Samson in a corner initially and didn't think about the fact that Samson's most critical need was not his sleeping space, but his workspace?

"It's a fantastic workshop because it's filled with your creations, Sam." Samson blinked, then blushed, shaking his head. "Are they . . . working well for you?" Jo added hastily, thinking of how being tied closely with her destructive magic in the Society had begun to take its toll on his own powers.

"No issues." His tone assured her that he understood the underlying meaning of her question.

"Good, I'm glad to hear it." Jo wasn't sure if she could handle her magic breaking down another person after Nico.

Takako refocused them once more. "So, what did you need Samson for? Let's not dally. Who knows if the cops are coming."

"Cops? Why would—"

"Pan attacked Jo."

"What?" Samson's head whipped back and forth in confusion. "Are you all right?"

"I'm fine." Jo swallowed and forced herself to take an extra breath—forced an extra three seconds of thought into what she was about to say next. She had to get them—and keep them—on track. "Sam . . . Do you remember the first time I was in your room? When I helped you find weak points in the new seismograph machine you were working on?"

Samson nodded.

"You showed me your personal room too." It was a setup not unlike what he had now, Jo realized—a small bed shoved off to the right side of the entry and a much, much larger workspace. "In that room, you had some of your personal projects—arrows."

"Yes?"

"There was one arrow. An arrow you didn't want me to touch."

"I know the one you're talking about . . ." Samson seemed on guard. His hands began to twitch. The lack of tactile sensation caught up with him as he reached over to the table, grabbing the nearest bauble.

"That arrow—"

"Is special," Samson interrupted in rare form. "I still have it."

"What?" Jo and Takako seemed to say in unison.

"It survived the end of the Society?" Takako whispered, solo.

"Yes . . ." Samson gave a small nod. "Everything I made in the Society is gone. Perhaps because I didn't make it?" He went from nodding to shaking his head to shrugging. "It was in my room in the Society when I woke there, just as it was in the room where I woke up in this timeline. It seems to follow me."

"Can we see it? Just see it?" Jo's voice bordered on desperation, but she didn't care in the slightest. "Please?"

Samson's eyes darted between them for what seemed like forever, until he finally nodded. "Okay."

Jo's heart was in her ears as she watched him shuffle around the table. Along the wall of windows that overlooked Yorkton there sat a pile of heavy-looking crates, one of which Samson approached and opened. It was an odd contrast: the modern city illuminated behind the trunks that could have been from the set of an old fantasy film.

"It was a gift," Samson said, straightening, a quiver in both of his hands. His knuckles had gone pale with how tightly he was clutching it. "A gift . . . that's all I remember." When he returned to them, he placed the quiver on the table. Samson opened his mouth to speak, but was stunned into silence as Takako walked right up to it.

As if in a trance, Jo watched the woman move with precision and certainty. She had never seen Takako be half as bold as she was about to be. Even Samson stared, slack jawed, his words forgotten.

"This," Takako whispered, going right for the arrow Jo had been entranced by. It stood out from the others—slightly longer, with a slightly thicker shaft of pale wood, and a plume that seemed to sparkle with its own light.

"Taka—" Samson never finished whatever objection he was about to voice.

Right as he moved, Takako's fingers closed around the end of the shaft. Pure white light overtook the arrow, blindingly bright. As she lifted it from the quiver, the light seemed to drip off like molten, white hot metal, fizzling and disappearing as it met the table. In its wake, as though it was fresh from the forge, was an arrow made of pure gold.

At the same moment, all of Jo's past memories and discoveries finally clicked.

"A golden arrow," she whispered. "A golden arrow!" Her voice seemed to dislodge the other two from their trance, if only slightly, as both of them turned in her direction with yet-gaping mouths. Jo was quick to try to explain, though the thoughts seemed to whizz through her head as though they were arrows themselves, impossible to pluck from the air in any kind of order. "My research. Don't you remember, Takako?"

"You asked me about archer deities."

"Yes! It came up, across mythologies and timelines. It was even in Eslar's story book." At that, Samson gave a small nod of affirmation. "I remember . . . The Goddess of the Hunt, back in a time of gods. She was working with other gods to try to fight against Oblivion. But . . . it wasn't going their way. Pan killed her. That was when Snow and I—our past selves—decided to try to reboot the world to kill Chaos."

"Did a goddess give this to you?" Takako asked Samson.

"I think I'd remember." Samson shook his head almost violently.

"Can I see it?" Jo held out a hand.

Takako extended her arm, holding out the golden arrow toward Jo.

"Thanks." Jo reached for it, and the moment her fingertips brushed the gold, memories that did not belong to her flooded her sight.

*Hunt, swathed in the furs of her kills and with dirt on her face, bestowing the arrow on a man she called Champion, so that none of the other gods would know of its whereabouts. The man was to kill Pan, but then . . .*

*The world shifted, and the man was without memory of the gods. As he lay dying, he passed it on to his son, who sold it to a collector. The collector's home was ransacked by thieves, who pawned everything off but the arrow. They held onto it, revering it for power and luck, before their hideout was burned down and the arrow was hidden in a bed of ash.*

*. . . Until a farmer discovered it while tilling the land. The farmer gave it to his daughter, and it was she who ultimately gave it to Samson as thanks for a night spent in his home during a storm.*

"Josephina?" Takako asked. Instantly, Jo knew it wasn't the first time her friend had tried to get her attention.

The visions faded and Jo shook her head. She'd barely touched the weapon, but her hand fell from it. She felt heavy, weary from the onslaught of memories. "It's Hunt's arrow."

"You're sure?"

"No doubt," Jo affirmed.

"Let me see it?" Samson asked.

A brief look of uncertainty shadowed Takako's face but she quickly held it out to Samson. He ran his own fingers up and down the projectile.

"Please don't disassemble it," Takako cautioned uncertainly.

"I don't think I could if I tried. The craftsmanship is just . . ."

"Divine?" Jo finished with a small if tired grin.

"If it is something designed to bring down Pan—Oblivion—then why didn't Pan destroy it while she could in the Age of Magic, or the Society?" Takako asked.

"I don't know." Jo thought aloud. "Perhaps she couldn't?"

"Or perhaps she didn't know what it was," Samson suggested. "You saw the protection slide off the arrow when Takako touched it. Which, why . . ."

"Because Takako is of the Champion's lineage," Jo whispered. "*That* was the magic that lingered within her through the ages." After the visions had seeped into her mind as if they'd been her own memories, it was impossible not to sense the similarities in magic between the original Champion and the young woman before her.

"So now what?" Samson asked. "If this is what takes down Pan, then what next?"

"We need a bow," Jo offered, and Takako nodded her own agreement. "Samson, can you make one?"

On cue, the crafter lifted his head. "I can, but first I'll need something."

"What?"

"Not what," Samson corrected. "*Who*."

J o didn't waste time knocking on Wayne's door, and instead barged in without warning, much to the man's startled and flailing dismay.

"D-Dollface?" Wayne blinked as much of the sleep from his eyes as he could, though he was clearly disoriented. "Is everything jake? Are we under attack?"

"Sorry to bust in like this," Jo apologized sincerely, even as she made a quick route to the nightstand to turn on a light. His room instantly filled with a painful brightness. At first, Wayne just continued to blink, letting his eyes adjust, but eventually, he noticed that Jo wasn't the only one in his room. His face contorted first in confusion and then concern.

He forced his gaze back to Jo. "If we need to hightail it for a bit, I have a bunker."

"Might not be a bad idea," Takako muttered.

"Why?" Wayne asked before Jo could get a word in.

"Jo was attacked."

"I'm fine." She tried to stop the concern from sprouting before it could take root. "More importantly, we have a plan."

"A plan?" Wayne quirked an eyebrow at her and on reflex, she glanced over her shoulder towards Takako. The golden arrow, the best clue they had to defeating Pan, was still nestled in the palms of her hands, as if the Japanese woman were cradling it like a child. Wayne looked from Jo to the arrow and back before taking in and letting out a deep, weary breath. "I think you have a lot more to explain than just this plan. But maybe first, you could let me put on some clothes?"

Before Jo could agree that was the best course, the phone at Wayne's bedside table rang.

"Who . . . no one ever calls that line," he muttered, reaching for it. Jo's heart began to race as he ran a finger over the obsidian backing.

A voice appeared to emit from thin air. "Mister Davis, there are some of the King's Guardians here."

"King's Guardians?" Wayne glanced back to them. Jo had no idea what "King's Guardians" were but she could guess it wasn't going to be anything good.

"Yes, they want to ask your guests a few questions."

"Go ahead and send them up."

"Wayne, no—" Takako hissed, stopping short when he held up a hand.

"Yes, sir."

"Give me a minute or two, however. I need to dress."

"Understood." The obsidian disk went dark and the sensation that filled the air along with the voice vanished.

"What did you all do?" Wayne turned slowly back to them.

"Pan's after Jo. You can't let them in."

"We're not going to be here by the time the elevator arrives. Go, pack your things. We have a minute, maybe."

Jo wasn't sure if it was the panic of the situation, or the fact that Wayne gave them no warning before moving to throw off his covers, that had them scurrying from his room. Pack their things? Takako hadn't really unpacked and Jo didn't have anything, which fortunately left their hands free to help keep Samson as he worried away everything he wouldn't be able to take in such a short period of time.

In the back of her mind, a timer ticked down. Every second seemed to fly by and every movement seemed to crawl.

"Are you ready?" Wayne said, breathless, a backpack over his shoulder.

"Just where are we going?" Takako asked, lifting one of Samson's boxes as though it were filled with air and not pounds of tools. She clearly wasn't too hung up on the "where" since she was already following him out of the room.

"Remember that bunker I mentioned? There's a secret elevator that leads to it in the basement . . . It also has its own exit to the street le—"

"Myrth!" Samson interrupted suddenly. "We're going to Myrth!"

"What?" Everyone paused, stopping in lock-step.

"I have a workshop there. It can be a hiding spot. If you can get us out." He looked to Wayne.

"I don't know if trying to leave the country is the best idea . . ." Takako muttered.

"Money finds a way," Wayne insisted. "And it's out of reach of Pan."

"Yes, but—"

Jo's head jerked away from the conversation. She could have sworn she'd just heard the soft *ding* of the elevator. Her hands went slick with perspiration, forcing her to adjust her grip on Samson's trunk.

"There's no time to argue," she interrupted. "Myrth is fine. Samson will have his workshop; he can make the bow."

"Bow?" Wayne looked for an explanation there wasn't time to give.

"Not quite . . ." Samson's fingers curled over the box he was holding. "I'll need—"

Banging on the door interrupted them all.

"To work it out later!" Jo hissed.

"This way!" Wayne started forward hastily. They all but sprinted through his penthouse to a far back room where he revealed a secret panel. With the sounds of shouting and more banging in the background, he moved his hands over the magical device to reveal a secret elevator.

The four stepped in, watching as the doors closed behind them, and feeling their stomachs rise up into their chests as the elevator descended away from the safety of Wayne's penthouse and toward the unknown.

# READY TO JUMP

**M**yrth spread out before them like an exotic tapestry unfurled.

As the tiny airship began its descent into the city proper, Jo stared in wonder at what would have been, in her time, a coastal city on the Strait of Gibraltar. It was still that, she supposed, a coastal city bordering a narrow sea between one continent and another. But that was where the similarities ended.

The city was a towering landscape of spires with domed and slanted roofs. Lush foliage created emerald contrast as they sprouted from between the white and cream buildings, topped with not red (as she would expect of Spanish Mediterranean architecture in her time) but bright cerulean clay tiles. Great birds with silver plumage and bright blue heads stood out against it all, flying from place to place and dropping off messages.

Jo stood at the edge of the airship railing, taking it all in. As they continued descending, she could see the flecks of white in the birds' feathers, and the splashes of rainbow color in the various flags suspended over doors and balconies. She was so engrossed, she didn't hear Samson approaching until he was at her side, elbows on the railing next to her.

"What do you think?" he asked.

"It's hard to think." Jo laughed softly. "It all seems so magnificent and so . . . impossible."

"A far cry from the Spain you knew."

"A few thousand years of alternate magical history will do that." The first few days of the trip were spent cramped together in a small hold as they waited to clear Aristonian customs and be smuggled out of the kingdom. Jo had spent much of that time reading, per Takako's suggestion. It passed the time and, after all, there was so much to catch up on. Be it her age or newfound interest, she found herself much more invested in this world than she had been in her high school history classes. It was like finding where she was always meant to be.

"They call those skywings." Samson pointed. "The way the elves tell the tale, the early families were gifted the birds by the goddess." *The* Goddess. Jo remembered reading about that. Interestingly enough, the elves had evolved into a monotheistic religion. She couldn't help but wonder what they'd think when they found a demigod on their doorstep. "These birds were made for them, to suit their long life spans. They live as long as a member of a certain lineage draws breath, acting both as spirit guardians . . . and convenient messengers."

"I see." Jo's eyes continued to scan the cityscape. As the airship turned, they got a glimpse of the sea. "That's . . ." Her words trailed off at the splendor of what she beheld.

At the edge of the city, stretching into the water, was an arc-shaped building. From either end, a walkway stretched, joining together to form a single road. This road, lined by giant sapphire statues that glinted as though they were moving in the sunlight, led across the strait—The Sapphire Strait, as it was known in this time—to what Jo knew as Africa, but was now the Luanian Empire. She was trying as much as possible to expunge the past names she knew in exchange for what was before her: a completely different world that just happened to share some similar continental shapes to the world she'd been born into.

"That's the Sapphire Bridge," Samson finished for her. "And the only way into the Luanian Empire. The other wards around the continent are virtually impenetrable."

"How do they ward a whole continent?"

"The magic of the elves." Samson shrugged. "They've been around centuries longer than the second oldest race—the fae."

"And the fae are said to be an off-shoot of elves," Jo recalled reading. Samson looked somewhat surprised that she knew the fact, so Jo added, playfully defensive, "Takako's not the only one who can do a bit of research, Sam."

His eyes wandered back out toward the city and the Sapphire Bridge, the massive structure quickly disappearing from view as the airship turned yet again. Samson rummaged through his pocket for one of his preferred cubes of wires and screws.

Jo watched as he fussed with it, eyes focused on something else entirely. She felt his magic radiating in unsettled waves, but Jo didn't inquire. If he didn't want to say, she wouldn't force him to. Instead, she opted for another distraction.

"Where's your workshop? Can we see it from here?"

Samson seemed startled, but quickly answered. "Not quite. It's a bit off in that direction." He raised a finger and pointed just diagonally beyond the bow of the airship. "It's small, but we should all be able to fit."

Their conversation was cut short by one of the smugglers poking his head out of the narrow door that led on deck. "We're gonna be dockin' soon. You should get under till we sort out customs."

"Customs? Again?" Jo mused as they stepped into the equally narrow passageway through the ship.

"It's nothing difficult. Should only take a moment on a vessel this small," Samson assured her. "I'm sure the crew has done it a thousand times."

Takako and Wayne were already curled up in the small cargo space positioned between cabins and the bridge—low in the hull of the ship. The few feet between them managed to look as wide as an arena as they sat squared off against each other like two fighters about to take the ring. Wayne curled his fingers into fists, where Takako gripped at the strap of the single-arrow quiver Samson had made her (a quiver that now never left her back).

"What did we miss?" Jo asked as she settled into her own space, Samson closing the hatch securely behind them.

Wayne opened his mouth to speak but Takako managed the first word.

"He wanted to pass us off as passengers and get off promptly. I insisted it was better to stick with the plan."

"*Crew*. I said pass ourselves off as crew."

"Takako is right." Jo sighed softly. "They said we'd just have to wait until nightfall and then they'll unload."

"I am not made to be shoved in a corner. I travel first class or not at all," Wayne huffed.

"Clearly not, Mr. Bigshot." Jo enjoyed the way he contorted to avoid her gaze. The trip had been the hardest on him. At first, he'd seemed thrilled to exercise some of his less-than-savory connections to get out of Aristonia. But that also meant stepping out of the comfort zone he'd settled into; this was the first time Jo had ever met a version of Wayne not surrounded by luxury.

They passed the rest of the descent in silence, rocking back and forth with the other illicit goods as the ship slipped into port. *Was it even called a port when dealing with airships?*

Jo pulled her knees to her chest, rested her forearms on them, forehead on her forearms, and closed her eyes. She was now an ocean away from Snow. An ache sank into her chest, flowing through her limbs with every slow beat of her heart. It solidified in every corner of her body, weighing her down.

*I'll come for you soon*, she wanted to say. But kept her mouth shut as the sounds of heavy boots ascending the gangplank rattled the side of the airship. Muffled voices could be heard over the sounds of feet shifting and boards creaking.

". . . on behalf of the Elvish government, we're going to need to see your papers."

A sudden jerk of movement grabbed Jo's attention.

Samson looked intently up at the floorboards, narrowing his eyes as if trying to peer through them. Jo wasn't the only one who'd made note of the odd expression and uncharacteristic mannerism. Takako glanced between her and Wayne, who merely shrugged.

". . . afraid your documents are out of order."

"Those documents should be fine."

"You don't seem to have the new papers. No matter, we should be able to assist you in procuring them."

Samson leaned forward with an agonizingly slow movement that the rest of them mirrored so they didn't make a sound. When they were almost nose to nose, he whispered, "Those aren't elvish customs."

"How do you know?" Takako breathed in reply.

"Wrong accent. All wrong."

"Are you sure?" Wayne asked.

Samson nearly loosened a braid with the furious nodding of his head. "I . . . I know the accent. I lived here before I—I—"

"We believe you." Jo placed her hand on his. The man's stuttering forced the volume of his voice to rise. Samson's throat clenched as if he was trying to swallow down his anxiety.

"Now what?" Wayne asked.

"Nothing changes. The safest thing is still to wait here until—"

Takako was interrupted by the sounds of a struggle. The interior of the ship rumbled as the unmistakable sound of a body being slammed into something above reverberated down the walls.

"What? Who—" The man's question was cut short by a gurgle, and another scream was suppressed.

One of the earlier voices of the "customs" officers finally spoke. "Search the ship. They're smugglers. There's a secret hold here somewhere. Find them."

"Still safest to wait?" Wayne asked Takako sharply.

"Now what?" Samson began to pat around him, no doubt looking for something to occupy his hands. They came up to his chest, where he began to mess roughly with his own fingers, lacking a bauble to fidget with.

Without a word, Takako reached up to remove the tie from her hair, letting the dark, pin-straight strands fall around her shoulders. Careful not to startle him, she held the hair tie out in front of Samson's hands, waiting for him to take it. Samson let out a soft breath, taking the hair tie eagerly, and began to fuss with it.

"Can we fight?" Wayne asked, again pitching his question to Takako.

"I can, but I can't guarantee I can keep all of you safe," she murmured, no doubt trying to calculate the odds in her head. "Sounds like there are four of them."

Jo closed her eyes, trying to block out the panic surrounding her and the sounds of what were no doubt Pan's men closing in on them. They'd followed her across the sea. Pan knew where they were. Or, perhaps, Pan's influence was so wide she'd merely covered all of her bases in every port she could. Who knew what Pan knew, what she was capable of, how far she would go.

All Jo could focus on now was the feeling of the ship around her, and deal with the immediate threat of the four—Takako had been right—pursuing them.

*Destroy them*, her magic seemed to whisper. It was the same feeling she'd had in Yorkton. But these men were different; they weren't like the chaotic, twisted version of a person. These were willing servants with only mere traces of Pan's corruption. In theory, they weren't beyond redemption.

Did she care? They'd sided with Pan. She should have no issues killing them on the spot and yet . . . something about giving into thoughtless murder felt like letting Pan win—*like letting Oblivion win.*

There also wasn't time for her to have an ethical conundrum.

"I can break us a way out," Jo said hastily, opening her eyes once more.

"Break us a way out?"

"Then they find us," Wayne hissed.

"Not if I break enough in the process that we can slip away in the chaos that follows."

"Can't say I'm following, doll."

A loud crack interrupted their conversation. The sound of wood splintering, breaking, and giving in was worse than an alarm clock on the first day of school. It grated against Jo's magic, as if some part of her was upset that something had been broken and it wasn't her doing.

"I think we're out of time. Just hold on."

*Controlled demolition* was the singular thought that ran through Jo's mind. Her magic surrounded every corner of the vessel. Like a sixth sense, Jo understood its construction, every support and load-bearing wall.

Such a little flex of her magic reaped such big destruction.

The airship's sides popped like popcorn, bolts flying off. A large crack ran down the length of the ship. Boards splintered away and whole sections collapsed.

"A hole is going to open there." Jo thrust out a hand, beginning to move in the same motion. "Get ready to jump. I have no idea how high up we're docked."

To her team's credit, they didn't hesitate.

The front of the ship cracked and fell away before them like a hatch opening. Takako was the first one out, followed shortly by Samson. Wayne stalled, but only briefly, before leaping awkwardly down to a pile of boards that had fallen like a ramp before him.

Debris fell around them like confetti as they tumbled to the ground that was—thankfully—not too far away. Shouting rose from within the airship and outside, but dulled briefly the moment Jo felt her body hit the ground, hard. She sprang back into action, expecting the pain to linger but feeling better than before.

The rest of her team didn't quite bounce back in the same way, but they pulled themselves together nonetheless.

"We need to go." Jo tugged on Samson's elbow.

"My supplies . . ." Samson swallowed, looking back toward the crumbling ship. With one more brief glance, he shook his head and ran forward, toward where Wayne and Jo had already begun pressing along the hull of another airship.

"Stand back, stand back!" someone with a thick accent was saying— an accent Jo now assumed to be Elvish.

"There's people trapped. Call healers!"

The four kept moving in the tight space between the hulls of airships and the ledge at their side. With the ruckus behind them, they went unnoticed, slipping around the hull of the fourth ship and up onto the platform where passengers, crew, and staff were running.

"This way," Samson said, keeping his head down.

Just like that, he led them though the lavish terminal with a flash of something Jo guessed was akin to a visa in her time, and a quick exchange of some words in what must have been Elvish. The real customs guard was more focused on the commotion at the platform than inspecting things too closely, and he waved them through to the busy central receiving area for the airship port. Beyond that was a giant cul-de-sac filled with vehicles, birds, and even a horse or two (if you count rainbow colored, equine-looking creatures with chicken feet as horses).

That was where they all stopped and seemed to take a collective breath of fresh air.

"It's only about an hour walk from here," Samson said, starting for the exit.

"I'm done walking, and sneaking, and being smuggled. It'll be faster if we get a car."

Before any of them could object, Wayne gave a confident wave and heralded what must pass for a taxi here in Myrth. Albeit, the nicest taxi she'd ever had the pleasure of riding in. The interior was made of a strange leather, one she'd only ever seen in the Society in Snow's room, and Jo wondered if she'd now find out what animal it came from.

The driver donned a pair of gloves, dotted in obsidian and sapphire, and gave a nod after Samson finished speaking. The second they came into contact with the wheel, both his digits and the dashboard glowed and the car began to move—powered entirely by the man's magic.

Jo tilted her head back, sighing again, letting the sights and sounds of the city wash over her as if she weren't still on the run. Men and women of all shapes and sizes went about their business. She realized she had assumed that all elves were dark skinned like Eslar, but that proved categorically untrue. She saw every skin tone imaginable, coupled with every hair color.

As they passed an outdoor theater, Jo witnessed a man orating a story, casting bright illusions that swept over the crowd. They drove through an upscale area where the men and women seemed to wear endless strings of sapphire and silver. And, for just a second, Jo got a glimpse of the long road that led to the Sapphire Bridge.

"Like this, it should only be about ten more minutes." Samson twisted around his front seat to tell them.

"Good, the sooner we can get inside the better," Takako muttered.

"Agreed," Jo mumbled, closing her eyes and letting the rumbling of the car fill her mind. It served as a poor distraction. All she could think of was the feel of the leather under her palms, and the memories of Snow's room.

# IF YOU DON'T, I WILL

In no time, they were parked in front of a decent sized and homey looking building, cerulean tiles dotting the roof to complement the terracotta and Cherrywood of the facade. The door was painted a vibrant teal and boasted a sign that said, "Commissioned Craftswork, Enquire Within." Jo's heart clenched when she saw the small attempt at a painted bird in the corner.

"Here we are," Samson mumbled, getting out of the car as Wayne took the liberty of paying the driver. "It's not very large inside . . ."

"I'm sure it's great, Sam," Jo assured.

"And, if not, we can get a hotel," Wayne muttered as they stepped into the cluttered work room.

"Not very large" may have been a slight understatement.

The workshop had one clear space that Jo could only assume was Samson's equivalent of a front desk, and even that was threatened by a litany of screws and baubles at its edges. Every other space was overflowing, lost beneath a mix of trinkets and unfinished projects. It left a pang in her heart, how similar every space Samson occupied tended to be, as if he was holding on to something too tightly, trying to keep a part of himself liminal and unchanging. An indirect kind of stability.

"You three can stay in the loft. I have a bed over here."

"Or a hotel."

"We're not getting a hotel," Takako insisted. "We need to fly under the radar."

"Yeah? Just like Jo's demolition was under the radar?"

"We were out of options." Jo didn't spare him a long side-eye. "Hand-to-hand combat wasn't going to be less conspicuous."

"It doesn't matter now." Takako sighed, running a hand through her hair. "Look, it was a long journey to get here." She was right about that; four days of travel had never felt so long. "We're here, in one piece, and hopefully out of Pan's reach."

"You said the Luanian government doesn't much like working with Aristonia?" Jo asked Samson.

"Not with anyone. They like to stay out of things. And I don't go by Samson here. We should be safe . . ." he said hastily, as if trying to predict their next concerns.

"Still, we shouldn't stay here for too long if we can avoid it." Takako walked over to one of the tables, resting her hand on it. "How long will it take you to make the bow?"

Samson hummed and grabbed for something off a nearby table. It wasn't sufficient, because he promptly reached for something else. In the span of about thirty seconds, he was in full-blown reorganization mode.

"You can't, can you?" Jo whispered as the fact dawned on her.

"I can!" Samson turned quickly as though she'd greatly offended him. "I can make it. I just need a special material to do it with."

"I can get you whatever you need. Money is no consequence." Wayne never passed up an opportunity to flaunt his wealth and the influence it gave him. "What do you need?"

Samson shook his head, deflating further into himself. "*You* can't get this material."

"Oh? Try me," Wayne challenged. Jo wondered if he was oblivious to the fact that Samson was on edge (and had been since they started on their way to Myrth), or didn't care. She didn't know which was worse.

"No. No, no, we . . . I—we *need* Eslar for this," Samson argued through a frown, not quite looking at anyone. His hands were clenched into tight fists at his sides, trembling just enough to be noticeable. His magic spiked and tensed, though Jo was certain she was the only one who felt it. It wasn't the reaction any of them had expected, the following breath of silence proof that they'd all been a tad caught off-guard by it. And that silence was enough for Samson to deflate a bit, looking up at Wayne with a tired but determined glint in his eye. "An arrow is worthless without a proper bow and the only design I can assume will be strong enough, and magically powerful enough to balance this arrow, will be made of a branch from the Life Tree on High Luana."

"High Luana? You never said anything about getting there." Wayne moved to storm over to Samson but Jo stopped him, and whatever he thought he was about to do, with a straight arm.

"Okay, I read about High Luana—down south, where the elf royalty lives." A nod from Samson prompted Jo to continue. "Why are we freaking out about it now?"

"Getting to Myrth is one thing, doll. Getting to High Luana as non-High Elves is downright impossible. It's where the most ancient elves live —the originals, as they claim. Even elves have a hard time getting there."

"This is why we *need* Eslar," Samson insisted once more.

"Let me guess . . . He's on High Luana?" A nod from Samson. "Of course."

"He would be," Wayne muttered.

Eslar's absence was beginning to make a lot more sense. "So if we can't get into High Luana, we get him to bring us what we need?"

"Great, everything hinges on a stubborn, stuck-up elf." Wayne threw his hands up and they promptly fell onto his hips. He turned away with a heavy sigh, as if unable to look at them any longer.

"Leave that to me. I'm sure I can get through to him," Samson pleaded.

"We trust you, Sam," Jo reassured. "Do what you need. But as quickly as possible, please." She didn't think she really needed the last bit, but was compelled to add it all the same.

He gave a small nod, lowering his eyes. "I'll do my best." Just once, she wanted him to channel Wayne's confidence to the point of arrogance. "In the meantime, just . . . make yourselves comfortable."

~

COMFORTABLE PROVED TO BE AN IMPOSSIBILITY. The loft was packed to the brim with tools, crates, and supplies, leaving little room for them to exist—not to mention sleep. As a result, Jo, Takako, and Wayne had all taken to spending the majority of their time in an odd hybrid space nearby —part restaurant, part bookstore, part concert venue.

She and Wayne had already set up in what had become their corner couches. Takako was the last to join them, book in hand. She perched with a steaming mug of something thick, green, and earthy smelling—something Jo hadn't yet been brave enough to try.

"Samson says he'll need a few more days." It had been Takako's turn to ask today.

Jo's stomach dropped, her magic crackling beneath her skin in rebellion. Even though Samson wasn't here, she wanted to argue, wanted to tell him they didn't have a few *more* days, not when Snow was . . . when they didn't even know if he . . . But Jo pushed it all down.

It had only been three days since they arrived.

Jo took a breath, letting it out slowly, and then looked up at Wayne and Takako, startling a bit at the look of concern on their faces. She cleared her throat, taking another bite of what she'd come to think of as an Elvish empanada. It was a pasty sprinkled with what looked like glitter, but with a rich, savory, meaty flavor—a deviation from the candy-like appearance that she'd been pleased to discover the first time she'd tried it. "Fine. We can wait a few more days."

Takako and Wayne shared a look before nodding in agreement.

Except, two days later, there was still no word.

"What's he even doing?" Wayne huffed, sitting back in the booth of a fancy bar and lounge they'd splurged on a taxi to get to. The scotch he ordered, which had probably cost as much as their fare, sat untouched in front of him, his arms crossed firmly over his chest.

"Making contact with High Luana in general is no easy feat, let alone one specific individual," Takako reasoned, but even her voice held a sort of flat disbelief. She was drinking a bright purple cocktail out of a swirling martini glass, a cherry-looking fruit changing rapidly through various neon colors at the bottom.

"You had smartphones back in 2005 that could contact anyone across the globe," Jo fumed. "We had biobands in 2057. And these, whatever they are, can do the same thing, right?" She fished one of the obsidian disks Wayne had bought her to play with out of her pocket and placed it a bit roughly on the table in front of her. "So what makes contacting one elusive elf so goddamn difficult?"

"Might want to dial it down there, dollface," Wayne hissed under his breath, and it wasn't until that moment that Jo realized how loud her voice had gotten, how much she'd been inching forward in frustration.

Takako wasn't wrong; Jo had been reading as much as possible about High Luana at night (in-between trying to actually learn some Elvish). It was the farthest spot of land in the Luanian Empire from any other non-elf territory, literally separated by a continent and a sea. Still, her point about the phones should be valid . . . She let herself slump back down in her seat with a dejected huff, grabbing her own cocktail from the table and taking a long drink.

"And this is why we're not letting you ask him for updates anymore," Wayne muttered.

The liquid inside her glass was perfectly clear sans an iridescent slick on the top. Though no ice kept it cold, it was chilled to near biting perfection and slid cool and calming from throat to chest to stomach. Jo shivered at the sensation, licking the berry tang from her lips before speaking again, voice more restrained.

"If we don't have anything by end of day tomorrow, I'm demanding news."

"We have no choice but to give him more time," Takako tried. Jo couldn't identify the undercurrent in her voice, but it made her less willing to argue.

Still, she couldn't help mumbling under hear breath, "We don't *have* time."

~

ONE DAY BECAME TWO. Two became four. And Jo's ability to give Samson the benefit of the doubt waned completely. Eslar, and by association Samson, were the only things currently standing between her and finding Snow, making sure he was alive, saving him from whatever torturous position Pan had left him in after the Society had been destroyed. The longer they lay in wait twiddling their thumbs, the more likely it was that Snow was suffering a fate Jo couldn't even bear to think of.

It was clear Samson knew something was up the moment Wayne and Takako left without Jo.

"Jo . . ." Samson whispered her name, and it killed her how nervous it sounded, especially after she'd worked so hard for so long to garner his trust. But she couldn't keep waiting like this, not without understanding *why* at least.

"What's going on with Eslar, Sam? Why haven't you been able to contact him, really?" Jo tried to ask gently.

As expected, Samson winced, a near full-body, knee-jerk reaction, though whether it was to Jo's questions or to the mention of the elf, she couldn't tell.

"I've t-tried, been trying, honest." Samson ran a shaking hand through his hair, the other hand reaching blindly for the nearest bauble, fingers trembling as they began to rearrange its varying pieces. "He's not . . . I can't get a hold of him."

"I'm sure you've tried." Jo walked up to him, placing a hand on his shoulder and hating the way it tensed beneath her touch. "But it feels like we're wasting so much time."

"He's very busy," he said, standing up straighter, and Jo could almost see a physical wall going up between them. "And very far, that's all. It takes time."

"But you've *had* time," Jo groaned, hearing the whine creeping into her own voice, unable to pull it back this time. Samson looked at her for a moment, face crestfallen and eyes holding something heavy in them that made Jo's heart ache.

"Give me one more day," Samson offered after a moment, and though Jo wanted to argue, wanted to demand right now, she could see something in Samson's posture, in the expression lining his young face, that said not to. "My last attempt to contact him was fruitless, but I have a plan for the next time." The words sounded forced, and she could tell he was already emotionally drained by this conversation.

"Get in touch with him, Sam, and get him here. Or just get the material you need, I don't care which." Jo paused, a dangerous idea crossing her mind. But desperate times called for desperate measures, and this felt like nothing if not desperate. She was done waiting. "If you don't, I will."

# SAPPHIRE BRIDGE

Jo sat in their usual café once more.

Today, the linens of the sofa were annoyingly bright and the dishware frustratingly brittle. Jo didn't know what she was putting in her mouth—some pastry slathered in a honey-like substance that left a bitter taste on the back of her tongue—but she ate it diligently. All of her mental energy went to three simple ideas: chew, swallow, and don't immediately lash out the moment she heard the name Samson. Or worse: Eslar.

Wayne sat down heavily next to her. He took in a deep breath but no sound came out. His mouth just hung open for a long moment, until, finally, "Now listen, doll—"

"Out with it, Davis."

"Jo—" Takako started.

"*Now*." She didn't want to be cajoled. She didn't want to be soothed. She wanted results.

"He says he needs—"

Jo set down her cup far too heavily, hearing fractures crack around its handle. She didn't even want to let him finish. "That's it, we've waited long enough." Magic crackled beneath Jo's fingers as she tightened her hands into fists against the table's surface. "If Eslar isn't going to play nicely, neither am I."

"Jo—" Wayne was on his feet as Jo started for the door, calling after her. "Don't do anything rash!"

"I'm *done* not doing anything rash." Jo threw her hands in the air. "I'd rather this blow up in my face than spend another minute not doing anything at all."

Takako rushed to catch up with her, stopping her on the sidewalk. "This, whatever it is you're about to pull, could alert *Pan*." Takako said the name as though it would act like a spell and instantly pull Jo back in line.

"Then let her be alerted. Let her come and face me here if she dares to risk the ire of the Elves after all. They already have no love for Aristonia thanks to Pan's own mischief, so I doubt they'll do anything to aide her or Snow.

"I'm done waiting," she declared. "I'm going to High Luana, *now*. Go tell Samson to let Eslar know, if he wants to prevent even a little of the destruction I'm about to bring."

Takako stared at her, mostly in disbelief, before finally letting her go. The woman turned, sprinting away in the direction of the workshop. Who knew if Samson could get to Eslar in time? Jo didn't really care. Nothing would change her mind.

Jo hadn't realized how tight the leash on her magic was until she let it go.

There had been a subconscious dampening of her abilities, no doubt. Perhaps it was in part because she had woken up with expectations of humanity as her "natural state". But here, in Myrth, and with all that had transpired, Jo had cast off that expectation. She was *not* human, she was not even *mortal*. She was Destruction, and an Age of Magic was about to know what happened when a demigod was dropped among them.

Her time wandering the streets of Myrth in an endless holding pattern had given Jo an opportunity to learn the layout of the city some. More importantly, she remembered the brief glimpse of the Sapphire Bridge from her arrival. That was her destination. The point that connected the outpost of the Luanian Empire in which Myrth was seated —the only place that non-elves were allowed to tread—with the Empire proper.

It was simply a matter of crossing the bridge.

Though nothing would be simple about it, she was certain. In a way, she'd been planning for this moment from the second she broke the airship. It was as if, in the back of her mind, she'd known it would come to this: Jo was meant to destroy her path forward.

Before her was a large building that arched into the sea. Its four floors and massive windows shone in the sunlight. In front was a large wall and gate—a manned checkpoint. Men and women waited in a line that stretched along the length of the wall, all elves waiting to go home.

"Sorry to ruin your day," Jo whispered softly but sincerely. Even if she was prepared for what was about to happen, and even if she wouldn't regret it in the slightest, she had never truly wanted it to come to this.

Jo lifted a hand and felt her magic unravel like a fisherman's line. It spun out from the tight coil of her control and flew into the universe, ready to do what she had been born to do—destroy.

In a split second, Jo analyzed the gate before her. It broke down before her eyes, lifting its skirts and showing all its most delicate areas. And with a thought, she let her magic do as it willed with that knowledge.

The immaculately woven, wrought iron gate groaned and buckled. The hinges pulled loose from their bolts in the stone wall; the iron fell with a cacophony of clangs as it disjointed at each of its ornately designed connection points. It was as if Jo had her fingers on the hands of time and spun the watch forward until the gate arrived at its natural point of eventual collapse.

There was screaming. Somewhere behind her, she heard a, "The hell, Jo?!" but she couldn't be sure. The people in line ran, and the guards scrambled in confusion.

"Stop right there!" someone screamed at her.

Jo's eyes scanned the wall. Archers were taking their positions. Gunmen were crouched in a semi-circle around the opening.

All of them could be torn apart.

*Mortals were such fragile beings.*

Jo pushed the thought from her mind; even more than Pan's men, she did not want to kill innocents. They posed no genuine threat to her and, more than that, she didn't actually want to make enemies. Though she may have crossed that metaphorical bridge long before she had begun crossing the physical one.

"I'll give you one chance," she shouted back. "Drop your weapons and let me through. I could care less about the Luanian Empire; all I want is one man: Eslar Greentouch. Give me him and I'll be happy!"

Jo watched as the elf she assumed to be some kind of general took a breath, no doubt about to scream the order to shoot to kill. She still didn't exactly know if she could die, but she wasn't going to find out here.

*They'd be far less deadly without their weapons.*

With a thought, Jo watched as every weapon simultaneously self-destructed. Guns misfired, bows snapped, arrows splintered and fell harmlessly to the ground as the strings they were attached to gave out. One or two soldiers reeled, but there appeared to be no major damage and no loss of life. Jo continued forward.

There were the makings of chaos now, the makings of a situation she knew would make Pan dance in glee. As much as Jo loathed the thought, it was clear why, and how, they could join together. Destruction and chaos were the in-breath that would exhale total oblivion.

"Let me through!" Jo said again. "Give me Eslar Greentouch or passage to High Luana, that's all I ask."

"Stop her!" the general shouted once more.

Jo balled her hands into fists. She'd raze the whole thing to the ground if that's what it took. But that wasn't her objective or desire.

Leveraging the chaos to her advantage, she ran.

She pumped her legs like she never had before, in a sprint that turned the world into a blur. With a leap, Jo cleared the yet-crouched soldiers (all of whom were still trying to make sense of their broken weapons) and landed gently behind them. There was another gate in front of her, another checkpoint.

Jo lifted a hand—rinse and repeat.

This time, rather than falling harmlessly to the ground, the iron exploded. Jo watched as it flew from its origin and scattered across the wide paved courtyard between the outer wall and main building. Once again, people were rushing to stop her, but they weren't fast enough. That, or their weapons broke the moment she passed.

Through the gate, the arc she'd seen from the air was on full display. Right or left? *It didn't matter*, her magic told her, and Jo chose right on a whim, running toward the stairway that led toward the bridge directly in front of the gates she'd just destroyed.

Across the bridge was Luana. Across the bridge was Eslar. It didn't matter how far he was; she'd leave a wake of destruction on her path to get to him.

She should feel tired, Jo realized as she crested the top of the stairs. But she wasn't the slightest bit out of breath, or even fatigued. Pausing, Jo looked behind her. Everyone seemed so far away, so slow moving and stilled. They'd never catch her if she didn't want them to.

Not more than twenty bounding steps in, the first of the sapphire statues began to shift. Two giant elves, easily five stories tall, coming to life. One wielded a sword, the other a staff. The gem they were crafted of shone like starlight, glinting through the cracks in their bodies as they walked with ground-shaking steps onto the bridge itself.

*This is old magic*, Jo realized as the first raised its sword. It was far older than the magic of the gates. Older than anything she'd ever felt before—save for Snow and Pan's rooms in the Society.

The sword screamed as it cut the air, the lumbering statue bringing it down onto the bridge. Miraculously, the surface didn't even crack, though Jo could feel the rumblings of the pressure down into the very foundations.

She leapt onto the sword's edge, sprinting upward. The sapphire golem was too slow to shake her, and by the time it tried, she was already on its shoulder. Jo scrambled toward its head—toward the shining point her magic sight had highlighted for her from her vantage point on the ground.

"So this is what holds you together." Jo stood poised on the crown of its head. Dropping to a crouch, she slammed her palm onto its forehead, magic pushing far beyond where flesh met sapphire. The stone cracked under her fingers, spider webs extending from crown to foot.

The golem crumbled like rain, and Jo was sent falling with it.

She felt the moment her body hit the stone of the bridge below. It was as if every organ exploded at once, every bone splintered and shattered into a thousand pieces, every inch of connective tissue pulverized. And yet, in the destruction of herself, she found life. Like a rubber band spread too wide, Jo felt herself expand and collapse, bouncing back stronger than she'd been before. There were no wounds to mend or limbs to regenerate, just the sudden flash of pain turned energy and power. A little giddy with the realization, she jumped to her feet, turning and sprinting toward the distant end of the bridge.

There was a whole sea of golems to cross.

One after the next, the guardians stepped forward to meet her. They attacked her with swords and staffs and daggers. The sixth had magic beams that made finding its creation point—its *weak point*—a little tricky.

By the seventh she was panting, but still had more than enough air in her lungs to scream, "End this, Luana. I don't want to destroy your history."

There was no response, just a sea of sapphire dust behind her, and more giants ahead.

After the eleventh, Jo screamed again, tilting her head to the heavens as if someone, somewhere, could hear her. "Are we really still going on with this, Luana? All this just for one man? How stubborn can you really be?"

Another sword swung for her.

Jo leapt, catching it on the broad side of the blade, clinging to the outer edge—dull from spending years in the rain and elements. The statue lifted the weapon, as if confused by her presence on the sword point. Jo used the opportunity to sprint up, landing her palm in the shoulder and feeling the same satisfying crunch from within.

She landed, hard. She felt her bones break and the air leave her body and was all the more alive for it. She rose to her knees, then her feet, and resumed her sprint.

At the fifteenth statue, Jo could see land in the distance, and a whole lot of bridge left to cross. Her mind had begun reorienting the purpose of this effort. Perhaps she wouldn't need to find Eslar after all; perhaps she could take on Pan herself with this much practice—hold the woman down while Takako just stabbed the arrow through her heart.

Jo clenched her hands into fists, ready for the next set of warriors, but they never came.

She lowered her eyes, looking not at the suddenly still sapphire giants, but at the bridge. There, in the distance, was a group of people. Ships—

gilded in gold and bearing bright blue sails with the seal of the high elves on them—had been anchored.

"Does your offer to end this still stand?"

"It does," Jo shouted back.

"Then come, and let us parlay like two civilized parties. We hear you're looking for Eslar Greentouch."

# SAMSON'S PAIN

The water splashed in waves against the boat's hull, sending sprays of mist up from beneath to tickle her face. It cooled instantly as. the breeze whipped about the deck, a slight chill running down Jo's spine. They'd been on the ship to High Luana for a couple of hours now, and had taken to wandering the Elvish vessel with a frenetic sort of energy, the adrenaline still high in all of them. Eventually Jo had settled on the upper deck, willing her heart to slow, but she couldn't shake the itchy feeling of "hurry up and wait."

They'd finally managed to get a step forward, after much, much too much time wasted, but Jo couldn't find any success in it. Not when Snow's safety was still an unknown, not when Eslar's involvement was still uncertain, not when she may have just caused a diplomatic rift that could start a war, and most certainly not when Samson looked about a hair's breadth away from throwing himself overboard.

In fact, Samson had grown more and more reserved the longer they were on the ship. It was almost as though, the closer they got to High Luana, the more panicked their craftsman became. To Jo's magical eyes, it was as if he was shattering from the inside out, spider web cracks inching across his chest, shoulders, back, just waiting for a single strike. Though she still wasn't sure what was troubling him, Jo couldn't help feeling guilty for all the stress she'd put him through as a result of her antics.

She wanted to know Snow was all right, she wanted to put an end to Pan, but she also wanted to keep her team—her *family*—safe. Samson might be physically safe, but she was doing very little for his emotional and mental well-being.

"Sam?" Jo risked a soft whisper, and though she'd expected him to recoil in shock, it still hurt. He had clearly not seen her approaching from around the corner of the deck. "Sam, I'm sorry." She dove in before he could scramble away again—like he had when they'd first boarded—though the look in his eyes said he clearly wanted to. She made to reach for him, but held back at the look of anxiety marring his features, hugging her hand to her chest instead. "I'm sorry I've put you through so much."

He was silent for several long seconds, looking back out at the water. Heaving a deep breath, he let it out with precious few words. "I was trying to reach Eslar."

"I know you were," Jo said hastily. "I knew that. But I just . . ." And damnit, there was nothing she could do to stop the sudden tightness in her throat or the blurring of her eyes. "I need to know he's okay. We're so close, and we have a plan. But the waiting... And Eslar's stubbornness—it wasn't you Sam."

"You're worried about him." Samson saved her from herself by saying what she couldn't. There was no doubt as to who he meant. It certainly wasn't Eslar.

Jo lifted a hand to her face, shielding her eyes. She hadn't realized just how terrified she was for Snow until that moment. She'd been assuming the whole time that Samson was the crumbling one that she could see right through him. Jo had never bothered looking in the mirror. "I have no way of knowing, Sam. And I'm so . . . I'm scared that he's—That if we don't hurry, he'll be—"

It took the feel of arms wrapping around her in a loose embrace for her to realize she'd gone silent beneath the weight of unshed tears. Samson's arms were strong, if a bit hesitant, and Jo melted into them, willingly taking the offered comfort.

"You've gotten your wish, Jo," Samson whispered into her hair, holding her a bit tighter. She buried her face in his shirt, smelling motor oil and something sweet yet spicy, like hot chocolate spiked with cayenne. "We're on our way to save him. He'll be fine." Samson let go of her for a moment then, holding her out at arm's length. Though it was a bit awkward (he couldn't seem to figure out if he wanted to use his knuckles or fingertips), Samson lifted his hand to wipe a streak of tears from her cheek. "Snow is strong. After you destroyed the Society, he saved us all by making this world, didn't he? He'll survive long enough for us to save *him* too. Don't you worry."

There was something sad in Samson's voice; in it, Jo detected a level of defeat that was palpable, like a man walking to the guillotine. And as sickening as it was, Jo felt her magic leaching into that weakness, breaking apart exactly what was making Samson shatter, exactly what Samson had been so afraid of. It was as if she naturally wanted to level the field, make him as vulnerable as she felt.

"Sam," Jo whispered, "you know my worries . . . now, tell me yours. What happened between you and Eslar?"

Samson jerked back as if burned, pulling completely out of her touch. Jo wanted to follow him, wanted to pull him back in and soothe away the look of betrayal on his face, but she knew these words were important. And a part of her, somewhere deep where the shadows hid, told her Samson needed to talk about it. He'd been needing to put it out in the open for a while and they were running out of time before he was confronted with Eslar's presence once more.

"You don't . . ." Jo paused, letting her magic formulate the words she needed to say, but likewise letting her desire for Samson's trust and comfort guide them. "You don't have to tell me, if you can't, but I can see that something happened. And I wanted you to know you can talk to me if you want to and need to before we get to High Luana." Then, reaching forward with a cautious and steady hand, Jo grabbed Samson's wrist, sliding down to link their fingers together with a gentle squeeze.

Samson looked from their joined hands back to Jo, conflict clear on his face. He seemed near tears. Keeping this secret was destroying him, Jo realized, the sensation potent and buzzing beneath her own skin. Talking about it may be its own form of breaking down, but part of her knew that if he got it out, it would destroy him less. So she held fast, silently luring him in.

Eventually, Samson seemed to relent. With a breath, he squeezed her hand back tight.

"He doesn't want anything to do with me now that he doesn't *have* to have anything to do with me," he said, so soft that Jo could barely hear it. His fingers were already trembling in her grip. "With . . . W-With us. With the Society and . . . and all this. With Pan. I tried, but—" Samson took a shaky breath, looking a little like he was about to pass out. As carefully as she could, Jo led Samson to one of the comfy chairs spread about the deck, kneeling at his side to keep their hands together.

"There's no rush, Sam," Jo offered, settling in to wait, her free hand resting against his knee. "The elves say we have at least two more days until we reach High Luana anyway. You have time. Just go slow."

Samson took another breath, a deep inhale that seemed wet with brimming tears, and a quiet, grounding exhale through his nose. When he looked at Jo, he seemed less anxious, and older than she'd ever seen him. Suddenly, she thought she could see every year of the countless hundreds he had lived.

"Why doesn't he want anything to do with us?"

"He's afraid."

"Afraid of what?" As far as Jo was concerned, the only thing anyone should fear was Pan.

"Afraid of losing his world again, his people, his culture. He sees the Society as the catalyst for . . . for the last time he lost it all."

Jo pressed her lips together, mulling over her next question. "When you say 'lost it all,' you mean his wish?"

"No, that was the first time he lost it all—his wish that brought him to the Society," Samson whispered, never breaking eye contact with Jo. "The last time was my wish." Her blood ran cold, even as anticipation and intrigue licked beneath her skin. "My wish caused the end of the original Age of Magic."

Jo . . . hadn't been expecting that. Luckily, once the floodgates had opened, Samson wasted no time elaborating.

"There was a war," he said, and then laughed dejectedly to himself. "There's always a war, isn't there? But I . . . I wasn't a soldier. I was a fletcher, watching my fellow countrymen die, watching villages burn, and I . . ." Samson shivered, no doubt remembering the sights and sounds of death, the stench and pain of a war he'd never wanted to be a part of. "The war was between those who had magic and those who did not. And I thought that maybe, if I begged, if I wished hard enough, I could—" His words failed him for a moment. But with a harsh exhale and a tightening of his jaw, he finished. "I wished to remove all magic from the world. I thought if I wished for it all to be gone, every last trace of it from everyone and everything, there'd be nothing to fight over anymore."

"It didn't just take the magic away, did it?" Bile rose at the back of Jo's throat, her stomach twisting violently. "It also removed the magical peoples and creatures, too, right?"

"I didn't know that I'd . . . I didn't mean for it to *do* what it *did*. I hadn't realized that—" Samson babbled, burying his face in the free hand not linked fiercely and painfully with Jo's. "I had never meant for something like that to happen, but I . . . I couldn't take it back. S-Snow said the deed had been done—it was when we learned about the dangers of forcing a transition without closing the Severity of Exchange. He'd forced the jump and it completely made a new age. Maybe if he'd hadn't? But the damage was done. Eslar blamed me for the erasure of his people from the first moment I woke in the Society."

Jo remembered her first week at the Society, and Eslar's passing comment about a time when Elves had existed. There were also the comments about Snow, how shifts with wide Severities of Exchange could be . . . violent. She'd been too new, too green to catch any subtleties between Eslar and Samson at the time, but now every remembered interaction between them seemed weighted.

What must that have been like for Eslar, watching a wish decimate his entire race? To have to live with the one at the root of such genocide for decades, generations? But to find the cause not to be a wretched soul, but a good-hearted man who made a scared and hasty choice that too many paid for?

"You and Eslar though . . ." Jo paused, trying to find the right words. "You always seemed so close."

"That took years and *years* of apologies." Samson sniffled through tears that seemed determined to fall even through his fingers. "It was a century before I could even get him to pass the salt. Eventually . . . Yes, we found a quiet peace and I thought it may have been enough. But how could have it had been?

"Now, the elves have returned—he's got people back. He's got his *home* back now. And . . . I thought that maybe, maybe he'd l-let me apologize once more, g-give me a chance to finally s-settle this so that we could move forward and put it all behind us for good." With a quick swipe at his eyes that did nothing for the snot and tears streaking his dark features, Samson looked at Jo with a weary smile. "I know I don't deserve closure, but I had hoped for it. We spent so many years together . . . there was so much time and he seemed like he . . . Not that you ever get over something like that. Perhaps, if I hadn't been the one to ask him for help, he'd have listened to your plea. Perhaps if I hadn't been selfish, if I hadn't wanted it to be me to bridge the gap, he would have offered his assistance in all of this far sooner. And for that . . . For that, Jo, I am sorry."

His words were filled with guilt and longing and pain, and Jo felt her own magic mingle with his, taking in the despair and destruction as if she could remove it from deep within him, spare him from it all. She eased him into another hug, allowing tears to soak into the fabric of her tunic as she rubbed soothing circles into his back.

It was obvious now, where all Samson's anxieties about contacting Eslar had originated. Still, he'd tried. For the team and for the mission and for Snow, he had tried and tried and tried. And while much was still left unsaid, that had to count for something.

If nothing else, Samson's pain and guilt counted for Jo, and she would find a way to make them count for Eslar, too.

# A ROYAL AUDIENCE

Two more days on the ship to get to High Luana were proving to be two too long.

Wayne and Takako had spent the first portion of the trip gambling with the elves and then the second portion avoiding the elves due to Wayne's cheating. After Sam had confessed his secret to Jo, they'd spent the better part of the evening together, doing nothing at all. Jo appreciated the quiet companionship and she had a feeling Samson felt much the same, because he sought her out the day after, and the day after that.

Finally, High Luana came into view.

Mountains stretched up from the sea, and above them towered a giant spire. It stood offset from the main island, connected by an arching bridge made of two colossal sculpted elves linking outstretched hands, palms upturned, as though they were holding the bridge itself between their loving arms.

"Is that—"

"The castle where the king sits? Yes." The tall elf cut her off. "The bridge to it has stood even longer than the Sapphire Bridge." He gave her a long side-eye.

"My assurances still stand. Bring me to Eslar Greentouch and I won't destroy another thing of elvish make. Despite what you and your men may think, I am no enemy of the elves."

A curt nod was his only response.

Jo allowed herself be distracted by the swiftly growing scenery. The more she thought of divinity, the more she thought of Snow. And that was a dangerous path to let her mind go down. Despite herself, her hands balled into fists.

*Hang on. Just hang on,* her heart pleaded into the universe, as though he could somehow hear her. He'd sacrificed enough. Now it was her turn.

The brilliantly blue sea was cut off by a strip of white, and the beaches turned into emerald foliage or jewel-bespeckled towns. The waters became crowded as they neared closer and closer to the island. Fishermen stopped their work to watch the Imperial vessel speed by. They stared in fascination and . . . worry. Jo wondered just how much word of her had gotten to the rest of Luana, or perhaps more importantly, what words were said when it had.

Their ship sailed right under the massive bridge she'd seen from the distance. Jo twisted, looking up till her neck hurt and then some as they passed beneath. It was truly a marvel to behold and she wondered if Samson saw the same thing she did: utter perfection in craftsmanship. The only thing that was going to bring the bridge down was if she attacked it with the brute force of her magic. It was as if the very land had been coerced into shaping itself into the foundation for the bridge and the giant castle on the other side.

Past the bridge, they began to slow, pulling into a sheltered inlet of docks. The four of them gathered at the end of the gangway before a group of elvish guards in suits of armor that nearly covered them from head to toe. The man whom Jo presumed to be the leader was the only one to speak.

"If you'll follow me this way."

They wound up stairways on stairways, working their way up from the sea to the towering bridge. They were about halfway when Wayne stopped on one of the terraces, hands on his knees.

"Just go on ahead, I'll catch up," he panted, breathless.

"We can't leave you behind," the leader elf said, matter-of-fact. "We can wait for you to catch your breath."

"Or leave me where I fall," Wayne muttered.

"What was that?"

"Nothing." Wayne straightened, wiping the sweat from his brow.

"I could carry you," Jo offered. After the physical feats she'd accomplished on the Sapphire Bridge, Jo didn't think Wayne on her back would slow her down one bit.

"I'm not that out of shape, dollface. Wouldn't want to crush you." He motioned toward the next set of stairs. "Carry on, then."

They had to stop two more times, but Jo's offer to carry Wayne seemed to keep pushing him all the way to the top. Even Samson and Takako had requested a small break each, though Takako's training as a soldier seemed to give her the greatest stamina, after Jo and their Elvish guides in ranked order. Jo couldn't help feeling oddly proud on the woman's behalf. It was late in the afternoon by the time they crossed the last stair. Wayne was the first one to mutter "Oh thank god" the second both of his feet were at the top.

This high up, the wind blew unimpeded, almost violently tossing Jo's hair. She raised a hand, pulling it back from where it whipped her face to get a better look at the city compacted into a basin of sheer cliffs. From the sea, it looked as if the bridge to the Luanian castle ended at a forested ridge. But the trees and ridgetop concealed a whole city within—a city of shallow pools, domed gazebos, hanging gardens, and all the lushness of a high society that had thrived uninterrupted for thousands of years.

Seeing High Luana, remembering Eslar's room, knowing what Samson had told her, all came together in an odd form of guilt. He finally had what he wanted—what he'd witnessed being blotted out from existence—his home. And now they were going to demand he remove himself from it and risk his life.

*No.*

Jo turned, looking up at the giant spire that loomed over it all, as though it were a watchtower for the whole world. They were coming to demand he remove himself from this home and risk his life *for* it, to protect it. She was no more pleased than he was about the situation, but that didn't give any of them the ability to ignore it, either.

"Think the elves are compensating for anything?" Wayne leaned in and whispered, motioning upward at the spire.

"You're going to get us in trouble," Jo hissed back.

"More trouble than a demigod bent on destroying the world and the thing you did to their bridge?" he said, deadpan.

Jo looked forward, determined to ignore any further remarks, and focused instead on the two giant silver doors that swung open soundlessly. Samson looked at them in awe as they passed through. The hallway was wide enough for everyone to walk side-by-side if they wanted and still have enough room. The roof was taller than any she'd ever seen before, tall enough that it was cast in shadow, tiny floating motes of light the only thing guiding their way forward. Especially once the doors closed behind them and plunged the hall into darkness. The lights descended one by one, falling to the floor, outlining the path for them to continue on. It was as beautiful as it was pointless, since there was only one way to go.

The hall dumped them into an even larger room. The floor was inlaid with silver, and made of stone fitted so perfectly that it was impossible to see the grooves with the naked eye. Thousands upon thousands of lines of elvish script traversed from one wall to the next, though Jo could only pick out a few words and one or two simple sentences with her elvish study so far.

Six columns, fat and reminiscent of the strange-looking trees she'd seen on their arrival along the beach, supported a vaulted roof. At the end of them, seated on simple thrones made of silver, was an Elvish man wearing an ornate headdress of silver. Next to him was a woman, and two younger looking boys sat on either side of them.

Their group was marched right up to the throne, stopping only when their leader dropped into a low bow. Jo didn't know what elvish custom dictated, but a little bit of decorum couldn't hurt, she decided. So she gave a small bow of her head, rising when the elf did. He spoke in the lifting tones of the elvish language and the king gave a nod.

Closer, Jo got her first good look at the elvish royal family; it wasn't what she had expected. These were ancient creatures, bent on the survival of their species and cultivation of their history before all other things. But they looked almost . . . modest.

Nothing like the storybook elves from Jo's history, the king had short, almost messy hair that was black as coal. His ruddy skin, clearly inherited by his sons, almost matched Samson's. He wore a simple silver tunic, cinched low with a wide sapphire belt. It complemented the blouse the queen wore with silver trousers. Jo hadn't been expecting trousers; she was used to cultures modeled on ancient times harboring an unnecessary obsession with gender roles and expectations. But perhaps the gender roles and norms Jo knew, and the ones here, were different.

"Which of you is the one they call Josephina?" The king spoke nearly without any accent at all, his English practically flawless.

"That'd be me." Jo took a step forward.

"Word has reached us that to a . . . vehement degree, you have demanded to speak with our Grand Healer."

*That's certainly a way to put it.* Jo kept the remark to herself, opting instead for a simpler, "It is a matter of dire importance."

"I would hope so," the queen said softly, crossing her legs and leaning back in her chair, looking bemused about the situation. "It will take a century to repair the Sapphire Bridge."

Jo should feel guilty. But she didn't. If anything, she just felt slightly angrier at Eslar for forcing them all into this mess with his stubbornness. Then again, she didn't *have* to start destroying the bridge . . . Her head hurt if she tried to tally up the scores for "who messed up more".

"Tell me, why should I not just strike you down here and now for waging war against the elves?"

"Because I am not waging war," Jo insisted.

"It certainly appears that way."

"I was given no other choice to get the attention of your—" *How did he phrase it?* "—Grand Healer. We had made every attempt to contact him through conventional means."

"So you expect to go unpunished?"

That was something Jo hadn't considered. Punishment was likely fair. But Jo didn't find it very threatening. She bit back a sigh.

"You want to 'punish' me? Be my guest. Let's see how well that works for you." Jo shrugged. "Could be interesting, I suppose, because I've found there's very little that harms me. Locking me up would just give me a fun puzzle to break apart. And the longer you keep me here, the more at risk you all are." *Be it from Pan finally catching up, or the end of the world*—Jo kept the thought to herself.

The king gripped and let go of his arm rests as if he were giving them a massage. "I am willing to forgive your transgressions." Spoken like a man already backed into a corner, making it sound like it was his idea to be there all along. "On one condition."

"I didn't come here for conditions." Jo put her hands on her hips. "I was hoping we could have a productive working relationship."

"I hope for that as well." The king stood. "But to achieve that, you must tell us what strange magic you used to break our wards and level the work of our people as though it were a mere initiate's exercise. This information will be valuable to us in rebuilding and could perhaps expunge the damage you've done." *And give him an opportunity to write her off as a sort of test, or human wrecking ball making way for new improvement, to his people.*

Jo frowned. It wasn't that she didn't want to work with him... "There's not enough time for that."

"I have lived for over five hundred years. I am very patient."

"Even if I told you, you wouldn't believe me. There wouldn't be enough time for you to understand, and unfortunately we don't have five hundred more years for you to let it sink in." Her hands fell from her hips, as though pulled by the weight of disbelief at yet another hoop before her. How hard was it to just give her some time to talk to one elf?

"You presume too much to speak to the king that way," their tall escort cautioned.

"Fine. I presume a demonstration of my powers will be good enough? Maybe then you'll see why you should've just taken my word?" Jo cracked her knuckles, mostly for show.

"Don't do anything rash," Takako whispered as their escort quickly said something in elvish to his king.

But the conversation was interrupted by the loud shutting of a door echoing through the hall, followed by a simple statement in an all-too-familiar voice.

"You should know better, Takako. Our Josephina has yet to master the art of not being rash." All eyes turned. Eslar gave a small frown at seeing them. "You never knew when to quit, did you?"

# IMPATIENT

For as much as Eslar's tone betrayed annoyance, Jo liked to think the exasperation didn't quite meet his eyes. He looked much the same as she remembered, though no longer wearing casual 2050s fashion.

Now, as he approached their stunned little group, a long robe flowed behind him, lined and accented in the oceanic tones that Jo was now learning to be the particular color scheme of those with import in Luanian society. His long black hair had been braided back from his dark face in intricate weaves, making the silver and sapphire jewelry lining his pointed ears and pinned throughout seem more prominent.

They had called him their Grand Healer, but to Jo, he looked equally as royal as their king.

"You've certainly put in a surprising amount of effort to get here." Eslar broke the stalemate that had followed his arrival. "Clearly my silence had not been answer enough to whatever request you plan to make."

Jo winced, not liking the way his tone shifted from indifferent to cold, though she held hope in the way his eyes took each of them in one at a time. Surely, despite his self-induced isolation from his former team, he would have missed them, *right?* Even just a little bit?

"We had hoped you would change your mind once you actually heard the request. And since you wouldn't give us the time of day over the phone—or disk—we had to come here to deliver it in person," Jo threw back, though Eslar's wandering gaze had finally shifted down the line of their group and onto Samson. Jo couldn't even be sure Eslar had heard her, not for the way his focus narrowed down to the craftsman as if he were the only one in the room.

At first, Jo's skin prickled at the attention, a need to protect Samson from any backlash rising like static electricity across her skin, especially after learning his truths on the ship. But the more she looked between them—the unspoken words on Eslar's tongue and a cocktail of emotions on Samson's face—the less protective she felt. In fact, the longer they stared at each other in silent communication, the more she just felt like a voyeur.

A couple of times, Samson opened his mouth to speak, but at each attempt he found himself losing the courage. He seemed relieved to see Eslar, maybe even antsy with nervous excitement, hands twitching against the hem of his shirt. But he also looked a little like he was going to throw up.

"Master Greentouch?" It was the king who finally sought to bring an end to the lingering quiet, the authority in his voice making Jo tense. And she wasn't the only one.

She wouldn't have noticed had she not been paying such close attention to the two men, but at the sound of the king's interruption, she saw both of their shoulders tighten, Eslar's back straightening as Samson hunched into himself more fully. She took solace in the fact that, at least for a moment, they must have been relaxing in each other's presences.

"Yes, my liege?" Eslar finally cleared his throat. Though the tension had fizzled some, it hadn't broken, and the Grand Healer and the Craftsman continued to lock eyes, a line of weighted communication passing like a tangible thing between them.

"Perhaps it would be best if you lead your *friends* somewhere where you can speak more privately and no longer trouble the crown with personal matters." The king emphasized the word *friends* in a way that left Jo more than a little miffed. This was clearly not the first time he'd had a conversation with Eslar about them, and it left Jo wondering how much of their initial interaction was for show. Eslar didn't comment, his back still to the rest of the group, but the tension had in no way left his shoulders.

"We have rooms prepared for you all in the East Wing," the queen added, this time addressing Jo directly. "We do hope they'll be to your liking." There was kindness behind the queen's eyes that Jo found comforting, even if her words still glistened with ice.

"I'm sure they'll be more than sufficient, your highness," Jo replied with another minute bow of her head. "We appreciate your continued generosity." She tried not to let sarcasm drip into the sentiment, but the slight rise of the queen's eyebrow suggested Jo hadn't succeeded.

"Our request has not been overlooked, Josephina Espinosa. We will allow you an audience with our Grand Healer—" The king's gaze shifted to Eslar, probably commenting on his interruption before any deal could be struck. "And in return for all the forgiveness and hospitality which we have shown you, we expect an eventual explanation of your rather . . . devastating magic."

A weight sank in Jo's stomach as she held the king's stare, her eyes narrowing into a glare. If she had to give them another "example" of her power, she would. But she also couldn't sacrifice their plan further by being hot headed, even in the face of the king's poorly veiled animosity. She'd known what she was risking when she destroyed the bridge, after all. As if to emphasize her thoughts, Jo felt Takako reach over, a subtle shift of her hand, to rest her fingers against Jo's wrist. Not a warning or a plea, but a reminder. They had Eslar, they would have their chance to appeal to him; no need to be rash.

Jo took a breath and closed her eyes for a moment before looking back to the king. "We'll see," she said, offering him what she hoped was more smile than grimace. The king didn't comment, finally shifting his focus back to Eslar.

"If you would, Master Greentouch."

Eslar bowed his head with a monotone, "Of course, sire," and began to lead the group out of the throne room. Wayne, Takako, and Samson followed without a word, Samson trailing a bit behind, but Jo spared one more glance at the royal family before following suit.

Through the doors on the right-hand side of the throne room, the group entered into a narrow but no less luxe hallway. Eslar didn't look back and his shoulders were so rigid, they formed an impenetrable wall.

"Your rooms will be in here," Eslar said when they arrived at a set of double doors at the far corner of the courtyard they'd been traversing. He opened both doors and led them rank and file into a common area.

It was an incredibly spacious setup, the windows along the far wall—bordered in swirling, branch-like patterns—only adding to the inviting openness. In the center of the room, flanked by two more open doors to the left and right, was a sitting area that boasted three couches, a chaise, and a long table that stretched toward the windows. The furniture was intricately carved in deep mahogany and covered in blue velvet.

Through the doors, Jo could see more furniture, including a four-poster bed. The bedding looked immensely plush, a pristine white duvet accented with embroidered swirls of green and no doubt filled with some type of feathers. The pillows looked equally as soft and inviting, if not more so. All in all, a very impressive place to rest.

Takako would certainly enjoy it.

Jo, on the other hand, took solace in the fact that the living room had an entire wall dedicated to shelves upon shelves of books (hopefully with some in English). She wouldn't have been surprised to count somewhere near a thousand or more on the floor-to-ceiling spread. Jo could already feel herself unconsciously dragging her eyes over each title, waiting for something of use to stick out to her.

The book that had helped lead them here had belonged to Eslar, after all. If they needed more information, more insight into their ever-changing plan, Jo's best bet would be this wall. At the least it'd stave off the boredom.

The elf stood behind them, still hovering in the doorframe as if he couldn't decide if he was really going to go through with talking to them, or if he was going to try locking them away and running. As if sensing her train of thought, Eslar crossed his arms over his chest and walked up to her, only barely breaching her personal space but looming over her nonetheless.

"You all wanted my attention so desperately," he said, voice cool and aggravatingly unemotional. "Well now you have it. After all that's transpired, what could you possibly need me for?"

Jo was struck with the sudden desire to tangle a fist into the collar of his tunic, to drag him down to her line of sight and demand that he stop being so indifferent about their arrival. Sure, the Society hadn't been kind to them, but they'd survived together. They'd bonded and grown and loved and lost. *Together.* Did that mean nothing to him? Now that he had his people and his status and his world back, did their trials mean nothing? Her magic was practically yelling at her to dismantle Eslar's truth, to rip deep into his mind and heart and find proof that he had cared.

But as much as it probably showed in her eyes, Jo said nothing. Not without taking a deep breath, willing her magic to settle back into her core. Arguing right off the bat would do no one any good.

"The Society itself might be gone, but we're not done fighting." Jo dove right in, willing herself not to mirror Eslar's dismissive pose. "I know having magic back, having your *people* back, is important to you. As it should be. But as long as Pan lives, none of it is safe."

As if it were involuntary, Eslar's gaze shifted over Jo's shoulder to where she knew Samson stood. She hoped she hadn't thrown the poor guy under the bus in some way, but Jo knew it was something Eslar needed to hear.

"We've come up with a plan to stop her, but we need your help to do it."

Eslar looked back at her for a long moment before speaking. "What makes you think, after a year of silence, that she intends anything so grandly malicious?"

"Because . . ." Jo hesitated, trying to figure out the best way to phrase it that didn't condemn her to the already reluctant elf, but really, there was no way to skirt blame on this one, was there? "Because I'm back. She's looking for me and will do anything to get me. And if she finds me before we have the means to defeat her, that's the end for us all."

Eslar raised an eyebrow at that. "And how, exactly, is that?"

"If she gets her hands on me and forces us to return to one being . . . Oblivion walks the earth once more."

By the look on Eslar's face, Jo knew he understood; knowledge of the Age of Magic, of the old gods and their demigod counterparts, had been scattered throughout his stories. Now it was come to life. She was one half of the monster from his people's fairytales.

"Then you are—"

"Destruction. Yes," Jo said, biting back a cringe. "And Pan is Chaos."

"And how much of this is actually about Snow?" Eslar's expression had resumed its look of careful stoicism, but Jo could see the judgment behind it regardless. So she swallowed back her defensive response and instead bared her soul.

"I won't deny that . . . that part of me wants to see him safe. Just as much as you no doubt want to see this world and your people's place in it safe. Snow is my counterpart in every sense. I was—" Jo felt the words lodge in her throat. The thought of Snow, still trapped, still so far out of reach, made her heart clench. "He was literally made to be with me. And being apart, not knowing if he's safe under Pan's constant presence —*hurts*. It's terrifying and painful and I've never wanted anything more than to know he is safe.

"But I need to know that all of you will be safe too. That this world will be safe. And none of you—none of us—will be, so long as Pan lives."

Once the words were out, Jo felt oddly exhausted, her chest aching and her throat sore. She could feel that tell-tale sting at the back of her eyes, the corners blurring with unshed tears, and she forced herself to look away. It was Wayne's attention that fell into her line of sight then, and she hoped the plea in her eyes was enough for him to pick up where she had left off.

Wayne nodded once, focusing on Eslar; the ache in Jo's chest eased.

"We have a weapon we think will work against her," he said. "An arrow Samson's been carrying through the ages. We have reason to believe it's the arrow that once belonged to the Goddess of the Hunt."

Recognition flickered across Eslar's face.

"All we need is a bow," Takako chimed in.

Eslar eyed Wayne and Takako each in turn, still somehow managing to look unconvinced. "And you expect to find such a bow here in High Luana?"

Though it sounded like it physically pained him to do so, Samson was the one who answered Eslar this time. "I can c-craft one, I think, that will be strong enough. I may need help. I don't know yet. But I do know that I will need a special material that can only . . . that can only be found here."

Instead of looking at anyone in particular, Samson's head was down, eyes locked on his shoes. He wasn't fidgeting with anything, but his hands shook at his sides, as if the simple act of talking was dragging him closer and closer to the edge of panic. Jo was overwhelmed with the desire to reach forward and hold one of those trembling hands, but to her surprise, Wayne beat her to it. He stepped easily into Samson's space until their shoulders were pressed together, just enough physical contact to know Wayne was there but not enough to crowd. It seemed to calm Samson down some, though his voice still shook as he went on.

"I know th-that it is unfair of us to ask this of you, Eslar. It is unfair of *me* to ask *anything* of you, and for that, I am sorry. I am so, s-so sorry." Here, despite the way his eyes filled with tears, despite the trembling plea in his voice, Samson looked up, capturing Eslar's gaze with a determination Jo could never remember seeing on the man's face. "But we can't do this without you, Eslar. Please. We need your help to get them to say yes and help us."

Jo looked from Samson to Eslar just in time to watch the look of surprise fade from Eslar's eyes. There was something beneath his expression that Jo couldn't quite identify, a loose thread he was unable to tuck away, and though part of her knew she could use her magic to pick at that thread until the elf unraveled before her, she held back. This was between them.

For a long and agonizing moment, Eslar simply continued to hold Samson's gaze, a silent battle warring between them much like it had when they'd first arrived. But unlike then, it didn't take the crude clearing of Wayne's throat for Eslar to break their connection. As if finally seeing something on Samson's face, Eslar blinked, back straightening in what Jo would almost define as disappointment.

"I will need . . . time," he said, already heading towards the door. "Someone will be along shortly with dinner." He didn't bother turning to face anyone as he said it, his voice as expressionless as Jo had ever heard it. The look on Samson's face was utterly heartbreaking. Despite the urge crawling like fire-ants beneath Jo's skin, she didn't follow Eslar out.

No one did.

# BROKEN TABLE LEG

"Time?" Wayne balked. "Time? He's had a whole—"

Jo caught Wayne's wrist before he could bolt out of the room. Wayne spun, his momentum redirected. But Jo didn't let go.

"Leave him be," she cautioned. "At least for now."

"We came all this way and you just want to let him act like this?"

"I think we have to." Jo's attention shifted to the door. Two soldiers had positioned themselves on either sides of the double doors leading to their chambers, pulling them closed. There was the sound of a heavy lock clanking, engaged from the outside.

"The hell is this?" Wayne reeled back to the door. "Now we're locked in like prisoners? So much for being honored guests." He wrenched his hand from Jo's grip.

"Calm down. It's not like we can blame them for being skeptical of us and, beyond that, I don't think we can be locked anywhere." Jo started for the bookshelves. "Given that we have a man who can make any bet happen with the guards, a woman who could shoot for the vulnerable part of the locks and never miss, a crafter whom I'm sure could make a key or some other mechanism to open the door . . ." She paused, just for emphasis. "Oh, and the demigod of Destruction."

"Takako doesn't have a gun right now to shoot with," Wayne muttered, but it was obvious in his posture that he was just clinging to his tantrum.

Jo turned to roll her eyes at him, but stopped when she saw Takako reach into her coat, and deftly pull a small handgun from a harness Jo hadn't realized she'd been wearing.

"You think I go anywhere without a gun?"

Jo barely managed to bite back her laugh, an awkward cough taking its place.

"Fine, you can all be relaxed with this." Wayne threw his hands in the air, stomping over to a sofa that he proceeded to throw himself onto. "I'll be over here, being the voice of reason."

Takako snorted at the notion, crossing over to the windows.

"Seriously, where does Eslar get off being all high and mighty?" Despite appearances, Wayne was clearly not done.

"Well, he is a *high* elf." Takako's grin was apparent in her voice, and the burst of laughter Jo had originally attempted to smother broke free. Even if Takako was only resorting to bad jokes for the sake of lightening the mood, it was both unexpected and gratefully received.

"Puns? We've resorted to *puns* now?" Wayne groaned, throwing an arm across his face in a way that reminded Jo of one of those heroines in her mother's favorite old movies, taken by the vapors and in desperate need of a lie-down.

With a final snort of her own, Jo left them to their banter, and looked instead to Samson, who still hovered as though completely lost. "Sam, can you help me with something?" Jo asked, loud enough to call him from his stupor, but soft enough that it wouldn't earn Wayne's and Takako's attention.

"Wh— *oh*, yes." Samson hurried over, shaking his head. "What can I help you with?"

"What do you think of Eslar?" she whispered, now working to keep the conversation entirely between them, purely because she had no interest in garnering any further remarks from Wayne.

"Me?"

"You know him better than any of us." Jo shot the man a small smile that had him looking promptly at his toes. She turned back to the shelves to give the illusion of scanning the books. The motion served a dual purpose: she could avoid both arousing Wayne and Takako's attention, and putting unnecessary pressure on Samson.

"I think . . ." Samson faltered. Then, in a sudden burst of energy, he took a step toward her. It was a little too wide, a little too hasty. He was suddenly close enough to be awkward but, for possibly the first time ever, he didn't seem to notice. "I *don't* think, Jo, I *know*. I know that I can convince him to help us. Now that I'm here. Now that I can speak to him, in-in person . . . I know—"

"I believe you," Jo soothed, covering his hand with her own as it clutched desperately at her sleeve. "I know you can, too."

"But with other people . . ." Samson's eyes drifted to Takako, Wayne, and ultimately landed on her. "He . . . I don't think he'll listen. He'll feel like we're ganging up on him. He always felt like the odd man out as the only non-human."

After their interactions today, Jo was inclined to believe it. To Eslar, she was sure they looked like a gang, here to bully him into submission. Even if Jo was willing to do that, everything would go much more smoothly if the elf was on their side of his own accord.

"Grab a book, Samson, and read with me," Jo said, reaching toward the shelf. She was forming a plan but didn't want to spook him. "And don't stop reading, not even when everyone else goes to bed."

Samson looked at her for a long moment, his lips parting around a question. But ultimately, it remained unasked; he gave a small nod. "I think I'd like that."

The two of them positioned themselves together on the couch, their noses in books. Jo had found a good primer on the elvish language and Samson had an unsurprisingly good command of it already.

Jo kept her head down as Wayne bemoaned how "she never used to be like this" and how bored he was and how she should, instead, go make trouble with him amidst the "easily connable" elves. Takako kept to herself, occasionally cleaning her firearms, but Jo could tell confinement made her antsy as well.

They broke for dinner when it was brought to them, returning to their couch as night filled the sky outside and a soft glow filled the lamps of their chamber. Takako and Wayne made an attempt at figuring out an elvish tile game they found on the bookshelf, but even that was eventually abandoned, and, by the looks of it, without much progress.

Instead of books or games, Jo found herself distracted by the small obsidian disk Wayne had bought her back on Myrth, as Samson was fidgeting with an intricate gauntlet.

"This is the strangest thing . . ." she muttered, glancing over to Wayne and Takako as the former gave a mighty yawn.

"What about it?" Samson looked up from his work.

"I can't figure out how to break it, and it's driving me insane."

"It's likely because you can't see it."

"What?"

"Your restriction. You have to see something to use your magic on it, right?" She nodded. "Well, you can't actually see it like that."

"I still don't understand." She tapped the disk, as if to point out that she (obviously) could see it.

He held out his hand and Jo passed over the thin, oblong disk. He placed it in the palm of his left hand, holding it between them. With his right hand, he gestured upward from his palm, pulling his fingers together as if tugging something out from the stone itself. And, to Jo's amazement, an image did appear. It was multi-layered and composed of simple lines and interconnecting shapes that glowed faintly in the air. "This is the magical makeup of the item."

All at once, what had eluded Jo for days now fell into place. She instantly knew how to break down every bit of magic the stone had to offer. "How did you do that?"

"You can do it with any obsidian—at least, any obsidian that isn't warded against intrusion. It's a sort of magic conductor in this world that can be impressed upon, not unlike a computer, I suppose." Samson closed his hands and compressed the image back into the disk. "Let me see your hands."

Jo obliged and Samson drew a few quick symbols with his fingers in the air over her palms. There was the faint outline of light as they seeped into her skin, and then nothing. "What was that?" she asked when he finished.

"It's a basic charm imprinted on you. It should allow you to pull apart obsidian workings as long as they're not warded . . . and even then, knowing your magic, you may not have a hard time of it. Why not give it a try?"

She did as told, and pulled out the same framework Samson had. "How do you know how to do this?" Jo whispered in wonder, looking at all the magical pathways at work inside the tiny disc.

"In my Age of Magic—which really wasn't *that* different from this one, just a few thousand years earlier—humans were the youngest race. Most had no naturally occurring magic within them. Other young races were similar, with very little or no magic." Jo recalled what he had said a few days earlier about the war of magic being between the haves and have-nots when it came to magic. "Those without had to develop charms and spells to draw magic from other sources, house it, and then give it a structure to do with what we wanted."

"What else is different between your Age of Magic and this one?"

Sadness flooded his eyes and before Samson could answer with what would no doubt be equally sad words, Wayne stood.

"Well, I think I'm going to go to bed. It's the only way to put an end to the longest, most tedious day ever. Of my many, many lives," Wayne announced dramatically. "Last chance to have some fun, doll."

"I can't tell if you're asking me to come to bed with you, or to stir the pot with the elves," Jo responded without looking up from the disk.

"Both, ideally?"

Jo just shook her head, and Wayne departed for the room to the left of the entry—designating it as the "men's dorm" with his choice.

Takako stayed with them a little longer, idly skimming a book selected seemingly at random. But eventually, she yawned more frequently than she flipped pages. Bidding them goodnight, she headed off herself.

Silence settled on the room.

After one more, long hour, Jo closed her book, set it to the side, and stretched. "Well, shall we, then?"

"What are you going to do?" Samson asked, looking tired but alert. Even though he questioned, he still followed her to the door without hesitation.

"I've been thinking about that a lot today . . ." Jo came to a stop at the door. "I know we could just break through and *demand* to be taken to him." She saw the objection on Samson's face and cut it off at the pass. "I don't want to do that either. I'd like to speak to him without a fuss."

"So, then . . ."

"I'm going to create a small diversion, send the guard over to investigate. Nothing serious . . . I just think one of those lovely tables holding those precious vases in the hall is going to lose a leg."

"You can do that from here?" he asked, awe apparent. "You don't need to see it anymore?"

"I think I have that covered. If I'm right, we'll move when the guards do. I'll destroy the locking mechanism on the door and we'll go through quickly. So, just stay close to me."

Samson gave a determined nod, one Jo mirrored back to him before she dropped down onto her hands and knees. She placed her cheek on the floor, peering through the slit she'd been watching the sun shine through for the better part of the day. One eye closed, and squinting, Jo could barely make out a table leg in the distance. But it was enough.

Taking a breath, Jo remembered what she'd seen of the tables earlier. Their make and design flooded her mind as her eyes narrowed on her target—a connection from the leg to the table, a point where the glue could be loosened—and just like that, pegs came free.

A crash echoed from the other side of the door, followed by the scampering of the guards positioned outside.

"Now!" Jo hissed and jumped to her feet, putting a hand on the door and feeling the inner mechanisms holding it closed crack and break. The door swung open and Jo immediately headed right, half-pulling Samson along with her.

They were down the hallway in a blink. With every step they took, her plan seemed to progress without a hitch.

Side-stepping into an alcove, Jo dared to look back.

The hallway was empty.

"I can't believe that worked," she breathed in relief.

"Let's not count our screws till they're tightened."

"You're right."

"Where to?" Samson asked, daring to look around himself.

"This way . . ." Jo started them down another hall, then quickly turned, ducking into a room that switched back, connecting to a stair.

"How do you know this?" Samson whispered.

"The elves were proud enough of their castle to include a book on its history in their library for guests. Even if I couldn't read it, I could look at the pictures." Jo paused only long enough to shoot him a grin.

Samson flashed her a broad smile, one that looked filled with relief and triumph. "I wondered why you picked up something entirely in Elvish."

"I think . . . it's one of these," Jo whispered as they finally came out on a landing high up in what she presumed to be the North Tower.

"Which one?" Samson asked.

"I don't—" Jo stopped in her tracks. She stood a little straighter, feeling a small amount of tension evaporate from her shoulders.

There, on one of the doors, in elegant script was the name "Eslar." It was not a perfect copy, but it was too perfectly reminiscent of another door to be pure chance. For a man who gave the impression of hating everything the Society had been, he had found an odd way to honor it.

Jo knew Samson saw it too by the look on his face. His eyes grew wide and glassy. His arms were limp at his sides.

"Well, go on . . ." Jo nudged him. He didn't move at first, but when he finally did, it was to look over at Jo with something akin to terror on his face.

"Will you wait here?" he asked, suddenly frantic.

"Yes, I will." Jo stepped down onto a lower stair, sitting low and close to the wall where she hoped she'd be out of sight.

Samson hovered alone in the hallway until his chest puffed and his back straightened. He balled his hands into fists and marched over to the door, muscles in his forearms tensing as he raised a hand. Then, with the lightest of touches, he gently rapped on the door.

A sliver of light appeared like a spotlight on Samson, and the door opened.

# THE PERSON I LOVE

**E**ven with her eyes rooted firmly in front of her, Jo had no problem envisioning that initial exchange. Their breaths, their words, the slight shuffle of their feet—Jo could see it as if it were projected on the wall before her. It was Eslar who spoke first, as anyone would have expected. He muttered Samson's name in what sounded like surprise. The only response to reach Jo's ears was silence, a brutal heaviness that stretched long enough that Jo felt her own pulse speeding up, anxiety on Samson's behalf becoming not only palpable but almost suffocating.

"How did— What are you doing here, Samson?" Eslar spoke again, and Jo winced at the way the warmth leaking into his earlier surprise had vanished, replaced by a demanding cold. Samson must have heard it too, judging by his shaky inhale.

"I needed to see you," he said. There was a tremor beneath his words, but no stutter, a strength built upon the foundation of a newfound determination. Jo wished she could see it unfold instead of just listening in. "I need to speak with you in private. Can I come in?"

A beat of silence, then another; Jo's eyes staring straight ahead, unblinking, as if that might help her hear the words left unsaid. With the sound of the door shifting on its hinges, Jo exhaled a quiet breath of relief. A few seconds later, Eslar's door shut with an echoing click.

Jo crept forward, inching toward the door. She felt like a creep, but Samson had asked her to stay, so the least she could do was continue offering her silent and secret moral support. Not to mention, she wanted to be ready if Eslar decided he was going to turn on Samson, because Jo certainly wouldn't let that slide.

Inching up to the door, Jo prayed that Eslar felt safe enough this high up in the castle not to put any sort of wards on his room that would alert him to her presence. Pressing her ear to the door, by the crack on the floor, Jo could hear their conversation clearly.

"I told you I needed time to think this over," she could hear Eslar saying.

"We don't have time," Samson sighed. "We know of the dangers and we have a plan to go up against Pan, but . . . But without your help and the help of High Luana, we have nothing. And that means Pan wins."

"Would that be such a bad thing?"

Jo's eyes shot open, her jaw falling slack. Surely he didn't mean—

"For all intents, Pan has already won," Eslar continued, though his words did nothing to loosen the twist in Jo's gut. "But even so, the last year has been . . . You can't expect me to risk a second chance like this, can you?"

"You know I would never ask anything of you if it wasn't important," Samson begged. "And you know I would never ask you—I would never ask you to give up everything, especially after losing so much already because . . . because of me. But this isn't about loss. This is about keeping everyone safe. You have to see that."

"I see a hot-headed demigod with a one-track mind leading you all down the path to ruin."

As much as she wanted to slam down Eslar's door and argue his comment, Jo swallowed back her spike of frustration and leaned more heavily forward, pressing her ear completely flush between the floor and the crack beneath the door.

"There's peace here, Samson. The Age of Magic *exists* again. It's not perfect, and it most certainly wasn't the culmination of anything ideal, but —" Here, Jo heard a quiet intake of breath, a shaky exhale. "We've been fighting for so long. How could you possibly want to step foot back in the arena?"

"Because I know it will keep this world safe," Samson replied easily, not even a waver to his voice. "Because I know it will keep *you* safe. Whether you want me around or not."

"Samson, please, you know I never—"

"Eslar, wait." Samson cut him off in a way that felt impressive for the mild-mannered craftsman. "I know my wish caused you centuries of heartache, something I can never attempt or expect forgiveness for. But I thought . . . I had *hoped* that, with the return of the Age of Magic, you might—*we* might—be able to set it all aside once and for all and focus on all that we found good between us..."

"Samson," Eslar whispered, and Jo almost startled at the intimacy laced into the syllables of Samson's name.

"It wasn't my doing, this second chance of yours," Samson continued, not waiting for Eslar to speak. "It was none of our doing but Jo's and Snow's. And now that Jo has returned to this reality, Pan's stasis of lying low won't last; she's already hunting us. I expect she'll find a way to come here too." A sharp inhale of breath from Eslar at that revelation. "Plus, we owe it to Jo, don't we? She broke the Society; she's the one who gave us this, after all."

"So now we are to risk someone's safety just to repay a debt we never asked for?"

"This is the best chance we have to *ensure* your people's safety, Eslar. This is the best chance we have of keeping *everyone*—"

"I wasn't talking about my people," Eslar interrupted this time, and Jo felt her throat catch. "I wasn't talking about the safety of everyone else. I was talking about *yours*."

This time, when the silence stretched, Jo couldn't help but hold her breath, wishing she could see their faces if only just to understand the silent communication they must have been sharing. Eventually, another sigh filled the emptiness.

"Forgiveness, in a sense, is something I never expected to give, Samson," Eslar went on, voice strained but filled with purpose. "But it was also impossible to maintain animosity towards you. Not just because of our close quarters and your guilt, but because of your kindness, your need to comfort." If Jo didn't know any better, she'd have said Eslar laughed a bit to himself at that, though it was a sound she'd never heard escape him before. "I wanted to hate you. And you know that I tried but . . . But I could only attempt to hate you for so long before I failed. Before I learned the nature of your wish and why it was made. Before I learned more about *you*."

"I wanted you to hate me too," Samson replied, sounding so, so small. "Part of me still does, even if I keep following after you like this. And . . . And I'm overjoyed, Eslar, beyond ecstatic to see the Age of Magic returned, even if it wasn't my doing. Even if it doesn't change what I did. So . . ." Jo imagined him squaring his shoulders, his voice coming out stronger, despite its pleading tone. "So I refuse to be the reason it gets taken away from you again."

"You wouldn't be the—"

"If I can help," Samson pushed, volume rising, "if there's something I can do to stop Pan and save everyone but I *don't* . . . Then I'm just as much at fault as I was the first time. If I have the chance to do something, if there's even a slight chance this might make the world safer for the . . . for person I . . . I l-love, then how can I—"

Samson's words cut off beneath a soft, muffled noise, and Jo felt heat rising to her cheeks. She'd known there was something between the two, something visceral and important to them both, but somehow, she hadn't stopped to consider love. Now that she did, however, she couldn't help but remember every moment they'd chosen to spend together instead of being alone, every moment they'd stood just shy of too close, every time they'd shared a private conversation as if no one else in the Society had been in the room.

But more than that, Jo found herself remembering those fragmented moments right before Snow had remade the Age of Magic, when she'd been pinned to the fractured Door, Snow held out of sight, the rest of the team in wounded shambles. She could see Samson's face as clearly as if she were witnessing it all over again, the look of anguish on his face as he cried over the unconscious form of their healer. How she'd never seen the love there before, she had no idea. It was so obvious it was almost painful to look at, especially with all they'd been through.

She'd seen herself in Samson's eyes then. If something were to happen to Snow . . . she couldn't even process such agony.

As slowly and quietly as she could, she got to hear feet, suddenly feeling much too much like a voyeur. Before she could turn back the way she came, however, Eslar's voice, deep and filled with a longing, made Jo's heart ache.

"That's what I've been trying to do, Sam," he whispered. "That's all I've ever been trying to do."

Jo hurried her steps after that, not wanting to eavesdrop any more than she already had. Whatever else needed saying, she had no doubt they would say it. And when the time came, Samson would surely be able to find his way back.

# DAYDREAM OF LONGING

When Jo finally made it back to their quarters, it was with an odd mix of pride, heartache, and happiness for her friend that left her somewhat distracted. The guards grumbled at her, but didn't look exactly surprised. Perhaps they'd received the memo that trying to keep her locked up was a bad idea.

"Welcome back, doll," Wayne said from where he sat near the wall of books. His voice was a bit hoarse and low, though whether it was from sleep or because he was trying to keep his voice down for Takako, Jo couldn't tell. She was too busy nearly jumping out of her skin. She managed to bite back her yell of surprise.

"What are you doing still awake?" she asked, trying to keep the accusation out of her voice. So much for a covert operation.

"I heard you guys leaving and got worried," he answered, no hint of judgment or even defensiveness. Jo felt herself relax a bit beneath the words, a trickle of guilt crawling up her throat. "Thought about following you, but I didn't want to throw a wrench in any plans."

"That . . ." Jo said, clearing her throat as she walked up to him, rubbing a hand along the back of her neck. She felt tense all of a sudden, sore in a way she hadn't felt since waking up as a fully-fledged demigod. "That was probably a good idea, thank you."

"So?" Wayne raised an eyebrow before leaning back in his seat. He gestured to the one next to him and Jo didn't hesitate to take it. She felt like she'd just chugged three RAGE energies after being awake for three days straight; exhausted and yet wide-the-hell awake.

"So," Jo parroted, letting out a groan as she sank into the plush cushions.

"So what were you guys up to?" he elaborated. Though Jo had leaned her head back into the seat, closing her eyes against the warm, yellow light of the reading lamp, she could still hear the smirk in his voice. "I'm assuming you two played jail break so you could go see Eslar. How did it go?"

Jo couldn't help but replay their conversation, the emotions running heavily enough between the two of them to be nearly tangible even from the other side of the door. Then, without meaning to, Jo found herself remembering the sound of silence, what was clearly a muffled kiss bringing the conversation up short. The blush that Jo had managed to walk off as she'd snuck back to their quarters rose to her cheeks once again. She sat up, blinking away the image.

"I think it'll be fine by morning," Jo offered, clearing her throat when she caught herself mumbling. She wasn't embarrassed, far from it, but she also didn't quite know how to process the information. She was happy Eslar and Samson had been reunited, but she was worried, too. If this whole ordeal, and by association Jo, somehow managed to come between them and what they'd just finally managed to act on after who-knew-how-many-hundreds of years, Jo wasn't sure she'd be able to forgive herself.

"Well," Wayne interrupted, "I'm glad you're all right. I'm assuming Samson is too?"

"Yeah." Jo let out a snort before she could stop herself; Wayne's eyes widened a fraction. She shook her head but couldn't keep the grin off her face. "He's all right."

This time, it was Wayne who cleared his throat, looking away with a blush that shone far more prominently on his pale skin than it probably did beneath her light brown tone. It was a small victory, but one that brought with it a familiar sense of camaraderie.

"Glad you two made progress then." Wayne sniffed when Jo only continued to grin at him; it was obvious he knew that she and Samson weren't the "two" who'd made progress at all.

When he got to his feet, Jo felt almost disappointed to see him go. Unlike her, he needed his sleep now. Being left alone with her thoughts every night was starting to become exhausting, especially when, more often than not, she found herself thinking about Snow and how far away he still was. They were getting closer by the day, but it still wasn't enough. It wasn't his touch or his embrace or his words of comfort whispered into her skin.

Once again, Jo felt the phantom pull of longing, like a physical rope binding the two of them together, making their separation a heavy, tangible thing.

"I'm going to bed, dollface." Wayne pulled her back to attention once more, and this time, when she looked up at him, his face was knowing, eyes a little sad. Jo felt something tug at the center of her chest. She smiled up at him, hoping to convey some of her gratitude for his company. Judging by the wink he threw her, the sentiment might have been lost in translation. Especially when he added a half-teasing, "If you get bored of reading, or doing whatever else it is you do... I'm a light sleeper."

Jo rolled her eyes, but the smile never left her face. "I'm sure I'll be well entertained," she said, gesturing broadly at the bookshelf behind her. Wayne just shook his head, shoving his hands into the pockets of his sweatpants.

"If you change your mind, you know where to find me," he added, turning towards his and Samson's empty room. "I'm sure we could both use a little stress relief."

Jo felt the laugh escape her before she heard it, leaning back into the chair and running a hand down her face. They both knew she wouldn't accept his offer; her relationship with Snow was something beyond even mortal comprehension now, a bond that Jo couldn't, and wouldn't, disrupt. Which made Wayne's offer all the more comforting. Like old times.

"Have fun with your hand, Wayne," she called to his back, softly enough for him to hear but not loud enough to wake Takako in the room over. She watched his shoulders shake with his own silent laughter, said hand coming up to wave at her from behind before he vanished into his own room.

In another life, maybe, things could have been different for them.

Bathed in the warm glow of the elvish lamp, Jo let her mind wander back to Paris. Where before, it had left a pang low in her belly, the memory now was mostly a comfort. He'd been there for her with Yuusuke and her re-formed family, and had taken her mind off of the stress of the Society in the best of ways.

They had fit well together.

Maybe, if she was just Jo, not Destruction, not one half of Oblivion, she would follow him to his room, ease herself into his offer for stress relief like she had in Paris. Maybe, if she had met him in another life not burdened by demigods and magic and their lives hanging in the balance of it all, they might have wound up finding each other, being together—no Society, just them. A sort of simple, playful relationship that could've happily extended across years.

Jo's heart clenched, a painful twist that had her sitting up in her chair, a hand already pressed firmly into her chest.

It had been the thought of being with anyone else, she realized with start. Just the thought alone of being with someone other than Snow had been physically painful.

In fact, Snow had settled so completely into her mind that she hadn't even realized how frequently she thought of him. That pull she felt, drawing her to him, was a near constant thing, dulled only by distraction and determination to breach that distance. Even now, with Wayne's joking offer still hanging in the air between them, all she could manage to think of was Snow.

All she *wanted* to think of was Snow.

Snow's hands on her face or in her hair or caressing her hip. Snow's lips against hers or pressed gently to her temple, her forehead. Snow's voice whispering comforts and moaning her name. The more she thought about him, the tighter that rope pulled, and as if it could somehow lead her to him, Jo let herself follow it.

It was hard to explain the sensation, like her magic was wandering freely, tracking the trail of breadcrumbs to where her other half might be. She imagined it was akin to astral projection—some true part of herself wandering while her physical form remained still. Jo's body grew lax as her mind took over; every thought became hot and desperate, a neediness spreading the closer her magic got to that other end of the rope.

She pictured Snow's fingers caressing her face, tracing the length of her body, tangling in her hair. She pictured herself beneath him or on top of him or just tucked in next to him, borrowing his warmth. She pictured —no. She *felt* the thrusting slide of him inside of her, the curl of his tongue between her thighs. She could taste the words of promise and love pressed humid and sticky to her collarbone and neck. She didn't even realize she'd slid a hand beneath the waistband of her pants, chasing the mounting pleasure.

Eventually—the closer she got to the end of the rope, the closer she got to a pleasure she'd been missing almost as much as the one who gave it to her so freely—she felt the images blur. It was less vision and more sensation, like all of her memories coalescing around a singular path. The path that led to Snow.

If she could have spoken, she would have called out his name. If she could have touched, she would have tugged him in close and never let go. If she had been standing, she would have collapsed beneath the burst of all consuming pleasure she felt building, spreading, dragging her under.

Jo hardly knew what she was doing, her fingers wet and sticky, her magic spread thin in an attempt to stretch farther than should be possible, but she kept going, chasing and chasing and begging and reaching for—

All at once, the world collapsed, like a camera capturing two overexposed images at once. She could feel a hand inching atop hers where it lay trapped between the fabric of her jeans and the center of her own pleasure. She felt fingers join hers to rub slow, teasing circles. She thought she might be dreaming, maybe hallucinating, but something in the crackling magic around her told her otherwise.

Hot breaths tickled her ear, soft, wet lips dragging against her neck. Jo tilted her head back, exposing herself for him, for his touch, for Snow, Snow, *God, Snow I miss you, I need you, please—*

*"My love,"* Snow's voice moaned against the dip of her jaw, his voice echoey and disjointed, real but somehow not real enough. His touch felt the same, a constant pressure but somehow not there at all. Jo could almost cry at the realization, at knowing that, the moment she opened her eyes, that touch would be gone, Snow would be *gone*. If he was even really there at all.

But her pleasure was mounting regardless, her body and her magic and the very essence of her being longing for release, for Snow to wring ecstasy from her body and soul the way only he knew how.

*Don't go.* Even in silence, the words floating in the magical space between them, she could hear the heartache in them. *Please don't leave me again, Snow. Please.*

*"I'm sorry, my love."*

The words shivered in tandem with her body, a gasp escaping her throat.

*At least let me know that you're safe. Has she hurt you? Are you alright? Snow, please tell me you're all right.*

An arm wrapped tightly around her as long, familiar fingers dipped past her entrance with a deft curl.

Jo broke.

*Please, Snow. Please I— I need— Are you— I can't— Snow . . . !*

Jo was too busy drowning in waves of pleasure to worry about it. And yet, she still felt unsatisfied, her body and mind already lamenting the dwindling connection they'd somehow managed to make. Jo clung to it, riding the aftershocks and pulling at the rope between them with every ounce of strength still left in her. It wasn't enough.

*I'll find you, Snow. I'll save you, I promise,* she called into the remnants of their connection. If it had even, truly, existed.

Jo's eyes snapped open, burning and rimmed in the beginnings of tears. She was back in their quarters, chest still heaving and body still twitching beneath the shock of such a powerful release. Jo pulled her hands away from where they'd been white-knuckling the armrests of her chair, startled to find she hadn't even really been touching herself. She ran one of those shaking hands over her face.

Too quickly, the high faded, the desire to be held overshadowing any afterglow with a heavy ache, a desperate sadness. She wanted to *actually* be with Snow, not just in some liminal space their magic (or even her mind) might have created. She wanted to hold him, to know he was safe.

But the question of his safety was the one thing he hadn't answered in their interaction, and the fact had Jo on edge until dawn.

# KING'S DEAL

Jo stood at the window, eyes closed, the morning sun breaking over the horizon and onto her face.

In her mind, she envisioned a book—the same book she'd been reading (or trying to) for the better part of the night. She'd known its every page and had her fingers on the parchment for hours.

Her brow knitted as she tried to recreate the book with exacting precision in her mind. Lines weaved together, forming the outline, then filled in with color as she tried to simulate an exact replica. She tried to ignore the feeling of the sunlight, the sensation of the breeze coming in salty and crisp off the ocean, and only pay attention to the book—without actually looking at it.

Inhaling through her nose, and out through her mouth, Jo imagined the first page tearing at the corner as if someone pulled on it too vigorously while flipping it. Not completely off, not the whole book, just the first page. She could almost hear the sounds of the fibrous paper pulling, stretching to the point of ripping. A bead of sweat rolled down her neck with the mental effort.

Doors opening behind her broke all concentration. Jo turned, looking not at the figure standing in the doorway, but down at the book on the table she'd turned her back to so that she'd avoid all temptation to peek. It was just as it had been. Hesitantly, Jo reached out, flipping open the cover to the first page.

It was pristine, unblemished, not a tear to be found.

*Damn.*

So perhaps her restriction was something she couldn't "learn" her way around after all. Jo had been experimenting with her magic all night. After the *interaction* with Snow, she wanted to test the limits of what she could and couldn't do—further hone the abilities she had as a demigod so that when the time came she'd be ready.

The man in the doorway cleared his throat and Jo's eyes flicked upward. "Good morning," she said when it became apparent that he was waiting on her to make the first move.

"His supreme highness, King Silvus the Third, has generously extended an invitation for you to break fast this dawn with him and Master Greentouch," the man said, projecting his voice to a near shout.

"How generous," Jo said, wincing at the noise as it shattered the morning's quiet.

The door to the room the men were sharing opened and Wayne blearily poked out his nose, muttering, "Could you keep it down?"

"The king has most generously said we can go to breakfast this morning with him," Jo paraphrased before the herald could repeat another ear-splitting shout.

"The king?" Wayne looked to her.

"And Eslar." Jo couldn't help but notice that her use of Eslar's name in such a casual manner set the herald's eye to twitching.

"Okay, how about in an hour or, better yet, three?" Wayne gave a yawn.

"Eslar?" Samson pushed past Wayne, stepping into the room. Jo was surprised to see him up, given how late he'd been out.

He hadn't said anything when he returned to their suite of rooms. Jo had been perched on the couch, fumbling with her obsidian disk, trying to make sense of the layers of magic Samson had helped her see. Samson had given her a small smile, and a nod, but said nothing as he dragged his feet to bed. As much as Jo had wanted to ask then, she'd assumed there would be ample time for her questions this morning after Samson got a few hours of shut eye.

Then again, Eslar calling them for breakfast may well be answer enough.

"They expect your presence promptly." The way the elf said the last word left little room for misunderstanding. "Promptly" actually meant *now*. "I shall wait for you while you freshen up."

Takako emerged. "What's going on?"

"Do you sleep in your clothes?" Wayne asked from across the room.

Takako looked down at herself in a way that seemed not just dismissive but annoyed. "No."

"Then, how?" He motioned to her meticulous attire.

"I heard noise. . . You didn't think I'd open a door without being ready to face whatever might be on the other side, did you?"

Jo didn't bother fighting back a smile. The way Takako handled this strange new world, taking everything in stride as though nothing would stop her. It was admirable, to say the least.

"Fine, I'll go get dressed," Wayne huffed, following behind Samson.

It took Wayne the longest to get ready. Jo had resorted to fumbling with her disk yet again while Takako and Samson made small talk. Samson didn't bring up their adventure the night before, so neither did Jo. And they both kept quiet about their interactions with their respective lovers.

When Wayne stepped out of the room once more, he was dressed impeccably from head to toe—tailored pants in a charcoal gray, vest to match overtop a crisp white shirt. His hair had been coiffed in its usual fashion, not a strand out of place.

"You know we're just going to breakfast, right? Not a gala." Jo stood, pocketing her magical trinket.

"Breakfast with a *king*." Wayne adjusted the knot of his narrow tie. "Gotta look the part, dollface."

Outwardly, Jo rolled her eyes. Inwardly, she assessed the clothes she wore. It was the same pair of cotton pants—the closest thing she'd found to denim in Myth—she'd been wearing for a day now. She had the sense in the night to change her shirt, but it was another plain tank top, much like the ones she'd always worn. Overtop was a flowing tunic—an evlish upgrade from her usual hoodie—that she'd discovered mixed in with her other clothes she'd brought. It was perhaps a not-so-subtle nudge by some persnickety elf that her clothes were sub-par.

She didn't know what part she looked, but it certainly wasn't demigod.

"I guess we're ready?" she said both to the group and the elf that had been sent to summon them.

"If you'll follow me."

For some reason, Jo had expected them to be going for a long walk through the castle. At the very least, she expected them to be going to some grand dining room. But the minute they left their rooms and turned the corner, they were practically at their destination.

The inner courtyard they had walked around the day before had been repurposed as a makeshift dining area. Set along a winding path to the center of the courtyard were posts that arched overhead like shepherd's hooks, fragrant white flowers strung atop them with ribbons of lilac. Elves stood with their heads bowed between the posts on either side—twelve in total—as if waiting for any reason to be of service.

"If this is the royal treatment he gets, I can see why he doesn't want to leave," Wayne muttered. And, judging from the small glance from a servant as they passed, she wasn't the only one to hear.

The path ended in the center of the courtyard. Pavers created a checkerboard circle of black and white, surrounded by low shrubs completely covered in the same tiny white blooms they'd seen on the makeshift pathway. At the center of the patio was a silver table, rectangular, set with six chairs.

The king stood in front of his chair at the far head of the table. Eslar stood at his right. They were both dressed in layers on layers of flowing fabrics in silvers and whites, with navy seaming and ribboning at their edges.

"Thank you for joining us," Eslar said. The king merely continued to stand, as though the world should sing praise for his mere existence. He certainly was not going to thank them for taking breakfast with him.

"Thank you for having us." Jo made it a point to speak to Eslar over the king. She had no issue with the noble, but she also felt no inclination to kiss the ground he walked on.

"Please, sit." Eslar motioned to the chair next to him, and the three on the opposite side of the table.

Samson went straight for the chair at Eslar's right. Since Jo had been leading the pack, she ended up seated to the left of the king, Takako beside her, and Wayne close to the opposite end of the table. They all sat when the king did, the servants that had been waiting along the path immediately stepping into motion to bring them a variety of foods. Unsurprisingly, Jo didn't find herself particularly hungry. But she picked out a few of the pastries and interesting-looking sliced fruits that intrigued her, doing her best to not offend the king beyond the affront her mere existence caused.

"Master Greentouch has informed me that it is of the utmost importance to assist you in your quest." Well, that sounded hopeful. "However, he was unable to give me a satisfactory reason why." Significantly less hopeful. The king turned to Jo. "Perhaps you can further illuminate why, *exactly*, you are here."

Jo wiped her mouth with her napkin, even though she'd only taken two bites and there was nothing on her lips. It gave her a second to figure out what to say. But all clever options left her, so Jo opted for the most original thing she could think of—the truth.

"It is difficult to explain. . . But I carry a—" How to word it that was both honest and not insane sounding? "Very ancient power. A power that only two others in this world carry."

"And those two are?" Well, he wasn't immediately writing her off, surely that was a good sign.

"You know them as King Snow and his Grand Advisor, Pan."

The king leaned back in his chair. "You are asking me to go to war with Aristonia?"

"Nothing of the sort," Jo insisted. *Though if he didn't help them, Pan may bring a war.* She managed to keep that thought to herself, continuing, "We merely require some aid and then will be on our way."

"And how do you think that aid will be perceived?"

"No one has to know."

The king let out a low chuckle. "If I give you a bough of the Life Tree, it will be known that the Luanian Empire has assisted you in what amounts to aiding a revolution."

"I don't want a revolution," Jo insisted, taking it as a good sign that Eslar had told the king that much already. "I don't want to see Aristonia and Luana fight. I don't want to see King Snow overthrown."

"Then what do you want?"

"To kill Pan." Jo didn't mince words, and she could've sworn she saw the glimmer of appreciation in the king's eyes for it. He leaned back in his chair, looking only at her.

"Killing the main advisor to a ruler is as much a sign of war as anything."

"Not when the king hates that advisor." Jo bit back further commentary on Pan. She didn't want Snow to seem weak, even if the time jump at the end of the Society may have left him in a vulnerable position.

"How do you know this?"

Jo faltered. Should she explain that—

"Josephina was his consort," Eslar answered for her.

"Excuse me?" Jo didn't know which she disliked more—the term, or the carefree way Eslar had dropped it.

"Is this true?" The king looked to Jo.

"I. . ." She glanced down the table, as if one of the others could offer a response. They were silent. "We . . . have been intimate," she confessed, feeling like a teenager put on the spot about her boyfriend. "More than that, I love him, and he loves me. You could say we were meant for each other."

"Then how have I never heard of you before?"

Eslar cleared his throat, directing all attention to himself. "Do you remember, my lord, when I told you of the dreams I had of my past lives? Of the knowledge I gained there, and the companions?" The king nodded. "These are the reincarnations of those companions and, as a result, I believe her past relationship with King Snow still lingers in his heart."

Well, that was a way to explain it, Jo supposed. But Eslar had been around in this new Age of Magic longer than anyone, and had to reconcile being in a prominent position at that. Waking from a dream was as good an excuse as any.

The king brought his fingertips to his lips, tapping them in thought. He looked from Jo to Eslar and back. Finally, speaking to Jo, he said, "Where does your mysterious power come from?"

It all came back to that, didn't it? "The goddess," Jo answered, as honest as she could be. She knew the elves held firm to monotheistic faith, and trusted he wouldn't ask *which* goddess. When he didn't, Jo doubled down. "I'm sure it's unconventional for a non-elf to say. But you must believe me that it's by her will that I *must* destroy Pan. If she is left unchecked, a great misfortune will befall not just Luana but the entirety of this world."

For several seconds that felt like hours, the king considered this. It was long enough that Jo was left wondering if she'd stepped too far. If, in her attempt to secure his help, she'd merely guaranteed his ire.

"Then I shall grant you this boon as a personal measure of faith—not one of state. Should any ask, the fact will be perfectly clear that this is not an action on behalf of the Empire, and that the Life Tree is at the discretion of the royal family and our holy mission to guide the elves in our faith." Jo had no objections, and the king continued. "You may have two weeks. This centennial cutting will go to your work." He gave a nod to Samson and the man nearly jumped out of his seat, though whether it was at the attention or excitement at finally getting access to the material, Jo didn't know. "I will offer you a workshop and access to the knowledge of my expert bow makers.

"In two weeks, you shall return to Aristonia, and never speak again of what happened here on High Luana."

"That is more than fair." Far better than anything Jo had hoped for.

The king motioned for one of the servants. "Following breakfast, show the Master and his companion to the lower-level workshops."

"Well, isn't this berries," Wayne chimed in.

"Berries?" The king blinked in confusion.

"Don't ask," Jo said with a shake of her head and a smile that she couldn't hide.

"We have the craftsman, the material, the arrow, and the marksman. Now all we need is a plan," Wayne continued.

"I will leave you to that, as I have no interest in being a conspirator in whatever action you take with my boon." The king stood and Eslar stood with him. At a small hand gesture from Eslar, the rest of the group rose as well. King Silvus departed, pausing to speak to the herald who had initially summoned them. "See they are given free use of the workshops and other basic facilities. They are not permitted in the royal wing. Any other questions of permission come right to me."

"Yes, my lord." The man gave a low bow and with that the king departed, two servants scampering to be at his side.

"We shall be off, then?" Eslar said to Samson.

"Yes!" Samson nearly burst from his skin, quickly grabbing at Eslar's elbow to walk arm in arm like an eager child. Eslar, to his credit, did nothing to shrug him off. If anything, Jo caught the ghost of a smile as they passed.

"And where does that leave us?" Wayne asked, looking to Jo.

However, it was Takako who responded. "War tactics are my area of expertise . . . but there's something that's not."

"What?" Jo asked.

"Archery."

# COMING OUT ALIVE

The archery range was elaborate to say the least.

The area was broken off from one of the main courtyards, bordered not by fences or ropes, but by rows of interconnected trees, their trunks literally woven into each other in a crisscross pattern that nearly looked artificial for its near-perfection. It was as though, for the centuries this range had existed, the trees had simply chosen to grow that way in deference to the courtyard's purpose.

The border of woven trees permitted glimpses of the ocean beyond; targets were placed inside the range at varying distances. Some were close enough that Jo assumed they were for elvish children in their early stages of training, but some were so far away even she had a hard time making out the bullseye.

Takako had chosen to start with some of the middle targets, closer than she would have for shooting, but farther than one would expect of a novice. Even with Takako's precision magic, Jo was curious to see what her aim would be like with a weapon so far from her element—and timeline.

"For training purposes, you will acquaint yourself with a standard longbow," a female elf dressed in a form fitting pair of trousers and cinched tunic explained. She handed Takako a sleek looking bow, already strung, and curved on both ends. When they'd been deposited at the archery range, they were left in the care of the royal archer and her unmatched expertise. She seemed less than thrilled to be offering that care to them.

Still, unfazed, Takako grabbed the longbow at the grip and positioned it the way the archer instructed. It took some fumbling to get the arrow to stay nocked, but eventually Takako managed it and aimed.

Jo felt the buzz of magic in the air at once, could taste it like static electricity at the back of her tongue. Jo could almost imagine Takako's eyes layered over with crosshairs, her magic allowing her to envision her target with scope-like precision. If the archer felt it too, she made no move to interrupt, a look of boredom on her face. The elves, for whatever reason, seemed to be immune to sensing the magics of the Society's members. But Jo was far from bored, practically leaning forward to watch magic meet arrow meet target.

With a breath, Takako drew back her arm, bent at the elbow. Jo watched her muscles strain, pulling the bowstring to tension. Fingers rested briefly against her lower jaw-line at the anchoring point, and then, on the exhale, she fired.

The arrow released from the bow with a satisfying *twang*, and though Jo shouldn't have been surprised, it easily found a home at the very dead center of the bullseye of Takako's choice.

"Still got it." Wayne whistled in appreciation as Jo clapped Takako on the back. When she glanced over at the royal archer, it was to find a look of barely veiled surprise. And maybe even something resembling appreciation.

"I will leave it to you, then," she said, gesturing to a booth with more arrows and bows in case they wanted to practice different distances, styles, and resistances. "If you require any more assistance, I'll be on the other end of the field."

Jo got the impression the archer hoped they wouldn't take her up on that.

Takako was already readying another arrow by the time Jo turned back around. "I'm not surprised you took to this so easy, but I'm relieved," Jo said, watching Takako experiment with different stances, sometimes aiming in an arch, sometimes keeping the arrow pointed straight forward.

"It's not easy," Takako replied bluntly, her eyes never leaving her target. "My magic is used to the mechanics of a firearm. These weapons are organic . . . it's like they're filled with their own power. It's as if I have to ask permission to hit the bullseye."

As if to accentuate her point, Takako closed her eyes. Her magic spiked in a way that had Jo pulling in a shocked breath, then, without opening her eyes at all, she released the second arrow. It flew in perfect form towards the target, then avoided it completely, embedding itself in a secondary target a good twenty feet behind the first.

Another bullseye.

"Whoa," Wayne blinked, shielding his eyes from the sun as if it would make them understand what they'd just seen any better. Jo could understand the sentiment.

"My magic. . . It's used to being in full control of the weapon, not sharing it," Takako explained. "It's not as easy to command precision, but it's manageable."

"Do you think it will be harder with whatever fancy wood the elves are giving us?" Wayne asked, and Jo turned to him to elaborate. He shrugged. "If a regular old bow has some sort of organic magic Takako's got to jive with, then the king's boon-bow-life-magic-tree-thing-that-Samson-makes will probably be wrought with it, don't you think?"

Jo had to admit she hadn't considered that. When she looked over at Takako, already aiming another arrow, this one a bit longer and with more elaborate fetching, the woman looked indifferent towards the notion of any added difficulty.

"I think Samson's arrow—the lost goddess's arrow—will help appease whatever magic the Life Tree imbues into the bow," she said, letting fly another perfect bullseye. "It wants me to be in control—I could feel it, and the projectile is far more important than the weapon. It never fights me in hitting my mark."

Jo took solace in the fact that Takako sounded confident enough for all of them.

After a few more practice shots, and one particularly hilarious attempt at archery by Wayne, they settled into more practical conversation, doing their best to pick apart the logistics of their plan.

"I wish I had access to a rooftop," Takako hummed, scratching at her temple with the arrow head, lost in thought.

"Why?" Wayne asked, leaning against one of the posts at the end of the field and munching on what could have been an apple were it not bright purple.

"I need to emulate a higher vantage point. My guess is I'll be acting as a sniper while you all make me an opening."

"Fair point." Wayne frowned, as if wondering exactly how they were going to be able to do that. "But first we need access to *her*. I doubt she's going to let us just waltz into Snow's castle and ask for a duel."

A thought began to form, slowly but with promise. "She might not let *us* in," Jo said, half to herself, half to the group. "But she'll let *me* in. It's what she's been seeking from the start, after all."

Takako loosened her tension on the arrow she'd been about to fire, looking to Jo with a start. "You can't go in there alone."

"I probably don't have a choice." Jo tried for a comforting smile, but even she could tell it came out defeated.

"And what do you plan to do when you get in there, huh?" Wayne crossed his arms over his chest, staring Jo down. His concern was almost sweet, but Jo held her ground. "You think she's going to let you out once you're in her trap? If Snow couldn't escape, what makes you think *you* can?"

All at once, that slowly forming thought solidified, a sense of rightness pulling the words from Jo's mouth. "She will let me in without suspicion if I agree to rejoin with her."

"And recreate Oblivion?" Takako blinked, mouth falling slack. "But why? Isn't that what we're trying to prevent?"

"Because that's when she'll . . . *we'll* be most vulnerable. If you just shoot Pan, she keeps living. As long as I live, so does she. But if we're one being . . . you can take Oblivion out for good. I don't see why the arrow wouldn't work on a full-fledged god." Jo let her magic filter into her mind, testing her idea for cracks. "I'll get inside, find Snow, and the two of us will find you guys an opening. Then, once I rejoin with Pan. . ." Jo looked at Takako. "You shoot."

For a breath, Takako and Wayne exchanged a glance. Then, without a word, Takako nodded, picking her bow back up and taking aim once more. Wayne, however, was far from done.

"But that'll kill you too, dollface," he said, barely above a whisper. Jo shook her head, her next words simmering in that same sense of magical rightness.

"You can't kill destruction with destruction, Wayne." Jo remembered the sensation on the Sapphire Bridge. How every fall and scrape and bruise didn't yield death, but life. Ironically, the only person who may be able to kill her was Snow. "I'm sure my magic will still exist, set free again from Oblivion." She wasn't, but it sounded nice to say. "Snow can make anything, even worlds. I'm sure he can rebuild me, too."

"I don't like all this guesswork, doll. . . What if you're wrong about all this?" he pressed, brow creasing in worry. But when Jo opened her mouth to reassure him, she found that she couldn't.

What if she was wrong? Her magic affirmed that the plan would destroy Pan, but what if bringing back Oblivion meant Jo wouldn't exist anymore as her own magic? What if, in killing Oblivion, Jo died too? It was a small sacrifice to make for the sake of an entire world . . . and yet. . .

Jo realized then that she hadn't given much thought to the possibility of not coming out of this plan alive. She wanted to survive this. She wanted Snow and her *both* to survive this. But she hadn't stopped to think about what might happen if things didn't go according to plan. Or rather, if them going according to plan meant Jo had to make a very important decision, one that meant giving up everything and everyone she loved so that they'd be safe. So that Snow would be safe.

She wanted to be certain. She wanted to square her shoulders right now and tell them that, if it came down to it, they would follow the plan and that would be that. If it was a suicide mission, so be it. If it meant saving everyone, Jo would make that sacrifice.

But when she finally spoke, all she could manage was a strained, "We'll think about that when we come to it."

# TO PROTECT

Jo found herself torn between utter contentment and agony.

Physically, at least, she was content. High Luana was possibly the most comfortable place she had ever been. Her every need was accounted for. Better than accounted for, actually; the elves had a keen knack for predicting what her needs would be before she even knew them herself. And, if they were wrong, all she had to do was ask. It seemed like no request was too much, and it was hard not to have a sort of competition evolve to see if she could conceive something to ask of them that would be too difficult for them to procure.

But if it was a competition, Jo was losing.

Yes, High Luana was comfortable from a physical standpoint. And if she turned off her brain she could find herself content to reside in such a location for an extended period of time. The problem was when she was thinking.

Because when she was thinking, she found herself obsessing. If she wasn't obsessing about the plan to vanquish Pan, then she was obsessing about what it meant for her continued existence. And if she wasn't obsessing about *that*, she was obsessing about Snow's safety.

There was an agonizing sort of quiet that came out of Aristonia. For a kingdom that took up nearly a quarter of the world, news was slim, and it was the lack of information that led her mind to wander down every dark path, every sinister avenue of Pan's creation. Surely, after the incident at the Sapphire Bridge, it was safe to assume that Pan knew Jo was in High Luana, now? Yet, if she knew, she had made no moves since Jo's arrival. It was unnerving to think about, if Jo let her mind wander too far.

So Jo made every attempt to keep herself occupied.

In the mornings, she would go down to the shooting range with Takako—the woman was nothing if not determined to practice with every bow ever conceived. After she had worked through every specimen the elves could dredge up from their armory, she began to practice shooting in different positions, left-handed, right-handed, perched, crouched, from behind corners, and even hanging upside-down. She had yet to figure out how to simulate a snipers' vantage, though she pestered the elves daily to somehow devise one. Just watching the girl shoot until her fingertips bled and her arm guard was torn through filled Jo with both comfort and pride. If their plan failed, it would certainly not be because of Takako.

In the afternoon of the second and third day, Jo, Wayne, and Takako all went down to the main city of High Luana. Of course, they weren't permitted to go alone. A company of no less than four Elvish knights accompanied them through the city. Jo found it to be a little excessive, borderline paranoid, but she had to pick her battles, and so far she had won all of the important ones when it came to the elves.

The city was a sort of variant on Myrth. There were similar blue tiles on all of the rooftops—which led Jo to believe they were a synthesized material, rather than a naturally occurring one.

She dared to ask the elves that accompanied them about it. On the first day she was met with no success, but a new member of their crew on the second day seemed charmed by her interest in Elvish society and architecture. He ended up taking it upon himself to be their personal tour guide, and another day passed full of distractions to keep Jo's mind from dark places.

However, four days after their breakfast with the King, Takako announced that she was not going to the shooting range. She did not want to over-strain her body, and risk damaging it in some way in advance of their confrontation with Pan. It was a respectable decision, but after a particularly hard night—one during which every question Jo tried to ignore by day had returned to her mind with a fierce kind of insistence—it was not what she wanted to hear.

That was how Jo found herself, for the first time, in what had become Samson's new crafting room.

The room was positively massive. Jo suspected that Samson had never worked in a room quite so large before, judging from the fact that his tools only radiated in a small circle outward from his general work area, and there was still much open table space waiting to be cluttered. In fact, the crafter himself looked small in the room, his orange hair straining away from the braids he usually kept woven tight to his scalp, wafting like little flames atop his head.

He looked small, but Jo had never seen his shoulders quite so straight. She had never seen him stand so tall. Samson moved with deft confidence from table to table, material to material. Every now and then, he would walk over to the corner of the room, lift up a silver bell, and ring it. An elf would promptly come to attend him. They would flutter away on light feet, and returned with whatever it was Samson had requested. The crafting continued in an unbroken dance of magic and wood.

"Why does he have three bows?" Jo asked Eslar. They were sitting on the edge of the room, far away enough from Samson not to disturb him. The other man didn't so much as look up when Jo spoke.

"He's testing different design elements," Eslar answered. "He wants to be absolutely sure in his approach to the bow before he works on the branch from the Life Tree. There's no going back if he gets it wrong."

"What *is* the Life Tree, exactly?" Jo couldn't help but ask.

"Do you remember what I told you, back in the Society?" Eslar said without so much as looking up from his book.

"You told me a lot back in the Society."

"In my room," he clarified.

Jo thought back to that day. She had been coming off the grief of Nico's death and looking for any possible way to destroy the Society. While she had succeeded in that mission, it wasn't entirely because of the information Eslar had given her, and as a result she found herself struggling to recall the details.

"Regarding the pillars." Eslar helped her along.

"*Oh*," Jo said, the interaction coming back to her with clarity. She was reminded of the pillar the Society had rested on, the one she had destroyed. "Yes . . . yes, you said the elves fed magic into the pillars through rituals. Pillars . . . pillars of the earth?"

"Not quite, but you have the fundamental idea."

"So how does the Life Tree factor into this?"

"In this world, this Age of Magic, the Life Tree does not die. It only grows here, on High Luana, and is said to have been planted by the goddess herself. Every century, at Springtide, the elves cut a bough from the tree and offer it, not to a pillar, but upon an altar. They say this ritual is the reason why all elves may live their near-eternal lifespans. So that much seems to have remained the same."

"If we take this year's cutting, what happens to the elves?" Jo didn't feel the least bit guilty for their actions. After all, if they didn't stop Pan, it didn't matter how long the elves would live if the world was purged into oblivion.

"That was a matter of discussion." Eslar finally looked up from his book. "But the consensus seemed to be that we had not missed a ritual yet; perhaps it would be a good experiment. At worst, I imagine some of the older elves will die. But most, who are young, should have no trouble weathering another century. I do imagine though, that many will be praying to the goddess to help see us through this time."

Jo watched Samson as he measured out a new string of line and inspected how it fitted at the ends of the bow. He tried a new knot, one she had not seen him tie before. She spoke without taking her eyes off of him. "What do you believe?"

"Do I believe in the goddess?"

Jo nodded.

"As the Grand Healer of High Luana, I'm obligated to tell you that of course I do."

Jo snorted; she saw through him. "It's just us, you know. You don't have to put on an act for me."

"It's not an act," Eslar said defensively. "I do actually believe that at some point, there was a goddess. After all we've seen, how could I not?" After a moment, he added, "Looking at you, how could I not?"

Jo had no response.

"The tree is certainly magical, that much can't be denied. And the power is . . . great. I've never seen its like manifested in anyone other than Snow, Pan, you, and the arrow Samson has carried."

"So you knew about the arrow? In the Society?" Jo clarified.

"Do you mean I had seen it? Yes, I had. And, as I said, I knew it possessed great power. I had a suspicion that it might even be a relic from Snow's time. However, that was all it was—a suspicion. I could never find a way to affirm or deny, seeing as the truth was a mystery to Samson himself."

Samson continued on, none the wiser to all of their discussions. Every time she watched him work, she found herself in constant awe. The man was so unassuming, yet he did everything with unparalleled mastery.

"I'm lucky you're both on my side," Jo blurted out.

"Pardon?" Eslar had apparently gone back to his reading, as his head jerked up to look at her.

"I'm lucky to have you both on my side."

"Well. . ." He trailed off. Eslar didn't seem to know quite how to handle the praise. "I certainly think you are."

Jo gave a small laugh. "At least you teach me how to be modest."

"I've taught you far more than that."

The statement opened up a new pathway in Jo's mind. It was something she had never quite considered before, but seemed completely obvious on review. Eslar was the oldest among them; he was the first one to join the Society and saw the rise and fall of just about every age after. He was around even when Snow was still learning what the Society was.

"Did you know?"

"Did I know what? Really, Jo, you must get better about pronouns and ambiguous questions."

"Did you know who I was? Who Snow and Pan were? Did you know about the Age of Gods?"

"I knew about the Age of Gods, yes. Snow had told me that much when I first joined. But everything else? No. Though, I had my theories." He leaned back in his chair, closing his book with only a slight huff of resignation. "Snow and Pan were always different—as I said, their magic was unlike anything else. And when one is granted all the time in the world, one finds oneself learning . . . *a lot*. And not just through history books, but by bearing witness. There's a different sort of knowledge you gain from that."

In just the short time Jo had spent at the Society, that was a lesson she had easily learned.

"I noticed there were some things that persisted, no matter what was wished, no matter how the world was rebuilt, and no matter who or what was in power. I imagined those things to be somewhat like the arrow. Somewhat like all of the overarching stories of divinity that seem to overlap in impossible ways—impossible, unless they were all rooted in some kind of truth. Why I imagined only certain books followed me in identical copy into the Society and why I gave them particular value."

She had found herself following similar lines of logic in the final days of the Society. It was amusing to realize they were so close in their thinking when it seemed as if they had always been so far off in a fundamental way. "Was that why you gave me the book?"

"Yes," Eslar said with a nod. "It was more of an experiment than anything else. I was trying to draw conclusions, see what was there. While Snow certainly wasn't going to tell me anything, there is enough written on his face and in his actions for me to know that my senses about your magic were not off; you were different as well."

*Snow*. The name was its own arrow to her heart, an arrow fletched with longing and struck from pure want.

"I want to protect him," she whispered.

"As he wanted to protect you."

"He wanted to protect the world." She didn't know why she was trying to divert the topic away from herself. Snow had told her his motivations in forming the Society: to save the world from Oblivion, certainly, but that had not been the only reason. If that had been his only motivation, then he would have merely assisted the other gods in destroying both her and Pan in one fell swoop.

Eslar merely gave a low hum by way of response. Then Jo followed his gaze. No longer did he stare out over the room with a hazy, unfocused gaze. Now they had settled on one man.

"We will protect the world, this time," Jo said softly.

"We will," Eslar agreed without hesitation. "The world is finally as it should be, and I will not see it lost again. I will protect my people. . ." He was silent for a long moment, as if gathering courage. His voice dropped lower; he clearly didn't want to be heard by the room's other occupant. "And I will protect him."

It was there, in the mirror of Samson's words that she'd heard through the door days before, that Jo let the conversation die. There was no more to be said. Even though they had only talked for a few minutes, it was enough to give her mind information to chew on for hours. It seemed that with Eslar, there was always something to read between the lines.

One thing was clear: The root of all of this—all of the hardship they had endured, every wish that had ever been made—was the determination to protect the ones they loved.

# MISDIRECTED ASSASSIN

Two more days passed with relative ease—a week in total, and just long enough for them to be lulled into a false sense of security. Just long enough for them to believe that, somehow, they had actually gained the upper hand on Pan.

But that delusion came crashing down with the blast of warning bells sounding throughout the castle.

Jo had been sitting up, studying the Elvish tile game that neither Wayne nor Takako had figured out yet (she was determined to be the first). She'd spent the preceding hours trying and failing to use her magic on items outside her line of sight. Reading had also begun to grow boring. Sure, she was fascinated by her new world. But Jo had never really been much of a reader to begin with, and fascination alone could only take her so far.

As soon as the bells rang, she was on her feet. She didn't know what they meant, but she could safely assume it wasn't something positive by the frantic pace at which they echoed throughout the castle. A shift in the atmosphere set her on edge. The door to her left burst open, revealing Takako in its frame. She looked directly to Jo.

"What's going on?"

"I don't know," Jo answered honestly. "But I have a guess and I don't think it's good."

As if to underscore the assessment, at that moment, a figure appeared in the window. Jo felt it, as much as she heard the sound of two feet landing on the windowsill. She saw Takako's reaction as if in slow-motion. The woman was reaching for her gun as Jo turned to face what-ever—or whoever—had put her in attack mode.

The creature—man, woman, or some other beast altogether—was lithe and spindly, unnaturally so. Its long gangly arms almost reminded Jo of spider's legs. Its actual legs were curled under its torso, but the length from hip to knee betrayed immense height. The creature seemed to be wrapped in shadow that mimicked Pan's in feeling. Jo squinted, trying to make out a solid figure beneath the shifting, almost anamorphic smoke that shrouded it.

The creature turned its head, looking directly at Jo. Its eyes glowed a faint vermilion, the light seeming to leave trails in the darkness like demonic fireflies. When it opened its mouth to speak, the shadows retreated, revealing two rows of jagged teeth.

"You," it hissed.

And without any further warning, it lunged for her.

Gunshots rang out, the bullets seeming to sheer off of the creature's fog-like armor. The two shots sparked against the magical shield as though they had met metal, ricocheting away and falling to the ground as rose petals—removing all doubt for Jo that Pan's chaotic magic was in play. The creature threw back its hand, and with it the shadows retreated to unveil thin-looking skin and deep crimson veins pulsing beneath it.

Underneath the assassin's fingertips, magic formed. Jo could sense it before she saw it. Light drew under its palm and when it suddenly balled its hand into a taut, fist the light condensed into a spear-like beam, extending no more than a foot from its palm.

It lunged, slashing with its short-sword of power solidified.

Jo dodged with the same deftness she had used against the behemoths on the Sapphire Bridge. However, unlike that fight, her target was much smaller and more nimble. More shots rang out, and bullets whizzed past the side of her head. Were it anyone else shooting, Jo would have yelled at them for taking such reckless aim right over her shoulder. But Jo had nothing more than the utmost faith in Takako.

Jo spent the time Takako had bought her with her shots—a few seconds, *ample time*—seriously looking at the creature. She allowed her magic to work through her eyes, allowed her mental pathways to be charged by the power that seared every nerve in her body. Every synapse fired, each working with a singular goal—to understand the very essence of the magic she was witnessing.

It didn't *quite* work; Jo didn't actually understand what it was she was seeing, but she did have the very keen sense of how it could be undone. Jo reached out a hand before her. Her fingers uncurled as though she were letting a bird fly from her palm. Her magic took wing. She felt it as though it were a harpoon gun, shooting from her forearm and aimed from her fingertips, the rope of her magic unraveling from the tether at her elbow.

The spell, command, intent—whatever Jo could call it—hit its mark.

She saw the moment her magic sunk into the creature's shield. It struck it dead in the center of the chest, shooting outward along invisible fracture lines. Had it been wearing a physical piece of clothing, Jo would have sent her magic along the seams; instead, it ripped every invisible stitch in an extraordinary fashion.

The spell of protection sheared away, fading harmlessly into the air. And leaving the body of a bipedal, humanoid male behind.

He was left mostly naked, having not anticipated someone completely removing his entire spell of protection. He wore nothing more than a tight, black wrapping around his loins. The skin covering his entire body had the same deathly pallor as she had witnessed on his hand, spider-webbed veins pulsing shallowly underneath the surface. His eyes continued to glow, and his teeth were just as jagged.

He hissed, as though the cool night air burned his skin. It was the last sound he ever made as Takako's next bullet finally hit its mark. Whatever the creature was, it was not impervious without its chaotic shield, and it fell to the ground in a heavy slump.

Jo witnessed the man's demise on two levels. She saw him physically oozing blood out of the wound in his chest. But she also saw him with her magic sight. She saw the frayed lines of his existence unraveling before her eyes. Without hesitation or remorse, Jo allowed her magic to help them along. She allowed herself to do what she couldn't back in Yorkton when Pan had first sent one of her agents. She helped this one be undone.

At that moment, the other door burst open. Wayne was standing at the ready.

"What's going on? What did I miss?"

Jo's eyes darted from the body to him; the scuffle had felt much longer to her but had no doubt only taken seconds. "Another one of Pan's men, from the looks of it."

Wayne looked down at the corpse on the floor for the first time, not even bothering to hide his cringe. "A man, or a monster? The hell *is* that?"

The final set of doors was thrown open and armored elves poured into the room. They had swords at the ready, though they quickly sheathed them when they saw the body. Behind them was a familiar face.

"Is everything all right?" Eslar asked.

"Yeah, though I'm going to need more bullets," Takako muttered. "Stupid magic shields."

"Are you all right?" Jo asked back, noticing a flush to his cheeks.

"Yes. There was one in my room as well, but I dispensed of him." For the first time, Jo wondered what Eslar could actually do in a fight. What did he fight with? Magic? Weapons? Some kind of weird reverse magical healing potion combination? She supposed that if everything with Pan transpired as they planned, she would eventually find out. Eslar crossed the room, kneeling by the corpse. "He is certainly dead."

"Thank you for that assessment," Wayne remarked dryly. "I can see why they made you their top healer."

Eslar gave him a nonplussed look but his eyes shifted to Samson, who now stood in the doorframe. The two shared a long look, and some kind of soundless communication. Because all Eslar said was, "Everything is fine."

"What even is that thing?" Wayne asked again.

"Dark elf," Eslar answered grimly. "Elves who have sold themselves to the dark arts. Usually, or rather unsurprisingly, under the tutelage of Pan. . . Or the great wizard of Taristin."

Jo made a mental note to ask—or read—about Taristin and their great wizard whenever she next found herself with free time.

"So it was another attempt to get Jo, then," Takako said.

Something didn't sit quite right with Jo and she spoke up about the nagging feeling, trying to put her finger on what, exactly, it was. "If this was about getting me, then why go after Eslar, too?"

"Maybe because she hates us all?" Wayne offered unhelpfully.

"Or hates that I'm aiding you," Eslar murmured.

"Why just send one? She knew we'd dispatch him quickly and it'd make no difference. . ." Uneasiness grew in her, but Jo couldn't tell if it was situational or a result of trying to get into Pan's headspace.

"Unless she wasn't trying to get you to come back this time?" Samson's tone was confused, questioning. He was simply following the end of Jo's logic. But hearing someone else say it, hearing the words spoken aloud, gave her mind the clarity it needed.

"She wasn't trying to get me," Jo repeated in a horrified whisper. "This wasn't about me at all!" She bolted for the door.

"What's going on?" Wayne called from somewhere far behind, clearly struggling to keep up.

"It's a diversion!" Takako shouted back.

Jo looked at the woman at her side and gave a small nod, glad someone was both physically and mentally keeping up.

Pan knew she wouldn't be able to take Jo by force from the fortified and warded castle of High Luana. But if she had been able to infiltrate it in some way, then she already knew they were there to procure a weapon. With any luck, however, she didn't know about the arrow.

Her feet picked up faster underneath her as Jo rushed toward Samson's workshop, praying all the while that she was not already too late.

# FINAL DEMAND

Jo's prayer went unanswered.

She made it to Samson's workshop first, all but breaking down the door in her attempt to get inside. Not that it mattered; the door was already practically knocked off its hinges. Jo's stomach dropped, her pulse quickening even before she'd managed a properly look at the room inside.

Or, rather . . . what was left of it.

Takako was right behind her, skidding to a stop just inside the door frame before walking up to Jo's right side. "Damn it," she hissed, and when Jo spared a glance at her out of the corner of her eye, it was to find the woman in full attack mode, ready and waiting for another attack. "Is the bow—?" She started to ask, eyes scanning the room, but Jo cut her off with a firm shake of her head.

"It's gone."

Takako's gun lowered a fraction from where it had been raised to her shoulder, head bowing just slightly in pained frustration.

Jo shared her sentiment, her own rage near to boiling over at the sight of the wreckage before her. Samson's workshop had been completely ransacked, tables overturned and half-done projects destroyed, some nearly unrecognizable. Whoever had been given the task of demolishing Samson's work had not been picky, executing a full-scale obliteration instead of focusing on specificity.

Though it was obvious their objective had not been destruction, but theft.

Jo felt her blood run cold at the sight at the center of the room, a broken pile of all of Samson's other bows surrounded by a literal circle of debris that was obviously meant to draw their focus. The only solace was that fragments of the bow made from the Life Tree were nowhere to be found—it was the only thing that managed to escape the destruction. Jo could have laughed at the sick and twisted irony, but she was instantly distracted by the feel of a hand at her hip, her arm, the sensation of being shoved frantically aside.

Samson's momentum didn't stop in the doorway, his feet stumbling forward beneath him as he took in the state of his workshop, the littered remains of his work.

"N-No. . ." He gasped, face deathly pale and legs wobbling beneath him. Still, he dragged himself around the perimeter of the room, shaky hands picking up pieces of shredded material and broken tools. "No, no, no!" There was an aura of devastation around him, as if his magic were grieving just like he was, and it kept Jo rooted firmly in place—no matter how much she wanted to comfort him.

By the time Wayne and Eslar and a compliment of guards finally snuck in behind them, Samson was as much a wreck as the room. His whole body went slack the moment he saw the pile of broken bows, the most important part of their plan now missing—a literal circle of destruction left in its place.

It was no surprise that Samson collapsed then, falling hard enough to his knees that Jo winced in sympathy. Though Samson showed no physical pain, only the mental anguish of a promise of hope laid waste.

The moment Samson's knees hit the floor, Eslar was in the room and at his side, wrapping an arm around the crafter's shoulders. His grip on Samson's upper arm was tight enough that tips of his fingernails had gone light green, his hair falling into his face as he bowed his head.

Samson barely seemed to notice, clutching the remnants of the bows in both hands hard enough that Jo was certain he was giving himself splinters. "I sh-should. . . I should have b-been here, I. . . I could have s-saved it, I would've never let—"

"If you'd been here when they attacked, you would have been killed for defending it," Eslar tried to reason, but Samson just jerked against his hold, looking at Eslar with wet, frantic eyes.

"I could have fought them off! I could have saved the bow! I could have. . . I c-could have—"

"We thought they were going after Jo," Takako said softly, her voice the only counterpart to the sound of Samson's labored breathing. "We had no way of knowing she knew about the bow."

"We sh-should have," Samson hiccupped as he clutched the broken bow to his chest. When he bowed his head, tears fell, soaking into the wood and feathers and painting them in splotches of darkened wet. "We should have assumed. Pan, she. . . Pan knows e-everything."

For some reason, Jo's magic recoiled at that, writhing somewhere deep at the back of her mind in rebellion. Pan had been one step ahead; she had foreseen the beginnings of their plan and cut them off at the pass. But she refused to believe the evil, candy-haired demigod knew *everything*. They couldn't afford to think that way.

"Can you make another one?" Wayne risked asking, a clear reluctance in his voice, as though he were afraid of interjecting. And rightfully so.

Samson's head shot up at the words, face stricken with guilt and fear. "I. . ." He started, but Jo could practically see the words lodging in his throat. "I don't. . . I. . ." Slowly, Samson held the pieces of various mismatched bows out in front of his chest, panicked eyes skating over every surface. Jo could feel tiny spurts of magic, but it was dim and withered; not even Samson's magic knew how to make this right. But as if he was too strangled by guilt to admit it, Samson just shook his head, eyes stuck wide. "I can. . . I could maybe. . . I don't know, I—" He swallowed, once, twice, before looking up at the elf all but cradling him in his arms. "E-Eslar, I—"

"It's okay, Sam," Jo said, taking a step forward only to be frozen still by the seething rasp of Eslar's voice.

"Another?" he bit out, pulling Samson in closer at the same time that he glared up at Wayne, a look so vicious it caused Wayne to physically startle backwards a step. "Of course not, you imbecile. There is only one. There could only ever *be* one, unless you want to wait another century and hope the elves will give us that bough too." Samson had bowed his head once more, though he rested further into Eslar's arms this time, wood and twine hanging loosely in his limp fingers. "Samson cannot make another," he added, and Jo almost scolded him when she noticed Samson tense. But Eslar pulled back then, just enough for Samson to look him in the eyes. "And we shouldn't expect him to."

It was surprise that flitted across Samson's features first, then relief. Eslar's eyes softened as they watched some of the panic ease out of his shoulders.

The relief was short lived, however.

"The bow wasn't the only thing Pan left behind," Takako interrupted, and Jo followed the sound of her voice to the far wall of the workshop, a piece of parchment literally stabbed into the table where the bow had been with an ornate, obsidian dagger. Because even Pan wasn't above the occasional cliché, apparently. Takako had chosen not to touch it, which was wise, but Jo held no qualms. If it was in some way warded or maybe even set to explode, Jo would be safe. Pan might have been overdramatic with the display, but she wasn't sloppy.

"Everyone take a step back," she said as she approached, just in case. Takako hesitated, but everyone else did as told. Jo smiled at her friend with as much confidence as she could muster. "It's just paper. I'm sure I'll be fine." Takako nodded, but she still kept her gun drawn, standing a bit closer than the rest of them.

Without wasting time, she reached out and ripped the parchment free.

When nothing happened, Jo turned back to face the group. She didn't have to tell them it was a letter from Pan, but she knew it was only fair to read it aloud; they all deserved to know what was about to happen next.

"'To my darling other half—'" Jo started, not even bothering to hide her cringe. "'As well as to all those who travel with you. Though I admire your resilience, I hope you can see now that your efforts are futile. As is your escape from any and all inevitable consequence. On this, I speak directly to King Silvus, to the elves of High Luana, and more specifically, to Grand Healer Eslar Greentouch.'"

Jo raised her eyes from the paper, first to spare a quick glance at Eslar, who was looking at where Samson had fiercely intertwined their fingers together, and then to the elvish guards by the door. They looked unsettled, though they did not make to leave. Jo cleared her throat before going on.

"'Your effort to aid the rebellion on the Aristonian Empire has not gone unnoticed. In offering your assistance, you have aligned High Luana with a known terrorist to our kingdom and have therefore administered a declaration of war. As such, the Kingdom of High Luana and all surrounding Elvish Kingdoms will be condemned to Chaos.'"

Jo could pretty much hear the King saying "I told you so," but she didn't let the thought fester, too distracted by the following line.

"'That being said, all may be forgiven on the grounds of one, simple request. An invitation of sorts.'" Jo had no problem hearing Pan's voice suddenly peek through in the letter, her sing-song cadence sardonic and twisted, even in writing. "'My dear, dear Destruction. If you wish to prevent this Chaos from befalling our dear friend and his people, then join me for an evening in Aristonia's Grand Castle.'" Jo's stomach soured at the thought, churning like curdled milk. Pan demanded their attention even from thousands of miles away.

Not that she had ever truly escaped Pan, Jo realized. With a single letter, Jo could feel their connection grow—Pan's magic was laced in the curved script like perfume soaked into the parchment. Unlike the rope pulling taut between her and Snow, this one she wished desperately to loosen. Ever since they had been first split from Oblivion, all those years ago, Jo had never been more than a half-step ahead of Pan.

"'A single evening is all I ask of you, Josephina Espinosa,'" Pan's final words declared, though it was obvious there was still much written between the lines. "'RSVP to my invitation and High Luana is safe, even protected by Aristonia should a future war arise.'" Jo didn't like the threat there, but nothing could be done to ameliorate it.

Finally, after it felt as though Jo's voice had gone raw from reading—though in reality it had been no more than a page of script—she brought the deranged announcement to a close.

"'My final demand is that you come alone,'" Pan had written, and though Jo had expected it, the implication still left her choking out the last word, requiring her to swallow once before continuing. "'Between the two of us, I'm sure we can work something out. Until then, my darling. Yours truly, Pan. Grand Advisor to the King.'"

# NO OTHER OPTIONS

"This is obviously a trap, right?" Wayne said what they were all thinking.

"Obviously," Eslar said, holding the letter. He'd stepped forward to take it from Jo after she'd finished reading it aloud. Now he inspected it as if some hidden meaning might be secreted away in the parchment itself.

They were all quiet, simply staring at the unassuming note, as if willing the words written on it to change. Well, all of them except for Samson. He was busy bustling about the workshop, trying to right things that had been toppled or tipped. It was a fruitless effort; no matter how hard he tried, he couldn't seem to get things just how he wanted them. It was as if the crafter could *feel* the invisible hands of the people who had ransacked his lab. But it gave the man something to do to keep his mind off his anxiety, so they let him bustle to his heart's content.

"So we're not actually considering just going back on her terms, right?" Wayne asked. When no one responded he repeated, "Team, we're not actually considering it, *right?*"

"What choice do we have?" If no one else was going to say it, then Jo would. "She has us between a rock and a hard place on this one. As Samson said, it's not like we can make another bow and we gave King Silvus our word Luana wouldn't get wrapped into this."

"But we also know that she isn't going to go after you, that she *can't* go after you while you're here. We have time and we still have the arrow —which maybe she doesn't know about yet. We still have the upper hand."

"He's not completely wrong." Takako almost grimaced as she said the words, as if the mere idea of agreeing with Wayne brought her some amount of physical pain. Jo stifled a laugh at the sight; this was certainly not a time for laughter. "We know she isn't going to make the first move."

"Or she already has," Eslar added. "And she will make good on her threats to Luana."

"Either way. . ." Takako motioned to the letter, unflinching at the mention of war. "She's at a stalemate when it comes to Jo. As long as we have the arrow we're a threat, and the bow is useless to her. Furthermore, as we already established, it's not in her best interest kill Jo. We can bide our time. We can think of a new plan."

Jo placed her hands on her hips, looking at the letter as though it were about to come to life and turn into something that she could actually fight. But there was no monster here for her to do battle with—only words scribbled down on a piece of paper by a madwoman. There would be no simple way out of this scenario.

"I can't imagine the elves will let us stay much longer after this." As if sensing the entirety of Jo's attention weighted on his hand, Eslar shoved the letter into an inner pocket of his robes.

"Rightfully so," he muttered. Jo didn't voice a disagreement.

"We could go to my home," Takako offered without hesitation. "My family would take us in. It's not much, but it's in the mountains and fairly off the radar. At the very least, it would give us a place to regroup without threatening Luana."

It was a good offer, but it only delayed the inevitable. "No," Jo said before anyone else could get an idea. "We're going back to Aristonia."

"What?" Everyone seemed to say all at once.

"Dollface, did you miss the part about this being a trap?" Wayne asked.

"I have no doubt it's a trap. But I also have no doubt that we have no other real options." Jo shook her head and every other possibility vanished, unviable. "If we go and hide somewhere else, she'll just find us again and wreak havoc there. I wouldn't be surprised if every time she'll find us faster and the devastation will get worse." Jo looked to Takako. "I'm not going to bring that on your family." And then to Eslar. "I'm not going to bring that on anyone's family. And you all know that's what she would do.

"Plus, it's not like we'll be able to make another bow. We'll just be delaying the inevitable."

Luckily, no one objected. Which was a relief; Jo didn't have to bring up how Snow had told her of the chaos Pan had reaped during the Age of Gods in an attempt to find her.

"So, then, you're offering yourself up to her on a silver platter? After being on the run for weeks, you're giving her just what she wants, just how she wants it?" Wayne threw his arms in the air. "Then what was the point?"

"The point is what it's always been," Jo said sharply. "And the plan is as it's always been—for me to join with her and then for Takako to kill Oblivion. We're just changing the how and when a little bit." Her mind tried to account for all the variables at once. Jo was certain she came up short, but they had time (even if it was precious little now) to revise. She could count on Takako to smooth over the kinks.

"I go in and figure out where she has the bow. This won't be like the Society—I have all of my powers." Jo tapped her chest. "This isn't like when the box was opened and my magic was just set free. It's *in me* now; I have it here. She's not going to take it by force or wrench it from the ether. If she wants us to join, it still has to be on my terms."

"But even if she can't force you to join her. . ." Wayne's words trailed off. He looked at her with a sad, lost gaze, as though he could barely bring himself to think what was left unsaid, let alone say it.

"There's no way she's going to let you leave," Takako finished for him. "Once you're in, there will be no way out. She'll know she just has to keep you long enough to wear you down."

"I know that. Trust me when I say I'm no more enthused by the idea of being Pan's prisoner than you are. But it's a risk I'm willing to take to get the bow back. Eventually we were going to her anyway; nothing has changed *that* significantly," she tried (and failed) to reassure them.

"How will you get the bow back?" Unsurprisingly, it was Samson who asked. The only thing that could draw him from the trance of cleaning his workshop was the desire for his lost work.

"I'll find a way. Trust me, Sam, I'll get your creation back," Jo swore to him, though it did little to quell the panic in his eyes.

"Let's say, hypothetically—and it is a big hypothetical—" Eslar started, ever the voice of optimism. "That you manage to get in unscathed, you're not forced in some way that we don't yet know about to join with her, she hasn't already destroyed the bow, *and* you can locate it . . . then what?"

"Then I'll find a way to let you all in."

"How?"

Jo shook her head. She wanted to throw her hands up in the air. She wanted to shake the elf and all of his questions until he rattled. Yet her voice remained level, and Jo remained calm.

"I don't know yet, but I know I won't find those answers standing here. We have to return to Aristonia before Pan makes good on her promises for Luana."

"For the record, I think this whole idea is insanity." Wayne made his final stand.

"So noted in the record," Jo replied, a tired smile on her lips.

"Well, at the very least, that means I get to say I told you so right before the whole world is literally plunged into oblivion."

"Just once, you should try being optimistic," Jo called after him as he left.

"We'll figure out a plan." Takako grabbed Jo's shoulder and gave it an encouraging squeeze. "I'll go pack my things."

Then it was just Eslar, Jo, and Samson in the workroom, as it had been merely days before, the elvish guards long gone. Samson continued to titter about the state of his benches, otherwise oblivious to their presence. Jo started for the door, foolishly believing they were finished.

"Josephina." Eslar stopped her, always one to have the last word.

"Using my full name, *hmm*? Well, this must be serious." Jo folded her arms over her chest and turned.

"This plan is reckless."

"And I've already established I understand that risk."

"Do you? Because if you fail, we all lose."

"If we do nothing, we all lose as she plunges the world into chaos. There is no way out of this that doesn't end with Pan. It's always been that way." Jo stood her ground.

"I don't fundamentally disagree with you." He surprised her, because it certainly sounded like he disagreed with her.

"Then. . ."

"Make sure you're doing this for the right reasons. When the time comes, you can't be distracted." He leveled his emerald eyes against hers.

"Snow, you mean." Jo said outright. "You mean to say, 'don't be distracted by Snow.'"

"Are my concerns unfounded?"

Jo couldn't suppress a laugh, though it sounded cold even to her ears. "Eslar, this isn't a zero-sum game. Everyone else doesn't lose because I'm worried about Snow. And my not worrying about Snow doesn't mean everyone else will win. I'm about to walk into the lion's den, alone on terms that are far from my own. I don't think it's exactly the wisest choice to try to decrease the number of reasons that I'm invested in making sure I get out of there alive. . . Or, at the very least, see this thing through to the end for his safety *and* the world's."

Eslar opened his mouth to speak, but a hand on his elbow stopped him. Neither of them had noticed Samson walking over to Eslar's side.

"That's enough," Sampson said softly. He met Jo's startled eyes. "I believe in you. I believe you can get the bow back."

Jo knew better; blind faith on its own wasn't enough. But in that moment, with his faith in her, she too believed that it would be as simple as they all said. She too believed that the world still had a fighting chance.

# UNCONVENTIONAL TRANSPORT

"It cannot be denied that your time here has been . . . a hindrance on my kingdom." The king addressed Jo and the rest of her team—but mostly Jo. The royal family, as well as what must have been nearly two dozen royal guards, were there to see them off—the king's way of offering the last word before wiping his hands of the whole affair, Jo assumed.

Following the infiltration of his palace, the king had been all too eager to send them away. Now, they stood just outside of two large gates which led to the elvish carriage deck, and their ticket out of High Luana. While it had been explained to her in some detail, Jo had yet to fully comprehend what that ticket was.

"We appreciate all of your help," Jo said, instead of the multitude of sarcastic comments she wished to impart. Even if their help had been begrudging, the High Luanian royal family had stuck their necks out for them. "I'll do my best to make sure it isn't wasted."

"I trust you will," he sniffed, as if to say, *Better see to it that you do.* Jo barely managed to hold back her sigh, taking the king's words as their final interaction, motioning for Wayne, Takako, and Samson to follow her towards the gate.

"Before you depart—" The king's words cut her off mid-stride, and Jo looked over her shoulder at him with an eyebrow raised. He looked as indifferent as ever, though the corner of his lip twitched as if in protest of what he was about to say. "High Luana recognizes the risk you are taking on its behalf, on behalf of this world, should you be believed. As such, we also wish to allow our Grand Healer to accompany you. As an act of good faith."

At that, Jo actually turned to face them all in surprise. It had been touch and go as to whether or not Eslar was planning on joining them. On the one hand, he'd offered the assistance they'd requested, albeit with unfortunate results, and Jo could see him choosing then to stay behind, to be with his people and separate himself for good from all lingering memories of the Society—to leave the rest up to fate. But on the other hand, Jo could see him being reluctant to let Samson walk into imminent danger without him, even if he had the rest of the team to back him up.

When Eslar walked up to them, however, personal effects in hand, it was a wonder Jo had ever thought he'd stay behind at all.

"Wasn't sure we'd ever see you again, Doc," Wayne smirked, clapping Eslar on the arm, though the elf seemed none too pleased by the casual contact.

"Yes, well," Eslar sniffed, tightening the strap of his bag across his chest. "You came all this way to acquire my help. Who's to say, when situations get difficult, you won't require it once more? I'm simply cutting the burden of travel off at the pass, especially since my king has most graciously given you a fliorth as transport."

Jo bowed her head to hide the grin threatening to take over her face. It was obvious in the way he situated himself next to Samson and in the looks they shared that his reasons had nothing to do with logical efficiency. His real motivations were far simpler. And more selfish.

Not that Jo blamed him. Though she did resist pointing out the irony of him almost outright criticizing her for the same thing when it came to Snow.

"I'm glad you're coming," Jo said. Even with their hardships and differences, they were part of the same team. They all wanted to see this danger come to an end. Pan was their problem to solve—*all* of them.

"I promise to take good care of your Grand Healer, King Silvus," Samson spoke up, to the unmasked shock of everyone present, including Eslar. In fact, if Jo didn't know any better, she could have sworn she saw a slight tint darkening the elf's cheeks. Samson had said *I*, not *we*, and Jo had no doubt it was not by accident.

The king cleared his throat and made a motion toward one of his guards, clearly unsure what, if anything, would be a fitting response.

"To account for outside variables, we've arranged for a day's worth of supplies for your trip as well as travel arrangements," one of the king's royal guard spoke up at last, everyone gathering up their personal effects to follow him to the gated entryway. "When you arrive at the Aristonian capitol, there will be representatives of High Luana there for a final customs check. They have already informed me that the Aristonian Crown has permitted your visit." The last three words were said with a twinge of suspicion, but the guard continued. "From then on, we will consider interactions between our Kingdom and your group at an end."

Jo held back a shudder at the mere mention of customs following their last interaction, choosing instead to offer the king one final bow.

"Fair enough, your highness." Then, straightening her back and squaring her shoulders, she added, "Should this plan of ours succeed, know that you will have placed yourself in the favor of King Snow himself."

King Silvus did no more than raise an eyebrow at the proclamation, but Jo could see genuine intrigue behind his eyes. Despite her feelings toward the elvish king, Jo figured she may as well try her hand at diplomacy—so she didn't make things worse for Snow, at the very least, when everything ended. That was the note she left on, finally making her way towards the gate that led out toward their departure platform.

The carriage deck was massive, taking up the entire rooftop of one of the largest castle-towers. She imagined it to be at least the diameter of one of the super aircraft carriers from her time. In a way, it reminded Jo of a gigantic helicopter pad, though instead of any aerial methods of transport she might have expected in this world (planes, airships, maybe even dragons), it was filled with what appeared to be grand and spacious-looking carriages.

Each had a different color scheme, but adhered to a very particular design—swirls of metal arching in patterns along the roof and doors. In a way, they almost reminded Jo of the storybook depictions of Cinderella's carriage she'd seen as a girl. Most seemed to be empty, mechanics and maintenance workers bustling about and fine tuning. But one, a ways down the dock, was currently in the process of being hooked to the creature that would actually bear the burden of transporting them across a continent and an ocean.

The beast was twice the size of the carriage in both length and width, its back stretching in a long, spiked slope that extended a good few feet above the carriage's elegant rooftop. Its build reminded Jo of a lion, feline in body and face, but sturdier and with a muscular girth that seemed almost elephantine. Along with leathery, black skin and long, translucent wings, it had bright blue scales shifting along the length of its back and legs. At first, Jo assumed it was armor, but the closer they got, the more she could see its organic makeup. Add that to the large, opalescent claws and the protruding fangs, and it was truly an intimidating sight.

This beast was clearly an evolutionary predator playing at being domesticated in the way it regarded the elves checking its hookups . . . and the way the elves warily regarded it right back. Jo wondered what type of symbiotic relationship had to form to make such an unlikely alliance possible.

"Right this way, please." One of the elves on the carriage deck stepped forward to escort them over to the beast and carriage. This elf was wearing a long robe with buttons fashioned down both sides, a hat perched atop his head in matching accents of blue and green. Either he was their bellboy or the captain, Jo couldn't be sure. "Please leave any large belongings here and we'll have them stowed for you," he said, pulling a level that lowered a large panel from the bottom of the carriage. "I would like to stress that under no circumstances should you leave your carriage at any point in the flight. A fliroth has never failed to bring its passengers safely to their destination."

They finally reached the carriage and, as if knowing they had been speaking about it, the beast turned and its nostrils flared, as if getting in a long smell of them. Jo hoped it didn't think they smelled good, because its claws were even larger up close. "Now, if you please. . ." The man pulled open the door to the carriage, pulling out a stair from within for them to ascend.

"Well this is . . . something," Wayne mumbled under his breath as he placed his briefcase on the floor by his seat.

The inside was as elaborate as the outside, designed in a way that resembled a fancy, ovular train car. Small couches were set up along the side walls on either side with tables in between. Lamps hung above the long sweep of curtained windows, casting the car in a warm, orange glow. A spread of drinks and snacks were stacked at the far end on the top of what appeared to be a well-stocked bar. She should have been accustomed to the opulence after spending nearly two weeks with the elves, but Jo couldn't help suddenly feeling kind of. . . under dressed.

"Fliroth carriage is the most ancient form of transportation in Luana. A true honor to be traveling as such." Eslar puffed his chest, as though *he* had been the one to bestow this upon them.

"So the king said," Takako murmured as she sat, clearly in apparent awe of the surroundings.

"We'll be taking off in five minutes," their elvish guide announced suddenly, barely giving them time to respond before he was collapsing the stairs and sliding the carriage door shut.

"Might as well get comfy, I guess," Jo said, still staring at the door.

Wayne wasted no time, moving from his seat to one of the lush couches and plopping down with a groan. "At least we can guarantee a good thirteen hours of peace before all hell breaks loose," he said, leaning his head back and kicking his feet up onto a table.

Jo walked up to the couch opposite Wayne and took her own seat. She rested her elbow at the armrest, looking out the window at the other carriages and elves that bustled around them.

"Don't jinx us," Jo said, folding her legs underneath her and willing herself to get comfortable. "For all we know, Pan could be waiting to shoot us out of the sky."

"Seems counterproductive," Takako said, turning to aim a smirk in Jo's direction. "But not unlikely. Knowing her, she'd do it just for laughs." She was already busying herself by unpacking a few of her guns onto a cloth she'd laid on her own table. Tools for dismantling and cleaning them soon followed. Samson and Eslar settled into their own set of couches, conversing in low voices that Jo would probably be able to hear if she tried, though she opted to give them their privacy. Though, given how their fingers had interlaced on the sofa between them, they may not care about privacy any longer.

"Either way—" Jo's thought was interrupted by a soft *oomph* as the carriage lurched forward. Her eyes turned as the world became a blur, trying to catch a glimpse of the beast at the helm taking long strides to get them airborne. "Either way . . . whether Pan attacks now or later, the plan is already set in motion."

Jo felt the moment the carriage became airborne, a hollow sensation deep in her stomach. It was just before the stone of the castle tower disappeared from under them and was replaced by the depths of the sea. High Luana's vast landscape blurred past, the whole carriage jerking violently for a moment as the creature turned before settling in a glide. In one solid lift-off from the carriage deck, they were making their way with impressive time up towards the clouds. What had felt like years of waiting and inaction to Jo had come to an end.

They were moving forward, back to Aristonia once more.

And finally back to Snow.

# TOGETHER AGAIN

"If it can't be taught in eight hours with a captive audience, then it can't be taught at all." Wayne threw his tile down, frustrated.

"You haven't been learning for eight hours," Eslar corrected, leaning back in his chair. "You slept for the first four, you drank for the next two, slept for an hour again, complained for an hour about how long our journey was taking, and then decided to sit down and learn tarith." Tarith, Jo had learned, was the name of the elvish tile game they had all been trying to pick up for the past two weeks. Naturally, Eslar seemed to be somewhat of a master at it. "And even then, you've only spent a collective two hours of the past four actively trying to *learn* the game."

"I've been trying," Wayne insisted, folding his arms over his chest and looking like a pouting child. "You're just not a very good teacher."

"Or you're not a very good student," Samson said without missing a beat, not even looking up from the gun he and Takako had been working on.

"What was that?" Wayne turned in his seat. Jo couldn't stop herself from laughing. "What?" He turned to her. "Is something funny?"

"Yes, you."

"It's not like you've had any more luck than I have. You gave up an hour ago."

"I didn't give up," Jo insisted. "I just got bored and wasn't too proud to admit it."

"It looked like giving up to me," Wayne huffed.

Jo just rolled her eyes, no longer indulging the conversation. The truth was, she'd stopped being able to focus about an hour ago. She knew they were close to Aristonia, though how close was impossible to tell—traveling by fliorth was unsurprisingly low-tech; there were no in-flight maps. Instead, all she had was the vast ocean, and the eventuality of seeing land on the horizon.

"Wait, what are you doing?" Wayne turned back to find Eslar packing up the tiles and board.

"I assumed you were done."

"No, you and I are going another round. I'll get it this time."

Eslar looked skeptical, but before he could insist on putting away the game, the carriage dipped downward. Jo pressed herself to the window, looking for any sign of Aristonia.

"Look, there." It was Takako who spotted it first.

The Kingdom of Aristonia took up what had been North America and Greenland in Jo's time. She spent a few hours at the start of the flight looking at maps Eslar had found in a cabinet. For the most part, as Jo had first suspected, the continents and general layout of the world was familiar to her. However, there were some minor differences. Jo had no idea why they were there—what magical occurrence had led to what had been Canada and Greenland being connected by a land bridge, for example— but she took it in her stride as just another thing to accept with this new Age of Magic.

Getting up from her seat, Jo made her way over to Takako's window on the other side of the carriage. The woman quickly moved aside, giving her room to look. Jo squinted into the sunlight; sure enough, there was land on the horizon, quickly drawing closer.

The capital of Aristonia was near the southern tip of the land. Craggy bluffs reached upward from the ocean in the same color as the ancient blues of ice that one would find deep within a glacier. The landscape was coated in white: White snow on mountain peaks. White ice reaching out into that Arctic cobalt canvas.

The ice and water stretched tendril fingers into the mainland, as if reaching and trying to reclaim the land itself for the sea. They flew over capes and fjords, their shadow racing across land and sea below. Then, as if by the same magic that made its presence sustainable in such a harsh environment, civilization appeared.

"Do you think calling it Goddik was a little too on the nose?" Wayne murmured the name of the city under his breath.

"What?"

"*God*dik. As in, god. Gods. Demigods. I don't know, perhaps I'm reading into it."

"Would it really surprise us?" Takako asked. "Given who probably came up with the name?"

Jo gave a noncommittal hum, her mind and focus now completely consumed by the spiky black castle that reached upward, as though it were made of frozen black fire. Pan was somewhere in there, waiting for them, waiting for *her*. But more importantly, so was Snow.

Her heart seemed to skip a beat, as if to say, *I'll be there soon.*

The creature banked again, descending further. It seemed to know by instinct where it needed to go. Jo wondered if there was some sort of system that the elves had that only the beast could hear. Or did the beast have more sense than she had given it credit for, and this entire time it had carefully charted out their flightpath, fully understanding who it was carrying and where?

They were questions Jo would never get an answer to, for the Luanian customs elves seemed eager to wipe their hands of them the second they landed. She could ask Eslar, assuming he would tell her, but that would dedicate brainpower to something that wasn't finding her way to Snow. It was as if landing in Aristonia had given her a devoted sense of tunnel vision, her heart and mind stretching along that rope of magic and longing with renewed vigor.

They had just cleared the customs building when the fliorth took to the skies once more, carriage still attached. Jo paused, watching as it quickly ascended into the heavens, turned, and headed back the way it came.

"It really is incredible," she whispered.

"It is," Eslar said, equally as soft. His voice was filled with longing and sorrow; mixed emotions were no doubt rampant in him at the sight of the last connection he had with his homeland leaving without him.

"How about that one?" Takako asked, pointing at the first hotel she saw.

"That'll work."

They checked in. Wayne paid for a room for him and Takako to share. Eslar paid for one on his own to share with Samson. The hotel clerk looked suspicious of his new patrons, but didn't question. Even though it was the capital of a major nation, Jo couldn't imagine people often made their way up here for pleasure. Especially not with Pan's reputation casting a pall over the landscape.

If she had been the owner of the hotel, she would've been thrilled for a walk-in.

They all crammed into Wayne's room. It was an extremely tight fit, but doable. This wasn't exactly a trip meant for leisure, and the likelihood of anyone spending significant time in the room was slim. Once everyone was seated—on beds, the chair, and even the desk—Jo decided to speak. It seemed like they were all waiting for her to anyway.

"Well, if she lets me go, I'll know where to find you all."

"She's not going to let you go," Wayne muttered. Just once, it would be nice to hear him as the voice of optimism. But under the present circumstances, pragmatism was likely far more valuable.

"I know. Which means you all need to look for my sign, for when I have the bow."

"What sort of a sign?" Takako asked.

The question had been in the back of Jo's mind as they were flying in, and Jo was pleased with the solution she'd come up with. "There are flags flying on almost every tower of the Castle, so no matter where I am, I should be able to see at least one. I'll go for the tallest one, break it clean off, shred the flag—something obviously unnatural. And if I can't get the tallest, I'll do one of the others."

"Then what?" Wayne asked.

"Then you guys will have to find a way in." Jo folded her arms over her chest. "I'm sorry I don't have much more of a plan than that, but at the very least, after the Sapphire Bridge, I think it's safe to say that I can break down any wards standing in your way."

"And then we'll find you in the castle," Takako continued. "Get the bow—if you don't have it already. And take out Pan."

"What if you're imprisoned?" Wayne asked. "Somewhere that you can't see these flags?"

"Then I'll break out. You know nothing can hold me back."

"Nothing except for whatever another demigod can concoct. She's done a good enough job of holding back Snow across time."

"Wayne," Eslar spoke up, using his best Team Mom voice. "We're all well aware of the flaws in this plan, but unless you have a better one, or even a useful suggestion, I think you should try to focus . . . *quietly*."

Wayne sighed heavily, hanging his head. "I'm sorry," he said to the group, scratching a hand through his hair before straightening back up. Then, looking directly at Jo, he added, "I'm just worried about you is all."

"I know," Jo said softly, meeting his eyes. "And I appreciate that Wayne, I really do. But we have no other choice. We have to do this."

He nodded, one sharp jerk of his head. Then, in front of everyone, he got to his feet, stepped forward, and pulled Jo in for a tight embrace. Whispering low, and directly in her ear, he said, "Be careful, and come back. Got it, dollface?"

There was a small waver to his words, or perhaps that was the hitch in her own breath, Jo couldn't tell. Either way, she hugged him back, fiercely. The moment he pulled away, he was replaced by Takako. And then Samson.

Eslar. . . wasn't really much of a hugger. But Jo took the firm handshake and long gaze, knowing they were just as good.

They ran over the details of their plan one more time, minimal as they were, and then Jo started out of the hotel alone.

The walk to the Castle couldn't have been more than ten minutes. Goddik was dense, but not large. However, with every step, time seemed to move more slowly. As the castle in the distance grew, so did Jo's nerves, and when the first ward pushed against her, Jo was already eager to break it. Anything to alleviate some of the pent-up anxiety coursing through her veins like its own form of magic.

The shattering of the magical barrier protecting the outer rim of the castle looked to Jo like a rainbow turned to dust—there was no doubt whose magic created it. Jo was ready to tear the whole building apart. She wanted the satisfaction of breaking everything brick by brick. Or magical obsidian shard by magical obsidian shard—she couldn't really tell exactly what the castle was made of. Whatever its makeup, it looked eerily similar to the obsidian disc in her pocket.

Two guards, swathed in the same shifting shadow as the assassin had been, came out to meet her. The shadows retreated from one of their mouths and a feminine voice spoke through rows of pointed teeth.

"She has been waiting for you."

Six words.

Six words summed up a millennia. They summed up a war that dated back to the Age of Gods. They summed up what would be the end of their world, either in the triumph of Pan's ultimate demise, or the failure of Oblivion being reborn.

Pan's shadow minions led Jo through the outer wall, across a narrow courtyard, and through another protective wall that led to a drawbridge. Wind howled over the iron spikes that reached up from the deep pit the drawbridge was suspended across, as if they were hungry for blood. The portcullis was raised, just for them, and was still clanking as Jo entered the final courtyard. As soon as they passed, it closed with a heavy *bang*, shutting out the outside world.

But Jo wasn't focused on what had been lost outside; she was too focused on the new sensations of magic seeping into her skin the moment she walked into this inner sanctum of her enemy. Across the courtyard, perched on a ledge next to a gargoyle, was the painstakingly familiar visage of a woman-child. Long hair, stick straight and bright orange, blazed like fire in the wind, striking a strong contrast to the black castle behind her.

Pan stood, and a scarf of bright yellow with pink polka dots unfurled. It fluttered behind her as she skipped over to Jo. With a wide grin, Pan grabbed both of Jo's hands, and before Jo could pull away, she began laughing, all but bouncing on the balls of her feet.

"It is so good to finally have you with me."

## CHAOTIC CASTLE

"I can't say the same." Jo pulled her fingers from Pan's; it took a massive amount of restraint not to wipe her hands on her shirt. But she wouldn't give Pan the pleasure of seeing her squirm.

"Don't be like that." Pan twirled in place and Jo watched as her dress went from short to long, changing color from a soft pink to a deep amber. In the same movement, she grabbed Jo's elbow. "It's good to be together again. Don't you feel it too?"

Jo wanted to say that she didn't. But there was an undeniable pulse between them that had never been there before. Every time Pan touched her, even in the lightest of ways, Jo felt the spark of magic crackle underneath her skin. It wasn't like the magic she felt with Snow—with him there was a deep sense of rightness, almost like sinking into a warm pool. With Pan, it was like lightning: sharp, fast, and terrifying for how powerful it felt. It was like the first drop in a roller coaster, or the rush of taking a life in self-defense—all adrenaline, all danger, all immense and thrilling power. It was something that she already knew would leave her wanting if she let it.

The taste, no matter how intoxicating, was something Jo did not want to acquire.

"I want to see Snow," Jo demanded.

Pan made a soft *tsk-tsk* sound and shook her head. "Not so hasty, darling. We just got together again! He doesn't get to hog you the whole time. . . I want to catch up. Come, walk with me."

Jo didn't really have much of a choice; Pan was already pulling her along.

With a wave of the woman-child's hand, a door in front of them opened. Pan led them into a narrow hallway lit only by ominous, green glowing orbs. The door closed behind them, plunging them into the dim twilight of Pan's castle.

"So, what do you think?"

"What do I think of what?" Beneath where Pan clung to her elbow, Jo's hand was clenched so tightly it shook. But if Pan felt it, she said nothing.

"This new Age of Magic."

*Incredible*, was the first word that came to Jo's mind. But Jo didn't share this assessment. She didn't want to betray any emotion to Pan. The more she said, the more ammunition she gave.

"It's certainly very different from my own time."

Pan puffed out her cheeks, making a noise that expressed her discontent. "You're acting so different from when you were in the Society. I think I might have liked you better as Josephina, Destruction."

A jolt ran up Jo's spine at the sound of her divine name. It was immediately followed by anger—anger at the notion that she was no longer considered Josephina. That, by gaining her power, she lost everything she had been.

"I am still Josephina," Jo insisted to them both.

Nothing could ever make her give up the memories of her mother and grandmother. She would never stop missing the feel of breaking *cascarones* over her friends' heads during Easter and watching the confetti spill into their hair and onto their clothes. She would never stop loving the sight of luminarios lining the walkway to her mother's house during the holidays or the perfume of rich foods and flowers lining her *abuelita*'s *ofrenda* during Dia de los Muertos.

Even after she'd grown and her *abuelita* had passed, Jo had clung to those memories. Even as she'd joined Yuusuke in a life of hacking and lawlessness, those days, those memories, had made her who she was. Every moment from Juarez to El Paso to Dallas to the Society had combined to make her the woman standing before Pan, here and now.

And regardless of past lives, that woman was still Josephina Espinosa.

"I'm not so sure about that," Pan said with a giggle as if she could hear Jo's thoughts. "Tell me, whose face do you remember better: your own father's, or the one the mortals called Odin?"

Jo refused to answer. At the mere name, Jo's mind brought forth a clear image of a king among gods. But her father's face? Hazy and shadowed.

Then again, she was never really that close to her father anyway. When was the last time he'd even come to visit? Her mother's face, her *abuelita*'s? Those were crystal clear. Pan wasn't getting into her head so easily.

"I'm not in the mood for games, Pan," Jo said dismissively, trying to convey her clear displeasure.

"Then what are you in the mood for?"

"I want to see Snow."

"Yes, yes." Pan rolled her eyes. "I will take you to your precious Creation. But before then—on the way to him," she corrected, with a placating smile, "there are things we should discuss."

The hallway ended at a door, and on the other side was a sitting area. The decoration was so mundane that Jo was almost surprised. For some reason she had expected the entire interior of the castle to be the equivalent of a carnival fun house designed by someone high on LSD and pixie sticks. Pan led them to the other side of the sitting area, and through another door. This one led to a spiraling staircase and then a hall lined with windows.

"What is it that you want to discuss?" Jo asked, simply to break the uncomfortable silence. Pan kept staring straight ahead, an unnerving smile on her face.

"Our future."

Jo barely bit back the remark that Pan had no future. Only she, or neither of them, would exist before the week was out—and the sooner the better. But for the time being, Jo tried to force herself to take a measured approach. There was no reason to arouse suspicion in Pan, or her ire.

"Well, go on." Jo looked out the windows.

From above, the castle looked as it was one solid structure. In actuality, there was an inner courtyard—a great room, more like. The castle zigged and zagged around it, and Jo was reminded once more of a ring of frozen, black fire. Giant archways supported a glass ceiling that was barely transparent from above. The floor looked like compressed pebble or stone, and there was no furniture, no décor, and no indicator as to what the room's function was.

"I'll start with a question," Pan said, smiling up at her like an excited child. "What age are we in?"

"The Age of Magic," Jo answered as if they hadn't talked about the fact already.

"Good!" Pan clapped her hands together. Jo enjoyed the brief reprieve of the woman-child's hands being off of her. It was short-lived as Pan quickly grabbed her elbow again, pulling her in close. "And what age did we come from?"

"I came from the Age of Man."

Pan huffed out her cheeks again. "You know that's not true! Well, your body may have . . . once," she clarified. "But what age did we *really* come from?"

"The Age of Gods." Jo put aside her need to defend the history she remembered as Josephina Espinosa for the sake of getting Pan to her point faster.

"Exactly. I think you can see the problem," Pan said. She opened another door, led them through a bedroom, into a closet, and behind a shelf that opened to a hallway eerily similar to the one they had first entered.

"Let's say I don't."

"This is no longer the Age of Gods."

"Yes, meaning?" Jo was more than ready for Pan to arrive at her point, practically clenching her teeth to keep herself from demanding that she do.

"Meaning we are losing our power with every day that goes by."

"What?" Jo blurted the word. But she didn't know if it was more directed at Pan, or the room they now stood in.

It was a mirror image of the first sitting room they had walked through —mirror, literally. The ornate sofa Jo remembered being to the right, was on the left. The tapestry looked as though it had been flipped. Even the rug was oriented in the opposite way. Instinctively, Jo looked to the door across from her—were she standing from that vantage, the room would look as it had.

Or perhaps it was all in her head.

"I know, what a pity, don't you think? It makes one wonder what Snow's plan was when he ended the first Age of Gods. Would he have split himself, stored his magic, and joined you as a mortal? Or would he have joined *with* you, Creation and Destruction, to form a perfect god, strong enough to withstand and change the age around them back to one of gods? I'm not sure if he could do that, but maybe he would've tried?"

There was a long silence, long enough that Jo realized she was waiting for response. "I don't know."

"He didn't tell you?" Pan exclaimed with a whine. "He won't tell me either. I've asked him."

Pan led them through yet another door and up yet another staircase. At the top of the staircase there was a door again. Jo could feel herself getting dizzy from each transition, all of the doors and hallways starting to blend together, looking the same. Especially when, through another, Jo was faced with the same, near-identical sitting room.

"Either way, this is not a place—an Age—for demigods like us."

"You seemed to have no trouble existing in the Society."

"Of course we didn't—it was a place outside of time, our own little safe haven to wait for you. And you, you were born mortal, separated from your powers and immune." Pan paused, half-stepped in front of Jo, and raised up a hand to give her a condescending little pat on her cheek. "The Society was a reality without ages, fed by the power of destroyed worlds. But here we are now."

"So you're saying that even as demigods we will eventually—"

"Die," Pan finished for her. "Not really godly, is it?" She stopped in front of the tapestry in the sitting room, pulling it aside to reveal a mirror. Then, with a mighty squeal, Pan pulled open the mirror to reveal yet another hallway lit by the same green orbs. She stopped, mid-track, raising her hand to her chin in thought. "And you'll die faster. But it'll still take a while, long enough to have some fun."

"Why would I die faster?" If Pan was trying to confuse her both physically and mentally, she was succeeding.

"You see, after we ended up in this age, I decided not to make another Society. It was an interesting experience, but not something I would want to do again. It took far too long, and I think this route will be much more effective in convincing you to join me—or, doing it by force when you become weak enough."

Jo kept her mouth shut, following behind Pan on blind faith that they would eventually end up where Snow was.

"But I did manage to pull Creation into another little bubble of mine."

Jo stopped, her heart suddenly in her throat. "What did you do to him?" she whispered.

"Nothing major," came the no doubt false assurance. "I just tethered our magics together. Oh, goodness, I can see you don't understand. . . How should I put it?"

As Pan thought, Jo felt the rising need to punch her. It took everything she had to keep both hands, clenched and white-knuckled, at her sides.

"You see, Snow, as Creation, can continue sustaining these bodies of ours. If it were just him, he might even be able to survive off his own magic in this world. But sustaining two demigods. . ." Pan pointed to herself and then held up two fingers. "I don't think it will be enough. But maybe it will! I think, though, that eventually, both of us will die as well, just much *much* slower than you."

Jo was seeing red. She took a deep breath through her nose, and let it out through her mouth, trying to calm herself down. There was one sliver of hope here, Jo tried to reason: the knowledge that even if Jo was killed after joining with Pan, Snow would manage to live on.

"Don't look so upset." Pan motioned for Jo to follow again, and begrudgingly, Jo did. "I have a solution for you." Jo knew it was coming before Pan said it. "Join with me. If you do, then as a full-fledged god, we should be impervious to the fact that our structure was not meant for this world. And if I'm wrong in that, we'll just destroy it."

Jo opened her mouth to speak, but Pan cut her off with a small smile and a single finger pressed against her lips.

"I wasn't done," she said, almost tenderly. "Because I want you to know that if this is what you choose, we can let Snow live. We both get what we want: I get our ancient power once more. And you get the demigod you claim to love."

Jo's world went still. It almost sounded like a good option. For the briefest of moments, and against her behest, Jo's mind actually considered it. Could she live as Oblivion? What if she could control Pan's urges and not destroy everything in the process?

"Don't answer now," Pan said with a knowing smile. "Because now, I'll give you to your Snow. As a gesture of good faith."

She motioned to the door at their side. Jo hadn't even realized they'd stopped walking. She stared at the door, heart fluttering in her chest.

"This doesn't change—" Jo turned back, trying to get the final word, but Pan had vanished into thin air.

Opening the door, doing as Pan wanted, felt oddly like making a deal with the devil—a mistake Jo had made once in the recreation room and had vowed never to make again. She also had no proof that Snow was even on the other side. And yet—

Her hand fell on the door latch, pushing it open.

# I'M HERE

All at once, Jo was hit with a strong sense of déjà vu, strong enough that she had to grip the door frame against a wave of unexpected vertigo.

Whether it had been Pan's failed attempt at comfort or a twisted mind game (Jo assumed the latter), the room was set up to be a near-perfect replica of Snow's old room in the Society. In fact, if Jo allowed herself to pretend, she could almost be convinced that they were back there, that it still existed, that none of their trials since its destruction had happened at all, and what had once felt like prison was now a safe haven. But the small inconsistencies kept her in the present: the darkened floor beneath her feet, the black frames enclosing the art on the walls, the dim lighting and bright purple fire in the ostentatious fireplace at the center of the room.

Or the fact that, upon her first, frazzled sweep of the room, it appeared to be completely empty.

Jo instantly went on the defensive, magic pulsing in preparation for whatever mental war tactics Pan had intended to use this room for. Was it a distraction? Was she trying to use familiarity to get Jo to let her guard down? *Fat chance.* Even with distant memories of Snow clinging to the phantom image of this room, Jo would have no problem blowing the whole place to—

"If you have nothing to say to me, then I request you leave me to this prison in peace," a voice, achingly familiar in a way the room could never be, broke through the tense silence and pierced right through Jo's heart. She followed the sound to a window, just out of her line of sight, overlooking Aristonia. And standing in front of it, his back to the door and his eyes locked on the world outside, was Snow.

Jo's magic drained away in a rush, the need to attack replaced with the need to be near him, to comfort him, to be comforted, to touch, to hold, to feel. Every inch of her reached out with the overwhelming need for him, like her very essence was begging for him to turn around, to come to her. Even as she leaned heavily against the door in momentary shock, frozen in place by the sight of him (at last, *at last*), the rope between them tightened and pulled. If she tried hard enough, she could lasso him up and pull him close without moving so much as a muscle.

Even more than she could see it, her eyes dragging over his form without shame, she could *feel* the moment his magic sensed hers, the moment that rope pulled taut on his end too. She was reminded of their moment while she was in High Luana, the feeling of his presence all around her and within her, his hands over hers despite the distance. But this time, it was more potent. This time, there was no distance, and the sensation of their magics intertwining and mingling nearly took Jo's breath away.

Snow seemed to feel it too, his back tensing before all energy seemed to drain from his shoulders, his arms wrapping around himself in a desperate kind of embrace. He hung his head and let out a shaky breath, but didn't turn away from the window.

At first, Jo was confused, her feet finally pulling her away from the doorframe and forward, both her and her magic wondering why he wasn't holding her yet, why they weren't falling into each other yet, as they should be. But then Snow's hands tightened around himself, as if he could feel her worry and hear her concern.

"My love," Snow whispered, and his voice sounded so pained, filled with a longing that didn't make sense. She was right here, *right here*. Unless. . .

To prove it to them both, Jo crossed the room in an instant, arms wrapping around Snow's waist from behind. He felt so real under her hands, the smell of cloves and citrus and the crispness of winter filling her nose, the plane of his back sturdy against her cheek.

At first, she felt him stiffen, though whether in shock or confusion, she couldn't tell. She just held him tighter and whispered, "I'm here."

Snow remained quiet, though his arms loosened enough to fall to where Jo's had settled, fingers wrapping gently around her wrists. "You can't be," he said, barely a whisper and filled with so much doubt and pain that Jo felt it in her own chest like a physical ache.

"But I am," Jo insisted, pulling out of his slack grip to trace a hand up his chest and over his heart. "Can't you feel me?"

Snow didn't answer, one of his hands following hers and gripping tighter, more desperately at her fingers, digging his own nails into his chest. Jo let him cling, even if she could feel in the tension of his body and the weak thrum of his magic that he still didn't believe her, like he couldn't allow himself to, couldn't bear it if he was wrong.

Jo was struck instantly, and in a more agonizing rush than ever before, by the state of him. What had Pan done to him? What had he seen, been put through? Had she tortured his mind with images of Jo? Had she locked him in solitude with nothing but his own thoughts for company? How long had he been alone, waiting for her? Or had he assumed she would never come back, hoped for it even, taking solace in memories and expecting them to be all he would ever have.

*No more,* Jo thought, both as Josephina Espinosa, the girl from the Lone Star Republic who had fallen in love with a mysterious wish granter, and as Destruction, Creation's bonded and eternal love. Jo let the thought flow between them, hoping Snow could feel it. *You will suffer no more.*

Though she could feel Snow's reluctance beneath her hands, she pulled away from him, only just long enough to gently tug on his shoulder and turn him around to face her. Jo's breath caught in her throat at the sight of him, still so beautiful and ethereal despite the shadowed look in his eyes. He seemed to look through her, even as his gaze scanned her face, and Jo swallowed back the agony and hatred for Pan that threatened to break her focus.

With as kind and gentle a smile as she could manage, Jo lifted a hand to cup Snow's face, thumb brushing against his cheekbone in soothing strokes. "I'm here, Snow," she said again, grabbing one of his hands to mimic the gesture against her own cheek. "I'm right here. For real this time."

Snow blinked once, twice, as if trying to clear his head, but the furrow of his brow never lessened and the clouded haze never left his eyes. When he tried to shake his head in disbelief, Jo trailed her hand to the back of his neck, fingers scratching at the shorter strands of his silver hair.

"This isn't like the last time, Snow," Jo whispered, pulling just enough to inch him down and closer, a request beneath her touch, her words. "I came for you. And I found you." She leaned into his space, lips barely centimeters apart. "This is real, I promise."

If she thought being in his presence had felt overwhelming, kissing him was like drowning in a sea of pure rightness, like her whole life had been in grayscale only to have watercolor bleed into every crevice at once. Even her magic seemed to rejoice, sparking both literally and metaphorically around them both as Snow's magic swirled and fluttered in graceful counterbalance. Jo wasn't sure how long the kiss lasted, but when she pulled away, the haze had finally lifted from Snow's eyes.

In fact, for a long moment, he didn't seem to know how to process the realization. Even as his other hand rose to her face, both hands cradling beneath her jaw in a reverent sort of awe, he didn't quite seem to allow himself to believe.

When he finally spoke, it was barely above a whisper, voice rough. "You. . . It's really you?" he asked, the last word getting caught in his throat. Jo nodded beneath his grasp, smiling as she lifted one of her hands to his own and leaned into his palm.

"It's really me."

"How?" Snow breathed, bottom lip trembling as much as his words. "Why?"

"You really thought she could keep me away?" Jo aimed for lightheartedness, but she could feel the sting behind her eyes, Snow's face blurring around the edges of her vision. The relief of seeing him, of feeling his cooling touch against her face, suddenly hit her in full force. Especially when Snow dropped his hands to pull her into a fierce hug, wrapping himself around her and pulling tight until every plane of their bodies touched.

"You shouldn't be here," he said into her hair, though the awe in his voice betrayed him.

"I know," Jo said, hugging him back just as fiercely. "But I am."

"It was foolish of you to come here."

"Probably," she said, knowing he could hear the joy in her voice too. "But I'd do it again."

"Why?" The word held more weight than any they'd shared so far, not just a question so much as a deep rooted need for confirmation, for four words Jo had no problem whispering into his ear.

"Because I love you."

A sigh of relief got lost in her hair, Snow's whole body relaxing against her as if the last shred of doubt had vanished, leaving him deflated. When he finally pulled away, his gaze was watery and his smile was formed of a new kind of disbelief, one Jo could tell her own mirrored.

"You're here." Snow huffed out a laugh, amazement overshadowing all other emotion. Jo breathed him in, feeling that rope between them go slack at last, its job finished.

"I'm—"

Jo didn't get a chance to finish parroting the mantra, Snow stealing it away with another kiss, this one deep and insistent, filled with a determination Jo hadn't felt in possibly literal ages. She gave in easily, slotting herself against him as close as she could and returning the kiss tenfold.

Snow moaned against her lips, one hand tangling in her hair as the other inched down to the small of her back, dragging her closer still, the hard length of his body molding against her like two puzzle pieces slotting into place—two lovers of godly design finally reunited.

At first, Jo was certain the all-consuming sensation of his touch, his taste, was because of distance at last collapsed, because of time apart finally brought to an end. But the more they kissed—the more their touches lingered and traveled—the more Jo started to sense something intoxicatingly different.

*This is the first time*, Jo realized with a rush of anticipation, arousal pulling low in her gut and mixing with the warm glow of intimacy and love until it was an indeterminate cocktail of sensation and emotion.

This was the first time they had seen each other, first time they had *touched*, since Jo had accepted her status as demigod and settled into her power and name. The first time being fully in the real world, as they were meant to be. This was not just Jo and Snow making love after tragedy had kept them apart. This was also their first time together as Destruction and Creation.

Jo's magic pulsed and thrummed at the realization, and if she focused, she swore she could feel it like a sentient lick of energy searching out to Snow's magic and tangling with it. As if Snow could feel it to, he looked down at Jo where he'd sprawled her out beneath him on his bed, and a cloud of lust filled his already half-lidded eyes. This time, when he dipped in to kiss her, it was as if his magic was tingling against her lips, waves of it washing over her naked body as her magic stroked along Snow's skin.

By the time Snow's hand reached between her thighs, she was already aching and desperate, back arching off the bed at the simplest touch. She wanted to beg for him to go faster, to give her more, but she also wanted this moment to last forever, for time outside this room to stop and allow them the taste and feel of each other for an uninterrupted eternity.

Still, she moaned in pleased approval as Snow crawled down her body, kissing and nipping at sensitive skin the whole way, until he could replace his hand with his mouth. Jo cried out, hands moving instinctively to tangle in his hair, not pulling but simply giving herself something to hold. Each swipe of his tongue was electric, her body bucking beneath his teasing ministrations until she felt herself teetering over the edge, her mind spinning at how soon he'd managed to bring her to this point.

"Snow," Jo panted, thighs trembling around his head with the need for release, heat coiled so tightly it was a hair trigger needing barely a touch more and she would—

Snow pulled away with a hot, shaking breath against her inner thigh, and Jo barely held back her whine of protest, instead opening her mouth to ask why he'd stopped. Before she could, however, he mumbled one word into her flesh, a shiver running up her spine at the sensation.

"Creation," he said, soft enough that Jo shouldn't have been able to hear it, though he might as well have yelled it for how firmly it settled in her ears. "Please," he kept going, kissing to the crook her knee, and back down. "After all this time, I just. . ." He looked up at her then, silver hair falling over one of his eyes, the other capturing her gaze with a ferocity that was almost tangible. Jo felt her breath catch, her heart stutter. "At least here, at least now. Would you call me by my name?"

Jo's tongue felt heavy in her mouth, her heart pounding with more than just strain and anticipation. She ran a shaking hand through his hair, keeping her eyes on his. Even before the word left her, it felt right. It felt *perfect*. "Creation," she sighed, smiling softly at the perfect image of him just inches away from where she wanted him most, where her whole body screamed for him almost as loudly as her heart did for him every minute of every day. "My Creation."

Snow's eyes fluttered closed as if the words alone had given him pleasure, an exhale leaving past parted lips that tickled Jo's skin and sent a fresh wave of need through her. But Snow stayed still a moment longer, seemingly basking in the echo of Jo's words. Then, he opened his eyes once again, looking up at her with more love than she'd ever seen written on his face. Jo was surprised her heart didn't stop at the sight.

"My love," he whispered with another kiss to her inner thigh. "My everything." A kiss lower, breath ghosting over the ache at her core. "My Destruction."

The feel of her name, her true name, on Snow's lips sent a burst of pleasure through her almost as powerful as the feel of his lips and tongue returning to their purpose. It took barely a single bit of pressure, a finger slipping past tight wetness, before ecstasy claimed her. It was a pleasure unlike any other, her body singing with it, her magic dancing with it. She could feel the rush of it all the way from the crown of her head to the tips of her curling toes.

By the time the pulses of pleasure died down enough for Jo to return to her senses, Snow was placing kisses to the inside of her neck. She could feel his own need pressing lightly against her as if in request, and even with the aftershocks of such an intense sensation still wracking her body, Jo felt her desperation for him double. She wasn't even sure if she formed words or simply reached for him with a begging whine, but all at once, he was sliding deep inside her, filling every inch of her that had longed for him since the moment she'd awoken in this new Age of Magic.

"Creation," she gasped as he began to thrust, first slow and deep, then with a harder, more demanding pace. When she called out his name, she felt his hips stutter, a groan of his own catching in his throat. So she said it again and again, reveling in how perfectly it rolled off her tongue, how deliciously it seemed to effect the man, no the *demigod* she loved. "Creation, my Creation, please—!"

"Destruction. . ." Snow groaned, lips dragging against the juncture of her neck and shoulder, teeth scraping against the sensitive skin there. It seemed as if every inch of her was sensitive and aching and desperate for him, needing him closer, needing him within her and around her for now and for always. When he sucked a bruise into her pulse point, Jo keened, wrapping her legs around him to get him deeper, wishing vaguely that his mark might last, that a part of her status as demigod didn't mean such easy healing. She wanted to feel him inside of her for days, wanted to look in the mirror and see where he'd marked her in the heat of the moment.

Jo wasn't sure what other words she might have laced around his name as his thrusts became sloppy and quick, or what she might have called out as his hand finally wormed between them to work her blissfully over the edge a second time. All she knew was that with their magic intertwined, even in the daze of her own release, Jo could feel Snow's pleasure, could feel the moment he'd fallen over his own precipice. She clung to him, held him through it, and whispered his name over and over again, "Creation, my love, my Creation, I'm here," until they both stopped trembling and she was certain he believed it.

# THEIR PLAN

They'd fallen silent after that, content to simply enjoy the warmth and presence of finally being back in each other's arms. Jo snuggled into his side, head resting on his shoulder, and lifted a hand to his bare chest, fingers tracing loose patterns against his skin. When he hummed in contentment, she could feel the vibration of it all along her body.

"Just once," Jo whispered, stopping to splay her hand over one of his pecs, fingers lightly fanning out to brush against a still-hardened nipple. "I would like to have sex with you when the world isn't falling apart."

A deep chuckle vibrated beneath her hand. The bed shifted as Snow rolled over, his arm falling on her waist, pulling her closer to him and trapping her hand between their bodies. There wasn't much space left to begin with, so Jo appreciated the indents his body made on hers.

"What if you no longer desire me when the world is not falling apart? How shall I find you in my bed if I cannot use desperation to have you running to me?"

She could hear the joke in his words and it brought out a laugh of her own. "Perhaps you won't be able to. Seems a poor reason though to leave the world in a near-constant state of worry and chaos."

"For you, it would be worth it." He kissed her forehead, her cheek, her jaw.

Jo's eyes fluttered closed and she sighed softly, feeling reality seep back into her. Despite the fact that it had been turned into something of a joke, she really did want to see how things would be between her and Snow without the weight of the world continually crashing down between them. She didn't think it'd ever be easy. Relationships, from what she'd seen, never were. Plus, Snow didn't really seem like the type to relax on a beach for the rest of his life—no matter how deserved it may be.

Her eyes opened again, the room coming into focus over Snow's shoulder. She had no idea what he would be like without living at the end of Pan's leash. But she wanted to know, and there was only one way to do that.

"Is it safe in here?" she asked delicately.

"Safe how?"

"Will she know what is said? Or are there wards like your room in the Society?" Jo clarified. Breathing under Pan's roof would likely never be safe.

"I've placed my own protections that I do not believe she can penetrate."

It wasn't an absolute like Jo had hoped for, but it was the best she was going to get. The feeling of sand slipping through the hourglass was beginning to creep up in the back of Jo's mind. Wriggling away, Jo sat, gripping the edge of the bed, as if bracing herself for what needed to happen next.

"She'll come for me soon."

"I have no doubt," he agreed, grimly. Jo felt Snow move behind her. He appeared at her side, fingers lacing with hers. "Why are you really here?" he asked, finally, rephrasing his earlier question. "You know it's not—"

"Let's not waste the precious time we have talking about what I should or shouldn't have done." Jo caught his gaze. "I'm here now. I've rolled the dice on this."

"What, exactly, did you roll the dice on?" he asked, simultaneously tucking a stray piece of hair behind her ear, his fingers brushing down her cheek as if he was still trapped in wonder at her mere presence. "You're not safe here."

"I know, but no one is safe if I do nothing. Pan said she's using your magic to keep existing." His expression told her everything, so Jo spared him an explanation and continued. "She also told me that if I join with her and form Oblivion, we can exist on our own, and she'll let you live with us." Snow pulled away from her as if burned.

"She's lying to you," he said quickly, rolling to sit up in bed before getting hastily to his feet. Jo fought to keep her focus on what Snow was saying when his naked backside loomed ahead of her. It became significantly easier when he wrapped a silken robe around his god-like form. "There is no way that once she gets what she wants, she will let me live. Beyond that, if you join to form Oblivion once more, then you will be something—someone—else. Who knows how your wants will change, if they are not lost entirely. And—"

Jo stopped him with a touch on his elbow. Snow blinked, clearly startled even though she hadn't exactly been quiet about getting up off the bed and walking over to him.

"I know all that," she said gently. "I know she's lying to get what she wants—that she'll do whatever it takes to get what she wants. Which is why I came here with a plan."

"What plan?"

It was Jo's turn to dress as she spoke. Snow returned to the bed, watching intently, a look of pure appreciation on his face with her every movement. Once more, she had to resist distraction, and not give in to the quickly refilling tank of molten need that sat low in her stomach.

"The Society is here."

Snow blinked, clearly taken aback. "*Here?*"

"Well, the team is outside, in Goddik."

"What do you hope to do?" The way he phrased the question told Jo he did not suspect that she was going into this blind—a fact she appreciated.

"We have the arrow from the Goddess of the Hunt."

Snow stared at her as though she had just grown several tails. Then there was a swift intake of breath, and a whispered "*What?*" Followed quickly by a "*How?*" that brought him from the bed back to his feet.

"Samson had it this whole time."

"Impossible. I would've been able to sense. . ." He came to a full stop, movement and speech. "She shielded it."

"I was hoping you could clarify how even Pan doesn't seem to know about it," Jo folded her arms, leaning against one of the pillars that surrounded the fireplace at the center of the room.

"When Hunt said she would make a weapon, she kept the details secluded from the other gods, afraid that the information would somehow get back to Pan—rightfully so, because it did. The only thing she assured us was that Pan would not, under any circumstances, know of the arrow's existence—it was to be shielded from her touch. But perhaps I. . . Perhaps it was shielded from her gaze as well."

Jo's eyes ping-ponged across the room, following Snow as he paced. "She gave it to her chosen champion. When I touched the arrow, I saw its history," Jo clarified at his immediate confusion. "He was going to take the arrow and slay Pan with it. Or, try to. But when the Age of Gods ended, he forgot this purpose . . . he only remembered that the arrow was important and passed it on to someone else. Who passed it on to someone else, from generation to generation. . ."

"Until Samson. And it followed him into the Society as the current champion," Snow pieced together, almost correctly.

"Not quite. It followed Samson into the Society, yes . . . but not because he was the champion."

"Then who?"

"Takako."

"Of course." Snow sat heavily on the bed, bringing a hand to his forehead. "Her ancient lineage of magic came from Hunt's champion. Why it persisted all this time. . ."

"And why her magic is what it is," Jo finished for him. "Takako is ready to be the champion, and we have the arrow. So—"

"You set out to make a bow," Snow interjected.

"Yes. How did you know?" A frown pulled on her cheeks. No matter what the reason, Jo didn't think it was a good one.

"Pan came to brag to me about thwarting your plans. Gloating about whatever chaos she's creating is a sort of pastime for her." The distant look that glossed over Snow's eyes told Jo that she didn't want to know what else Pan had done, or forced Snow to endure knowledge of. "She said she was going to bring you and that she'd taken what you were making—a weapon. Which I'm presuming to be a bow now that I know you have the arrow."

"It is. We went to High Luana and got a bough from the Life Tree to carve it."

"The elves agreed to that?" Snow said with equal measures of shock and pride.

"We convinced them it was in their best interest, and they had little choice." Jo pushed off the column, crossing over to take his hands in hers. "Snow, we can end this." She omitted the words her mind treacherously would not let her forget—that to end it could mean her death. Jo didn't want that weighing on Snow. She didn't want him trying to talk her out of the decision, or hesitating. He knew Pan could not die as long as she lived, so surely, somewhere, he also knew what was on the line. "But I need to find the bow. If she bragged to you about the bow then she likely didn't destroy it, right?"

He nodded. "I don't think she would destroy it. Pan is a hoarder. She enjoys the feeling of possessing too much."

That sounded about right. "Then, do you know where she might be keeping it? Once I get it, I'll bring down the walls and let in the team to finish her."

"I cannot cross the threshold of that door." Snow nodded toward the entrance Jo had come through. "At least not without Pan's invitation. Sometimes, it leads to throne rooms where I give messages to the people, maintaining the illusion of my rule—but never anything else."

Whatever frustration she felt toward not knowing the arrow's location paled in comparison to the visceral anger at Snow's treatment. "I will kill her," Jo muttered under her breath, never more resolved.

Snow squeezed her hands tightly. "But I have some ideas."

"You do?"

"I know enough from the Society and before. . . She usually likes to keep things squirreled away in a central treasure room." As he spoke, Jo's mind filled with images of Pan's room—the horde of treasures condensed at her innermost sanctum. After all the illusions had vanished, all there had been was Pan and her treasures.

"I think I have an idea. . ." Jo whispered, clarity dawning on her.

Just when she opened her mouth to speak, there was a knock on the door. Jo glared angrily at it, gripping Snow's hands even tighter, as though she could cling to him hard enough that she wouldn't be taken away. His hands went slack and Jo looked back in a panic she couldn't fight.

"You have to go," he said quickly. "Don't fight it, do what must be done, stay focused."

"I'll come back for you," Jo whispered hastily, as if everything they said could suddenly be heard.

"I'll be waiting," Snow said, as if there were anywhere else he could be. It made the words all the more sorrowful.

Jo's heart broke as she walked for the door, and rage filled the cracks. She gave the handle a mighty yank, feeling the whole thing strain under her touch. It was a satisfying reaffirmation that, yes, even Pan's magic could be broken. Jo had been ready to unleash her anger at Pan next, but she stopped short.

There was a man on the other side of the door.

He had skin that looked to be made of some kind of steel or alloy, and all-black obsidian eyes. He wore what could best be described as a child's interpretation of a butler's uniform, comedic in its ostentatious parts that didn't quite go together. His coat had capped sleeves that poofed up to his ears in a balloon of fabric. It was double-buttoned, a long silver tie running down the center and extending nearly to his knees. His shorts reminded Jo of what she'd seen boys wearing to prestigious private schools when she was a kid.

"She requests your presence for dinner." His lips barely moved when he spoke, like an automaton or a puppet, the jaw hinged at the corners of the mouth and sliding down from the chin rather than the ears.

"I am inclined to take dinner here," Jo protested. Even if she didn't have a choice, she didn't want to start a habit of going willingly. She would be trouble for Pan up until the end . . . whatever and whenever that ending was.

The butler looked at her blankly and then repeated in the same sort of hollow, echoing voice, "She requests your presence for dinner."

"I said I was inclined—"

"Jo," Snow stopped her with a deep utterance of her name. A hand slipped around her waist, tenderly, as if seeking one final embrace before she was pulled from him. He moved to kiss her shoulder and from the corners of her eyes Jo could see that his gaze never left the threshold of the door—the barrier that confined him to his room. With just one look of frustrated resignation from him, Jo wanted to say plans be damned and shatter it now. "Go on ahead. There's no point in fighting."

*There's no point in fighting now,* she mentally corrected. The time for fighting would be soon enough and when it came, Jo would not hesitate for a moment to unleash her full wrath on the world.

"Very well," Jo said finally. "Take me to her."

The man nodded. His head spun first, a full hundred and eighty degrees around to face the opposite direction. His body followed in an uncomfortable pivot. Without a word, he began walking away.

Jo gave Snow's hand one more squeeze, and then felt it fall from her waist.

By the time she looked back, his door had already shut, and unnatural shadows had begun to obscure it from view.

# DRESS FOR DINNER

She followed behind the strange creature without question.

It wasn't that Jo didn't *have* any questions; she had quite a few, in fact, what it was and how it came to be in Pan's service, for starters. What kept Jo silent was the fact that she didn't think that asking her questions would actually get her anywhere. If the creature answered her, she was sure it would either be something vague and immaterial, or so specific as to be devoid of meaning for Jo—someone still learning the particulars about Age of Magic she now resided in.

But if she had to describe the man in her own terms, it would be a stone marionette. As she looked more closely at the grayish skin on the man's arms, she realized that it was not metal, as she previously thought, but some kind of dark, smoky quartz. It looked hard, and picked up the light as though it were mirror-polished.

She was so distracted by trying to pick it and its strange magic apart that Jo didn't notice she was now in a completely different hallway.

Gone were the halls she'd first walked through with Pan. There were no orbs to light the way, but glowing strips on either side of stone walkways where the floor met the walls. They looked like carved channels, some kind of luminescent liquid flowing down them. It cast an eerie reddish haze that caught on every bottom edge of the stone walls, which looked almost as if they were bleeding as a result.

The hallway reached a dead end and the creature came to a prompt stop.

"Where to now?" Jo reached over its shoulder, tapping on the wall. "Don't think we can go this way, unless you want me to break it down."

She heard a soft grinding noise as the man twisted his head once more.

Jo took an involuntary step backward, still not entirely accustomed to that ability. His body followed and then he stood, immobile, for a long minute, just staring at her with those blank eyes.

"Turn, please," he instructed.

Jo turned to find the hallway she had been walking in was no longer the same. Sure, it had the tracks of light, the bloody glow, and the stone walls. But now, clouded windows let in the orange glow of sunset along her left side. Along her right were a series of doors, all nearly identical.

"Third one, please," the man said from behind her.

Jo took a few wide steps. Not because she was eager to get to dinner with Pan, but because she had no interest in keeping the man at her back longer than necessary. The more distance between them, the better.

"All right, Pan, let's get this—" Jo spoke as she swung open the door, expecting some kind of dining room, but was stopped short the moment the room registered.

It was not a dining room. More like a glorified closet. A glorified, *empty* closet.

There were racks to hang clothes, shelves, and shoe cubbies on every dark-wooded wall. The carpet was a plush red velvet that muffled their footfalls as Jo and her guide entered. Directly across from the door was a mirror, and hanging in front of it was a single article of clothing—a dress.

"She requests that you dress for dinner."

"I am dressed," Jo protested.

"She requests that you wear this."

"I know what she wants." Jo walked over to the dress, grabbing the hanger and running her hands over the thin silk. "She wants to humiliate me."

In her entire existence, Jo didn't think she'd ever worn something so extravagantly impractical. And she meant her *entire* existence, because Jo was fairly certain that even as a demigod, she had worn more utilitarian garb. This, however, struck a balance between "female escort" and "got in a fight with a pair of scissors and lost." Jo didn't take issue with either in concept, but neither was *her*.

"She requests that—"

"I heard you the first time." Jo held up the dress by its spaghetti straps. "Did she say where the rest of it was?"

"This is the dress that she has requested."

Jo sighed, clearly getting nowhere with the man. She was beginning to suspect that his sentience was an illusion and he really was one of Pan's machinations. Regardless, she had no interest in tormenting a creature who was likely as much of a prisoner as she was.

"Did she say what would happen if I didn't wear this?"

There was a long pause, and Jo was expecting yet another variant of the same expressionless mantra. But he surprised her. "In my experience, if one must inquire, one doesn't want to know."

Snow's words rang clearly in Jo's ears—*there's no point in fighting, yet.* So she'd wear a revealing dress. She'd let Pan have this battle for the sake of the war. Her friends were counting on her and the sooner all this ended, the better.

"Could you turn around, please?"

The man obliged as he had before—first with his head, then shoulders.

Jo stripped down, shivering as her bare skin met the air. Surely it couldn't be that much colder than Snow's room, could it? It felt downright frigid and she felt the tingle of an icy phantom finger run down her spine. Perhaps it was just the feeling of being so vulnerable in Pan's lair getting under her skin.

The dress didn't offer much in the way of feeling less vulnerable. Jo's arms were completely bare, as was her back, and most of her front, given the drooping V of the neckline. Its hem sat high on her thigh, just barely low enough to ensure everything was covered.

Straightening her shoulders, Jo stole a second to compose herself. This whole thing was to break her down, make her feel off-kilter. It didn't matter if she walked into the room naked. Pan wasn't the one in control of Jo's feelings, and Jo was determined to show her that.

"All right, let's go."

The man's head spun, no doubt verifying that she had put on the dress as it promptly swiveled back forward. "This way, please."

He opened the door and, once more, it was not connected to the hallway Jo had used to enter. The marionette motioned for Jo to step through, but made no effort to do so himself. A strange sort of magic pulsed from the room beyond and Jo had every suspicion that it was not a place the man could go, even if he wanted to—and even if he were able to act on his own desires (which Jo was beginning to doubt).

Jo stepped into the dining room alone.

"Well, this looks more like what I was expecting," Jo muttered under her breath.

The room was a dreamscape of part-medieval hall, part-Versailles palace. The floor was the same dark wood as the closet's shelving. It, too, was polished to a mirror-shine and reflected the ornate chandeliers that hung in a row of three on the ceiling. Where Jo expected most chandeliers to be electric (magic, perhaps, in this age) or candle lit, these were neither. In an odd reverse, they dripped glowing orbs of light that occasionally fell, disappearing before they made contact with the table below.

The table could've easily sat eight—perhaps ten. But there were only two chairs with place settings, one at each end.

"I'm so glad to hear it," Pan said from where she was perched at the far end of the table. She was seated on the wide top of the wingback chair, her feet swinging happily and bouncing off the tufted navy velvet. "I want you to be happy here. Want *us* to be happy here."

Jo made no comment, heading directly for the chair at the opposite head of the table.

"I see you're wearing the dress. It looks nice on you."

Still, Jo said nothing. The sooner this was over, the better. Jo would give Pan no encouragement if she could avoid it. The last thing she wanted was to give the woman the impression that she was actually enjoying herself.

Jo inspected the silverware as she sat. It was ornate, gold, and carved in a similar pattern as the moldings throughout the walls and ceiling of the room. Jo squinted at the walls, trying to make out the paintings that hung in the heavy, gilded frames. But every time she got her focus, they seemed to shift like a mirage. In a way, never being able to make out an image was far more unnerving than seeing something disturbing.

She examined her plate. *Eat and get it over with*, Jo thought, willing the empty space to fill with food.

Movement drew her attention back to Pan.

The woman-child jumped down, both feet landing on the seat with a small bounce. The multicolored ruffles of her dress floated in the darkness, shimmering from orbs of light that continued to vanish between them. Reaching down, Pan picked up her glass and lifted it into the air. As she did so, it filled with a deep crimson liquid.

Jo noticed the same liquid filling nearly to the brim of her own crystal goblet.

"Let's begin, with a toast to us." Pan held out her glass expectantly.

Trying to feel as though the action was an indication of war rather than defeat, Jo lifted her own glass, and drank the bitter, metallic liquid.

# EAT UP

"Isn't this charcuterie just delightful?" Pan cooed, plucking a small, yellow berry up from her plate between middle finger and thumb and placing it to her lips with a long, drawn out, nearly pornographic moan. "They've really outdone themselves, haven't they?"

Jo didn't bother to ask who "they" were, too busy examining the odd array of finger foods laid out on a tray before each of them, what Pan had proclaimed to be their first course. Jo also didn't bother to ask how many courses were planned; even one was too many.

Starting from the left corner of the tray and all around in a perfectly organized spiral, were slices of something purple and gooey, the yellow berries Pan was currently devouring, cubes of what looked like uncooked chicken meat, a single leaf-like object that kept twitching, and a literal puddle of something grey and rotten-smelling.

Jo poked at one of the cubes with her golden knife, wincing when the cube deflated with a hiss like a popped balloon, dribbles of black ooze spurting out of the hole like blood from a wound. Jo swallowed back the involuntary prickle of nausea and put her knife down. She could always just spend the meal sipping the weird, metallic liquid in her goblet, but the more she looked at it, the less she wanted to.

It was going to be a *long* dinner.

"Well?" Pan's voice brought her back to the table. Jo's eyes snapped up, not to find Pan sitting all the way across from her anymore, but in the chair just to the right of her original placement. Jo hadn't heard her move seats, but she chalked it up to her mind being occupied by the unappetizing fare before her.

"Well what?" Jo asked, keeping her voice indifferent.

Pan frowned, popping one of the meat cubes into her mouth and biting down. To Jo's disgust, a line of dark black fell from her bright blue lips to make a trail from mouth to chin, one she made no effort to wipe away. "You haven't told me what you think of your food yet."

Jo looked away, not dignifying that with a response. "You haven't told me yet what I'm *doing here*," she countered instead. "Why did you do all this?"

Instead of an answer, which Jo really never should have expected, Pan responded with a piercing squeal of delight. Out of reflex, Jo turned towards the sound, tensing when Pan was now seated halfway down the table on the left-hand side—though there was literally no way she could have made it there naturally.

The cause of Pan's squeal was apparently the plate in front of her, no longer the odd platter of finger foods, but now what appeared to be a rather large, perfectly ordinary looking steak. She was cutting into it with a vigor that reminded Jo of a starved animal ruthlessly tearing its prey to shreds. It wasn't until Pan paused to take a long swig from her own goblet that Jo realized she'd been near mesmerized by the sight.

"You should really try your filet!" she said, resting her elbow on the table and a hand against her cheek. Eyes glittering with mirth and messy lips pulled into a vicious grin.

Jo looked down at the plate before her, perfectly aware that despite no one having come to remove her tray, a new course now sat before her, identical to Pan's. Regardless of how Pan's eyes on her made the hair on the back of her neck stand up, Jo picked up her fork and knife, cutting into the meat.

There was no other way to describe the sound that filled the room other than a scream of bloody murder. It was loud and violent and terrifying, Jo's utensils falling out of her hands in her shock. At first, Jo looked frantically around the room, wondering where the noise was coming from, the acoustics and the volume making it impossible to tell. But as the scream went from a deadly yell to a pleading cry, Jo felt her stomach drop and mouth fall slack.

The steak in front of her heaved with the sound of screaming and bursts of desperate cries from between every line of the muscle. Jo pushed the plate away from her, adrenaline coursing through her veins even as she remained frozen to her seat. Slowly, the screams tapered, the cries growing hoarse, and Jo was forced to watch, horrified, as the filet of meat eventually quivered, stilled, and grew silent.

"Whoopsies," Pan hummed. "Looks like yours was still screaming a bit. My apologies. The chef doesn't always get the temperatures right."

Jo couldn't tear her eyes away from the plate, the dish looking disturbingly normal now that it had stopped its very sentient-like cries.

She swallowed thickly, considered reaching out and pushing the plate away, but she couldn't move her hand, didn't want to. What if she touched the plate and it, too, started screaming or crying? She knew it was all a game—that Pan was playing tricks with her, messing with her mind—but she couldn't deny that it was working.

Right now at least, heart still thrumming in her ears, Jo was scared.

Out of the corner of her eye, Jo saw the silhouette of someone walking up to her chair. She startled, still on edge, and turned to see who might be approaching. For the second time in as many minutes, Jo felt her stomach drop.

Even after so long in the Society, even after all the changes she'd seen the world go through in its transition back into a new Age of Magic, she would never forget the sight of her friend's face. Her first friend, and—in another life—her best friend.

"Yuusuke?" Jo choked out, voice thick with fear and confusion and still-pulsing adrenaline. He stood before her, dressed in a similarly outlandish butler's uniform, this time in a bright green that reminded her of his once-ubiquitous, beat-up pair of headphones. His black hair was slicked back and his face hand been done up in makeup, but despite all that, he looked exactly the same as she remembered. Except for one thing: his stare might have fallen on her, but she saw no recognition there.

"Yuusuke, what . . .?" she started, nearly rising from her seat. *What was he doing here?* Had Pan remembered her first wish at the Society and brought him here for revenge, for bait? Was he a hostage, like Snow? He didn't seem to know who she was, but was that Pan's doing, or a consequence of their new world? She watched him move, as if on autopilot, to pick up her plate, and something in her heart broke. "Yuusuke, are you—?"

In a flash, Pan was suddenly directly to Jo's right. And a knife was pierced directly through Yuusuke's hand.

Yuusuke buckled, the first glimpse of true emotion flashing across his face before he cried out in pain. "Now, now, *Yuu*—" Pan purred Jo's childhood nickname for her friend. "She's obviously not done with that yet."

Jo was out of her chair in an instant, ripping the knife out of Yuusuke's hand and dropping to her knees at his side. She took her napkin and wrapped it tightly around Yuusuke's bleeding hand, blood soaking into the fabric almost immediately.

"What the hell are you doing?" she shouted at Pan from over Yuusuke's shoulder, but Pan had already switched seats again, now positioned unnervingly at Jo's back. Jo kept her focus on Yuusuke despite the way it made her skin crawl to let Pan out of her sight. Except, when she looked back to her friend, the cries had stopped and his face had once again grown devoid of all emotion.

A soft sound grabbed her attention, a chitter, a squeak, and when Jo looked from Yuusuke's face to his chest, she saw his uniform bulging.

Wiggling.

All at once, the buttons on Yuusuke's ridiculous butler outfit burst open, a swarm of rats crawling from the gaping hole. Jo fell backwards, raising her hand and the bloody napkin to cover her face as the rats swarmed over her in an attempt to flee. It took only a matter of seconds, but they left Jo panting and stunned in their wake. When Jo finally opened her eyes, looking past the blockade of her arms, it was to find Yuusuke's butler outfit rumpled but complete in front of her.

Jo took a breath, trying to get her heart to slow, only for the napkin in her hand to jerk wildly in her grip. When she dropped it in a fresh moment of panic, it was to the sight of a wounded rat, hole through its side, dragging itself as quickly as it could out from under the napkin and towards the door.

All at once, the terror and confusion in Jo's blood boiled over into a rage, pushing her back to her feet. She spun three-sixty until she locked eyes on Pan, pointing at her with what she was glad to see was a perfectly steady finger.

"Enough of this, Chaos!"

To her immense satisfaction, Pan actually froze in surprise at the sound of her proper name, though it was an expression quickly hidden by glee.

"Oh come now, Destruction," she sing-songed, voice playful and light as she too got up from the table. "I'm just having a little fun. You used to like my fun, a long long time ago."

"Was any of that even real?" Jo demanded as Pan stepped closer, slow, lilting footsteps practically dancing into her personal space. "Was that really—"

"Does it matter?" Pan cut her off, close enough now that she could feel the odd magical presence surrounding the woman-child. And the way Jo's own magic responded to it. . . It was an intoxicating sensation, like feeling the ground rumble beneath the wave of an explosion, or seeing a star implode and become a black hole. It was devastating and visceral and—

Jo took a step back, realizing that Pan had raised a hand as if to touch her, nails glistening neon yellow in the space between them. Understanding washed over Jo instantly.

They needed to destroy Pan before it was too late, before she lured in Jo's magic and never let go. Jo shuddered at the thought; she didn't want to be a part of this chaos any more than she had to.

"Oh dear," Pan sighed with a histrionic pout. "It seems that display really upset you." She almost looked legitimately put out by the idea, though Jo wouldn't have been surprised if it was all an act. "Unfortunately our magic is becoming more erratic, you see. More . . . intense." As if to emphasize this point, the floor shifted like shuttering blinds from a dark wood to a bright and blinding white, the table melting into a literal puddle of multi-colored paints that splashed about the empty canvas around Jo's feet. Dishes and cutlery clattered into the puddles. Jo felt the paint seeping into her shoes, dampening her socks.

"So what?" Jo asked, voice level despite the rising air of disturbing energy soaking into the very essence of the room.

"So," Pan held out the 'o' for a long while, twirling about in the paint and making a mess of both the floor and her clothes. "I can sustain myself on Snow's magic for a good, long while. But sadly, it's not enough for three." Despite herself, Jo's breath caught in her throat.

All at once, Pan stopped her messy spinning. "This is an Age of *Magic*, Destruction. Not *Gods*—don't you remember that?" When Pan turned around then, she looked almost demure, the ruffles in her dress hanging less puffed up, the bright neon colors muted. Her hair had fallen over her shoulders in rainbow waves, but even those seemed lackluster in comparison to her usual level of outlandishness. "You must join me soon, Destruction. Or I fear you might find yourself unraveling completely."

Jo didn't quite know what to do with the seriousness in Pan's voice, or the look of seemingly genuine concern on her face. But as quickly as it had come, it was gone, replaced once again by flashy colors and a bright pink smile. As she skipped up to Jo's side, the puddles freezing in place mid-splash, Jo felt her mind and magic waver, thrown off by the complete one-eighty. Enough so that she didn't manage to move away in time before Pan was pulling her into a tight hug. She smelled like burnt sugar and gasoline.

"Why don't you . . . *sleep* on that, huh?" She giggled into Jo's hair, planting a kiss on her cheek that tingled with pins and needles, like her face had fallen asleep. Yet, all the same, Jo found herself leaning into it, her body yearning for something she didn't recognize but had once, she was sure. With a final squeeze, Pan released Jo from the hug and stepped away, snapping her fingers.

The whole room went from the mess of paint and ruined dinner to darkness, then blinked back into existence with an entirely new identity.

Though, perhaps not *entirely* new, Jo noticed as she turned around to take in her surroundings. Judging by the layout and the furniture, even the dull globs clinging to ceiling, it was obvious she was in the same place. Though perhaps if the place had aged a thousand years in a second.

Everything was covered in dust and cobwebs, cracks lining the walls and the broken remnants of the fancy tables and chairs. The large portraits which once held shifting mirage-type paintings were now either completely black or ripped from their canvases entirely.

The door at Jo's right creaked open on hinges that sounded as if they'd gone many, many years unused, and Jo caught sight of a butler's outfit beyond it. She held her breath, walking into the wash of light pouring in from the hallway, and sighed in relief when it wasn't Yuusuke but the marionette once again.

"To your room, madam," he said, ushering her towards the hall with a jerking motion that made it look as if he'd dislocated his shoulder. Jo didn't argue, didn't bother to give the room even another glance before following her orders.

Much like before, the halls shifted and changed as they passed, room after room blending into one another in a way that should have made her dizzy. But Jo kept her eyes on the golem's back, allowing him to lead her to whatever room Pan had "graciously" provided for her. Jo struggled to regain her footing, to level her mental state.

The best she could do was continue with the plan, though it was becoming painfully clear that getting a message to her team wasn't going to be easy. Especially when the golem finally led her to a room with no windows and only one door. So much for breaking one of the flag poles.

"You will be summoned," the marionette said, never setting foot inside Jo's room; she wondered if he was contained within the halls and nowhere else. "Until then, you have been instructed to rest."

"Yeah, sure." Jo shrugged, watching as he closed her door, and unsurprised to hear him lock it. With a huff, she sat heavily onto the bed, comforter plush but scratchy beneath her fingers. However, her old clothes were there. *How kind.*

As it was, she was without a means to contact the others, and only a vague idea as to where Pan was keeping the bow. She'd found Snow, and though it both filled her with rage and heartache to know what he'd been put through, to know he was so close yet still so far, seeing him again was like a boost of adrenaline, a surge of motivation that pulled her back to her feet with a determined breath.

The original plan was the best thing they had, even if it was still mostly evolving as they went along, and it was the least she could do to try and keep it playing out. She'd gotten inside, she'd found Snow; now all that was left was finding the bow and sending out a signal.

She just hoped that total destruction of Pan's precious castle would be enough to get their attention.

# TIME TO DESTROY SOMETHING

Snow's words replayed in her head as Jo paced the tiny box that was her room.

*Pan kept her treasures in a vault, a room, a safe place at the center of it all.*

Those thoughts layered atop the memory of her visit to Pan's room in the Society—the only time Jo had achieved an in-depth look into the workings of the magical fortresses Pan surrounded herself with. But there was something more, adding a depth to her understanding that even Jo didn't want to consider too closely.

It was a quiet reassurance nearly purring in the back of her mind that she knew what Pan had done because they were one being; they were born of one mind and had never deviated too far from each other's thoughts.

Jo stopped her pacing. She closed her eyes, mentally summoning the central courtyard she'd seen earlier—the one void of decor and function. *The room was an illusion,* Jo decided, *one of many*. It was a house of mirrors, reflecting outward distorted images to keep people from finding what was truly within. But something about that room seemed significant to her. Something about that room in particular was central to everything else.

"They call me a demigod." Jo looked at her hand, balling it into a fist. "I should see if it really holds true."

She had come here for one purpose: to end it. No amount of fanfare or distraction was going to change that. Resolved, Jo turned to the door. Magic churned within her, faster and faster until it felt like she was at the eye of a storm that would be unleashed on the whole building. She would start as usual—by dismantling and cracking at the seams. But Jo was prepared to unleash a hellfire of wanton destruction, caring not for how things were decimated so long as they *were*.

Jo gripped the door, ready for a lock, ready for it to resist her.

But it did not.

It swung open soundlessly, miraculously revealing the same hallway she'd seen before. Jo stared at it, somewhat angry that Pan couldn't even let her have a dramatic start to the end.

Jo shrugged the idea away, running down the hall. The less she had to destroy—for now—the better. The longer Pan could be ignorant to Jo's movements (assuming she didn't already know them), the longer Jo would have to locate the bow. But first, she had to get to Snow.

Jo skidded to a halt at the end of the hall, a dead end creeping up out of nowhere. Like she'd done with the marionette earlier, Jo turned in place to reveal a new stretch of hallway. She sprinted between the orbs, pushed through the door at the end, and was met with the first sitting room she'd seen upon entering.

"I choose . . . you." Jo pointed to the door opposite, pushing through it and into another hall.

She repeated the process two more times.

On her fourth try, Jo came to a stop at the end of the hall with the dead end. But this time, she didn't turn around. Jo stared at the wall in front of her, forcing herself to think of what Pan would do. She was certifiably insane, but she could calculate a long game better than a chess protégé.

Pan knew Jo would come for Snow, for the bow, and to end things once and for all. Pan knew she would ultimately escape her room—the unlocked door was practically an invitation. Which also meant Pan knew that Jo would fall prey to her maze and reach this point of frustration.

*She knows I'll break something*, Jo thought to herself, not daring to say the words aloud. If Jo had been herself from a year ago—headstrong and hot-headed—she would've walked right into Pan's trap and destroyed the wall before her. And why not? It was barring her path. All the doors in the room were unlocked—there was no need for her to break them.

Jo's eyes dropped. In truth, Pan might think Jo would do any number of things. But destroying the floor from underneath her feet? Jo didn't think that would be among them.

Pushing her magic downward and into the floor, Jo felt the fractures increasing just before the large, satisfying *crack* that sent rubble and magic scattering.

Biting back a scream as she fell, Jo braced herself for impact—braced to bounce back the moment her body would be destroyed. Her magic worked in the same fashion as it had before and Jo landed hard, feeling the bones in her shins shatter and using the momentum of it to send her sprinting forward—her body as good as new in the process.

This hall felt different than the one above her. She'd landed in another one of Pan's mazes, but one a little closer to the castle's center. Here, the chaos seemed to writhe and struggle to keep its foothold. It was almost as if an invisible comb was trying to pull out the tangles and yank it into order.

Snow was here.

Using his magic like a homing beacon, Jo broke through the walls and windows and doors that would hold her back. But that wasn't all Pan would throw her way, apparently. One of the shadow creatures she'd faced before at High Luana stood at the ready, blocking her path ahead. Jo remembered what Eslar had said—these were elves who had sold themselves to the dark arts. This wasn't like the first man who'd been a civilian tainted by Pan's magic. This man stood here by choice.

She didn't even waste her breath offering to spare its life.

Jo launched in for the offensive, throwing out a wave of magic. The creature's shield unraveled, then promptly bounced back together—it seemed Pan had made some modifications. Startled, Jo was almost caught flat-footed as the thing charged.

Dodging to the side, Jo stomped her foot down as she caught her balance. It sent a shockwave of magic into the floor that crumbled the stone beneath the man's feet. He barely had time to look at her before he was falling and Jo didn't waste her time looking to see where he landed.

She started running again, only to come to a sudden stop mid-hall. Turning to a wall, she pressed her hand into the stone.

*Creation*, her mind, her magic, and her heart, seemed to say in unison.

The wall blasted inward with a cloud of dust.

"My demigod prince, I've come to rescue you." Jo took a shot at the dramatic, because why not?

Snow's reaction was decidedly unenthused. "What're you doing?"

"I'm breaking you out."

He looked nearly frantic. "But—"

"There's no time, Snow. We'll get the bow. I'll let the team in. We end this."

"The team is here!"

His confused panic suddenly made sense.

"What?" Jo whispered. The dust settling on the bedspread they'd made love atop mere hours ago suddenly seemed loud, as though every minute speck landed with an earth-shaking rumble. "*Here?* That's impossible. They're out—"

"Pan left not long ago. She came to make sure I was . . . aware. That she has you and the team, and that she's successfully playing you both."

*The team.* Pan had the team. Well, of course she did. "We were so stupid!" Jo agonized aloud. She reached up, grabbing her hair with a colossal cry of frustration at the ready, then stopped. "No . . . this can work."

"What?" Snow pulled one of her hands from her hair, taking it in his own, drawn as much by a need to comfort her as to assure himself that she was real.

"The team is here, in here already, we just have to find them. Pan meant to trap them—to show off how strong and in control she was. But all she did was bring us together. And if *you* didn't know about the—" Jo stopped herself short, not daring to say the word *arrow*. His room had been compromised by the large hole in the wall, after all. "—the special thing."

"Then she still—yes, I understand. But how will you get to them?"

Jo thought about this a moment. As they stood, speaking, she could feel ripples in the magic throughout the castle. It was as if Pan was trying to redesign things on the fly. But Jo wasn't about to give her that chance.

"I'm going to get the bow." Jo gripped his hand tightly, pulling him close and planting a firm kiss on his mouth. "You use the cracks in her chaos to find the team."

"If you can destroy her magic, perhaps I could create passages through it," Snow reasoned as she was pulling away. "When I get to them, then what?"

"Then find me! I think it'll be easy to tell where. I'll get the bow and then keep holding her off!" Jo started running down the hallway once more, stopping at a window. She put a foot on the ledge and the glass shattered outward. As the wind howled, whipping her hair, Jo took a long look at Snow. Who knew if it would be her last? She ignored the twinge in her chest, the sudden extra weight around her heart, and grinned. "Good luck, Creation."

"Good luck, Destruction."

# A CHEAP MAGIC TRICK

Jo jumped through the window and fell onto a lower balcony. She could've sworn she'd been in the basement of the castle not a moment before, but what made sense anymore? In Pan's topsy-turvy castle, nothing did.

But that was fine. There didn't have to be any rules, because Jo wasn't going to play by them. She was making her own from now on.

Looking over the edge of the balcony, Jo saw the greenhouse-like rooftop of the strange room she'd seen before—the room she suspected held Pan's treasures, and the one she had deemed her goal. She could fall right down onto it, but that was assuming Pan didn't have any other tricks up her sleeve. Instead, Jo turned inward, turning the doors to the room beyond into splinters with a look.

She stepped into the decimated room, eerily similar to the dining room Pan had entertained her in not more than an hour ago. Jo had two missions: The first was to get to Pan's treasure room. The second was to break as many things as she could, so Snow would find the opening he needed—if he couldn't create it himself. Or perhaps her destruction would yield the fodder for him to craft a door. Jo was still learning how his magic worked, but either way she relished in the opportunity to wreak more havoc on Pan.

The doors across from her opened, more shadowed assassins rushing toward her. Jo didn't even bother with them. Instead, she rushed to the table between her and the dark elves, meeting it before they did. The moment her fingers came into contact, it exploded into shards of wood for them to impale themselves upon.

Jo knew it wouldn't work; if Takako's bullets couldn't penetrate their shields, then wooden spikes couldn't either. But her aim was to slow them down—and she did, if only by a fraction of a second. By the time they even noticed she'd moved, Jo had rushed through the doors to her left. The second they closed, Jo looked at the keystone of the arch above the door and forced it to crack to the base on either side. Fissures spread outward with a surge of magic light similar to a lightning strike, bringing the whole wall crumbling down.

For the first time since entering the castle, Jo saw daylight. It streamed through the hole in the wall like a ray of hope shining on an otherwise desperate situation. Climbing over the rubble, Jo stepped outside onto one of the narrow glass-like ledges of the castle's many spindly towers.

Knowing what was on the inside, knowing Pan, Jo looked at it as if for the first time. It was obsidian, much like the disk she'd looked through with Samson. Jo held out her hand, thinking of the framework he'd helped her access, and raised it.

Like an architectural sketch visible only to her, the castle's magical structures laid themselves bare. She couldn't make sense of what was inside the room, but she could see its structure. And if she could see it, that meant one thing.

"This is going to break beautifully."

Jo started from one of the flagpoles and worked her way down. With a mighty heave of power, she felt the castle rumble and the tower come crumbling down. Turning her eyes to the next one, Jo exerted the same force, watching as it was reduced to glass-like shards.

After the third fell, a familiar rooftop was exposed.

*There.* Pan's treasure room, finally accessible without layers of magic concealing its true nature.

Jo took a leap, not caring for the crunch of her ankles or kneecaps as she landed. She was Destruction; she could find life in death itself. In her own way, she was eternal.

Making her way across rooftops and ledges, Jo found herself on the top of the greenhouse-like roof. Crouching, she placed her hand on the semi-translucent stone. She didn't even brace herself for the impact among the dagger-like shards of crystal.

As she stood, Jo heard a slow clapping sound.

"Well done! Looks like you made it all the way here," Pan's voice echoed from the opposite side of the room. "Too bad it will mean very little in the end."

"The only end is yours, Pan," Jo threatened, instantly feeling like some comic book hero brought to life. She had no reason to talk to Pan and she wasn't going to be lured into it again.

"Well, the bow is right here. So take it." Pan motioned to a pedestal in the center of the room. "Or, you can join—"

Jo started running.

"I didn't even finish my dramatic declaration!" Pan half-screeched, half-whined.

She barely got several steps toward the center of the room before a wall suddenly jutted out from the floor. Jo skidded to a stop, stumbling, tripping, bracing for impact only to fall through it like a mirage. Another one of Pan's illusions.

"They're not coming." Pan's voice echoed as Jo peeled herself off the floor.

She looked around the room and took it in for the first time—it was just like in the Society. There were shelves upon shelves lining the perimeter, stacked with all manner of trinkets and tokens. Jo saw rows of military medals between platemail she'd associate with a knight in medieval times. There was a whole train engine that looked to be made of jade next to a life-sized sculpture of some muscle-bound woman swathed in silks.

"Join with me. End this," Pan all but commanded. "End it all!"

Once more, Jo didn't reply. She turned her head toward the sound of Pan's voice, locating it in the cavernous room, and set the shelves behind her to exploding. Their contents scattered the floor, rolling to clutter the room.

"I really liked that one!" Pan screamed, picking up a platter from the ground. "You'll pay for that!"

She threw it like a Frisbee and midair the disc morphed, taking on a saw-like silhouette. Jo held out a hand, letting the teeth bite directly into her flesh. It gave her enough of a rush of power that she spun easily in place, sending the disk right back. But before it could hit Pan, it transformed into a raven and flew away.

*Chaos and Destruction, an even match for no one to win.*

Jo looked back to the bow, more resolved than ever. She couldn't end this, which meant there was only one person who could, and one plan that even had a chance of working. Putting her trust in Snow and the others, she pushed forward.

Another projectile was thrown at her and Jo didn't even bother redirecting; she merely dodged. But Pan had closed the gap faster than she expected, and the other woman caught her wrist, wrenching Jo close. Their noses were almost touching.

"Join me," she hissed. Jo could feel the heat of her breath, the spark of magic that bounced between them, turning into something dangerous. *I may want to,* a voice whispered in Jo, more tempted every minute. "End this and join me."

"I will end this," Jo vowed, finally breaking her silence. With a grunt, she yanked her hands free, feeling her bones snap and twist away from Pan's unrelenting grip.

Jo began running again, and Pan attempted to thwart her.

Back and forth it went, but Jo gained on her step by step until her hands landed on the bow. A magic not unlike Snow's coursed through her from an origin that Jo could only suspect was the Life Tree. Like Snow, it was an antithesis to her that was as calming as it was alluring, in a far more wholesome way than Pan.

But the trance was only momentary as Pan yanked on the other end of the bow.

"Do you think you can defeat me with this?" she screeched.

Jo didn't answer. Instead, she pulled on her end and forced her magic toward Pan with the express intent of breaking the demigod's wrists. It didn't quite work—there was something about Pan that her magic refused to harm. But it was enough to startle Pan, who let go completely. Jo's force over-compensated; off-balance, she tripped, falling backward, and lost the bow in the process.

The wooden implement clattered across the pebbled floor of Pan's treasure room to the opposite side of where they now stood. It came to a stop, landing against a large piece of golden platemail and what looked to be a geode as big as Jo's head, cracked open and scattered on the ground. Jo looked to it, panting, and then back to Pan.

Pan's eyes were on her, her cat-like irises narrowed to thin vertical slits as sharp as daggers. Her shoulders heaved up and down with her ragged breathing and her hair seemed to change color with her every breath— blue, purple, pink, green—a kaleidoscope of shifting magic. Then, with a ruffle of bows and ribbons, Pan moved.

Jo was close behind, dashing in the direction of the bow. It seemed to ooze light and life in staunch protest to the chaotic world around it.

She had to get to it before Pan did.

Lengthening her strides and pushing her legs as hard as they could go, Jo cast a hand in Pan's direction, unleashing her magic. The ground beneath Pan's feet rippled, pebbles breaking upward, free from the mortar, in shrapnel of stone. Pan responded with a jump and a snap of her finger, leaping through what were now rose petals falling harmlessly to the ground.

"Try again," she snarled.

With nothing more than a look in Jo's direction, the silver medals scattered at her feet unraveled and slithered, turned from ribbons into cobras. Jo reared back, stalling. She looked at the metal, reducing it to white-hot molten pools she quickly leapt over.

"Gladly," Jo grunted.

She threw everything she had at the roof overhead. With a look, it fractured, raining translucent black stone down on Pan. Pan stopped scowling as she leaned down. Gripping at a ribbon on her sandal, she tugged it free, the shoe falling lose. Pan wove it through the air like a whip and it slashed through the hail of stone nearly completely.

*Nearly.*

With her nemesis caught in the debris, Jo made her final steps, preparing to lunge. She was so close to the bow. She could feel it now, almost taste the magic in the air. And then—

"Jo!" Snow's voice called.

Jo's head whipped around at the sound of her name spoken on the tongue of her other half, her *wanted* and *beloved* other half. Snow was standing at the far corner of the room—where a stone tunnel had been crafted impossibly through the rubble. The other members of the Society were clamoring over the debris around him, Takako in the lead. Relief soared through her at the sight of them—safe and sound, if not a little bruised and beaten. She saw tears in Wayne's clothes that she had no doubt he would kill someone for (hopefully Pan), and some blood on Samson's face that *Jo* would kill someone for (also, hopefully Pan).

But *no one* was killing Pan when all their eyes were off her.

Jo never even saw it coming.

It felt like a claymore digging into her side, tearing her from the edge of her flesh nearly to the naval. It stole the wind from her lungs, stalling her, knocking her off balance. She rolled, feeling the muscles in her abdomen tense as magic pulsed in her brighter than before. Rearing upward, Jo was ready to launch the next attack. But her magic never left her body.

Pan stood over her with a heart-shaped scythe in one hand and the bow in the other, twirling it impossibly between her little fingers.

"I can't destroy it—not my magic," Pan admitted, loud enough that her voice carried across the decimated remains of her treasure room. "But I can change it."

In one movement that seemed like nothing more than a blink, Pan tossed the scythe aside and gripped the bow, thrusting it out before her. There was no flash of light, no sound to herald the end of the world. Pan simply uncurled her fingers, and the bow was transformed into nothing more than doves and confetti—an act that could've been done at any time, but Pan no doubt waited until just that moment, her intended audience gathered in rapt attention.

The hope of the world died like a cheap magic trick.

# THE FINAL MOMENTS

**N**o.

Jo watched the confetti fall, some of it landing in her hair, on her outstretched hand. It wasn't over. It couldn't be over. There must be something else they could do. . .

But not without the bow. That had been the crux of their plan. Without it, they had nothing.

They'd think of something else. They'd come up with a new plan. But with what time? What could they possibly do now and with no weapon? There had to be a way. It was over. It couldn't be. Not like that. Not. . . Not so suddenly. Her thoughts were dangerously scattered and chaotic. Jo had no draw to pull them back together or she'd risk losing herself.

Jo lifted her head and watched the doves fly up and away, wishing she could do the same. There was no escape now; Pan had them all trapped. The hopeless truth of it filled her lungs and stole her voice. She couldn't breathe.

"This is pointless. Fun, but pointless," Pan giggled, walking right into Jo's line of sight. Jo kept her gaze steadily trained on the doves overhead, diminishing white specks in the sky. When Pan noticed the lack of attention, she glanced over her shoulder, frowning. With a click of her teeth, the doves bloated to impossible size and turned into balloons that drifted out of sight on the breeze. Jo forced her gaze to attention, though not without throwing Pan as murderous a glare as she could manage.

"This isn't over." She thought she might have heard a rustle behind her, the sounds of commotion from her friends, but she kept her focus on Pan, drawing herself shakily to her knees.

"Oh but it is," Pan said sweetly, reaching out to place a hand beneath

Jo's chin. "You've played your little game of rebellion. Even I admit I had a bit of fun with it. But it's time to stop this now, my darling. It's time give up the charade and join me."

Jo's magic spiked at the idea, though whether it was in temptation or revulsion was hard to say with Pan's touch against her skin. So Jo shook that touch away, backing up. "We'll stop you." Pan frowned at Jo's words, her catlike eyes shimmering red. Despite the warning signals crackling down Jo's spine, she pressed on. "We haven't lost yet."

If Pan's magic had been a fire, everyone in the room would have burned beneath the onslaught that suddenly filled the room.

"Enough of this nonsense!" Pan suddenly stood before them in swaths of elaborate armor, her hair a flyaway mess of rainbow strands caught in a perpetual whirlwind. But it wasn't the costume change that had everyone falling into stunned silence so much as the look of pure, unbridled rage on her face. "Stop being such a *fool!*" She reached back out towards Jo, grabbing her face in a vice-like grip and squeezing her cheeks enough to bruise the flesh—if Jo had been mortal still. In an instant, Pan was back to her normal self, ruffles and colors and all. "I mean seriously," she giggled again, releasing Jo's face. "What are you going to do without your precious bow?"

And she was right, wasn't she? No bow meant no weapon. No weapon meant no shot. No shot meant no chance to vanquish Pan. It had been a plan with no failsafe because it couldn't have one; even Samson had said there was no other material from the start. Everything up until then was a last resort in a war that none of them had asked to be a part of.

Except, it was a war that *Jo* had asked them to be a part of. The members of the Society hadn't needed to fight, and might not have if she hadn't dragged them back into the fray. She'd led them all to failure, hadn't she? Just like she had with Nico.

"That's it, my sweet," Pan hummed, her tone soothing as she covered the distance between them in a single step and wrapped her arms around Jo's shoulders. "You know you've lost. So just let go, *hm*? Just do what your magic has been begging of you, destroy it all—these petty friendships, your pathetic life, this sad little world. I promise, it'll feel good."

As if in counter-argument to her words, Jo felt the lick of familiar magic against her own, not Pan's wild and fiery blend of chaos, but the swirling rush of a bonded soul easing its way beneath the cracks in her confidence. Still somewhat slack in Pan's embrace, Jo let her eyes drift towards the sensation of it, capturing Snow's eyes at once.

He stood within a circle of his own magic, eyes already searching out Jo's gaze. The moment they connected, the soothing reach of his magic began to ease her away from the chaos, willing her own magic to fall back into a semblance of order, safely out of Pan's reach.

He was trying to counter-attack Pan's sway, pulling in the opposite direction—a game of magical tug-of-war.

Jo could see the rope between them in beams of light, felt it wrap around her like a blanket, warm and comforting and desperate for her safety. It heightened her senses and called out to her in a way that Pan's did not.

"You think your pull is stronger than mine?" Jo heard Pan hiss, the words themselves slithering into her ears and attempting to block out Snow's call. Jo felt suspended between the two of them, Pan's magic seeping into her skin, dark and sticky like tar, while Snow's tried to wash away the chaotic darkness clouding her mind. It was growing impossible to tell herself apart from the whirlwind of magical sensation.

In fact, within the storm were even tendrils of her team. She could feel Wayne's magic in a distant thrum, even Eslar's and Samson's too, their magics so intertwined it was near impossible to tell them apart. She could hear their fear and taste their desperation, but among all that, with a sudden spike of recognition, she could also feel their hope.

Which was when Takako's magic tickled her senses.

While Snow's magic called to her like a song, and Pan's called to her like a demand, Takako's was a beacon on the horizon of a dark, vast ocean. And as if Takako's magic had shouted her name, it drew Jo's focus instantly.

Takako held the arrow nocked between the middle and index fingers of her right hand. Her left was curled into a relaxed fist, space between her fingers as though she was holding something invisible. The shaft of the arrow rested on her left pointer finger as she slowly raised her arms, drawing back in an invisible string.

Muscles tense and bulging, Takako stood in a perfect firing stance, her arms aligned in front of her in a way that looked ridiculous, and had Jo been unable to feel the swelling thrum of magic coming off of the woman, she would have laughed. But as Takako braced her fingers against her jaw, Jo could almost see the magic rippling in the air in the shape of exactly what they needed.

*A bow.*

Pan seemed to sense the shift of magic too, her whole body tensing before she yanked away from Jo, her attention suddenly consumed by Takako. Out of reflex, Jo grabbed Pan's wrist, keeping her from moving forward, and putting Pan's chest in the direct line of fire at Jo's side.

But that wouldn't be enough. Not nearly enough. It was a truth Wayne had forced her to accept at the onset of their journey—their journey to a conclusion she hadn't wanted to face.

"Where. Did. You. Get. *That?*" Pan growled in clear recognition, an inhuman sound as she tried to rip her arm out of Jo's grip, but neither of them moved an inch. Jo could already feel her magic giving in, keeping them both rooted in place, and by the way Pan flashed a surprised look in Jo's direction, she could feel it too. Jo had expected elation, maybe even a smug sort of giddiness. What she hadn't expected to see on Pan's face was relief. Maybe even . . . pride?

"Do it, Jo!" Wayne yelled, the first words to break through Jo's haze, which opened up the floodgates for a cacophony of sound, most of which came from Snow. Not from his voice, but his magic. It begged and cried against the feeling of being replaced, and Jo tried not to listen. She already knew how much it would hurt, knew that in many ways, what she was about to do could be seen as a betrayal to all he had endured for her.

Especially if it didn't work—if she didn't come back.

So Jo focused on her own magic, on how it twisted and writhed around Pan's wrist and upward, sinking into her skin in veins of color, electricity crackling along every inch of their skin. Jo could still see Takako over Pan's shoulder, poised and ready, and when she mouthed the words *"I won't miss,"* Jo could have sworn she heard them in her soul.

Pan was so consumed by the sight, the sensation of their magic sewing together into one, that she didn't notice Jo's last, desperate glance over at Snow, her love, her fated half, her Creation. He'd stopped struggling, knowing perhaps that it was too late to stop the process when she'd willingly opened herself to it. But that didn't mean Jo's heart didn't break at the look in his eyes, the devastation and the pain. But not anger. At least there was that.

"I love you," Jo whispered, sending the words to him on the last tendril of her magic that had not given itself over to Oblivion.

Once she knew he had heard, once she saw the recognition on his face and the beginnings of her name on his lips, Jo closed her eyes and made her choice. She gave in to the riptide that had been working to pull her feet out from under her from the first moment she'd entered the castle.

Takako was their champion, and she would not miss. Even as Jo slipped away, that faith did not waver. That faith freed her to spend the last moments of her awareness—the last moments of her existence as a sovereign entity, unencumbered by the mad will of Pan or Oblivion—on the only thing left that mattered.

Snow. He was her love; their bond had transcended ages, and he would be the last thing Josephina Espinosa's eyes would ever see.

# REUNITED

"*C**almase, calmase. Estas bien, mijita. You have nothing to be frightened of anymore. I am here.*"

The words were both familiar and strange, filtering past Destruction's ears like a whisper. Part of her wanted to cling to them as they drifted by, but she had no means with which to grasp them, and no recognition of why she desired to do so. Even still, the voice soothed something in her, the words sparking a deep comfort low in her being.

"*Calmase, estas bien,*" the voice had said. "*Calm down. You're alright.*" Be calm, do not cry, do not fret, you are safe.

But the calm did not suit Destruction, just as it did not suit Chaos. There was no calm or safety in Oblivion, so what use did she have for it? And what right did the voice have to demand it of her?

"It wasn't a demand, it was a comfort. *Abuelita* had to comfort us a lot back then."

The new voice was more familiar but still strange, like listening to a recording of herself. And where the last voice had drifted past before Destruction could properly grasp it, this one echoed loudly, wanting to be heard—waiting to be recognized.

"I don't remember the nightmares anymore, but they probably had to do with you," the new voice continued.

Nightmares felt like Chaos's doing. Too abstract for Destruction, too inefficient.

"We would dream about things we didn't understand, things we wouldn't understand until much, much later. And if our parents weren't around to ease us back into sleep, then *abuelita* would. Her voice would keep the monsters away."

There were no monsters anymore, only gods.

"You are right, my darling," another voice, the most familiar of them all, eased into Destruction like a drug. Arms wrapped around her from behind, looping around Destruction's waist in a tight embrace. "There are only gods. Would you like to be one?"

There was a power simmering to life between them at those words, a power that Destruction both did and did not understand. Something about it tugged a distant part of her mind, like a warning. But Chaos's arms tightened around her, her chin resting on Destruction's shoulder, and all warnings were forgotten. The path before them was illuminated and easy to follow—they simply had to take that first step.

*"It has been an honor working alongside you, Josephina Espinosa."*

A memory. One Destruction did not own, but which held something visceral and painful nonetheless. Her heart ached with it, and Chaos's arms loosened from around her waist, though they did not vanish completely

"It was my fault," that voice from before whispered. *Jo's voice.* Ink-stained fingers and a warm smile flashed behind Destruction's eyes. The taste of coffee coated her tongue.

*"It has been nothing short of a blessing getting to know you."*

That pain in Destruction's chest grew, overwhelming even the illuminated path before her, drowning it in a warm glow, like sunlight.

"They were the last words Nico ever said to me, filled with kindness until the very end. I will miss him every day."

But Destruction wouldn't. Why would she? These memories weren't hers. What was an end, if not a celebration of the final break?

"You are one and the same, my love."

Creation's voice. Destruction had no problem recognizing him, even if he sounded far away. She tried to turn towards it, to take a step closer, hear him better, but for some reason she remained rooted in place.

"My Destruction," he said, sounding even farther, as if fading away. "My Josephina."

*Josephina.* The name settled over her own like a second skin. She could hear her *abuelita* singing lullabies in Spanish, could see lines of code floating in front of her vision. But she wasn't Josephina (was she?), and when Creation spoke again, it was so far away she couldn't hear it.

"Are you ready, my darling?" Chaos hummed, voice clear in Destruction's ear. But something kept her from stepping forward. Even with the path once again illuminated before her, even as Chaos's embrace tightened until it was almost painful, something kept her rooted in place.

"You don't want to leave me behind," Jo said, voice sounding as if she were standing just inches from Destruction's face, though only the path lay before her, empty and bright.

Destruction wanted to argue with the voice, wanted to demand it let her pass, but she stayed silent. She wasn't sure she could speak at all anymore. Josephina could speak though, and despite herself, Destruction listened.

"You don't want to forget. You don't want to lose me. That's why you can't go forward."

Ridiculous. Destruction had no use for Josephina's memories. Joining with Chaos was her purpose, becoming Oblivion was her design. Why would pointless memories keep her from righting a centuries-old wrong?

"Because it would mean losing all of them too." Her team, her friends, the family Josephina had found in a world outside of time. "And you don't want to risk losing him."

She could no longer hear his voice, but she could feel the memory of him as clearly as if it were his arms wrapped around her instead of Chaos's. She could feel his lips against hers, his hands on her skin, and every nerve within her was suddenly calling out not for Oblivion but for Creation. For Snow. Jo ached for him, so Destruction did too, and all at once, it became unclear which of her was which.

"But we're doing this *for* him," Destruction said in Jo's voice. "Even if it means losing him."

Chaos's arms tightened and a giggle spilled from her lips, tickling at Destruction's neck with honey-sweet breath.

"Then we know what we have to do." For a moment, it was as if Josephina Espinosa stood before her, blocking the path from Destruction's view. It felt like looking at her own reflection and seeing a memory. A beautiful memory that she would hold on to for as long as Oblivion allowed.

Jo stepped aside, letting the path shine before them, and Chaos's laugh filled Destruction's ears. This time, stepping forward was easy. Even as she and Chaos began to merge into one, Destruction had no trouble walking the path. Even as her steps began to feel more weighted, power fracturing the ground beneath her with each step, it was easy.

Every movement was so, so easy.

It wasn't even about giving in, really. This had always been the outcome. It was just a matter of finding her way back together. The leisurely pace down the path became a skip, a twirling jog, a sprint. Her magic twirled with her, around her, licking at her heels and helping her speed down the path until she could see it: an actual light at the end of the tunnel where the world awaited her return—*their* return.

It had been too long, too *long*. And as the path came to an end, but a single step left for her to take, there was no hesitation.

Oblivion's heart soared at the feeling of existence, her body somehow both weightless and settled into the gravity of her new world. It was euphoric, intoxicating, and for a fraction of a second, she could do no more than breathe it in, her eyes falling lazily back open.

If her old and fractured memories were any indication, not even a second had passed, Takako still poised to fire in her direction. It was a laughable display. To assume any weapon held the power necessary to destroy her, Oblivion was almost insulted. Hunt had always been foolish, no better than her beasts. *Best remind them of who they were dealing with.*

"You think that little toy of yours can stop *me*?" she called out in a voice that could shatter the very foundation of the bedrock itself. "I am Oblivion! I am a *god*!"

"And I'm the Champion sent across the ages to take you down," Takako replied, not even bothering to raise her voice. Not that she had to. The arrow flew the moment the words registered, a lifetime of knowledge and experience rushing through Oblivion's head. *Champion,* Takako had called herself. For the first time in her new life, Oblivion's heart skipped a beat, just in time for the arrow to pierce it.

# OBLIVION

Beads of sweat traced the outline of hair on the nape of Snow's neck, rolling down under the collar of his shirt.

Every drop of magic and focus was wrapped around Jo and Pan in a desperate attempt to combat Pan's sway. He could see the swirl of magic like a rainbow whirlpool, though he didn't know if it was visible to only him, or if the rest of the team could see it as well. Frankly, he wouldn't have even known they were standing next to him were it not for their muted words.

For him, the only thing that mattered was Jo. It had been the only thing that mattered throughout the whole of his existence. He had been made for her—for this—to shield her magic and keep her wholly separate. Then, he'd fallen in love, and after that it was hopeless to expect him to do anything less than make every sacrifice he could for her—from ending the Age of Gods, to surrendering himself to Pan, and now this.

He was a horse that would run until its heart exploded and legs gave out, not daring to stop even a moment sooner.

Which made it an even more bitter pill to swallow when he felt the current of her magic shift. Jo would leave him, he realized. While he'd been expecting her to resort to desperate measures, he'd never expected her surrender.

It wasn't until he could feel her slipping into what promised to be a swift descent that she finally looked his way. Despite the confusion, despite the agony of loss, his heart stuttered beneath her stare. His chest ached at the thought of losing her, but the idea that she was sharing her final moments with him, in the only way she could, was a thin spackle to the cracks of his breaking heart. There wasn't long now until she would be gone, and he would fill his sight with her for every last moment.

"I love you." Her lips formed the words, silent amidst the chaos but loud within his ears, his mind. One of the few remaining wisps of her magic broke free from the rising tide, just long enough to reach out for his presence.

Then, her eyes shifted. Briefly, barely, a small change in focus that Snow almost missed. He fought to tear his sight from Jo, fearful of what it would mean when he looked back—if she'd even still be there at all.

Takako stood at his side, sure-footed atop a fallen bookcase leaning against a pile of rubble. Snow squinted at her, his mind struggling to make sense of what he was witnessing. She held her arms steady, muscles taut, and in her hands was the glittering outline of a bow, one made purely of her magic's design.

And the arrow that he had seen crafted ages ago was suspended between it. The arrow that had been made with the power to kill a god.

Snow's attention jerked back to Jo the moment he felt her magic slipping free of the protective well he'd been shaping for her. A soft "*Please*" may have escaped his lips as he searched for her eyes. But it was too late.

It was over in barely a second, swirls of rainbow colored light dancing over Pan's hair and Jo's skin, spinning about the two of them until its speed obscured them completely, the sheer luminosity of it blinding. All it took in the end was a blink against the barrage and suddenly Pan and Jo were no more. In their place was a being Snow had only ever heard tales of, in whispers between him and Destruction, in words of warning from those who'd created him.

The rubble bit into his knees as he collapsed onto it, hands swinging limply at his sides. Magic swelled in him, making him whole in a way he could barely remember being, for the first time in eons—fully untethered from Pan. For Pan was no more, Jo was no more; there was only Oblivion now, and what looked to be the end of all things he'd ever fought for.

The sheer oppressiveness of her power aside, what truly brought him down in a way that no man or god or demigod had ever been able to do before was the curve of her jaw, the lift of her cheek, and the fullness of her lips. He could see her—Jo, the woman he loved, the woman he'd been made for. But he could also see Pan in the slit of her cat-eyes, in the opalescent hair flying madly about her head.

"You think that little toy of yours can stop *me?*" Oblivion spoke with Jo's lips, the sound a rumble that seemed to come from the very heavens. Yet even in the sound, his ears objected, trying to pry apart Jo's voice. "I am Oblivion! I am a *god!*"

"And I am the Champion sent across the ages to take you down," Takako's voice pierced the cacophony like a bullet through the center of one of her targets. Or perhaps, more accurately, like an arrow through the heart of a god.

Snow wanted to close his eyes the moment he heard the magical *twang* of the bowstring. He was scrambling to his feet as the arrow shot through the air, curving true and powerful toward its target. It hit Oblivion square in the chest, piercing with an ease that should not have been possible. Her torso curled in on itself at the impact, the slits of her eyes narrowing to almost nothing as she lowered them to take in the arrow now embedded in her heart.

"*You. . .*" She gasped a noise that sounded like a chainsaw on a chalkboard. "You think that can stop me?" Oblivion lifted a trembling hand, gripping the shaft of the arrow. Snow watched as she yanked it from her chest. "Hunt was a f—"

Her final words were cut short by a scream that shook the world.

Magic filled his vision and licked like flames beneath his skin. It was as if the goddess had been tapped like a keg. Magic poured out with all the brilliance—all the chaos, all the destruction—of fireworks. She leaned backward, her spine bending at an unnatural angle, arms dangling, as though she were held up by the magic being torn from her body.

Then, she crumpled, and it was over. It was finally over.

And Snow ran.

"Snow, wait!" Takako called.

"We don't know if she's really—" Eslar began to say behind him. But Snow paid them no mind. If Oblivion wasn't dead, she would ride again to kill them all, and his distance from her would only buy him seconds.

Snow skidded to a stop, falling, scrambling, half-crawling to the corpse of the god. Her skin looked brittle, the light within no longer contained by it. It was as though she was burning alive from within and would soon be reduced to ash, scattered by the breeze.

"No," Snow whispered, tilting her face upward. The wide eyes were still Pan's, but the cheeks his hands cupped were Jo's. "It can't end this way. Not after everything we did."

For a brief second, so quick he could've missed it, her eyes gained focus. She looked at him in a way Pan never had and Oblivion never could.

*Destruction.*

"What must I do?" he whispered to her, to the world. "I would give my life for you now, if I could."

"You . . . can." Jo's voice, his Destruction, spoke. In an instant, there and gone. The focus in her eyes was beginning to vanish.

"I—" And it hit him. Oblivion was very much dead in his arms, and yet she was still there, the faintest of echoes trying to scream against a growing silence. Holding the limp form of the fallen god closer, Snow closed his eyes and reached deeper for that sensation, that spark of life that felt distinct and undeniable. The one that mirrored his own.

He felt no trace of Pan, no inkling of Oblivion, but just as he began to grow doubtful, worried that the feeling had been nothing but a symptom of his own grief, he sensed it. Jo was still there, burning up the last of her magic like a dying star.

"I'm sorry, Snow," Eslar's hand fell heavy on his shoulder. Snow hadn't even heard them approach. He could feel Takako's magic, still buzzing about the air after firing the arrow, and beneath that, Samson and Wayne's, familiar and dulled by their own confusion and heartbreak.

"This isn't over yet." Snow hastily laid the limp form down. Sure enough, her skin was beginning to crack and fly away in the breeze. He didn't have much time before the final casing holding in Jo's magic was gone. And then, *she* would be gone.

Unless he made a new casing for her.

"Eslar, I need you to do something for me."

"Snow?" The elf seemed startled, but already resolved.

"No one else can." He'd done it for her. When the time had come to end the Age of Gods, Snow had been the one to see Destruction split in two. He'd seen the process once before. "I need you to use the same ritual the elves would use to sever my magic and imbue it in a new form."

"What?" Eslar balked.

"Like the pillars at Springtide." For as panicked as Snow was, his voice was low, quiet, and he never took his eyes off of Oblivion's slack form. "Do it."

Eslar was at his side in a second. With a reluctance that bordered on physical pain, Snow tore himself away from Oblivion's face to stare into the eyes of his first friend, his first confidant. The first member of the Society. Eslar's brow was furrowed in concern, his expression distraught, but Snow rested a hand on his shoulder in brief reassurance and pressed on.

As pointless as it might have looked to everyone else, he knew what must be done for him to have a hope of a life worth living—a life with her.

"What are you going to do, Snow?" Samson asked, voice soft yet no longer filled with its usual tremor. There was grief there, Snow noticed, a sort of muted hope overshadowed by a sense of doubt that tainted and spread.

"I'm bringing her back," Snow offered, persistence soaking into his voice, his magic, and then blocking the rest of the world from his mind.

There was no point in holding anything back. He'd give it all to her. Snow reached deep, and held out his hands in the air in front of him as Eslar began to chant at his side.

As if Snow were sculpting from invisible clay, light shimmered under his thumbs as he drew them through the air. He traced the outline of her face, sculpting her every curve from memory. His magic eagerly filled in the blanks, creating a doll of light and life from nothing—pure creation.

Snow kept Jo in his mind all the while, the glint in her eyes and the tantalizing pull of her smile, the soft curves of the body he'd become intimately familiar with in more than one life. He thought of her voice, both as Destruction and as Jo, remembered the softness of her hair and the bite of her sarcasm. He held tight to her memory as if nothing else mattered.

And then he let it go.

"Now, Eslar!"

It wasn't a painful thing. His magic was taffy under the elf's hands. Eslar pulled and drew. Despite Snow's willingness, his magic reacted to the sensation defensively, unable to be soothed. It was like trying to convince himself to undergo a surgery without painkillers; his magic was used to being whole, and being ripped apart was met with vehement resistance.

Yet the ancient magics of the elves—handed down to them by the gods themselves for the sake of tending to the world in their absence—came through once more. Eslar pulled. He pulled and Snow willed his magic to heed his commands. As if sensing his intent at long last, his magic gave way. No longer a demigod, but a mortal. No longer one person, but two.

The sensation left him feeling hollow at first. He slouched and fell into something hard and sturdy; orange hair tickled his cheek. But as he opened his eyes, he looked to the hovering shell of Jo he had made, praying this final bid worked.

Magic filled the floating form of his love like a paint by numbers. Her long, dark hair bore streaks of vibrant color, her tanned skin glowing despite the lack of genuine life. His magic welled in the doll, filled to the brim thanks to Eslar's efforts.

"What now?" Eslar panted. "Snow, I did all I could."

"No. . . wait . . ."

A soft whisper of her magic chose the moment of his doubt to make itself known, followed by the familiar warmth of her presence pulsing from the fading outline of Oblivion and charging toward the magic he had imprinted in the doll to draw her essence like bait. It was a wave of sensation after that, her magic spilling into the new host with a weak but determined vigor. He could sense it settling beneath the doll's skin—*Jo's skin*, bringing color to her pallor, life into her dormant heart.

The world became real for her; she became real. No longer hovering, her bare foot touched down on the stony floor. Jo stood, naked as the day she was first born; on this day, she was born again.

"S-Snow?" she whispered, her eyes on his hunched form foremost.

"What happened to me? Did I bounce back like bef—" Jo looked down at herself. "Why am I naked?"

The sentiment broke the deathly chill of panic with the bounding laughter of relief.

"Here you go, dollface." Wayne shrugged off his coat. "Though, for someone just come back from the dead, sorry I don't have something a little more flashy."

Even as she slid her hands into the sleeves, her eyes stayed on Snow. "What did you do? I thought my destructive magic would be impervious."

"Your magic was. The physical form . . . not so much."

"Then?"

"I split my magic to make a host for you. Your magic . . . filled it," Snow simplified.

Awareness widened her eyes and she quickly crossed the gap between them, raising her hands to his cheeks to gently cradle his face. Watching her move was enough to make his eyes go watery. "Then, if you split, you're not a demigod anymore?"

"Neither are you," he affirmed.

"You did that for me?" She still sounded fragile, unused to her new body and voice, but she sounded alive. She was *alive.*

"I would do anything for you," Snow said, meaning every word of it. He would do anything for Jo, for Destruction, for his other half and truest love. Even living out the remainder of his life as a mortal. A life with magic, yes, but not the infinite well of forever to draw it from.

Still, as long as he shared his life with Jo, no matter how long, it would be worth it. He would split his magic a million times, and she would still be worth it.

"What does this mean?" Jo asked after a long moment of tense silence, gaze still hazy but regaining its usual brightness. Snow didn't care, not while she was living and breathing within his arms. But still, he gave her an answer.

"We live, my love. We simply . . . live."

"We'll be back as soon as we can to come and see you and Jo," Samson said, pulling in for a tight hug.

Takako returned the embrace, feeling a little smile work its way onto her mouth at the mention of her and Jo, but no Snow. As if Jo would go anywhere without Snow again now that they had each other. Or, perhaps, that was just the craftsman's way of communicating his priorities.

"What about me?" Wayne huffed from Takako's side.

"You too, when you're here."

Wayne rolled his eyes at the implication that he was not worth his own trip, but hugged Samson anyway.

"We will not be leaving High Luana often," Eslar added, tempering the expectations Samson was setting. His familiar, no-nonsense demeanor was oddly comforting, something Takako had always appreciated in the man. Yet, despite his words, he took a step toward her, holding out a hand. Takako gripped it firmly. "However, we may be able to make an exception for a royal wedding, should one ever happen."

Takako gave a knowing grin.

"Wayne, do not cause too much trouble."

"I was never the troublemaker," he insisted to a wary-looking Eslar. "That was entirely Jo."

"You can only use Jo as an excuse for the last year and change of the Society, not all your antics prior. I do recall when you were meddling with an illegal—"

"Okay, okay, I get it," Wayne stopped Eslar hastily. "No need for details, old friend."

*Old friend.* The words stuck with Takako. Here they were, four people who should've never met. Four people who'd shared little in the way of mutual interests, thrust together in such an impossible situation that they'd had no choice but to become friends. She'd once resigned herself to seeing these faces, and no others, for the rest of her life.

Now, there was a new age upon them. They all had choices before them, paths they could take. Still, something drew them together. The ties that bound them would persist, and Takako certainly didn't find herself upset at the thought.

Takako gave a wave as Samson and Eslar were ushered into a vehicle and carried away, nothing more than the residual haze of magic left behind. She and Wayne stood in the central courtyard for a long minute, saying nothing, merely looking at where their friends had once been. It was time for them all to start anew—as they'd tried to do when they'd first woken in this Age of Magic—but with no godly threats looming over their very existence.

"And then there were two," Wayne finally muttered.

"Not for long." Takako put her hands in the pockets of her pressed trousers, feeling where the rough starched wool met the inner silken lining. They were standard-issue for the Aristonian army, something Takako was not *exactly* a part of. But she was also not exactly *not* a part of it, either. Her new post straddled the line between garnering respect in Aristonia and not committing treason against her home country. "You're leaving soon too, aren't you?"

"'Fraid so. I should get back to Yorkton, make sure my executives haven't destroyed my company. I like being rich far too much to see them squander my success." Wayne turned, starting back for the castle. Takako followed suit.

The castle was almost done being rebuilt—construction with magic was far hastier compared to purely manual labor in Takako's time—a time that was slowly fading from her consciousness. Takako was letting it go without struggle. The world she'd been born into was gone; she'd accepted that in the Society with every granted wish. Now, it seemed like a natural evolution to settle into this reality in its entirety. She could actually put down roots here, after all; it wasn't as though timelines would be changing again.

"I'm surprised you're not taking her up on her offer. Head of the finance department sounds . . . prestigious," Takako said, throwing a brief smirk in Wayne's direction.

"She shouldn't give out every cabinet post to her friends, and you already accepted Champion." Wayne gave her a wink.

"Champion is not a political position. I am not Aristonian, so it cannot be. It's more of an award of—"

"Easy there, I'm just joshin' you. Either way, you're right, I should get to finishing up my travel arrangements," Wayne finished.

They came to a stop just inside the now perpetually open castle gates. They overlooked a recessed central courtyard—the same place Oblivion had died—that was slowly being transformed into a grassy garden. The destruction of the castle had been written off to the public as surprise renovations gone wrong. At the same time, there was a quiet mention of Pan being "out" and Jo being "in" as Snow's royal advisor.

Aristonia on the whole seemed so thrilled with the changes that no one probed too deeply. Of course, there were always conspiracy theories online for Jo to find and the rest of them to get a laugh at. Even when the truth was seemingly impossible, fiction could be made to sound stranger (and oftentimes more hilarious) than fact.

"I'm sure I'll see you again soon," Takako said with a smile, their rooms in opposite directions.

"Likely for that eventual wedding." Wayne looked across the garden. "Can't believe Snow wouldn't lock a woman like that down."

"Women aren't meant to be 'locked down'," Takako reminded him, though she'd heard the expression before and saved Wayne the unnecessary explanation by continuing. "And it isn't for lack of trying . . . after all, it's Wednesday. I'm sure he just made another attempt."

"I don't understand them." Wayne shook his head.

"Understand those two? I don't think we ever will. But wanting to live a little without Pan and the Society pressing on them . . . that at least is clear enough to me."

At that moment, the disk in her pocket pulsed with magic. Takako pulled it out, recognizing the frequency. Her eyes skimmed the message on its surface.

"I'll leave you to that," Wayne said, already starting to walk away.

"Sorry! It was from my family."

"It's all right. I'm not leaving until the end of the week, I just decided. We can have a rematch at tarith with a nightcap tonight."

Neither of them really knew how to play the elvish tile game. They seemed to have more fun arguing over made-up rules than actually trying to learn the game properly.

"It's a deal." Takako turned in the other direction and put Wayne from her mind. She had other, more pressing things to worry about now.

Takako strolled upward through the castle, amazed at how much transformation could transpire in a mere month. Originally, she had thought the castle looked like obsidian stalagmites, jutting unnaturally from the ground. Now, the color of the stone had changed to a pearly white, bright blue glowing deep under its surface. It was a reflection of Snow's magic, Takako had reasoned.

Or it was merely an aesthetic illusion to cast away Pan's lingering darkness. Either way, the outer casing still pulsed with magic and the inside had been transformed into an equally bright (and far more logically constructed) space.

The one thing that had remained the same were the puppet-like creatures. Pan's assassins fled like rats, retreating to their next hideaway to lurk until a new, powerful leader no doubt organized them. But that would be a problem for another day. The puppets, however, had not been destroyed when Pan's magic dissolved.

They had lingered about the castle, listless, until Jo made the decision to accept them. Now, they played an active role in upkeep and restoration. Takako was wary of anything that changed loyalties so quickly, but they seemed harmless enough, merely happy to have a purpose. She wasn't sure how she felt about them stepping aside with a bow, though, every time she passed. It was worse when the other (more sentient, living, breathing servants) did the same. Takako wasn't used to such deference.

She came to a stop outside an unmarked door in a quiet wing of the castle. Servants, and those closest to the royal advisor, knew it was her true office—not the fancy ceremonial desk she was forced to use during meetings, to maintain appearances. This was where the woman felt most at home.

Takako gave two raps on the door.

"Come in," Jo's voice called from inside.

The room was a total wreck. Where the rest of the castle was beginning to reclaim order from chaos, this room was chaos incarnate. Perhaps Jo had the tiniest bit of Pan within her still. If Pan's only lingering mark on the world was a messy room, Takako reasoned, they'd done all right.

Clothes were strewn about the floor, and boxes stacked on boxes spilled over with pieced-together technology, wires dangling from them like gutted beasts. At the center of it all was the woman herself. Jo was lit up only by the neon glow of the monitor in front of her, her eyes glued to the magical script flowing across it.

"Still working on learning technomancy, I see." Takako closed the door behind her.

Jo turned, a can of RAGE ENERGY at her mouth. "It's being a pain. The whole 'magic meets technology' thing is nonsense."

"So you've said." Takako looked at the drink more closely. "Where did you get that? Weren't you lamenting how this age didn't have that particular flavor?"

"His newest proposal." Jo wiggled the can before taking another sip. "Thinks he can win me over with caffeine."

"I think he's already won you over."

"Don't let him know that." Jo didn't even bother hiding a grin as she spun in her desk chair.

They all knew it was only a matter of time before a royal wedding happened. Even Jo had said as much the first time Snow offered to make things official in that decidedly mortal way. But Jo had requested they spend some time *being* mortal first, just living without the Society or Pan.

Takako had thought it sensible, but she suspected it may have disappointed Snow at first. He proposed for the second time not long after. The third proposal came even faster after that. It was now a weekly thing, more like an inside joke than anything else.

"So, what can Aristonia's chief advisor help you with today?" Jo grinned over the can. "Come to give me an extra set of hands again?"

She had been, originally. Takako fumbled with the disk in her pocket, feeling somewhat guilty. Everyone was leaving all at once. . .

"There's something I'd like to ask."

"Shoot." Jo's expression told Takako the pun was intended, and Takako couldn't suppress a chuckle.

"I have received a message from my family."

"Oh? How are they?"

By way of answering Jo's question, Takako pulled her disk from her pocket, reading aloud.

"We had not heard from you in some time, and given all that has transpired in Aristonia, the family wants to make sure you're all right. Your sister's children miss you. It would be good to have a call soon. Don't be like your cousin Hiro; he left for the Kingdom of Zakon nearly three months ago and hasn't been heard from since.

"All is well here," Takako finished.

"You should go back and see them," Jo said with a smile, prompting Takako to wonder if she could now read minds. "I'm sure they'd like that."

"It wouldn't be any trouble? I had promised you I would—"

"Don't worry about it." Jo shook her head, turning back to her computer. "I have enough to keep me busy for a while. You can go over the Aristonian military with me when you get back. But take as much time as you need."

"Thank you." Takako almost felt compelled to give the other woman a hug. Instead, she let the gratitude of her words hang in the air before turning for the door. She didn't have much to pack, but like Wayne, she should still do that and square off her travel arrangements.

"Oh, one thing though."

"Hm?" Takako hummed, turning.

"If you end up going down to Zakon to find your cousin—"

"I doubt I will," Takako interjected. "Hiro has always been a bit of a wild child for his parents. This is hardly the first time he's pulled a stunt like this. I'm sure he'll be back soon, talking about how he 'found himself' in some remote mountain village."

"Still, if you do, be careful." The genuine caution in Jo's voice caught her attention. "I'm sure it's nothing . . . but I've been seeing weird reports pop up online about merfolk attacks down there."

"Merfolk attacks?" Takako repeated. "I haven't heard anything."

"It's just rumors right now. Who knows if they're true. No reporting seems to confirm. . ." Jo glanced up at her. "Still, be careful."

"I will," Takako vowed. It was easy to make such a promise. While she had jumped head-first into research about her new world when she'd first woken in this new Age of Magic, there was still much to learn, and ignorance bred caution.

In a time like this, when elves were real and dragons streaked across the sky, who knew what could happen?

# ABOUT THE AUTHOR: ELISE KOVA

ELISE KOVA has always had a profound love of fantastical worlds. Somehow, she managed to focus on the real world long enough to graduate with a Master's in Business Administration before crawling back under her favorite writing blanket to conceptualize her next magic system. She currently lives in St. Petersburg, Florida, and when she is not writing can be found playing video games, watching anime, or talking with readers on social media.

She invites readers to get first looks, giveaways, and more by subscribing to her newsletter at: http://elisekova.com/subscribe

Visit her on the web at:
http://elisekova.com/
https://twitter.com/EliseKova
https://www.facebook.com/AuthorEliseKova/
https://www.instagram.com/elise.kova/

# ABOUT THE AUTHOR: LYNN LARSH

LYNN LARSH considers herself to be a serial hobby-dabbler. She got a bachelors degree in music (which she used for all of four months), studied aerial acrobatics and classical piano for many years, worked briefly as a stunt woman in a Wild West stunt show (it's a long story), and eventually settled down into the bar tending business in St. Petersberg, FL. When she's not acting as a purveyor of fine libations, you can find her diving head first into her newest venture as a New Adult author, or simply writing Voltron fan fiction on Archive of Our Own.

Visit her on the web at: https://www.lynnlarsh.com/

# ACKNOWLEDGEMENTS

BOOK ONE

## Elise's Acknowledgements

LYNN—Not only have you been my best friend and confidant for nearly a decade, but you have also helped make this book happen. Without you, it wouldn't have been the story it is. Thank you for adding your creativity, voice, and depth to this work… And for putting up with all my neuroses. I can't wait to see what we make next!

ROBERT—My dear, you have been a huge support to us both in this process. Thank you for showing up to signings with all the things I forgot, for feeding me when I didn't have time to find food, and for never batting an eye when it was a late night.

CAITLIN, MELISA, and MI-MI—Your insights as beta readers not only transformed this manuscript, but took it to a level not even Lynn and I could have imagined. Thank you for working with us!

MOM, DAD, & MER—As you three know best, this was a particularly hard year for me. But, no matter what happened, I was blessed to know that I'd always have the safety net of your love and support. Thank you for always being there.

MARY—Thank you for helping me continue to write books like this by (sometimes painfully) keeping my hands, wrists, and shoulders in top condition.

REBECCA—I'm honored by every book we get to work together on. Your critiques for this manuscript really pushed it to become a fantastic story truly worth telling. Thank you for everything.

THE TOWER GUARD—Can I ever write a book and NOT include you in it? No, the answer is a solid no. You are the most amazing support team an author could ever ask for. You keep up with me enthusiastically and are always there to encourage me when it gets tough.

~

### Lynn's Acknowledgements

~

TEAL—For constantly putting up with my self-confidence issues and reminding me that a lack of notes on a fanfic does not mean I'm a bad writer. Even if it's 60,000 words of a Voltron, college music AU I spent a year on.

ANTONIO—For making me want to get better by constantly wanting to better yourself. And for late night, real talk, wine sleepovers. That too.

TWINSIE—For giving me those little moments of escape and comfort that I would shatter without. Also Haikyuu. Nice kill.

ELISE—For helping me get here. Seriously, I would never have made it this far without you. Full stop. The Monday happy hours helped too, though. AND PEGGY.

# BOOK TWO

## Elise's Acknowledgements

MY EDITOR, REBECCA—I do not think a manuscript will go by where I do not thank you. Your patience, professionalism, and pushing me to always do better is critical to the creation of my stories.

LYNN—Thank you for all of your hard work on this project. I believe so much in this world we're building and have had such a great time building it with you.

ROBERT—I can never seem to find enough words for you, my dear. But I'll keep writing books until I get close.

CAITLIN, MELISA, and MI-MI—Thank you for continuing to work with us on beta reading. Having your eyes on this project early has been so helpful.

AMANDA—You're an absolute gem. Thank you for all your support. I can't wait for the next signing I have in Austin so I can catch a ride with you again.

EMILY, HETAL, LINDA, MEGAN—When the call went out, you each stepped up to help me re-tool book one and give me new insights on what needed to happen to make book two even better. Thank you for your support and friendship.

THE TOWER GUARD—I can't say enough how much you all help me and shape my work. Your never-ending support is the foundation of my survival as an author. It's dramatic, but I do not think I would be anywhere close to where I am now without having you there as readers, as feedback, and as friends.

DANIELLE—My books would each have the worst synopsis in the world were it not for you. Thank you for always being so such a good friend, whether it's professional advice, or just rambling away on Twitter.

MOM and DAD—Thank you for your never-ending support and interest in my work. I so appreciate the "CT" and proofreading around the world. Love you both.

MER—Thanks for helping make my new office, and the home around it, amazing. I'm so much more productive because of it.

∾

### Lynn's Acknowledgements

∾

ROBERT—For always being there when I need someone to lean on, for playing checkers with me when I feel like running away, and for being totally and completely awesome.

BLAINE—For being so supportive of my ventures in another field, for housing us at our first book signing, and for being the literal best boss a person could ask for.

THE WILLARD'S BEER COMMUNITY—For being the most kind and supportive group of people a debut author could hope to surround herself with. To everyone who showed up at my first signing, to everyone who bought a book, and to everyone who left a review, you have all of my thanks and more.

ELISE—For continuing to put up with my shit.

# ALSO BY ELISE KOVA

~

### THE AIR AWAKENS SERIES

A library apprentice with rare elemental powers. A sorcerer prince with a dark past. And the magical bond between them that will change the future of an Empire.

*Series complete!*

**READ NOW:** http://getbook.at/AAGG

~

### THE LOOM SAGA

Recently listed by Bustle as one of the 15 new fantasy to read for Game of Thrones fans! Dark fantasy, grit, enemies to lovers, in an epic new world.

*Series complete!*

**READ NOW:** http://mybook.to/TAOL

9 781949 694079